Bram Nielson Collection

i

Ron Mueller

Bram Nielson Collection

Books and Stories by Ron Mueller

The Taelo Series

Taelo: The Early Years
Taelo: The Golden Feather
Taelo: Journey of Discovery
Taelo: Dangerous Passage
Taelo: Condor Clan Slingers
Taelo: Circumvention
Taelo: The Journey of Sages
Taelo: Collection
Taelo: Future Leaders Journey

A Taelo Story:

White Swan and Quiet Pheasant
The Child's Name
Floating Cloud
Quiet Rabbit
Busy Bee
Little Otter & Talking Wren
Broken Spear
Burley Bear & Meadow Flower

Science Fiction

The Savitar Series:
> Journey's End
> Savitar
> Confluence
> Savitar Collection

Bram Nielson Series
> The Fold
> The Message
> Fold Wormhole
> Negative Fold
> Ripples in Time
> Bram Nielson Collection

Single Science Fiction Books

> Current Past and Future
> The Event
> The Door
> Viajante 7

Ron Mueller

<u>Fiction Series</u>

The Alex Evercrest Series
The River Front
The Girl on The Grill
Missing
Maggot
Racist
Votive Candles
Windy City
Country Road
Pool of Blood
Sins of the Daughter
Body Parts
The Skull Collector
The Vanishing
The Shadow Fighter
Moonshine
Grief's Trajectory
The Magic Touch
Northern Lights
Alex Evercrest Heroin Collection
Alex Evercrest Collection Two

A Brian Oneil Novell
Hawaiian Phoenix
Moon Curser
Death Broker

The Problem Solver Series
Solutions
Drug Lords
Border Crosser
Problem Solver Collection

Imagination by Courtney Huynh and Chloe Parker

Bram Nielson Collection
By: *Ron Mueller*

Around the World Publishing LLC
4914 Cooper Road Suite 144
Cincinnati, Ohio 45242-9998

This story is a work of fiction. Names, characters, places, and incidents either are products of the author's imagination or are used fictitiously. Any resemblance to actual events or locales or persons, living or dead, is entirely coincidental.

Bram Nielson Collection Copyright © 2023

ISBN 13: 978-1-68223-950-6
ISBN 10: 1-68223-950-0

Distributed by Ingram
Cover Picture by: @ShutterStock
Cover Design by: Ron Mueller

Ron Mueller

Bram Nielson Collection

Table of Content

Fold

Ron Mueller

Table of Content

Bram Nielson Collection

Ron Mueller

Bram Nielson Collection
The Fold

Chapter 1: Conscripted

At five in the morning the far and faint twinkling starlight and the hint of the Cheshire moon provided the only light. Bram moved cautiously as he took each step up the narrow foot path he had made through the ragged greyish green leafed sage brush of the desert.

A slight breeze put a chill in the air. He was glad that he had on his warm windbreak it held back the surprisingly frosty chill of the desert air.

At this time in the morning all vegetation looked black to his eye and seemed to challenge the existence of the path he had made in the days since he had arrived at the camp, that he thought of as his personal gulag.

The sharp brown glass like particles crunching beneath his hiking boots spoke of some ancient volcanic activity in the region.

He envisioned the large boulder, which was his destination, being pushed by the glacier for thousands of years until one side was worn flat. This flat area had become his morning throne.

The large commanding boulder appeared ahead and loomed above him. Using several projecting knobs and several pock holes, he climbed up and claimed his East facing throne.

Soon after his discovery of the boulder and while sitting and waiting for the sun a friendly desert mouse befriended him and joined him each morning to watch the sunrise. His little friend always waited until the morning sun was ready to warm them both. He was a great listener, and they got along admirably.

The sun broke over the far horizon and Bram turned his face to let the morning light fall on and warm it. He watched as Einstein, the name he had given his small, brown fluff of a desert mouse, scurried up and sat by his side.

In the flat valley below lay the airfield, the few houses with yards, the helicopter hangar and the expansive block building that housed his apartment, his lab and housed the rest of the people in what had become his home. The facilities were new, luxurious, and well appointed. He knew the whole complex had been built specifically to house him and everyone that was there to keep him in and to make his stay comfortable.

He had been surprised when told that a chef would cater to everyone's desire. He knew that his current life was more lavish than he had ever experienced.

His previous years had been much more utilitarian. He had been an assistant professor living in Boston. He had discovered that the combination put him on the edge of starvation.

Yet, being held in luxury against his will and not being told where he was made him feel like a well-kept prisoner.

They would not tell him where in the world the compound was located. This was a point that irritated him and made testing of his theory more difficult.

He was dead set on finding out where he was being kept and on changing how the program, he was the center of, was managed.

For the last one hundred and eighty days, with the exception of a few trips east or to other secret locations, this had been where he was "kept and protected."

He had established his morning routine that began by greeting the morning sun, then feeding and talking with Einstein and then hiking out into the desert.

He had logged many hours among the sage brush. He had surprised many unwary jack rabbits or had been surprised by the rattle of an angry rattlesnake upon whose territory he had encroached.

He learned that rattlesnakes were sluggish in the morning cold but chose to wear high leather boots with a metal lining slipped in.

The warmth of the sun and the aroma of a cup of hot mint tea held between his hands, slowly wore away the early morning chill.

The sun rose slowly and created a shadow that pulled away from the base of the boulder he was sitting on.

He had positioned a timing stone. When the shadow hit that stone, it was time to leave for his hike in the desert.

Einstein and he had shared many a morning in this manner. Bram thought he and the mouse would have been well known to each other had they been able to converse.

The routine was consistent.

Bram would arrive just before sunrise and climb to his perch. As the sun broke over the eastern horizon, the mouse would poke its nose out from a hole at the base of their mutual boulder and climb up the boulder and sit with him.

Bram had told Einstein all his woes at least once, maybe more. He had asked him for advice and to review his scientific theories. He now felt an attachment to his lone desert mouse and always brought it a morning treat of biscuit or cookie crumbs.

The mouse would turn his head and seemed to agree with many of the complaints and comments Bram threw his way.

The surrounding desert, with its sage brush and yellow desert flowers was his one escape from himself and the government that was now "helping" him fulfill his goal.

He was virtually their prisoner. Well treated but monitored and tightly confined.

Sitting out on this boulder or hiking through the desert was a victory that he had gained by consistently refusing to work if he was not given the time to get out.

He was sure he was being monitored even when he sat on his boulder. He wondered if those monitoring had seen him talking to Einstein. If they had Bram figured that by now, they would have taken him away in a straight jacket.

Each morning, he would wish his mouse well and he would then head out on a brisk walk away from the complex in a specific compass heading. His first four excursions had been the main compass headings of North, East, South and West. For the last half, a year he had gone out hiking on one degree increments clockwise away from North.

Each time after approximately an hour, a helicopter would arrive and tell him he must return to the lab. The first few times he hiked back. Then he began to ride the helicopter back. This saved him time and he enjoyed bantering with the pilot. She seemed to be about his age. He wondered how she had been chosen for this duty.

This morning, day 185, he was now traveling south plus five degrees. He was slowly plotting a circle with the center being the site of his lab.

Bram carried the instrumentation that transformed him into an altimeter. He was creating a detailed topographical map of the terrain around the lab. This information had already reduced the possible location of his lab to just three areas in the United States.

On a daily basis, in a morning project meeting, he requested the information about where he was, and he was always politely refused.

He continued to ask about the location every time there was a meeting. He had decided that until the program leaders changed their mind about how they handled the team he would not provide them with any more information about his space-time Fold breakthrough.

He thought of his breakthrough as having stumbled on the knowledge that when activated would change how travel through the universe would be achieved. He was close to opening the universe to humankind.

He was not going to let his breakthrough remain a secret but publishing the concepts of his ideas in a leading scientific journal had gotten Bram into his current situation. He had been sitting at his desk running his fingers through his hair in frustration when the doorbell rang. He looked through the peek hole and saw a very beautiful woman dressed in a black business outfit. He opened the door, and she introduced herself as Ms. Erica Wilson with the US government.

Her shoulder length black hair that swept over a perfectly formed ear and exposed the right side of her smooth, flawless face placed her looks in the beautiful woman category. Her smooth introduction, smile and greeting put her in the good sales ability category.

Her smile though clearly was not genuine but lit up her face.

He took it all in as he listened to her polished introduction and her pitch about how his article had captured her imagination. He wondered about her imagination since he had not described anything that might be imagined but he invited her in and pointed to the couch.

She explained she was with NASA and invited him to come to Washington and share his knowledge with her team. The invitation was enticing and of interest to him. When she highlighted Elizabeth Miller renowned the theory of Ethical Behavior in Science as a member of the team and a person he had read, as a member of the team, he agreed to attend the meeting.

He asked a few questions about his theory, and it was clear that Erica had little understanding of his article, but he was excited that his work had been deemed significant enough to get him invited to a NASA team meeting. It was important enough to send their project leader to personally recruit him.

Erica informed him that the meeting was for the following Wednesday. He was to review his article with a team that was focused on the same problem. She asked if he could make the meeting, as she reached into her purse. She hinted that there was a hefty salary if he made the team.

He said that the timing was very tight, but he would attend. He was about to tell her not to ruin things by trying to buy his participation but thought better of it.

Erica pulled out an envelope and handed him a plane ticket and hotel reservations as she stood to leave. She informed him that he would be met at the airport and escorted to the meeting. It was clear to Bram that she had come prepared for him to say yes.

He stood looking at the tickets in his hand as he realized that over the weekend, he would need to arrange to have his classes covered by his graduate students. He had not expected anything to happen this fast.

He looked out the window and watched as Erica got into a black limo. He was surprised at her ride. It seemed to him that she was well connected.

The weekend was a scurry of calls to his graduate students as he assigned them to cover his lectures.

On Wednesday as Bram was getting ready to leave to the airport, he was met at the door leading down to the street by an individual in a dark blue suit. Bram was intent on getting out to the walk where he expected to be picked up.

He excused himself and proceeded down the steps. He was followed down the steps and out to the edge of the walk.

There the man continued to engage him and invited him to meet with the president of the firm that was interested in funding his research. After giving Bram a card with the time and place for the meeting at a posh restaurant in Boston, he walked to a black limo and departed.

Bram had the card in hand as he got into the car taking him to the airport. He noted that the article had stirred the interest of more than the US government. He wondered what funding a private firm would pay.

He now had doubts about Erica's team.

Clearly people thought his idea was important. He had two people that had come to his apartment and that alone gave him cause for concern.

He wondered why was there this sudden interest in his theories?

The flight to DC left Boston early. He took note that if things didn't go smoothly with the US government, he now had a private company that was interested in supporting his research.

As Erica had promised when he walked into the arrival area, he saw a person holding a sign with his name on it. The sign welcomed him and had Erica Wilson written below his name.

He had not checked luggage, so he walked out with his escort to a waiting grey Ford sedan.

He was taken to NASA Headquarters at East Street Southwest. He felt good that NASA was so interested in his work. Its reputation was another reason that he had agreed to the meeting.

He wondered what group he had interested and what they wanted with his breakthrough.

He went through security and then was guided down a long corridor around several bends and finally guided into a meeting room where he was seated at the end seat on a long table.

Bram noted that all the seats had been taken. He looked down the table at the rather handsome Asian heritage person sitting directly across from him. Erica was sitting to that person's right. Bram recognized only one person from the rest of the people at the table.

The meeting was called to order, and everyone gave a brief introduction of themselves. Jeffrey Mikelson sitting at the head of the table, introduced himself as the Space Technology Mission Director. He was currently leading a program named STCP (Space Time Continuum Program). He welcomed Bram and then asked everyone to introduce themselves.

As Bram listened to the introductions and watched the team's interactions, it seemed to him that this team had been formed quickly and had done little work together.

When Elizabeth Miller, a person who he had admired and followed for years and now sitting to his left introduced herself, Bram stood and extended his hand. He said that she was one of the persons who had inspired him.

They shook hands and Elizabeth pulled him in for a hug. She whispered that it had all been set up for him and that NASA wanted him badly, but it was real. Bram smiled at her and nodded his head. If she was on the team then Bram was certainly interested.

After the introductions, Bram was asked to go through the presentation that he had brought with him.

The five-slide presentation that he presented to the team confirmed his suspicions. The team was of top talent, but they didn't seem to know each other and seemed to only know what he had written. He noted that the few questions asked were general and lacked depth.

He thought that the team was fresher than just churned butter. He now understood Elizabeth's whisper.

He concluded his presentation and after a final question and answer session, everyone on the team but Jeffery and Erica left the room.

Elizabeth patted him on his shoulder as she past him on her way out.

It was clear to Bram that the meeting had been rehearsed and that the participants had each played their part. He knew that the two persons remaining in the room were the decision makers.

Bram put his left hand on the spot that Elizabeth had patted. Bram knew Elizabeth, was globally known for her focus on human ethics in space exploration and would not have participated if she had not thought it important.

Jeffery made him the offer to get on team.

Bram was surprised that there was no small talk, and the offer came with a title, the highest government ranking and pay possible and a signing bonus.

Bram was offered the technical leadership of the team.

The salary offer was more than twice as much as his current salary and the signing bonus of five thousand dollars made it even more attractive. It made him wonder if the offer from private industry would be significantly more. When he asked for time to think about it, the atmosphere in the room changed.

Jeffrey and Erica looked at each other.

The answer surprised Bram.

Jeffrey quietly said, "No!." We are aware of an offer that might have been made to you this morning and we know about several additional offers that will come with conditions that would seem to be more attractive than the one I just offered, but each would make you their captive.

We are concerned about you and about the US national security.

Bram listened as Jeffrey emphasized that he was giving him everything that could possibly offered, and it was an offer that could not be refused.

Bram realized that he was not being asked but told that he was on the team. Jeffrey went on to inform him that he was immediately being put under government protection because of the importance of his scientific work.

He had been given best possible deal but the choice about joining was not an option.

Bram asked how it was possible that he had been noticed by so many organizations at the same time.

Erica assured him that he was already on the most wanted list of people to either recruit, abduct or eliminate. She shared that his actions since his publication had been monitored and that he was put under guard since the moment she had met with him.

Two men in black waited outside of the meeting room. Jeffrey introduced them as FBI bodyguards that would guard him until he interviewed and selected four that would live with him. They escorted he, Jeffrey, and Erica to lunch.

There they briefly discussed the arrangements that were being made on his behalf.

He would retain his position on the MIT staff, but he would be posted as taking a sabbatical.

That was the end of lunch.

He and his two men in black were flown to an undisclosed location. He arrived in the dead of night and was escorted to a spacious and well-appointed corner apartment on the top floor of the building. He walked slowly through his new two-bedroom apartment that had a huge common room and large open veranda.

It was an apartment that could have been featured in one of the luxury apartment magazines. It made his apartment in Boston seem like a squatters shack.

The spacious exterior deck provided a place to sit and enjoy the desert view at sunset and it was large enough for him to practice his Tae kwon do and Aikido.

Windows formed two walls of the apartment. He was using one room for his office and the other, that featured a shower stall, for his bedroom. The apartment came with someone to cook his meals and with another person to clean it periodically.

It was clear that if he were a prisoner he was a pampered one.

He was, by his own estimation of the circumstances, a valuable asset that was getting the best treatment possible but, in all respects, he was now a prisoner of the government. He wondered if it was the same situation for the rest of the team.

He would soon find out who would be staying at the compound with him.

He decided to enjoy his deck and sit and relax.

When his belongings arrived, he arranged his meager belongings and developed a schedule that he would follow.

He recalled both of his martial arts master's asking him what he planned to do with the capability and knowledge they were giving him.

He replied that he planned to do good.

They both seemed pleased with his reply. He really had no clue why he felt the need to pursue these martial art skills, but he had become a third-degree black belt in each.

Now he put the exercises to work to reduce the stress he felt by his current situation.

Tae Kwon Do and Aikido became his early evening exercise routine.

He added the early morning hikes into the desert to his exercise routine.

That is where he met his confident and counselor Einstein.

He thought about the fact that he had been given a brain that had a capability that was taking him on a journey that if he succeeded would be change the world.

He wanted that to be used to do good.

This morning like all the mornings for the last six months, he said good day to his pet mouse as he left the boulder. Bram then focused on his footing as he walked carefully down the rocky slope. This was his one hundred eighty fifth radial hike away from the compound. At the bottom, as he rounded a ragged boulder about twice his height, he came to a dark gapping opening. A cool breeze washed past the beads of sweat that had already formed on his brow.

The breeze surprised him. He was not sure what he had discovered but he was intent on exploring it. He pulled out his flashlight and entered the ten-by-ten-foot cave entrance.

The breeze meant that there was another opening somewhere ahead. He let the breeze guide him through the dark cave. His light bounced off the smooth well-worn ancient path and he slowly made his way forward.

He realized that what he was doing would certainly confuse his routine helicopter pickup pilot.

Amy began suiting up, it was time to retrieve Bram from his radial hikes away from the compound. She was not sure why he went out on his morning walks, but she had come to believe he was mapping the surrounding areas. Anything else made little sense to her.

She rated her current assignment as an easy one but very visible. She had heard this assignment was high up on the recognition list of special assignments, so she had volunteered in hopes it would look good on her service record. She was one of a short list of volunteers and she was the only female.

The assignment was not highly sought since it was an assignment that put a person in the middle of nowhere. She however was happy to have gotten the assignment.

She knew her performance ratings had always been high. What she wanted was a gold star in her record to improve her chances at getting accepted into the space program. She wanted to be an astronaut and the barriers leading to that opportunity were many.

She finished suiting up and walked out to her helicopter. The red beauty sat on its skids on the landing pad. The tail rotor with a shark like fin above the bright red rotor shrouding and the long thin white tubular connection to bright red main body brought a dragon fly to her mind.

But her toy had a sleek body that could host at least seven people and if necessary, it also had a winch to lift a person from the ground. It was the best ride she had ever piloted. She looked forward to each of her morning flights.

Amy climbed into the cockpit, went through her flight checks, and brought the engine to life. She slowly lifted off the pad and headed out on the heading of one hundred eighty-five degrees toward the south. She dutifully added the one degree each morning. She had figured out Bram's pattern.

She soon knew something had changed. She had flown out slowly, so she could spot Bram. This had become a normal morning routine. She would spot him hiking through the desert. He would wave at her as she passed over him and then she would swing around, land and he would approach and jump into the seat beside her. He always had a desert flower or some other small trinket to give her.

Today he was nowhere to be seen.

Her immediate reaction was alarm. Had he fallen down some ravine?

After several circular search runs, Amy made a call back to the base. She asked if Bram had returned to the base. A few moments later she was informed that he was in his lab.

Amy cursed under her breath and headed back to the landing pad. She was pissed. She figured Bram should have let her know that he had not taken his normal hike.

Amy took off her helmet and carefully hung it on its hook. She was fuming mad at Bram. For more than six months she had made this same flight and she had always found him. After the first two weeks he had always flown back with her. It had become like clockwork. She wondered what had happened to change the arrangement.

Still mad, she decided to go ask him what had happened and if the change was permanent.

A second person was also going to find Bram.

Erica was free to come and go from the compound as she pleased. She did not have to be at the compound but none the nonetheless she was upset that Jeffrey had given Bram a salary that was at least twenty per cent higher than hers and he had put him in the best apartment. She privately had her eyes on it and had been planning to move into it. She figured she deserved it. Instead, she had been assigned a one bedroom on the second floor. Jeffrey told her that she would only be there part-time and did not need anything more.

Damn him. She was the one who was supposed to be in charge of the project logistics.

He was getting the best of everything.

She bit her tongue and moved into an apartment she felt was below her paygrade.

She was sitting in the meeting room where she held her daily meeting when she was on-site. She watched as Bram, Marcus, Elizabeth and Mallica walked in chatting. They seemed to have developed a good working relationship.

It had become clear to her that Bram did not need the support of any of his team in the realm that he was working in. He was quite independent and engaged the rest of the team in philosophical discussions but seldom in the science he was engaged in.

Elizabeth seemed to be the exception but when Erica asked, she was clear she had no clue about the math and science that Bram was developing.

Erica decided she needed to have more control of what Bram was doing. She needed a timeline to the completion of his work. She would insist on a work plan from him.

Bram saw the look on Erica's face and knew that she was going to push. She would be trying to get control of the science part of the effort. This was a part of the project that Bram knew she had no clue as to what was happening.

He did not want her involved.

He put her in the category of a person too self-engrossed and not really interested in the science but interested in control of the environment around her.

She was only interested in getting herself recognized and rewarded.

Bram categorize her as self-aggrandized. He saw little use for her in the scientific arena.

He decided to try to shock her. He had determined the location of the base. He was ninety-nine with six nines after the decimal point sure where the compound was located.

He stood and looked at Erica but instead of asking his normal question about where the compound was located, he gave a latitude and longitude and stated that it was the location of the compound and gave the specific altitude of the room in which the meeting was being held.

Bram looked at her and softly said I know where I am and unless you quit playing games with me the rest of the world will know as well.

There was total silence in the room.

For the first time in her life, Erica did not know how to proceed. She had never faced anyone like Bram. Why was it so important for him to know where he was?

She put up her hand as if to deflect what he had said. She wanted to shout obscenities at him, but this was beyond what she had anticipated. Her self-control won out.

She canceled the meeting and said that she was bringing Jeffrey into this discussion.

Bram nodded and said he was pleased to meet with them both.

The sky was still a somber grey the next morning when Bram climbed on his boulder and looked down at the compound. The lights gave the complex an eerie shimmering appearance as the early morning mist began to rise.

The scene really looked like area 51 in all the sci-fi movies. In this case, Bram felt like he was the alien. He knew that the upcoming meeting focus would be on him.

The sun slowly drove the grey mist from the air and filled it with its clear rays of warmth.

The morning came awake like sleeping beauty after her lover's kiss.

Einstein came out of his hole for his morning treat. Today he listened to Bram's analysis of what would transpire at the coming morning meeting.

Bram left the rock and headed out at one hundred ninety second degree clockwise from North.

The morning air was brushing past him and hitting him on his right cheek. Now that he knew where the compound was located, he could almost predict what his hike would encounter. The few surprises were made up of boulders and cactuses that rose up in his path. But the elevation and the up and downs were visible in his mind's terrain map.

The location had never been of any concern to him other than as a lever to pull that would cause the mouse trap to open.

It would make it easier to test the space-time Fold transmitter, but he could have done it without knowing his current location.

He had patiently baited the trap so that he could force a change.

He heard the chatter of the helicopter and gave a wave as it passed overhead. Amy had told him he had scared the hell out of her when he had disappeared on his 185-degree hike and had not let her know he had found another way back to the compound.

He had promised not to scare her again. He was becoming very fond of her and enjoyed their morning chatter on the way back to the compound.

Marcus watched as Amy and Bram walked toward him. He was there to warn Bram about Erica's continuing bad mood. She had almost bitten his head off when he had given a simple morning hello.

He greeted Amy and then turned to Bram. He quietly told him the situation and that Jeffrey was already in the meeting room with a fuming mad Erica.

Bram smiled as Elizabeth joined them. He always felt better when he had his morning hug from her. She was old enough to be his grandmother. Her mind was the most powerful one in any room she was in. Bram used his interactions with Elizabeth to clarify his mind.

He let out a mental sigh of relief as Mallica joined them and they walked into the meeting room together.

Bram greeted Jeffrey and said good morning to Erica who was seated to Jeffrey's left. He was not surprised but disappointed that she did not reply. He concluded that Marcus had been right about her current mood.

Bram purposely chose to sit to Jeffery's right, so he could look directly at Erica. He also took noted that Elizabeth chose to sit next to him. It was clear to him that everyone expected sparks and fire.

Jeffrey opened the meeting by describing Erica's frustration with the behavior of the team. He went on to describe the concern over Bram's determination in constantly requesting the location of the compound.

Jeffrey listened to Erica, as she vented her fury at the disrespect she felt was being shown by Bram. Jeffrey said he understood her frustration but was surprised at her intense emotion. He thought to himself that it was clear that she would not last in the long term if this was how she felt.

He turned his attention to Bram to find out about his interested and focus about the location of the compound.

He looked at Bram and asked what the issue could be.

Bram looked around to each person on the team and then focused alternately on Jeffrey and Erica.

He began by stating that he cherished his freedom. He made the point that the breakthrough he was working on would affect the entire world. He went on to state that changes needed to take place if he was to continue his work.

Bram stood up and described how he envisioned the breakthrough being managed. It would be managed similar to the joint space station or Antarctica. It should be a concerted effort by a team made up of representatives from all the major countries of the world.

Bram sat down and asked if such a team could be formed.

Jeffrey looked to Erica and saw her face was a livid red. It seemed clear to him that she did not think much of Bram's vision.

He in turn stood. He looked at each team member and asked each to state their opinion of Bram's proposal.

Elizabeth was first to support the idea. Then the entire team supported Bram's approach.

Ok, I will pursue this program change with my superiors. However, I would like to reserve the right to time the sharing of any breakthrough so how and the timing of the information can be planned and controlled.

Now what is the fixation about knowing the location of the compound? You have driven Erica crazy with this constant request.

Jeffrey sat and looked at Bram.

Bram looked across at Erica.

He asked her how hard would it be to ask someone to meet her if she didn't know where she was.

It would be impossible she blurted out but what the hell does that have to do with your request.

Bram leaned back as she leaned across the table as if to grab him.

He looked at Jeffrey and asked him the same question.

Then he looked at the rest of the team and asked them as well.

Elizabeth smiled.

She stood and took a piece of paper and made two round spots on it. She then slowly folded the paper, so the two spots met. She pointed out that she was able to do it because she knew where each point was located. It required her to know the location, so she could properly Fold the paper. She went on to say everyone should think of the paper as the fabric of Space.

Erica slapped the table and shouted, "Why the hell didn't you just say so?"

Bram knew he could have made a similar point, but he had wanted to bring the issue of how the project was managed to a head. He also knew that he didn't need to know the location at all.

He stood and stated that now it was time to talk about freedom. He was not going to continue to work on the concept and had not for as many days as they had been in the compound.

He stated that the team should be free to come and go as they desired. He made the point that top security was provided to many people who were doing much less important work.

"Who the hell do you think you are," Erica blurted out?

She looked to see if Jeffrey was as mad as she was and was surprised that he was completely relaxed.

Jeffrey remained seated, but he was nodding in agreement.

He let the team know he agreed on both points. He asked the team to leave the room. He asked Bram to stay.

Jeffrey looked from Bram to Erica.

He made the observation that the two of them seemed to interact like oil and water and that it was clear to him that the technical side of the project did not need overseeing.

Bram would lead that part of the project.

Erica would manage the project resources and logistics of the effort.

The three of them would have weekly meetings to ensure a successful outcome for the effort.

Erica stood and left the meeting room without saying a word. She went out to the plane that would take her back to the DC area.

Jeffrey stayed to verify that Bram would continue his work in earnest.

Bram agreed but highlighted that they had not set up a work plan that would lead beyond the invention of the hardware to implement the breakthrough. He needed assurance that he would be involved all the way through the first use of the space-time Fold capability.

Chapter 2: Elizabeth

Elizabeth had given Bram a squeeze on the shoulder and winked at him as she left the meeting room.

She had covered the bullshit about needing to know his location to do any of the work he needed to do.

She was also aware of the ton of work he had been doing in building a variety of electronic control systems.

She might not understand much of what he was doing but she was certain that he was making progress. His behavior and attitude indicated that he was moving steadily ahead. His private workshop was a series of tabletop experiments.

Bram had invented a magnetron like honeycombed chamber that created the space time Fold.

Interacting with Bram made her wish she was forty years younger. She would have loved to be one of the people that would make the first trip to some distant star.

If she were forty years younger, she would certainly have been vying with the young helicopter pilot for his heart.

The daily conversations they engaged in were all focused on the ethics and impact of the ability to instantly leap across hundreds and thousands of light years.

Bram was of the view that such an action should be done in unison with all the people of earth.

He was keenly aware that his technological leap would leave the current development of the space program in the same position as the discontinuity the advent of the car created for the buggy makers.

Tremendous financial business crashes would occur. People at all levels would suffer. He felt those at the bottom of the ladder would suffer the most.

He had shared with her that he would not disclose the mathematics and the method of folding the fabric of space until a global approach was agreed to.

Even then he would try to limit the scope that would be shared.

A balanced, secure global group like the United Nations Security Council would need to be formed. He doubted the countries of the world could come to an agreement in time to be part of the implementation of the Fold capability.

They would need to come together to guide the long-term implementation of Fold destinations and potentially the interactions with intelligent life that might be discovered.

He had also expressed his concern about the actions various companies and countries might take to either gain access to or to gain control of the effort.

He was not sure Jeffrey and Erica were ready for such an onslaught. He placed himself in the too naïve to know what to do category.

The question Bram had posed for her was if Jeffrey wielded enough power?

Elizabeth had come to one realization.

Bram was the most disciplined and fair individual she had ever met.

Thinking about Bram took Elizabeth back to her days on Coochiemudlo Island in Australia.

She and her husband had lived there for twenty very pleasant years.

The Island was in Moreton Bay and was shielded from the Pacific by several larger islands.

Ron Mueller

Her morning swims were invigorating. Her daily morning and evening walks were soothing, and they provided time to think and ponder.

She was the typical Australian pad-old lady. Her husband went to work each day and expected his breakfast, lunch, and dinner ready and waiting when he walked through the door.

Twenty years of living with her mate had taken a toll on her. She had fought back and developed herself by reading the classics. She then continued her mental journey into exploring the sciences.

Her husband had stayed mentally where they both had started their union. He came home one afternoon and demanded a steak instead of the soup and salad she had prepared.

She complied and prepared steak, fried onions, and asparagus. She ate her soup and salad. He got up from the table after only eating half of what he had served himself.

He told her the food tasted terrible as he sat down in his recliner.

After clearing the table and cleaning the kitchen she came into the study to see if he wanted coffee or tea.

She discovered that he had passed away while sitting in his recliner.

She called the police. She did not know what else to do.

She immediately felt liberated, and she always felt guilty that she celebrated his death as the day of her freedom.

The year after his death she entered the University of Southern Queensland. She sold her home of twenty years and rented one on Fleet Street in Toowoomba. She bought the home based on its location. She was within an easy bicycle ride through the Japanese garden to the university. She would not need to own a car. She wanted to grow her mind and to live a simple life.

Her move of a little over one hundred fifty kilometers might as well have been a move of a thousand miles.

She went from being a pad-old lady to a reborn old lady of forty-eight.

She was at last free to pursue her own way. This thought did not escape her. Even though she had been comfortable and able to pursue her mental growth, she had been living an empty life. She recognized that it lacked a clear purpose.

Her educational goals were like a cross-stitched scarf.

On the one hand, she enjoyed the penetration of the minds psyche and intellect. She marveled at how the mind functioned and ticked and the personality each person developed to protect the being that was sculptured by the choices they either made willingly or were pressed into making based on their fear.

She had concluded that fear was the prime lever that formed a person's personality and guided many of their actions.

Her interest in the expansion of mankind into space and the science involved with astronomy and space drew her into the cross-stitch of the fabric she was weaving for herself.

This fabric was a mix of studies in many fields. Her advisors did not know how to advise her. It was clear to her that she was a student anomaly to her advisors.

She earned a Bachelor of Science degree in Spatial Engineering.

She was not satisfied. She went on to get a master's degree in Phycology.

She then applied to the most prestigious schools around the globe.

She was surprised by her aggressive approach.

She did not really expect to break into the next upper tier of universities.

Several months went by and just when she was about to look for work, she was surprised to get accepted to Oxford. She must have read the acceptance letter at least twenty times.

Each time she would laugh and hold the letter up and shout.

It was a shout of victory.

It was a shout against her fears.

Elizabeth realized her move to England and attending Oxford would deplete her finances.

She feared becoming destitute.

She began to write and submit articles in hopes of selling them to various publications. She hoped to make a small living to finance her PhD.

Her submittal to the Quarterly Journal of the Royal Astronomical Society was accepted!!!

The submittal was for a series of articles focused on the ethics of travel by humans into the vast areas of space.

This was more than she had hoped for. It would not pay her way, but it would give her more credibility as a published author.

She submitted articles to at least twenty additional magazines. She was accepted by at least a half dozen. She was able to establish a credible story arc that was accepted by each of the magazines. Each had a slightly different slant. Each flowed easily from her fingers and to her typewriter.

Each magazine provided a small but steady income that together was a significant income that made her quest for her PhD a much surer and comfortable journey.

She sold the possessions she could and gave the rest away. She left Australia and made the move halfway around the world to England. She had only one large chest and a small suitcase with her.

She arrived at the city of Oxford. Oxford was a city of almost ninety thousand and had a vibrant environment that was a mix of about forty percent factory working people and forty percent university students and the remainder in various supporting office and store work functions.

She learned that the university was teaching as far back as 1096, making it the oldest university in the English-speaking world and the world's second-oldest university in continuous operation.

She also learned that the University of Oxford was spread throughout Oxford. It did not have a centralized campus.

Elizabeth rented an apartment that was close to and convenient to the parts of the University she would be attending. She purchased a new bicycle and then began her pursuit of her PhD.

A short time later, Elizabeth was completely surprised by being chosen by the Royal Astronomical Society to receive a grant that covered her expenses. The grant was like found gold. It made her life that much easier.

She continued to publish and to explore the concepts and implications on human space travel. She was able to consolidate all her writing into a single manuscript that was more than five hundred pages long.

It became a best seller among the scientific community. This meant it sold at least a thousand copies. It did not, however, pay her living expenses. She knew she had been very lucky to have received a grant. And it did get her invited to several scientific conferences. The conferences in turn made her name recognized in the world of science.

It took her several years to earn her PhD. With her PhD in hand, she became a guest lecturer. She traveled to Amsterdam where she lectured for a year.

Then it was on to MIT where in the second year there, NASA approached her to engage the NASA leadership in a series of discussions on the ethics of human space travel and the risk posed on the persons sent out into space. The offer was not employment but came with a significant stipend. The stipend was large enough and renewable on a yearly basis that she would be set for life.

Elizabeth accepted. It seemed she would be spending time with people interested in the same field as herself. She was not exactly clear about her role, but it seemed that her book was the reason for the offer. She thought more highly about her book after that. In the end it had paid for all of her effort in writing it.

It was Jeffrey who had made the offer. He engaged with her in the topics covered in her book and seemed to be deep into the concepts presented. She enjoyed his perspective and was impressed with his passion for the topic.

She spent a great deal of time over breakfast discussions with him. He sponsored several workshops with a variety of government leaders. A few weeks later Jeffery asked her to be on a team working on the topic of folding time and space. She had no clue how or what the topic entailed but she was willing to be part of the effort. She did wonder where in the world Jeffrey had come up with that concept.

Elizabeth came back to the present. She had just met Bram. It was clear he was being forcefully recruited and that everything about the team Jeffrey had pulled quickly together had been aimed at him. She was about to leave the meeting room. She knew Bram was in a trap. She wanted to help him.

She made a comment to Jeffrey about his personal quest and that of the ethics of the situation.

She continued to look at Jeffrey and made the simple statement.

"Let's have breakfast and discuss the ethics of this meeting."

The look on Jeffrey's face let her know he understood her message to him.

Chapter 3: Project Control

Jeffrey sat calmly as he watched the team members leave the meeting. He understood Catherine's comment and its implication. The many breakfast discussions on the ethical concerns associated with individual countries trying to use space travel and technology to gain the upper hand on the politics of the earth grew in fertile ground. He had wondered and worried about this from the beginning of his assignment.

Bram had clearly stated that this project was beyond the boundary of any one country. It must be a global effort. He felt the same. He had come to that conclusion some time ago. He had not acted on in because it was unclear how he could clear the formidable barriers he clearly saw ahead.

It was clear Erica was not listening. For her it was a matter of control, of being in-charge. It was "her" project. She was not looking at the larger longer term as it applied to the world.

Jeffrey was about to make a radical change. He was not sure Erica would accept the change. She was a hard-charging individual. Hopefully, she was still flexible enough to accept a role that had less overall control but was essential to the success of the effort.

He gave Bram new respect for how patient and methodical he had been to bring the issue out in the open. He hoped Bram would be as effective in making the effort a global one.

Jeffrey thought about himself. He in fact had folded his time and space.

He had grown up in the German section of Shanghai.

He had played in a time that no longer existed. He had gone to school a few city blocks from his home. The family's living quarters where above his father's shoe shop. They never had many material goods, but they ate well, and he played with friends out in the street in front of his father's shoe shop.

His mother insisted on him eating breakfast and then he went to school.

His favorite eatery was the noodle shop less than a half block from home. He would come to the noodle shop for lunch and then return for dinner at home.

Looking back, he thought of it as a great way to have grown up.

His mother had insisted on and enforced a rigorous study regime. He got away with doing little work with his father by claiming the need to study. His mother always backed him up.

It worked. He was the number one student in his high school class.

He received a scholarship to attend the University of Shanghai. He was good at book work and excelled but he had no clue what he wanted to do. Once again, his mother's guidance, to get a degree that could make good money, paid off. He graduated top of his class with an Engineering degree.

His engineering degree opened the door to go to work for a Global Western company. Their salary offer had been four times what any Chinese company offered.

He had changed his name from 杰佛瑞 (Jié fó ruì) to its western equivalent, Jeffrey

The teamwork, fair treatment, culture, and the attitude of the people in the company invigorated him. He excelled and went smoothly and consistently upward.

He had assignments in the US, Europe and then back to China as a Vice President.

He ran out of corporate ladder to climb. The work became less enjoyable, the environment much more political and the people around him seemed desperate and not motivated by their work or environment. They were not having fun. He was beginning to wonder about his own motivation.

He again folded time and space and made the leap away from the corporate ladder to his current position at NASA.

He had been aided by the desire of the US government to diversify their leadership. He realized it was proving to be a very challenging leap. He was on a slippery slope and needed both spiked ice boots, ice hammers and someone to hold his safety line.

He hoped that Bram would be that someone.

He looked at Erica and saw the same desperate need to succeed he had seen in the corporation he had left. She wanted to feel the surge of power when she was in command. He felt a little sad for her. The need for power usually preceded a fall.

He looked at Bram and recognized a person who had total confidence in his actions and was centered on fundamental principles of honesty, integrity, and the belief that everyone was valuable.

Bram was fighting the system of secrecy and confinement.

Jeffrey was sure he would win.

Jeffrey looked back and forth between the two. He said, "let's make some changes."

Both Erica and Bram looked at him in silence.

He asked Bram how he wanted the project to be organized. He could see Erica's face go red in anger.

Bram looked at Erica and carefully thought through his next words.

He had nothing against her.

She was smart, capable, and very aggressive.

He wanted her to see that there was more to the work they did than who was in control.

He began by surfacing the need for global participation. He verbally speculated that getting participants from the various countries would be a monumental task. It would require someone who would recognize the attempt to place spies that would be recommended with the legitimate placement of top scientific talent.

He stated that it would take someone that would confront those who were not honest or not acting with the true intent to make the project a success. The intrigue and the political machinations would be a challenge for anyone, and it would take someone who had a tough backbone, commitment to success and who would make the tough calls.

Bram pointed out that Erica had such capabilities. He went on to say that she would be the perfect person to negotiate with each of the world's country representatives.

He continued by saying she would also be the perfect person to stand the onslaught of the news media. She would be the best public face the project could possibly field.

Bram then looked at Jeffrey and made the point that he too would be in the spotlight on the world stage and would need to back Erica. The two of them would need to collaborate and negotiate and maneuver the politics of the entire program.

Jeffrey would need to face the internal US government challenges while Erica would need to face the global challenges.

He then recommended Elizabeth as the person to manage the technical and scientific team. She would be a tremendous asset as the three of them took on the world.

He saw the look of surprise in both Jeffrey's and Erica's faces. He knew they had been expecting that he would name himself as the leader of the technical team.

He smiled, nodded, and said, "I want to be left alone to accelerate the program through my discoveries." I don't need help. I need support.

I will need a top project manager to ensure the hardware and equipment for the project come together in record time.

I will need technical help in the field of electronic hardware and in the field of sensors and data gathering and analysis but only when I ask for it.

I don't want to participate in meetings to discuss the details that need to get done. My mind dies in such meetings.

I need the space to maneuver and experiment. I don't want to wait for approval of my actions. I want to make and prove the breakthroughs and then get on with improving them.

Jeffrey looked at Erica and asked, "What do you think?"

He then went silent and waited for a response.

Erica looked across the table at Bram. She came to the realization that her feelings and understanding had just changed.

She had a new respect for Bram.

She thought he had wanted her job. Instead, he had promoted her into the most visible role. It was a role she was already looking forward to and she was already trying to figure out how to make it a success.

She realized that she had just experienced a life change and undergone some life-changing personal growth in this new understanding of the environment and the people around her.

Tears came to her eyes. She stopped to wipe her eyes.

She nodded and thanked Bram for recognizing her as the person who could make the team into a global one.

She quietly said she would be honored to do just that.

Jeffrey looked back and forth at the two.

The world had also changed for him. He felt they now had a team.

He felt a sense of relief.

Perhaps the oil and water aspects of the two could be leveraged to enhance the chances of project success. He knew the hurdles ahead were high, but he now had confidence that together they would clear them.

He stood and extended his hand to Erica and thanked her for expanding her vision.

He thanked Bram for his persistence and his global vision for the project. He called for a lunch break and called for a meeting of all site personnel after lunch.

Jeffrey walked out of the meeting and located Elizabeth. He wanted to have a brief conversation with her to make sure she agreed to lead the technical team. It would mean a little more work on her part, but the technical direction would be mostly in Bram's hands.

He invited Elizabeth to lunch where he shared the outcome of the meeting with Bram and Erica.

Elizabeth was not surprised and was pleased with Bram's view of the future direction of the break-through Fold effort. She agreed to her role in the short-term.

The long-term role was questionable. As the team grew it seemed that she would need additional help.

Jeffrey assured her she would have a proper support staff to handle all the requirements for the team.

To Jeffrey, lunch tasted wonderful. He would later remember that feeling and realize he could not recall what he ate.

Later after lunch, Jeffrey approached the podium and looked out at all the site personnel. There were somewhere around thirty military personnel with duties of providing services, guarding the base, and up keeping the one helicopter assigned to the base.

He knew Amy as the pilot of the helicopter.

Bram had shared her desire to be an astronaut. Bram had also asked that she be recommended to be in the next class.

Jeffrey had agreed to make it happen.

He marveled that it took so many people to support a technical team of only four people. He shrugged his shoulders when he thought about the additional set of people back in Washington.

He looked at Bram and realized there was only one person that they all looked to for success.

This realization put one more action he would need to take.

As tight as the attempt to isolate Bram had been, he was not protected properly. He would need night and day bodyguards. Jeffrey decided he would immediately approach the FBI for such help.

He looked around and shared that some changes were going to occur. In the short term the site would continue to function as it had.

Jeffrey made the point that Marine Major Edward Sharp would retain all his current responsibilities.

No changes were expected in that arena.

He announced Elizabeth's change in role but did not mention the broader changes. He needed to evaluate and come up with how the team was going to function. These changes were going to come out later. He had lots of organization redesign work to do before making any observable changes.

He thanked everyone for the great job they were doing.

He then asked Elizabeth to say a few words.

Amy was sitting in the first row. She sensed that much more than putting Elizabeth in charge of the technical team was happening. She looked over at Bram only to see that he was wearing his poker face. This was all she needed to know that there was more.

She made up her mind to somehow corner him and find out the real scoop.

She would get it out of him when he went out on his next desert walk. He was due for his last walk the following day.

She intended to sit with Einstein and Bram. She would enjoy the morning sunrise, scratching Einstein behind the ears and while listening to Bram explain what was happening

Chapter 4: Breakthrough

Time slowed to a crawl, slower that a snail inching its way along a wet garden steppingstone.

The meetings had come out better than he had expected. Change was in the air.

Bram went to watch the sunrise from the perch on top of his boulder. Einstein, his pet mouse, came out to sit with him and listen to his explanation of how the meeting had progressed.

Periodically Bram would credit Einstein for helping him clarify what had been accomplished and how the project should proceed.

Einstein seemed to understand and would turn his head when asked a question.

The heading for today's hike was three sixty degrees clockwise. Each compass degree represented a calendar day. This was his one full year at the facility.

Getting agreement to have the program become a global effort made the morning seem to be more peaceful. He was ready to attack his work with more vigor and knew that he would make the breakthroughs he still needed to make.

Jeffrey had let him know that agreement on making the effort a global one had been accepted but it would be carefully controlled so it would not affect the effort.

Erica had enthusiastically engaged in getting the bios of potential team members from countries around the world.

He thought all seemed to be going well.

Bram's discussions with Amy had gone to a deeper level. She shared that she had been accepted into training as an astronaut. She had expressed mixed feelings about leaving her current assignment, but she was still eager to become an astronaut and get a chance to go into space.

Bram took his hike heading on the three hundred sixty degree on the compass. An hour later Amy landed the helicopter to take him back.

On their return, Bram invited Amy to watch the sunrise with him the next morning.

Bram walked slowly to his office. He was eager to continue his work but once again the rest of the day went by at a snail's pace. He had the breakthrough and had a working model.

He had figured out the physical design of the transmitter. It looked like a honey combed magnetron. He powered it up and the combination of the oscillating chambers and the enveloping magnetic field created a Fold that linked two special three dimensional coordinates. The chambers dimensions and their oscillating frequencies translated his mathematical equations into the magnetic space time Fold.

Amy walked away wondering about the timing of the sunrise invitation. She had shared the fact that she was going to accept the invitation to be trained as an astronaut.

She spent the day cleaning and re-cleaning her helicopter. She had no idea what Bram had in mind, and it made her nervous. She knew she was attracted to Bram but was not ready for any type of personal commitment.

Bram spent the day preparing for the next morning. He encapsulated two apples and two bunches of grapes in two clear plastic bubbles. He set them aside and completed the work on the two boxes that to the eye of an observer would appear to be square aluminum suitcases.

The content of these suitcases held the electronics and magnetron he had personally designed and had the lab machinist and computer specialist build.

The following morning would be his maiden test of being able to Fold time and space.

He wondered what the team would later think about his minimalist approach to testing a world changing breakthrough.

In the late afternoon, he set the two bubbles, one on each suitcase and left his lab.

He met the rest of the team for dinner. The conversation escaped him. He was wrapped in the fabric of time and space.

He was living tomorrow.

He knew it would be hard to sleep.

Early the next morning he walked by the lab and briefly looked in. What he saw excited him. His system seemed to be acting as he expected. He was hoping to see success at the destination of his morning walk.

He walked on past the lab to meet Amy.

Then together, they walked to the boulder where he hoped the verification of his efforts would be waiting.

He was having trouble controlling his breathing and his pace. This was the moment he had worked so hard to get to.

This was the proof of his many months and years of driving himself both mentally and physically.

Amy walked into the empty lobby and gave a small groan. It was five in the morning. She was not a morning person. She hoped Bram would not keep her waiting in her morning misery.

She smiled as he walked in on the tail of her feeling sorry for herself. He seemed wide awake and chirpy. How that was possible was beyond her.

She could see excitement on his face. She hoped that she was not going to be ice water on his good feelings.

Bram walked in and gave Amy a hug. This was the first time he had greeted her in this manner. It was how the team greeted each other every morning.

It was not until he had done it that he worried about whether it was a proper greeting.

He decided to get up to the boulder before saying or doing anything else. He headed for the door with a follow me over his shoulder.

The star's twinkling and the Cheshire moon provided meager light for the ten-minute walk through the dark. Once on the trail, Bram could make the walk with his eyes closed.

This morning, he was having trouble making his way.

He was on his three hundredth and sixty first trip along the trail.

This time it was different.

What was ahead would change how mankind controlled the world, controlled travel in space and across the Universe. It would most certainly change his life.

This time he was straining to see what was on the boulder. Finally, he could make out the top of the boulder.

He came to an abrupt stop. He asked Amy what she saw.

Two balls floating in the air was her reply.

Her response was what he hoped to hear.

He took her hand and walked up to the boulder and helped her up. She took a seat to one side of the two bubbles. He got up on the other side.

Amy commenced to pass one hand under the bubble on her side. She asked how it was possible that they were floating in the air.

Bram moved his hands under and around the bubbles.

This was a first for him and he too wondered how the bubbles remained in their position. It was the position and elevation he had specified in the space time location of the algorithms running on the computers located in each of his suitcases in his lab.

How the two bubbles floated in the air would require more analysis on his part. He pushed on his bubble and got it to move but when he let go it returned to its original position.

Bram Nielson Collection

Bram told Amy that one bubble was for her and one for him.

He opened his bubble and took a big bite of the apple that was inside.

Amy continued to look at her bubble.

All she could think about was how it was possible.

What was the trick to make the bubbles float in thin air?

How had the bubbles been placed here?

She wanted to ask these questions, but she knew that Bram was enjoying his success at getting the bubbles to this location.

Bram told Amy to enjoy her breakfast fruit.

He told her that she was the first to witness the breakthrough he had been working on.

He would tell her more right after the sunrise and after greeting Einstein.

Amy was surprised at the globe holding an apple and a bunch of grapes. She twisted open her globe and popped a large purple grape into her mouth and let the sweet juice infuse her mind. She smiled and went to think, "her disoriented and twisted mind." She felt relief when it struck her that it was not about romance, but it was about science.

She looked at Bram and knew she was looking at a genius. One that seemed to care and look out for all the people around him. One that took the greatest breakthrough that could possibly be made as a moment to share with a lowly helicopter pilot.

She watched the sun slowly break above the horizon and felt the warmth of the first rays on her face.

She scooted away from Einstein as he came out of the hole at the base of the boulder and quickly climbed to sit between them but really next to Bram.

Bram took a napkin from his pocket and opened it. The remains of a cookie drew Einstein to the napkin. He thanked Einstein for helping him with the breakthrough.

Bram turned to look at Amy.

He repeated her desire to go into space. He then made the point that he would need a pilot when bubbles like the ones holding their apples and grapes took people across the universe.

He told Amy she could be that pilot and told her to go get the astronaut training but to come back to help design and then to pilot the bubbles that would cross the vast distances of space.

Amy was overwhelmed. She also wondered how she would be selected to be the pilot of such a craft. There would be many candidates that would out rank her for the job.

She asked Bram why he was so certain that she would be able to be the pilot of such a craft.

Bram understood her concern about being able to come back as that pilot of the first across the Universe spacecraft.

He stated that he would determine the passengers and crew of the first few trips across the universe. If she wanted, she would be the pilot on one of the two initial spaceships to cross folded space.

Amy sat trying to take everything in. She had been worried about some romantic advance but was now being rewarded for their current friendship with a future offer to be among the first to cross space.

She was also aware that Bram had let her be the first to witness his success.

This was more than she had ever expected.

She scooted over to sit next to Bram and gave him a hug as she thanked him.

She then said she was going to leave him with Einstein, and she would go to get her bird ready to pick him up.

She was going to go to her helo and scream her head off.

Her world had taken on a new meaning.

She was having trouble breathing as she stumbled back to her domain.

Ron Mueller

Chapter 5: Participants and Master Plan

The tension in the room was as strong as black phantom pepper sauce on a bleeding steak. It burned just to breathe the air.

Bram looked from one strained face to another. Meetings like this had been going on for months and little progress was being made. He had now sat through two of these.

He had no clue how Erica had survived so long.

He had received a request for him to join her in handling the situation. This had been a great surprise to him. He learned that more than two thousand names had been proposed. Every country had at least one entry. The larger countries had multiple candidates.

Erica had no clue on how to select the right candidates. She had been told select between fifteen to twenty candidates. She had finally concluded that she needed someone to help her reduce the number of candidates.

Her meeting with Bram had at least reduced the stress to where she was not contemplating shooting herself.

Bram seemed to think the situation was normal. Maybe for him but she was at the end of her rope. The representatives from the various countries were at best pushing hard and at worst they were just plain assholes.

Bram laughed when Erica vented her frustration. He made the point that he had been certain that he did not want the job of selecting the candidates but that he would be glad to help figure out how to evaluate and select the best candidates.

Bram had not only spent two days in unpleasant and contentious meetings, but he had also reviewed the list of candidates and was no more able to make selections than Erica.

Since the candidates were from the fields of astronomy, physics, math, and a variety of other related sciences he decided to get the whole team involve. He went one step farther and put Amy on the list of people who would review the candidates.

He did not anticipate her knowing anyone on the list, but it provided a way for her to be noticed.

He knew that would be important later.

Bram anticipated the rest of the team would have some say about certain candidates.

He sent his request for total team participation to Elizabeth.

When Elizabeth received the request, she immediately called the team together. The team agreed to take a shot at the more than two thousand names.

They discussed the request.

Both Mallica and Marcus confessed to not knowing any of the names on the list.

Elizabeth admitted she knew only four names on the list and had heard some information about another dozen.

The three of them agreed to split up the list and review the resumes, look at publications and the exposure on the web.

They agreed on Bram's suggested priority process.

First, they had to get candidates from all the countries on the UN security council.

Then any candidate that had been published in their field.

Then one from each of the five major religions.

Then one from each country by population size.

Bram also wanted; a planetary scientist, an earth scientist, a helio-physicist, an astrophysicist, a chemist, a biologist, an astronomer, an engineer, and a historian.

Elizabeth asked if there were any other consideration that Bram might have that could make the selection process a little more complicated.

He laughed and replied that if he thought of any others, he would let her know.

Amy received Bram's request and wondered how she had been selected to review the list of candidates. He must certainly know that she would not know anything about the candidates. She also noted that he had copied most of the NASA and Army command.

She realized that he had put the spotlight on her. She had grown up as a Lutheran and submitted her long-time pastor's name for the religious representative position.

She thanked Bram and gave him her one candidate as part of her reply. She made a point of mentioning her commitment to space and to her continued desire to complete her astronaut training. She copied the distribution that Bram had used.

Thank you, Bram, went through her mind as she pressed the send key.

Jeffrey reviewed all the messages with a focus on the expanded team. He believed Bram was orchestrating the situation so that the choices made would have a solid selection process that could be explained.

He was surprised at how well Erica and Bram were getting along. He was aware of the strain Erica had been under.

Bram's approach had provided an explainable means of managing the process.

He faced a similar storm within the US political and military hierarchy. Every agency and military branch wanted control of the Fold program.

He was keeping them all at bay by leveraging his connection with President Natorly.

He would keep Bram in mind when it came time to break down the next barrier.

He asked his administrative support to set up a meeting with Bram and Erica. He needed help and would explore his next steps with them.

Elizabeth cursed quietly under her breath. Bram had set them up with a lot of work. She smiled and asked Mallica and Marcus about their progress in prioritizing the list of candidates.

Mallica complained that she had spent more time than she had expected in researching each candidate.

Marcus just said ditto.

Elizabeth echoed Marcus.

After a quick discussion, she agreed to send their composite list to Bram. It added some depth to the information, but it said that Bram was to make the final selection.

Jeffrey's requested meeting was a Saturday morning breakfast meeting. There were no weekdays that worked. His support had found a secure location on the base. The normal kitchen crew would cater the breakfast.

He was sure it had been a long week for all of them and felt some guilt about a Saturday morning meeting.

Guilt yes, but the need was great.

He met Bram and Erica in the empty parking lot. He apologized about taking part of their weekend and then led the way to the breakfast meeting.

Jeffrey suggested they eat breakfast first and get into the meeting afterwards.

He noted that conversation was non-existent, and he wondered how the meeting would flow.

Bram Nielson Collection

Bram had reviewed the recommendations and finalized the list as best he could. He was ready to layout the way forward as he saw it. He hoped that Erica had worked through an initial master plan for the massive work that remained to be done.

When the after-breakfast coffee and tea was set up, he stood and after filling his teacup said he was ready to share his participant selection, to share a rough work logic and a list of things that needed to get done for the project to move forward.

Erica was relieved. She wanted the participant selection to end. She wanted a normal project with logical actions and steps that she could manage.

Anything to bring the chaos to an end.

Bram left the planning wide open for her to step into.

Her response to Bram's statement that he had a participant selection list was that she was all ears.

Jeffrey echoed Erica.

Bram expressed the fact that he was glad to be able to close the participant list. He handed out the list of seventeen names from twelve countries to Jeffery and Erica.

He also stated that he did not need any of them for the Folding of time and space effort. The global team was a way to engage the other countries but until the Fold effort became a reality and was ready for sharing the global team should not be brought together.

He noted the surprised look on both Erica's face and on Jefferies face.

He apologized and said that he still held the view that the Fold program should be a global effort, his participation of selecting a global team had convinced him that it would just add chaos to the program.

His current team was all he needed.

Bram then suggested they develop a plan to build the space bubbles, the data collection, and analysis systems that would be required.

He highlighted the bubble construction as perhaps the critical path but that was something that Erica needed to handle.

Once again Bram surprised Erica. He was very clear on his capabilities and what he preferred his focus to be.

He said that delaying setting up the Global group freed her up to do what she liked best.

Erica was surprised with the sudden change in direction but immediately agreed and felt a sense of relief. She stood and walked to the white board and began asking the questions that would lead to a project master plan that would ensure a winning logic to guide the remainder of the effort.

Jeffrey shook his head and thanked Bram for simplifying his world and wished that he would have done it earlier.

Bram agreed that he too should have reached that decision earlier, but he had shared his conclusion as soon as he had come to it.

He then responded to Erica's questions and identified the need for two plastic bubbles each to house twelve people. They would need to have the supplies to sustain the twelve crew members for a year.

Four members would be data collectors. They would manage and maintain sensors and telescopes in the visual, the infrared and x ray spectrum.

Four would be data analysist.

One would be an instrument maintenance specialist.

One would be in command.

The remaining two would be the pilot and co-pilot of the bubble.

A third system of data collection would be housed on Earth.

The additional selected participants would utilize the data for analysis. Some of them might or might not go out in the bubbles.

He looked at Jeffrey and let him know all was ready as soon as the bubbles were done. He would need to get his time-space Fold equipment enlarged to make a sufficiently large Fold and to move the bubbles to the Fold location.

Bram identified two support items. He needed a company that would work with him to test his extrapolation of the power required for his space-time folding equipment.

The other need was to design the transport bubble he envisioned.

Jeffrey asked Erica if she had enough to get started and would she work with Bram to get more detailed on his needs. She replied yes but she would need more people to get all the work done. She was especially worried about the time it would take to construct the bubbles.

Jeffrey looked at the draft work plan that Erica had put on the white board.

He pointed to several of the task items and had Erica put NASA, Boeing, and the Air Force next to them. If speed was required, he would see if he could leverage existing resources that were already contracted and active.

Jeffrey felt great about how the three of them were working together.

He highlighted that he would need to get an increase in his budget.

He thanked both Bram and Erica and suggested they meet again on the following Wednesday.

Chapter 6: Power

Bram could not determine the amount of power he would need to Fold space around the structures of the space vessels. The amount of power to simply move an apple and some grapes had blown the power supply. He went through his equations several times trying to figure it out how he could determine the power required.

He could not determine it mathematically.

He had decided to try moving different blocks of steel of specific sizes through a Fold and monitor the power draw for the series of folds. He would then have the data to determine the power supply the project would need. He was certain the power requirement would be extremely high. He needed to quickly learn just how high.

Bram looked out at the collection of steel blocks he had shipped in for his testing.

The first one was a one by one-foot cube.

The next was a three by three-foot cube.

The next was a ten-foot cube.

The largest was a thirty by thirty-foot cube.

Viewed from the side they looked like the base of an asymptotic curve. This he thought was an appropriate view.

Once he was able to move all these cubes from one point to another, he would have the data to determine the mathematics to design the actual space time bending power unit and magnetron units on the scale he would need to move his plastic bubble spaceships.

His concern was how steep the asymptotic power curve would be.

His new lab was located outside of the Seattle area in an abandoned National Reserve helicopter hanger. To Bram it seemed like a huge facility. His steel blocks seem like tinker toys relative to the size of the hangar. He later learned it was not the size of the hangar that was of any concern, but the size of the power supplied to the hangar.

He was alone in this endeavor. He did not know how to engage someone to help him.

Well, he was not alone, he had a crew of twenty technicians working on building, the transport power supplies and a local machine shop making the space Fold magnetrons. He was having successively larger power supplies and space Fold magnetrons made for each size of steel cubes

Two bodyguards now accompanied and shadowed him day and night. There were four bodyguards. Two for the daylight hours and two for the nighttime.

Jeffrey had informed him that there was credible intelligence that numerous groups, countries, and companies were looking for him and that several subversive groups had interest in kidnapping him. This information was troubling to Bram, but he was focused on getting his space bubbles powered.

The attempt to move the one by one-foot cube had blown the power supply and the site transformer for the hanger. His control unit was also toast.

That clearly demonstrated his lack of knowledge of the power draw.

The power company upgraded the substation by tripling it in size. Bram asked that his power supplies were also tripled in size.

The rest of his technical team had remained in the original desert location. He talked to them daily and was trying to get them to help in defining the power requirement.

Once a week the entire team lead by Elizabeth met to discuss their activities.

Bram, Erica, Elizabeth, and Jeffrey had a separate meeting each week to review the program master plan. Erica was keeping everything moving. She laughed and commented that Bram was creating the critical path by regularly blowing up his work.

It was not his work plan that he was blowing up. He was now being guided by the power company crew supervisor and being shown a whole substation that he had recently blown up. The power surge when he tried to create a Fold to move his three-foot block of steel through had not only blown out the substation but had blacked out the three surrounding counties.

The power company refused to set up the substation again. They suggested he find a site that was located near or at the power generation site that had the capacity to support his power needs.

Bram returned to his office and called Mallica and gave her the data from the first two experiments and asked her to calculate the power required for the ten by ten and the thirty by thirty-foot blocks of steel.

Mallica spent the entire night working on what the power requirement would be. She extrapolated that it would take at least one thousand megawatts.

Mallica qualified her estimate by stating the parameters for the asymptotic curve she had developed. She was not sure of the accuracy of her estimate. She feared it could be more and she did not know if the distance of the Fold would need more power.

Bram thought about this huge power requirement. He needed to be as close to the source of power generation as possible. He also needed to be isolated from the general public population centers.

He called Erica and requested a location that would allow him to use the output of an entire power plant with at least one thousand megawatts. He made the point that the power requirements might be even more for the crafts being built. He doubled the power request.

Bram was surprised at how fast Erica and her staff located a plant that had that much power. They settled on a site south of the Dalles hydroelectric plant on the Oregon side of the Columbia river. They would need to erect a new building, but it would be surrounded by at least two thousand megawatts. The dam provided power to a wide area but there were one thousand megawatts that was sold and flowed out on the grid. When the time came for the use for the power, the grid could adjust to cover it.

Erica called Jeffrey and assigned him the task of making the site available for the Fold project. She specified the building size, erection location and time to completion. She was confident Jeffrey could make it happen. She knew that he had a direct line to the NASA director and had visited the White House several times.

Jeffrey listened to Erica. He then put in a call to Bram, so he could hear for himself about the power need. Bram shared the experiences he had so far with blowing up substations and the fact that the power company had told him that the current location prohibited them from quickly giving the site any more power than they had made available.

Jeffrey then put in a call to the US Army Core of Engineers District Commander at the Dalles site. He asked who the final decision maker would be if he were asked to accept a project that might take all the output of the Dalles hydroelectric plant.

President Natorly was identified as the one needing to make the decision.

Jeffrey put in a call the John Morgan the NASA director. It would take both of them to convince the President. John would have to share the vision for NASA if this technology panned out. Jeffrey would share the Fold program objectives and share some of the specifics of what a Fold meant.

John listened as Jeffrey explained the need for the large amount of power required to Fold time and space. He went on to explain how much total power that would be needed was not yet clear. Jeffrey gave the current estimate to be two thousand megawatts to be continuously used during the time needed to see the mission through the Fold. He had doubled what Bram had told him.

John responded that the suggested location provided a good base and agreed that another two thousand megawatts should be installed as backup. The request would be for almost a billion dollars for the current location. A second location should also be included and be planned.

Jeffrey was surprised at how quickly John accepted the need and how quickly he planned to act. It was only a week later that they were set to meet with President Natorly. Jeffrey knew who the best person would be to convince the President.

The following week Jeffrey entered the White House meeting room and looked around the table. The entire cabinet was there. He had been asked to present the project to the group, but he had no clue how to communicate the details that would be needed to convince President and his team to support the project.

Bram walked in with him and took a seat beside him. Jeffrey stood and introduced himself. He proceeded to give a general introduction of the Fold project and then introduced Bram.

Those sitting around the table were silent and did not seem to understand and were not looking very supportive.

Bram knew that none of the people in the room understood the concept of Folding time and space. They certainly would fall asleep if he went into the math and science of the project. He had thought about how to communicate the need for the tremendous power to Fold time and space and had arranged that with the White House maintenance supervisor.

A demonstration would be the best way to get the support the program needed. He slowly and dramatically put his brief case on the table. He looked in the case at the bubbles placed in their holders. He took out a thick massive power cord and connected it to one that had been made available by the White House maintenance supervisor. He told everyone around the table to pay attention and reached into the brief case and pressed a button.

The lights in the room dimmed and flickered. A small bubble appeared and floated in front of President Natorly. He pointed at the bubble. Then he repeated the process two more times. Each time the lights flickered and dimmed. A bubble appeared in front of the Vice President, and the Chief of Staff.

He asked each of them to verify the bubbles were indeed floating in the air. The three did as requested. President Natorly pushed his with his finger and then let go. The bubble returned to its original position.

Bram asked each to grab the bubble and open it. He made the point that each bubble contained a candy kiss that was intended to persuade them to support the Fold program.

Bram took out a candy kiss for himself put it in his mouth. He stated that everyone in the room had just witnessed the process of folding time and space. He pointed out the dimming of the lights before each bubble had appeared. He explained that the bubbles had traveled from his briefcase through space to float in front of each person.

He then asked the White House maintenance supervisor to share the amount of power that had been consumed. The response was that a whole month of power had been consumed.

Bram smiled when President Natorly said his support could be had for one more candy kiss. He reached into the briefcase, placed a bubble in the appropriate location and pressed the button. The lights dimmed, and a bubble appeared in front of the President. Bram watched as the President passed his hand under and around the bubble.

Why doesn't gravity cause it to fall the President asked?

Bram answered that it was a great question and one for which he had no answer.

He volunteered that as soon as he solved that problem he would get back to him.

President Natorly looked around the table and said the project had all the support it would need. All resources of the US government would immediately be made available.

Jeffrey complimented Bram on his presentation. He then turned to the President and thanked him for his time and that funding was needed immediately to prevent the delay of the "Fold in Time" FIT project.

The reply that the funds would be released immediately to NASA pleased Jeffrey.

Bram was surprised at how quickly funding had been agreed to. A billion dollars seemed to be something that would take months to get.

On the way to the airport, Jeffrey complimented Bram on the way he had used the Fold breakthrough to get President Natorly to open the purse strings.

On his return to the west, Bram decided to go out to the new site and get the lay of the land. He would also go and check on the progress being made by Boeing on getting the bubbles built.

Amy learned from Elizabeth about Bram's funding success. She was close to the completion of her astronaut training. She would be one of two females in her class. Patricia Fleming, the other female candidate, had become a friend during the training. They had supported each other as each felt the bias against them by the male astronaut students in their class.

There were no scheduled space flights for them anywhere in the near future, so Amy asked Pat if she was interested in a side adventure. Pat asked what that might be. Once she learned of the specific details of the Fold project, she was not only interested she was eager to be included.

Bram recognized the ringtone on his phone and greeted Amy with their familiar greeting of *Babe.*

He stopped what he was doing and sat down. His bodyguards sat down on each side. They were in an empty field surrounded by power stations and overhead power lines. He listened to Amy and agreed to interview Pat.

He replied that he was planning to attend the astronaut graduation ceremony. He would interview Pat during his time at the graduation ceremony.

Bram stood up and thought about his relationship with Amy.

He really liked her but was she the one?

It was unclear to him.

He decided that time would tell. He looked around at the new location that would house the space bubbles and be the project's command center. He decided it was certainly secluded enough that any new construction would go unnoticed outside of the immediate community.

He returned to his Portland hotel and decided to drive up to the Boeing factory just south of Seattle.

He not only had bodyguards, but he was assigned a limo. He rode in back where he could relax.

Though he had planned to take in the view, he was soon asleep in the comfortable back seat.

Bram Nielson Collection

His two bodyguards sat up front. The four assigned to guard Bram took turns in their day and night coverage. Bram knew that the current set of bodyguards were temporary until he interviewed the potential long-term applicants. He got along with the current set, but they all had families in the DC area.

Bram was met by Jose Estrada the project manager for the construction and assembly of the two bubbles. Jose was accompanied by Ester Mannerly, Jose's NASA counterpart. She reported directly to John Morgan the NASA director.

Bram was informed that the four half shells for the space bubbles had just arrived and were being put into their assembly position at the very moment. He was led out to the assembly area. This was one of the locations where the Boeing 787's were assembled.

It was clear to Bram that two assembly locations were set up. The four-story plastic bubble halves were being placed into position. They were mounted above a very large forty by forty-foot square, low-slung platforms. The bubbles were held in place by two cables that suspended them at what would be the center of a wheel like living and work area.

Bram followed behind Jose and Ester as they led the way to the first assembly area.

Bram took in the crew of about twenty personnel. He learned they were immediately starting to install the telescopes and sensors that he had specified.

He walked over and examined the sensor and computer equipment. He asked how they had been obtained so quickly and learned that NASA had redirected them from the next four space shuttles.

Bram asked how they planned to move the spheres to the launch location.

Ester smiled and replied that she had been told that he would take care of that problem.

Bram laughed. He realized that would be a great way to test the Fold power requirements.

He asked that the co-ordinates for the very center of each bubble be determined and sent to him. Yes, he replied that he would take care of getting the spheres to the launch location.

Bram spent the rest of the day with Ester inspecting the bubbles and the equipment to be installed.

The three of them agreed to meet for dinner. Bram made sure that the dinner was for seven people. He was making sure his protection team was well fed. Bram enjoyed the dinner, and the genial conversation shared by all of them. He was pleased with the two of them having been selected to manage the assembly process.

He was headed for the airport and a night flight to Houston.

As he climbed into bed, Bram knew he was getting spoiled. He was on a private plane on the way to Amy's astronaut graduation. On any other airline it was called the red eye special. On this plane Bram figured it was just special.

His guilty feeling did not last long. Bram was almost immediately asleep

Ron Mueller

Chapter 7: Fold Pilots

Bram slept throughout the four-hour flight. He was awakened just prior to landing and took a seat. He looked out the window to see that the sun was threatening to come over the far horizon.

Bram did not feel even a bump as the plane landed. He complemented the pilots for the smooth as glass landing as he passed them on his way down the steps.

Bram looked up at the still visible stars. His watch showed it was five in the morning.

He was bracketed by bodyguards as he went to the waiting limo.

Bram learned that they had landed at NASA's private airport. It was not even shown on the normal Houston area map.

The driver commented that he and his partner would be with him during his stay. They drove to the Villa where he would stay. It was a three-bedroom furnished condo that had been recommended by John Morgan's support. The driver stayed behind the wheel, but his partner quickly stepped out to open the door of the limo and proceeded to get the bags out of the trunk.

Bram's guards talked briefly with the limo driver. Two of them got back into the limo. They were staying at a nearby hotel and would return in the evening.

Bram stopped long enough to thank the driver and his assistant. He asked their names and was told it was Jim and Joe. He again thanked them by name and then went into the condo.

Bram was impressed by the open feel of the condo entrance area. Two bedrooms opened to each side of the entrance hallway. The kitchen area was to one side of the hallway and the living room was on the other side. A third bedroom was to the right and a fourth bedroom was to the left.

Bram took the back-left bedroom. The two guards staying with him for the night each took one of the other bedrooms.

The sun was threatening to light up the far horizon and it was making the few clouds turn into pinkish yellow fluffs in the morning sky. Bram thought that it was the making of a wonderful day.

His two bodyguards entered and quickly checked out the apartment. Then they cleared Bram to go on his own.

He wandered through the suite to take in its layout. Once he had wandered around the suite, he stood looking out as the sun slowly rose on the far horizon.

The smell of fresh coffee reminded him that he had a busy day ahead. He was ready for a long hot shower and then he would go on to breakfast to meet Amy.

He was expecting a very hectic day.

The restaurant where he was to meet Amy and Pat for breakfast had a great view of the Gulf and when he entered it was empty. He and his guards had entered just as the restaurant opened and had selected the two tables that seemed to have the best view.

He ordered a pot of tea and some honey to sweeten it. He took in the view and when the tea arrived, he put in the honey and slowly stirred it. He sipped on the tea as he waited.

Bram came awake as he took in the two very good-looking women entering. One was Amy, her dark hair framed a calm and serene face. She looked very different in her current outfit versus the military garb he had always seen her in. Her friend, Pat, had long curly red hair, freckles and green eyes that immediately caught his attention. She too had the looks that would turn heads.

His two bodyguards and the four other persons now in the restaurant all stopped to look at the two women. Bram stood and waved to get the attention of the two.

After introductions they all sat down. After a brief discussion they ordered breakfast. Bram felt an immediate attraction for Pat. He took note that she was as direct and as confident in herself as Amy. The two were a contrast in looks and in mannerisms but both were stunning in their appearance

Bram put his evaluation of the two into a back mental compartment. They both impressed him.

Bram wanted to make sure of the schedule for the day and asked to go over it.

The graduating astronaut class had only six persons. The ceremony would be held at the NASA main training area at one in the afternoon and then there would be a dinner at the training center's director's home.

Bram had received his formal invitation more than a month ago and had sent in his acceptance.

He mentioned that he would attend with four bodyguards, and he hoped that it would not cause any problems.

He invited Amy and Pat for lunch at the Galveston waterfront. Amy accepted but Pat declined saying she had a couple of things to do before the graduation ceremony.

After breakfast Amy and Bram went to the NASA space center. There Bram followed the flow of the space program development. It was clear to him that his breakthrough was the next S curve of improvement in space technology. The current rocket technology would suffer the same fate as the horse and buggy when the automobile came on the scene or that the propeller plane faced when the jet engine was developed.

Bram listened to Amy describe her training routine. She shared that Pat had finished first in the class and she had finished third. He congratulated her on her performance and said that it qualified her to command one of the two, Fold, modules.

They returned from their walk and took seats facing the Gulf. They sat making small talk until it was time for lunch. After lunch they departed to the graduation.

Bram estimated that there were about fifty people attending the graduation and that the graduation class of six was greatly outnumbered. Half of the people attending were family and friends and the other half various officers, a state representative, and several sponsors for the astronauts.

Bram sat quietly and observed the reactions of each of the astronauts. He seemed to be Amy's only sponsor and that one of the state representatives was Pat's sponsor.

The ceremony lasted for about forty-five minutes. Afterwards there was some small talk among all the guests as they shared some hors d'oeuvres and drinks. The gathering did not last long. Except for the graduates, the rest of those attending did not know each other and were soon leaving from the gathering.

Bram walked with Amy and Pat out to the parking lot. They agreed to celebrate with a few drinks at a local night spot not far from the apartment that they shared.

The ten-minute drive to their apartment gave Bram time to contemplate on the accomplishment of the two women.

On the way to their nightspot, he heard them talking about the end of their training. They both commented on the fact that no space missions were planned, and they would probably be old ladies when the next one would occur.

Bram liked the fact that the background music at the nightspot remained low and allowed for small talk and periodic serious discussion. Part of Bram's discussion was Pat's interview. He was interested in her background and experiences.

Amy reminded them it was time to go to the Astronaut graduation dinner. Pat let out a small groan. She voiced the hope that it would not be too boring.

Bram stood up and led the way out to their waiting limo. He thought about Pat's comment about the dinner being boring. He knew that he would not be bored escorting the two of them.

Bram's limo took the three to the base commander's home. The limo easily held all of them in the spacious back seating area.

The dinner turned out to be a backyard barbeque. A cooling breeze kept the outdoor venue comfortable. The NASA training commander had selected only those close to the graduates to be invited.

John Morgan, NASA director gave a small speech about the future of space travel and the expectation he had of the new astronauts. He made the point that several of them would get a chance of a lifetime.

The dinner of steak, grilled shrimp, grilled asparagus and grilled corn with a mixed side salad and the backyard venue made for a more relaxed meal then Bram had anticipated. He made a point of sitting next to John, so he could request both Amy and Pat join the Fold team.

John expressed his concern in taking in rookies for the piloting.

Bram replied that independent of age or gender everyone was going to be a rookie. There were no Fold veterans. He pointed out that he was not sure what a Fold pilot would do.

John nodded and said he understood Bram's view, but the other two pilots he was recommending would be based on seniority and their performance in the NASA space program. He made the point that he was accepting a hot potato by naming the two women to be the pilots.

Bram said he understood and that having two long term NASA astronauts made sense. He was satisfied with the acceptance of the two astronauts he had requested.

Bram, Amy, and Pat were the last of the guests to depart the dinner. They thanked Major Wellington for choosing such a relaxing way to host the new astronauts.

Bram shook John's hand and reminded him of the request he had made.

His two guards and the limo drivers had discreetly enjoyed the backyard barbeque. The limo drivers commented that they had never attended an astronaut graduation, but they would try to be the drivers when Major Wellington again hosted such an event.

Bram made the comment that if he returned to Houston in the future, he would ask for them by name.

Bram wished he were staying another day, but he had arranged to go on to the East coast and meet with Jeffrey and Erica. He had also agreed to interview the FBI candidates that had volunteered for the role of being his permanent bodyguards.

He would then return to Seattle and meet with Ester and Jose to monitor the arrival and positioning of the main control and living quarters sections of the space bubbles. Together the three of them would make the acceptance inspection of those sections. The internal components of these sections were also arriving and would also need acceptance inspection.

Once on the plane, Bram ordered a ginger ale. He sat for a while thinking about Amy and Pat. He knew that in the future he would need to sort out his feelings about each.

After takeoff Bram walked to the back and got into bed. He knew he would need all the sleep he could get.

<u>Chapter 8 The First Fold</u>

For Bram, the months after the trip to Houston both flew and dragged by. He saw the work on the bubble as an Indy car going at breakneck speed around the track. He experienced the work on the Fold apparatus and equipment as moving at a snail's pace. The snail's pace was riddled with various and dramatic explosions as power supplies overheated when trying to move an object to a Fold coordinate. Bram was finally confronted by the Boeing power utility manager and informed that the power company would no longer deal with the surges that he was causing.

He resigned himself to wait to the time he would have access to enough power to complete his Fold transmission development.

Bram turned his attention to working with the crews of the two bubbles and began conducting simulated launch trials.

John kept his word to Bram. Amy and Pat had received their assignment by NASA to the Fold program. Two senior astronauts, Daryl Nazda and Harold Redat were teamed up with them as their backups. Bram instinctively assigned Pat and Daryl to Bubble 1 and Amy and Harold to Bubble 2.

Bram surprised Elizabeth by asking her to be in command of Bubble 2. Elizabeth gave an uncharacteristic shout and with tears in her eyes she rushed Bram and gave him a hug that made it hard for him to breath. Bram listened as she whispered into his ear that he had just fulfilled her personal dream of going out into space.

The bubbles became known as Bubble1 and Bubble 2. On his next visit from the NASA headquarters, John commented to Bram that the names were very clear but lacked creativity.

The building of the launch facilities at the Dalles hydroelectric plant had become the project bottle neck. The bottle neck was not the Launch building but the power generators, the power line infrastructure and the gas turbines that would back up the hydroelectric dam power.

Bram had pressured Erica to make it happen. Erica in turn forced the redirect of all the orders the turbine manufacture had to the Fold project. The manufacturer had objected but Erica invoked national security and made it happen.

Bram was pleased with the tour of the computer hardware and inspected the facilities that each of the two-bubble analysis teams occupied. Each bubble analysis group had a separate office area.

He really liked the large theater sized screen that was the center piece of the common gathering area. This was where everyone would gather during the observation periods. Bram felt the pull of the screens like the urge to jump when standing on the edge of a cliff.

Bram encouraged every participant on the team to select and decide on the observations to be made at the selected Fold locations.

It was Pat that asked if a powerful enough telescope to view the other side of the hole was part of the package. Bram listened to the discussion that followed and agreed with the team's recommendation that one Bubble should focus on the long-range mapping with a powerful telescope and the other Bubble should focus on the closer area of space.

Elizabeth took on the role of organizing the analysis teams. She spent her days working with each team on the aspect of the data gathering and the subsequent analysis to be done on the data. An initial analysis would be done at each Bubble and the data would be sent out in a continuous feed back to Earth. This transmission would not always reach Earth before the Bubble returned but it would be the safety valve in case of a major disaster.

Bram commented that any message sent out from across the universe might never be received. He made the point that Earth may have perished in all that time even if the message was traveling at the speed of light.

It was clear to him that the team needed to think differently about how data should be backed up.

Bram focused on the work with the Bubble one and Bubble two crews. His initial focus was on how to use and repair the sensors and the computer data gathering programs. He also worked through how navigation would take place.

The Fold was totally computer controlled but both systems had manual overrides that were the responsibility of the navigators. He made sure that Amy, Pat, Daryl, and Harold received training on how to program in new coordinates and what the home base coordinates were.

He was eager to get to the Dallas site. Erica had told him that the Fold program was also building homes to house the entire Fold personnel. He learned the housing area was at the entrance to the Dallas power plant area. His house would be first and would be at the top of the hill of the complex. She let him know that they were building on a hill side that had a great view but that looked more like the desert that they had left behind that what land should look like in Oregon.

Elizabeth joined Bram, Jose, and Ester on the inspection of the completed Bubbles. Bram's specification that the bubble was to maintain as close to one G rotation as possible had resulted in an expanded section and a composite shape that looked more like a spoked motorcycle wheel and tire with a globe at its center. The work and living area were on the inside of the outer tire like area. The bubble sensor area was connected in the center of the wheel by eight tubes that created the spokes. Bram noted that the center bubble area would have no gravitational pull orientation.

The week-long inspection tour of each wheel section was Jose's responsibility.

Bram briefly reviewed the plan with the four of them and clarified the process. He knew each day would be at least twelve hours long. He wanted a brief walk-through tour and then planned to step back and concentrate on his Fold power problems.

Bram commented that the name originally used for the two space vehicles no longer applied and the team should be thinking about better names.

Each day Bram noted that the wheel was rotated so each quarter of the wheel could be thoroughly inspected. Jose had an inspection checklist for every room and installation.

The control room and systems were checked first. Elizabeth, Jose, and Ester were the primary inspectors.

The plumbing and living area checks were done by activating each item. The lighting, showers, faucets, and stool were all tested. Each wheel occupant had their own small room. A common eating area able to hold the wheel team would function as both an eating and meeting area. Several minor defects were found in each area but overall, the work had been well done.

Bram had Amy and Pat, and the other NASA pilots simulate their control actions. Bram evaluated the system response by attaching his computer to the control system.

Bram was impressed with the thoroughness of the checks and the immediate response to the defects list the team generated.

He invited the inspection and support team out for a steak celebration dinner.

At the dinner Bram suggested a name change from Bubble One and Two to Space Wheel One and Two. He watched the expressions on the faces around the table and knew that he had missed the mark.

After some discussion Amy and Pat suggested USS Hood-Wheel One and USS Rainier Wheel Two. Their suggested names were immediately accepted.

Bram passed on the names to Jeffrey and asked him to verify that these names would be acceptable.

Bram didn't know it, but the inspection was the calm before the storm. On the weekend following the completion of the inspection, almost two thousand demonstrators showed up at the gate leading to the hanger where the crafts were housed.

Bram was on what he had declared was his recovery weekend at his new Dalles home when he received Jose's call about the demonstrators. Bram felt near the point of exhaustion and was planning a hike in the Mt. Hope National Forest with Amy and Pat.

He watched the video Jose shared and read the signs the demonstrators carried stating in large letters that the world would end if the project continued. He noted that the demonstrators had a large banner showing Earth exploding. He listened as they shouted that the project would be the end of the world. He wondered how the demonstrators had found out about the project and how they had learned where construction was taking place.

He called Jeffrey about the leak. Jeffrey said he would investigate where the leak occurred but made the point that leaks were hard to track down.

Bram shared his thoughts of where the leak might have come from. He shared them in the order of probability; President Natorly's office, someone in the Boeing construction group, someone in NASA. He was certain it had not come from anyone on the designated Fold team.

After Jose's call he drove out to the new Fold site and toured the facility. He took in the massive six-inch thick powerlines that swept down from a series of towers. They curved gracefully down to two dozen transformers each the size of nine sea containers standing on end next to each other. The power lines ran from there to the hanger that dwarfed all other structures in the area.

Almost everything was ready for the bubbles to be moved in. The remaining item was the installation of the ten-gas powered two hundred fifty kilowatt generators. Their mounting pads and power hook ups were ready and waiting but it would be another two weeks before the generators would start arriving and another month to get them all installed.

However, if all the power from the dam were utilized, Bram figured he would be able to transport the vessels from the Seattle hanger site to their Dalles hanger launch site.

Bram called Jeffrey to suggest they accelerate the day for moving the crafts to the launch site. It could be done as soon as all the current power being generated by the dam was made available.

Jeffrey agreed with the timing change and said he would have Erica make the power available.

Bram immediately called Amy and Pat and had them take their copilots and get their Wheels ready to move. He called Elizabeth to let her know about the move of the Wheels and asked her to take command of both wheels. He told her it would be their first Fold, and she would be in command.

He let her know that he was staying in Dalles to control the move. He wanted to make sure everything was in control on the Dalles end.

Erica bent arms and called in favors. She faced what seemed to be a wall, but she made the power available. More and more she was becoming a fan of Bram's bold moves. She loved the action that seemed to follow his development of space travel. She was happy that he had stuck it out even when she had been extremely frustrated.

A few hours later after getting the OK to go call, from Erica, Bram listened as Pat hailed Amy over the ship-to-ship communication system. She looked around to the six people behind her. Her copilot gave a thumbs up. Pat declared the USS Mt. Hood, Wheel-One ready.

Amy declared that the USS Mt. Rainier, Wheel-Two was ready for Fold.

Elizabeth stated that as commander of the fleet she was ready.

Bram at the Dalles launch site checked that everything was ready at his end. He had walked the entire power system with the power supervisor and decided that everything that could be done had been done.

Bram looked at the two crafts at the Seattle launch site. They appeared on the left side of the Dalles's auditorium forty-foot by sixty-foot screen. The right side showing the inside of the Dalles receiving site was blank.

Bram was seated in the back of the auditorium with his auxiliary control system running on his computer. He decided he needed to install a more substantial control booth at the back of the auditorium.

Pat would be the first to activate the Fold from her Mt Hood control system. This was a duplicate of Bram's back up.

Bram told Pat to activate whenever she was ready.

Pat had practiced the simple act of pushing the activate button at least a hundred times. She knew that a monkey could be trained to perform this simple act.

Yet her palms were sweating.

She pushed the button.

She thought it had not worked.

Then she looked out the window to see a group of cheering people.

The lights in the hanger dimmed and the giant screen blinked. Then a cheer went up as the Mt Hood appeared in the Dalles hanger.

A cheering group rushed out to the Mt Hood, Wheel-One. They were the ground support crew for the Mt. Hood.

Bram had a very different experience than everyone else. A shiver had run down Bram's back when the lights dimmed. He had experienced this when he lost power and lost his three-foot steel cube. He had never recovered it and had no clue where in the universe it might be. It was not at the coordinates that he had set for it to go.

He was keenly aware of the loss that would have been suffered if the power had failed. He called the power crew and asked them to check the condition of all the lines and the transformers used for the transfer.

Not much later he was informed that power lines and transformers were at the top end of their temperature ratings and one of the transformers had cycled to prevent itself from blowing up.

Bram called Elizabeth and Amy and told them there would be a delay in the Fold of the USS Mt Rainer, Wheel-Two.

He let them know that he would authorize the next Fold when the local power system reached its normal operating range.

Amy asked if the Hood was OK. And then she asked of the Rainer what the crew should do?

Elizabeth ordered everyone to go for a walk and then have lunch.

She was not about to sit while waiting. She knew it would only make her nervous.

Bram Nielson Collection

Bram joined the power crew for a tour of all the equipment that had been stressed. He ordered fans and cooling systems be deployed to bring temperatures down and keep them from going offline on the next transfer.

In Seattle, Jose stood on the back of the flatbed truck and looked out across the entrance gate to a gathering that had continued to grow to at least ten thousand protestors. He had been sent out to reassure the crowd that they would be able to go into the hanger to verify that it was empty. His loudspeaker comments to the crowd had been met with jeers, boos, and Bronx cheers.

A short time later he was appraised about the delay. He was now worried about losing control.

He decided to broadcast the local music over the speaker system. He then had his support team contact all the vending food trucks they could and asked them to come out and feed the crowd. However, he specified that no alcohol was to be served. He made sure that the trucks knew that the food tab would be picked up and paid immediately and she should give the vendors the code to get paid.

He was hoping to delay any aggressive actions by the demonstrators.

He hoped that the transfer of the wheel would take place soon. He did not want a riot or the crowd trying to break in.

The arrival of the food trucks had an immediate calming impact on the demonstrators. The scene, though still tense turned into more of a large party atmosphere. People were eating hot dogs and hamburgers and talking with each other.

Back in Dalles, it became clear to Bram that the transformers that had over heated were the original older ones. The new transformers that had been installed were temperature controlled and had both air coolers and air-conditioners. They had stayed in their control range.

Bram immediately called John to see if the older transformers could be replaced with newer air-conditioned versions. He knew that he would need to manage with what he currently had but was pleased to hear that John would have it on order immediately.

Though it seemed like a year for Bram, four hours later the second Fold was a duplicate of the first. He noted the power draw was at sixteen hundred megawatts and that the overheating occurred again. It was clear to him that the issue was the age of the equipment associated with the Dalles Dam facility.

Bram greeted each member of the Fold teams. Pat had asked about her Fold and about the delay for the second Fold. Bram told her that it had been a close call for both Folds. When Amy asked about the delay, he told her of the overheating of the power grid.

Bram's report of the two successful Folds sent a wave of relief through all members of the Fold program. The Fold team received calls from Jeffrey, John and at the top was a call from President Natorly. All expressed their pleasure and pride in the success of two successful Fold events.

From the bed of the truck, he was standing on, Jose announced that top management had finally authorized the opening of the facility. He apologized for the delay and had the gates opened. He had the food trucks move to each side of the hanger doors.

The hangar doors opened to show the vast expanse of the interior. The building was empty.

Jose stood looking at the emptiness and felt a shiver as he realized the magnitude of what had happened. He would have to ask Bram what had caused the delay.

He thanked the protestors and invited them to have drinks and snacks courtesy of the company. The demonstration changed tone, and the gathering ended up looking like a fair event.

Bram looked at the two wheels perfectly positioned in the Dalles hangar. He walked around each just to take in their structure. He felt a sense of relief but also a nagging that he had overlooked something important.

Erica planned a success celebration. She had arranged for a canvass to hang from ceiling to floor and hide the wheels. On the outside, a catered dining area was set up. Excited conversations sprouted up between those mingling on the floor. The Fold success had everyone excited.

Erica had specified the menu that featured the choice of steak, local salmon, and shrimp or chicken as the main course.

Jeffrey, Erica, and John had all flown out for the success celebration. Jose and Ester had driven down from Seattle.

Bram had continued his analysis of the transfer. He was mentally exhausted, but adrenalin was still driving his energy.

Elizabeth came by to escort him to the dinner where he was the star participant. She knew that Bram was still reliving what he had referred to as the dimming of lights and lives of the Fold soul.

She was proud to have participated in Bram's achievement of the breakthrough he had promised and had the fortitude to act to defang the opposition. All the team members had expressed their willingness to take any risk associated with the first Folds.

Bram walked into the celebration area with Elizabeth on his arm. It was clear to him that she was currently in control.

He knew he was still overwhelmed by the Fold event.

He thought of the success as an Angel balancing on the point of a needle or a barefoot walk across a razor's edge.

He knew they had all been more than lucky. If they realized or not they had experienced a miracle.

He felt and breathed lightly as he thought on how close to losing it all they had been. He would needed to make sure that this risk was eliminated.

He took in the cheer of all those who had gathered for the celebration and let the grey thoughts be washed away.

He accepted the kind words of President Natorly and the praise from Jeffrey.

When asked to speak, he stood in front of the gathering silent for a few seconds and pointed to them and quietly commented that they had all been a key part of making it happen and that as a team they would continue to have success.

He sat down and then wondered what the next challenge would be.

Chapter 9: Mt. Jefferson Remedy

It was clear to Bram that he was in an after-success slump, and he needed to escape the environment of the Dalles facility. He wanted to do something with the team other than work on Fold.

He mentioned visits to the Mountains that the two wheels were named after. The team had discussed going to Mt. Hood but had taken the advice of a local Dalles born technician who said that the camping and fishing was better in the lakes around the foot of Mt. Jefferson.

Pat had researched the choice and had been impressed with the variety of activities available. She recommended that the team take the shorter trip and spend more time relaxing than sitting in a van. Her suggestion was accepted, and she made the arrangements.

They left the housing complex after an early breakfast. The white peak of Mt. Jefferson could soon be seen rising impressively up into a clear dark blue sky. It slowly disappeared as the van drove closer and the peaks disappeared beneath and behind tall soldier-like pines that seemed to be guarding them.

Bram, Amy, Pat, Jose, and Elizabeth sat in their comfortable captain chairs in the back of the conversion van.

Two of the four new bodyguards, Zoe and Eric sat up front. The other two, Bob and Thomas were following in a separate car.

Erica had pushed Bram to interview and select four permanent guards that would reside with him in his new home. He had done as requested and hoped that he had selected well and that they would all get along. They were all young agents that were looking for an assignment that would have some adventure other than always guarding an old man in an office.

Elizabeth had agreed to the fishing, but she wanted to have a nice shower and bed when the stars came out. She commented that she wanted to enjoy fishing not survive it.

She jokingly said she would save survival for the Folds like the last one that Bram had put them through. Everyone laughed and agreed with her.

After reviewing all the B&B's in the area, they selected an Inn along the Rushing river. Its location, the room availability and the surroundings made it the first choice. The friendly greeting, from Mary the owner, to a call from Pat sealed the choice.

It was a leisurely drive from Dalles to the Rushing River. They checked in early and chose to have a late lunch. Then those who chose to, each were on their own. They could do some fishing and gather later for dinner.

Bram passed on going fishing and chose instead to sit on the porch and relax. His B&B host, Mike, brought out the tea Bram had ordered and joined and engaged him in idle conversation. He shared the story of starting the B&B with his wife Mary.

Periodically Bram politely commented but he was deep in thought about the Fold activities. The constant nagging about having missed something seemed to be incessant. He seemed trapped in an analysis do loop.

Jose and Amy walked alongside the river and chatted. Amy had conflicting feelings about the situation she found herself in. She was struggling with her feelings for Jose and for Bram.

She had invited Jose so she could get to know him better.

Jose had made a very positive impression, and it was clear to her that he was seeking to be more than just her friend. Her attraction to Jose clearly let her know that she welcomed his interest.

Bram attracted her, and she saw him as a true friend, but was he more?

She knew she was confused.

She decided she would seek Elizabeth's advice about the situation. She dropped back to where Elizabeth was throwing rocks into the river.

Elizabeth chuckled when Amy asked her for advice about her mixed feelings. She skipped several more, flat rocks across the water before looking at Amy.

She responded that she had no good advice. Her advice was to slowly stir the pot and examine what the spoon brought to the surface.

She advised to relax and let nature take its course.

Amy thanked her for such sage advice. It really did not seem to be of any help, but she didn't say anything.

She walked just upstream from Elizabeth and threw her fishing line into the river. She immediately hooked a large trout. She admired her catch but then unhooked it and threw it back into the river.

The simple act of unhooking the fish and letting it go helped her make up her mind in how to handle her situation.

His cup of tea in hand, Bram sat on the porch and rocked slowly back and forth in his rocker. His mind was racing through all his space Fold calculations.

His recent success and accuracy gave him confidence in his calculations.

But he knew that a small error in any of his numbers would be significant in the gigantic Fold of time and space across the galactic distances.

He concluded that he should first try a Fold across the solar system before proceeding to go across galaxies. Even then he worried about any minor miscalculations.

And the nagging feeling about missing something just kept growing.

Pat cast her line and in and began reeling it in with slow jerky motions. The surprisingly strong strike almost pulled her into the river, but her left boot found footing on a small boulder below her.

Her catch made a strong upstream run and then reversed course and tried going downstream. Pat continued to slowly reel her catch in. She was in no hurry, and she was enjoying the play of the fish.

Her patience paid off and soon she had an almost three-foot long salmon in the shallow waters at the edge of the bank. She decided it was a keeper that should grace the dinner table that night. She carefully slipped her hand into the gills to pick the fish up. She struggled to get it up the bank.

Elizabeth volunteered to take the pole and reeled it in. Pat struggle as she walked back toward the B&B.

The red hair, light green blouse, trim dark green shorts, knee-high socks, and black booted long legs caught Bram's eye, but it was the chest to ground length of the largest fish Bram had ever seen that kept his attention. The fact that someone as petite as Pat was able to hold it off the ground impressed him. She was much stronger than she looked.

He came down the steps to help her carry the fish to the side, kitchen door. There Mike greeted them and helped put the fish on a wood block table. He congratulated Pat on catching one of the largest fish he had recently seen coming from the Rushing River. He asked how Pat wanted the fish prepared.

Pat asked to have the fish scaled and served whole. She went on to ask if carrots, sweet potatoes, broccoli, and onions could be place around the fish and the entire tray baked in the oven. She described how she wanted the fish to be presented at dinner.

Once Mike agreed, Pat excused herself and said she was going to shower and change clothes, so she would not smell like a fish.

Bram watched as Pat walked out of the kitchen.

Mike commented that she would make a good catch.

Bram quietly agreed with Mike and returned to the porch to continue his musing. As he sat down, he watched as Jose and Amy walked toward the house.

He was aware of Jose's feelings toward Amy. He also took in Amy's relaxed and easy conversation with him. Emotional clarity came quickly to Bram, and he felt more relaxed than he had been for some time.

Mike and his wife Mary joined the team for dinner. The baked salmon was placed in the middle of the table. Mike had baked a potato and prepared a mixed salad for each person. He poured a glass of Muscat wine for each person and made a toast to the catch of the day.

Mary held up her glass and greeted everyone to the M&M, Inn and wished them all a good stay. She thanked them for filling the Inn in the off season and that they were welcome to come back as often as they wanted to relax and enjoy the area around them.

Bram looked around the table and knew he had the friends he had always wished for. He was not yet sure of his new bodyguards and was having to get use to them being somewhere in his presence wherever he was.

Later, as he was sitting and watching the day slowly ebb away into a grey that the Rushing River was disappearing into, Amy came out to talk with him.

He immediately knew what she was seeking. He clarified to her that he would always be her friend but that she was free to seek the partner that would be her soulmate. He said that he was all for happiness.

Amy gave him a hug and thanked him for making it clear and easy.

The rest of the weekend was a blur in his mind. He had gone fishing, hiking, and just relaxed on the veranda.

Pat carrying her giant salmon on that first Friday evening and his talk with Amy were the two events that stood out about the weekend.

His last thoughts were about his ability to ensure the success of the Fold project.

Ron Mueller

Chapter 10: Fools Rush In

The fishing and hiking had worked wonders in reducing the stress Bram had experienced after the two Folds to move the Wheels to their launch locations. It had also allowed him to clear the deck on the romantic side of his life.

Now he was back in his house. It was in the back of the new gated community built for the people associated with the Fold effort.

It had the highest elevation of all the homes and a had a good view of the apple and pear orchards to the South and the West. It also had the view of the power grid and transformer stations, and the buildings associated with them to the North and the East.

He and his four bodyguards would all live in his five-bedroom home. It had been specifically designed for him and his bodyguard's occupancy.

It looked down on the entire fenced in community.

The large kidney shaped swimming pool and the spacious common dark green recreation facility had strategically placed parking lot designed for the electric golf carts that provided the transportation to that was used in the community. A small fire truck, an emergency rescue vehicle and another car were parked in the top corner of the lot.

He could see the playground equipment and the sand volleyball courts, one on each side of the rec building with the playground equipment next to the pool area..

He only had a glimpse of the baseball diamond located in the back corner of the grounds.

The soccer field was hidden behind the new row of maple trees.

The grounds had been transformed from a few old trees and a straggle of grasses to a series of three and four-bedroom homes and lush green lawns with tree lined streets. There was enough room for at least two hundred homes. About one hundred homes were completed and occupied.

A four-story apartment building on the backside of the recreation area and pool was almost complete.

The new community had a recreation leader, Melisa Etrius, that was an analyst by day and a neighborhood organizer by night. She was determined to get everyone to know each other. She had scheduled a series of weekend events for several months in advance.

She had come to Bram and asked him to fund these events.

Bram thought this was a great idea. He agreed to fund the expenses for the food and entertainment.

He gave these events visibility by having the community events highlighted in the weekly Fold News published by his staff.

Bram walked or jogged on the way to work each morning. His bodyguards participated each morning and joked that Bram was wearing them out and would need to replace them as they wore out.

He joked back that they needed to start paying him for getting them into shape. He was pleased with the attitude of his four bodyguards. He was relieved that they got along so well.

He had always been something of a geek and had often been excluded by his classmates. He knew that was why he had pursued and excelled in his martial arts classes.

He still practiced his Aikido moves but did so in the privacy of his spacious bedroom.

Since he often worked late, he was often driven back by his bodyguards. This cycle became a well-practiced routine for Bram.

Getting the electrical power system beefed up was the current delay in scheduling the next Fold. Bram had decided a Fold across the solar system should be the next step.

The pause nagged Bram, but he was using it to clarify what the two Wheels would be looking for and in laying out the analysis that would be a key part of the effort. The first Fold target was a location roughly ten thousand miles from Neptune.

In astronomical distances this target was like standing across the street from the Empire State building.

The Fold was delayed for a month until the new power generators were available. The delay would allow for the testing of the power systems that were being improved.

Elizabeth guided the teams to define the observation targets and the types of analysis to be carried out on Neptune and the surrounding area. The teams associated with each Wheel all participated.

Bram opened his eyes and let them get use to the dark interior of his windowless room. The lack of a window was one of the downsides of his security. A late sleep in was part of his Saturday and Sunday routine.

The dark seemed to amplify the question of what he was missing. He knew that he needed something to change but he did not know what.

Weekdays it was up at five, Aikido practice and then on to work. Breakfast on the workdays was at the site. There he always randomly sat with whoever he had not yet had breakfast with so he could get to know as many people as possible.

Today was Sunday and there was a community gathering planned that he was looking forward to.

He decided that he would fry two eggs over easy and make two pieces of dark bread toast with goat cheese and ham or sausage.

Bram got up and after brushing his teeth went down to get his first cup of coffee before making breakfast. He stood sipping it as he looked out the two-story high windows. One view looked out over the apple and pear orchards and the baseball diamond. The other view was out over the complex. At the center was the swimming pool, recreation center, picnic area and the new apartment building. He was looking forward to the grill out planned for lunch.

Bram turned to prepare breakfast. Zoe. She pouring a cup of coffee. She asked him if he were interested in a couple of over easy eggs. He was about to answer when Eric walked in and declared he would love a couple.

Bram watched the interaction of Zoe and Eric. It was clear to him that the two had hit it off and were becoming a pair. This he thought was good.

He knew that Bob and Thomas each were carrying on long distance romances with their interests back East. He wondered how that would work out.

Bram wondered about his own romance potential and decided it was time to relax.

He took Zoe up on the eggs and accepted two sausage patties and the toast that he had planned to eat.

After breakfast he retired to his office, sat down with a book in the Alex Evercrest series by Ron Mueller about a black female detective in Cincinnati. He was about a third of the way through it. He enjoyed the flow of the stories and was always trying to guess how each episode would end. It was clear that the author had no idea where the story was going.

Bram always contemplated his actions if something like the story line would happen to him. He realized that the author and he had many of the same traits.

The pool party and grill out was well underway when Bram left the house a short time after that start time. Bob and Thomas had stayed behind with him. Zoe and Eric had gone down earlier to see if they could help in setting up and manage the outing. They had also wanted to get a quick swim in so they could be at pool side when he got there.

Bram was taking note of those sitting out by the pool. The only shade was provided by strategically placed umbrellas, but most chairs were out in the sun and occupied by those trying to get a tan. He saw Pat in the shade of one of the umbrellas. The bikini she was wearing made it clear to him that she liked bright lime green. And he couldn't help thinking that she also had a great body.

The parking area was full, and a few families were unloading their water floats and trying to get their kids in control and on the way into the swim area.

It didn't register that there was a strange pickup in the lot.

Suddenly, very loud shots rang out.

Everything seemed to go into super slow motion for Bram.

He briefly saw three persons at the top of the parking lot near the pickup before he was pulled down by Bob. Thomas was already firing at the shooters.

A mad scramble was going on around the pool. Zoe was in prone position also firing toward the gunmen. Additional shots came from the corner of the recreation center.

Bram saw a clear path to the side of the car just uphill from the shooter's pick up. He rolled downhill and then ran to the side of the car. The firing became a back-and-forth volley.

Bram waited until the shooting from his bodyguards stopped. He then jumped up and ran toward the shooters as they began their response fire toward the pool. He was within striking distance when the shooter closest to him sensed him and turned and brought the rifle to bear.

Bram continued his forward motion but turned his back to the shooter and stepped into the shooter's chest. He closed his left fist and forcefully slammed it back into the shooter's nose. He could hear the bones breaking. The force of the hit drove the nose bones into the shooter's brains. The shooter was dead on his feet.

The shooter's rifle had fired one shot that hit the back window of the car Bram had hidden behind.

Bram was surprised with the result of his attack, but he held the shooter up by the waist band with his left hand and grasped the rifle falling from the shooters hand, with his right. He turned and fired at the other two shooters. He missed both! They both began to raise their rifles to return fire. Bram was surprised as both went down in a fuselage of bullets. The back of one shooter's head exploded into a red blossoming spray. The other shooter's chest seemed to grow holes the size of large grapes.

Bram looked around to see his four bodyguards rushing forward all firing until their guns were empty. He would long remember Zoe in her blue string bikini firing her gun until she had clicked three times on empty. The two gunmen had gone down, and silence replaced the sound of gun fire.

Bram knew Zoe was on full adrenaline as she immediately went into the protect mode and asked what the hell Bram was thinking by rushing unarmed toward the shooters.

Bram replied that he was thinking about the kids in the pool.

He noted that his adrenaline was about as high as when the lights had blinked during the first Fold.

He turned and ran toward the pool area.

Two people sitting by the pool had been shot. Their wounds were serious, but the team doctor was immediately tending to their wounds as they waited for an ambulance to arrive.

Bram turned and went over to the grill and rescued the grill's contents that had been abandoned. He selected a brat and commenced to put relish, mayonnaise, and mustard on it. He then took a beer out of the cooler and sat down in the shade of one of the umbrella tables.

Melisa, the neighborhood event organizer, came and sat down with him. She pointed out to the kids in the water and quietly said, "I don't know if they saw what you did. I have it all here on my cell phone. You rushed in where angels would fear to tread."

Bram smiled and replied, "Yes fools rush in."

He lifted his beer and took a sip. He knew he was trying to recover from the shooting event.

Zoe went up to the house and got dressed. She returned immediately and located Bram. She shook her head when she realized he was sitting and talking with Melisa as if nothing had happened.

Most of the people of neighborhood were standing by the pool fence looking out to where the soldiers and the police had cordoned off the top part of the parking lot.

Zoe watched as two ambulances arrived. The Fold doctor and some helpers had moved some umbrellas to shade the two who had been shot. Both were conscious and talking with the Doctor.

Zoe decided that her role was back to watching out for Bram.

Bram asked Zoe if she was ready for a brat and a beer. He knew she would turn down the beer but was pleased that she asked for a hamburger.

Bram went to get the burger.

Melisa showed Zoe the action she had filmed. She commented that she had never seen an FBI agent in a bikini leap over a pool fence while shooting at an attacker. She asked where the gun had been kept.

Zoe took in the scene as Bram made his unarmed attack of the three shooters. He had been quite skillful in taking out the first shooter. It was clear he had been better in hand-to-hand than in firing at the other two attackers. She figured it was hard to hold up a dead body and shoot at the same time.

Bob and Thomas were immediately moving in, but Bram was blocking their ability to safely take a shot. She beat Eric over the fence. He was firing as he leaped and followed her. Their bullets were the first to hit the other two remaining shooters. Then all four were emptying their guns into the shooters.

Bram looked at the four of them as if he wondered where they had come from. He dropped the shooter he had killed. He looked out at the pool and then ran toward the pool entrance gate. He called out to the kids in the water. He took in the scene and then walked toward the abandoned cooking grill.

Zoe thanked Melisa and asked to have the video sent to her. Zoe knew that there would be a detailed follow-up, and the video would help to clarify the situation. She asked Melisa to check to see if any of the other folks at the pool had gotten any video as well.

Eric was the next to join the three. He declined Bram's offer and said he would get it himself. He looked at Zoe and told her that the two of them had the watch duty of some crazy guy at the pool.

Zoe chuckled. "Crazy brave," she commented.

Her respect for Bram was at an all-time high.

The four were soon joined by Elizabeth who had just stepped out of her house when the shooting had started. Jose and Amy were the next to join. They pulled over another table.

When Pat appeared Bram immediately remembered why he had gone at the shooters. Pat had been sitting in the shade next to the two who had been shot.

He knew she must be suffering from shock. He had forgotten about Pat when he came down to the pool area after the shooting.

Bram got up and walked over and gave her a hug. It was clear to him that she had been crying. She responded by again crying. Bram was not sure what he could do other than hold her.

She looked at everyone at the table and simply said, "I was the next to be shot."
Thank you for saving me.

Bram followed by saying that no one would get to shoot at one of his Wheel pilots and live to talk about it.

Ron Mueller

Chapter 11: Ready

Bram was not asked for permission for the erection of a ten-foot chain link fence topped with razor wire that went up the following week around the entire housing compound. The pristine housing complex looked very much like a deluxe prison camp to him.

He knew better than to object.

The army guards with their full body armor, machine guns, and night vision equipment was a step beyond what Bram had anticipated.

Again, he knew better than to complain.

The same fencing closed any open areas around the Dallas Power Station and the army had been tasked to guard the station.

Jeffrey called to explain the heightened security. He explained about intercepted messages indicating there were multiple groups trying to disrupt the Fold effort.

It was still not clear how the information had leaked but the heightened security had been a Presidential decision.

Elizabeth took the lead in getting the gas-powered generator installations accelerated. She was as eager as Bram to launch the next Fold. Her daily inspection tour became the talk of the installation crew. She was a tough inspector but when she arrived so did her crew with coffee, bagels, and donuts.

She promised the installation crew a full steak dinner for them, their significant other and their immediate family if they could beat their current schedule.

It was soon clear that she had inspired them to beat the schedule by at least a month.

Bram decided to use the extra time to test the whole system by moving each Wheel out of the dome to the open field immediately outside and then move it back in. He wanted to identify any significant issues while still in Oregon and not somewhere out near Neptune.

He made sure to have the field raked and all large stones removed. He toured and personally inspected each gas turbine generator unit. He made sure to include inspecting the fuel supply for each unit. He then followed through to ensure the fuel supply had been properly sized to last for a year.

He then inspected the power grid from the gas turbines and the connection to the Dallas hydro generators. All the transformers and power lines were new. They should not be needed but having them ready was a must for Bram.

Pat was accompanying Bram to work each morning. She had taken up Tae Kwon Do and was taking lessons at a local Tae Kwon Do Dojo, but it was the work out she got with Bram each morning that was accelerating her progress. Her feeling of helplessness was slowly diminishing. She still woke up from nightmares of getting shot but those too were less and less frequent.

She and Amy were sharing a two-bedroom apartment, and their evening routine include Yoga, which helped give her a deep sense of peace.

Bram seemed to understand and coached her in a calm and nurturing way that worked for her. She came over from her apartment for coffee and then went with the team on their jog to work.

She not only had a heightened feeling for Bram. She knew she was in love with him. She had watched the videos, and it was clear that he had been the first to act to take out the shooters.

He had been unarmed but fearless.

The morning trips to work were more trying since the shooting. Bram had two personal bodyguards and two Marine guards in full body armor that accompanied he and Pat to work each morning. The Marines were impressive as they jogged in full body armor and a full backpack.

When he drove home at night, the Marines went in front in a Humvee with externally mounted machine guns that was also an impressive sight.

To Bram the Dalles environment had changed for the worse. He now felt super constrained and recalled his feeling in the original compound in Arizona.

Pat was slowly recovering from the shooting incident and coming back to the strong person Bram knew. This gave him a satisfying feeling.

He was in the wait mode in their relationship. He would wait until both upcoming Folds took place.

Amy noted the changes in the people and the work environment. There was a little more tension in the air, but everyone seemed to be focused on making sure their co-workers were OK. This was good to see and feel.

She too was a little more on edge, but her personal life had taken the direction she desired. She and Jose were truly meant for each other. They got along well and had fun being around each other.

Amy was as relaxed and calm as she had ever been. She was trying to help Pat get over what she knew was classic PTSD. Any unusual noise seemed to trigger Pat. She knew Pat risked losing her status as pilot if she did not overcome her current situation.

Elizabeth was very aware of Pat's situation. She had breakfast with her every morning for the last month. She saw a steady improvement and felt that Pat would be fine.

She discussed the situation with Bram. He suggested they touch base again after the Fold test they would be doing in the very near future. They would evaluate Pat's performance and decide prior to the Solar System Fold.

Bram extended an invitation to Pat to go fishing in the Rushing River. They would stay at the same Inn. He wanted to take her back to a time he had seen her full of confidence.

She asked who else was going fishing?

He replied, it would be just the two of them, Zoe, and Eric and two Marine Guards. He laughed and added that was as private as it would get for them. He went on to share that he had rented five rooms because Zoe and Eric would share one room.

Pat smiled and agreed to a weekend fishing trip. She said that she would love her "*private*" time with him.

The Marines drove their Humvee. Zoe drove their black SUV. Bram and Pat sat comfortably in the back in the captain chairs and enjoyed their iced sparkling water. They all listened to some jazz and hardly spoke a word on the way.

Bram was mentally reviewing the coming week's Fold. He had made sure the timing was such that no satellites would be able to spy on them. He mentally reviewed his discussion with Jeffery and John. Both had voiced their concern about Pat.

Bram had staunchly defended her and assured them he would have her ready.

The Humvee driving into the parking lot made a statement that was hard to miss. The armed Marines that jumped out caught Mike and Mary by surprise.

Bram rushed forward and apologized for not having given them any warning. He went on to introduce Zoe and Eric as two additional bodyguards. He finally pulled Pat into the group and recounted that Pat was the one who had provided the main course last time.

Mike asked what Bram had done to warrant such heavy protection. He went on to say that the Inn had no other guests, so it should be safe.

Bram suggested they all move into their respective rooms. He made the point that it was still early in the afternoon, and he wanted to go fishing.

He was soon out on the porch on the easy chair he enjoyed on his previous trip. Both Mike and Mary came out to sit with him. They were curious about the heavy security that was following him about. They knew that he was working on a secret project but that was all they had learned on his last trip.

Bram let them know that he was being protected from potential attackers. He reiterated that he really had come up to go fishing.

Mike chuckled and made the point that he had brought along the big fish catching lady, so he had to believe him.

He asked whose catch she was.

Bram smiled and replied that he hoped he had the big one this time.

Pat came out wearing the exact outfit she had worn on her first trip to the Rushing River. She too wanted to catch fish. One was sitting in front of her, and she hoped one was waiting in the river.

Zoe and Eric came out immediately behind Pat.

Pat waved her pole and said, "let's go."

Bram got up and followed Pat. They were passed by the two Marines who were still in their fatigues and brandished their two machine guns.

Bram called out to go left at the bank.

Pat flicked her line out into the river. She was in the exact spot of her previous success. She noted that she was in the exact same position with her foot on the stone.

Then her heart stopped as a helicopter flew past. It was flying low and following the river.

The tug on her line brought her back to the fishing line now moving swiftly upriver as if to follow the helo. She focused on her catch, but her ears listened to the two Marines. One was checking in and finding out about the helicopter. He kept repeating a four letter swear word over and over.

Pat kept her focus on her fish. The Marine hung up the field radio and turned and said they had to get out of sight. The helo that had gone by had been high jacked from the army group at the Dalles site.

Pat had her fish up to the bank. One of the Marines was about to cut her line. At the top of her voice, she shouted for him to stop. This caught him by surprise, and he stepped back. She reached down and lifted her catch by the gills.

Bram reached out and caught the other gill. Together they both lifted the fish from water. Pat then cut the line and tossed the pole to the still surprised Marine.

Bram led the way to the side kitchen entrance. Mike looked at the fish and smiled. He went on to say, "You have the touch. You only go for the big ones. I will prepare this the same way as the last."

Pat thanked Mike and told Bram that she was going to take a quick shower.

The two Marines told Bram that they would probably need to leave the B&B. They looked over to Mike and asked if there was a place close by that would offer protection.

Mary asked why in the world would they want a place of protection?

"Mam, a high jacked Army helicopter flew past us as we fished. It has enough fire power to totally demolish this Inn. We need to move to a safer location. We've called for backup. Both the Army and the Marines are responding but meanwhile we need to move as soon as possible.

Bram looked at Mike and Mary and asked again about a good hideaway location away from the Inn.

Mike looked at Mary and said in an inquisitive tone, "the mine shaft tunnel?"

"Yes, we have that set up as our storm and survival location. Let's go there," Mary replied.

"Let's bag the fish and the other things we want for dinner. We can cook everything at the mine," Mary went on.

The Marine Sergeant urged everyone to get moving immediately.

Bram was turning to go and get Pat. Her appearance in the doorway surprised him. She looked stunning in a black blouse and dark green khaki pants. Her red hair seem to be a flame illuminating her face.

She stood in the doorway and then asked, "What kind of trouble are we in?"

Zoe was the one that answered that they needed to immediately leave the Inn and go to a shelter that belonged to Mike and Mary.

Pat commented that thanks to Bram she was ready to take on the bad guys in hand-to-hand combat but now she would need to learn to shoot to be really ready. Then she asked what was holding them up.

The hike to the mine shaft entrance took only a few minutes. The night had enveloped the valley in a pitch-black veil. The Moon was behind the mountain and doing little to help them see the way. Mike was in front with Mary leading the way.

Mike took off the chain hanging across a three-inch thick oak wood door. He told everyone that he had made it himself. He had figured that the shelter would need a heavy-duty door if it was to protect Mary from a raging storm. He then opened the bolt lock holding the door closed. He led the way in with his flashlight. Mary herded the group into the shelter.

When everyone was inside, Mike closed the door and locked it from inside. He put a steel bar across the door. He then flipped the switch, and the lights came on. He pointed at the lights and commented that he had run underground power lines in. He also had a backup generator if necessary.

He pointed at a heavy-duty locker and commented that he also had a small arsenal to defend himself if necessary.

There was a table with four chairs, a full gas cook stove with an oven, an old refrigerator, a kitchen work area, two double bunk beds. The entire shelter area had a plastic plank floor, and the walls were stone. Mike was proud of the shelter. He had tried to make it as practical and as comfortable as possible. He had also put in a large supply of dry food that would last for a couple of months.

The Marine sergeant called in his coordinates, then signed off and turned off his radio. He looked around and gave a low whistle.

He commented that this was as comfortable of a hideout that he could possibly dream of. He went on to point to the entrance tunnel leading to the door and said he and his partner would set up their equipment there.

He went and set up his machine gun on a tripod and positioned it as close to the wall as possible. His partner did the same along the opposite wall.

Mike was already preparing the fish and vegetables to put into the oven. He commented that he and Mary had dibs on the lower two beds. The top two were available.

Bram looked at Pat and raised an eyebrow. She smiled and said she would love to share.

Zoe and Eric had already thrown their packs up on one of the beds.

Dinner was a spread-out event. Mary, Mike, Bram, and Pat sat at the table for four. Zoe and Eric stood at the kitchen counter and the two marines found boxes to sit on and positioned themselves at the entrance with their backs to the wall.

Pat thanked Mike and Mary for the great dinner and a wonderful place to hide out.

Bram climbed up into the bunk above Mike. Pat climbed in after him. This was as intimate as they had ever been.

Bram absorbed the warmth of Pat lying beside him. He looked at her and was pleased that she was looking directly back. Pat put her hand on his chest and leaned in and kissed him. Their eyes never left each other. Bram smiled and whispered, "so much for waiting until after the Fold missions."

He did not recall falling asleep. He only recalled feeling warm inside.

It seemed that almost immediately, Bram was knocked out of the bunk by a roaring explosion that ripped through the shelter.

He instinctively put Pat behind him as he moved in the dark along the wall toward the front part of the shelter.

Mike was thrown out the back of his bunk. He immediately made his way to the gun locker. He had two 308's, two shot guns and two forty fives. He sat on the floor and loaded them all.

Mary crawled up beside him and took one of each of the weapons and then crawled forward. Mike did the same.

Bram accepted the 308 that Mary handed him. Zoe accepted the gun Mike offered. He and Mary both preferred the shot guns. Pat took one of the forty-fives.

The sergeant had put the refrigerator on its side across the entrance area. His partner had tossed two grenades out through the entrance. For the moment all was quiet.

Mike began pushing crates of dried goods up to the marines. They immediately began positioning them across the entry way.

The dull deep thuds of a heavy-duty machine gun firing into the shelter area was followed by the boxes being shattered and exploding into flying splinters that flew back into the shelter.

Bram tilted the table on its side and positioned it, so they would be protected from the flying debris and ricochets caused by the heavy-duty gun fire.

The two marines suddenly stood up and let out a continuous round of machine gun fire. They must have been successful in hitting the operator of the heavy-duty machine gun. It fell silent.

They threw two more grenades and then went into a prone position on each side of the entrance.

Through the grey of the early morning dawn six dark figures rushed the entrance.

Bram and Zoe stood and fired their 308's. Eric was firing from a prone position. Bram ran out between the two marines who were firing from each side of the entrance.

He was firing his weapon as fast as he could work the bolt.

The dark figures in front of him went down in the hail of fire that they must not have anticipated.

The two marines jumped over the barricade as they continued to send short bursts of gunfire out. Zoe and Eric followed. Instinctively they spread out to the sides of the entrance. The marine corporal ran and secured what turned out to be a heavy machine gun (HMG) and verified that the three operators were dead.

The Marine sergeant checked out the downed attackers. He hit several with the butt of his gun. Three were apparently dead. There were two more dead by the machine gun location.

The Marine corporal zip locked the three live attackers' hands behind their backs. He then disappeared as he went into the woods to make sure there were no other attackers.

Three helicopters suddenly appeared. One swooped in and six armed men dropped down on lines.

The Marine sergeant shouted over the rotor noise and shouted not to shoot that they were friends.

Bram turned and handed his empty 308 to Mike. Mike took the 308 and then gathered the other guns and returned to the gun locker.

Bram turned and greeted Pat as she came out of the shelter that was now surrounded with Marines at the ready.

Pat said she did not know that being a Wheel pilot was going to be this exciting.

Mike returned and was looking at what was left of the door he had been so proud of. He pointed to Bram and commented that it was going to cost extra for the entertainment.

The entire group including the two marines went back along the trail to the Inn. Marines were now posted along the entire trail.

Bram was immediately thinking about how he would need to change the system test for the coming week.

Bram noted the two helicopters in the parking lot and that the Humvee and black limo were gone. He figured the third copter was probably parked in the open field on the other side of the river.

Bram knew the return trip would be on one of the copters in the parking lot. They had been instructed to gather their belongings and prepare to leave.

Mary gave them all a hug. Mike said he would love to have another salmon dinner with them, but he would meet them somewhere and bring the fish. He figured it would take a while to recover from their visit. He went on to say he was going to bill Bram for a new door, interior cave refurbishing, a new refrigerator and stove that were now Swiss cheese and with a smile he said he was going to use top dollar wages to calculate the labor cost.

Bram replied that the next fish dinner would be at his house. He would send the invitation out in about a year. He took Pat's hand and followed his Marine Sergeant guard out to the waiting helicopter.

He would report that Pat was recovered and ready to pilot any vessel she was assigned to.

It was clear to him that his fishing expedition though much more exciting than he had planned had been a complete success

Chapter 12: Team Recovery

Bram jumped into the helo, took a seat, and put on the headset given to him by the copilot. He watched as everyone else took a seat and put on their headsets. Pat sat next to him. Eric and Zoe sat across from them and their two marine guards sat across from each other on Pat's left side.

Mike and Mary guarded by two marines waved to them from the edge of the parking lot.

Bram took in Mount Jefferson and the surrounding mountains. The dark green Douglas-firs stood as straight as the Marine guards and seemed to be guarding the way to the brilliant white cap of Mount Jefferson. He put his arm over Pat's shoulder and pulled her toward him and pointed out and commented on the beauty that surrounded them.

The helo flight back to Dalles only took about thirty minutes. As they descended, Bram could see that cameras had been mounted along the fence and guard towers had been erected.

He saw an armored vehicle that seemed to be driving around monitoring the fenced perimeter. The equipment all had US Marine signs on them. He learned later that the Army guards had already been replaced.

Bram looked to the community complex and saw that cameras and guards had also been added. There were no corner guard towers at the community perimeter but two of the towers from the power facility looked down into the housing complex.

He knew he would soon be talking to Jeffrey and John about the upcoming test he had planned. He would suggest using the facility in Washington as the test location. That venue would make the test invisible to anyone watching the Dalles site. He wondered about who had ordered the change in security and who was managing it.

Only a few weeks earlier he would have been against it all. Now he realized that it was going to be necessary to ensure the safety of the people involved in the Fold effort.

They got out of the helicopter and were met by a Marine and told they were there to transport Bram and company to the VA Health Care Facility that was located only a half mile away as the crow would fly but about five miles by road. Bram could look out and see the facility from the power area parking lot. But he knew it was a five-mile ride by road.

The EMT briefed them that they would all undergo a comprehensive examination. A team of Marine doctors had been brought in and the VA facility was being used to provide medical support to the Fold team.

Bram became aware of the ringing in his ears. He was surprised he had not noticed it earlier. He looked around at each of the others and realized they all had scratches or other small wounds. His two marines as he was now thinking of them had several deep scratches along their cheeks and neck. They had been in the immediate area where the rocket grenades had exploded.

He followed the EMT to the emergency vehicle and got in. They all sat oriented in the same positions they had been in the helo. The lights came on and they were off to the VA facility that was within sight, but they would need to go around the highway to get to it.

It was Monday following his return from his "Fishing" trip. He resumed his early morning workout and then jogged into work. He was accompanied by Eric and Zoe as well as Pat. They were all led by their two marine guards.

He now began using the first names of his two Marine guards. The sergeant was Orlando, and the corporal was Caster. They smiled when Bram began calling them by name.

His support, Lacy, informed him that he had a ten o-clock morning call with Jeffrey, John, and a Major General Lester Tilson. She said that the General had been assigned to oversee security and team health care for the Fold project.

Bram thanked Lacy. He poured himself a cup of tea and then sat down and listed the topics he thought should be covered during the meeting. He planned to let Jeffrey lead, but he wanted to be ready. He placed a call to Elizabeth and asked her to come to the meeting.

At ten sharp the phone rang. Elizabeth and he each had a cup of tea in front of them. Bram had shared with Elizabeth some of the events that had led to their current situation.

Jeffery opened the call by introducing the General and letting Bram know that John and Erica were also sitting in on the meeting.

Bram replied with, may all be well with all of you," and let Jeffrey know that Elizabeth was on the line with him.

Jeffery then asked Bram to fill them in on the details of the attack that had occurred.

Bram jokingly asked if Jeffery wanted to hear about his recent fishing trip and the size of the fish he had caught. He went on and made fun of the Marine style of fishing with rockets and hand grenades and the type of fish they caught. Bram then claimed the Marines were mad at the Army for giving terrorists helicopter gunships, so they pushed their Army friends out.

General Tilson laughed. He commented on the fact that he had received information that Bram had vigorously fished with his two Marine buddies and caught more than all of them put together.

That surprised Bram. He had indeed been shooting at the attackers, but he did not know that he had hit anything.

The General went on to compliment the entire fishing team on their resilience and ability to protect themselves.

He sent compliments to be given to FBI guards Eric and Zoe. They would earn gold stars in their evaluation reports.

His two Marines would also be recognized for their actions and probably get the promotions they deserved.

Bram replied that he was pleased with the recognition his protectors were receiving. He said they deserved every bit of it and more. He let the General know that he would appreciate having his two Marine fishing partners stick around until the Fold effort ended.

The General commented that he had talked to the two just before the call and they said they would like to do just that. They commented on the fact that they had never protected someone who attracted so much attention but needed so little protection. They figured that since they had finally achieved a first name relationship they should stick around for a while.

Bram chuckled and replied that indeed he wanted their protection, especially if he ever went fishing again.

The General asked if there was any concern with the security arrangements.

Bram looked at Elizabeth and raised his eyebrows. He replied that it certainly was an upgrade, but he had his eyes on making the success of the Fold project a reality and would leave security to the General.

The General went on to inform Bram of the fact the that the airspace above the Dalles Power Station area was now restricted. The landing and takeoff pattern from the Regional Airport had been changed to exclude the runway that utilized the airspace above the power transmission area.

Bram commented that seemed to be a very serious limitation and perhaps would affect the airport and the local economy.

The General commented that negotiations to build another runway would begin in a short time.

Jeffery then suggested they discuss the upcoming Fold test.

Bram suggested the hangar where the wheels were built be used as the place to Fold the two Wheels. They would stay there in the powered mode for a week and then Fold back to Dalles and stay in the powered mode for a week. Once back, Bram also wanted to test whether the Wheels would stay in position if power failed. He planned to position the Wheels a sixteenth of an inch off their holding stands and then cut power.

Elizabeth said she supported the tests as described. She wanted to add a disembark activity while in the Boeing dome.

They all agreed on both Bram's and Elizabeth's suggestions.

Jeffrey then raised the question about Pat's mental condition and readiness.

Elizabeth spoke up and said she had breakfast with Pat on a daily basis. It was apparent to her that Pat had come back from her fishing trip as the strong person she had been before the first shooting. The action during the fishing trip had strengthened her. Elizabeth left out the part about the new bond between Bram and Pat. Knowing Pat's feelings for Bram was the reason that made Elizabeth speak up.

The General reinforced Elizabeth's assessment. He quoted the Marine phycologist as having found Pat one of the strongest most balanced people she had spent time with.

The general went on to say he had asked the same phycologist about the stability of a certain Fold genius. She claimed doctor-patient confidentiality, refused to answer based on the persons obstinance.

Bram took the line and commented that he too had wondered about Elizabeth's genius stability, but that in the past he had let it pass. She seemed to him to be doing OK.

Erica had been on the phone all morning. She had talked to Zoe, to Elizabeth, to Pat and Amy and to Eric. She had gleaned the fact that Pat and Bram had stepped up to a new level in their relationship. She had sensed the old but now a much more powerful and confident Pat. She wanted to support both Pat and Bram and make sure there was no question about anyone's fitness.

She stated the fact that the Fold team was stronger and more powerful after the trying events that had taken place. She looked forward to the success of the upcoming tests and to the success of the entire Fold effort.

Jeffrey looked over at Erica and smiled. He saw a complete transformation and growth in a person that only a few months before he had been ready to replace. She was ready for more.

Jeffrey closed the meeting and said they would resume their normal weekly meeting on the following Monday.

Bram pressed the off button on the speaker phone. He looked at Elizabeth and commented that it seemed the call had gone well.

He then asked about her request to get out of the Wheel when at the Boeing dome.

Elizabeth gave a small laugh and said that she planned to take her crew to the best restaurant in Portland.

What was he planning to do with his crew?

Bram walked around the desk and gave Elizabeth a hug.

He asked if he could come with her to dinner.

Chapter 13: Fold Community Aftermath

Like a bear in hibernation, the Fold neighborhood quit its outdoor habitat and hid in their safe domains. The shootings by the pool had a dramatic negative impact on the outdoor neighborhood activities. It carried over into the work area. People were not interacting well.

Bram asked Dr. Serena Windal the Fold phycologist to design some group programs that would help them get relief from the shooting incident.

He also suggested she take on anyone wanting help.

Bram made a point of walking through the neighborhood after lunch each day. Since he was not allowed to walk alone, the group was made up of Orlando, Castor, Eric, and Zoe or on other days it was Bob and Thomas. Orlando and Castor were always out front.

The marine guards that patrolled the fence and walked the streets got to know and wave to all of them.

The fishing trip battle had made Orlando and Castor heroes to their marine brethren.

Bram noticed that all the Marines would salute him as well. He had participated in the shooting but did not have a clue at the time that he had any effect. It was only when Major General Tilson shared Orlando's and Castor's battle report that he discovered how effective he had been. He credited an adrenaline high for his actions.

Whereas the battle at the Rushing River had solved one problem, the shock of the pool shootings had created a major problem and had brought total paralysis to the once vibrant and active community.

Bram stopped by Melisa's house to talk to her and see if she would organize another grill out. He offered to make it a steak and shrimp affair with games and prizes for the kids.

She shared that she had been afraid to push for another event. She felt so bad for the two who had been shot. She was also a little intimidated by all the armed marines.

Bram agreed with her that it was a daunting situation that they had to overcome. He went on to make the point that she could play a key role in helping everyone deal with the situation.

He suggested the kids get to know the Marines by name. He proposed giving five one thousand-dollar prizes for the kids that submitted the most signatures of the marines first.

He said that he would talk with Edward Sharp, the site Marine Commander and make sure every guard wore a large name tag.

Bram said he would award the guard that got all the kids names in first a dinner out with a friend or better half.

Melisa agreed to invite everyone to another pool side grill out. She would make it a grand affair if he would also fund a music band to play.

Bram readily agreed with her request.

The couple that had been shot had recovered and had chosen to come back to work early. Bram met with them to ask for their help in getting the community back to its once active and fun lifestyle. He asked them to help sponsor the next outing. They each agreed to do so.

They thanked him for his action in taking the shooters out. They also ask Bram about what had happened to have the Marines come in to be the guards of both the Fold facility and the neighborhood. He briefly explained what happened when he went fishing.

Wow! So, there are more bad people after us, was their reaction. They asked if there was any other way they might be of help.

Bram suggested they share their experience on the Fold internal web site information system. This would help everyone process the shooting incident. He asked them to connect with Melisa and see if they could help plan the coming event.

Bram was surprised that the personnel on the Fold effort had not heard about the attack at the Rushing river. It spoke volumes of the tight control the Marines had over the situation.

Pat suggested to Bram to have a folk singer perform with any band that Melisa chose. She felt it would enhance the mood.

She joined Bram on his next neighborhood walk. This time Melisa came out to walk with them. She shared that Marine Commander Sharp had already agreed to support the next outing and he already had the Marines wearing large name tags. He also had established the contest to award a prize to the first five Marines to turn in all the kid's names.

There was also a prize for the Marine that turned in the most names of the residents. Melisa went on to share the fact that there were two marine bands in the guard unit. One was a pop band, and the other was a country western band. The commander said he would make sure they were both available. Bram laughed when he learned that the Commander said that the fees for the bands would be covered by the Fold program budget.

That budget was Bram's budget!

Pat went on to ask Melisa to see if there was a folksinger among the Marines.

Dr. Windal was surprised that her individual patient schedule immediately filled after she started to have daily lunch session presentations on incidents such as the shooting by the pool.

She asked Bram whether it was appropriate to have morning and afternoon Yoga and Tai Chi sessions so that the people in the Fold program could attend.

She did not wish to upset the normal workday, but she thought it would make it easier for those who had kids to attend during the working hours. She suggested that the pool area facility be used. She made the point that in that way those taking the classes would be at the location of the attack.

Bram thought that it was a great idea and told her to go full steam ahead.

He approached Major Sharp and asked if any of the Marines would like to teach swimming. Bram had discussed this with Pat, and they had decided that having swimming lessons would be good for the kids and it would be an activity that got parents back in the habit of going to the recreation center.

Bram engaged the Fold team educators that had established a school inside the Fold community. They had classes set up for students of every age. Most of the classes were on-line but every student had a real teacher guiding them and interacting daily with them.

Lacy was studying the population of the Fold team that lived in the closed community. She, herself had recently moved into one of the new apartments. The move made it much easier to come to work and to work late if needed. She personally felt safer moving into the facility.

Bram wanted to know the demographics of the personnel. He was interested in the number of stay-at-home moms and their skills and talents. He wanted them to be able to contribute to the Fold effort at the level they chose.

Bram Nielson Collection

Bram was also interested in the number of kids that resided in the Fold community and the programs to engage them. He was willing to sponsor fishing, hiking and any other outdoor activity and to have the most popular movies brought in.

Bram knew he had ignored the community but was now determined to have it prosper as part of the Fold program.

On one of Bram's after lunch walks through the neighborhood, Melisa walked up to him and introduced him to a young lady, Maryanne and a young man, Terry. They were both in their high school senior year and were looking for a community project that they could put on their applications to the universities to which they planned to apply.

Bram greeted them and asked them to walk with him. He began to ask them questions about their interests and about their grades in math, science, and history. He asked them about the universities to which they were planning to submit their applications. Maryanne reminded him of Mallica or maybe a young Elizabeth. She was more interested in how people perceived and reacted to events around them. Terry was more into the technical aspects of how things worked.

Bram suggested that Maryanne have interviews with, Elizabeth and Dr. Windal. Once the interviews were complete, a project would be designed for Maryanne to work with one of them.

He went on to suggest that Terry have interviews with Lori Middleton and Remi Hardwood. Once those interviews were complete, he also would get a project assignment.

He then suggested they expand their applications to the Ivy League schools and perhaps to schools like Oxford or Cambridge in England.

Bram commented that scholarships and grants would be available if they were accepted into one of their choices.

Maryanne and Terry walked away excited about the projects they would get in the Fold program. They knew it would be a key element of their application strategy. They also were now thinking more broadly about their schools of choice.

Bram asked Lacy to set up meetings with the parents of both Maryanne and Terry. He wanted them to know that the program would pay for the kid's college expenses if they maintained a B average or above. He also asked her to write an article for the Fold news highlighting this benefit.

The Sunday picnic schedule began at eleven and was scheduled to go on past dinner time. Bram and company arrived early and helped to get everything set up. However, Lacy had arranged for her parents to cater the event and there was little to do but sit by the pool and relax.

Bram noted that Marines were posted around the parking lot and the pool facility. The neighborhood families began arriving and soon the pool was full of the kids splashing and playing.

Melisa joined Bram and shared that the folk singer turned out to be one of the stay-at-home moms.

Bram shared that Pat had commented on the singer's great voice and asked that when she stopped singing that she join the group for a drink.

Orlando and Castor had recruited two Marines to guard Bram and were in the pool enjoying a beer and talking to all the kids.

His four FBI guards were sitting all around him in their swimsuits. Each of them had a gym bag at their feet. Bram figured that was where their weapons would be.

Bram put his lawn chair back, took in the music, and reached over and took Pat's hand into his. He imagined the commercial with two people, holding hands, sitting on lounge chairs on the beach, looking out to the ocean as the sun began its descent.

He fell asleep to the melody and the melodic vocal of the folksinger.

Chapter 14: Fold Bubble Scouts

ℛe-establishing a vibrant, happy community had taken longer than Bram had expected. The pool party and the involvement and help of almost every person in the community made a huge impact. The kids and young adults were surprisingly effective in changing the feel of daily life. The Marines and their engaging participation also made a huge positive difference. Melissa became her old self and took the initiative to schedule events out into the coming months, so people could see and plan out the coming six months. Bram was pleased to step away from the community issue.

The fence around the community and the marines patrolling the fence kept the community in isolation. But every home had one or more large screen monitors and linkage to the internet. The internet was strictly controlled to ensure that the outside could not "break" in.

Bram's primary worry, the power requirements for the project now received his full attention. The power requirements for the Fold was an enormous worry. It literally kept him up at nights.

He had been successful in the transfer of both Fold Wheels to and back from the Portland site. He had kept the power on for the entire time and was continuing to do so. He toured the electrical power supply every week. He talked to the maintenance crew to understand the maintenance requirements for such a system.

The gas-powered generators were running normally and showed no signs of stress. The new transformers were staying in their normal operating temperature range. The system had a fifty percent backup capacity just in case any component failed, and it was designed to bring the backup power online before the system power dipped too low.

The Fold to the edge of the solar system would stay in place for six months. The Fold across the galaxy was currently scheduled to last close to a year. Bram needed perfect performance from the power system.

The time frame and the need to have everything remain flawless bothered Bram. It made the mission dependent on what he considered a vulnerable power system. His original concept was to have the Fold power system be part of the Wheel. Bram's desire to have people in the Fold Wheel was the reason for the extreme power requirement.

Now that the time was near, he was having second thoughts. He was potentially risking the lives of people who he cared a great deal about.

He had not given them a choice.

Pat had become his confessor. She laughed when he first shared his concern. She commented that if he told the people who were assigned to the Wheels that they had a ninety percent chance of dying, every one of them would still want to go.

She then asked if there was a way that the risk of having a problem could be reduced?

That discussion resurfaced Bram's original design of having the power aboard the Wheels.

He replied that the ability to have an onboard power source or have shorter stays would reduce the risk.

Bram scanned the huge workshop that he had built as part of the Dalles structure. He had staffed it with one of every skilled profession from welders, electrician, electrical techs to computer geeks.

The staff of twenty in the lab so far had done little work. They had become familiar with their area and the equipment available to them. The manager of the area immediately reacted when Bram walked into her office.

In case you don't know my name, I am Lori Middleton she said as she stood up. She went on to ask if he had some real work for her team to do, to make, to build or to program. She said her team was going bonkers waiting to contribute to the Fold effort.

Bram took an immediate liking to Lori. He said that yes, he had an idea that he wanted them to help with. He asked if there was the possibility that the folks in the shop could meet?

Lori asked her support to call everyone into the meeting room. She went on to ask that lunch be brought in.

Bram followed Lori to the meeting room. There he got some help in hooking his computer to the large screen that dominated the one end of the room.

Bram looked around at the people in the room. He recognized many of them from having breakfast with them. He asked everyone to introduce themselves by giving their name and their specialty area.

Bram listened to each and repeated their name and specialty. Once everyone had introduced themselves, he shared one piece of information that would be new to all of them.

He had been fishing but had never caught a fish!

That caused some laughter, and someone commented that they had heard it was dangerous to go fishing with him.

Bram agreed and focused on opening a power point slide deck. A diagram of a sphere with a camera mounted inside appeared.

Bram stated that he wanted to build a sphere with a camera inside. He wanted the camera to be smart. It should focus on objects as specified by a computer program. The camera needed to be able to rotate to a position to get the best shots possible. All of this should fit in a two-foot diameter sphere.

Once the first sphere was tested, Bram said he wanted a dozen more.

Lori asked Bram if he could give her team about an hour before the team responded. She wanted the team to brainstorm and see what they could come up with.

Bram replied that they could take as much time as they needed. He would be in his office working on what the camera would be recording.

Lori called Bram about two hours later and requested he again meet with the group.

Bram returned to the meeting room. Three easels had been put to use. One had a list of questions. The other two had diagrams of spheres.

Bram noted that the team must have several very good artists. The spheres and the camera looked almost real.

The first question was if the sphere was free to rotate in space?

Bram replied that he was not sure. They could test this in the lab. He would Fold a small sphere to a specific location and the team could check it out.

The next question was how long the sphere would be at its location.

Bram said that on the first placements, each sphere would stay long enough to slowly rotate and take pictures of all the surroundings. Then it would return. The time would be determined on the speed of the camera rotation.

A fourth question was whether any communications out of the sphere was required.

Bram replied that all pictures should be stored on memory and that at this moment in time he felt the sphere would often be so far away that it would return ahead of any signal it might sent out.

Bram Nielson Collection

The final question was if the camera should be only in the visual frequency range?

Bram's reply was that the other camera frequencies would follow. This would either be in additional spheres or as separate cameras put into existing spheres. He stated he was open to their recommendations on all of his replies.

Lori asked the team if the answers changed any of the conclusions the team had reached.

All members were either silent or responded with a no. The only thing that was highlighted was that the behavior of the sphere would determine the final design.

Bram had brought the Fold transmitter he had used for the Presidential meeting. He asked if the lab had a sphere he could transmit.

While the team looked around the lab, Bram determined the Fold location of the table he had been shown.

He was handed a small Florence flask and was asked to send it out upside down.

The flask neck fit perfectly in the hole that was in the brief case send location.

Bram pressed the Fold button, and the Flask appeared floating two inches above the surface of the target table.

The entire team converged on the table, and each took a turn moving their hand around the floating sphere.

Remi the design engineer grasped the flask neck. He was able to move it but when he let go the neck and the flask returned to its original position. He did this several times and the flask always returned to its original position.

Lori looked around at the team. She turned to Bram and said that she could have his first bubble done by the following week.

Bram then asked if the team would examine the various size Fold transmitters and recommend the size that fit the bubble that was being built. There were three larger power supplies than the one in the suitcase in existence and they were all on site.

Bram returned to his office. He now had a clear plan on how to proceed. He would deploy the cameras as scouts. He would get the visuals of the location that he had selected to take the Wheels. This would allow for better planning and dramatically shorten the time that the Wheels spent in the Fold.

He located Elizabeth and shared his current thinking on how to move forward.

Elizabeth listened to Bram. She watched his movements and realized that he seemed relieved and energized. He began by sharing his fear of losing power while they were in the Fold. He went on to explain his current approach with a set of scout bubbles.

Instead of having the Wheels stay out for months, the scouts would go out and collect the initial data. The Wheels would follow and focus on the areas selected from the footage brought back by the scouts.

Her reaction was positive. The approach Bram had chosen was a very practical one and one that she could easily support.

The next day was Friday. Elizabeth called a meeting of the entire team to share the new approach.

She and Bram walked into the meeting together. She called the meeting to order and shared the new approach in how the upcoming Fold events would be managed. This change would delay the Wheel Fold about two to three weeks.

During the meeting Pat suggested that a Scout Analysis team be established. She volunteered to get it setup. Amy volunteered to help. Bram voiced his support and asked to participate in defining the Scout Team membership criteria.

Elizabeth agreed with setting up the analysis team. It would help her when she shared the change in Fold timing with Jeffery and Erica at the next leadership meeting.

Ron Mueller

At the end of the meeting, Bram suggested a Columbia River Fishing outing and asked who wanted to go with him.

The entire team, almost in unison, shouted, "You must be joking."

Chapter 15: First Catch

Everyone that had volunteered to go fishing met at Bram's house at five Saturday morning.

Bram had coffee prepared.

Three white vans arrived shortly after everyone had gathered. The vans would transport them to and from Celio Park.

Breakfast and lunch were part of the fishing trip package. Each seat in the vans had a box holding an egg, cheese, and sausage breakfast sandwich. A hot cup of coffee was in each cup holder of the van.

Bram and Pat led the way to the vans. Zoe and Eric were in the lead and Bob and Thomas walked behind Bram. Amy and Jose followed on Eric's heels. The rest of the group was comprised of Lacy, Lori, Orlando, Castor, Edward, and Ester. The outing would be comprised of three vans, three boats and twelve people.

Bram made a point to thank Lacy for her super ability to arrange the fishing trip on such short notice. She had pulled off a small miracle in successfully setting the trip up.

Lacy thanked him and made it clear that her father, uncle, and brother owned the boats. They had been the only ones available and were willing to do it for free. The vans were new and had been provided by the local car dealer and Bram owed the dealer advertising airtime. She said she would have arranged a fish for everyone to catch but she had no connection in that area, so she wished everyone good luck.

It was a short drive to Celio park where they would cast off. Bram was one of the few that stayed awake. His eyes stayed on the black waters of the Columbia river, that in this location was called Celio Lake. These were the waters above the Dalles Dam. It was hard to make out the far bank in the grey black of the early morning, but occasional lights appeared like low lying stars. The stars overhead were still shining, and they reflected up from the dark waters. Celio Lake became a mirror of the stars above. The heavens were still dominating the morning.

The bright lights in the parking lot and those casting their rays at the landing dock blocked the view of the Celio Lake but put the three sleek, low profiled, black fishing boats with 250 hp outboard motors in the spotlight.

Bram stopped to take a picture of the three boats and commented on how stunning they looked. The team agreed.

Lacy introduced her Father, Ted, her brother, Luke, and her Uncle Cedric. Ted said it was a pleasure to take the group out. He went on to claim that the three boats would show the group the best fishing they had ever experienced. He told them that Lacy had worked with him to assign everyone to one of the boats. He looked at Bram and told him since all the firepower would be with him, he would be in his boat, and it would be the most crowded.

Lacy then called out the names of the people in each boat. A safety discussion went on at each boat.

The proud boat owners also gave a brief tour of the boats. The live well and the bait boxes were the first to get shown off but the storage box with the makings of a variety of snacks got the most response from the team.

The plan was to return to the landing area for a picnic lunch. Ted's and Cedric's wives were bringing out spareribs, salad, and drinks.

Ron Mueller

Bram looked out to the East at the rays of sunlight chewing at the edge of the dark grey of the morning. The far side of the Celio Lake was still enveloped in black with a few lights twinkling their existence.

The captain of each boat lowered their propellers into the water and started their engines. Bram had expected a roar but heard the low purr of an angry lion instead. He relaxed and concentrated on Pat's warm head on his shoulder.

The three boats, in a triangle formation, cut smoothly through the water. The air rushed through Bram's hair. He was sitting with his back to the left side of the boat with Pat sitting next to him. Zoe and Eric were sitting together facing forward. Bram noted that they were wide awake. Orlando and Castor lay prone on the bow, Bob, and Thomas, sitting between he and Zoe, were sitting with their eyes closed.

Bram closed his eyes and cycled through the air blowing across him, the purr of the lion pushing the boat and the gentle pull toward the back of the boat.

The next thing he knew was Ted telling everyone it was time to get their poles into the water.

Bram looked at the flat platform at the bow of the boat and the one behind the L shaped seating area. He was unsure where he should go. Ted solved the problem by pointing to a seat he put up in the center of the bow. Bram went up on the bow platform. He stated that he had never been fishing before. He watched as Ted's eyes went wide and a smile spread across his face.

"My gosh, I have a virgin on my boat," Ted shouted out at the top of his voice as he pointed at Bram.

Bram had not expected the outburst. His cheeks turned red when everyone shouted that Ted must be kidding.

Bram listened carefully as Ted explained how to cast and slowly reel in the line. Ted asked Pat to fish from the center, out the open right side of the boat. He asked both Orlando and Castor to fish out the left side and assigned the rest to share the back platform.

After a few initial problems, Bram got the hang of casting and reeling in the line. He took a moment to look around and saw that everyone was focused on their own fishing. He relaxed and started trying to target his casts.

The sudden jerk and pull on his line almost caused him to fall out of the boat. He recovered and listened to Ted tell him to take it easy, keep the line tight but be in no hurry to pull the fish in. Bram immediately understood that keeping the line tight meant the fish was slowly being pulled in toward the boat.

Bram was finally looking down at what he thought of as a huge fish.

Ted handed Bram a large net with a long handle. He instructed Bram in how to bring the net up along the fish so that it would envelop it. He then instructed Bram to put the pole in the holder and use both hands to lift the fish up and onto the platform.

Once the fish was out of the water Ted opened the front live well and skillfully put the fish in.

Bram took out his phone and took a picture of his first fish. Ted commented that it was a good size and would make good eating. He went on to say that everyone wanted to catch the big fish, but the bigger ones had a stronger fish flavor that he didn't like. The size Bram had caught was just right.

Bram felt good and decided that it was time for another cup of coffee and a snack.

He asked Orlando if he wanted to fish from the bow.

The fishing was as good as promised and everyone caught a fish.

Bram went back to fishing and by eleven when it was time to head back for lunch, he had three fish to his name. He had caught the largest and the most fish on their boat. Ted praised him on his fishing ability and his luck.

Bram Nielson Collection

Bram smiled and replied that in his case it was all luck and to being brought out to where fish were dumb enough to bite on his line.

As his boat and the two others approached the dock, Bram spotted a Humvee parked at the far end of the parking lot.

He looked at Orlando and asked if this was his doing? Orlando smiled and gave the excuse that the marines had been jealous and had come out to the park to fish from the pier.

Ted led the way to four picnic tables that were covered with food. He introduced his wife Rita and his sister-in-law Marial. Rita welcomed them and pointed to the table.

Bram looked at two trays stacked with barbeque sauce covered ribs, a tray of corn on the cobb, a large bowl of potato salad, a bowl of loose-leaf lettuce covered in tomato, cucumber, and onion slices, a tray of white, brown, and black bread slices.

Bram commented that this was beyond anything he had ever expected but he had no problem in digging in to such a feast.

He approached Rita and Marial and pointed to the Humvee at the end of the parking lot and asked if his Marine guards could take part in the meal.

They said they would be pleased to feed them as well.

Ted went to Orlando and asked him to invite the rest of his friends for lunch.

Ted commented to Bram that Lacy had shared the events of the attack at the pool and then the attack when he had gone fishing at the Rushing River. She had also shared that this was the first time since then that they had all had come outside of the fence that had been put around the entire area.

He was wondering how Bram felt.

Pat was sitting next to Bram and looked at him. She knew that she felt safe inside what she now thought of as the compound. She was interested in hearing his take.

Bram had not thought about what the situation looked like from the outside. Only a few people from the outside community worked inside the compound. He paused for a moment before replying.

He admitted that he had never thought about the situation from the Dalles community's perspective. He went on to say that he embraced a supportive community.

He also pointed out that the work inside the compound was top secret but a very positive development for everyone on Earth. It had nothing to do with battle or war.

Ted replied that Lacy had said almost the same thing and that she could not say more. She did say it was not weapons work or war robots or anything like that. She had also made the point that she liked living at her apartment next to the swimming pool and the other facilities.

Bram told Ted it was a breakthrough, and he was making sure the world would benefit.

Ted said thanks for giving him this much information. He looked around and called out that it was time to get in some more fishing.

Bram walked over to where Rita and Marial were sitting and thanked them for one of the best meals he had recently enjoyed. He then joined Ted, and they led the way back to the boats.

The sun was now on its decline but at the hottest point of the day. The wind coming over the bow and the wind shields pulled Bram's hair across to where it looked like a sheet of paper. Pat raised her left hand to play with it. She complemented him on his explanation to Ted.

Ron Mueller

Bram watched the Oregon shoreline passing by. It seemed to go downstream. The illusion was strengthened by the puffy clouds overhead that seemed to be flowing downstream as well.

Ted dropped anchor about fifteen minutes above the spot where they had first fished. He declared it as the spot to catch the big ones. He went on to say he didn't have room for any little ones.

Bram once again took the bow by himself. It was clear that the beginner was being given the space he needed.

Bram caught two good sized trout almost immediately. Then his luck ran out. He stopped to take a break and decided to watch how everyone else was doing. Orlando again willingly took the bow spot. Suddenly Pat let out a yell and was almost pulled overboard. Ted gave her a recovery hand but then stepped away.

Bram stepped over into the center area and put his arms around Pat's waist. It was clear to him that she was struggling to maintain her footing. He reached around and grasped the pole with his right hand.

Pat kept the line tight and was constantly pulling her fish in. Ted looked out from the bow and told Pat that she had one of the larger gars he had recently seen. Pat gave a gasp when the fish was finally alongside the boat. It seemed to be almost as long as the boat.

Ted pulled out a pole with a curved hook on the end. He asked Eric to help him lift the gar out of the water. Zoe, Bob, and Thomas got off the back deck to give the two more room. The gar put on a valiant fight, but Ted and Eric finally pulled him onboard, and Ted hit him on the head with a hammer. The gar spanned the entire width of the boat.

Bram snapped pictures with his phone and sent it to all on the Wheel team distribution. He had never imagined that anyone could catch a fish this size with a fishing pole. He pointed at Pat and put his arm out and made the motion of flexing his muscle. He asked Pat to lay down next to the gar so that he could take a picture of the two together. The gar was the same length as Pat was tall. It was another great picture to share with the team.

The team all caught fish. It was more than any of them wanted. Ted agreed to take all the fish that the team did not want.

Bram wanted to keep his first fish. He planned to bake it the way Pat had specified at the Inn. Most team members kept one of their smaller fish.

Then all the extra fish, a big amount, went to Ted and his team.

The trip back to the pier was relaxing. Bram sat with his arm around Pat and took in the scenery of the surrounding area.

<u>Chapter 16: Continued Threats</u>

Getting the giant gar off the back of the boat became a three-person job. It took Ted, Luke, and Cedric to get the large gar off the boat and onto the pier. They set up a tripod stand to hang the gar. Bram took several shots of Pat standing by the tripod. His large salmon was hung up next and Pat took pictures. The picture taking went on for at least half an hour as everyone captured their catch on camera.

Pat and Bram returned to the house and carried his salmon in together. Pat had given her giant gar to Ted. She had asked for a small piece that she could try later. Pat, Bram, Zoe, and Eric all worked in the kitchen to prepare a dinner that would feature his salmon. Zoe and Eric had also kept a fish each. The two together had caught the most fish.

John and Thomas decided the house had enough fish and gave their catch to Lacy and family. They also made a point of staying out of the kitchen and enjoyed a beer as they watched the rest preparing diner.

Elizabeth had gushed about her catch and had brought home three smaller trout. She was glad to be home for a refreshing shower. She was looking forward to the salmon dinner at Bram's house. She would take over a bottle of white Muscat Wine.

Jose, Amy, Orlando, and Castor all came to dinner. Jose and Amy arrived with two bottles of Riesling. Orlando and Castor arrived with a cold case of beer each. They all made their way to the refrigerator. Orlando went over to the ice-filled cooler and put in as many bottles as he could. He then joined John, Castor, and Thomas to watch the dinner being cooked.

Amy and Elizabeth volunteered to set up the table. Elizabeth had John and Thomas put in the two-expansion table leaves so that the table would be large enough for it to seat all of them.

The fish had been much too large for the oven tray. It was cut in half and cooked on two trays. The dinner consisted of a tomato, cucumber, onion and lettuce salad, corn on the cob, grilled sweet potatoes, and a mix of other root vegetables and the baked salmon. The Riesling was served with the dinner and the Muscat as a desert wine. Desert was a mix of three ice creams: coffee, caramel vanilla, and raspberry chocolate chip.

Bram had invited the Stetson family, but they had declined saying they had a lot of boat and fish cleaning before they could think about eating. They made it clear they would love to come over on some future date.

The talk around the table was about the great fishing trip they had enjoyed. Elizabeth commented that the team needed three tries to get things right. This had been their third and very successful uninterrupted fishing trip.

The dinner ended, and the talk continued into the night. Finally, everyone realized how late it was getting and everyone went home.

Bram came awake on Sunday and knew that he had dreamt about the Fold. He wished for some other topic to command his dreaming, but he knew that until the next big idea came along, he was stuck with the Fold.

He got up and prepared a pot of coffee. He filled his large mug and decided to walk the perimeter of the housing area. He was on his way out the back door when Zoe yelled for him to wait up. She and Eric each carried their coffee as they joined him.

Zoe wanted to know if Bram was really planning to walk by himself.

Bram made an excuse about it being Sunday and besides there were enough marines inside the compound to defeat a small army.

Bram walked slowly as he mulled the problem that had been in his dreams. The bubbles were always anchored at the co-ordinates that they were given. A Fold to a planet moving at the speed the planet traveled around the sun would have only seconds of a few minutes of video. He needed to change the feature of being anchored to a specific co-ordinate.

Bram caught the glint of the Sun on some far object. He stepped behind a tree and looked again. The sparkle was still there. He told Zoe and Eric to casually move behind a tree. He asked them to look out directly across the fruit trees to the other side at the barn area.

Bram waved one of the perimeter guards over and asked him to look at the glint coming from the fruit farm barn truck loading area.

The guard took a quick look through his binoculars. He called in the suspicious glint.

Bram watched as a helo swept swiftly in from the west. It must have been on patrol along the river. There were several shots fired and two Marines dropped out of the helo to the ground. He asked the marine to share his binoculars. He was able to see the two marines climb up one of the semi-truck trailers. A body lay on top.

The guard tapped Bram on the shoulder and informed him that he was requested to return to his house.

Zoe and Eric took positions in front and rear as they walked back the long way down to the pool area and back up to the house.

Bram had refused to return immediately to the house and had chosen the long way back, so he could work through his idea that had formed by the blinking from the dead shooter. He spent the rest of the day mulling over various ways to implement his idea.

The next morning, in the dark grey of the coming day, six figures, only one looking awake, jogged along the road to work. Orlando and Castor in their full battle gear led the jog toward the office. Bob and Thomas jogged behind Bram and Pat. Bram was humming as he kept the pace set by the two marines.

Bram was eager to get to the office and work on his idea for moving the bubbles to keep up with their targets. One way was to manage multiple sequential Folds. This was his short-term fix. He continued to work through his Fold equations trying to see if there was a way to make the position fluid with time.

Bram entered the building and split from the rest of the team to go to the shop area. He was surprised to have Zoe and Eric follow. In the shop he found a partially complete camera and its multidimensional drive.

The bubble lay in two halves on another table. The computer lay next to it. It was clear to Bram that assembly was close at hand. He would try his multiple Fold idea with this first unit and evaluate the impact on the power system.

Zoe asked what he was building.

Bram replied that, it was a surprise, and it was time to get breakfast. There he saw Lori sitting down and asked if he could join her.

She laughed when he immediately asked how building the bubble was going. She responded that she knew he had already been to the lab and knew the answer to his question. Then she asked about his fishing trip.

Bram smiled. He liked Lori. She was easy to interact with. He told her about the trip and how good the fishing had been.

Lori responded that Lacy and her had breakfast on Sunday and that Lacy's father had said it was one of the best fishing days he had ever experienced.

Bram Nielson Collection

Bram then asked Lori for a favor. He wanted to send some gifts to the Stetson family and wanted to go around Lacy, so he would not put her in the middle. He said that the gifts would be for the kids and grandkids in the family. He wanted to know what bank the family used. After Lori agreed to find out, Bram excused himself and went to the Monday morning leadership meeting.

Elizabeth was just finishing the normal good morning, how are you part of the meeting when Bram walked in.

Edward Sharp, site Marine commander was first on the agenda. The bright blink Bram had spotted on the previous day had indeed been a sniper. Ed figured the early morning sun was giving the sniper problems in seeing through his scope. When the Helo came in from behind the sniper, he turned and fired. The bullet glanced off the front of the Helo. The immediate returned fire killed the sniper. The who and the why were still being investigated. There was no identification on the sniper. The owners of the fruit farm were cooperating and had no idea who the sniper was. They agreed to allow the truck area to be monitored.

Bram knew that a small place like Dalles would immediately have a rumor with some version of what had happened. He suggested that a PR team come in and give an explanation about the Fold program and ensure the community that good stuff was being done inside the compound.

The message to the community had to be good.

Jeffrey agreed and asked if NASA might have a good PR team. John replied that he was sure NASA could do something along the lines suggested.

Bram requested that Laci, his support be included. She had grown up in the community and had a big well-known family. She would make a good spokesperson.

Bram brought up the point that he seemed to be wearing a target on his back. He felt that somebody in the know was guiding the attacks. The effort to get to him must be well funded and high up in the political ladder.

He asked if someone on the Fold team had good enough connections to get the FBI to investigate.

To the surprise of everyone Erica spoke up and said that she had the connection that the team needed, and she would call in favors to find out who was behind the action to subvert the team's efforts.

Bram gave a small chuckle and said, "Please let the investigators know I am the good guy."

Elizabeth guided the discussion toward the Master plan.

Erica then went into the detail of the power reliability trial requested by Bram that was coming to an end. It was very close to the time to make the first Solar Fold. The initial results indicated that the gas power generators had very high reliability and the backup switch over was accomplished with no power dip.

Bram chose to share the small bubble scouting Folds he wanted to throw into the mix. He went on to explain his idea about the scouting with the small bubbles and then strategically positioning the Wheels.

Erica asked how long this would delay the Wheel Folds?

Bram responded that there would be no delay. He did say that he might want some additional resources to staff the Bubble Scout Fold Program. Bram envisioned a Bubble Fold team that managed bubbles around each of the planets and bubbles that scouted ahead of the Wheel Fold.

The meeting ended with Elizabeth agreeing to a meeting in the following week to develop the plans for the Bubble Scout Fold Program.

Elizabeth took Bram's arm and guided him to the Wheel team meeting room. She called a meeting of both Wheel teams and asked Bram to explain what the Bubble Scout Fold Program was about.

Ron Mueller

<u>Chapter 17: Bramlets</u>

Bram looked around the meeting room. It was hard to believe that he had just come up with this new concept and quicker than a bramble weed being blown across the desert in a windstorm, it had become a whole program.

He had gone to bed thinking about how to best utilize his, frozen in specific space coordinates, space balls and had gotten up to see if he could test his concept. What he had seen in the lab meant it would be possible to test the concept in a couple of days.

He still had to share his second concept with the lab team to see if they could quickly put together a self-powered version of a bubble that would still be significantly smaller than a wheel but could be programed to do multiple folds on its own.

The second bubble would need to be big enough to encompass the power transformer unit and a power source small enough to fit in the bubble. This would be a breakthrough if it did not have to return to the original Fold location.

Bram envisioned a ten-foot diameter sized bubble.

His final endeavor was to get help in the mathematics of the Fold equation to see if the Fold object could be moved without having to constantly Fold to reposition itself.

Bram wanted the object to be able to propel itself in any direction of interest. He either wanted to use a rocket system or perhaps a time altering technique.

He walked up to the white board and wrote down the three items:

Bubble Ball Scouts and their use

Multiple Fold Bubble Ball Scouts

Self-powered Bubble Ball Scouts.

He then thought about the resources he needed to pull in to help him review the math.

He wondered what Mallica had been doing for the last several months. He felt guilty about not having assigned her to do something meaningful. She was part of the team he had more-or-less abandoned in the original team space in Arizona. He had also left Marcus, another great resource languishing there as well.

He wondered if they were interested in coming to the Dalles site

The various members of the team began to come in and almost to a person they each asked what was up or don't tell them about another postponement.

It was clear to Bram that everyone was ready for some Fold action.

Bram listened as Elizabeth clarified the reason for the meeting as discussing an enhancement to the Fold effort.

He was surprised when she clarified that they would do multiple shorter strategic jumps because he had developed the Fold Bubble Scout.

Bram looked around the room. He started his update by stating that everyone in the room was the cause of his development of the Bubble Scouts. He went on to state that his biggest concern was the safety of the Wheel teams.

He told them of his near heart attack when the power fluctuated on the very first Fold, when they brought the two Wheels to the current Dallas location. That event had caused him to demand replacing all the old transformers in the existing Dalles power grid and to wait on the new gas-powered generators for the next Wheel Fold.

He went on to share that the current test of the power system had increased his confidence, but he was still putting twelve people on the line on the next Wheel Fold. He went on to clarify that the longer they remained in the Fold the higher the probability of a problem.

The scout bubbles provided a way to look around at the site being targeted for a visit. They allowed for a way to take a best guess and then adjust once the scout verified the chosen coordinates.

They also allowed for the relocation of a specific Fold. If by bad luck the coordinates were in the middle of an object, no major loss, no lives lost.

The scouts could also reduce the time spent on any Fold by collecting all the general data before the wheels arrived. The Wheels would go in with a specific set of targets picked from the scout data.

Bram stated that he was mad at himself for not having started first with the Bubble Scout approach.

The question about a Fold schedule was one common theme the team seemed to have and asked repeatedly?

It was clear to Bram that the team was negatively affected by the delay.

Bram explained that the Wheel Fold had been planned for six months. It was still scheduled that way. He however made it clear that he was now thinking each Fold would be more like two weeks, but perhaps each time at a different Fold location. He would let them know. It depended on how the scouts worked.

The next question was when would they know?

Bram answered that question by telling the team that the first bubble scout would go to the first designated solar location on the coming Wednesday. On the following Monday, the Wheels would go to the location the scout had visited unless he and the teams wanted to make coordinate adjustments.

Elizabeth and the team began reviewing what remained to be done to be ready for a Monday Wheel Fold.

Bram excused himself saying he needed to go to the lab to see how the first bubble scout was coming along.

He walked briskly down the hall toward the lab. Zoe commented that he seemed extra energized and wondered what he had eaten for breakfast.

Bram took in the entire lab crew gathered around the larger of the two stainless steel tables. There in what seemed a totally assembled state was the first scout bubble.

Remi proudly pointed to the bubble and declared that it was ready. He and several of the lab team had worked over the weekend to make sure they could get the bubble done.

Bram walked up to the worktable and put his hands on the two-foot diameter sphere. He suggested that the lab team name this first bubble scout.

Lori said she would work with the lab team on the name. She wanted to make sure Bram knew about a short coming to this first scout bubble. She pointed to the camera and the internal space and asked what Bram saw.

Bram looked at the bubble and its interior. He said it seemed a bit crowded but very practical and functional.

Lori made the point that the bubble had only a four-hour power supply. The battery would take almost four hours to recharge.

Bram agreed that was a limiting factor. He let her know that he had heard about a Japanese scientist that was claiming he had doubled the life of the conventional lithium type of battery. He asked Lori to follow up on that opportunity.

Bram went on and recruited the entire lab team to become the first Bubble Scout handling team. He made the point that there would be many more bubbles made of different sizes. They would all face the problem of having enough power.

Bram Nielson Collection

Bram asked that the bubble be placed on a stand between the two Wheels. He declared high noon the next day to be the first Fold for the bubble.

Bram ordered a new power line to be brought in straight from one of the spare generators. He allocated an office, which looked out to the bubble, to be the new headquarters for the Bubble handling team.

Bram went to his office with the computer that controlled the bubble and programed in the coordinates for the Bubble Scout's Fold. He also programed in the camera motion for each of the four hours it would be at the Fold location.

Lori asked that he provide her lab team with some guidance on what he was expecting them to do as a bubble handling team.

Bram gave a chuckled and told her he would send his two lead Wheel Pilots, and they would tell her what her lab team needed to do.

He made the point that one of the key actions was to get the Bubble Scout recharged and sent out again. He let her know that he had programed the computer for six launches and the camera orientation for that many.

He asked if the first scout had a name yet?

Lori responded that the vote was occurring at this very moment, and she needed to get back, so she could put in her vote.

The power line from the generator to the bubble launch location took much longer than Bram had allotted. The electrical maintenance manager refused to take any short cuts. He estimated that if the installation crew worked all day and through the night the power line would be in place by Wednesday afternoon. It was the best that he could do.

Bram had little choice and thanked the electrical crew for their hard work. He let them know that he wanted them to do it safely and to make the power source as reliable as possible.

He followed the electrical maintenance manager who insisted that Bram verify the work that would be done.

Later, while Bram was sitting with Pat, Zoe, Eric, and Amy in the cafeteria Lori approached. She had a large grin as she said she wanted to share the name given to the first Bubble Scout.

After a big pause she shared that it had been named Bramlet One. The one had been added because the team already knew that Bram was planning to have them develop additional ones.

Everyone at the table laughed. Zoe said it was so appropriate and right.

Bram knew his face was turning red. He said he wanted the lab team to know that he appreciated their naming the bubble after him. He wanted them to know how great it was to have them be able to turn his idea into reality in such short notice.

Pat and Amy engaged Lori about getting the lab team trained. They also wanted to know if the lab team would be making more of the bubbles and could the Wheel team members help.

Bram left at the same time Pat and Amy followed Lori back to the lab. He was on his way to his office to make a call to Mallica and Marcus. He now had a sense of urgency to get them out to Dalles to help him dig into the mathematics involved with creating the Fold. He felt that he had missed something important and continued to miss it on every run through the math and physics. He was somehow blind to what he knew had to be a huge, short coming.

Ron Mueller

Chapter 18: Problems with the Math

Bram returned to his office and placed a call to Mallica. Her surprise made him feel even worse than he already felt. He had forgotten about her and Marcus back in the original Arizona location. He asked how she was doing. After some reconnect chatter he asked if she were willing to come to Oregon and help him review the math associated with the Fold.

Her resounding, "Oh my god yes," made it clear that she felt left out. She made the point that Marcus would love it as well.

Bram told Mallica that she and Marcus could come out as soon as they wanted. There were two new three-bedroom homes available for them that had just been completed. They were available for immediate use. If they needed to get them furnished it would all come out of the Fold budget. He could hear Mallica saying, Yes, Yes, Yes, over and over again.

Mallica said that she would be there by Monday. Bram said that would be fine.

After hanging up Bram went out to Lacy and let her know about Mallica and Marcus. He asked her to work with them and get them moved into the new homes.

Lacy said that she would do so.

She then thanked Bram.

When he asked what she was thanking him for.

She said for the Stetson Educational Trust that had been set up. She let him know that she and her Dad had accepted being the trustees. She also made the point that having it designated for use with schooling and the future generation was the only way her Dad could have accepted the money.

Bram smiled and said that it was great. He let her know it was a forward payment. He was sure with good guidance the trust would do well. He wanted her to make sure her Mom and Dad got the credit. They created the money that was now in the trust.

Bram returned to his office. He sipped his tea and thought about how small gestures had huge impacts.

A short time later Elizabeth came to his office. Her excuse was that she wanted a cup of tea. She made herself a cup and took a couple of sips before she moved carefully into the topic she had come to discuss.

She was worried about what she perceived as his current protective attitude toward the wheel teams. She felt he had to disassociate his personal feelings from the role he was playing as the technical lead. It was her role to worry about the well-being of the teams. She wanted to know what his issue might be and how she could help.

Bram looked steadily at Elizabeth without saying a word.

He wanted to give her a hug. He decided to do just that. He was sure he surprised her and smiled as he sat down and took another sip of his tea.

He decided to share his current concerns about his Fold concept, its short comings and what he considered his biggest mistake.

It was not yet lunch time but close enough that he called out to Lacy and asked her to order in lunch for he and Elizabeth.

Elizabeth asked if this meant that Bram was going to talk a lot?

Bram smiled and replied that she had asked, and he was going to share everything that had been eating away at him.

First, he let her know that he had asked Mallica and Marcus to move out to Dalles.

She commented that it was about time. She had meant to bring that up some time ago, but their exciting fishing trips had always distracted her.

Bram said fishing had certainly distracted all of them. He went on to highlight that another concern he had was the fact that he was sure he was missing something in the math and the implementation of the Fold. The fact that he was missing something meant that the entire team could be at risk.

Elizabeth agreed with him.

She pointed out that the entire team knew there was a great risk in the Fold technology. She made the point that the team had talked about it, and they were willing to take that risk.

They appreciated his concern but reiterated the fact that it was not his role to limit them based on his concern.

Bram replied that she should assure the team that he had put their asses on the line several times already. He had done so with little concern and certainly had not limited the team.

He wanted Elizabeth to communicate to the team that he would continue to be aggressive in his deployment of the Fold. He also wanted them to know that if he found any problem, he could not fix, he would stop the Fold program until he could fix the problem.

His lack of knowledge should not be the basis for risks that need not be taken.

Elizabeth agreed to share that with the teams.

Bram then went on to describe the first problem he was trying to overcome. His Bubble Scout idea was his attempt to solve a problem that caused him concern.

He pointed out that the two Folds that the Wheels had experienced were short Folds in Earth's atmosphere. Earth was a clean environment compared to where they might end up, in an across the solar system Fold, or a Fold across the Universe.

He went on to state that now he would not allow a Fold to either location without scouts going first and checking out the area around the Wheel Fold coordinate

Elizabeth asked for clarity about the first Bubble Fold. She asked if Bram would call for a delay in the Wheel Fold if the Bubble scout trial failed?

Bram replied that if the bubble scout failed, the Wheel Fold would be delayed.

She made the point that no one would be leaving early on the following day. The Wheel teams would all be eagerly waiting for Bramlet One to return from its first Fold.

Bram made the point that he would certainly be there at return time.

Lunch arrived. Bram had ordered a half of a Reuben and a squash soup. Elizabeth had ordered a shrimp and scallop spaghetti in white sauce. They both took a moment to arrange their lunch before continuing.

Bram brought up his next concern about his understanding of the mathematics and science of the Fold. He knew he was missing something.

This made him worry about long Fold deployments. The unknown missing Fold problems or mistakes might show up with time or perhaps with the distance of a Fold. He welcomed anyone that wanted to get involved in the inquiry and investigation of the science behind the Fold.

Elizabeth chuckled. She said that Mallica and Marcus had been playing with the Fold math and were stumped in how you managed to get anything to work. She went on to say that she did not know anyone even close to Mallica's capability. She would open the door to everyone. She was sure there would be interest but that no one would last more than a few minutes when they got into the math.

Bram thanked Elizabeth for helping him unload his concerns.

Bram Nielson Collection

Lacy came into the office. She apologized about having listened in, but they had left the door open. She went on and said that she might know of someone that could engage in the math.

She said that her sister, Linda, was a social worker who worked with kids that had special problems. Her sister insisted that this one kid had an exceptional mind but that the system was not equipped to handle her. Would Bram see if she was as brilliant as her sister insisted?

Bram was surprised. He agreed and asked when he could meet with the girl Lacy was talking about.

Lacy put up her hand as she got her sister on the phone. She looked up at Bram and asked when he could see her.

Bram thought for a moment and wondered if it could be done during the wait for Bramlet One to return from its Fold.

He wondered if the girl could meet here at his office during the time Bramlet One was out scouting.

Lacy replied that would be a great time. She would arrange for the transportation and the passes for her sister as well.

Bram looked at Elizabeth and asked if she would like to be present during the young girls visit.

Lacy brought in a card with the name of the young girl. She also let Bram know that she was physically misshapen, and wheelchair bound.

Bram spoke up and said that he would be glad to go to the girl's place to do the interview.

Lacy laughed and said that she had already heard from her sister, Linda, that the trip to the facility would be the highlight for her and for Zuri.

Bram suggested that they planned to start with Zuri meeting everyone that would be standing by waiting for Bramlet One's return. He went on to suggest that they make it into a waiting party. He asked Lacy to set up the event and send out the invitations to everyone.

Elizabeth stood up. She had a smile on her face. She always found being around Bram was full of surprises. A few were terrifying, but most were good surprises.

She left wondering how this interview of Zuri would turn out. She knew many social workers who believed in some poor soul but most often the individual was so damaged and limited that there was little hope. She hoped that it would not affect Bram negatively if it did not pan out. She would keep a close eye on this situation.

Bram knew immediately that Elizabeth was concerned about his interview of Zuri. He would know almost immediately if Zuri's mind was filled with brilliance or if there was only gibberish. It was clear to him that brilliance would not solve Zuri's problems, but it could open the door to a very different world for her.

Bram was glad the day was over. It was time to get home. He wanted to share his thoughts with Pat and of course his four bodyguards. He thought about the events that transpired in just one day. He knew that it didn't get better than this.

Ron Mueller

Chapter 19: Mallica's Arrival

He chose to walk home and enjoy the sunset. Pat was holding onto his elbow as they walked and talked about the events of the day. She had enjoyed working with the lab folks. She commented that it had been the most productive day since their fishing trip.

She let Bram know that Lacy had brought in a "small" chunk of the Gar she had caught. It was large enough to make two meals for all of them. She went on to say that she was planning on cutting it into steaks and grilling it in the oven for dinner.

She pulled on Bram's arm and asked if he was listening.

Bram looked at her and smiled. He replied that he was indeed listening and looked forward to eating her Gar.

He pointed to the Sun slowly setting behind the low mountains to the west. He let her know she was missing a beautiful orange, purple and gray sunset.

Orlando looked over his shoulder and asked if the dinner included the two most powerful and effective Marine guards on the ground?

Pat jokingly replied that the two he was talking about were probably already eating their dinner. She then asked if he and Castor might be interested in having dinner with the rest of the poor people that had to put up with Bram?

Bram's mind wandered back to Zuri. He had also been reminded that Marcus had a family that he was bringing with him and that Mallica had place of her own. Bram was pleased that Lacy had made the appropriate arrangements.

It reminded him that she was due a pay raise.

Bram seemed to be making a rapid run through all the events of the day and the forks in the road each of the events seemed to create.

He was glad that he was surrounded with very talented people.

He looked forward to dinner but by the time it was over he was dead on his feet. He excused himself and went up and after a quick shower fell into bed and immediately fell asleep.

Bram woke up to Pat's head on his shoulder and her arm across his chest. He let out a slow breath and took in the warmth of Pat's cheek. He looked over at the large green numbers on the alarm. It was five in the morning.

Bram knew it was time to get up, but he allowed himself to absorb the feeling that seemed to embrace his soul. He slowly extracted himself from the bed and headed for the bathroom.

Bram thought he would be the first to the kitchen and coffee, but Zoe greeted him as he came down the stairs.

Bram said a polite good morning and headed straight for the coffee. It turned out he was just ahead of Eric.

He knew it was their turn on guard duty. A moment later Orlando and Castor made their appearance at the kitchen door. Bram commented that it seemed to be a waste of good talent in that it took four of them to get him awake and on the way each morning.

Pat added that it took five of them to keep him operational.

Bram gave her a hug and handed her a cup of coffee. He then called out five minutes and he was heading for the door.

Orlando began singing a cadence about Bramlet One this is your day, Bramlet One hey, hey, hey. Bramlet One to space today, Bramlet One this is your day. Castor took up the wording and added his own twist about Bramlet One was making hay, Bramlet One was on the way.

Everyone else but Bram added something additional and then they all sang the verses together.

Bram enjoyed the camaraderie but did not add any additional lines to the already ridiculous wording. His mind was on the events that would transpire on this day.

The cafeteria was empty when Bram and his guards entered. The Cafeteria had the coffee ready, and the manager greeted them as they all poured themselves a cup. She let them know that this morning the menu had waffles, sausage and eggs any style ready to go. Anything different would take a little time but the kitchen was ready, and she knew that oatmeal would be out shortly.

Bram asked that she let him know when the oatmeal was ready. He led the way to one of the tables and sat down. He was happy just to relax and watch the crowd slowly come in.

The electrical maintenance manager approached Bram and asked if he could sit with him for a moment. He wanted to share the progress in getting the power line setup.

Bram welcomed him and then listened as the manger proudly told of the super work his team had done. The manager went on to let him know that everything would be ready by one.

Bram thanked him and told him to thank the rest of the crew as well.

The next person that caught Bram's eye was a real surprise. Mallica stood in the entrance doorway looking around.

Bram raised his hand and waved until Mallica waved back. Pat got up and brought another cup of coffee to the table. She gave Mallica a hug and asked when she had arrived.

Mallica got introduced to all the people around Bram. She joked about the fact that Bram seemed to have increased the number of people it took to keep him going.

Bram stood up and gave Mallica a hug. He told her that it was good to see her, but she was not due until next week.

Elizabeth walked in and greeted Mallica and thanked her for coming out early. She looked at Bram and nodded and said that she was the reason Mallica had come early. She went on to say that she thought it would be a good idea for Mallica to participate in interviewing Zuri.

Bram let the implication sink in. He conjectured that Elizabeth was worried about the emotional toll that he might experience from the interview.

He valued Elizabeth and her instincts and figured she was probably right. He wanted Zuri to have that genius that would change her life and help him identify the barriers to his Fold vision.

A second opinion of someone of Mallica's mental capacity would be a good check.

Elizabeth engaged Mallica and soon led her away for a tour of the facility, the wheels and the Bubble Scout named Bramlet One.

He heard Mallica laugh as she repeated the name, *"Bramlet One."*

Bram turned his focus back on having breakfast and prepared his oatmeal. This morning, he chose to use black pepper and mix in a soft-boiled egg. He noted that the cafeteria was doing a much larger business than usual. He figured that the word about the launch of Bramlet One had brought the folks out early to get their work done so they could relax at the Bramlet One picnic gathering.

Bram Nielson Collection

Pat let him know that she and the rest of the team were going to the lab to assemble additional Bramlets. The lab had acquired enough bubbles to make a dozen. They were short on camera's and the wheel crew had relinquished the spares to get the scouts done.

Bram said freeing up the cameras was a good idea. He let Pat know that he would make the rounds as soon as he had met with Mallica and Elizabeth.

Lori arrived just as Bram was getting through breakfast. She wanted to make sure that the launch would be at two and that the computer seemed to be working well and that the battery was at its peak charge. She let him know she was nervous about being the person in charge of the launch of Bramlet One.

Bram smiled and assured her that he would not hold it against her if the Bramlet One blew up when she pressed the launch button.

Bram returned to his office and stood looking out the window. The sun had long cleared the mountains. It was a crisp clear cloudless morning. He cranked open two of the high glass windows and enjoyed the cool air falling in to embrace him.

He stood silently looking out at the far snow-capped mountain peaks to the East. He turned to the set of windows that faced West and the lower mountains that blocked his view of what he imagined would be the Pacific. He loved the landscape around Dalles.

The knock at the door brought Bram back from his mental travels.

Elizabeth led Mallica in.

Bram greeted them and asked how the tour had gone.

Mallica responded that she was amazed at the progress the team had made. The wheels were amazing. She went on to say that she thought that Bramlet One had quite a resemblance to him. Its interior was jam packed and its capability amazing.

Bram laughed at her dig and thanked her for coming early.

Ron Mueller

Chapter 20: Bramlet One

Elizabeth guided the discussion to the interview of Zuri. She wanted to understand how the two of them would know if Zuri had the potential to be of help.

Mallica looked at Bram and proceeded to give her thoughts. She would be looking for some understanding in basic math or in some ability to process a mathematical question such as the adding or multiplying two numbers. She did not expect her to be able to process complex equations, but she needed to be teachable. Zuri would need training to get to the level that Bram would be expecting so she would need to be able to comprehend new concepts.

Bram suggested they continue their conversation while they walked to the housing area and visited Mallica's two-bedroom apartment that she had requested versus a house.

Lacy had let him know that it was ready and Mallica's suitcases were in the apartment.

Mallica was surprised at the entourage that accompanied them. Orlando immediately made the point that he had changed his allegiance from guarding Bram and would look out for her instead.

Mallica smiled and turned to Bram and asked if his Marine guards were worth having.

Bram commented that Castor seemed OK, but he was not sure about the other one.

Zoe piped up and made the point that the FBI had decided to reinforce the protective coverage to four because of that concern.

The friendly banter went on until they approached the four-story apartment building. Mallica had a fourth floor, corner apartment. Lacy claimed it was the best one in the building.

The entire group crowded into one elevator.

Castor and Orlando were the first ones through the door of the apartment and told everyone to wait. They went in with their guns at the ready and checked out the entire apartment and the outdoor deck.

Mallica let out a long breath as she took in the exquisite arrangement. A plush cream-colored couch that had reclining seats on each end faced a huge, curved TV screen. A pale blue-gray patterned rug accented the space between the two. A matching cream-colored recliner was located on the far side of what Mallica immediately labeled the living room.

She looked at the table on a dark oriental rug just behind the couch in a large open area. A delicate, purple, and white orchid at the center of the table accented the space she labeled as the dining area.

Immediately inside the apartment door and slightly to the right was a large white marble island with a deep large single sink. To the right was a stainless-steel refrigerator, more white marble countertop, a microwave, and smooth surfaced stove and more white marble countertop.

This was Bram's first visit to any of the apartments. He was pleased that it immediately impressed him.

He led the way to the roomy deck. Lacy had pointed out that a screen blocking anyone from looking in had been put on the deck and all the windows. The person inside could look out and those on the outside would not be able to see them.

Mallica walked through the apartment and returned to the point between the entry and the living room. She commented that Bram should have invited her earlier.

Bram made the excuse that the apartments had just been completed.

She thanked him for having her now and then asked that she be given time to get unpacked. She would come back to the Bramlet One celebration later in the afternoon.

Bram agreed and told her that a car would pick her up in time for the return party.

The black SUV dropped all of them at the entrance to the main office complex. Once inside, Bram headed straight to the Bramlet One launch area.

There, Bram encountered the electrical supervisor in the process of doing the final inspection of the power panel and the power line to the scout launch pad. The electrical crew was standing by so Bram took the opportunity to thank them for the great work and to invite them to stay around for the refreshments Lacy had arranged.

The electrical supervisor pointed to his watch and said that the crew wanted an extra beer for being fifteen minutes early.

Bram smiled and thanked him for the super effort and that if each person let him know the beer, they enjoyed the most, he would make sure they each got a case.

Lori was waving to Bram from the control room. It was clear she wanted him there.

Bram made sure everyone cleared the launch area and walked toward the control room. He looked up and saw Pat and the two crews of the Wheels all standing by in the observation area. He was sure everyone in the building was present to see Bramlet One disappear.

Lori greeted him and guided him to the launch table and pointed to the launch button. It had been appropriately labeled "Launch."

Lori pressed a button on her phone and a drum roll blared out. Bram looked at his watch and exactly as it turned to one, she pressed the button. Bramlet One disappeared and a loud hurrah could be heard throughout the building.

Bram chuckled because to him it was all a little too dramatic, but it was satisfying.

His phone rang, and Jeffrey, John and Erica complimented him on a successful launch. They along with President Natorly had watched via a video link.

Bram was surprised by the call since he had not thought about inviting any of them.

A moment later President Natorly called to compliment him as well.

Bram left the control room and went out looking for Elizabeth. She had to be the one who arranged for the remote viewing. She was doing a great job at making the Fold team look professional! He wanted her to know how much he appreciated her help.

By two everyone in the building and all the Marines not on duty were gathered on the far side of Wheel number two.

Lacy had arranged for three food vending trucks to come in to cater the event. One truck featured Mexican food, one truck feature Asian food, and one truck was all about steaks, sausage, burgers, and hotdogs.

Bram's observation was that the Marines were going to make sure every truck did a good business.

Major Sharp approached him and thanked him for making sure all of his Marines enjoyed this impromptu celebration. He emphasized all and let Bram know that he was rotating all the Marines through. The only restriction for those on duty was that there was to be no drinking.

Bram Nielson Collection

Bram wondered how much his impromptu celebration was going to cost. It didn't matter to him, but it peaked his curiosity.

Lacy walked up to Bram and let him know that she had invited her sister and Zuri to arrive early. She asked if he would be upset if the entire Stetson family made an event of it.

Bram almost choked on a sip of ice-tea. His first question was if the family had been cleared for the visit.

She pointed to Zoe and said that she had cleared them before the family was allowed to take them on the fishing trip.

Zoe saw Lacy pointing and walked over. Bram asked her about the Stetson family. Zoe assured him that all but the one standing with them had been cleared at the same time and had signed a confidentiality agreement. She smiled and said that Lacy had received a top-secret clearance.

At that moment Linda Stetson pushed a wheelchair bound Zuri through the door. Bram walked over and knelt to greet Zuri.

Zuri looked at him and through a twisted smile said hello and identified him as the man who knew how to Fold space and time.

Bram knew instantly that he had found the genius he was looking for. He replied that he needed her help in figuring out what he was doing wrong. Her smile sealed her fate. As far as he was concerned, she was in.

He described the foods that were available and asked her what he could get for her?

Elizabeth appeared and took the Stetson family in hand. They all got some drinks and then she took them for a tour of the hanger area.

Bram walked along and periodically got down on his knees to talk with Zuri. His observation and the questions that Zuri asked kept reinforcing his initial assessment.

Orlando escorted Mallica into the hangar area. He had picked her up early. Mallica thanked him for bringing her to the hangar. She picked up a glass of ice-tea and walked to where Bram was returning with Zuri.

Bram made the introductions and suggested they all take a table and chat. He went on to tell Zuri that Mallica was the resident mathematics genius that would be working directly with her. She would be the one that would spend the most time with her. He told Zuri to cut Mallica some slack because if she didn't like Mallica he would have to find someone smarter and that would be very difficult.

Zuri gave a loud, "Ha." She signaled with her hand for Mallica to lean in. She whispered that Mallica was beautiful and probably as smart as she looked.

Mallica was surprised by the comment. She thanked Zuri and looked around to see if anyone had caught what was whispered. The crowd had drowned out the whisper. It seemed clear to Mallica that the small person in the wheelchair was mentally in full control.

Five was the return time for Bramlet One. The catering trucks left the area, and the party broke up. The observation area was full of folks still enjoying the party.

Bram and the lab crew were in the control room waiting for Bramlet One to reappear.

The stand for Bramlet One seemed to flicker and then blank out. Then it seemed to slowly take shape.

Bram listened to the intake and gasp as the team absorbed what they saw on the stand. He also noted the absolute silence that followed.

He knew immediate action needed to be taken and shouted out orders.

Ron Mueller

Chapter 21: Bramlet One-Sad Return

Bram rushed out of the control room. He shouted for the transport cart and assigned six people to put on anticontamination gear. The cart was to have a nitrogen filled enclosure.

He approached the grotesque object that was part Bramlet One and a part that looked like a stubby moray eel trying to eat it. The black granite like boulder was slightly larger than the Bramlet. Bramlet One was half in and half out of one side of the black granite moray eel.

He noted that the observation area was almost empty. The Wheel teams were gone.

The wait seemed to take hours, but Bram noted that it was only a few minutes past five. It seem like hours to him but only a few minutes had passed!

Six alien looking figures in the anticontamination gear were rapidly pushing a cart toward Bramlet One.

Lori came to stand beside Bram. She commented how amazing it was that Bramlet One managed to return. She made the point that it meant the computer was still functioning and that the power source safety margin had been up to the job.

Bram agreed with her and commented that he would need to analyze what the computer had registered and what had been recorded. The shimmering and power surge were probably due to the extra power need to handle the mass of the boulder. He would need to know the amount of power consumed for the return.

Mallica brought Zuri out to where Zack was standing. She repeated the observation Zuri had shared that sending out Bubble Scouts was a wise move by a wise man.

Bram agreed to the wise move but added by a person who should have known earlier to do it in that manner.

He knelt and whispered that it had been pure luck.

He looked up as Pat, Amy, Elizabeth, and Marcus approached.

Pat and Amy said they would be glad to delay that Wheel Fold until Bramlet Two could verify a safe Fold coordinate.

Bram laughed and went on to poke some fun at them.

He pointed out that the coordinates for Bramlet One were the exact location in the Wheel where the crew sat. He went on to make the point that the coordinate was the coordinates of the Primary pilot seat. Pat and Amy looked at each other.

Pat made the comment that the coordinates he had chosen were diabolical.

As he looked at Pat, Bram was so thankful that Bramlet One had taken the hit.

The coordinates were not the pilot seat but the exact center of the bubble at the center of the wheel. None the less, the size of the Wheel meant that other debris could have been in the same location.

He looked at Zuri and told her that how an object moved to the specified coordinate was a mystery to him. It was a mystery that needed to be solved. Another mystery was how the power from Earth was able to reach through the Fold and power the object in the Fold. And why if the power made it why was it that communication could not also make it?

They all listened as Zuri responded that she would think about these questions, but she would need help in understanding the math and science Bram had used to create the Fold in the first place.

Mallica let Bram know that she was taking Zuri home. She had talked to Zuri about staying with her at the apartment. They would ask Zuri's parents for the approval.

Bram commented that it would be great if that could happen. He knelt and thanked Zuri for having stayed for the return of Bramlet One. He watched as Orlando pushed Zuri toward the SUV.

He turned to Elizabeth and asked her to arrange for a self-powered wheelchair for Zuri. He also asked her to arrange a total medical evaluation at the best clinic that handled cases like Zuri's.

Elizabeth gave him a hug. She let him know that she too was very impressed with Zuri. She agreed to get her the best care possible.

Pat took Bram by the arm. She led him toward the lab. She quietly told him she was taking him to look at Bramlet Two, Three and Four. She told him that the Lab team and the Wheel teams had been working on making more Bramlets.

She went on to tell him that even now as the lab team was examining Bramlet One, Lori was urging the rest of them to finishing another Bramlet to be sent out as early as the next morning.

Bram thanked Pat for letting him know. He had a surge of new energy as he realized that the next bubble scout into the Fold was that close to being ready. He let out a deep breath and gave Pat a hug.

Bram entered a lab that appeared to him to be a beehive in action. He noted that everyone was engaged and concentrating on their work.

Bram walked over to where Bramlet One was housed in a sealed containment where it could be handled without being contaminated any more than it had originally been. He noted that a small chip had been taken from the boulder and would be processed for its composition. It was clear to him that the lab team had the examination clearly in control. They had cut open the top quarter of the bubble and were extracting the computer. He asked that he be called when it was ready for examination.

Pat again took him by the elbow. This time she guided him over to an area where the wheel teams were gathered around three worktables. He looked at the center of each worktable and noted that each was almost at the exact point of completion.

Bram was surprised at seeing Remi the lead lab engineer supervising the completion of the three bubbles. He would have anticipated his wanting to be involved in examining Bramlet One.

He asked Remi as much. Remi replied that getting another Bramlet out was a much higher priority than figuring out how Bramlet One had survived.

Bram agreed with him and asked about the timing of the availability of another Bramlet.

Remi looked at the people around the three tables. They had all stopped to hear what he would say. He looked around and smiled as he said, "If the Wheel teams had applied themselves with more intensity earlier, they would have been ready now, as it is, once they saw what happened to Bramlet One they are much more enthusiastic about getting their Bramlets online. He said that there would be three Bramlets ready by the morning."

Someone added, "and it would go even faster if we had a better coach."

Remi groaned and asked who had come up with a way to double the battery capacity for Bramlet Two that would double the time a Bramlet could stay in the Fold.

Bram laughed and thanked all of them for their super effort. He would try to find better co-ordinates for the subsequent Bramlets. He also mentioned that he had a different scouting behavior he would share in the morning.

He looked at Marcus and asked if he would be able to help in defining better coordinates?

Marcus gave an affirmative shake of his head.

Bram announced that ten a.m. would be the launch of Bramlet Two.

He asked Pat if she was staying. She responded that she was. Bram thanked everyone again and walked out of the lab.

He had decided it was time to go home and continue work after dinner.

Castor stood by the Limo with another Marine. He explained that Orlando had requested to guard Zuri. His request had been granted and Corporal Donna was to be his replacement.

Bram welcomed Donna and told Castor to let Orlando know that he would not be invited to the next fishing trip. Castor laughed and said Orlando would probably not even notice. Castor pointed out that Orlando had his eye set on Mallica, and that Zuri was the official line for the change.

Zoe laughed and said that love conquered all and that Orlando, though a tough guy was no different. She took Eric's hand and got into the back of the SUV.

Bram agreed with Zoe and said he understood and knew the feeling. He asked Donna to tell them about herself.

Bob and Thomas had kitchen duty and were in the middle of getting everything ready. They welcomed Castor and asked who the new Marine might be. They invited both to stay for dinner.

They said they had been present for the return of Bramlet One and wondered how long of a delay that would cause? Would Pat be joining for dinner?

Bram answered the last question first. He suggested they put away a small amount of dinner for Pat just in case. He went on to announce that there would be no delay in the in the Fold program unless the launch of Bramlet Two suffered a similar fate.

Donna found it hard to concentrate on dinner since the team members grilled her.

Zoe commented that it was good to see a woman up front guarding Bram.

Donna joked that she had volunteered when she heard that going fishing with Bram was bound to be very exciting or very successful.

Bram was enjoying the dinner, but he wanted to spend some time in thinking about how best to scout out a Fold point. He excused himself and invited Marcus to join him in his study. Bob got up and led the way and Thomas followed in back. Once in the study, Bob walked over to the tea pot and asked who wanted a cup.

Bram replied that a tea would be great.

Marcus chose a bottle of cold water.

Together they then studied the location near Neptune. Bram decided that he had been too aggressive in locating Bramlet One at only three thousand miles from the surface.

Marcus suggested that something around one hundred thousand miles in front of the planets path would be aggressive enough.

They determined the coordinates that would place Bramlet Two one hundred thousand miles in front of and the same distance inside its orbit. They developed six sets of coordinates that would be used for the six folds.

The coordinates would be the center of a Wheel as it had been for Bramlet One.

It was approaching one in the morning when they finished programing everything into his laptop. He and Marcus agreed they would review their work in the morning before loading the coordinates into Bramlet Two.

Thomas and Bob had been playing cards while they waited. When they saw Bram closing his laptop they got up and cleaned up the coffee/tea bar area.

Zoe and Eric were still up and agreed to escort Marcus to his new home.

Thomas and Bob led the way to Bram's bedroom. It was strategically located and had no windows.

Zoe and Eric's bedroom was across the hall to the right side. Bob's bedroom was to the far end of the hallway and Thomas's bedroom was to the front.

Double curved steps on each side of the front entry area led up to a hallway that made a sharp right turn that was followed by a left turn. Bram had analyzed the layout and agreed that it provided him with maximum safety.

Additionally, the house had three safe rooms. One in the basement, one on the first floor and one in Bram's room. They were stacked one above the other and connected vertically so that Bram could, if necessary, go down through the safe rooms and get down to the basement and be whisked out of the house.

After Bob had cleared the room, Bram entered after saying goodnight to his two guards. He stood under the shower for a long time, as he once again reviewed the following day's agenda. He looked at the clock as he climbed into bed and groaned. It was almost two.

Zoe's knock at the door was the next thing he heard. Once again, he groaned. It was almost eight. Now he was late.

Bram jumped up and quickly got ready. By eight thirty he was going down into the basement to get into the SUV. He kept conversation to a minimum and was eager to get to programing Bramlet Two.

Pat and her team were in charge of Bramlet Two. Her bloodshot eyes spoke of having stayed up all night, but she and her team were exuberant that their Bramlet had earned the number two spot. She gave Bram an uncharacteristic public hug and a kiss on the cheek.

Bram thanked them all for their dedication.

Marcus had been in the lab ahead of Bram. Bram took a moment to introduce him and thank him for his help in determining Bramlet Two's coordinates.

Someone quietly commented that after looking at Bramlet One it was good that an expert coordinate definer had joined the team.

Bram looked around to see who had made the remark but laughed when everyone put up their hands.

He shared that Bramlet Two would make at least six Folds throughout the day. Except for the first that would last only ten minutes, each Fold would be an hour long with an hour between each subsequent Fold. The coordinates would always put Bramlet Two, one hundred thousand miles ahead of the planet.

Remi added that such a schedule would allow recharging the battery each time and Bramlet Two could continue such a schedule indefinitely.

Bram agreed that if more Folds were needed, he would certainly take advantage of the improvement of Bramlet Two.

After programing and closing of the bubble, Bramlet Two was ready for launch. It was moved out to the launch position.

This time the Launch was from a nitrogen filled chamber and each return would be back into the same chamber.

Bram suggested that the whole team press the launch button. He enjoyed the teams loud shout of Fold before they pressed the button.

He knew that the wait time would be like the ten minutes at end of a tight football game.

He decided to get a fresh cup of coffee.

Chapter 22: Bramlet Two

Small tables one for each person had been brought into the launch office. This allowed everyone to have a seat while waiting and provided a way to do some work. The room remained filled with Wheel Team One members. Elizabeth sat silently to the right of Bram and Marcus sat to his left. Neither said a word.

The anticipation in the room bubbled over like oatmeal boiling too fast and about ready to spill out of the pot.

It was heavy and tense.

Nerves were sparking like broken power wires in a storm.

Bram was sure that like his, every mind was on how Bramlet Two would return from its maiden journey.

Bramlet One had surfaced a huge problem. The environment in those far off Fold coordinates that Bram picked was an unknown. Up to this point the coordinates had not even been discussed.

The previous Fold successes had hidden the type of problem Bramlet One had suffered.

Bramlet One had gone out into far space. It had left the protection of the Earth and its risk-free environment. A new sense of danger had been realized and everyone wanted a way to reduce the risk of repeating the event.

Bram looked around. Most of the team was dozing. They had all spent the entire night getting Bramlet Two assembled.

The clock seemed to have gone on professional football time. It was on the last ten minutes of the game speed of a tied game.

He could feel his heartbeat match the beat of the wall mounted clock.

He realized that he was into an adrenalin high.

He felt Elizabeth take his hand and someone else put their hand on his shoulder as the last minute began ticking down.

He looked up to see Pat looking out intensely at the Bramlet launch chamber. The chamber was a nitrogen enclosed containment vessel like the one Bramlet One still occupied.

Then as if by magic a shimmering produced Bramlet Two. The suited crew ran out and wheeled the cart away toward the lab area where it would be briefly examined, and camera memory dumped.

An eager stream of potential examiners gushed out of the launch office, and everyone made their way to the lab.

It made Bram think of the scene one always saw of the football players jogging to their locker rooms.

The camera video from Bramlet Two was put up on the screen and the view of the blue planet was spectacular in its clarity and detail of the surface.

Even as they were enjoying this initial success, John Morgan, the NASA Director informed the group the Scout Bubbles would be equipped with more sensors. NASA wanted a more complete understanding of what was being captured.

He looked around to a beaming Remi and asked how big a scout bubble would need to be to have the equivalent of the sensors that was housed on a Wheel?

Remi replied that with the right camera capabilities and radiation sensors the bubbles might be in the three-foot diameter range. This would allow for more battery capacity needed to operate the additional equipment, but it would still limit the time a bubble could stay out.

Bram asked Remi to take the lead and get one ready as soon as possible. The target date would be to have it available before the Fold across the Universe. He commented that the current bubbles would be used for a Solar System Fold.

An hour later everyone was in the control room for the second Fold of Bramlet Two. This time Pat pressed the Fold button. It was not as dramatic as the previous Fold and the room emptied as soon as the launch button was pushed.

The Wheel teams all retired to their Wheels to get some sleep while they waited for the next hour to pass by.

Bram led the way to his office. He was tired but relieved. He asked Lacy to show Marcus to his new office.

The two agreed to meet back in the launch room for the return of Bramlet Two.

Bram called Mallica to see how she had fared.

Mallica said that Zuri's parents wanted to meet and speak with Bram and the other leaders of the program. They wanted to make sure their daughter was not taken advantage of, and they were very interested in what could be done for her. Their initial reaction was very positive, and she felt good about them.

Mallica commented on how much Zuri had taken to him.

Bram agreed that it was good that the parents would want to make sure their daughter got the best treatment possible. He asked Mallica about her evaluation of the parents.

She replied that they were well educated. They had both graduated from Ohio State. The mother had a degree in mathematics and the father had a master's in mechanical engineering. They provided a very positive environment for Zuri. They were struggling financially because of Zuri's medical needs.

He asked Mallica to investigate the availability of a house in the Fold community for the entire family. It would be good to give Zuri a stable home environment. He also asked that Mallica ask the FBI for top level clearance for all of them. He stated he would have a job for the two talented parents.

He and Mallica agreed to a weekend lunch at his house. Having it there would reduce the security effort and it would allow the family to see the community that would be available to them.

Bramlet Two made its multiple one-hour cycles. It performed flawlessly. The visual data that was captured was sent to the IT analysis team at the end of each Fold. It was being immediately reviewed by a host analysts. Word came back that it was beyond anything they had imagined they would be able to learn about Neptune in their lifetimes.

Bram was pleased with the enthusiasm the IT folks were showing.

He on the other hand was only taking a quick look at what was seen on each cycle. He was more concerned about making sure that Bramlet Two was executing all the commands as he had programed into it.

He was becoming more confident that he would have safe coordinates for the two Wheel Folds.

He asked about any additional Bramlets that were ready to go and was surprised that there were six more ready.

He looked at Marcus and asked if he were thinking what he was thinking.

Marcus replied he would not presume to try to guess what Bram was thinking.

Bram replied that they could send an array of Bramlets out and ensure each Wheel space was free of debris.

Marcus agreed that it would be a very good idea and agreed to set up the coordinates so there was a three-point clearance check for each wheel and one for Bramlet Two that took in the view of the six Bramlets. This would provide a double check of the chosen behind the moon coordinates.

Except for a crew of six from the lab, Marcus and he were the only ones to see the final four Bramlet Two cycles. After the last Fold he asked that Bramlet Two and the other Bramlets all be prepared for Fold instructions and be ready for launch on the following day.

The next thing Bram did was to verify that the current power supply was ample. He then asked the power superintendent to set up six more Bramlet launch power supplies.

Bram spent the wait time reviewing his Fold equations. He was verbally talking through the equations. Marcus was politely listening and pointing out the points where assumptions had been made. Bram noted several points where he chose to use a constant versus a variable to make the equations link. He wondered out loud which constants needed to be variables.

Marcus replied that he had no clue what he was being asked.

Bram knew these would be the areas he would seek Zuri's reaction and comments.

He then asked Marcus to pick a location across the Universe that he wanted to send Bramlet Two. The two of them would do a quick scouting trip to see if the Fold would take them to where Marcus chose the Fold to be.

Marcus whistled silently and said, "you seem to be able to expand scope, change actions, and just decide and then do what you want?" Has anyone challenged you on your independent, lone wolf approach?

Bram replied that if he asked permission there would soon be a whole group of people who had no clue about the Fold, trying to guide the program. He chose to act and then inform. He pointed out that so far it had worked. He also said that as soon as the Fold program was registered as a success, he would most likely be pushed back from the forefront. He said that he was almost ready for that.

Marcus said he would have the location coordinates by morning.

Mallica had spent the day and by late afternoon she knew she had run into a time barrier with having Zuri's parents being checked out by the FBI. Late in the afternoon she went to Bram's office to share her frustrations.

She nodded at Marcus and asked if she could have a moment.

Marcus asked if he should leave.

Mallica said no and started to vent her frustrating day.

Bram listened for a few minutes then put up his hand to stop her.

He called Erica and brought her up to speed on the issue and asked her to see if she could increase the importance of the background check and get it accelerated. He made the point that the family had been thoroughly investigated to get their US entry visa and they were both Ohio State graduates.

Erica readily agreed to go push the system. She was sure it could rapidly be done.

She informed Bram that he had the enthusiastic support of NASA and President Natorly and could get about anything he wanted. She made the point that his success was going to be a huge political boost for President Natorly in the next election.

Bram thanked Erica and went on to say he had also asked Elizabeth to seek all the medical help that was available for Zuri.

Erica replied that she had talked to Elizabeth earlier in the day and had connected her with a Mayo Clinic specialist in Minneapolis. She was sure Zuri would get the best care available in the world and that money was no barrier.

It was clear to Bram that his Fold successes had opened the resource door.

Mallica had taken the opportunity to make some tea. She handed one to Bram and smiled. She went on to say that success certainly opened many doors.

She recalled the year that Bram had walked out into the desert to determine the location of the compound at which all three of them were being held. His persistence then had made all this possible.

Bram looked at Mallica. He agreed with her and went on to apologize for leaving her and Marcus there for so long.

Mallica nodded in agreement and went on to say how demoralizing the lack of action on his part had felt. She said that Elizabeth had made sure everything was OK and had kept both Marcus and she connected.

Marcus had a harder time because his family was back in the Boston area, and he felt that he was not contributing to the Fold project while at the same time cheating his family. He almost dropped out but again Elizabeth assured him that he would be pulled in as soon as you realized you needed help.

Bram nodded.

He agreed and stated that now was the time he was seeking help.

He needed it with the math associated with the Fold.

He needed help with the astronomical locations to send the bubble scouts.

He needed help with the technical development associated with all the hardware and the power consumption the Fold required.

He nodded again and agreed he needed help.

He realized that the Fold effort was growing beyond his personal ability to control the many aspects that needed attention.

Elizabeth poked her head in the door. She asked if she were interrupting anything personal.

Bram smiled and got up walked around the desk gave her a hug and then went to get her a cup of tea.

He asked Elizabeth to sit down and share her good news.

Elizabeth wanted to know how Bram knew she had good news.

Bram pointed out that the smile on her face had broadcast good news.

Elizabeth went on to tell of her discussion with a Dr. Morgan Sewal. Dr. Sewal was globally known and recognized for working with children around the world who suffered many of the same problems that Zuri faced.

He had agreed to come out to meet Zuri and do a preliminary evaluation. Elizabeth said she took the opportunity to invite him to come over on the coming weekend.

Mallica had told her of you arranging for the family to be at your house for dinner.

Elizabeth went on to say that she had invited Dr. Sewal to attend dinner.

Bram looked to Mallica, Marcus and then back to Elizabeth. He asked who was cooking?

Elizabeth laughed. She said she had thought about that and had asked Lacy to arrange for the dinner to be catered. She said that she had counted twenty-two people that would attend. That included Jeffrey, Erica, and John who were planning to fly out and to arrive on Friday.

Elizabeth went on to say that Lacy had asked whether her family would be allowed to cater such an event. She had given Lacy the preliminary OK based on his approval.

Bram put his hand on his forehead and said quietly that it seemed to be a good time to prepare for his background role.

He looked at Mallica and asked if she were ready to assume guiding the Mathematical review of the Fold equations? He wondered if Zuri's mother would be a good participant in that effort.

102

He looked at Elizabeth and asked if she would be OK with stepping back from being the technical supervisor and becoming the guide for Zuri's care and education.

She would retain her command of Wheel Two.

He asked Marcus to become the lead in determining the location and coordinates for the across the Universe Folds and to oversee all Folds.

He would ask Lori to be the lead in managing the Solar System Folds. Marcus would be her coach.

He would ask Remi to be the lead in developing and production of additional bubble scouts.

He would ask Jose and Ester, the previous project managers of the Wheels to retain those positions.

He looked at Elizabeth and asked her to identify and suggest people for the many other roles he was sure he was forgetting. He wanted folks like Amy, Pat, and their backups to be put in meaningful and appropriate Fold program roles. He went on to say he was totally biased and needed to keep his hands off their assignments.

Mallica agreed to lead the analysis.

Elizabeth nodded and said that the change would be welcome and probably be much more to her liking. She commented that it was clear to her that Bram was stepping back as well and that was good. It was time to utilize Erica's project management skills.

She suggested he should think about another fishing trip. He could arrange to take Zuri.

Marcus said he would agree to his role, but his family would need to be invited to go fishing.

Bram evaluated what he had just said. He had instinctively positioned the key people. He was determined to keep the Fold program moving forward as rapidly as possible. If its management was going to change, he would make sure it would fall forward as he envisioned.

He then asked Elizabeth to work with John Morgan and have anyone associated with the Fold effort be relocated to the Dalles site. He wanted to be able to keep the Fold information secret.

Bram stood up, stretched, and declared that it was the seventh inning, and it was time for a beer, a hot dog, and a bag of peanuts. He then walked out of the office.

Ron Mueller

Chapter 23: Leap of Faith

The grey light of the sun outlining the various peaks of the Rocky Mountains painted a black zigzag-like surface ahead of Bram as he and his entourage of guards jogged on the road to the office complex. On this morning Marcus and Pat were jogging besides him. He had agreed with Marcus when he had commented that five thirty was an ambitious time to go to work. He asked Marcus if the opportunity to identify the point across the Universe where the two Wheels would make their maiden interstellar voyage gave him any energy to jog the distance. He pointed out that Marcus would personally press the launch button to send Bramlet Two and the other Bramlets to that location.

Marcus groaned and replied that he would try to keep up. He said he had the coordinates and maybe Donna or Castor could just take them and put them in.

Bram felt good about having engaged Marcus and felt bad at having forgotten him out in the desert compound for the past year. He wished Elizabeth had spoken up but with the flurry of situations that had happened he could not think of a time that he would have paid attention or cared.

He felt good. The Fold team had acted to keep the program on track.

He felt good. The people around him were great and they cared about the Fold program as much as he.

He felt good. He was sure that Zuri would provide the new insight and perspective that he was missing.

He felt good.

He called out to Castor and asked if he had a Marine jogging ditty about feeling good.

Almost immediately Castor had all of them chanting about feeling good to the beat of their jogging. The other marine guards they encountered as they got to the office area joined in as they went by. They called out that they felt good too.

Marcus, Pat, and he were the only ones at breakfast.

Marcus said he had asked his kids about where on the other side of the Universe they wanted to go.

They asked if they needed to stay in the Milky Way or could they go to another galaxy.

Marcus said that their question caught him by surprise. He decided that for now they should stay in the Milky Way.

He was aware that the power consumption of executing the Fold still needed more evaluation and decided they should take one leap of faith at a time.

His current thinking was that the order of the Fold sequence should be a Solar System Fold, then a Milky Way Fold to the nearest potentially habitable planet, and in the near future a Fold to another galaxy.

Bram commented that he was pleased that Marcus had such a bright group of resources to consult. He would be sure to thank them for their guidance.

Pat put her hand on Marcus's wrist and said that this was the highest praise he would get from Bram.

Bram smiled and raised his cup of coffee.

After breakfast Pat led the way to the lab area. Bramlet Two was parked in its nitrogen filled containment besides Bramlet One. The other Bramlets were contained similarly and were standing in a straight row along the wall. The sight of all the Bramlets parked side by side reinforced the need to be thorough in checking out Fold locations.

Bram logged into the local hub that communicated with the Bramlets. He asked Marcus to enter the coordinates that the Bramlets would go to.

Marcus explained that he had considered four locations. They were the most recently found exoplanets. They were Proxima Centrarui b at approximately 4.2 light years distance, Ross 128 b at about 11 light years, Luyten b at about 12. light years and Wolf 1061b at 13.8 light years.

He had let the distance be the guide to his choice. He wanted to send Bramlets to all the locations in the very near future. He commented that this would give them a chance to monitor the power draw as the distances increased.

Bram replied that Marcus should enter the coordinates of all four and that the Bramlets had the opportunity to set a new world record for distance traveled in one day.

Marcus let out his breath and replied that he indeed had coordinates for all the Bramlets.

Bram commented that if all the Bramlets made it through all four-Fold coordinates it would blow the lid off the everyone's expectations.

He went on to say that they would wait until the Bramlets made all their Folds before sharing any information.

He pointed out that if the Bramlet Folds were successful, Marcus would have his hands full in handling an ever-expanding Fold program and asked if he were ready?

Marcus made the comment that maybe he should have settled for the quiet life out in the desert compound.

Pat reacted to the banter by asking if the two were just going to talk or were they ready to get on with the Fold.

Bram and Marcus replied, "let's go do it."

The power meter registered a significant rise in the power consumption as the Bramlets made their first multi-light year Fold. The power increase seemed in proportion to the distance of the Fold but well with in what one power generator could handle.

Marcus commented that if the power draw was somehow proportional to distance then one generator seemed to be the capacity needed for the more distant Folds.

Bram agreed with Marcus. He took the precaution of checking with the power generator superintendent to ensure additional power would automatically come online if needed.

Bram returned to his office during the hour the Bramlets were deployed.

Lacy entered and said she wanted to give Bram a quick update on the dinner arrangements for the next day.

She shared the menu that would feature Salmon and Gar as the fish. Lamb would be the red meat. There would be a mixed fresh vegetable salad. Sweet potatoes and cooked carrots would round out the menu.

Bram said the menu sounded great. He wanted to make sure that this would fit Zuri and her family's diet.

Lacy said she would double check with Zuri's mother. She went on to inform Bram about rearranging the lounge area in his house and setting up a long table to seat everyone.

Bram Nielson Collection

Bram raised his hands and replied that he was OK with anything and everything. He laughed and said dinner was beyond his control. He would stick with the simple stuff like monitoring the Fold.

Lacy responded to his comment. She said that indeed the Fold was much easier and more like eating a piece of cake, "sometimes a little crumbly but it had frosting and was sweat as a piece of cake."

Bram agreed with her. He asked whether she could also arrange for another fishing trip for two weekends after the dinner.

He then excused himself so that he could get back to the Fold launch office and get frosting put on his cake.

Marcus had not only programmed in the coordinates for each Fold, but he had also provided guidance to the camera motion. His goal was to guide the picture taking so that the resulting images could be oriented. At this point Marcus had no clue how to aim the camera. Once these initial shots were examined future guidance could then be managed in a controlled fashion.

Bram agreed with Marcus's approach. Together they examined the results from the Proxima Centrarui b Fold.

Bram realized they could spend hours examining the footage they had brought back. He brought the viewing to an end by declaring it was time to send the Bramlets out to Ross 128 b.

The power draw for the Ross Fold increased proportional to the increase in distance but it too stayed well within one generator's power.

Bram now had the information to calculate the power draw for the bubble scouts based on their size and distance. He would soon have the similar requirements for the power requirements for the Wheels.

He decided that the first Wheel Fold would be out close to the Moon. This would give him two power requirement points for the Wheel folds and the opportunity to make sure that the Fold out to Neptune would be within the power that was available.

He mentioned it to Marcus and the two worked together to put the moon Fold location on the dark side of the moon. It would not be detectable from Earth.

Elizabeth, Amy, and Pat listened to Bram as he explained the change in the Wheel Fold sequence he was planning for the coming week. The fact that he had added a Fold close to the Moon was seen as a great precaution and well accepted. This was especially true when they learned that they would only stay at the Moon Fold location for two days. They would then take a day off and then make the Fold out to Neptune.

Everyone on the team thanked him for his caution but voiced the fact that they were ready.

Bram asked that the changes to the Fold schedule not be shared. He knew he was moving fast and adjusting schedules as the scouts provided additional information.

He and Marcus reviewed that footage the Bramlets brought back from Wolf 1061b. They had calculated all the upcoming Fold locations for all the Bramlets and the Wheels during the day. They decided that it was time to decompress and get ready for the Saturday dinner event at Bram's house.

Bram and Marcus walked back to Bram's office.

Lacy informed Bram that Jeffrey and Erica had just arrived and were in his office.

Bram took a deep breath and walked into his office.

Jeffery stood up and walked over to shake Bram and Marcus' hand. Erica did the same, but she gave Bram a hug.

Bram asked how the trip out to the west coast and the drive down had been?

Erica replied that it had had been a long trip but other than that it had been fine. She said that Lacy had been very helpful and had arranged to have their apartments ready for them. She went on to say that they had decided to come by his office before going there.

Bram replied that he was glad to see them. After asking if they wanted anything, he went on to say that he and Marcus had just finished sending Bramlets to four distant places that were from four to thirteen light years away.

He went on and said that Saturday evening's dinner would feature unedited views of Neptune and these four across the galaxy visits.

Erica gave a small laugh and commented that it was almost impossible to keep up with him and the Fold progress.

Jeffrey commented that he was pleased and that the speed of the Fold progress was taking everyone by surprise. He asked if Bram needed anything to keep things going.

Bram decided that this was the moment to share the changes he had decided on.

He looked at Erica and said that she was really needed at the Dalles site. He explained that he was stepping out of the role of managing the technical activities.

He needed more time to study and improve the Fold equations and the process. He was recruiting Zuri Juma, a seven-year-old savant, to provide an outside fresh evaluation of his work.

He had asked Mallica to manage the review and be a mentor to Zuri.

He had asked Elizabeth to step back from being the technical project manager and manage the medical care for Zuri. Elizabeth would retain her position as Captain of Wheel Two.

Marcus would determine the Galaxy and beyond Fold locations and coach Lori Middleton on her role as Solar system Fold locations leader.

Bram went on to explain that he had asked Elizabeth to work with Erica to make these changes and then make sure the remaining team members all got recognized and rewarded for all the great work by getting strong career building assignments.

He was staying on as the Captain of Wheel One. He made the point it was the only role that took so little time that he could afford to stay there for the near future.

He went on to say that Erica could have any home in the Fold complex that suited her and that was available.

Once again Erica commented on the speed of change in the Fold project but said that she would be pleased to take a bigger role in the Dalles location. She commented that it would be a relief from the haggling that occurred on the East.

Bram stood up and suggested they all ride together to the Fold community area. They could continue their conversation tomorrow over a late eight in the morning breakfast.

Chapter 24: Project Alignment

The short ride back to the Fold housing area allowed for only a brief follow-up conversation. This is what Bram had planned. He wanted Jeffrey and Erica to have the evening to think about the changes he had described. He let them both know that there would be a food menu in the apartment at which they were staying, and that the cafeteria stayed open until ten and would deliver the food to them.

They both thanked him and then exited and went to their apartments.

After dropping them off he let Marcus know he was welcome to the breakfast, but his presence was not required.

Marcus thanked him and said he and family would come over for the dinner and the space movie.

After Marcus got out of the SUV, Zoe and Eric moved from the very back and sat next to Bram. The SUV proceeded to the basement of his house.

Eric commented that he thought Bram had done an excellent job of managing his boss.

Bram gave a chuckle and added that it was not Jeffrey but Erica that he was trying to manage. She was excellent at her job, but she often wanted to step in and manage what other people were responsible for.

Zoe replied that while Bram was around, Erica would most likely stay between the lines of the road.

Bram thanked her for the kind words. He went on to say that Erica had been the one that had made first contact with him and at that time had greatly influenced his decision to work on the Fold project.

Jeffrey had sealed the deal by simply informing him that he had no other choice.

Bob greeted them as they came up from the basement. He let them know that he was just finishing getting dinner ready. He said the meal consisted of grilled chicken, mac and cheese, some grilled asparagus and a side salad of mixed lettuce topped with small tomatoes. He said it would be on the table in fifteen minutes and asked who wanted some Muscatel.

Bram said it all sounded good, could he have about twenty minutes so that he could take a quick shower.

The conversation at dinner was about the number of guests that would attend dinner on Saturday. One main concern was for the team to review the guest list and make sure everyone had been cleared.

The Juma family seemed to be the only guests that might not have their clearances, but Zoe felt confident that the family was not a threat.

Bram let Zoe know that Erica had indicated she expedited the clearance process, and that Zoe should look to see if there were any outstanding messages about that situation.

Zoe asked if Bram was willing to share what he had been doing with the Bramlets during the day?

Bram understood Zoe's curiosity and described sending the Bramlets across the Universe. The fact that the Bramlets had gone from four to fourteen light years across the Universe and brought back some astounding pictures was historic. He pointed out that those sitting around the table would be among the first to know. The Saturday dinner entertainment would be the showing of a few minutes at each location.

Pat had been silent until that moment. She looked around the table at the in-the-headlight kind of stares each of the protection team members exhibited. She commented that she too was amazed at the speed that Bram was using the Fold capability. It was historic and seemed to leap forward at the speed of a winning drag race car that did not have a stop parachute.

Bram asked who on the team would like to help him select the photo segments from each location.

Every hand including Pat's went up in the air.

Bram suggested that maybe the more fun thing would be for them to select the scenes and surprise him at tomorrow's dinner with the choices they made.

Pat and Zoe both said that the idea was a great one.

Bram smiled and said he would spend his time having breakfast with the boss and then go on with his reexamination of his math. He said he wanted to be sure it was safe before he got on Wheel One and let Pat push the launch button.

Pat joked that it was about time that he thought about the safety of the crew.

Bram got up and carried his dishes to the sink. It was his turn to rinse the dishes and put them in the dishwasher. He had insisted they all take turns at kitchen duty. He had designed the daily kitchen chore list of one cook and three of them as cleanup crew. During the week this only applied to dinner. On weekends it applied to all three meals. He was pleased with how well the team made it work.

After dinner Bram went to his office. Pat brought in two large mugs of tea and sat down beside him on the two-person recliner-couch. He chose to recline. Pat put her back to his side and opened the latest book she was reading.

Bram had his eyes closed and was once again going through the Fold math. He put his right arm over Pat's shoulder and absorbed the comforting warmth her body transferred to him. It was hard for him to concentrate on Fold equations, and he soon dozed off.

Pat felt the change in Bram's breathing and realized he had fallen asleep. She figured the events of the day had sapped his drive. She felt total contentment. It was a feeling she had sought. When she met Bram, her yearning was immediately satisfied.

At midnight Pat nudged Bram and suggested they go up to bed.

Pat guided a sleepy Bram up to their room. He threw his slacks on the chair and got in on his side. Pat soon came back to the bed and got in on her side and scooched over and put her head on Bram's chest. She gave him a kiss on the cheek and then settled in with his arm around her.

The next morning Bram fought through a dream about his Wheel flying off out of control and heading into a blackhole. He awoke with a jerk. He decided his dreams were much too real as he wiped sweat off his forehead.

He went into the bathroom to get ready for the day. It was already eight. He was glad he had agreed with Erica for a late nine or nine thirty breakfast.

Pat was at the stove getting ready to cook some pancakes when Bram finally came into the kitchen.

Bram gave her a hug and said he was surprised they were the only ones up.

Pat corrected him and said their four FBI guards already had breakfast and were in the basement welcoming Jeffrey, Erica, John, and a Dr. Morgan Sewal. She went on to say that breakfast would be pancakes, bacon, eggs over easy and either coffee or tea.

Bram thanked her for being ambitious enough to feed ten people. Then he headed to the basement door to welcome his morning breakfast guests.

Jeffrey led the way with John close behind. Erica and Dr. Sewal were talking and briefly said good morning as they came in.

Bram said good morning to the FBI four and then led the way to the breakfast eating area.

John and Dr. Sewal had traveled down from Portland in an SUV that Lacy had arranged to pick them up.

Bram welcomed everyone and made sure everyone had been introduced and asked Pat to share the breakfast offering.

He then asked how Jeffrey and Erica had faired with dinner the night before.

Erica said she chose to just have a salad and now she was ready for a big breakfast. She said she would take one of everything and a cup of coffee.

Zoe brought the coffee and tea pot and filled each cup based on each individual's desire.

John said that he and Dr. Sewal had been on the same flight and had breakfast on board, but he was ready for some over easy eggs, bacon, and some toast.

Dr. Sewal said he would take the same as John.

Jeffrey said he would take what Bram planned to order.

Bram looked at Jeffrey and smiled. The two had in previous breakfasts discussed Bram's favorite breakfast being two pancakes, with two over easy eggs with three strips of bacon on top and drowned in maple syrup.

Pat had made brief notes of all the orders. She said she knew the last two orders by heart. She would add Erica to that list.

She began with John and Dr. Sewal's breakfast.

Zoe served them as soon as it was prepared.

Bram suggested that each person dig in as soon as they got served. He commented that breakfast was best when it was hot.

Erica dug in as soon as it arrived. She was on her second cup of coffee. Her comments about the breakfast were all positive.

Jeffrey got his next and immediately put the pads of butter between the pancakes and two on top. He then smothered it all in Maple syrup.

Erica copied his preparation on the three quarters that was still on her plate.

Bram did the same as Jeffrey had done. He looked to Pat and asked if she was going to join them at the table.

Pat sat down with just a cup of coffee for herself. She commented that breakfast was either very good or everyone was too shy to talk.

Bram saw that Dr. Sewal's plate was empty, and he was now just sipping his coffee. Bram thanked him for coming on such short notice. He went on to describe Zuri and that she was brilliant, probably a Stephen Hawking-like person. He hoped that Dr. Sewal would be able to improve her life.

Dr. Sewal replied that Elizabeth had made a similar comparison and had persuaded him to come out immediately. He thanked Bram for inviting him to dinner. He was eager to meet Zuri, and he would certainly do everything in his power to improve her life.

Bram again thanked him.

He then turned to John and asked if NASA was ready to up their contribution to the Fold effort. Bram went on to specifically state that he did not want supervisors. He wanted contributing team members.

John replied that he had been waiting to be asked. He had a host of great people all chomping at the bit to get closer to the action. They were all wanting to be on the court and taking shots. He said that there were no bench warmers or sideline coaches.

Bram nodded and thanked John. He asked that all the current folks associated with the Fold effort be relocated to Dallas so that the information could be contained.

He asked John to help Remi establish bubble building contracts with some reputable companies. He pointed out that they had a leading company that had the Wheel building contract, but NASA needed to take a position on bubble building. At this time, the bubbles were being assembled on location. Remi Hardwood was the engineer leading that effort. He would be a great resource and potential future leader of such an effort.

He turned next to Erica and asked what she had decided about moving to Dalles.

Erica smiled at Bram and replied that if he would have her over once a month for a breakfast like the one she just had, she would make the sacrifice and leave the DC arena immediately. She said that she personally was ready for some field action and that the atmosphere back east was getting way too political.

Bram promised to give her as many breakfasts as she might want.

Jeffrey looked around the table. He commented that the Fold project seemed to manage itself. He wondered what he might do to help.

Bram looked at Jeffrey and commented that his role was going to get much tougher once the world realized how powerful it made the country that controlled the Fold process. He pointed out that even if it shared the results, the US currently controlled what was seen and how the program was managed.

He asked Jeffrey whether his support team back east was strong enough to influence and guide the US administration that was in power? He went on to ask which military branch wanted to control the program?

Bram's final comment was that Jeffrey should let Erica be his Fold Project manager and lock everyone else out and keep them on the other side of the fence.

Jeffrey commented that he had asked and gotten a clear message of what he should do. He agreed with Bram that the political aspects were getting tougher. It seemed that the Fold's early success had surprised almost everyone.

There was opposition for whatever reason, but probably they were financial ones, and that opposition seemed bent on stopping the program. A Fold success antiquated every space technology currently being use. It would put the rocket building business into the same situation that buggy making had experienced when Ford began mass producing automobiles.

He pointed out that Bram had introduced the next dramatic economic change and was continuing to do so at breakneck speed.

Bram looked around the table and saw everyone nodding their heads in agreement. He commented that the financial and cultural situation on Earth would take a momentary hit. He pointed out that John would be seeking to establish many business contracts. The world would quickly recover and benefit financially.

He then shared his major concern that he might expose Earth much like a prairie dog coming unsuspecting out of its den and being fanged by a rattlesnake.

He needed to ensure that there was not a rattlesnake waiting out in the universe that would sink in its fangs into Earth.

Jeffrey looked at Bram and agreed that the finances would quickly balance out and that the changes that had been suggested made the Fold effort much stronger. However, the short-term impact was a barrier that might prove insurmountable.

Eric commented that a catering truck was parked out front and that it was probably time for breakfast to end.

Bram stood up and thanked everyone for their participation in the Fold effort. He said he was looking forward to the dinner and a continuing discussion on how the world around them would change but benefit everyone.

Chapter 25: Team Problem

After everyone had left, Bram retired to his office. Zoe and Eric were his shadow for the day and sat on the sofa reading. Bram had spontaneously spouted his concern about exposing Earth. It had not been something he planned to say. He was now working through the various risk scenarios that some belligerent or scared, intelligent alien culture might pose.

He looked to Zoe and Eric and decided that they were probably always thinking about the various situations that's put him at risk.

Bram excused himself and asked them to help him identify the various risk scenarios that they would be concerned about and how they would prepare for each.

Eric said that would be great. Zoe agreed but she said that Thomas was the risk scenario freak among them. She suggested they invite both Bob and Frank to join in on the discussion.

Bram agreed everyone's participation was welcome.

Pat entered and became alarmed as Zoe ran out and called for Frank and Bob.

Bram signaled her over and explained that he had ask for help in identifying the risk scenarios that the Fold program could put Earth into.

Pat let out her breath and said the first risk would be the heart attack for the unsuspecting. She sat down in the recliner and sipped on her tea. She figured this would be a work session in which she would be able to understand and perhaps participate.

Eric, Zoe, Frank, and Bob took seats around the office. Frank expressed the fact that he had been discussing this exact point with the team. He wondered why it had taken so long to get to this critically important topic.

Bram restated his request. This time he asked that each risk that was brought up should be accompanied with at least one counter measure. The risk should be written down and pinned to the note bar that ran around the room. All the risks should be identified and then on a second round all would be reexamined.

Zoe agreed to be the scribe and to put each sheet up.

Bram listened as the four began their risk identification. He only intervened when they began to argue about a specific risk.

The risks were interesting and informative. They were,

- That a bomb would be attached to the scout and would explode on its return. The bomb might be big enough to blow up the earth.
- That an external tracking device could be put on the scout and provide the aliens with a way to follow it back.
- That the aliens put germs or viruses on the scout that would then attack humans when the scout returned.
- That an alien computer Trojan horse could be put into the scout and that it would spread around the world.
- That the scout would be captured and would give the aliens a technology they did not currently possess.
- That the scout would give Earth coordinates to the aliens.

This would give them the ability to launch a variety of attacks.

Bram thanked the team for their morbid view of the alien culture. He had not thought about any of the scenarios. He admitted that he had been on "the raise your open hand and say friend," scenario.

He made the point that he could immediately implement having a sensor that made sure nothing was attached to the scout. Additionally, the scout was now launched from and returned to the inside of a sealed chamber, so any external viruses or germs would be detected. This chamber could be enhanced into a bomb explosion containment chamber. He would ask the computer experts about enhancing his software defense and a way to test the software for any changes on each Fold return.

He admitted; he was not sure about blocking any back tracking of the coordinates. He would put this on his list to work with Zuri as they reviewed the Fold equations.

He took in the expression on everyone's faces and commented that they had done a great job. He asked if they would they like to continue and lead a more thorough defense effort?

Zoe spoke up immediately that she would love it. It would make life so much more fun. They would need to get it cleared by their bosses. She pointed out that Bram's request would make acceptance an immediate reality.

Bram agreed to get Erica to make it happen. He then suggested they take a break and see if there were any snacks that they might enjoy prior to dinner.

Lacy greeted Bram as he came into the kitchen. She quickly re-introduced all of her family. She said that her Father was out getting the grill ready. Rita said hello from where she stood in front of the oven. Marial said hello from where she and her husband, Cedric were setting up a series of tables that would be pushed together to form one large table that would take up the entire recreation area. Luke, Lacy's uncle was busy erecting a large viewing screen.

Bram welcomed everyone and thanked them for responding to Lacy's request. He then asked if there might be a snack that the team could take away for an impromptu picnic down by the playground.

Lacy led the way out to where her father was at the grill. She asked what he was grilling? Ted responded that he had brats, hot dogs, and some chicken wings.

Bram shook Ted's hand and gave him a hug. He asked for a couple of chicken wings for each of them and a dog for himself.

Ted responded that it was great to see Bram and Pat again and that the Gar she had caught was still being eaten.

Everyone made a choice and the six of them headed for the playground. Almost immediately Bram caught sight of a drone hovering above one of the trees. He asked his four bodyguards if any of them had a silencer on their gun.

Zoe and Frank responded that they had.

Bram gave them the coordinates of the drone and told them that unless they had been informed that they should expect a drone they should shoot it down.

He watched as the two shot the drone out of the air. He thought that Zoe had been the one to hit it.

He called Major Sharp and informed him that a drone had been shot down. Then "Ed" as he liked Bram to call him said he would immediately send a team over to investigate.

Bram called one of the marine guards over and pointed to the drone and asked him to have all the guards look around for someone, inside or outside the fence that might be around with a drone control unit. He should guard the drone until the investigation team arrived.

Bram went to the nearest picnic table and sat down. He opened the basket of chicken wings and then took a bite of his hot dog. Pat sat down next to him, and Zoe and Eric sat across the table in front of him and Thomas and Bob sat one to each side of him and Pat.

It was clear to Bram that they were in their defensive protect positions.

No one at the playground noticed anything unusual. Melisa their neighborhood event organizer waved and walked over to say hello. She did not notice the Marine guard who was guarding the shot down drone.

Bram decided not to say anything and instead offered her some chicken wings. Melisa declined and said she needed to get back to her kids.

Bram looked over at Zoe and said they needed to work on the risk scenarios associated with being a part of the Fold program and come up with additional counter measures. It was clear to him that so far, the Fold team was being naively defensive. He went on to say he wanted an offense.

He asked Zoe to work with Erica in setting up an FBI counter offensive unit.

Zoe agreed that something needed to be done but commented that she was not sure getting the FBI involved was the right step.

Bram watched as the Marine investigation team gathered up the small camera drone. They spent a few moments talking to the guards and then quietly left. Bram's request that the investigation team be discrete had been clearly followed and no one at the recreation center noticed anything unusual.

Eric made the comment that they were being watched. He suggested that all the dinner guests arrive by SUV and enter via the basement. He pointed out that the catering truck was parked in back and was out of view. He suggested that extra Marines be posted discretely and out of sight around the perimeter of the yard for the afternoon and evening.

Bram thought that Eric's suggestions were very appropriate. He asked Eric to make the arrangements with Major Sharp.

Pat suggested that they get back to the house and finish selecting the clips that they would show their guests.

Bram thought that it was a great idea to get back to the house. He stood up and headed up the hill toward his house.

He sought out Lacy and after explaining the situation he asked her to have the guests be brought in as Eric had suggested. He let her know about the extra guards and asked her to make the arrangement to feed them.

Lacy commented that he seemed to be a magnet for attention. She would inform the family of what was going on and then to make all the arrangements for the guests and those around that were guarding them. She said she was going to go ahead and arrange an escort for those leaving later for the airport.

She suggested that they needed a broader security net that was outside of the compound.

Bram was getting discouraged by the success of his adversaries and nodded his head in agreement. He decided that some of his Bramlets might be put to good use as perimeter snoopers.

The guests began arriving and were mingling around the kitchen, the eating area, the front entrance and sitting area. Marcus and his family were the last from the compound to arrive.

Then Zuri and her parents arrived.

Zuri was carried up the stairs by Orlando and Castor.

Mallica escorted Zuri's parents and introduced each. She made a point that Nuro, meaning born at night, had a master's degree from The Ohio State and Jina whose name meant victorious had a mathematical degree from the same university.

Bram shook hands with each of the parents and then got down on his knees and gave Zuri a hug and welcomed her. He called Dr. Sewal over and introduced him to Zuri.

Dr. Sewal got down on his knees and said hello.

Bram stood up and suggested that Lacy take control of getting everyone seated.

Ron Mueller

Marcus approached Bram and said that he really did not want to say anything, but his wife insisted that he tell Bram that she thought his greeting of Zuri was inappropriate. She wanted to let Bram know that she did not want him near her kids.

Bram was taken aback. He did not know how to reply. He looked at Marcus and then over to where Myla his wife was standing. He replied that he would seek additional opinions and get back to him.

He asked Dr. Sewal about the greeting and if he saw anything wrong with it.

Dr. Sewal replied that he would be doing the same once he got to know Zuri better.

He next asked Mallica and Orlando. They both said they had done the same thing he had done. Mallica wondered why Bram was asking. Bram explained about the message Marcus had given him from his wife. Mallica said she would talk with Myla and see what was up.

Bram thanked her and proceeded to take his seat. He knew that he had a real issue on his hands. He was almost sure there was a dark cloud in Marcus's wife's childhood. Bram made up his mind that it would either get resolved or Marcus would need a new assignment.

A name tag identified each person both with a name and a number. The number indicated the menu choice that had been selected. Salmon and Gar were the two most popular choices, but a few chose the Lamb. Zuri said that she had chosen Gar because she had been told that it was the one that Pat had caught.

Bram watched as the picture of Pat standing on the dock beside her Gar flashed up on the screen. He noted that she had on the same green blouse, shorts, and shoes that she had worn when she caught her record sized salmon on the Rushing River. He also noted his own response with seeing the picture.

After a round of congratulations, the table went silent as everyone ate their meal. Small conversations would pop up and then once again there was silence.

Bram proposed a toast to the Stetson family and the fine cuisine they had prepared. Everyone raised their wine or beers and gave a Marine "Hurrah."

Pat then announced that they would start showing the journeys the Bramlets had made.

She showed the launch of Bramlet One and explained about the celebration that was held. She then flashed a picture of Bramlet One as it now rested in a container sealed in Nitrogen. There were audible gasps around the table.

Bram commented that the Wheel teams went from complaining about he being too cautious and worried about their safety to saying they were fine with the delay that sending out the Bramlets to ensure the area for the Fold would be clear.

Pat then showed the launch of Bramlet Two and explained how both Wheel teams and the Lab team had worked together to have Bramlet Two ready the next day for additional Folds. Marcus was lauded for moving Bramlet Two to a more distant and safer position out in front of the Neptune orbit. She explained that those present were seeing footage so far only seen by a few others in the room.

Then Pat shared that the next four slides would show views that went multiple light years across the Milky Way and that now there were seven Bramlets in existence.

She explained that the pictures would show the four planets that had been discovered in the last four years and ranged from four to thirteen light years away. She stopped and looked around the room and quietly pointed out that they were the first to see them. No one outside the room had yet had a chance. She pointed out that this was a historic moment for all of them.

There was a round of applause and an exclamation about having gone out into the Milky Way with no warning announcement.

Bram pointed to Marcus and gave him credit for having selected and determined the coordinates for the Bramlets' Folds. He complimented Pat and the FBI team for having selected the views that had been shared. He said all the information was safely stored and backed up multiple times on multiple storage hardware.

He closed by saying that it was time for dessert and wondered what it might be.

Lacy announced that the dessert was three types of her mother's secret recipe pies.

She described one as a strawberry rhubarb pie that was required eating before one went to heaven.

She said the second was an apple raisin pie that would make you want a second piece.

Lacy claimed the third, a caramel cream pie would instantly put ten pounds around your waist even if you just looked at it.

Bram had watched Zuri to see what her reactions had been to Lacy's dessert descriptions. It was clear she had enjoyed the banter and understood what was being said.

He waited until Zuri had ordered. She chose the last saying she could use a good ten pounds.

Bram said he did not need the ten pounds, but he was also choosing the caramel cream pie.

Mallica had changed seats so she could sit and talk with Marcus's wife, Myla. It was clear to Mallica that there was some personal history that might include abuse as a child that was affecting her reaction to Bram's hug of Zuri. This was not just a guess. She had experienced that type of abuse.

She knew that the dinner was not the setting to pursue the issue, but she wanted to make some personal contact.

The dinner broke up and everyone was chatting and marveling at the progress that the Fold effort had made.

Bram asked Mallica to meet with Dr. Sewal and Zuri in his office. Nuro and Jina joined the group going into Bram's office.

Bram watched as Marcus, his wife and two kids went into the basement to get a ride home. He would need to talk with Marcus on Monday morning.

He got everyone situated and thanked Nuro and Jina for participating. He said that he would step out and let Mallica, Elizabeth and Dr. Sewal talk with Zuri.

He went on to say that the interview by Dr. Sewal was to ensure that Zuri got the best care that was possible.

He introduced Elizabeth as the person who would manage getting Zuri every possible thing that would improve Zuri's life.

He pointed to Mallica and said that she would be Zuri's advanced math instructor.

He then said he was going to leave the office but would return at the end and would like to hear from the Juma family about being part of the Fold effort.

Chapter 26: Zuri Makes the Team

Ted was leading the break down effort of the tables and chairs. Rita was arranging the leftover food and supervising the kitchen clean up. The dishes were rinsed but would get a final wash back in the catering facility. The cleanup action would stop, and they would all talk about the pictures of planets light years away that they had been allowed to see. It was something beyond what they had thought was possible. They had commented that Bram seemed like just another guy, but he must have some brain to have figured out how to instantly send an object across the Milky Way.

Lacy came over to Bram and asked why he had left the meeting in the office.

Bram replied that he had something more important to handle. He had come out to talk to Ted about something even more important than what was going on in the office.

Ted heard what Bram said. He looked a little amazed and asked what in the world would he know that could be more important.

Bram smiled and replied that Ted knew where to take him to catch fish. He wanted to schedule another fishing trip.

Ted laughed and said that Bram could go fishing with him anytime that he wanted but he would have to bring along his better half who really knew how to catch fish or anything else she put her mind to.

Rita said she could provide lunch, but the weather would probably not be very cooperative. She suggested their catering truck and the use of an awning.

Bram said he wanted to take Zuri fishing. She would be in an outing wheelchair. It would be a light structure, but it would need to be fastened to the boat so that it was stable and would not roll or move around. He went on to say that he would pay for any modifications that might be required. He suggested that four eye bolts placed on the edge of the flat area would be a way to anchor the chair. He suggested that Ted figure out the best approach and let him know.

Ted chuckled and said that it was good that he had talked to him and not Luke or Cedric because they would have turned down any suggestion about putting eyebolts in the hull of their boats.

He, on the other hand, figured any person that could provide guidance to a disoriented person like Bram would be a person that he would modify his boat to go upside down and backward if needed.

He told Bram not to worry, leave the simple boat modifications to him and that his boat would be equipped to safely take Zuri fishing.

He suggested a date two weekends away.

Bram agreed to the date.

Pat came out of the office and said it was time for Bram to come back.

Bram entered as Elizabeth was pouring some lemonade and offering bottles of water to everyone in the room. It was clear to Bram that she had taken control and that all was well. When she saw Bram, she asked Dr. Sewal to share his diagnosis and his recommendations.

Dr. Sewal replied that he would like to have Zuri come to Minneapolis to the Mayo clinic for a full evaluation. He would then generate a plan for long term care. He would personally supervise the fitting of a motorized chair that Elizabeth had agreed to pay for.

Elizabeth looked at Bram to see if there was any reaction on his part.

Bram looked to Nuro and Jina and asked about their current thoughts and would they agree to having Zuri be a full working member of the Fold program.

Jina smiled and replied that she and Nuro had never dreamt of such an opportunity for Zuri. She said that the Fold team atmosphere seemed so positive, and Zuri was very excited about the work that was being done. She went on to say that having the best care for Zuri was a dream come true for them.

Bram said that indeed the Fold team culture and atmosphere was inclusive and positive. He asked if the two of them would also like to be part of the team.

Both Nuro and Jina had tears in their eyes as they looked around the room. Nuro said he did not know what to say. What possible job could he do? What would Jina do?

Bram replied that there were many jobs available and there was a house in the Fold community with the Juma name on the mailbox. Bram pointed out that the following day was Sunday, so they should be able to take tour of the house.

Nuro and Jina got down on their knees and shared a hug with Zuri.

He heard Zuri say see, I told you I knew a person who worked miracles.

Jina stood up and gave Bram a hug. She said that yes, she wanted to be on the Fold team and would sweep floors if Bram asked her to. Nuro gave Bram a hug and said that he would prefer a role that utilized his skills, but he too would sweep floors if asked. He was all smiles.

Bram replied that Jina would be part of Mallica's Fold equation review team. The objective of the team was to figure out how to make key improvements that he had no clue how to make.

He pointed to Nuro and said the Bubble design team was going to need his skills.

Bram pointed at the clock on the wall and suggested they call it a day.

He invited everyone for a picnic lunch at noon the next day.

Dr. Sewal thanked him for the invitation but said that he had a flight to Minneapolis close to that same time. He looked at Zuri and told her that he would look forward to her visit in the next few weeks. He then got down and gave her a hug.

Bram again thanked him for having taken the time to come out and said that now he was their Mayo Clinic Fold member of the team. Bram said that the Sewal family was welcome any time and that they should think about a vacation in the area and plan to go fishing at that time.

Orlando was waiting outside the office. He wheeled Zuri to the steps where Castor joined in to carry her and the chair down the steps.

Elizabeth and Dr. Sewal said good night and followed them down.

Linda Stetson had waited to see how things would work out. She knew instantly that Zuri had made the team. She gave Lacy a hug and said that now she could go home.

Bram realized that Ted and Rita were also still present.

Ted said that the four of them were riding home together in a SUV that was blocked in by the SUV that was taking Zuri home.

Lacy grinned and said that was the family excuse for hanging around so they could all go home and celebrate the successful end of the Zuri saga that Linda had kept the family involved in for more than a year.

Bram looked at Lacy and said that maybe the Fold team needed a caring person like Linda.

Pat thanked the four and said their SUV was ready and pointed to the basement door.

Bram looked around at what was now as empty as the house ever got. He noted that Eric and Zoe were each standing on opposite sides of the room and that Bob and Thomas must have retired to their rooms.

Pat suggested they go to the office and unwind. She poured each of them a glass of Muscat wine.

Bram agreed that her suggestion and the wine made a great combination. He commented that Marcus's message from his wife, Myla, was still eating at him and he wanted to discuss it with the three of them.

Pat said she was not sure to what the issue might be and asked Bram to explain the issue to the three of them.

Bram explained that Myla thought that his hug of Zuri was improper and that a man should not hug a young girl in that manner. She had expressed to Marcus she did not want him near her children.

Pat looked at Zoe and Eric and asked if they had seen anything that Bram had done that was improper.

Zoe commented that nothing improper had happened and the Marcus's wife must have a problem.

Bram said that Mallica was going to look into it some more. He said he believed Myla, might have been molested as a child by some man. He looked at Zoe and went on to say that he would like the FBI to look into Myla's background and see if there was any indication of her being molested as a child.

He shared that he had scheduled a fishing trip two weeks out. He had decided that Marcus and family would either be on the fishing trip, or they would be leaving to a new assignment.

He went on to say that to go on the fishing trip, Myla would have to agree to get help for her problem and realize that she was inappropriately projecting her experience.

The three of them agreed that it seemed a fair way to handle the situation even though it seemed he had put it on a tight timeframe.

Bram raised his glass and thanked them for listening to his problem. He praised them on doing a great job in selecting the pictures to share with the guests. Their selection had blown everyone away.

He admitted that he had experienced a ying-yang dinner. The company, the food and the follow up meeting had all been great. He put the issue with Myla on the dark side and that it had ruined the otherwise highlight of the year.

Pat said sleep might help the situation and they should go and see if they could get some.

Bram agreed and rinsed and put his glass on the bar towel by the sink.

The next morning Pat was up early and discussed the Marcus situation with Zoe. She shared that Bram was really taking the accusation hard. He was afraid that Myla would poison the community if she did not quickly get help. The two agreed that they would work with Erica to expedite the FBI background check, and they should also arrange for immediate counseling for Myla.

Bram had reiterated to Pat that the only way Marcus would be allowed to stay was for Myla to get professional help in dealing with her issue.

Pat knew that Bram had planned to make breakfast for Zuri and her family. She had been kept awake much of the time by his tossing and turning. She was in the middle of getting things ready when Elizabeth came up from the basement. Jeffrey and Erica were right behind her. They said good morning and asked if they could help.

Pat accepted their offer and asked that the table get set and more coffee and tea get made.

Bob and Thomas were the guards for the day, and they helped everyone get organized.

Bram walked in just as everything but the final cook to order took place. He suggested that those who were ready should get their breakfast. He pointed out that it would allow the early risers to enjoy a leisurely conversation while he cooked breakfast for the later arrivals.

Pat said she would do the cooking if Bram took the orders.

He readily agreed and memorized each order as it was given.

Pat was always amazed at Bram's short-term memory. She also knew that he could retain whatever he decided was important.

It was clear to Pat that Bram had cleared his personal issue about Myla. He was back to the positive side that broadcast a warmth to everyone around. Sleep had been the right medicine.

Chapter 27: The Juma Home

Bram had put on his chef's hat and was busily filling the pancake, bacon or sausage and egg breakfast orders. Orlando and Mallica carried Zuri in on her wheelchair into the kitchen. Nuro and Jina entered behind the three.

Bram stopped what he was doing to greet everyone and to give Zuri a hug.

He stood up and asked everyone for their breakfast orders. He went on to boast that they had one of the best chefs in the world preparing their breakfast.

Jeffrey got up to greet the new arrivals and said there was plenty of room at the table. He took the chair at the head of the table and moved it to the side. He then helped position Zuri, so she could see everyone.

Zuri thanked him and commented that he seemed to be a very good boss.

Jeffrey replied that he was boss in name only and he was surrounded by bosses. He hoped that Zuri would be as good a boss as the rest.

The conversation between the two was the beginning of a rather long discussion about what it meant to be a good boss.

They all agreed that a good boss created a culture that valued, nurtured, and developed everyone. How the boss led by doing was another theme that was discussed.

Pat suggested they change the subject to what the Juma family wanted in a good home.

Jina commented that she had only seen the inside of Bram's home and it was beautiful. She would not expect such a wonderful house. She said that it appeared that all the homes were new, and she was eager to see the home with the Juma name on it.

Zoe came over to Bram and quietly commented that she had talked to Major Sharp and extra security had been put in place. She told Bram that he could walk over to the home that had been selected for the Juma family.

She volunteered that she and Eric would clean up after breakfast.

Bram thanked her. He smiled and commented that her offer to clean up was much more important than the info about security. He then carried his breakfast and took the seat by Zuri.

Outside grey clouds lay overhead in a thick blanket that made the day feel like the moment before sunset. A light intermittent drizzle blown by a slight breeze created the feeling that snow might be on the way.

Bram asked Zuri if she would rather be driven in the SUV. She replied that she wanted to see the neighborhood. A warm raincoat would be all she needed.

Orlando pulled out a poncho from his pack. It went over to Zuri and the wheelchair and slipped over her and the chair as if it had been designed for that function. He took out his knife and made two cuts so the handles on the wheelchair were exposed.

Bram smiled at Orlando and told him he had just earned a gold star and another fishing invitation.

Orlando commented that a good Marine was always ready but that fishing with Bram was always a bigger challenge than expected.

Mallica smiled and added that Orlando practiced being ready to a fault. She went on to say that he was always too ready.

Bram looked at Pat and quietly said that it seemed that Mallica and Orlando had bonded.

Elizabeth took Jeffrey's elbow and took the lead toward the Juma home. The single story, four-bedroom, ranch style home was located down the hill, below Bram's house. It was midway to the pool facility. It was one of two spec homes in the complex designed to house a wheelchair bound person.

When Bram asked if there was a home for Zuri, Lacy had immediately checked to see if one of them had been finished. She immediately designated it to be Zuri's.

Bram walked along side of Zuri and chatted with her as he pointed out the Fold neighborhood.

Jina was walking on Zuri's left side. She and Nuro shared one large blue umbrella and were commenting on the natural feel of the community and how impressed they were.

Bram noted that the ramp leading up to the front door was five-foot-wide and went across the front of the house and had only an eight-inch rise to the threshold. He admired the short deep green leafed hedge that edged the walk on the street side. It went around the eight-foot rounded landing at the front door.

The ramp was not visible from the street and the house seemed like any other house when viewed from the street. It was clearly a little longer and seemed larger than the two house on either side.

He wondered about and planned to look at the ramp leading to the backyard and the one in the garage.

Orlando shouted out "here we go" as he rapidly pushed Zuri up the front walk opened the front door and went smoothly into the foyer. He made a right turn and stopped in what he thought would be the living room. Beyond it was what he said was the dining room. He went through the dining room and to the left was the kitchen with an exhaust hood over a black glass stove top. The kitchen a refrigerator that was on its side and countertop high. There was as second one that was vertical and had bottom freezer, a vegetable drawer in the middle and the top had two vertical doors There was also an oven and microwave that could be operated by a person in a wheelchair.

The kitchen was open to the dining room but also open to a family room area. The circuit continued to another room to the left.

All rooms featured wide open areas that would allow a wheelchair bound person room to maneuver.

The way out to the back was through the kitchen eating area or through a wide door out from the family room. Both exits had a large landing area at door level with an eight-inch drop in a twelve-foot-long ramp down to a large tiled thirty by thirty-foot back yard tiled area that was surrounded by a flower bed. The tiled area had a wide walkway that went out to the driveway.

The home provided a wheelchair bound individual the ability to easily navigate all areas of the home and outside around the backyard and an easy exit to the driveway and garage.

Bram walked to the door at the back of the family room. It opened to the garage. The floor of the garage was at the same height as the floor in the family room. No ramp was needed.

He was impressed with the architect's attention to eliminating the barriers most wheelchair bound individuals faced.

Orlando took Zuri through a door from the family room into a large bedroom with a bathroom that included a roll in shower. He shouted out that they had found Zuri's room.

The roll in shower controls were outside the roll in area and at a level that could be reached by someone in a wheelchair. The sink and counter were also at a wheelchair height. The commode was in a separate room with hand bars and extra room around the commode.

Bram Nielson Collection

Jina and Nuro came out of the front two bedrooms that share a common bathroom between them. They had gone through the master bedroom that was to the back of the house through a short hall from the kitchen eating area.

They marveled at the accommodations in Zuri's room.

Everyone agreed that the layout and the accommodations were appropriate for housing Zuri.

Once again Jina had tears in her eyes. She commented that the house was wonderful and more than she ever dreamt of living there but she said she was not sure they could afford the rent.

Bram had not thought about rent. As far as he knew no one living in the Fold complex paid rent. He made a note about the fact that it was a great work benefit that he had not thought about.

He replied that the house was part of the benefit of working on the Fold project. He was met with more tears in Jina's eyes.

He smiled and said that to qualify for such a benefit, Zuri had to be to work by ten the next morning.

He told Nuro and Jina to work with Stacy and arrange the move to their new home and that they should report to work in two weeks.

He then announced that in two weeks there would be a weekend fishing outing and a picnic in the park to celebrate the Juma's move into their new home and the Juma family's enrollment into the Fold team.

Elizabeth suggested that they all return to Bram's home for some coffee and cake. Afterwards they would all go their separate ways for the rest of the afternoon.

Bram agreed. He was ready to spend some quiet time in his office to relax while he reviewed the Fold equations. He looked forward to having Pat sitting next to him reading.

Pat had watched Bram as he took in the home for Zuri. She realized that he had made a strong connection with Zuri and the potential he saw in her. She was warmed by his concern and his desire to open the world to the brilliant, but wheelchair bound young girl.

Bram noticed Pat observing him. He decided that once they were comfortably sitting on the office couch, he would ask her to tell him her thoughts about what she was so closely watching.

The grey of the morning was giving way to the sun that periodically flashed its rays through breaks in the cloud cover. The walk back up to Bram's house proceeded at a comfortable walking pace.

Bram looked at the smile on Zuri's face and decided that he would put this into one of his better days list.

Ron Mueller

Chapter 28: Marcus Ultimatum

Donna was running besides Castor and started singing a ditty about poor Bramlet One that had come back with something on its mind that just would not go away. Poor Bramlet One now locked away. She kept adding more miseries and then repeated the whole thing. The whole group went jogging through the dark misty morning repeating the ditty. She ended with a shot at Bram about not caring for poor Bramlet One namesake of the heartless one.

Bram enjoyed the ditty. It distracted him from the cloud that he faced. Once again, he had been awake much of the night as his mind chewed through the issue with Marcus's wife. He needed to convince Marcus of the issue's importance, and that immediate action had to be taken.

The aroma of coffee and the cooking going on in the cafeteria brought Bram to a better state of mind. He took two premade English muffins with cheese, sausage, and egg. He stopped to fill his mug with steaming dark black coffee and then went to his favorite table. The rest of the team joined him.

Pat, Eric, and Zoe took their normal seats.

Zoe was sitting across from Bram. She knew the agenda facing Bram. She shared her conversation with Erica. The two had met on Sunday and sent an urgent request to Erica for immediate action. They expected a quick report back by Thursday morning.

Erica had promised that it would be thorough and if the potential for abuse existed, they would know.

Elizabeth joined them and asked Bram if he wanted her in the meeting with Marcus.

Bram thanked her but said he would prefer to discuss this with Marcus alone. He was uncertain of Marcus' personal knowledge of why the hug had triggered Myla's reaction.

Pat wished him luck and let him know that both Wheel teams were getting ready for the Wheel Folds that would occur on Wednesday morning.

She also reminded him that he had essentially required Zuri be at work by ten.

Bram watched as Marcus came into the cafeteria. He went through the line and came out with two eggs and toast. He was going to sit by himself at another table, but Bram waved him over and pointed to the seats that Elizabeth and Pat had vacated.

Marcus was very quiet and commented that he had a notice from Lacy about a meeting with him right after breakfast.

He asked how Zuri's evaluation had gone?

He heard from Lacy that the family was moving into one of the units designed for someone in a wheelchair. He assumed that the evaluation had gone well.

Bram commented that things had gone well. He let Marcus know that Zuri was joining in on the review of the Fold equations. It would start at ten at his office.

Marcus figured the meeting in the office might be his last. It was clear that Bram had come to some sort of conclusion on Myla's threat about hugging children. He had personally been surprised at her vehemence. He had thought back at her behavior of him hugging the kids. It had become worse recently and he had no clue why.

He was worried about his meeting with Bram, but he was just as concerned about Myla's behavior. He needed to talk with somebody.

Bram led the way to his office and told Lacy that he did not want to be disturbed. He would let her know when he would be available. He asked her to break in if Marcus and he went on too long. He wanted ten minutes before the ten am meeting started.

He asked Zoe and Eric to wait at Linda's desk. Zoe went through the security check of the office and then gave the "all clear."

Bram made one more request that Lacy find a large nearby room that could be made into a wheelchair friendly office.

Marcus and Bram entered his office together. Bram suggested they get a tea or coffee and sit on the couch.

Bram went straight to the point and commented that he had checked with everyone that had seen him hug Zuri and no one had any impression of impropriety.

He asked Marcus about his opinion of the situation.

Marcus looked in at his cup of coffee. For him, the dark black coffee was a reflection of his mind. He had argued with Myla much of Sunday as he tried to find out what had triggered her reaction.

He was lost about what to do.

He looked at Bram whose penetrating gaze always was disconcerting to him. He saw what he thought was real concern. He shared his confusion and that he was not sure what to do. He went on to describe his miserable Sunday.

He volunteered that he was mentally exhausted.

Bram pointed out that Myla's behavior was not acceptable. If she were to express her current opinion about the hug she would be poisoning the culture of the Fold community.

He made the point that he worked hard at making it a culture of inclusion, fairness and of treating everyone as one would expect to be treated. Bram pointed out that it was a culture that he had worked very hard to create and one that seemed to be functioning the way he had hoped it would. He said that he was going to protect that culture.

Bram then said that Dr. Windal expressed the opinion that Myla's behavior suggested that perhaps Myla had been molested as a young girl. Dr. Windal had gone on to suggest it might well be someone in her family.

Marcus said that he and Myla had never talked much about her family. He had met her parents before their wedding, but they had always gone to his family get togethers. Now he wondered about Myla's not wanting to go to her family's get together.

Bram went on to say that he had asked the FBI to do a background check on Myla's family and that the initial report would be back by Thursday.

He also pointed out that he thought Myla needed some professional counseling. He looked at Marcus and said he really wanted Marcus to be part of the Fold effort but unless Myla agreed by Friday to get counseling, he and his family would be reassigned to the best alternate job that could be arranged. He made the point that the assignment would be outside of the Fold community.

Marcus knew that Bram always worked fast.

He asked if he could get some help in talking to Myla. He said that he was afraid that she would shut him out.

Bram asked if Mallica, Elizabeth or if Dr Windal, who was a female Marine, might be of help.

He agreed with Marcus that it would be Myla who would need to come to grips with her past.

Marcus asked how much time he had to get Myla to agree.

Bram replied that he had a fishing trip planned two weekends away. The Smith family would either be fishing with the rest of the team, or they would be reassigned and moving East. The venue depended on Myla's agreement to therapy. Bram said that he expected the therapy to go on for a long time.

Marcus held back his astonishment at the speed for the agreement to action. He said as much but agreed that something needed to happen fast. He said he would take all the help he could get.

Bram reiterated the fact that he wanted Marcus to be part of the team. He stated that he was not expecting resolution in two weeks but the start of resolving Myla's problem. He suggested that Elizabeth, Mallica and Dr. Windal meet and decide on the best approach in working with Myla. He pointed out that they needed to connect on a personal level.

Bram shared that he was aware that Mallica had experienced sexual assault as a child and was able to identify with Myla's reaction.

Marcus said he would take all their help and let them guide him. He had already had his unsuccessful argument with Myla.

He shared that it was their first real argument that ended up in a shouting match.

Bram let Marcus know that he wanted this to work out well. He would free up all the resources at his disposal to make it happen.

He pointed at the clock and said they would soon get their ten-minute warning about the next meeting.

Marcus asked if he could miss the meeting and meet with Elizabeth and Dr. Windal.

Bram suggested they delay the Fold equation review until later in the day or until the next day. He and Zuri would look over her office space that he was sure Lacy had found by this time.

This would give Mallica a chance to be part of the meeting Marcus wanted to have.

Marcus had tears in his eyes as he got up. He was overwhelmed and as he looked at Bram, he knew that he had a friend that was trying hard to help but who insisted on fast and effective action.

Bram got up and gave Marcus a hug. He commented that Myla was a strong woman who when presented with the facts would measure up. She would connect with Mallica.

Marcus said hello to the Juma family as he walked out of Bram's office.

Bram gave Zuri a hug and then shook hands with Nuro and Jina. He invited them into his office.

He asked Lacy if she had an office space that would be Zuri's office?

He also asked for Remi to come to his office to meet Nuro.

He asked Zuri how the rest of the weekend had gone.

Jina answered that they had gone out for a treat at the local ice cream parlor to celebrate their good fortune.

Zuri asked if she was really going to have an office to herself?

Bram smiled at her and said that yes, she would have an office similar to his. If she was smart enough, she would probably soon have one bigger than his.

He looked at Jina and Nuro and said that they would have offices like their counter parts in their field. He smiled and made the point that Zuri was the one that got the biggest office.

Jina replied that her office could be a closet, and she would be satisfied.

Bram smiled and said that they should all go and see the space that Lacy had located for Zuri. Afterwards, Nuro would go with Remi to see what he would be doing, and Jina would go with Lacy to her office.

Mallica and Orlando were standing outside the office when they came out. Mallica said good morning and then excused herself saying she was going to Marcus's office.

Orlando said hello to Zuri and gave her a hug and then pushed her down the hall as they followed Lacy.

Bram had a good feeling about how the week would go. He noticed that Zoe and Eric were missing and had been replaced by Bob and Thomas.

Orlando was whooping it up as he accelerated around the corner just down from Bram's office. Lacy called out that he had gone too far. She led the way into a forty-person meeting room. She said she had called in the architect, and he would be out to look at the space and then convert it to a wheelchair friendly office. He would use as much space as made sense and the rest would be turned into huddle rooms.

Bram said he liked her approach to getting the office ready. It should be at least as spacious as his and be wheelchair friendly. He said he expected it to be ready by the time Zuri returned from the fishing weekend outing. He reminded Lacy that Zuri would be back from the Mayo clinic and would be in her new motorized wheelchair by then.

He looked around and figured it was time for a tour of the lab and to review the Wheel readiness for the coming Fold.

Chapter 29: Myla-Self Realization

𝒯he walk out to the Fold Wheels was a welcome break from what had been a stressful morning for Bram. He took in the size of the Wheels and wondered if their full functionality would ever be used. His current plans made the Wheel living quarters almost useless. The Wheels might be useful for the longer across the universe folds or any longer-term exploration. For now, Bram wanted only the main bubble of the Wheel. The smaller bubble would mean less power use and would allow for more exploration at one time. It would also reduce the risk to those involved in the program.

He approached Wheel One and was greeted by Pat. She and the crew were doing a walk-through of the Wednesday Fold. Bram entered to look around and to see if there was room for one more.

He then went over to Wheel Two and was greeted by Harold Redat the backup pilot. He was taking the crew through a similar walk through. Elizabeth had assigned him the task while she worked with Marcus.

Bram was pleased with the readiness of both crews. He asked the two crews to procure HazMat type suits for the trip. When asked why, Bram explained that he wanted another layer of personal protection for the crew on the upcoming folds.

The lab was now a bubble assembly area. The lab team was divided into Bramlet One investigation and new bubble scout assembly. Remi was touring Erica and showing her the various bubbles under assembly. Nuro was busy with a team working on a three-foot diameter version. He took a minute to express his excitement of being part of the effort.

Bramlet Two through Seven were in their containment boxes. The team handling them commented that the Bramlets would be launched at noon to the location he had programed for the back of the Moon Fold area. They would Fold into the coordinates Bram had specified.

Once the Bramlets were back they would be prepared for the Neptune Fold.

Bram was pleased with the energy of everyone associated with the Fold effort. He decided to make a stop in the offices of the analysts. He had not visited with them for more than a week and wanted to hear from them about what they hoped they could get from the Wheel Folds.

Elizabeth had listened to Marcus and to Mallica, Zoe and the Fold phycologist Serena.

Serena had suggested a meeting between Mallica and Myla to see if Myla recognized she had a problem.

Mallica would see if Myla was open to talking to a professional trained to help her, but she did not want Myla to be defensive. Serena suggested she would hold off and plan to be a part of a second meeting with her if Myla was open to it.

Elizabeth asked Marcus to set up a lunch meeting between Mallica and Myla at some location away from the Fold area but that would provide some privacy. She said that lunch was on Bram.

Lacy called in the architect that she was working with on Zuri's office layout. Orlando was making sure that Zuri was in the right place as the architect first inspected Bram's office and layout and then proceeded to the large meeting room that was to be converted.

The architect commented that he would probably use the entire space for Zuri's office. He measured the room and said he would get back with some plans by Thursday for them to review.

Lacy thanked him and led the way back to Bram's office. She explained that Bram had changed his schedule, and she was not sure what to do with the two of them. She offered to let them wait in Bram's office.

Orlando looked outside at the bright sunshine. He asked Zuri if she was interested in a tour of the outside of the hanger area.

Zuri replied that she preferred the outside to waiting in the office.

Orlando replied that he was the best tour guide in the compound.

After visiting with the analysts Bram decided that he would ask Remi to work with Pat to add some eye bolts to the floor of Wheel One. He had decided to include Zuri in the first human transit across the solar system and across the Milky Way.

He stopped by Wheel One to let Pat know of his decision.

She nodded and said that Zuri would be a great addition to the crew. She said she would get one of the support mechanics to put the eye bolts in the floor.

He went to the lab and met with Remi.

He asked where Erica had gone.

Remi said she had just left and was headed to Lacy and his office.

Erica approached Lacy and asked about Bram.

Lacy replied that she had lost control of Bram's calendar and his where about.

Erica took the time to inquire about office space for herself.

She had reached her decision about staying and agreed with Bram's project role clarification for the individuals he had named.

She recognized that the application of Bram's Fold breakthrough was rapidly expanding and as well as accelerating.

Lacy looked up to see Bram approaching. She commented to Erica that she would find an appropriate office for her and let her know. She asked if there was any specific location that Erica might prefer.

Erica thought about it for a moment and then replied that somewhere close to the Lab area or Remi's office. She went on to say that if there was no space in that area then show her the available offices and she would select one.

Erica greeted Bram and said she was impressed with all the practical work that was getting done. It was amazing that the lab had become such a good bubble assembly area.

Bram agreed with her and complimented Lori and Remi for their rapid response to his bubble scout idea. He commented that he felt that the bubble scouts were life savers. They were a great way to keep the human participants from ending up like Bramlet One.

Erica asked if all his Monday mornings were so active.

Bram replied that he hoped that they would not all be like this specific Monday.

He commented that he had not faced such a serious problem as the one involving Marcus's wife.

He thanked Erica for getting the FBI to quickly do a check of any family sexual abuse issues.

He shared that Elizabeth was facilitating a discussion with Marcus, Mallica, Zoe and Serena the Fold phycologist. He said that he was not sure where that was going but that he had given Marcus notice that the issue had to be resolved in two weeks.

Erica commented that it seemed to be an aggressive schedule but supported his decision.

Bram thanked her. He said such an issue could not be allowed to permeate the Fold community. His requirement was that Myla had to agree to counseling. He knew she would have a long way to go to fully address her issues.

Erica had expected Zuri to be in Bram's office and asked about her.

Bram replied that he had no clue where Zuri might be but that she was with Orlando and would be doing something fun. He described Orlando as a super Marine guard and a person that he would trust his life to. He went on to say that he had lost him as guard to Mallica and Zuri.

Lacy called in that Zuri and Orlando had returned from their tour around the outside of the facility.

Bram stood and walked to the front of his desk as Orlando wheeled Zuri in.

They were both laughing at something Orlando had said to Lacy. They turned to Bram and Orlando said in a serious low tone, "Ready for work boss" and they both laughed again.

Bram was pleased that they both seemed to like each other. He looked at Erica and asked if she would join them for lunch.

Zuri asked what there was for lunch. Orlando commented that Bram made the cafeteria serve only healthy food and that Zuri might be disappointed.

Bram replied that the problem was that Marines had such poor eating habits and probably did not wash their hands before lunch.

Orlando laughed and followed Bram and Erica as they walked toward the cafeteria. He commented to Zuri that the brains of the outfit was really going low when he started to attack the Marines about their eating habits, and he acted like he was whispering in her ear and said he did wash his hands before lunch.

Erica marveled at the atmosphere around Bram. It was fun to be around the people that worked on the Fold effort. She thought about the political intrigue and backstabbing she experienced back in Washington. It would be a treat to work in the Dalles area. She would not miss the pressure of her office back east.

Orlando took pains to point Zuri to the food that was the richest and the ones he thought Bram would object to most. Zuri had a problem seeing the food that was out on the counter.

Bram saw her trying to see the food and made mental note to make sure that her new motorized chair placed Zuri high enough to see the food.

Elizabeth and Dr. Windal entered that cafeteria together with Marcus. They saw Bram sitting with Erica and asked if they could join him.

Elizabeth asked if Bram had met Dr. Windal.

Bram replied that they had only met briefly when the facility had first opened and then again after the shooting by the pool area had occurred and then again when she became a lunch time lecturer.

But otherwise, he had no idea who she was.

He laughed and asked how she was doing and were her skills being utilized by the Fold personnel.

Dr. Windal in turn laughed and replied that she wished more people would come in and talk with her and when was he going to take the time to get treated for his lifelong affliction.

Marcus listened to the exchange and knew that he wanted to remain in the atmosphere that permeated the Fold community. He commented that the morning had gone well. Mallica and Myla were having a lunch meeting. He hoped that Mallica would be successful in her meeting.

Bram commented that it seemed they had made good progress and agreed that he hoped Mallica could make a positive intervention.

He looked at Zuri and tilted his head at Orlando and went on to say that after lunch he had a surprise for Zuri. He asked Orlando if he could push Zuri out to Wheel One.

Pat had skipped lunch and was relaxing next to the ramp leading up into Wheel One. She watched as the entourage that surrounded Bram approached. The mechanical support technician and she had just completed putting in the floor eye bolts that Bram had request. She had been surprised that he had decide to take Zuri along but liked the fact that he was doing it.

She stood up and greeted the group. She said that she would lead the way in and then Zuri and Orlando would be the next ones in. She said the rest could follow.

Orlando followed Pat and pushed the wheelchair up the ramp.

Pat led the way to where the rings were located and instructed Orlando how to orient the wheelchair. Pat then adjusted the hooks and bound the chair to the floor.

She then stood in front of Zuri and gave her a salute and welcomed her as a crew member of Wheel One as a performance analyst first class. Zuri was to analyze the crew performance on the upcoming Folds to the moon and the galaxies beyond.

Zuri shouted out, "no way! Is it really true? Am I a part of the crew?

Bram knelt beside her and answered that it was true, and her real role was to think-deep and think-hard about what was happening during the Fold. The performance she should be thinking about was the Wheel One, Fold performance. He said that he still needed her help in making sure her parents were OK with her going out with the Wheel Fold on Wednesday.

He gave Zuri a hug and welcomed her to the Fold Team and to the crew of the USS Hood Wheel One better known as Wheel One. He told her she was the Admiral, and he was the Captain of the ship.

Chapter 30: Time to Step Up

Lunch for Mallica was a walk on thin ice. She needed to connect with Myla and get her to understand that she was fighting her own demon and overlaying it on other people. She needed Myla to accept help via counseling. Mallica knew that failure to connect and get agreement to treatment would result in Marcus getting reassigned. Her similar personal experience helped on how to approach Myla.

Mallica began by sharing her own personal experience of being molested as a young girl. In her case, it had been an older cousin, and it had devastated her. Her mother had finally believed her and had acted to get her out of the situation.

She asked if Myla might have had a similar experience.

Myla sat silently looking at her.

The moment lasted longer than anticipated and Mallica went on.

She let Myla know that if she did not get counseling, Marcus would be reassigned to a job outside of the Fold program.

Myla got mad and stated that was not fair to Marcus.

It was a reaction that Mallica had anticipated.

Mallica agreed but said there was no other option.

Myla said that she wanted to talk to the boss of the program. Mallica responded that the boss had already been informed and agreed to the requirement of her getting counseling.

Myla broke down and began crying.

Mallica breathed a sigh of relief.

Myla admitted that she had just recently recalled being abused as a young girl. She had suppressed it for so long she had forgotten about. Seeing Bram hug Zuri had been a lightning bold that brought it all back. It had gone to the bottom of her soul and ripped open a memory that she had suppressed. It was a shock.

She was afraid to tell Marcus.

Her safe warm world had shattered in that one moment before dinner on Saturday.

Mallica gave Myla a hug and told her she was with a friend who understood. She had a similar experience but had gotten help and still regularly sought that help. She went on to let Myla know that Marcus had been part of the team that had sent Mallica on the mission to get her to agree to get counseling.

She shared that Bram had been the one driving all of them to resolve the situation in a way that would help everyone.

And that Bram wanted her to be happy and that he wanted Marcus to be on the Fold team. Then Mallica made it clear that would only happen if Myla agreed to get on the path to getting healed.

There was what seemed to Mallica to be an endless period of silence.

She kept her silence as Myla cried silently.

Finally, Myla took a deep breath and quietly agreed to get counseling and said she would meet with Dr. Windal and learn what was needed.

She wondered if she could speak with Dr. Windal on the following day.

Mallica said that she would arrange it.

Mallica was drained but the outcome of the lunch made her eager to get back and share her success.

On her return to the compound, Mallica's first stop was Marcus's office.

When she walked in the tears in Marcus's eyes let her know that he had already talked to Myla. She and Marcus had become very close friends during their year at the initial Fold facility in the middle of the desert. She just walked over and gave him a hug. There was nothing else to add.

She asked if he wanted to come along to share the good news with Bram. He replied that he would join them in a moment. He said he did not want to go down the hallway crying.

Mallica said she would wait in her office until he was ready. She told him that he should be the one to inform Bram that Myla had agreed to get help.

Lacy had informed Bram that Mallica had returned from lunch and that she had gone to Marcus's office.

While he waited to hear from Mallica, Bram had called Nuro and Jina to his office to request their permission for Zuri to be part of the Fold team that would visit the back of the Moon on the coming Wednesday and then would Fold to Neptune and the Galaxy in the following weeks.

Nuro and Jina were chatting with Zuri. It was obvious Zuri had her heart set on being part of the Wheel One crew. She said she trusted Bram because he would have the seat next to hers.

Nuro and Jina looked at Bram and they told him that he had not played fairly but they were so proud that Zuri would be one of the first humans to make such distant trips. They just wanted to make sure he would bringing Zuri back safely.

Bram agreed that he had in his excitement rushed ahead and he apologized for not having checked with them first. He went on to say that sometimes he forgot how young Zuri was. He commented that he thought that her mind was well beyond his own in capability and interacted with her as if they were partners working on the same problem.

Lacy announced that Marcus and Mallica were waiting to meet with him.

Bram thanked Nuro and Jina and told them to take Zuri home and that they should all report to their workplace at the normal time the next day.

Marcus led the way in and simply said that Mallica had accomplished her mission.

Bram walked over to Mallica and gave her a hug and thanked her. He turned and gave Marcus a hug as well.

He went on to say that there would be a prize for the biggest fish and the most fish caught on the upcoming fishing trip. He stated that he expected the Smith family to win one of those two prizes.

He looked at Marcus and told him to go home and give Myla a hug and comfort her. He could take the next day off if that would help.

Marcus had tears in his eyes. He thanked Bram for pushing to get help for Myla. He would talk with Myla and decide about being with her on her first day of counseling.

Bram put his arm around Marcus's shoulders and guided him to the door and said, "see you later," and gave him a gentle push out the door.

Mallica had quietly observed how Bram handled Marcus. She knew why she had stuck around in the desert even when she had felt abandoned. Bram exuded a positive aura even when he was pushing everyone to work faster, smarter, and harder.

Bram turned to Mallica and asked for some more detail and her feeling about Myla's acceptance.

Mallica replied that she felt Myla had come to realize her actions were driven by her own demons.

Bram shared that Myla had sent him a message of apology and said that she had agreed to the counseling and had expressed the desire to start immediately.

Bram Nielson Collection

Mallica let him know that she had arranged with Dr. Windal for an appointment in the morning.

Bram closed his eyes and took a deep breath. He looked at Mallica and ask what she wanted as a reward for having saved the day.

Mallica smiled and said that she wanted a seat on the other side of Zuri during the upcoming Folds.

Bram laughed and replied that she was lucky that he had not yet recalculate the power draw expectation for the added weight on Wheel One. He told Mallica to check with Lacy and to report for her weigh-in at the same time that Zuri was getting weighed in.

Mallica gave him a hug and then asked if there was room on Wheel Two for Marcus.

Bram shook his head and replied that Marcus should weigh in with her but since she had extracted such a big reward, he was not sure she qualified for the fishing contests. He would have to think about that.

Mallica was all smiles as she walked out to check with Lacy.

Bram looked at the clock it was a little early but called Pat let her know that he was ready to call it a day.

Zoe and Eric came into his office and said that they realized that he would need FBI protection even when on the Wheel. They asked if he had he made allowance for the two of them to be there to protect him?

Bram rolled his eyes and said he would see but he felt that he was getting to the Fold power limits. He would let them know in the morning. He asked for their weights.

Pat walked in as he finished his comment and asked about weights for whom?

Bram replied that the FBI guards were pressuring him to accept protection even when on the Wheel.

Pat replied that he would probably need protection from the chief navigator.

Bram replied that is what he had told the FBI representatives making the request but that they had insisted.

He said he was going to walk home to clear his mind. On the way out he asked Lacy if the home service was going to be doing the cooking that evening. She replied that indeed the Stetson Catering service had arranged for a chef and kitchen crew to be on duty that evening. She said that by the time he got home dinner would be ready.

Castor and Donna were in the lead. Zoe and Eric followed behind. Bram walked silently holding Pat's hand.

Bram was tallying the various scenarios that were unfolding around him. He had pulled back just in time. It was time to let the Fold program grow. It was going to grow well beyond his ability to managed it. Once he had done the initial set of Folds, he would need to retreat into deeper development research.

He hoped that Zuri would be the mind that would provide or trigger new insights.

He needed to advance the capability of the objects being Folded.

He needed more sophisticated scouts.

He needed to work with Marcus in selecting the future targets.

He needed to get Jeffrey to expand the program and to get Erica to manage it.

He had brought the Fold breakthrough to the world. It was time for the world to step up and engage the future.

Ron Mueller

Chapter 31: Fold Virgins

Bram got home and realized that his first Fold to the back of the moon could not be scheduled for two days. The Wheels would be exposed within hours. They could only stay for the length of time the moon would shield them.

He talked to Elizabeth, Pat, Amy, and Marcus and together they agreed to multiple Folds. The new Fold schedule would be a better test of the power system than the original Fold sequence. He asked Elizabeth to explain the change to the rest of the Wheel crews. He smiled and suggested that the teams should have picked up on his mistake.

It was hard to describe his frustration. He found it hard to accept the fact that his Fold location was static and not dynamic. He was really looking forward to the additional research work that would occur when his equations were tested and revalidated.

He was sure that the different perspective that Zuri might trigger would change his understanding of how the Fold occurred.

Bram had no doubt that the design of the magnetron would be impacted, but at the moment he had no clue what that impact would be. He tried to imagine what physical change was needed to allow movement of the object in the Fold.

He wondered if an alternating current source in the Fold objects, would make it possible to create mini folds that would act to propel the object. In space, once motion was established it would be maintained. He decided that the way to create physical movement could be immediately tested in the lab.

Bram found it hard to contain himself. He called Remi to see if he were willing to do a little early evening bubble modification. After describing what he wanted to do, Remi suggested that he would do it early the next morning. He had to locate a dc to ac converter that could be put into one of the bubbles. He suggested they use one of the new bigger bubbles since it would have enough room to add the converter and the Fold transmitter.

Remi recommended the test be held after the two Wheels completed their Fold behind the Moon.

Pat had listened in to the bubble discussion and agreed with Remi's advice. She reminded Bram that he would have his hands full for the entire day. Their first Fold was scheduled to be at nine in the morning.

The evening seemed to pass slower than a duck trying to take off into the record headwinds of a one-hundred-year storm.

Bram felt conflicted. He was certain that his scheduled Folds behind the Moon would be successful.

What he was now eager to try was the concept of mini-Folds as a propulsion concept. Then he wanted to see if modifying the design of the magnetron could be the means of channeling the power flow to provide not only the Fold but also propulsion for the object being Folded.

Bram decided to spend the evening investigating the equations that led to the design of the honeycomb like magnetron. He wondered if his math might be expressed in a slight variation and if in that manner change the design.

Pat could tell that the morning Wheel Fold was not a concern to Bram. He was off into a world of his own. He was scrolling through the endlessly long Fold equation on his computer.

She wondered if he knew that he periodically talked to himself. He not only talked to himself, but he became two different persons that argued the different sides of a problem.

At this moment it was clear he was having a major internal struggle with himself. She had never seen Bram in this state.

A light was blinking in her mind reminding her that Bram really did have a different mind than the rest of the people around him.

She knew he she was seeing him during intense mental arguments as he envisioned another breakthrough in his Fold environment.

She got up off the couch and walked over to him and gave him a hug.

Bram was brought up out of the haze that had enveloped his mind as he felt Pat's hug.

The haze turned to a warm glow.

He turned and pulled Pat onto his lap and gave her a kiss. He thanked her for bringing him back to the surface before he drowned in the depths of his mind.

Pat believed him. He truly had been in a different world far from her reality.

She looked him in the eyes as she again gave him a kiss. Bram was looking back as if he could see her mind. She wondered if he had the power to do such a thing.

Zoe had watched the entire scene. She looked over at Eric and gave him a smile. She knew he had also taken in the exchange between Pat and Bram.

They had talked about Bram's relationship with Pat and about his intense sessions when he was somewhere in his mind. It would sometimes seem that he was frozen. His eyes often stayed open, but Zoe had played games to see if he was seeing anything.

Eric always tried to stop Zoe when she began testing where Bram might be and what he was seeing. It was clear to him that Bram focused inward when in his deepest thoughts.

Bram recorded everything that went on around him. He knew of Zoe's tests and games she played.

He let it go. He figured someday he would play a game with her and get even.

Bram decided that he would try to get some sleep. He picked Pat up and then gently put her on her feet and led her out of the office. He saw Zoe jump up to get to the door ahead of them.

Once in their bedroom, Bram went for the shower.

He planned to get it as hot as he could possibly stand it and let the heat cool his mind. He was onto something, but he did not know what. He had to let it go so that in the following days he could again find it.

Pat joined Bram in the shower, but the water was so hot she had to stand to one side.

Bram reduced the hot water and then pulled her to him. He found the perfect release for his brain's conundrum.

After a few moments, he led the two of them out of the shower and slowly toweled Pat dry. She did the same for him and then led him by the hand to their bed.

Five thirty came early the next morning. Bram came up out of the depth and absorbed the warmth of Pat's cheek on his chest.

He gently raised her chin and gave her a kiss as he slid out of the bed.

When he got down to the kitchen the entire FBI guard group was there and said good morning.

Bram had put Zoe and Eric on Wheel One and Bob and Thomas on Wheel Two. Mallica was on Wheel One and Marcus was on Wheel Two. He figured if he was willing to put Zuri at risk then he would not deny the rest.

The crew would all go down in the history books. How could he deny them that privilege when every one of them had made great sacrifices to help him?

The entourage jogging along the road was led by three marines followed by Marcus, Mallica, Pat and Bram. His four FBI bodyguards followed behind. This morning Orlando started a ditty about hiding behind the Moon,

Hiding in back, the dark side,
Hiding in the dark, not ashamed
Don't want to be seen, Feeling sad
So sad to feel so bad.
Bram, Bram, Hiding, Hiding
But we are all smiles to be
Hiding in back, the dark side,

He went on then to repeat it and then everyone repeated the words.

Bram found it hard to keep jogging. He wanted to stop and laugh. He threatened to leave Orlando behind.

Orlando included the threat in the ditty being repeated by everyone. Orlando added, "No sense of humor, only threatens his friend."

Bram and the whole group entered the compound laughing and had all the Marine guards looking their way.

Orlando greeted the van arriving with Zuri and her parents. He gave Zuri a hug, greeted Nuro and Jina and pushed Zuri toward the cafeteria.

Bram took his usual spot in the cafeteria. He gave Zuri a hug. She had the end of the table, Orlando sat across from Bram. He thanked Bram for including him on the Wheel folds. It was special, and he would always be grateful. Bram looked at him and said that he had missed that day at the cave and some poor unknown had taken his bullet.

Orlando smiled and simply said, "Yeah I guess I am lucky at that."

Pat was the one that simply said let's go Fold and stood up and walked out toward the Wheel holding area.

Bram followed behind with Orlando and Zuri.

The countdown for the USS Hood Wheel One and USS Rainier Wheel Two was controlled by Lori.

Elizabeth had given Bram a hug and thanked him for making her dream come true. He had also gotten a hug from Amy with almost the same words. He had heard the same from Pat.

Bram took a moment to thank everyone for their dedication and hard work. He pointed out that most of them were Fold veterans and only a few were novices like himself. He described that their first Folds were intended to test some new concepts close to home but then in the following weeks they would all cross the solar system and then go out into the Milky Way. He made the point that Marcus, their destination identifier, had already threatened to go beyond to other Galaxies.

Bram looked up to the viewing area and saw that Myla was standing in the observation area with her two kids. She looked down and mouthed a silent "Thank you."

Bram waved at everyone and turned and walked into the Wheel One control center and took his seat next to Zuri. He held her hand as Pat closed the Wheel hatch. He listened as Pat announced that Wheel One was ready for Fold.

The next thing he saw was the glow of the sun coming around to the backside of the Moon.

He responded to the small hand that squeezed his and heard Zuri give him a quiet thank you.

He had tears in his eyes. He did not know how, but his mind had taken him to a place that embraced a magic that would forever empower humanity with travels to the farthest places.

The End

Bram Nielson Collection
The Message

Chapter 1: Success Celebration

This was Bram's first Fold. He, Zuri, Orlando, Eric, and Zoe were the newbies in the bubble.

Bram sat next to Zuri looking out at the surface of the far side of the moon. He was explaining to everyone that what was most often referred to as the dark side of the moon was no darker than any other part of the moon. In the course of a month, Sun light fell equally on all sides of the Moon and that the lunar day lasted about two Earth weeks.

He then shared the fact that they were being shielded from the noise of the Earth and were in what was called the "radio dark." It was a location that was shielded from the noise of the Earth and the weak signals from the universe could be measured more easily at this location.

In fact, the systems on Wheel One were scanning out into the universe and when they returned to Earth the data would be closely scoured to see what they could learn.

He went on to have everyone look at the difference between the more heavily cratered backside surface and the fact that it lacked the maria or seas that made up the familiar man in the moon face.

He shared the fact that it was thought that the differences were caused by a wayward dwarf planet colliding with the moon in the early history of the solar system.

Orlando thanked Professor Bram for the great story that he had just shared.

Nuro squeezed Bram's hand and thanked him for giving them all a quick education about the moon. She said that it was all new to her and that she would have to do a little more study and research before the next Fold out to the edge of the solar system.

The Fold they were on was a top-secret Fold to test the ability to Fold over a long distance through space. In reality the distance to the back of the Moon was a miniscule distance as compared to the subsequent distances that were in upcoming Fold plans. The Fold implementation order was to go first to the edge of the Solar System, then to the nearest next solar system and finally to a different galaxy.

Since a Fold took relatively no time, it was possible to do the three planned Folds in the coming year. It could be done as quickly as doing them on three subsequent days but there was data analysis time put between each Fold. It would be important to analyze the data and apply any improvements that the data might provide insights about.

The successful Fold to the back of the moon pleased Bram. It was to have been the first Fold of the two Wheels but in reality, it was the third. The first two folds occurred in getting each wheel out of the Seattle area when a throng of rioters threatened to expose the technology that was a top US government secret. So, the official Fold that would be recorded for the history books was really the third one.

It was his first, but it was the second for each of the Wheel Crews.

He had let them all know that the people taking part on this Fold would have their names and biographies recorded in the history books.

143

He had been as inclusive as possible, but it was not possible to take everyone on the project. He took all the top players. He eventually would offer the Fold experience to all those who desired.

The Fold was a moment of relief for him but the lead up to it had been extremely stressful.

He had not intended the days leading up to the Fold to have been so hectic and stressful. He had envisioned a rather controlled, full schedule but one that focused on making the Fold to the back of the Moon safe as well as successful.

One concern was the safety of the crew members. Since relocating the Fold project to Dallas, Oregon he and his team had been attacked several times.

He and his close team had been attacked when they went on a fishing trip to the Mt. Jefferson resort along the Rushing River. He, his team, the Marines guarding him, and the resort owners fought and defeated a group of mercenaries that had arrived in a helicopter gunship and had a tripod large caliber machine gun on the ground. The battle had been fierce but ended in a few minutes as Bram and his two Marine guards took out the attackers.

The next attack had been at the Fold neighborhood swim party. Three shooters opened fire from the parking lot. Bram, unarmed, took immediate action, and killed one of the attackers and his FBI bodyguards took out the other two.

He had gone into action when he realized that Pat was the next target after the first two people had been shot.

A third attack, by a gunman shooting at him from a boat, had occurred out on Celio Lake during a fishing party. Orlando and Castor turned the attacking boat and its occupants into Swiss cheese.

The final attack had been thwarted when he reported seeing a flicker from the top of a semi parked in the orchard that bordered the Fold community housing. A Marine marksman killed the attacker from a patrol helicopter before he could act.

Bram figured that some rich and powerful people were trying hard to stop the Fold development from making any progress and he was the bullseye of the project.

These attacks had made him very cautious about everything associated with the project.

The attacks were disturbing and of concern to him but not as disturbing as being accused of being a child molester by the wife of his genius Astronomer and Fold coordinate planner, Marcus Smith.

He had worked hard at making the Fold community into a caring, sharing, and fun group.

The accusation if it was shared would have a very negative impact and he acted to immediately address and resolve it.

It turned out that Myla, Marcus's wife, had been molested as a child and had a hysterical reaction when she saw him hugging Zuri, a young autistic savant constrained to a wheelchair. He told Marcus to get help for Myla or both of them would be transferred to another project or job. It was a huge relief when Mallica got Myla to accept counseling to deal with the child abuse she had suffered. He was hopeful that with the counseling, she would resolve her mental issues.

After that he turned his attention to the planning of a celebratory fishing trip.

Lacy his secretarial support had worked out the schedule with her father for another fishing trip.

Bram had her invite several dignitaries all the way up to and including the President. He did not expect most of them to accept but he asked Lacy to make sure that she arranged enough fishing boats to handle everyone that accepted the invitation.

She let him know that her father, and brothers were all committed, and a picnic lunch would be arranged as well. They had all sent their greetings and had said that they hoped for another successful fishing outing without the associated fireworks of the last one.

On the Fold's return from the back of the Moon, Zuri commented that though she had learned a lot about the moon, she was a little let down that the Fold experience was no different than taking a ride in a car.

Bram gave a little laugh and said that he agreed with her and that the only thing that had made it the least bit interesting for him was Orlando constantly joking with her.

He said that getting the math and the means to make a Fold occur had been the part that had engaged him. Taking the ride out to the back of the moon had been very anticlimactic.

He asked if a fishing trip might excite her more.

That brought out an immediate and loud yes and she commented that the last time, her first-time fishing, had been a blast. She said that Orlando had really caught all her fish because she was too weak to pull them in. He would have her hold the pole, but he would reel in the fish.

She said that Captain Ted had done a great job in making the boat wheelchair friendly and he had made sure that she was safely strapped in. Then he had zoomed at top speed and made sweeping turns to give her a thrill sitting in her wheelchair. A ride in his boat was more fun than a ride in Wheel One to the back of the moon.

Bram said he agreed with her.

He then asked her if she wondered why the trip to the moon had been so short.

Zuri replied that she had no idea.

He then shared the fact that the current Fold was frozen to one coordinate location and could not move. He wanted to add the capability of motion to the Fold process.

Zuri looked at him and said that if he solved that problem, he would create a Fold wormhole that would turn Wheel One into a Fold spaceship. It would be a spaceship that could move through time and space free of the conventional limitations of the speed of light.

She asked what he was waiting for.

He looked at her and asked her for her IQ then reminded her that hers was much higher than his and that she was the smart one in the room that needed to solve the problem.

She gave a little laugh and joked that he was the smart one she was just the clueless one that asked the right questions.

Pat, Amy, and Elizabeth walked into the office and commented that the journey of Wheel One and Two had been anticlimactic and that it seemed surreal as if it had just been a dream. They commented that getting the two Wheels out of the hanger in Seattle into the Dallas hanger had been more exciting.

Bram said that Fold had been more exciting for him too since he had almost left them somewhere in-between. He made the point that he had no idea if an in-between existed or if the wheels would have just disappeared and never been found again.

Elizabeth looked over to Zuri and told her to watch out for Bram because he might have a great mind, but he often moved faster that the technology around him. She shared that she had gone and looked at the charred power transformers that Bram had fried when the first Fold was done. She said she had gone out and bought a dozen lotto tickets hoping to cash in on her good luck at being alive, but the lotto had won, and she was still poor.

Zuri smiled and said she would pay close attention to what Bram was concocting since even his fishing trips were more exciting than she had expected.

Lacy called and asked if Bram was able to meet with Myla.

He was surprised but he said that he would be free in about five minutes.

Pat said that she would take Zuri and look to see if anything had been done with her future office area and that afterwards she would have Orlando take Zuri home.

Elizabeth said she was going to see about the new Bramlets that were being assembled. She commented that the next set of Bramlet scouts for the Neptune Fold were almost all ready for testing.

Bram asked Lacy to send Myla in.

When she came in, he saw that her hands were shaking, and he knew immediately that she was very nervous.

He asked if they should shake hands or just go for a hug and put the past behind them and look forward to a long friendship.

Myla began crying but stepped forward and they hugged.

She began to apologize.

Bram stopped her and said that she should relax. He had no grudge and was not looking for an apology. He was looking forward to the long and good relationship the two of them would enjoy.

Myla thanked him and asked if there was anything she could do that would be appropriate.

Bram said that she should talk to Lacy on the way out and get the information about the upcoming fishing party and that he would expect the Smith family to catch the biggest fish.

Myla thanked him and said that she loved fishing, but she seldom caught one. She said that it was the sitting and enjoying the motion of the boat that pleased her.

Bram agreed with her and said that what he enjoyed most was to watch folks fishing, talking, and teasing each other about the one that got away.

He escorted Myla from his office and told her to stop by Marcus's office and let him know that his rather eccentric scientist was waiting to find out what the future travel plans would be.

He already knew the plan, but he wanted to have Myla stop and talk with Marcus before going home. He had told Marcus to finish what he was doing and then go home to Myla. He figured Marcus would figure out that he did not have a meeting with him.

Pat came back and said that Orlando and Zuri had left. She commented that Orlando and Zuri seemed to have bonded and become fast friends.

Bram said that in fact he had replaced Orlando with a new Marine guard, Donna because Orlando had suggested that Zuri rated at least one person guarding her at all times and he was stepping up and volunteering to do so. Orlando had been the one to recruit Donna, who seemed to have her eyes on him.

Pat gave a small laugh and suggested that they both stay out of the love triangle.

He nodded and said he had all he could handle with his own love affair.

He suggested that since it was a nice day they walk home.

Walking home was not a simple affair, Castor, and Donna the two Marine guards, in full battle gear, were in front, and on this day, Eric and Zoe his two FBI bodyguards were walking in back and Bob and Thomas the other two FBI guards were driving the van that was most often the mode of transportation in the afternoon.

The morning always consisted in a slow jog to work.

The attacks aimed at killing him had resulted in the current mode of increased protection. This had been the routine for several months.

Bram Nielson Collection

The level of security around Bram had always been high and though he sometimes felt constrained by it, the attacks that he had experienced made it clear that he was at the center of the bullseye to his adversaries and his adversaries seemed to have some deep political connections that surprised him. He wondered how he might find out who they were and see if there was a way to stop them.

The walk gave him time to think and to allow his mind to sort through what he needed to do to make the Fold program successful. He had stepped back from being the only one making it all happen and had split the responsibilities with various other members.

The Fold program's overall management on site was now being handled by Erica and back on the East coast by Jeffrey.

He had embraced the role of being the scientist that managed the data analysis and its interpretation, and he was the lead in making improvements to the Fold program.

Now all he needed was for his mind to open up and participate in solving the problem of developing a means to propel a Fold enclosure.

Ron Mueller

Chapter 2: Fishing

Almost every one of the team members signed on with Linda to go fishing. There was high enthusiasm among all the participants and a common groan when they found out the time that the fishing boats would leave the dock.

Lake Celio was really the Columbia River up stream of the Dallas hydro-electric dam. The river was somewhere around a mile across, and the current was slow and easy.

It was still dark when the boats left the Celio park docks. The moon light etched the far bank a dark black. Home lights twinkled as if the bank had its own stars competing with the millions of the ones overhead.

The rising sun was battling the night and slowly bringing in the day.

As it rose ahead, the seven boats went single file toward it.

Then the far horizon looked as if it had burst into flame and the sun rose red behind a thin layer of clouds.

The saying, "Red sun in the morning, sailors warning" went through his mind.

The rising white steam going up from the lake seemed to be trying to warm the cool and somewhat nippy air.

Ted gave a hand signal and the six boats behind him moved into a V formation. He began weaving back and forth and the other boats all followed and did the same. He was making it as exciting as he dared.

Zuri had thanked him for an exciting ride the last time he had taken her fishing. He planned to get her to thank him again. He was personally pleased that he had made a positive connection.

It was hard for him to treat her like he would anyone else. He needed to get rid of his lifetime feeling of alienation when he saw someone who was crippled. He needed to realize that the people in their wheelchairs had their own talents, ambitions, and dreams.

He loved fishing and so did Zuri. He figured that would give them a common bond. A good start. He shook his head; he was just an old foggy that needed to be around people like Bram and Zuri.

Bram was sitting next to Pat and holding her hand as they let themselves be absorbed by the moment. He alternated between watching the occupants of the other boats, enjoying the motion of Captain Ted's boat, and the feel the wind blowing his hair gave him.

The majestic scenery of the snowcapped mountains and the skirt of green forest that swept gracefully down to the edge of the water was spell binding. The experience seemed to tease his mind to let go of other thoughts.

The zigzagging brought him out of his daydreaming, and he paid attention to what was going on. He laughed when he realized that all the boats were copying what Captain Ted was doing.

He shouted out to Ted and asked if help was needed in guiding the boat.

Ted smiled and said he had no choice because he was following Zuri's order to make fishing fun.

Zuri shouted out that she had not given any such order, but he should continue doing what he was doing.

Bram noted that the seven fishing boats formed a V as they made their way eastward along the lake. He wondered what the formation looked like from an arial view. He looked up to see a small drone following above them. He pointed it out to Ted who nodded and pointed to himself and to the drone to indicate it was one of his.

Bram later found out that Lacy was the one flying the drone. It had been her idea to film the entire fishing trip.

Lacy had informed him that Jeffery and Major General Lester Tilson would be joining in on the fishing trip. She also let him know that every one of the big shots up to and including the President had sent him and the fishing party good luck and that they regretted not being able to join in personally.

Jeffery had called when he had landed and let him know that he and the General had been parked out on the tarmac for almost an hour waiting for some gate keepers to get to work and work the bridge that connected the plane with the terminal. The Pilot finally let everyone off via the planes own steps.

The fishing had just started when Jeffery and Major General Lester Tilson arrived in the eighth boat. They pulled alongside and apologized for having been late.

Bram let them know that no apologies were necessary but that they needed to get their lines in the water so they could try for one of three prizes, the largest fish, the most fish and the smallest keeper fish.

They both gave him a salute and their boat went out to the edge of the group and threw in their lines.

By noon everyone had caught a fish and Ted called a halt to the fishing and said it was time for the picnic to begin. He pointed to the darkening sky and said that it looked like a rain squall was coming in over the lake.

He called ahead and asked that the tent to cover the picnic area get set up in case they got rain.

The ride back was fast and straight. They all had their eyes on the black clouds slowly gathering down by the hydro-electric dam.

They had all just gotten out and helped finish putting up the very large tent when the rain started and soon it was pouring. The far side of the lake disappeared. It was hard to see to the end of the dock. The boats had their rain covers on, and all fishing poles had been put away.

Ted said that the amount of rain they had been getting was unusual.

The three grills were just outside of the tent and the three doing the grilling got wet every time they got a serving of what was on the grill.

Zuri was sitting by the edge of the tent looking out to the lake with her parents helping her eat. They were all listening to Orlando tell a story about the time he was on patrol and the rain had started. He made the point that the patrol was in the middle of the desert and had not come prepared for the rain that fell as heavy as the one that they were now sitting and watching. He went on to share that after the rain the desert was covered in flowers. It was as if a miracle had happened.

Bram enjoyed the story and noticed that Orlando had captured everyone's attention.

He took the opportunity to let everyone know that they would wait until after lunch and after the rain they would see who had qualified for the prizes that were being offered.

The tent and the food seemed to bring everyone closer. Pat commented that the rain only added charm to the event.

The thunder and lightning seemed to have the effect of making everyone speak softly. Rita, Ted's wife, asked if it was all right for her to play some music.

Lacy gave a small groan and then said that it would be country western, or old crooners singing songs of the sixties or before.

Major General Tilson said that it would be great to hear some music that he could understand.

The intensity of the rain lessened. The music was just what everyone needed, and the conversations seemed to well up like a dry sponge getting water put on it as everyone listened to Rita.

Bram then heard a loud explosion and as he looked back along the shoreline, he watched what looked like a small atom bomb's plume rising brightly up into the grey of the clouds.

Everyone under the tent quit talking.

He knew immediately that the location was back at the Fold property.

The silence was louder than the thunder and lightning that seemed to have risen.

Everyone turned and looked at Castor as his phone rang. He put it on speaker mode and answered the call. It was the Marine site leader calling to inform him that an attack on the compound had taken place but had been thwarted.

The explosion had been one of the attack vehicles exploding in the back of the compound area and other than being spectacular, the explosion had killed all the attackers that had retreated to it, but it had done no damage. He said that each attacking van had four gunmen and all but one of the attackers were dead.

He reported that USS Hood, Wheel One had been tipped on its side, but it did not seem to be damaged.

When Jeffery asked if they should return to the compound, Bram was about to say no, when Pat spoke up and said that they should finish their fishing picnic. She went on to say that if the wheel was not damaged, she would later do a Fold and then land to bring the Wheel back up right.

Major General Tilson asked the Site commander to have a twelve-person patrol sent to the picnic area and set up a defensive perimeter. He looked around at the group and said that it was just precautionary.

Bram looked out at the rain and the lake and said that if there was to be an attack they should be expecting the action to come from the lake.

Orlando suggested that they prepare for that possibility, and he asked if the Marine bodyguards had their weapons. He knew the answer but asked so that he could ask that of all the others would know that they had come prepared.

He then looked to the FBI bodyguards and asked them the same thing.

They all responded in the affirmative.

He then asked the boat captains if they would allow their boats to be used and got a unanimous response that they could but only if they were doing the driving and they got to shoot as well.

Bram watched in amazement as the boats loaded up and went out in the rain. He had been turned down when he had volunteered to go with Ted.

The General simply said that he could not justify risking either Bram or any of the other brains running the program.

Jeffery agreed and when he volunteered to go out, he was also turned down.

Rita said that she wanted those that were staying under the tent to round up all the extra tables that were in the park and bring them to the edge of the tent on the lake side and tip them so that they made a protective barrier.

She then went to the van and the trailer and returned with several shot guns and boxes of shells.

She handed one to Bram and said that she had heard that he was rather deadly in a gun battle and that her Ted had said that he was almost certain that once the rain let up there would be an attack.

Bram had a second set of tables tilted in the center of the tent and had Zuri and everyone else get behind the second barrier.

He asked that Lisa help Zuri to rest on the ground and instructed everyone to lay down flat if the fighting came their way.

The storm must have been listening because almost immediately after his announcement the rain stopped and as if it were providing better fighting conditions, the sun seemed to be pushing the clouds west along the lake.

Bram then saw what looked like a dark grey blanket being lifted from a fleet of boats coming in at full speed from the west.

Pat was looking through a set of binoculars and commented that there seemed to be more than a dozen and that two had what seemed to be heavy duty machine guns and two had mortars mounted on the bow.

Lacy excused herself and asked Linda to look after Zuri. She took the opportunity to launch her camera drone. She said she would take a closer look, and she could help guide the gun fire from their boats.

Elizabeth said she would talk with Orlando and Pat said she would talk with Castor.

Bram had several tables moved to the two launch ramps and had two shooters positioned behind each.

Rita and Marial were also out at the two tables to help support them in case of a gun battle.

Amy, the helicopter pilot turned wheel two captain became the play-by-play announcer and shared what she was seeing on the computer screen.

Bram quickly realized that their boats were outnumbered and out gunned. The only advantage seemed to be that Stacey was an expert in flying the drone and in providing critical information.

The two boats carrying mortars were sunk in the first round of fighting. Then those out in their boats were able to take out one of the boats with a fifty-caliber machine gun.

The remaining boat with the fifty turned toward the docks.

All the attacking boats that remained had shooters with either AR 15's or high-powered rifles.

Bram realized that the one boat that had a fifty-caliber gun was fast approaching the ramp area.

Lacy saw the same thing and her drone made a sweeping turn and returned to the tent area.

When the first round of the fifty caliber was fired, the splinters from the first set of tables flew past Bram as if they were sent to make him into a porcupine.

Lacy flew the camera drone directly at the gunman and turned so close to his face that he turned to avoid getting hit. She then took the drone on a sharp turn and flew the drone toward the boat driver and crashed it into his face.

The boat swerved and hit the end of the dock. The fifty-caliber gunman hit the grips of the gun chest first and was most likely critically injured but Bram's shotgun blast sent him flying back over the boats low wind shield where the shooter behind him accidently shot him in the back.

Bram rushed toward the boat in a continuous pump and shoot fashion and then the click of the trigger made him realize his gun was empty and he was now a sitting duck. He was about to jump into the water when Pat handed him another shotgun as she took the empty.

Rita had done the same back up with a second shotgun for the grill master that had done the same thing as Bram, but on the adjacent dock.

Bram continued on toward the boat as he pumped and fired. There was no response, but he made sure everyone was dead.

Lacy ran down the pier, jumped into the boat, retrieved her drone, did a quick check, and used some duct tape and then launched it and sent it out to the boats where the battle was still going at an intensive battle.

Bram stood and watched as she flew her drone as if it was a combat plane.

Stacy's harassing drone seemed to turn the tide, and the battle slowly came to an end as the only surviving attacking boat surrendered.

Stacy did a slow sweep of the boats and noted that all of their boats were full of holes, but the design of the boats kept them afloat. They might fill with water, but they would not sink.

Only Ted's boat had an engine that came to life and allowed him to slowly tow the other boats into the dock area. All the boats were tied bow to tail as Ted slowly pulled them back.

Bram had the ramp area cleared of the tables. He was about to get Zuri sent home when the Marines from the Fold compound arrived.

They took over. They had an EMT group with them and as the boats came in, they began checking on the wounded.

Almost everyone out on the boats had some sort of wound. They were treated and then those needing to get transported to the hospital were taken by the first unit. It was designed for battle conditions and could transport six and they were full as they departed.

Another EMT unit was on its way.

Bram was listening as Orlando was telling his version of the battle to Zuri. Castor kept throwing in color comments and Donna kept saying that they shouldn't try to pull the wool over a person's eyes who was ten times smarter than they were.

He saw that Zuri was really enjoying the banter.

Niro and Jina were standing next to him, and they commented that Zuri was really blossoming into a very social person and even with what had just happened they thought that she was where she should be.

Jina looked at him and said that she had not expected to see the dark side of such a bright mind, but she was relieved that he was a person of action.

Pat came over and pointed to Bram's leg and asked him if he knew he had a splinter the size of a chop stick that gone through his leg.

Bram looked down and realized that the shower of splinters created by the fifty caliper bullets had not all missed him. He was surprised by the size of the splinter and the fact that it was not bleeding.

Jina gasped when she saw the splinter.

They had all been so intent on listening to Orlando that Bram's injury was missed.

Pat had motioned to one of the EMT's and pointed to Bram.

He came over and asked Bram to come over to the Emergency Vehicle and get the splinter removed.

He wanted Bram to go to the hospital, but Bram refused. He asked them to remove the splinter and later he would go to the hospital.

The EMT went over to the General and after a brief discussion he returned and told Bram that removing the splinter was going to cause some pain.

By this time everyone was standing around watching.

Orlando was reassuring Zuri that Bram was going to be alright and that he was going to demonstrate the bravery of a Marine.

Bram reached into his shirt pocket and took out a large piece of hard jerky and put it between his teeth.

The EMT use some Novocain to numb the area around both ends of the splinter. After a few minutes he said that he was going to pull it out in one fast pull and that his assistant would put some gel and gauze to prevent the wound from bleeding.

Orlando began a chant.

> *Fifty caliper no big deal.*
> *Bram is shooting,*
> *Bram is real.*
> *Fifty Caliper missed the mark.*
> *Splintered the table,*
> *Angry table, Angry table,*
> *Tried for Bram but missed the mark.*
> *Little splinter, Little splinter*
> *Does not bother.*
> *Bram is real.*
> *Bram, Bram is a true Fold hero.*

Everyone at the outing took up the chant.

The EMT waited until "hero" and then swiftly pulled the splinter out.

The pain caught Bram by surprise. He bit down on the hard beef jerky and thought about a Fold to the Alien world.

Pat put her hand on his shoulder and asked if the contest was still on. She knew that Bram had used his powerful mind to ignore most of the pain and she wanted to distract him as the EMT's finished binding the wound.

Bram looked at her and smiled. He thanked her for being such a brave backup. It had saved his life.

Pat had not expected the reply, but she smiled and said that she always had his back.

He then replied that everyone had won and that they would all share first prize.

Chapter 3: Aftermath

It felt to Bram like the drive back to the compound took twice as long as the trip out to go fishing. An armored Marine vehicle was in front, and one was in back. There were three vans transporting the fishing party back to the Fold living area in the middle.

He was still recovering from the removal of the large splinter, and he was also feeling the emotional aftereffects of having shot and killed several of the attackers. He was feeling fine, but he was already thinking about the discussion he would have with Dr. Windal the Fold phycologist. He had no remorse about his actions so much as it nagged him that he was constantly under attack by an unknown but seemingly powerful group of people and that his side was constantly in a defensive posture.

He was also thinking about the action that Lacy had taken with her camera drone. She had played a huge part in thwarting the attack.

He wondered if she were up for a new role on the team. He would ask her and see if she would lead a team assigned to identify potential enemies of the Fold program.

He had voiced his concern before about always being on defense instead of being on offense. He figured that Stacy was the one that could lead a team to develop a Fold offense.

When the caravan arrived at the Fold work area, Bram asked it to stop by the gate area where two of the vans had been stopped. He took in the crumpled entrance gate.

He figured that the van had run through the gate at a high speed. He decided that the entrance would need to be redesigned to make it impossible to just run through at high speed.

The bodies of several of the attackers were still on the ground or in the bullet riddled vans. Bram looked at all the bullet holes in the vans, he looked around and saw all the bullet hits on the entry booth and he was sure that if he walked around the entry area he would find a ton of bullet casings from the guns that the Marines had fired.

He asked the Marine guards if any Marine had been wounded or killed. He was relieved to learn that there were no injuries on their side.

He was thinking of walking the rest of the way in but realized that the wound in his leg was flaring up. His protection group jumped out and helped him back into the van.

The driver drove toward the rear of the compound to where the remains of the third mangled and blackened attack van rested looking like a high diver that had missed the water and had instead hit the pool side headfirst. It looked like the van had a black accordion body design. Bram saw the blackened arm of the person who must have been inside at the time and several blacked bodies were still on the ground where the explosion had hurled their bodies.

The van then drove into the hanger where the two Wheels were housed.

He was processing the events of the day. He was sure that he had someone on the inside of the Fold organization that was giving information to his adversaries. He was sure he had a spy in the Fold organization. He thought through how he would expose this spy. He mentally put together a list people that would potentially have a reason to be the spy.

When he stepped out of the van, the sight of Wheel One laying on its side put the list out of his mind. He limped to the Wheels entrance ramp and pressed the open button. The ramp went to its down position. He was about to climb in to see if there was any internal damage, but Pat stopped him and said that she would see what the damage was.

Bram heard her laugh as she called out that the only damage was the broken Boston Starbucks coffee mug that Bram had given to her. She came out, shook her head, and commented that the attackers had lost their lives and the most they had accomplished was to shatter her favorite coffee mug.

She thought through how to get the wheel back to its upright condition as she exited and pushed the ramp's close button. She remembered the lab demonstration that Bram had done for Remi and the lab group to show them how the Fold process could be used to move a bubble. She realized that she could create a Fold inside the hanger and be able to get Wheel One back to its upright position.

Bram felt a hand on his shoulder and realized that Pat was talking to him.

She was telling him that she would do a Fold inside the hangar to upright Wheel One.

He let her know he would go online and order a replacement Boston Mug.

Pat started to laugh. She pointed to the Wheel and asked whether they were going to put it back upright.

Bram replied that of course they were and that her idea of doing a little Fold was right on. He said that the first Fold would be to an upright position one foot off floor and the second Fold would be to a position on the floor. He looked around and signaled to Marcus and asked him to determine the coordinates for the two Folds.

It was Marcus's turn to laugh. He shook his head and said that he had discussed getting Wheel One upright with Pat and he had the coordinates already programmed. He shared that the Fold would take almost no power.

Bram agreed and walked over to where Lacy was standing and asked her to set up a meeting with the Fold leadership to start immediately after Wheel One was back upright. He asked that she plan to attend as well.

Pat entered Wheel One and strapped herself into the pilots control chair. She called the control center and asked if everything was a go.

Marcus gave her the green light and she pressed the Fold button.

As the Wheel seemed to magically move into an upright position and levitated one foot off the floor, a cheer went up, from everyone that had gone fishing and were standing in the observation area. A second cheer went up when the Wheel moved onto the floor and was back to its upright position and Wheel One was secured with its holding cables.

Lacy let him know that she had arranged for the leaders to be in the meeting room and that everyone else was going home.

Bram took a moment and asked Lacy if she was willing to take on a new role. It would be a promotion, and it would put her in charge of a team that would focus on taking an offensive posture against the people trying to subvert the work of the Fold project.

Lacy replied that she was excited about being more active in the Fold project and that she would do her best to fulfill his expectations.

He deflected her question about the details of the role and said that they should go to the meeting, and she would learn what he had in mind.

The meeting room was uncharacteristically silent. Everyone seemed to be concentrating on their drink or silently looking around.

Bram walked in, sat down, and used the old line, "I guess you're all wondering why I called this meeting."

Erica smiled and quietly said that she hoped that this time it wasn't about her.

Bram gave a little chuckle and replied that "No," this time it was about the fact that the Fold team lacked an Offense and an Offense coordinator, and he was determined to change that situation.

He pointed to Lacy and said, "let me introduce, Lacy Stetson, the superior and excellent drone fighter that was a key participant in defeating the attackers. I am promoting her into the new position of Offense coordinator."

Today in the battle by the lake, Lacy single handedly put offense in the air with nothing more than a camera drone. She disrupted the attack and gave our side the upper hand. It was an arial performance that you will all need to watch.

Her actions saved the day.

I want the upper hand against those who have repeatedly acted against the Fold project.

I would like Lacy to lead a team of five, have an appropriate number of Fold bubbles and anything else that she and her team determine will make them a potent offensive force.

I now request that the rest of you work with Lacy and put the Fold offense team on the field. She will lead and manage but she should be coaching a professional and superior team.

Jeffery asked if a person in the meeting could be on the team.

Bram once again pointed to Lacy and said that it was up to her. She would review the qualifications of those wishing to be on the team and insure that the participant brought the resources that contributed to winning.

Bram stood up and said that he was now leaving the meeting, and Lacy would manage getting the Fold offense team established and organized.

He looked at Lacy and asked if his way of explaining her new role made it clear to her what he was asking her to do.

Lacy looked at Erica and asked if this is what she had meant when she commented that she hoped it was not about her.

Erica replied, "Yes and now you know how Bram can knock you off your pace."

Bram looked at Erica as he got up to leave, "It's her first moment in this new role, give her a hand and then get out of the way."

The conversation in the meeting room rose to a robust level as everyone began talking about the way to get to their adversaries.

Bram left the meeting room and was greeted by his Marine and FBI bodyguards. He uncharacteristically gave each of them a high five slap and said that it was time to go home and have a cold one and then prepare dinner. He looked at Donna and suggested that she check with Orlando to see if he wanted to join in.

The ride to the house was short but his Marine and FBI bodyguards carried on a constant discussion as each described their experience in the gun battle on the lake.

Bram knew that, like himself, all of them were still on an adrenaline high.

Castor pointed to two large red coolers, three cases of beer and a large watermelon and said that the picnic should continue when they got to the house.

He then lifted the cooler lid and said that the warm food was still warm, and they could all just sit back and continue the party.

Bram stopped him and said that the picnic should continue at the house, but he wanted all weapons turned in so that he wouldn't worry about having anyone animating the action of the gun fight that they had all survived.

That got a laugh out of everyone.

Bram led the way up the stairs from their basement parking area. He knew he was supposed to get his leg checked out, but he did not want to sit and find out from the Doctor that time would heal his wound and he could have pain pills if the pain was too great.

He was more interested in getting his protectors back into the partying mode. He thought that some watermelon and some of the grilled broccoli and baked beans would make a great snack.

He would then sit down in his study and think through his bubble problem.

The team insisted he have a beer with them as they all put their weapons on the dining room table.

Bram had to laugh when Orlando came in and said that he was still armed and would protect him if his regular guards were too drunk to do so.

After he had his "snack," he picked up his half-finished beer and said that he was going into the study to work through his current problem with how the Fold vehicles were frozen at the coordinates that they Folded to.

He had to laugh when the whole group in unison said that perhaps another beer would help to solve the problem.

Bram went into the study and turned on the pot to make some tea. Eric and Zoe had followed him in, and Eric came and took over getting the teacups ready for the hot water. He said that he was making a cup for himself, and Zoe and he would include Bram as well.

He said it was their day on guard duty and they had only taken a sip of their beers.

Bram thanked him and sat down at his desk. He turned on his computer and began going through the equations on the spreadsheet that he had created.

He could just as easily have settled into his easy chair and gone through the equation in his mind and if Pat had been present, he would most likely have chosen to do so. But since she was back working with the rest of the leadership team on how to set up the offense for the Fold project he chose to sit at his desk.

He had been reviewing his equation and the assumptions he had made to connect space position with time for more than an hour when Pat knocked on the door.

As she entered he heard the group in the dining room say, "Tell us that half a beer didn't knock him out."

Bram knew that his guards were enjoying the remainder of the day. He got up and gave Pat a hug and asked how things in the meeting had gone.

Pat commented that Lacy had taken charge and had done a great job on insisting that the focus stay on identifying the members of the Fold Offense Team. She had limited the number of members to one from each organization and insisted that each provide some expertise or connection needed to provide the team with the ability to take action. She had made the point that she was not inclined to work with a team that talked more than they acted.

Pat went on to praise Erica for supporting Lacy in how the members should be selected.

Bram asked if the group had provided the names of members to Lacy.

Pat shared that Major General Lester Tyson, John Morgan, Elizabeth, and Lacy's father Ted were currently on the list.

Brian thought for a minute and asked how Ted had gotten on the list.

Pat said that Lacy had made a call during the meeting and asked if her father had recognized any of the attackers. She then hung up and put his name on the list.

Bram asked whether she was going to stay in the office or go and party out in the dining room.

Pat pointed to her side of the recliner and said that she had all the partying that she could take and that a cup of tea and some quiet time was what she was looking forward to.

Bram turned off his computer and made her a cup of tea. He was now looking forward to having her lean against him and feel her warmth.

Chapter 4: The Bubble Problem

The next morning when Bram arrived at his office, Lacy was sitting at her desk. After greeting her, he asked her to come into his office.

He let her know that he had heard from Pat and early this morning from Erica what a great job she had done in guiding the leadership meeting and with organizing the Fold Offense Team. He then asked if she had any recommendations for someone to replace her and he said that he wanted her to remodel the room next to Marcus's and appoint it in the manner that pleased her, but she had to make it a better office than Marcus's.

Lacy admitted that the change was happening in a very fast but exciting way. She was a little overwhelmed at the role that he had carved out for her. She admitted that she had to overcome the fact that many of her team had positions that were at the top of the organization.

He nodded and said that he had thought about the change all the way from the picnic area until they got to the gate. Seeing the attack vans and the bodies and then seeing the wheel on its side had coalesced the idea of an Fold team offense. He wanted an attack team and as soon as that thought came to him, her attack with her camera drone and the expertise she demonstrated using it had made her his choice of who would lead that attack team. He made the point that his one desire was that she develop the expertise of the Fold Offense Team with as much skill as she had demonstrated flying the camera drone in an attack mode.

He told her that on her team, her members answered to her no matter where they sat in the organization hierarchy.

He suggested that she identify what she needed to learn. He let her know that he was not going to get involved in all the details that she would be working through, and she should look to Elizabeth for support guidance. He would be available as well but expected to only get called on if a barrier seemed insurmountable.

The vacant support position was one that he identified needed to be addressed before she would be able to assume her new role. He asked if she had anyone who might be able to fill the role. He made the point that it would be good if that person was already in the Fold organization.

Lacy was silent for a moment and then said that she knew of several persons capable of filling her positions. After a moment she asked if it could be someone in her family.

Bram smiled and said the Stetson family was in good standing with him and who did she have in mind.

Lacy said that it was her older sister, who had asked if she could interview for the position, when she heard about the promotion.

Bram pointed out that Linda was a social worker.

Lacy nodded and said that Linda had done a little secretarial support before becoming a nurse and going into the social work force. She was the smart one in the family and had always gotten better grades than her. They both had been on their high school lacrosse team, and Linda was seen as the leader of the team. Lacy gave a short laugh and said that Linda had expressed the fact that her younger sister had been the lucky one to land a job with the Fold Organization and that luck paid better than skill.

Bram said he was a believer in luck and that it was good to be lucky but usually luck was the result of good preparation and hard work.

He asked when Linda would be available for a personal discussion with him.

Lacy smiled as she said that she could be in his office in as little as fifteen minutes from now.

Bram replied that he was not going to cause someone to get a traffic ticket and that he would like to talk with Linda at one hour before the end of the normal workday.

He then tilted his head and asked what Lacy's new salary would need to be for him to keep her from jumping ship to one of the outside support organizations that he was sure would make her salary offers that might make her head spin.

Lacy replied that she was already getting one of the best salaries that she could imagine for someone with her skills.

Bram smiled and said that her sister was most likely going to get something close to what she was currently earning, but he expected to give her a salary closer to what Marcus was earning. He knew that Lacy had seen the pay level of several of his staff.

Her face went red. She pointed out that would mean that her pay would almost double. She said that she would love it, but she would settle for much less.

Bram nodded and said that when she got into her new role and experienced the intensity of the work, she would have a different opinion.

He said that it was time for her to call her sister, organize her transition to her new role and for him to meet with Zuri, Mallica, Marcus, and Jina and organize the review of the Fold equations.

He stood up and walked to the door, opened it, and waved her out.

Lacy walked out and immediately called Linda.

Bram could hear Lacy saying that yes, yes, she had the interview.

He was looking forward to having Linda as his new support. He had been impressed with her ability to recognize that Zuri was a mental genius and how she had persisted in telling everyone so. He had also noted that Zuri had a close relationship with Linda. He figured all Linda had to do was show up for the interview and she would have the support role that Lacy currently held.

It came to him that the Stetsons were slowly penetrating the Fold organization. By the end of the day, three of them would have active positions in support roles.

Orlando was joking with Zuri as he wheeled her into the office. He pointed at Bram and commented that he was the one that had twisted his arm and made him drink too much.

Zuri gave her soft laugh and said that Bram was too weak to twist Orlando's little finger let alone his arm.

Bram joined in and said that Orlando and his cohorts had consumed so much alcohol that he was amazed that Orlando was even capable of pushing her in and he would understand if Orlando were to pass out on the floor.

He then suggested that Orlando sit down and enjoy a cup of coffee or tea while the rest of the Equation Analysis Team (EAT) reviewed the Fold equations.

Orlando said that the review of the equations was sure to put him to sleep and most likely he would have nightmares. He walked to the door and said he was going to go to the cafeteria and make up a ditty about the EAT team that were trying to eat their way through the Fold equations.

Everyone laughed and Bram insinuated that he was probably going to engage in a pleasant endeavor while the rest of them drank tea or coffee and tried to stay awake.

Elizabeth called the EAT members to order and suggested they all get comfortable, and that Zuri would be expected to ask the why questions and as often as possible suggest a reason. Everyone else should ask questions for understanding or clearly state that they were lost and needed to be told what a specific part of the overall equation meant.

She then pointed at Bram and said that he would have to answer Zuri and the rest of them and needed to make everyone have at least a general understanding of the concept that each part of the equation represented.

It soon became clear that those in attendance were struggling like maple syrup sap trying to flow out of the tree on a cold winter day. Their sap, drip pan minds were mostly empty. The sap was just too thick.

Zuri was the only one that seemed to grasp the concepts and her why's caused Bram to stop and think about the reasons why he had linked certain parts of the equation together and what assumption had led him to do so.

Bram came to realize that he had been very lucky to have made the breakthrough. He thought back to his conversations with Einstein at the desert location when they sat together on the boulder where he had finally achieved the breakthrough. Einstein his pet mouse was still with him. He had the urge to share this fact but decided that would wait until he and Zuri were working through the answers to her questions and share it only with her.

After an hour, Elizabeth called an end to the meeting and suggested that they reconvene in two days or when Zuri had answers to all her questions.

Bram thanked Elizabeth for having led them through the hour. He thanked Jina for having recorded all the questions. Then he thanked everyone else for having added their questions.

Mallica commented that she felt that getting the answers to Zuri's questions would make a huge difference in her understanding the basics of the equation. She admitted that it was hard for her to understand how many of the assumptions allowed the connection between the concepts.

Bram nodded and said that luck had a lot to do with his success.

Zuri shook her head and added luck and a brain that worked in a nonlinear fashion. She then emphasized, "in a fashion distinctly different, and more like that of a savant on drugs."

He asked Zuri to stay for a few moments and then asked Elizabeth to let Orlando know that they were done but that he should wait about fifteen minutes before coming to get her.

Zuri was in the process of asking what he wanted to talk about when Bram raised his hand to stop her.

He walked over to his bookcase and opened a small door, and a small grey mouse walked out and got on his hand.

He carried it over to Zuri and introduced Einstein the coinventor of the Fold technology. He then described sitting on a large boulder in the middle of the desert in the dark, early in the morning waiting for the sun to rise. A few minutes after the sun hit the boulder, Einstein would come and sit with him and nibble on a piece of cookie.

He would always share the problem that he had with Einstein and ask for his advice.

Einstein never failed him and in time guided him to the Fold equation.

He explained that when he claimed not to know an answer it was because Einstein had never told him why an assumption would work.

Zuri had been gently petting Einstein, who had settled in her lap. She asked if she could give him a piece of cookie and ask him a question.

Bram gave her a cookie from the refreshment area.

Zuri gave a small section to Einstein and then asked why he had never explained the assumptions to the brilliant but definitely loony person named Bram.

"Oh, you say because you didn't think he was smart enough to understand. I get it from now on you want us to come to you with the questions needing answers and you will help us get to the answer. OK, you have a deal," Zuri said in a soft voice to Einstein.

Bram had a huge smile on his face when she lifted Einstein and place him in his hand.

There was a knock on the door as Bram put Einstein back into his palace and closed the little door.

He walked over and let Orlando in.

Lacy was standing right behind Orlando and when he wheeled Zuri out, she let him know that Linda had arrived and was ready.

Bram asked for five minutes and then to bring her in. He called up her resume and reviewed her work history. A picture of a very smart and hard-working person formed in his mind. He also was impressed with her focus and dedication to helping the most disadvantaged younger persons. He gave her a lot of credit for having insisted that Zuri was brilliant in spite of everyone doubting her.

He figured she had the job, but he wanted her to make her case and feel that she had sold herself.

The knock on the door caused him to rise and walk around the desk to greet Linda.

He went directly to the key question. He asked why she wanted the support role.

Linda responded that from all the stories that Lacy had shared working on the Fold project was the most challenging and provided the biggest opportunity to grow. She pointed out that Lacy was now moving on to a role that had not existed and that neither had ever dreamt of such a role.

Bram commented that such an opportunity might not happen again for a long time.

Linda smiled and said that she had only experienced a slice of the action that went on and it was a slice bigger than she had experienced in her whole working career.

Bram asked when she could start.

Linda said that she would ask Lacy to vacate her desk as soon as the interview was over.

Bram asked if she had any other questions.

Linda asked if she could move in with Lacy in her apartment.

Bram said that she could have her own apartment.

Linda replied that she and Lacy preferred to share since it would give them a chance to interact with each other every evening. Later if either of their situations changed one of them might want an apartment.

She gave a little laugh and said that neither of them had any love life and figured that it was because of their reluctance to be the weak member of a romance.

She then asked if he might want to change any support items.

Bram said that there was one small change that was due to the current effort of reviewing and improving the Fold equations. He normally ran an open-door office but for the duration of the review, he would like to have a scheduled ten-minute warning for the next item on his calendar. She would schedule, let him know and then give him the ten-minute warning when appropriate.

Linda thanked him for the opportunity and stood up and walked toward the door.

Bram asked her to send Lacy in.

Lacy was all smiles when she entered. She thanked Bram and let him know that she and Linda were going to have a celebration dinner at their apartment that evening.

Bram smiled and said it was an easy hire. He knew that Zuri would be ecstatic about his new support since she would also be her support.

Lacy agreed and asked what he wanted to talk about.

Bram nodded and said that he wanted to apologize for having underpaid her in the past for her talents.

Lacy spoke up and asked if he were kidding. She was the highest paid support on the Fold team and made at least twice as much as she could get on the outside.

Bram said, "Oh" as if he were surprised. He then asked if her salary would satisfy Linda.

Lacy let him know that she made twice the salary that Linda currently got.

"Oh," so you think your current salary would be too much for Linda, he asked?

Lacy gave a small laugh and told him to pay Linda whatever he thought was fair.

Bram smiled; he had enjoyed baiting Lacy. He let her know that Linda would start at her current salary.

He then asked what he should pay her for her new role.

Lacy nodded and answered, "Whatever you think is fair."

Bram threw out the figure that he had determined fit with the role into which she was moving. It was just below Erica's, Elizabeth's, and Marcus's salaries but almost twice as much as she was currently making.

"Wow," I am shocked, "Wow" let me catch my breath before I faint," Lacy said as she closed her eyes.

Bram felt good about everything that had gone on during the day and the ending was especially rewarding. He suggested that Lacy go and celebrate and let him get home and get some rest so he could work on the most important issue at hand.

Ron Mueller

Chapter 5: Change

It was clear to Bram that the change in his role was opening up more time for him. He wondered how the change was affecting some of his key people. He invited those closest to him to give him their opinion on the change.

He asked Pat and Amy to meet with him. Amy wondered what the meeting was about, and he said that he wanted to get the impression from the two of them about the organizational change impact.

Amy said that overall, it seemed that Erica had become a new person. She was still hard driving, but her current approach was much more into making sure that everyone was getting coached, developed, and was enjoying their work.

He knew Pat's assessment already but asked her for her impression. Pat smiled and agreed with Amy. She did not have the desert experience where Amy had described Erica as the wicket witch from the east but what she saw now was a caring person and one that was trying to embrace the social environment that he had created.

Amy then said that she had heard from Elizabeth that during the Fold equation review, whenever you didn't have an answer to a question about why or how you had decided to combine concepts, you always replied that only Einstein would know and that Zuri would often repeat, "yes only Einstein would know."

The only Einstein that I ever met was a little mouse that came and sat with us on the morning that you revealed that you had solved the problem of creating a Fold. We two ate our treat and Einstein ate his cookie crumb.

I went on to become an Fold pilot. I forgot all about Einstein until Elizabeth shared what was happening in the Fold review.

Is Einstein still alive?

Bram looked at Pat and said that he had shared the story about talking to Einstein with her, but he had not shared the fact that Einstein was the most experienced Fold traveler among them.

One of the side effects to going through the Fold seemed to affect aging. He said that Einstein had volunteered to be a Fold traveler, so Bram had used him to make sure the Fold process did not prove fatal to a living organism. He had Folded him more than a dozen times and other than his friend turning grey as he aged, he physically was not deteriorating.

Pat smiled and asked if he had Einstein in the office.

Bram got up and went to the bookcase, moved a few books, and opened the little door. Einstein sniffed his way out and hopped into Bram's open hand.

He carried him over and handed him to Amy. Einstein sniffed her hand and then curled up in her palm.

Bram pointed out that it was Einstein's way of greeting an old friend.

Amy had tears in her eyes as she handed Einstein to Pat. She said that her trip to the rock in the desert that Bram went to every morning had been the turning point of her life and she was still on the launch trajectory he had urged her to take and hoped that it would take all her life to reach orbit. Einstein is the jewel that I think about often and it doesn't surprise me that he is smarter than the mad scientist he coaches.

Bram gave a light laugh and agreed about Einstein being the genius. He was now in the process of coaching Zuri and he, as they examined the assumptions that had been made during the Fold equation development.

Bram went on to share that the reason that he and Zuri were examining the equation so closely was that their goal was to create the ability that an object in a Fold would be able to move the Fold coordinates from their Fold location but not have to use additional energy to do so.

Pat put up her hand and asked whether that would allow her to move positions at will.

Bram answered that Zuri described it as creating a portal that allowed the Fold vessel to travel through a time and space portal.

Amy shook her head and said that she was lost in how it would work but she was eager to see him succeed and if Einstein was the critical thinker, then she would bring him a cookie crumb every day if that would help.

Bram replied that Einstein had agreed to a strict diet and did not want to eat too many cookies and gain weight. He said that he had also volunteered to be the first to travel through the time-space wormhole as soon as what allowed that to happen was discovered.

Pat came over and gave him a kiss and said that she thought that he had told her everything but now she had learned that he had kept a secret.

Bram said yes he had but he lifted Einstein and pointed out that it was a little secret.

After they left Bram asked Linda to come meet with him.

It had been a week since she had become his and Zuri's support. He asked her how she felt about the week and whether the pay was adequate.

Linda had learned what her pay was going to be from Lacy when they both celebrated their new jobs. She was very happy to be getting her sister's old job. She was surprised at how much she was to get paid. Was the pay adequate? She then shared that it was a fifty percent increase over the pay she had received as a nurse.

It was more than adequate.

She finally verbalized that yes, the pay was more than adequate and that if Zuri and he did not generate more work she would need to bring in large books to read.

Bram nodded and said that she should embrace the moment and that it most likely was the quiet before the storm.

He then asked if he and Erica were still scheduled to meet.

He walked to Erica's office to meet with her. This was the first time for them to meet with just each other and it was the first time he would get to see her office.

He knocked on the door and entered when her heard Erica say come in. He took in a simple and efficient looking office. It seemed somewhat Spartan. He sat down and asked how the first week had gone.

Erica commented that she had no idea how he had kept things going on his own. The bubble assembly work alone could take all of her time if she let it. But she was also in the process of contacting the companies that they might choose to produce the future bubbles.

She asked whether any additional wheels would be needed.

Bram replied to the last question and said that if he and Zuri were able to make a breakthrough in the Fold equation that the wheel might be of interest but at the moment two wheels seemed to be two too many.

He said he felt bad about having started with them, but they had been successful and would be useful if staying out in a Fold for some length of time were the objective.

Erica then asked him what he was hearing about her leadership.

Bram replied that she was seen as a hard driver but one who seemed fair and developmental. He made the point that his informants were tough critics, and their positive assessment meant that she was doing a good job in her role.

He thanked her for having chosen to come to the Dallas Fold complex.

He asked her how she liked her living accommodations.

Erica was overjoyed at the comfort of and the view from her top-level apartment. She let him know that the tension overload that she had accumulated working in Washington was leaving her body on a daily basis. She laughed and said that she was waiting for a breakfast pancake, eggs, and sausage invite.

Bram felt relieved that Erica was making the transition into being the kind of leader he had always envisioned she could be. He was pleased to hear that she was finding the Fold environment to her liking.

He then invited her for a Sunday brunch. He said he was not sure who would be present, but he would make sure there would be plenty for everyone.

Erica thanked him and said she would put it on her really busy Sunday schedule.

Bram said his would be busy as well. He had breakfast, lunch, and dinner to deal with and maybe a dip in the pool.

He then stood and said that he was going to go to the bubble assembly area to get a look at the bubbles. He said the bubbles helped him to think physically about the mathematical concepts with which he was struggling.

Erica asked if she could join in on his visit.

Bram was greeted in the lab with a Marine "Hurrah" that had become a common way for the folks there. He gave the Hawaiian finger waggle and walked over to where Bramlet One was still in its chamber with the large black object merged in its bubble.

He asked Erica what was planned for Bramlet One.

She said that the following week Bramlet One would be taken to a sterile lab and disassembled. She said that there was a great deal of interest to learn if the plastic was merged with the asteroid material or if it had been melted and formed around the asteroid.

Bram said that he would bet on the two materials having merged all the way through and the shape of the bubble would be found in the asteroid.

Erica said she would let him know as soon as she found out.

Bram then went around the lab and asked if what he saw was the total production to date.

Remi said that they had started to put the bubbles out by the Wheel area. He wondered how many more his group should plan on.

Bram said that Erica and Marcus would be the ones that would determine how many more would be needed.

Erica replied that the current production was based on Marcus's projection of where he wanted to send the bramlet scouts. She was working the longer term and was working with external folks to set up production. That longer term need would be based on what the Fold expansion would look like.

Bram nodded and said that if he had anything to do with it, they would need a lifetime of bubbles, but he was not sure what the specifications would be.

Ron Mueller

Chapter 6: The Message

The team analyzing the Fold equation decided that viewing the equation on paper might be easier than viewing it on the large screen. Bram agreed that an analog way of seeing the whole equation allowed the assumption points connecting various concepts to be seen all at once. He suggested they move their review to Zuri's office.

Linda let them know that only the area around Zuri's desk area was complete. The window area across from her desk was due to get painted and a long flower tray would be built in front of it.

Bram asked Linda to have the contractor put some plywood across the windows and to leave the end walls open. He then asked her to find a large roll of thick white paper to put on the wall and across the windows to create a giant white board that he could write his equation on. He asked for several large black felt pens and some white out in case he messed up a part of the equation and wanted to correct it.

Linda commented that she had never seen white out and was surprised he even knew about it.

Bram laughed and let her know that he had gone to a sandstone walled, one room school for his first eight years. There he had used chalk on a black board. He had used his teacher's manual typewriter and often used whiteout because he was terrible at typing.

He asked that the work on the white board take priority and get done that day.

He then asked Linda to have a messaging tube like those used at the mobile banking stands installed between his office and Zuri's office and to locate the tube exit behind Zuri's desk. He said this would allow the two of them to send material back and forth and save them time. He added that he wanted the tube to be in the wall and basically invisible.

He and Zuri had come up with this as an excuse and were really planning to use it as Einstein's private subway system.

The next day he spent the day carefully writing the Fold equation on the white paper. Mallica, Jina and Zuri stayed and watched but Marcus excused himself so he could go focus on where he was planning to send the Bramlet scouts.

Bram started writing on the upper left corner at head height. He thought that the equation was complicated and long enough that he would be having to be on his knees writing to get the equation on the space that the paper provided.

When he got to the first connecting assumption, Zuri suggested leaving a wide-open space so they could add a linking equation that might be needed to create the Fold location motion.

Bram let her know he liked that suggestion and wondered how much space he should leave.

Mallica suggested leaving at least three feet of space.

Bram worked hard at keeping the equation going straight across the room.

Jina joked that it reminded her about her writing lessons where the paper had guidelines to guide the writer.

Bram stopped and asked if Jina would put the guidelines up so that he could concentrate on the equation versus on trying to keep it level.

At ten, Linda brought in break refreshments and asked if she should order lunch in.

Bram shook his head and said that he was looking forward to going to the cafeteria for lunch and that Linda should take the lunch order and make sure they had a table reserved.

By lunch Bram was only a third of the way through the equation.

Mallica commented that Einstein had written his $E=MC^2$ that had stood for most of a century and wondered why Bram's was so long.

Bram replied that the next layer of equations that Einstein had written as the proof for that equation was about as long as what he had written on the wall.

He made the point that his equation took everything that Einstein had done and merged it with the works of several other scientists and that he had to modify some parts of each of those equations. This meant that his equation was roughly three times longer than Einstein's proof equations.

By noon Bram had made it about halfway and the going was slowing down. Zuri commented that they needed Einstein's guidance, and everyone agreed.

Bram smiled because what everyone else had heard was not what he had heard. He knew that Zuri was telling him that she wanted to hold Einstein, the mouse.

He suggested that after lunch, he would continue on his own, and they would all reconvene in the morning.

Mallica thought that was a good suggestion and said she was going to check on the progress of the next set of Bramlet scouts and see how Marcus was doing with getting the coordinates ready.

Jina asked Mallica if she could tag along.

Zuri said since she was in her office she would sit, and watch Bram put up the equation until it was time to go home.

Bram led the way to the cafeteria and spotted Linda sitting at a table that she had reserved.

He had a leisurely lunch and then he pushed Zuri back to her office.

He then went to his office and carried Einstein back in his pocket and hand him to Zuri who held him in her lap and lightly stroked him.

He spent the rest of the day writing his equation along the lines that Jina had drawn for him.

Zuri would periodically pose a question to Einstein about the equation and Bram would answer if he knew the answer or he would write her question down on a separate easel that they had set up for that purpose.

He stopped writing when he came to the last equation link assumption. He figured that he had at least a half day left of writing and that the link was a good stopping point.

The next morning everyone was back in Zuri's office and Bram concentrated on writing the last series of equations. He was down to the last few mathematical statements when there was a knock on the door and Linda announced that Erica had called and let her know that she had received a call from analysis team saying they needed help and that she needed to meet with him.

Bram held up his hand and said that he would speak with Erica after lunch because he was at the end of writing his equations and it would take that long to finish.

Linda replied that she would let Erica know.

Bram wondered what the analysis team could possibly have found that would cause Erica to want to immediately talk with him.

He sped up his writing and by lunch he emphatically drew a large black circle and put the words "The End" at the end of the last mathematical symbol.

He looked around at Mallica, Jina and Zuri and declared that he was done writing and that now all they had to do was to step through each part of the equation and answer all the questions that they had captured on the chart pad, and they had to determine if the transition points were where they would be able to put transition equations that would alter the Fold from being stationary to one that would move allow movement in the desired direction that could be programed in.

He declared that after lunch they would get into the thick of things and see if they could make the desired breakthrough.

They were all just finishing their meals when Erica entered the cafeteria and came over to their table.

She was about to engage them when Bram put up his hand and asked that they all go meet in Zuri's office.

He pushed Zuri back to her office and once there he took a seat and asked about the urgent request from the analysts.

Erica said that the analysis team that was examining the tremendous amount of data from the first set of Folds that Bram had conducted with the Bramlets. The team had called her and said that they needed help in deciphering what they were sure was a message from an alien race.

They had sent her the recorded section that held the message, and they were asking for help in deciphering it. They admitted that they had hit a wall, and no one knew what to do next.

The meeting had gone silent. They were all looking at Bram.

Bram looked around the room and asked which branch in the road should the team take. Should they continue to work on the Fold equation, or should they see if it was a message from an Alien race and decipher it?

Zuri spoke up and said that they should address the message, but they needed first to determine if the message was fresh, and she clarified that fresh meant that it was within her lifetime and was not a message that was sent millions of years or longer ago. If it was fresh, they should decipher it otherwise they should focus on the finishing the work on the Fold equation. She commented that a million-year-old message was like finding a message floating in a bottle that had been thrown off a sailing vessel three hundred years in the past.

Bram nodded and said he agreed and then asked how they would determine if it was a fresh or ancient.

The room was quiet.

Zuri asked how many times the message repeated.

Erica said she had no idea. She had received only one copy of what the analysis team said was a message.

Bram suggested that they set up a meeting with the analysis team so they could learn what they had done and could answer any questions that the Fold team might have.

He asked Erica to work with Linda to set up a meeting for the following morning.

He let her know that the Review Team would generate a list of questions for the Analysis team, and they would finish the day reviewing the Fold equations and determining what the next steps would be.

He then asked Mallica to lead the preparation for the meeting with the Analysis Team.

Mallica excused herself saying she would work with Elizabeth and Jina on the meeting with the analysis team.

Bram realized that only Zuri was still in the office. He said that he was going to get Einstein, and they would set up the equation review so that they could return to it and determine how to dynamically connect the transition points in the equation. Then they would focus on setting up a test plan to determine if any transition point was the key to allowing them to create what Zuri had labeled a moving Fold.

Pat knocked at the office door and then entered. She pointed at the clock and asked if the two of them were going to call it a day.

She said that she had joined Mallica and had worked on getting ready to work with the Analysis team. She had listened to the one cycle of the message and wondered how that team had decided that it was a message.

Bram and Zuri both started to answer. Bram waved to Zuri to indicate she should answer.

Zuri said there was no way to know if it was a message until they listened to the entire transmission that was received and that even then it would be hard to determine if it was a message or if it was a random signal being generated by some rotating object that was emitting a radio signal.

Bram agreed and said that he planned to get the entire transmission and that he had the original saved in Dallas and they would make sure that no corruption of the signal had occurred.

He agreed that it was time to quit. He took Einstein from Zuri and handed him to Pat for a moment.

Pat asked if Einstein had helped to solve any of the questions generated by the Fold equation review.

Bram pointed to Zuri and said that Einstein had calmed her down enough that she had stopped shouting insults about how poorly he actually understood his own equation and assumptions.

Zuri gave a small laugh and said that talking to Einstein was the only way for her to come close to understanding what Bram had developed since he was somewhat smarter than either of them.

Bram took Einstein and put him in his pocket and said he was returning Einstein to his castle for the night and then he was ready to head home.

He asked Pat to get the van pulled to the door and notify Orlando that it was time to get Zuri home.

The next morning as they jogged into work, Bram asked that they think up a ditty about a message from space. Caster started with,

There are aliens out in space.
   They've no idea about the human race.
There are aliens in out space.
   They may be smart or maybe not,
There are aliens in outer space,
   They have no idea of what they now may face.
The human race, the human race, will make fodder of the alien race."

Bram was surprised at how fast the ditty came out and except for the last line he liked it.

Linda was waiting when he arrived and let him know that she had arranged a large table on the stage of the auditorium. She had determined that every member that had made the Fold to the back of the moon had requested a seat.

Bram asked her to establish the protocol that only he, Erica and Zuri would ask questions of the Analysis team members until they were at the end and then there would be an open question and answer period.

When they got to the table, Linda made the announcement.

Bram asked Erica to manage the meeting.

He handed Zuri an I-pad and said that the two of them could talk back and forth on it. He said that they were the code breakers and just like the ones made so famous in World War Two, the two of them needed to become as good as they were and needed to do it much faster.

Erica opened the meeting by having the Analysis Team introduce themselves.

She asked that they begin by listening to the entire message cycle.

The team leader replied that the entire message would take several hours and did they really want to start there.

Bram nodded in the affirmative.

Erica replied that they begin at the beginning of the message cycle.

The message indeed seemed to repeat but Zuri picket up that one passage only repeated every tenth time and each of the repeats in between seemed to have a slightly different tone at the beginning. She noted that the other nine distinct sections remained unchanged when they repeated.

She said that she believed the unchanged part was the message being repeated and the one changing was the key for them to unravel the message.

She was typing away as fast as her fingers would allow her to. She pointed out that the one repeating every tenth time was most likely the Rosetta stone that would allow them to decipher the message.

Erica picked up on the fact that Bram and Zuri were communicating with each other, and she was watching for signs of some sort of breakthrough. It was clear to her that they had discovered something, and she was dying to know what that might be, but she knew to keep out of their way.

It was hard for her to listen to what seemed to her to be a monotonous signal repetition.

Brian noted that most of the participants were having difficulty listening to the seemingly monotonous, repetitive signal. He wanted to share that there were slight nuances that would most likely lead to the ability to decipher the message.

He now began to wonder how he and Zuri would be able to determine when the message was sent. He did not want to spend time on a message that might be millions to billions of years old. If, as Zuri had suggested, that if it was fresh then they should focus on it and determine what was being sent.

She had jokingly suggested if it was a fresh message, she wanted to be certain that it was not a bogeyman race letting Earth know that they were on the way to ravish the planet.

Linda escorted her father, brother, and mother in as they set up some tables and put a variety of snacks and drinks out for everyone. They then returned with a variety of pizza's and a large bowl of mixed greens.

Bram thanked her for going the extra mile.

He was still trying to figure out how to time stamp the origin time of the message.

Linda pointed to one end of the table and mouthed the words, start here.

Bram suddenly had a flash of how to identify what was on the "Alien Rosetta Stone." He stood up and suggested they take a break.

Erica knew the look on Bram's face as she called for a break. As the team headed for the refreshment and pizza table, she approached Bram who was talking to Zuri.

She asked him what had just happened.

Bram pointed to Linda and said that she had solved the conundrum of how to decode the message.

Erica looked at him and said that she was confused since Linda had never said a word.

Bram laughed and agreed but he said that she had pointed at the end of the table and mouthed, "start here."

Erica asked how that had triggered Bram to ask for a stop.

Bram said that they had to go back to the beginning of the message and take a few steps back so they could start at the beginning. He said that he believed they may have started after the tutorial on how to decipher the Rosetta. They had to go back and get the very first part of the message and take a step back to get the start here section. Then they would be able to decipher the message.

He commented that the question of when the message was sent still needed to be resolved.

He suggested a fresh start on the following morning. He said that he and Zuri would spend the afternoon organizing their thoughts and on stepping back to the very first point of the message.

He also planned to have Marcus send a bubble out to that original location and see if they could look back farther and get the very beginning of the message.

Erica replied that she would manage the change, and he could get Marcus going on Folding a bubble to the desired location.

Bram thanked her and after asking Linda to have Marcus come to Zuri's office and to also bring some pizza to her office, he wheeled Zuri out of the auditorium.

Chapter 7: Time Marker

Bram had just handed Einstein to Zuri when Marcus knocked on the door. Bram walked over and opened the door and let Marcus enter.

Once Marcus had entered, Bram asked him to send out a bubble to the coordinates of the bubble that had picked up the message. He asked Marcus to pinpoint the direction from where the message originated. Once Marcus had those coordinates, Marcus should then Fold the next bubble at least half the distance to the origin of the message. While the bubble was in that location, he wanted a high-resolution picture of the stars and constellations in that area of space.

Marcus confirmed the request and said that he had several bubbles ready, and he would send at least two out simultaneously and try to get another one out to the halfway point.

He excused himself and said that he would be able to fulfill the request by late afternoon. He asked if he should share the results with the two of them then or wait until the following morning.

Bram said that he wanted the information that day.

Marcus let them know that he would get it to them immediately on return of the bubbles.

Once Marcus had departed, Bram took a wedge of pizza and pinched off a small piece, gave it to Einstein, and asked him if they were going to find out if the message was fresh.

Zuri responded that she wanted Bram to share what he had in mind with the information Marcus was gathering.

Bram replied that he was going to correlate the message origin with the star map of that area that was on record. He would then compare the message star pattern to the star pattern for that area captured by the bubble. If they were the same, they would have a fresh message and they would know how much energy they needed to assign to deciphering the message. He was also hoping that they had missed the very beginning of the message which he was sure would be a tutorial on how to read the message. He figured the tutorial would guide them on how to translate the Alien Rosetta Stone message.

Zuri asked how Linda's pointing to the end of the table and mouthing "start here" had triggered the action that he was now taking.

Bram replied that a few moments ago Einstein had replied, yes, to his question about whether the message was fresh. It had triggered the thought about the tutorial being at the beginning of the message, he had no clue why he had thought of it, but it just happened.

Zuri nodded and said that he had a weird mind that had allowed him to tie a variety of seemingly independent concepts together by talking to a mouse and now he had added lip reading to the mix. She said that she had no way to keep up with such a non-linear mind.

Bram made the point that the two were a good match since she would force him to take the kinks out of his thought process. He said they were like the couple where the man could eat no lean and the wife could eat no fat, so between the two they licked their platter clean.

Zuri gave a laughed and said that he had just proved her point about a nonlinear mind.

Bram poured each of them a cup of tea and then sat down. He suggested they listen to the message again and try to use its cadence to organize it into a structure that seemed to make sense.

It was late afternoon when Zuri suggested that they put Einstein back in his palace and get ready to go home.

Bram was returning to Zuri's office when he saw Marcus coming down the hallway in a slow jog. He asked him if the jog was meant to get him in shape

Marcus replied that he wanted to get the information to Zuri and him before the end of the workday and handed Bram four memory sticks each having the numbers one and two written on them. He said that the one labeled one was the message and the one labeled two had the star constellation picture taken from the bubble and it also had the star constellation as seen from the Hubble telescope. He went on to say that he had run a statistical analysis that compared the two pictures that showed them to have a ninety-nine percent correlation. This seemed to suggest that the message was a recent one, but he did not know how to define recent.

Bram then said that perhaps they had started out wrong in listening to the message and thinking it was a written message needing an Alien Rosetta Stone to break the code. He then share the fact that some forty years in the past when the Arecibo telescope had been rebuilt they had sent out a very simple message on the celebration event day meant to be assembled as a graphic and then interpreted. It had been aimed at a very specific star cluster and was still on its way and would be traveling there for another twenty-five thousand years. There had also been the records sent out on the voyager spacecrafts. The records were more elaborate and had music, laughter, and messages in text and in voice.

Zuri commented that she had not known about either. She then asked how they should approach the message.

First let's think about who they are trying to reach. We have a signal that seems to be coming at us but in fact we need to look to see if there is a specific galaxy behind us. We might also need to develop a three-dimensional map of where else they are beaming the signal. If they are beaming in all dimensional planes, then they seem to be trying very hard to get a response. It makes me think about a ship beaming a Mayday signal in all directions.

He asked Marcus to send out his Bramlets to determine the signal distribution pattern. Meanwhile we can start at the very beginning of the message to see if we can begin to decipher the signal.

Zuri said she needed to absorb the morning's lesson about historic space messages before trying to learn an alien language.

Bram said that he understood and that he was as hesitant as she about learning a space language or perhaps figuring out a space drawing or a multi-piece puzzle. That is when it came to him that the messages could create a flat puzzle and the breaks in the message string might be there to guide the layout of the puzzle pieces.

He shared that with Zuri who put up her hand and suggested he get the rest of the people who had volunteered to help decipher the message.

Bram gave her a thumbs up.

By ten everyone had gathered in Zuri's office. Linda had brought in another large white board that Bram had requested.

He went to the board and drew a large rectangle and then divided it into nine parts. He then had Linda print out each section of the message that seemed to be preceded by a number and place it on the board. The first three went across the top from left to right, the second three went across the middle and the last three went across the bottom.

He then asked the team to examine the signal to see if the pattern remained the same or if there was a difference. He asked that they slow the signal speed down so they could listen for differences.

Jina immediately commented that there were differences in each section. Elizabeth confirmed that she too could discern differences. Mallica and Erica shook their heads and said they were not able to hear the differences.

Bram nodded and said that he could not hear differences either, but he was going to count on Jina and Elizabeth to create the picture that he now was sure was in the puzzle and he was certain the puzzle would be the message.

Linda suggested that they break for lunch since Chef D'Carluca had sent her a message that he had made French Veal Cordon Bleu with mushrooms and scallions in a white wine sauce for the team and that it was on the verge of being ready.

Bram said he was ready as Elizabeth grabbed him by the arm and led the way out the door.

They were met by Eric and Zoe who immediately took the lead.

He looked back and saw Mallica pushing Zuri, so he relaxed and sauntered up the Hallway to the cafeteria.

Pat and Amy came over to the table and said that they had been invited to lunch and wondered if they could join the team in trying to translate the alien message.

Bram listened as Elizabeth said that she was eager to get the two to listen to the message to see if they could hear a difference between each segment.

Bram knew that Pat had a great ear for music and expected her to discern a difference. He hoped so. Having three persons able to hear a difference would be reassuring.

Chef D'Carluca came out with his team and served the Cordon Bleu.

Bram asked if there was something special about the day and found out that it was exactly two years since the pool attack.

The Chef pointed to Zoe, Eric and to him and said that he was recognizing the heroes that had saved the day.

Zuri gave a hand clap and the whole cafeteria responded in kind.

Bram acted as if he had forgotten the date but in reality, it was hard for him to forget anything that he considered significant. He had remembered but he had not expected anyone else to remember.

Pat came over to him and gave him a hug and whispered that he was a good actor, and she knew that he had not forgotten that it was the day that he had saved her life.

Bram smiled and thanked her for the hug.

He raised his glass of sparkling water and toasted Zoe and Eric for having both jumped the pool fence in their swimsuits and charged at two shooters who had long rifles and were shooting at them. He added that he had fallen down and accidently knocked into one of the gunmen and was lucky to have survived.

He had just finished the toast when Marcus entered the cafeteria and announced that he had sent out his Bramlets and had surrounded the source of the signal and all had returned with the same signal.

Marcus sat down and asked if there was enough of whatever they were having. Mallica said that she had plenty to share but Linda stopped her and signaled one of the cafeteria cooks and asked for an additional order.

Mallica commented that the two of them had spent a year isolated out in the desert and had learned to share everything.

Marcus asked if he should plan any more Bramlet missions. He said that if not he would really like to join the team trying to break the message.

Mallica said with his great musical ability he should definitely be part of the group.

Elizabeth answered and asked if he was good discerning slight differences in the flow of sounds.

Marcus replied that he thought so, but he was not sure why she was asking.

Bram explained that he thought each of the signal blocks held a different content and that the content would be graphical, but they would need to figure out how to interpret the sound.

Once back in Zuri's office, Bram asked that the message be played again and this time he wanted to go slow enough so that they could diagram each block with a different symbol for each sound. By going slow enough they were able to recognize the blank space between each sound. Elizabeth, Marcus, Pat, and Jina worked together to decide the symbol for each distinctively different sound. It soon became visibly apparent that some sort of alphabet was being used.

After the fourth block had been listened to it became clear that the alien alphabet was going to be longer than that of Earth's English alphabet.

Bram pointed to the number of symbols and commented that they had designated eighty-four different symbols. He said that the longest alphabet on Earth was only seventy-four letters long and that one of those languages was Vietnamese. He then pointed out that they were trying to put together a puzzle and puzzles were normally pictures. There were currently two active languages that used ideographic and pictographic forms of writing.

He said that Mandarin was an ideographic alphabet. It was a language that used graphic symbols that represented an idea or concept. He made the point that it was actually independent of any particular language, and specific words or phrases.

The other was Cantonese that was a pictographic alphabet. He made the point that it used pictorial drawings to represent concepts and ideas.

The Fold team had individuals that fit into each of the unique alphabetic groups. Bram decided these folks needed to be on the team.

Elizabeth pointed to the wall clock and said that it was time to close the meeting. She congratulated the listeners for having created a set of symbols for each sound.

Bram said he was going to recruit members that were on the Fold staff that were familiar with each and have them come and listen to the message.

He declared the following day to be free for everyone including Zuri if she decided to take it off.

Zuri responded that she was not going to miss out on her moment to become smarter. Everyone but Marcus agreed that they wanted to attend.

He said that he would spend the day reviewing where to send the Bramlets.

Bram asked Linda to set them up in the auditorium. He said that there would be ten additional people that he was inviting for the next day.

He let the rest of the team know that he wanted the early part of the morning until ten to interview the folks he was going to recruit. He wanted to make sure they could hear the nuances in the message. Then they would listen to the entire message again.

He listed the people that he was planning to invite and asked Linda to contact them before the end of the day and invite them to the auditorium. He let her know that she should let them know that it took priority over everything else they might be doing.

Chapter 8: Visual Language

Bram decided to walk back to his house and once again he was following Castor and Donna in their battle gear. He had asked them if it was really necessary, and Castor had responded that Bram should stop asking that question or show them his superman costume.

Bob piped up that Bram didn't have a superman costume but instead wore a bull's eye target on his back and that was why the FBI ran in back. Zoe and Eric were in the armored truck behind all of them and had heard the exchange and blinked the headlights.

Pat gave a pull-on Bram's arm and quietly told him he had asked for it.

Bram nodded but said he really worried about the weight that the two carried and that the heat was very oppressive.

He then went silent and concentrated on the Alien signal. He was feeling more and more positive that in the next several days they were going to break the message.

He had the resources; he had the right people now and they all had to listen to the tutorial and learn how to decode the message.

He wondered if they should have started with the tutorial but felt that they would have had to do the same thing and now that they were more familiar with the message, the tutorial should be easier to decipher. He also felt that having the additional new folks would make a huge difference.

Pat knew that Bram was off in a different world and walking in automatic.

It was his day to cook but she wondered if he were up to it. She thought it would be better for him to spend the time in his office and sit on the couch and think.

She sent a text to the team and asked who was up to take Bram's cooking duty. Everyone responded in the affirmative.

When they got to the house, they all entered through the basement garage. As they got to the kitchen, she pushed Bram past it into the office and said she wanted a cup of tea to go with her biscuit.

It was clear to her that he was still in his other state.

She took the cup when he handed it to her and had him take his seat. She leaned against him and asked what he was thinking about.

Bram was silent for quite some time and Pat wondered if he had heard her. She was sure he had but had put her question at a lower priority than what he was working on.

He finally said that he thought he knew what the message was about, but he had to think through it some more and he would wait until the following day and the next pass through that message.

Zoe had been standing quietly on one side of the office and Eric was on the other. She commented that she knew when Bram was in this mode that he was in she could do almost anything and he would not bother to react to her.

Bram opened his eyes and replied that he remembered every action that she had taken when he was thinking and someday, he would get even.

The call to dinner stopped the exchange and they all went into the dining area.

Bram reminded everyone that the following day was going to be grueling and that he planned to retire early, and they should make sure he did not oversleep.

The next morning, he asked for a ditty about the message from space from an Alien race that was presented as a picture puzzle or perhaps it was instead no puzzle, but a daunting threat caused by a dying sun.

They were soon jogging to the ditty, and he was asked several times why he had suggested the words.

Bram refused to answer and replied that he had dreamt the answer in his sleep.

Pat had wondered what Bram's tossing and turning had been about and now she knew that he had spent a good part of the night working on the message.

Bram led the team into the cafeteria and suggested they all have breakfast and then relax until Linda let them know that their new team members were all in the auditorium. He would then test the new members for their ability to discern the changes in the message tones. Then he would have the team establish symbols for each of the sounds. Once they were organized, he would have them listen to the Alien message from the beginning. Once their new members had listened to the entire message, he would call a break and then everyone would listen to the tutorial and then go through the message once more.

He said that he hoped to decipher the message by the end of the following day.

Pat asked if he planned to share what he thought the message said.

Bram shook his head and said he did not plan to until they had figured out the body of the message. He hoped to learn the alien numbering system and their alphabet and then he would be willing to make suggestion on the translation of the message based on what was appearing on the white board.

Linda walked into the cafeteria and let them know that she had assembled the one Vietnamese couple, the four persons that knew Mandarin and the four that knew Cantonese.

Bram stood and headed out toward the auditorium. Bob and Thomas jump up and assumed their body guarding positions.

Bram was always surprised at how his bodyguards were always at the ready.

He entered the auditorium and thanked the ten people sitting around the table for having responded to his request on such a short notice. He made the point that it was a historic opportunity and if they contributed to solving the Alien message, they would all be remembered in the history books.

He then explained that he would like them to listen to the message that everyone else had listened to and then put their take of the message in each section on the white board that corresponded to the section of the message.

The ten sat and listened to the message. They talked among themselves and then they let Linda know what to write in the section of the block.

Bram was satisfied with the fact that they all agreed that the message seemed to have the progression that he and the rest had identified.

At the end of message string, he listened to them discuss the fact that there seemed to be many characters to the message. Bram cut short a discussion of how many characters existed when it was apparent that the range the group was arguing about was from one hundred ten to one hundred eighteen characters.

He pointed at the wall clock and suggested they have the lunch that had been brought in. He then asked Linda to let the rest of the participants know that lunch was served, and they should return and spend a few moments with the new translation team members.

During lunch he explained to Erica that Marcus had been able to retrieve what he hoped was the tutorial that would help them decode the message. He asked her to explain this to the group and then take them through the very beginning of the message.

He asked Linda to capture questions, but that discussion about the question would wait until the end of the tutorial.

He explained that he wanted to focus on the tutorial and did not want to try to do that and lead the group.

He suggested that Erica keep the question-and-answer session short and focus on pulling out what each member had learned.

The Q&A session was brief.

The main request was to listen again to the tutorial but go through it very slowly because several of the team felt that they had figured out that there was a section that taught the number scale and there seemed to be parts where the alphabet was being explained.

The Vietnamese husband and wife team was certain that they had picked up on the alphabet portion.

The eight Chinese that understood Mandarin and Cantonese shared that they had to stop themselves from trying to use the pictorials that came to their minds when they listened to parts of the tutorial. They wanted to go slowly through those sections and see if they could break the pictorial code.

Bram suggested that they stop for the day and start the next morning and slowly go through the tutorial again and work on learning how to count and use the sounds used to count and apply that to the rest of the tutorial message.

Pat knew that Bram had an idea of the basic content of the message and that by the next morning he might have learned both the counting system and the alphabet. She was mentally preparing to sleep next to a person that would mumble to himself throughout the night. She had come to realize that Bram talked to and answered himself when he was working through a problem during his sleep.

Pat agreed with Bram when he suggested they walk home.

Pat always enjoyed the walk. The view of lake beyond the adjoining fruit farm was inspiring, the chatter between their bodyguards amusing and Bram's attempt to stay in the present was always interesting. He would periodically point out some view or comment on something that had occurred during the day to her and then he would return to his musings. She figured he was plotting how he was going to solve the problem he was working on.

This walk was no different and by the time they walked into the basement entrance to their house Bram came back to the present and suggested they relax for a short time before going into the study.

That night was as Pat had anticipated. She positioned herself slightly away from Bram and fell asleep.

She was surprised to find the bed empty when she awoke at four.

She got ready for the day and then went downstairs where she found Bram in his study on his computer.

She left and returned with two cups of coffee. She sat and watched as his fingers seemed to dance across the keys like a virtuoso playing a piano. She did not bother to try to engage instead she returned to the kitchen that now had all four of their bodyguards preparing their breakfast.

Zoe asked her where her other half happened to be.

Pat shared that she had lost him in the office where his computer had kidnapped him.

Castor and Donna made their entrance and asked the same question and then said they would love a cup of coffee.

Donna asked if there was a ransom that had been demanded to release Bram. The chatter took off in that direction and they all sat down in the dining area.

Pat knew that Bram would emerge as soon as he was finished with what he was doing or if it was getting close to the time when the morning session was to begin. Bram might be in his own world, but he always was early to any scheduled interaction in the normal world.

This time it was the normal world schedule that pulled him off his computer.

Bram walked out of his office and was greeted by all his bodyguards. He walked over to Pat and gave her a hug and kiss and thanked her for the cup of coffee.

He then said he would eat his breakfast when they arrived at the Fold site auditorium. He laughed when they all replied that they would be ready for their second breakfast by that time.

He nodded and said he appreciated their patience with his periodic upsets of their day's schedule.

On their jog in to work, he proposed a new limerick to jog to.

One, two, three, four an Alien counting lesson.
One, two three, four, count, count, One, two, three, four.
A, B, C, D, an Alien message.
A, B, C, D, learn, learn, A, B, C, D.
1234, 1234, ABCD, ABCD, Alien kindergarten, 1234, ABCD
Let's do it. Let's say it.
Let's do it all once more.

Pat knew then that Bram had solved the message, and she knew she would have to wait as he guided the decoding team on their learning journey.

Bram looked at Pat and let her know that he felt certain that he had made a breakthrough and thanked her for being patient with him.

Pat once again felt that surge of personal euphoria for having found such a dynamic and interesting soul mate. She reached up and touched his cheek as they continued the jog and singing the ditty.

Chapter 9: Solution

ᏌBram enjoyed the jogging limerick. He, however, kept thinking about what the message implied. He wanted the team to work through the message and come up with their interpretation. He felt strongly about the fact that the team would clarify any points that he might have missed. He felt confident on his understanding of the numbering system, but he had several interpretations of the visual parts of the alien language.

He was right on time, and everyone was at the table and most had a cup of coffee. He noted that Mallica and Elizabeth, Zuri and her parents had not yet arrived. He wondered what might be keeping them. Elizabeth was one that was usually early.

Orlando burst through the auditorium door and shouted that the "Star" had arrived then came weaving down the aisle toward the stage as he pushed the wheelchair in a weaving drunken like path. Jina and the rest were all smiles as they followed.

It was clear to Bram that something positive had occurred.

He waited until they were all on stage and then asked Zuri why she had kept Orlando away for so long.

Zuri smiled and said that Elizabeth had Dr. Sewal explain that he had set up a program that he hoped would improve her condition. But what had kept them was that he had received her motorized wheelchair and wanted to show her what it could do. She went on to explain that it was a beautiful maroon color and that it had features that would open up much of the world for her. She explained that chair would go up and down, would tilt at all angles. It had the ability to climb stairs, but she said she would want to try that out herself before being comfortable with that feature. She added that the umbrella feature was one that she was sure she would be able to put to use at the Fold facility. Then she added that she would be able to come in with Bram in the mornings and most likely be able to set a fast pace for the jog in.

Orlando pretended to wipe a tear away and said that he was about to lose his favorite job and would most likely be assigned to gate guard duty.

Bram played along and commented that the Corp would likely have to send him back to bootcamp for re-indoctrination before he was good for anything else.

He then walked over to Zuri and gave her a hug and quietly told her how pleased he was with the fact that she was getting the new chair.

He then looked around and declared that it was time to decode the message.

Zuri looked at him, nodded and then asked if he had already done it and he was just testing the rest of them for their ability to do so.

Bram had wanted to keep that information from the group, but he knew better than to deny that he had been able to do so. He replied that he had the basic message but there were some gaps that needed filling, and he wanted to solidify the alphabet. He pointed out that the visual elements were challenging, and he needed help there.

He said that he was not going to directly share what he knew until the team took a cut, but he reassured them that he would contribute to the decodifying by keeping it on track. He made the point that he was remaining open to better interpretation or translation of the language.

It took them all longer than Bram had anticipated and three days later in the late afternoon the message was displayed on the white board and there was one huge file on one computer that was shown on one of three large screens that had been set up on the auditorium stage.

The whiteboard showing the visual message was now standing in the middle of the three large screens. The screens displayed three-time lapse pictures of the solar system where the sun was dying and expanding.

The first visual showed the planet and the sun as it was at the beginning. Below the image of the planet and sun was an image that most closely resembled a skinny whale, with gill-like openings behind very large forward-looking eyes and almost halfway back two long arm like appendages came out the sides.

In the second visual the sun was twice as large, and the figure below was bottom side up and there was the number that equated to roughly one billion.

In the third visual the sun had encompassed the planet and the visual was shown as a pile of ashes.

Bram congratulated everyone on having contributed to solving the meaning of the message but also in having clarified both the numbering and the letter systems.

Earth had a numbering system based mainly on ten which corresponded to number of digits on each of the human appendages.

It turned out that the aliens had a numbering system based on the eight digits on the appendages that functioned like hands. They had a thumb like appendage and three fingers.

The numbering system seemed to have the same features as the one on Earth in the sense that it featured raising numbers by powers. Bram felt that they had the equivalent of a grade school understanding, but it was all that was necessary at the moment.

The alphabet with its visual elements was daunting. It was what had given the team the most problem. Bram felt that the Asian members made a huge contribution in extrapolating their own alphabets and visual languages and adjusting them to a world where there was no land but only water.

The late Friday discussion on the stage was about the difficulty in translating between English or any Earth language and what the group was now calling the Water World language. The Vietnamese couple commented that they had a phone AP that translated Vietnamese to English or any chosen language and vice versa. Why not have one to do it for the Water World language.

Bram replied that he was going to visit with folks in the IT department to see if any of them had that talent to program such and AP or could connect with someone that did.

Erica volunteered to contact the developers of the Vietnamese translation AP and see if they could re-apply it with some modifications and if they could do it quickly.

Bram told her that doing so would be great and if they had a local talent that could then own its maintenance and improvement, they would have a perfect match for a much-needed capability.

Elizabeth took the opportunity to announce that Zuri would be going to the Mayo Clinic in Minnesota for most of the coming month. While there she would be thoroughly evaluated by Dr. Sewal, and his team and a treatment program designed.

She would get her chair fitted and get trained on its use. She finished by saying that the entire Juma family would be staying there and enjoying weekends at various vacation spots that Bram had graciously asked her to arrange.

Bram asked Zuri if he could use her office while she was gone.

Zuri knew immediately what he was talking about and replied that her office was a good place for him to talk to Einstein about what to do and how to connect with the Aliens and that maybe Einstein could help him solve the problem with the Fold equations.

He thanked her and thanked Elizabeth for having so graciously arranged for the vacation spots. He had never asked her to do any such thing, but it was her way of letting him know that she had spared no expense in the arrangements that she had made.

He thought about the fact that he had a secret code with three separate women in the room: Pat, Elizabeth, and Zuri. He thought maybe he would ask the AP writer to make an Ap for each of them.

After the meeting ended, he immediately called the IT department and asked if someone there was into writing Aps. He was pleased to learn that there were programmers that belonged to an online AP writing network and who were currently writing some APs for the department of defense.

He set up a meeting with them and let Erica know about the meeting that he had scheduled a week out.

Erica thanked him and said she would see about getting the writer of the Vietnamese translation AP to be available that Friday as well. She said it would depend on where that developer lived.

Bram thanked her and asked if she were up to a three-pancake breakfast on Sunday.

On Sunday morning, Pat was at the range, bacon, and sausage sizzling in the black iron skillet with which she had a ying-yang affair. She loved the way it cooked the food, and she hated cleaning it and it was way too heavy, but it was her favorite because it held in heat and made it easy to make the pancakes.

She welcomed Erica in and let her know that Bram was in the study being guarded by Bob and Thomas.

Erica thanked her for letting her know but said she had dreamt about the pancakes and was going to stay in the kitchen and learn how to make them the way Pat did.

She wanted to make better friends with Pat who seemed a little reserved with her. She was not sure why since Pat had never been around her in her previous life as the witch of the Fold program. She still thanked the time when Bram had let her know that he was not interested in her role or any role dealing with the business side and that he really wanted the freedom to create the concepts and technology that would continually improve the program.

She marveled at what he had done and now he had the world on the verge of communicating with an Alien race and that might also have the technology to help them.

She realized now how cold and calculating she had been only a few years ago and how unhappy she had been and how happy she now was.

Pat let her know that the pancakes would be rolling out in about five minutes and asked her to set the table for eight.

Erica was about to ask who the eight persons might be when Orlando came in.

Orlando was in a good mood. He said that he had just put his princess and her parents on an early morning flight. He had thanked Bram for the breakfast invite and was looking forward to two eggs over easy, sausage links, buttered toast, coffee and one of the jelly filled rolls from the box of donuts that he had purchased on the way back from the airport.

He was surprised to see Erica, but he figured breakfast was a good time to get better acquainted. He was about to put the box of donuts on the table, but Erica handed him a serving platter and suggested they put them on display to make sure that there would be no leftovers.

He liked the idea and was about to pick out the donuts and rolls when Erica waved two plastic glove in front of him and made a joke about not knowing where a Marine might have had their hands.

He laughed and said that the line was, "the Navy guys washed their hands before not after touching treasured parts, whereas Marines just spit on theirs and rub them together before touching anything."

Erica replied that she definitely wanted him to wear gloves before touching the food.

Zoe had been listening to the exchange and agreed that gloves were required.

Pat asked Zoe to get Bram to the breakfast table and handed Erica a platter with half a dozen pancakes and a dozen sausages.

She then pointed at Orlando and said that his order was next, and he should get ready.

She was about to sit down when Castor and Donna entered the kitchen from the basement. She took out two plates, asked what they wanted and had them sit down.

She looked at the gathering and realized that no matter what meal they had at their home, the table was almost always full.

It reminded her that it closely matched the meals at her home when she was growing up. Her parents both worked, and the family was probably considered to be in the lower end of middle class but on Friday nights and on the weekends her house was the place where all the kids gathered for breakfast, lunch, and dinner. She remembered her mother saying that there was always enough food for good friends.

She was standing and enjoying looking at the group in the dining area when Bram quietly spoke to her as he went by to refresh his coffee. "Isn't it great to have a group of friends gathered around the table and enjoying each other's company."

She followed him back and sat down beside him. She then reached out for a roll but had Orlando slap her wrist and with his gloved hand asked which roll or donut she desired.

Chapter 10: Einstein Solution

ℵext morning on the jog into work Bram was quiet. He had figured out how he planned to evaluate the impact of each equation transition. He would ask Linda to set up a meeting with Marcus, Remi, and Lori with the objective of getting them to prepare for the various tests that he planned.

He was going to utilize the fact that a Folded object currently returned to its original position. This was somehow a feature of his current equation set. He was going to attach two bubbles with this programing to a larger one that would utilize his newly modified equation. If the larger one began to move on its own, it would pull the two smaller observation bubbles along with it. Once the larger one had about five minutes to move, the program in the large bubble would shut down. If it had traveled along the Fold wormhole the two smaller ones would then return to their original position and then they would time out and return to their positions in the launch hangar.

In this manner he would test the impact of each part of the Fold equation.

Orlando took note of Bram's silence and started the ditty,

    "Silent leader, Silent Leader
        Oh, so quiet on this day.
            A poor bubble is bound to pay.
  Yes, bound to pay!
  Yes, bound to pay!
      Pay, Pay, Pay
           For the leaders desire to play
  Bound to pay for the leader's silence today
        Step aside, step aside,
      Don't you dare get in the way."

The entire group took up the chant.

The ditty came through to Bram who smiled, shook his head to clear out his contemplations, and joined in.

The Marine guards along the way had gotten use to them coming by with a new ditty almost every morning and they always joined in for the period that they were within ear shot.

This morning Bram was going to start his day in his office. He would take a few minutes and share his thinking with Einstein and then go out to the lab and share his final plan there.

Linda was at her desk and greeted him.

He stopped long enough to ask her to call Lori, Marcus, Remi, and Erica and set up a meeting in the lab for nine.

He then went into his office and locked the door. He then turned on the electric water pitcher and prepared his teacup.

When he opened the door to the small door in the bookcase, Einstein came out and after sniffing his hand got into the palm.

He took Einstein over to his desk and placed him on the large glass that covered the entire desk and had a picture of the Milky Way below it. This was a picture that was permanently etched in his mind. He had learned that it was but one of perhaps billions of galaxies spread throughout the universe, but this was where at the edge, his solar system traveled.

Once he had his cup of tea in hand he slowly explained the plan to Einstein as he gave him little crumbs of a cookie. It seemed to him that Einstein always stopped to listen to the plan for the equation transition and would nod his head up and down in approval. That approval always earned him another crumb. The deciding test of Einstein's understanding was when Bram asked if he had missed anything, and Einstein shook his head in the negative. Bram gave him the remainder of the cookie and thanked him for listening and told him what a smart mouse he was.

Linda gave him his ten-minute warning.

Bram printed out copies of his equation test plan. It included sending out twelve bubbles in the next three days. It they all returned, then he would only need to modify six bubbles.

Lori and Erica were in a full animated discussion that Bram understood was about the great work that the lab had done and how the lab members would be able to train the personnel in the company being considered to mass produce them.

The room went quiet as soon as he was spotted.

He let them know the objective of the meeting, paused for a moment as the four read through the paper he had handed them. He then verbally described his test plan and asked how long it would take to prepare he bubbles.

Remi asked if Bram had the new program for the two lead bubbles and if he did, the Bubbles could be ready in two days.

Bram smiled and said that Thursday morning would be a perfect day to run the tests and that by Friday afternoon he would know if he had a chance at creating a Wormhole Bubble.

Lori commented that they had the two large bubbles that were to replace Wheel One and Wheel Two ready, and they could be modified to become the first two Wormhole Spaceships. She asked if she and any other volunteers could figure out names for these ships.

Bram chuckled and commented that she was, "getting the cart before the horse."

Erica said she wanted to be on the naming team, and she was sure every Wheel member and probably every member on the Fold facility would want in. She suggested making it a contest that everyone could participate in.

Bram shook his head and said that he was open to doing so, but first he had to create the equation that resulted in the wormhole capability and then he and Remy had to provide the battery power needed to ensure the ability to go along the wormhole and then return to the hangar launch site.

Erica suggested that she work with Linda to set up the contest so they would be ready when he successfully created the first wormhole.

Bram smiled and said that it was great to be working with such positive team members and wished that he could be as certain as they that he would solve the problem of creating motion for a bubble.

Remi stood up and commented that he was going out with his team to select the six bubbles and get them to start the modifications. Lori said she was going with him and followed Remi out of the lab.

Bram realized that Erica had stayed behind and seemed to be waiting until the lab members followed their bosses out the door.

Once the room was empty, Erica said that she had located the lead programmer of the Vietnamese to English translation AP. She said he was currently creating and testing various improvements of how pilots communicated with their sophisticated supersonic planes. She had set up a meeting the following day to see if he could create a Waterworld to English AP. She apologized about making the meeting appointment without contacting him first, but it all happened dynamically, and she did not want spend weeks trying to schedule the meeting.

Bram said the timing was perfect since he would be sitting idly by waiting for the bubbles to be modified. He suggested including the members of the translation team that was on site and if possible, including Zuri and her parents.

Erica agreed that the full contingent would be invited but the meeting time would remain fixed.

Lori intercepted him on the way back to his office and asked if he were going to request a bubble that could hold a member of the Waterworld.

Bram stopped walking and was silent for a moment. He then commented that one Waterworld being was about as large as an Earth Whale Shark. The human bubbles were designed to hold a team of twelve. So, the Waterworld bubble would need to be at least large enough to hold twelve of aliens. He said she should figure out the dimensions of such a bubble and let him know who could construct one.

Lori stood looking at him in disbelief. She shook her head and mumbled that she was sorry she had asked.

Bram agreed that it was a daunting task that they might undertake. He suggested she find out the largest sphere that could economically be produced and then suggest options.

Pat met him at Linda's desk and said that she had ordered a mixed salad in for lunch, and it was waiting for him at his desk.

Bram gave her a hug and thanked her. He said that he needed to decompress from a full morning.

Pat asked about his test plan and what else he had done in the morning.

Bram stood and got Einstein and handed him to Pat. He then suggested they call Zuri and her parents to share what he had accomplished during the morning.

Pat said that it was a good idea.

Bram called and asked if Zuri had a few moments for him to share what he had accomplished with Einstein's help.

Zuri gave a small laugh and said she would send her wheelchair driving instructor away for a short time. She went on to say that her morning had been spent on learning to use her wheelchair and she hoped his morning had been spent on learning how to move a bubble through space.

Bram told her he hoped she was having more fun than he had so far on this day.

She replied that running into walls and almost tumbling down some stairs had scared her, but she was otherwise having a great time learning how to use her new motorized chair.

Bram then shared how Einstein had approved how each equation transition was going to be tested. He approved of using the tiniest of motion change to ensure that the bubble didn't jump across the universe but only a few feet.

He then commented on having two normal bubbles being towed by the wormhole bubble so that he could retrieve all of them and continue testing the effects of the various equation sections.

Close to the end of the call Bram shared that there was a naming contest being held to pick a name for the wormhole vessels. He asked what the first prize should be.

Zuri suggested that he offer a bullet proof fishing boat to the winner and a gun mounted drone to the second and a common grenade launcher to the third-place winner.

Jina commented that she was shocked at the suggestions of her daughter.

Pat spoke up and said that she hoped that she would at least get third prize. It would make her feel much better equipped to go fishing.

Bram closed the call by sharing that on the following day there would be a meeting with the programmer of the translation AP to see if he was willing to program an Alien to English AP for the Fold effort, and they were all invited.

He said to expect a call from Linda who would share the specifics of the meeting. He went on to let them know that attendance was optional.

Chapter 11: Reverse

ꝃram spent the last part of the day reviewing the work that
had been done and had resulted in the Fold program being in a position that
would allow it to potentially provide aid to an alien civilization that was several
million light years away.

He wondered why a civilization that had learned to use the Fold to send out a
distress signal had also not developed the ability to build the equivalent of his
Wheels or the Bramlets. He speculated that a water world civilization made up of
whalelike inhabitants might not pursue the type of buildings and structures that the
much smaller animal that was human would. They might also not have faced the
multitude of predators and weather challenges that humans had to overcome.

He was certain that interaction with them would be one of learning and of
developing new technical capabilities.

He knew that a new habitable water world would need to be found.

The Fold capability would be central to that search. The ability for a Fold
vehicle to move along a selected trajectory would be invaluable in the search. He
thought about the power needs of a Fold vehicle and knew that he needed another
breakthrough in that arena.

He decided that he would see if Zuri would take on the project of coming up
with a new power system for the Dynamic Wormhole Bubble. He hoped that she
would look across the energy field and check out the claims of a breakthrough in the
nuclear industry.

He had read about the breakthrough in China where they claimed to be able to
create an energy source as powerful as the sun. He doubted it would be available in
time to make a difference.

On the way home he told Pat about getting Zuri to tackle the power problem.
He was surprised when she said that Zuri needed to get away from the Fold project
and experience as normal a childhood, as a child, of her intellect and her disabilities
would allow. She suggested asking Zuri's mother to tackle that assignment and
have her use Zuri as a resource.

Bram thought about the fact that he had failed to see Zuri as a child but had
focused on her superior mind.

He thanked Pat for having pointed out what he had failed to grasp and that now
seemed so obvious.

He made the point that he was sure that Zuri would still have a problem of
having a normal childhood since she would end up in some university as one of the
younger or perhaps the youngest students.

Pat agreed and commented that Elizabeth had found a program for genius
students. That university had a program that focused on merging the genius
students, the advanced courses and also arranging social events that brought them
together. Elizabeth had volunteered that she would attend the university with Zuri
and attend several of the classes that she did.

Bram asked if Jina was planning to stay with the Fold project.

Pat said that Elizabeth had convinced her that she should continue to reside at
the Fold housing complex and that Zuri would come home often and she could
continue her role as a resource in the mathematical aspects of the Fold effort.

He then said that he was now thinking of offering Zuri's modified office to
Mallika.

Pat gave a light laugh and said that she thought Mallika would love to have such a luxurious office that was larger than his, but she suggested that he make the office the center of communication about the message and about his bubble redesign testing. She made the point that it would provide a large area for information to be displayed. She suggested he invest in several additional large display screens.

He said that he would take her suggestion and get Linda to arrange the office to seat folks comfortably for design and translation activities.

Their conversation had transpired as they left work and rode to their house. Zoe and Eric had the guard duty. Zoe asked what Orlando would do while Zuri went to school.

Pat replied that he had decided to get his bachelor's degree. He planned to be Zuri's bodyguard during the day and take evening classes. She shared that he had put in a request to get a second Marine assigned to also guard Zuri. If that was approved, they would alternate times to allow him to attend classes during the day.

Zoe said that she hoped his request would be approved and then she added that she hoped that college did not dull his sense of humor.

Bram added, "Or his keen ability to come up with witty ditties."

Pat gave Bram a poke in the ribs and said that he should leave the witty ditties to others and concentrate on his simple Fold equation.

That night he had a dream where the bubble was going so fast through the wormhole that it left this universe and entered another. He kept trying to put it into reverse, but that section of the equation failed to activate.

Pat shook Bram awake and said that it was two in the morning and asked him if he knew where he was.

Bram embraced her and thanked her for rescuing him from the next universe. He said that he had found which equation had an error in it. He was not yet sure what the error was, but he would pursue it until he had found it.

Pat said she was happy for him to stay in her universe, but she was going back to sleep.

Bram gave her a kiss on the forehead and then focused on the black and the void of space and was soon asleep.

The next morning, he asked Linda if she was aware of Zuri going off to school. Linda nodded and said that she hoped he wasn't mad about her pushing for that.

Bram said he was not and that he had overlooked the fact that Zuri was still a child and socially not as developed as her super brain. He thanked her for pushing for that opportunity for Zuri and as a reward he was going to give her extra work.

Linda was used to Bram's dry humor and asked what her punishment was going to be.

He asked her to follow him to Zuri's office where he shared what he had in mind.

Linda said that it was a great idea and that she thought getting the architect that had set up the office to come in and see what he might suggest would be the next step.

Bram agreed that it was the way to proceed, and she should do it. He told her that he wanted to focus on the Fold equation for the rest of the day and did not want to be disturbed. He let her know that he had a lunch date with Pat at high noon and she should make sure he made it.

Linda said she would follow up and update him on what was happening with Zuri's office and that she would make sure he was not late for lunch.

Bram went into his office and got Einstein out and sat down and explained to him that he thought he had found the problem with the Fold equation that had been haunting him for months.

He asked Einstein if he had known that the problem was in the equation that provided the capability to go in reverse.

When Einstein seemed to nod in the affirmative.

Bram scratched him behind the ear and told him he needed to go and get voice lessons so he could talk so he could communicate what he knew.

He then got on his computer and pulled up the part of the Fold equation that dealt with the reverse feature and almost immediately he realized that one part that incremented in value only incremented upward. This meant that as it traveled in one direction it would increment up but when he wanted to go in reverse.

The equation needed to increment downward, and it needed enough power to negate the other sections of the equation that went in the opposite direction.

He studied how he could modify it so it would decrease in value and pull the bubble backward along the worm hole.

He soon realized that the parts of the equation that were pulling the bubble forward had to be turned off.

He wrote a reverse function program that provided a loop that would increment in the down direction until it got to zero value.

He wondered what would happen if it kept going into the negative and decided that would be one of the tests he would do after he verified he could get the wormhole bubble back to its original position.

Linda's voice on the speaker let him know it was time for him to break for lunch.

He looked at Einstein that was sitting next to the keyboard and told him that he was a genius and then put him back into his kingdom and closed the small door and put the books in front of it.

Pat waved to him from a table close to the windows of the cafeteria that had a view of Columbia River. She asked how the review of the equation had gone.

Bram told her that Einstein had solved the problem. He had written a program that he would try out that afternoon if he could get a bubble.

Pat reassured him that he could have any size bubble he wanted.

Erica walked over to their table and asked if she could join them. Once she had taken her seat, she commented that finding a company to quickly produce the bubbles was more of a challenge than she anticipated.

Bram asked if she had considered funding the establishment of a local bubble building company. She could hire one of the local entrepreneurs to run the business and then she would be able to have direct influence and more control over the production of high-quality bubbles.

Erica asked if he had someone in mind.

Bram suggested she check out Luke Stetson to see if he had the skill to manage a startup business. He was sure that his parents would provide great guidance on how to run such a business. He pointed out that Luke already had been checked out by the FBI and it would most likely be rather easy to get him a top-secret clearance.

Erica commented that her lunch tasted better than usual and that she would have to see about coming to lunch with Pat as often as possible.

Pat told her that she personally had bribed Linda to make sure she got Bram out of his office to eat lunch with her. She was sure that Linda would be open to Erica's bribes and all she had to do was hire her brother and she would have a tailor-made lunch time reminder.

Bram gave a small laugh and said that he was not that hard to have lunch with it all depended on when exactly they wanted to have lunch. He said he had to turn off his mind to be able to focus on food unless it was preceded or followed by gunfire. Then food was the first thing he thought about.

Erica got up and said that she was going to check out the availability of labor, materials and a building that could be secured. She wondered if that huge fruit barn that was within sight of the housing area might be available for the right price.

Bram said that was a great idea. It was close enough that the Marine perimeter could be extended, and protection could be provided.

Pat made the point that the power needed was also very near. The one item they needed to make sure of was that there were enough workers to staff the operation.

Bram suggested using the folks already making the bubbles as the startup personnel and ask them to recruit dependable local folks who wanted a great place to work.

Erica replied that she was now getting excited about doing something locally. She was going to get together with the Stetsons and see what came of it.

Bram suggested enrolling Lacy in that endeavor. He said that she had worked wonders in getting things organized for him in her previous role.

Pat excused herself and said she was going to give Remi a heads up about Bram's next request for additional bubbles to play with.

Bram added that she should tell Remi that he would need two sets of a two-bubble arrangement.

Bram returned to his office and focused on creating two computer control versions of how to activate reverse for the wormhole bubble. He had just accomplished this when Linda came up on the speaker phone and let him know that her sister was insisting that she see him.

Bram intuitively knew that she was coming because Erica had contacted her. He just hoped the two were not having a problem. He opened his office door and was greeted by a beaming smile on Lacy's face.

After giving him a hug, she handed him a pint of his favorite peach ice cream with extra cream. Then she thanked him for thinking of Luke and giving him the opportunity of a lifetime. She shared that Luke had earned a business management degree but had returned home only to find that it did little to help him locally. He had offers in other parts of the country, but she said that Luke wanted to stay near his family.

Bram could tell that Lacy was experiencing an emotional high because she had to stop and wipe tears from her eyes. He asked her why she thought he had anything to do with the good fortune that had come Luke's way.

Lacy replied, "because Erica had let her know it was your idea." She went on to let him know that Erica had become one of his staunchest supporters.

Bram gave a small laugh and replied that he had suggested Luke because he was a great shot and drove an immaculate black fishing boat.

"Yes and you gifted our family enough money that everyone will be looked after for years to come because we do such a great job setting up exciting gun battle-oriented fishing trips," Lacy joked back.

She then extended an offer from her mother and father to host a celebration dinner, but they wanted to use his dining room for it.

Bram replied that he would love to have them do so and he was counting on her to make up the invitation list.

He then said that he had to go to the lab to set up two experiments and that she should get busy planning the celebration dinner.

Pat, Lori, and Remi all walked over to Bram as he entered the Lab.

He looked around and saw that everyone in the lab had stopped what they were doing and were looking at him.

He joked that he was just stopping in to see if everyone was working hard enough.

Lori replied that they were worn out trying to adhere to his sweat shop management style. And they were all waiting to see if the two twin bubble set ups would satisfy him and keep him from imposing any additional restrictions on the workers in the lab.

She led him to the two large enclosures that held the two sets of one larger bubble and a smaller one tethered behind it.

Bram looked at the two then turned and put his computer down on one of the stainless-steel lab tables and transferred his two programs into the waiting bubble computers.

He asked that the first bubble be named Pat and the second bubble be named Lori. He looked at Remi and said that if they got bubble Pat and bubble Lori back then they would be renamed; Remi and Bramer and be sent out again.

He asked that bubbles Pat and Lori be taken out to the launch area and sent out to the coordinates he had programed in.

He said that if they came back in the next hour, then he would like bubble Remi to be sent out once the batteries in the Bramlets were recharged.

Lori turned to the rest of the folks and declared it was launch time and they all knew their part.

She then asked when bubble Bramer was to be sent out.

Bram watched as the Lab transformed into a beehive of activities.

He then let Lori know that Bramer would possibly never come back so he was delaying sending it out until the wormhole portion of the program was well underway. He shared that bubble Bramer would be going into what seemed to be negative space and that he had no idea what that meant or what would happen.

Pat took him by the arm and said that her role was to get him out of the way until it was time to launch. She suggested staying close by and he should relax and enjoy a cup of coffee or tea.

Bram suggested they sit at the back of the launch control room.

Pat asked him what made him think about such a thing as negative space.

Bram replied that when he had written the equation that pulled the bubble back from its forward path he had taken it into the negative values, and equation program had continued to function. However, since he had no idea what that would mean, he was going to experiment to learn what it meant physically.

He said that if he went negative beyond the zero point, he did not think the Fold would bring the bubbles back to the hangar landing area. He wondered where the Fold would end up on its return from the negative area.

Pat said that she was sure he would find out and that what he found would most likely be as astounding as creating a wormhole spaceship that could traverse the universe.

Ron Mueller

Chapter 12: The Price of Progress

The experiment went as Bram had expected. The Pat Bubble had to be deactivated and brought back as programed. The Lori Bubble had been programed so the pull part of the equation was decoupled and only the reversed equation was functional. It worked as expected.

He now knew how to set up the program so that it would function as desired and be controlled by both the computer and by a human.

He kept thinking about the negative test that he anticipated would take him into a totally new space environment but resisted the temptation to run that test.

The Remi bubble had been sent out with the enhanced design without the pullback bubble attached and was scheduled to return exactly at the end of the workday.

He had just heated the water for a cup of tea when Linda announced Erica's desire to update him.

Erica came in all smiles and said that she was looking forward to a pancake breakfast on Sunday.

Bram knew that she had good news. He asked if she wanted a cup of tea.

Erica said it was one of her better Friday's. She said that it seemed that getting the small bubble production situated in the fruit barn had provided a breakthrough for her. She credited Lacy with having helped in convincing the farm owners that a new building at the other end of the field would functionally improve their logistics of both selling apples locally and make handling distribution trucks more efficient.

Erica said that when she offered to pay the cost of the change, the deal was accepted immediately. She bought the parcel of land the barn and entrance were on and got agreement to a fence around it.

She stopped for a moment as she sipped her tea. Then she gave a small laugh and said that when she shared what she was doing with the aerospace leaders, the builders of the space wheels immediately offered to produce the large bubbles and would locate it in the same hanger where they had produced Wheel One and Two.

They had offered to help in securing the labor and had given reassurances that they would help staff the Dallas site with persons from both Seattle and Portland.

She went on and said that she and Luke had walked around the Fruit Barn and had decided that it was a perfect building for their needs. They were meeting with the architect on Monday to determine what needed to happen before production was moved into the Fruit Barn.

Then she asked what he thought of naming the new company, Fruit Barn Productions, LLC, and naming Luke as the President.

Bram leaned back in his chair and said that she had just broken his record for speed. He went on and congratulated her on making things happen fast and that he liked everything that he had heard.

He then said that she could have extra syrup for her Sunday morning pancakes.

She said that she was really looking forward to the pancakes and wondered whether she could invite three Stetson family members to breakfast as well.

"Well," Bram answered, "that would cost one trout for each of you."

The meeting ended as Linda let him know that he had five minutes until the Remi bubble was due back from its run.

He and Erica walked to the control room to watch the return.

The entire Lab team was still there, and Erica let them know that she had a great Friday end of the day message that would make their weekend that she would share right after they got Remi back into its position in the Lab.

Pat looked at Bram and asked who would be coming to breakfast on Sunday.

Bram rattled off the names. Then he went quiet as the Remi bubble appeared. He waited until the recovery team had moved it to the lab area and then he went out to inspect it.

Both he and Remi were standing in front of the viewing barrier and looking at the plant that was wilted and was apparently dead.

Bram knew that he had an additional problem to solve before he would be able to have humans traveling in a wormhole bubble.

He looked at Remi and said that it was good that he had suggested sending something live on his bubble's journey.

He asked if Remi liked pancakes and invited him to Sunday's breakfast.

Pat knew that because of the dead plant she would be sitting with Bram enjoying a book as he talked to himself with his eyes closed as he contemplated how to overcome his new problem.

Bram turned to her and asked what she thought the plants had died of.

Pat, Erica, and Lori all stepped up to take a look at the plant. They all agreed that the plant seemed to have died of natural causes. They conjectured that maybe a lack of water but most likely it had died of a natural cause such as old age.

Bram suspected that it had to do with time, and he needed to examine the Fold equation and see how it worked relative to time's passing.

He asked Remi to set up a precision mechanical clock with a backup that could be attached to a computer program.

Pat pointed to the door and said that it was time to go home and enjoy the weekend.

Bram saw that Erica had turned to join them and they all left the Lab together.

On the ride home Zoe asked whether he had heard about the ditty that Castor and Donna were working on about the wormhole that was going to eat Pat, but Bram saved her fat. The Wormhole tasted Lori and spat her back. Bram sent out Remi and his plant and it was shriveled dead when it got back.

Bram said that the Monday jog in would be an interesting one since they had the weekend to work on it and he was sure that they would share it with Orlando and give him a chance to smooth it out.

Once he got to the house he went up and took a shower and then retreated into his office.

Pat stopped by the kitchen and found out that everyone had decided on pizza and cheese nachos. The compound kitchen staff would deliver it as soon as it was ready. Mike said that they had agreed on three different kinds of pizza and had ordered enough for everyone.

Thomas said that the beer, wine, or soft drinks were in the fridge.

Pat grabbed two lights and headed back to the office.

She listened as Zoe was explaining that the Black-Eyed Susan plant that Remi had sent out was his favorite flower. She had asked Linda to order a new plant to replace it so that Bram could try again on Monday. She said she was all in favor of his success in keeping it alive on the next trial run and she would keep getting them delivered until he succeeded.

Pat sat down next to Bram who had listened, but she knew that he was already into his equation review and would not come back to them until he had found where time needed to be managed and manipulated. She was totally content to sit by him and read.

The next morning after a workout in the basement gym, she and Zoe were sitting at the kitchen table getting ready to indulge in some tea with a cookie or a sweet roll when the doorbell rang.

Zoe jumped up and said she had it. At the same time Thomas stepped out of the office.

Pat was surprised at their reactions, but she appreciated their vigilance. She heard Jina's voice and got up to greet her.

She invited her to share a cup of tea or coffee and a sweet roll.

Jina sat down at the table and then shared that it was hard for her to come back to the Fold facility and leave Zuri. She said that it was the first time she and Nuro had been away from Zuri for more than a day.

Pat said that she was sure it was hard, but that Zuri needed a chance to become independent and she pointed out that Zuri would have two people that would make sure that she would receive the best education and also do it in a safe environment.

Pat joked that Orlando would have the whole campus jogging and reciting ditties as they did.

Jina laughed and said that he already had two or three young men join him as he took Zuri to her first class. She said that she was sure that Orlando would change the atmosphere of the staid campus and would probably be the best recruiter of Marine Corp officers that the Marine Corp could ask for.

Pat said that she should send a message to Major General Tilson letting him know her impression of Orlando. She let Jina know that Orlando had requested a second Marine be assigned to guard Zuri so that he would have enough time to get a degree while he was at the university.

Jina said that she would do so as soon as she got home. Orlando was one of Zuri's favorite friends and the most connected to her on a personal level.

Zoe chuckled and said that Orlando connected with everyone on a personal level and was a favorite of everyone.

Jina then commented that Elizabeth was like the Grand Mother that she had always wanted Zuri to have. Elizabeth was already having a big impact on the social life of all the people that were somehow disabled but even more she had already made connections with the social life of what she called, "the spoiled socializers," and had set up events that included the disabled people.

Pat commented that Elizabeth was an extremely talented manipulator of the social and political scene and would make a huge positive difference for Zuri.

Pat then made the point that Jina and Nuro would need to focus on their own social development and prepare themselves for an independent Zuri. It would be a different Zuri than either of them or anyone who currently knew her would be expecting.

Jina put down her teacup and said that she had just enjoyed the best tea and cookie that she had ever eaten. She said she wished Nuro would have come with her.

Pat invited them to Sunday breakfast and then she would be able to talk to Nuro as she weakened him with buttered pancakes covered in maple syrup.

Jina said she would love to come to Sunday breakfast.

After Jina left, Zoe complimented Pat on how she handled Jina's feelings about missing Zuri. She said that she would keep that advice in mind for when her daughter went away to college.

Pat went into the study and saw Bram working away on his computer. He looked at her and smiled but then his eyes went back to the lap top screen.

Bram realized that he had just used up some of his emotional bank account, but he was more worried about killing the very person that held the account he just had drawn down.

He found that every one of the Fold equations had fixed time markers in them. He would need to make them all variables that only incremented at the pace of Earth time.

He marked every equation that had a time factor and then shut down his computer.

He decided to make a deposit with his favorite banker.

Pat was just getting ready to go for a walk and was surprised but very pleased when Bram came out of the office and asked what she wanted to do.

When they got outdoors, Bram was surprised at what a beautiful day it was. He had been in his office since early in the morning. He followed alongside of Pat as she said that they should go play some pool and maybe some ping pong and then grab something to eat from the snack bar, sit by the pool, and relax.

Melinda their neighborhood event organizer came over and said that it was great to see them. She said it was great that the Fold program was making such great progress. She asked if the expansion to the Fruit barn area meant that they would be getting more housing.

Bram shook his head and said he had no idea and that she should ask Erica what was planned. He said that even Erica might not have gotten that far yet in her planning. He commented that the part of the Fold project she was inquiring about would move slower than the news about its successes.

He and Pat started a walked around the perimeter of the of the compound but gave in to the request by the Marine guards to come back in toward the center because they were open targets out where they were walking.

Bram decided that at breakfast on Sunday he was going to ask Lacy how the Fold Offense Team was doing. He was sure that Lacy would have news of some sort to share.

Pat found the Sunday breakfast to be one that had several interesting aspects.

Jena brought up the fact that she and Nuro missed Zuri and that it was their first time to be away from her. Everyone reinforced Pat's earlier advice.

Soon after that, Erica shared the progress on bubble production and site expansion. She stopped when asked about housing and how it would impact the neighborhood and said that those aspects had yet to be addressed and now it would be on her radar screen.

Lacy then shared the fact that the Fold Offense had indeed been scoring against their opponents. She said that she was pursuing the money and had been able to freeze or seize several hundred million dollars that were in offshore accounts.

The offense had also identified several wealthy donors that had given money to several groups that had attacked the Fold compound or their members at the fishing outings. She was suing them in civil court and tying them up legally so that they would not have time to participate in actions against the Fold program.

She shared that currently her biggest worry was the smaller radical groups that resided in the northeastern part of the country. They could take radical action on their own. She had formed a surveillance group that was currently using thirty camera drones to monitor the groups they had identified. She was negotiating with the NIS to get them to track the online and phone activities of the more active and radical groups.

Bram thanked both Lacy and Erica for their work.

Linda pointed to her brother, Luke, and asked him whether he had any interesting news. Luke began by saying that his life was taking a big turn. The Fold bubble production barn was to be owned by his company that he was calling Fruit Farm Products LLC. He commented that the details of how he would, over time, become the sole owner of the facility was being worked out. He said it would initially grow to a two hundred employ company.

He ended by thanking them all for such an opportunity.

Bram Nielson Collection

Bram looked at Zoe and asked her what her opinion was about Luke getting such a break.

Zoe and Eric both shared the fact that they could think of nothing better to happen to person who had shielded her from a sniper during the last gun battle by standing in front of her and taking a bullet for her, than what was happening to Luke.

Zoe closed by saying she had dibs on being in his boat for the next fishing trip.

Bram thanked everyone for sharing and let them know that he had to get into his office and fix the mess he had as a Fold equation to ensure they all had a working future.

He heard the entire group say, "A very successful mess."

He got up and was pleased that the breakfast session continued. He noted that Pat was the one that was guiding the conversation. She knew that he enjoyed social interaction, but his threshold was much lower than most for social discussions that were almost always circular in nature.

He was off to make sure that he was not going to kill his willing explorers.

Ron Mueller

Chapter 13: The Meaning of Time

Bram entered his study and fired up his laptop. He was consumed with the thought of how time was a thread that ran through the fabric of the entire Fold tapestry. He had to figure out whether the time that the computer was using was Earth time or if it was the time that was passing as the Fold vessel traveled the wormhole. If it was external time then a lifetime might pass in a flash. He had to make sure that the time the passenger in the bubble experienced was based on the Earth clock time spent in the bubble.

He had to determine which time his Fold Wormhole bubble program was integrating?

The question on his mind was, how could he maintain the use of Earth time during a Fold wormhole trip?

Simple questions that could only be answered through trial-and-error physical tests.

He was sure that he would kill several more plants before he figured it out.

Even the reverse equation had a time thread. He figured if he didn't kill everything going in one direction, he might do it in the reverse direction.

He was glad that he had been lucky when he wrote the Fold equation, and it had no motion associated with it. Otherwise, his first Folds may have ended in death for all the Wheel personnel.

That thought sent a shiver down his back.

He took note that Zoe was uncharacteristically quiet and not playing her usual game of teasing him when he was deep in thought. He figured that he must be telegraphing his concern about what he had found wrong on the last run of the wormhole experiment.

He thought about the request he had sent Remi about getting the bubble ready for a Monday afternoon test. He stopped and sent him a text to let him know that the next test would be later in the week and Remi should not come in early on Monday to get the bubble ready to go.

He then told Zoe not to be so serious and that he would only be killing a Blacked Eye Susan on each of his failures to conquer father time.

Zoe nodded and said that she would order as many of them as he would need to figure out how to manage time. She wondered whether this affected the Fold team's ability to help the Aliens who had sent their message.

Bram replied that the response to the Aliens certainly would have to wait until he had solved the current time problem. He pointed out that the Aliens were not expecting a message from Earth and currently Earth did not have the capability to send a Fold message. He pointed out that currently each bubble had to return so they could get the information that had been collected. Even the Alien message had come back as a recording on the bubble's computer.

Zoe asked if a bubble could be Folded close to the alien's home world and the message beamed to them in a normal manner from there.

Bram smiled and said he liked the way she was thinking, and he had Marcus sending out probes so the space coordinates of the alien planet could be determined. Marcus would first send trial bubbles to make sure they sent the message to the right planet and that the bubble would not end up like Bramlet One with a boulder sharing the same space.

Ron Mueller

Zoe thanked him for sharing what Marcus was doing and said that perhaps if that was the way they delivered the reply perhaps they could ask the Aliens to share how they were able to send Fold messages.

Bram said that he liked brave bodyguards that were also smart, and he would keep her suggestion at the top of the list.

He suggested she engage Mallica who he had asked to see if she could learn how the message had been sent. He offered that a great question that would hook her was to ask if the message was made up of quarks that repeatedly Folded and whether the quarks might be transmitted like radio waves that were transmitted through Earth's atmosphere or whether up and down quarks might be used in some sort of up and down quark combinations that might periodically create hadrons as a way to transmit a Folded message through space.

Zoe smiled and said it was going to be all she could do to repeat the question that he had just suggested. She said that she had been recording his suggestion and would at least memorize it. She wondered if he had already asked that question of Mallika.

Bram replied that he had not.

He then smiled and said that when Mallika asked her how she had thought about such a question, Zoe should tell her that she had been taught that at the FBI academy.

Zoe laughed and said she was sure that Mallica would then figure out where she had really been fed that question.

He told her to ask the question anyway.

Bram looked at Eric and asked that he capture Mallica's face when Zoe asked the question. He said that he was sure that it would be one that the entire team would like to see, and Orlando would surely be able to make a jogging ditty that they would all enjoy from the interaction.

Pat, book in hand, had been standing in the doorway of the study listening and volunteered to go ahead of the two of them and have Mallica distracted with a few of her own simple questions. She laughed and said that her current surprised look was a shadow of what she thought Mallica's would be.

Bram took his laptop and sat down on the twin recliner and said he was ready for his reading partner.

Monday morning the jog to the work area was again rather quiet and no ditties were being sung.

Bram figured that everyone had heard about the shriveled plant, and he wondered how far up the chain of command the problem had been communicated. He was sure that Jefferey knew, and he was sure he would not send it any farther up until the two of them talked. He figured he had until Wednesday to figure it out or to describe the path he was following to figure out how to solve the problem.

The one thing Bram would not do was to send out any human on any Fold until he solved the problem with time. He kept thinking how lucky they had been to have had stationary Folds that locked in on a specific coordinate and how glad he was that Marcus had insisted on what at the time he had thought were exceedingly accurate coordinates.

He mumbled something about luck and was surprised when Pat quietly told him that luck had nothing to do with the success of the Fold program. She said that it was skill, fortitude, tenacity and as Zuri had describe it, his unusual non-linear brain.

The next day, before going to his office, Bram went to the lab. He felt a need to explain to Remi about how embedded the impact of time was in the Fold equation and that until he had followed every embedded path there would be no scheduled Folds and warned Remi that Zoe had ordered a dozen Black Eyed Susan's that would need care and watering.

He was pleased with Remi's reply that he should take all the time needed to solve the Fold equation problem and that until then he had all the time needed to water plants.

Remi said that he was also engaged in helping set up the Fruit Production plant and getting it up and running. He smiled as he commented that "time" was of no concern to him.

Bram left the lab and headed for his office.

Linda greeted him and let him know that he would have a standing room only dinner on the coming Sunday.

She let him know that because of the number of folks that had accepted her invitation, she had moved the dinner to the community shelter.

She said that Zuri was planning to attend as well.

Bram replied that the celebration might be premature since he did not have a Fold worm hole that humans could use.

Linda said that he had until Sunday evening to solve that problem but as far as everyone was concerned, they were sure that he would.

Bram asked that he not be interrupted but that he did want to be at the cafeteria at noon.

He went into his office and sent a note to Zuri letting her know that he was working on the problem of Fold wormhole time, and he would review it with her on the weekend if she wanted to get an update.

Almost immediately he received a reply saying that he would have fifteen minutes at breakfast at his house on Sunday morning if she could have pancakes, sausage and two over easy eggs. She said that things were going great for her, but she really missed their morning meetings.

He sent back an emoji check mark and a smiley face.

He then got Einstein out and explained the problem to him as he fed him cookie crumbs and told him that if he didn't supply the solution, he might be sent out in the next wormhole experiment. He chuckled as Einstein shook his head in the negative.

He said that he was just kidding.

Then he chuckled again when he thought about talking to a mouse.

He spent the next two hours working through the first equation string. He was modifying the equation so that he could control the time with a mechanical clock that put out a signal every one sixtieth of a second. This was a dramatic slowdown in time that before had moved at the computer speed of microseconds, but it created a time frame that he could easily track and control.

He would see if he could locate a more precise mechanical clock if the approach worked. He began linking each time-based equation to the clock. It was a simple but tediously slow reprograming process where each step needed testing to make sure the program still functioned. He realized that it would take him two full days with a couple more hours in the evening to get through the entire string of Fold equations.

Then he would want to review everything with Mallica, and he decided he should also add two IT specialist to make sure the program was fully operational.

He would have Remi prepare the Fold Wormhole bubbles for a Friday morning trial. Then he would spend the day running a series of tests that hopefully let him tune a functional, working control equation.

He would get Linda to supply some bait fish and some meal worms to test the ride with several living riders when the first flower came back alive.

When he got the ten-minute warning, he went out to Linda's desk and asked her to make the arrangements with the people and to provide the bait fish and meal worm.

Linda laughed about supplying the fish and meal worms and asked if she could throw in some crickets.

Bram said he was leaving it up to her since he might kill all of them. He then headed for the cafeteria.

Pat had set up the contest to see who could come up with the best snipped about Bram's Fold wormhole time problem. The lab group got so excited that Lori declared the morning a half day off and they all concentrated in coming up with hand drawn posters about time.

Pat had put up the posters around the cafeteria that the lab group and the wheel teams had made.

She had also asked Chef D'Carluca to prepare one of Bram's favorite meals.

Bram stopped as he entered the cafeteria. He scanned the signs and the sayings about time.

"Time will do all – of us in."

"Only a Bram can control time."

"We are spending time waiting for Bram to give us a Fold wormhole ride."

"Wasted time cannot be recovered."

"Time cannot be stopped or reversed, unless you are a Bram."

He took note of cartoon characters and the famous one of a character with a long nose looking over the wall that said, "Bram will sniff out time, he just needs to get over the Fold wall."

He asked Pat if she had supplied the colored felt tips and asked if any work got done during the morning.

Pat replied she didn't think so because Lori had given the entire lab the morning off and made it into a contest.

Bram asked how the winners would be determined.

Pat said that everyone had three votes, and they could distribute their votes any way they wished.

Linda and Lacy came in carrying their entries and asked if it was too late to compete.

Linda had a fishbowl with fish crying, a cricket with the words "why me" coming out of his mouth and a worm saying it was either a ride through a wormhole or a fishhook in his back.

Lacy had a picture of a camera drone flying down a worm hole shooting at the words, "time only gets one chance before getting "Bramed down."

Bram told Pat that he was putting one vote on Lacy's and one on Linda's entries and one on the nose over the wall.

Chef D'Carluca came out and looked around and did a mock shout about the mess that the Lab folks had created. Then laughed and put in his votes on the three posters that he liked.

He placed a Spaghetti alla Marinara in front of Bram and said that was all he could prepare in the "Time" he had available. And then laughed at his own joke.

Bram sat and listened as various folks came over and put in their votes with Pat. It seemed clear to him that the number one was going to be the nose. He wondered who had drawn it but decided to wait and be surprised by who it turned out to be.

Linda's entry seemed to be getting a large number of votes as well.

He asked Pat what the prizes were and was surprised that they were significant ones.

He asked who was paying for the prizes and laughed when Pat said not to worry it was coming from the Fold technical budget that was huge and bottomless. It was his budget, and the prizes were a full year's college scholarship, a gift of five thousand dollars to the food bank and three thousand dollars to the Dallas park budget to be spent on putting in a new hiking trail.

When he asked how they had come up with the prizes, Pat said that they had been ones that some of the lab folks had been wanting to gift.

He shook his head and said that he needed to get back to work and that she should somehow capture all of what was going on and put it out on the community network.

Pat liked the reaction that Bram had to the poster contest. She knew that the issue about time was Bram's current crisis, and she knew how significant it was by the amount of tossing and turning that she slept next to.

She hoped that he would solve the problem as fast as possible. She had not shared the fact that the folks at NASA, Jeffery's team and the folks at their large bubble production site were participating in the contest as well.

Bram decided to take a walk around the building to get some exercise before sitting himself down to continue the tedious task of modifying the equations.

He stopped and complimented Linda on her poster entry.

Linda let him know that she had contacted everyone, and they were ready for the review of the equation on Thursday afternoon and Remi would have the wormhole express ready to go on Friday.

That evening he learned that the contest ended at noon the following day and he was expected to hand out the awards.

He asked how he came to be the one to hand out the awards.

Pat laughed and said that it was his budget that was giving the awards, and he was the only one authorized to use the money as he saw fit.

He replied that he was associating with a devious person.

Ron Mueller

Chapter 14: The Fish Bait Solution

When Bram walked into a full cafeteria for Tuesday's lunch, Pat guided him to the podium that was set up by the windows where three easels held the winning posters that were covered by cafeteria tablecloths.

He was asked about his poster choices but said that he couldn't remember which ones he had chosen and that they had all been good.

Pat knew that Bram never forgot, and she liked the fact that he was being diplomatic in trying to keep everyone happy.

She asked Bram for a layman's explanation of how the solution to the time problem with the Fold equations was coming.

He began with the fact that he needed more "time" and that they had not given him enough "time" to get through all the parts of the equation that dealt with "time."

He shared that the basic problem was that if he were to send a baby through the wormhole and across the galaxy with the current set of controls, the baby would come back as dust.

He said that he was looking for some volunteers to send out to test his current solutions. He asked for any Fold Wormhole passenger volunteers to raise their hands. He then paused and waited. He laughed and said that he had so far only killed a flower but on Friday he would be sending out three fish, three meal worms and three crickets and hoped to get them back alive because Linda had threatened not to let her father take him fishing if he killed the bait.

He then asked, "Who wants to volunteer to take the ride after they comeback alive."

No one raised their hands!

Ya! I wouldn't want to go next either since all of them might be returning the day before their death.

So then, I will send three newly born mice and see if they return as baby mice.

He asked if there would be any volunteers if that worked. He was greeted by silence.

No. Wow, you all are a hard group.

I guess I will have to send out Wilbur the pig to see if he returns as a pig and not as cooked bacon.

He then asked, "If I am successful with Wilbur will I get any volunteers?"

Pat stepped out and said she would volunteer. The rest of the Wheel team members all shouted that so would they.

He thanked them and then said that it was "Time" to hand out the awards.

Pat explained that they would work up from third prize to the first prize. She stepped over to the first stand and pulled off the cover. It was a poster with a stick character with a voice bubble that had "Only a Bram can control time."

Once the winner came up to claim the cashier's check for three thousand dollars, Pat then went to the number two poster and revealed a drawing of a person with his finger on the hour arm and the saying, "Time cannot be stopped or reversed, unless you are a Bram."

Bram was pleased to see Lacy come forward to claim the five-thousand-dollar prize.

When Pat uncovered the first prize poster, the cafeteria erupted with a cheer. It was clear that it was the favorite for many people.

It was of a character with a long nose looking over the wall saying, "Bram will sniff out time, he just needs be able to get over the Fold wall."

When Zoe came forward to claim the prize, Bram broke into laughter. She had periodically tweaked his nose when he was deep in thought to see if he knew what was going on.

Zoe held up the certificate awarding her a one-year scholarship and said that she was going to become a mathematician so that she could help Bram solve his equation problems or maybe she would just go into the fifth dimension and disappear.

She received a round of applause, and someone shouted she should choose the fifth dimension and that it was less of a challenge then working for Bram.

Bram complimented all three for having won and went on to thank everyone for contributing to the Fold program.

He was pleased with the enthusiasm in the room. It provided him with the desire to successfully solve the time problem.

Erica came over to the table where Pat and he were eating lunch and complimented Pat on creating such a motivating event. She said that she had never been part of an organization that had as much energy and fun.

Bram smiled and said that she was now leading one and should enjoy it as much as he did.

She chuckled and said that Jeffery had threatened to promote her so he could have her job.

Bram nodded and said that Jefferey needed to move up so that he had more control of what was on the political horizon. He made the point that communicating with an alien race that looked more like a whale and inhabited a water world was going to be a huge political challenge.

He then excused himself and said that he had to get back to follow the thread of time through the Fold equation.

Erica asked Pat if Bram was moving too fast and maybe making too many chances.

Pat looked at her and said that, coming from her, it was a strange question because Erica had been with the Fold program from its beginning.

Erica nodded and said that Pat was right. She then asked if Pat was really willing to go out when Bram cleared people for the first wormhole Fold.

Pat smiled and said that she knew that Bram would not let anyone Fold anywhere until he was certain that it was safe.

She let Erica know that he looked back at all the previous Folds and kept saying that he had been lucky. She went on to say that he had tested his stationary Fold equation starting in the desert with apples, cherries, and candy. Then he had moved the effort out to a location near Seattle where he moved heavier and heavier weights until the power company stopped rebuilding the power station he kept blowing up, but he had worked his way up in weight to the point that he could Fold enough weight that he moved on to building the transports for people.

He built the bubbles that became wheels in shape because he envisioned months and perhaps years of the Fold personnel being on long term missions.

On the first Wheel fold from Seattle to Dalles he almost lost power when Wheel One Folded. He stopped everything until he could make sure he had enough reliable power before he would let Wheel Two-Fold.

I asked him what would have happened if the power had failed during either of the Folds.

He shook his head and said that he had no idea.

That is when he decided to send out smaller bubbles that only carried sensors and a control computer that was storage and had a built-in return program that it triggered after a given time.

When Bramlet One came back with a boulder embedded in it, he insisted that before the Wheels would again be launched, the coordinates of the Fold location would be checked out with a host of bubbles to make sure it was clear of any objects.

He then limited the first Fold to be out to the Moon to make sure that distance did not affect the Fold capability.

Pat paused and looked at Erica and repeated her question about Bram moving too fast.

She went on and said that Bram moved very fast and that the Fold program had outpaced and outperformed any developmental program she was aware of.

Pat then spewed out a series of questions.

Did he move fast, Yes.

Did he ensure the safety of everyone involved, Yes.

Did he constantly worry about making a critical mistake, Yes.

Did he move too fast, No!"

She concluded by saying, "He just moves at Bram speed and time."

Erica nodded and said that she had asked a stupid question. She said that she had come to trust Bram to always do the right thing.

Pat agreed and she said they should check with Linda to see how many pigs and of what size he had asked her to get.

They walked out together and went to Linda's desk.

Pat asked how many pigs Bram had asked her to get.

Linda crinkled her eyes and asked how they knew about the pig request.

Erica gave a laugh and said that they had bet with each other that he would ask to get three pigs each one bigger than the first one.

Linda replied that he had indeed asked for three pigs. The sizes were to be one hundred fifty, three hundred and five hundred pounds and he wanted them clean and ready to Fold on Friday afternoon. Linda said that he had told her she could skip getting them trained to be bubble pilots.

Pat smiled and said that Linda might have time to actually train the pigs since all they had to learn to do was to push a button.

Linda replied that Pat was the experienced pilot so maybe she could teach the pigs to push the button.

Erica said that she would leave it up to them to decide who would teach the pigs and turned to go to her office.

Pat asked Linda to give Bram a ten-minute warning when it was time to go home. She said he would continue what he was working on, in the comfort of his recliner where they sat together every evening.

Linda said that she would.

On the way home, Pat asked how far Bram had gotten with his Fold equation modification.

Bram said that he was about halfway through one version of the changes he was planning and that subsequent versions would be modifications to learn how to control the source of time being used and learn the effect of integrating time and distance. He said that the subsequent versions would be easy to do.

He commented that he was going to see if the two IT reviewers would do the subsequent versions so he could focus on sending out the various plants and animals. He said that the plants would be at the most risk, then the fish, worms and crickets would be the next at risk. If they survived, he would then send newly born mice to see that they did not age in their round trip. Finally, he would send out the three pigs one at a time to make sure that size did not matter.

Pat asked when he thought he would be executing the Fold wormhole missions.

Bram said that if everything went according to plan, they would begin after lunch on Friday and end by five in the afternoon. If he killed the flowers, then he would need to reschedule the remainder of the trials until he quit killing flowers.

When they were comfortably sitting in their recliner, Pat said that she would sit quietly.

Bram gave her a hug and thanked her for having made Monday a great day that had boosted his energy level and had broadened his Fold Wormhole validation process. He admitted that he had added the mice and the pigs after the cafeteria speech.

Pat watched Bram slowly going back down his equation wormhole. She worried that he would mentally wear himself out.

The next day when they arrived at work, she asked him to take hourly breaks and share his progress with Mallica or anyone else that he thought would be useful to keep in the loop.

She was pleased when he agreed to do it twice a day and at lunch.

She stopped by Linda's desk and asked her to give Bram a call at ten and three to make sure he got out of his office to go to whoever's office he was going to share progress with.

She kept track for the next three days to make sure Bram didn't get consumed with the Fold equation.

Every evening, she would sit by him on their shared reclining lounge and make sure that he got up and took an evening walk and talked to her.

She sensed that he knew what she was doing, and she took his quiet participation as approval.

On Thursday afternoon, she sat in the back of the viewing room and observed the review process. It was clear to her that only Mallica understood the basics of the Fold equation.

The two IT resources, though very capable programmers who understood how to write the program code for the Fold equation, were otherwise overwhelmed. They made several suggestions to improve the performance of the programing that Bram had done.

Bram thanked them and said that he would like them to make those changes immediately after the review and have the program ready to try on Friday morning.

Pat noticed how the two IT resources perked up and became more engaged. She was always impressed with how Bram could motivate and turn up the enthusiasm level as he turned up the level of work of those around him.

Bram suggested a ditty on the early Friday morning jog from the house to the compound that let Pat know that he was feeling confident.

Castor and Donna started the ditty, and then they were jogging singing:
"The Birds and The Bees, have nothing.
Nothing over the fishes,
Nothing over the worms,
Nothing over the crickets.
The Birds and The Bees, have nothing.
Nothing over pigs one, two or three.
Nothing over pigs one, two or three.
All will Fold.   All will Fold.
And live to be, live to be.
Very, very old
Pigs one, two, and three."

By the time they got to the door where they normally entered the building, Pat could hear the entire compound reverberating with the ditty that had been taken up by the Marine's guarding the compound.

It was clear to her that everyone had noticed that the ditty that had been missing for days was back. It was a message to all that things were back to normal.

Pat realized that somehow, the entire organization watched how Bram was acting and absorbed his mood.

She knew firsthand how his persona affected her but then she was the one that was in love with him. She smiled and guessed that in a way so was everyone else.

Pat was in the back of what had been Zuri's office. The room was in the process of being renovated into a more theater like atmosphere. Comfortable seats were arranged so everyone had a clear view of the screens. They were the original screens and behind them the wall mounted screens were in the process of being installed.

Linda was sitting next to her, and Pat told her that the room was going to be a super place to meet.

The room filled to the point that there was standing room only.

Bram entered and sat at the seat that was in the center and that had been kept open for him. He thanked everyone for coming and then turned to look at Linda, smiled and asked her why she had let the room exceed the rated capacity. He asked if she had provided enough refreshments to tide everyone over for the next four hours of lecture.

The room went deathly silent.

Linda smiled and replied that she would have let more people in, but these were the only ones willing to listen to him go through his boring equations and she had also run out of funds to provide more refreshments.

Pat watched as the exchange had cause everyone to smile. They knew that Bram was joking, and that Linda was readily returning his volley.

Bram looked around the room and welcomed everyone. He said he was just kidding about the four hours and that his update would take no more than the next thirty minutes and that afterwards they were welcome to spend time at the refreshment cart in the hallway to make sure that Linda had not wasted any funds.

He then turned to the two IT resources, introduced them, and ask them if they had been able to get the Fold programing complete and ready to go.

They responded that they had indeed made the changes, and they had tested it to make sure all the sections worked as intended.

Bram thanked them and then he activated the screen to show the test plan for the day. He had put a big question mark in red after the line that said,

"First Wormhole Fold returns with living plants?"

    Yes →send out the fish, worms, and crickets.

    No →go get a beer to cry in.

"Second Wormhole Fold returns with living fish, worms, and crickets"

    Yes →send out the baby mice.

"Third Wormhole Fold returns with living baby mice"

    Yes →send out pig one, pig two, and pig three

The mice and the pigs live to grow old.

The Fold team gets to live bold.

Pat marveled at the simplicity of the test plan. She knew that Bram had a ton of tests and detailed analysis that would happen, but the essence of the day was up on the screen in seven short lines.

Bram asked if there were any questions.

Someone asked if the pigs went out one at a time.

Another asked if there would be a total of six Folds.

A third person asked how long each Fold would be.

Bram replied yes to the first two question.

He then said that he would be increasing the Fold duration after fold number two, but all the folds would be of very short durations because he did not know how fast or how far a vessel in a Fold wormhole would go.

He said that the data coming back from each wormhole Fold would allow him to learn about the motion inside of the Fold wormhole. He pointed out that most likely the information coming back would keep all of them busy for the foreseeable future.

Bram looked around and said that unless there were more questions the update was over, and the action was now going to be out at the lab and the launch area.

He pointed to the clock and said that the update time had only taken sixteen minutes and that all the extra time could be spent enjoying the refreshments that Linda had spent most of his budget on.

He asked the two IT folks to follow him to the Lab where they would program the bubble for the first Wormhole Fold.

Chapter 15: One Step Above

It seemed to Bram that the entire site personnel were following him toward the Lab. He stopped at the Lab entrance and let everyone know that only the folks working on the Fold Wormhole Bubble would be allowed in the Lab. He asked the two IT folks to set themselves up in Lori's office. He then turned and walked back to where Remi was already getting the first plant ready. They had agreed to measure the soil moisture, take a picture of the leaves and they had measured the main plant stem diameter and its height. These were their control measures.

Bram watched as Remi secured the plant and sealed the bubble. Then they extracted air from the bubble and sent it to the chem lab to have it analyzed.

Remi signaled the lab personnel that were dressed to move the sealed bubble in its launch enclosure, to the launch area.

Bram then followed Remi out to the launch control room.

Pat had arranged for Linda to press the launch button as part of their continuing teasing of each other about teaching pigs to fly.

Pat said that she knew of a city where they had a flying pig contest that had selected the best flying pig entry, and that the winner had won a years' worth of sausage. She said that first contest had later turned into a yearly Flying Pig Marathon.

Bram interrupted the exchange and said that Linda should count down from three and hit the launch button.

The launch of a bubble was always anticlimactic because there was no noise. Only the disappearance of the bubble let one know that the launch had taken place.

Bram knew that he could have had the bubble return in less than a minute but he had set the return timer to ten minutes so the lab folks could turn around the analysis of the air that had been extracted from the bubble.

He took the time to explain that on every return there would be at least a thirty-minute period for initial analysis and then another thirty minutes if the Fold equation required tweaking.

He asked Linda to have the launches displayed throughout the facility on the information screens and suggested that everyone should follow their regular work routine.

He and Remi returned to the lab and discussed what they would do if there was any issue with the returning plant.

Bram pointed to the next plant and said it would be the next victim and they would follow the same process as before until the returning plant reading was the same as when it left.

Remi heard the call that return was one minute away.

They walked to the control room. They observed the return of the bubble and followed the crew rolling the containment to the lab.

Remi took a sample of air with an internal container and then opened the bubble and took the control measures. The soil was almost dry. The main stem was smaller, and the plant seemed to be drooping.

Bram was relieved that it had come back old but alive. He knew that he was on the right track and that he needed to refine the way time was being integrated. He let Remi know that in roughly an hour they would send out the bubble again with the next plant using a control program with some minor adjustments to the integration of time.

Ron Mueller

He excused himself and said he was going to ask the IT resources to make the modifications and then have them load the bubble's computer with the modified program.

The third flower plant to go out came back with all measures the same as when it was sent out.

Bram then asked that the fish, worms, and crickets be sent out.

They survived with seemingly no major issues.

The baby mice returned with their eyes open, and Bram once again adjusted the equation. He sent out the next set of three baby mice. They returned with their eyes still closed and seemingly had not aged but the lab workup that was to follow would be the definitive measure.

Bram now knew that he had the equation within the tolerance that he felt it was safe for the pigs.

The workday was almost over when the final pig was to be sent out. He had the time integration loop bias refined by a factor of one thousand. The refinement was made by changing the bias on the time equation and the numerical size of the change was now out to twelve digits.

There seemed to be no changes in any of the pigs, but Bram had asked the physical health lab folks to evaluate the health metrics of the pigs in detail. They said that they would need additional time for detailed analysis but said their initial readings indicated no impact from the ride.

Bram asked if they could get the analysis done by the following Wednesday and was pleased that it could be done if the Lab worked over the weekend.

He thanked them and suggested that after Wednesday they take the next week off and then prepare to analyze the human specimens that would go out next.

Bram looked at the three pigs, each in a controlled, clean environmental containment where they would be kept until they were moved to long a term farm where NASA kept all their experimental animals. He knew that the pigs, the worms, and the fish, would all live full lives and be studied for years to come. He was not sure what was to come of the two surviving Black Eyed Susans.

He thought about all the people that had gone through a Fold and knew that they too would be part of a lifelong health impact study.

He wondered what his legacy would be in the impact he was having and wondered how those individuals would remember him.

He walked out of his office a few minutes after five. He had taken the time to review his progress with Einstein and check with him what else he should do.

He credited his review with Einstein with reminding him that he had to check on the progress of how they would send back a message to the Aliens. He explained to Einstein that he had been so focused on solving the issues with the Fold Wormhole equation that he had not thought about the Aliens. He thanked Einstein for the reminder and put him back to his residence.

Bram felt he had gotten an insight how a message could be sent via the Fold process but first he wanted to review Mallica's progress in determining how the message had been sent by the Aliens via the Fold process.

He invited Mallica for breakfast on Sunday and was pleased to have her accept.

Linda gave him his normal ten-minute heads up and he packed up and walked out of the office just as she was getting ready to leave.

Thomas and Bob were standing by and led the way to the van.

Pat was already in her seat and after Bob got in the back seat, Bram got in and gave Pat a kiss.

Thomas shut the door and got into the driver's seat. After passing through the compound exit gate, he asked who they would have the pleasure of having for breakfast on Sunday.

Bram replied that he thought there might only be Mallica. He said that if Thomas had someone in mind, he should invite them.

Thomas replied that he had no one in mind and it really didn't matter who all would end up at Breakfast since it was Bob's turn to cook.

Bob thanked Thomas for his concern and said he was ready to feed anyone that sat at the table.

Bram reflected on the fact that his FBI and Marine bodyguards had become people that he considered his friends. He then gave a mental laugh at the fact that they were also the people that he spent the most time with. Socializing outside of the Fold personnel was almost nonexistent.

He would need to push for the Fold members to go on vacations away from the compound area.

He turned to Pat and asked where she would want to go on vacation.

She was surprised by the question. She thought for a moment and said that she would like to hike the mountains in Norway and stay in cabins along the trail and she would love to paddle board one of the fjords somewhere along the way.

Bram smiled and said that they could spend weekends there. They could travel by bubble and be there almost instantaneously.

Pat gave a small frown and commented that she had not thought about the impact the bubble technology was going to have on the travel industry.

Bram nodded and said that he had such a discussion with Jeffery and suggested that he develop a transition plan that could be presented to the President when the time came. He acknowledged it would have a dramatic impact on the world economy, on operations like NASA and all the transport and delivery businesses.

He foresaw a period of upheaval like the car industry had cause during its growth. He felt that the Fold impact would be a faster and more dramatic period of change that was more like the change the internet and the phone technology was having.

Bob commented that he had already been worried about having and raising children and now his worries had gone up astronomically.

Pat looked over her shoulder and laughingly said that he should use the Fold technology to search the world for his one and only so that he could worry about having children.

Bob nodded and agreed.

Bram had listened to the exchange and the request that Pat had made brought the idea of setting up a Fold travel agency for the people of the Fold community. He would bring that up with Linda to see if there was someone in the current community that could become a travel agent. As soon as he had that thought, Melissa's name popped up. She was always arranging the entertainment and other activities for the Fold community. She was a very good lab analyst, but she seemed to be better at getting the community to gather and enjoy themselves.

She seemed to be the perfect person. He envisioned her coming up with the destinations and Marcus determining the specific coordinates for the vacation Folds. They would have to set up the destination end so that the Fold traffic was invisible.

At breakfast on Sunday, Mallica thanked Bram for inviting her then asked if the invite had to do with the Alien message.

Just as Bram was going to admit that was the primary reason, Orlando made his appearance and asked if he was in time for breakfast.

Mallica jumped up and gave him a hug and asked who was watching the other woman in his life that he guarded.

Orlando replied that a new Marine guard had been added to the protection assignment and her appearance gave him the opportunity to return to the Fold community for a couple of days.

He made a joke about them needing his wit to send back an uplifting message to the Aliens. Maybe he could come up with a ditty that would put a humor into the reply.

Bram thanked him for such dedication and asked what he was thinking of having for breakfast. He was pleased that Orlando had arrived before he had answered Mallica. He watched as the two of them chatted and discussed what they would do for the time he was visiting.

Bram knew he had to find out Mallica's progress and then he could let her have time off with Orlando.

Meanwhile he would work through how he was going to generate neutrinos, the most abundant particles that had mass. He knew that the potassium in a banana generated them but that would be too weak of a source. He needed a stronger potassium source. He immediately thought of potassium chloride, KCl, a naturally occurring potassium salt used as a fertilizer. It would be inexpensive, and he could build a transmitter that would concentrate the neutrinos and then set up a pulse modulator so he could control the formation as the neutrinos were Folded into a message that used the Alien alphabet.

He laughed to himself about using such a cheap source material to create the world's first Fold message transmitter.

It was clear that everyone at the table had heard him laugh, since they stopped and looked at him and Pat asked what was amusing him.

He apologized and said that he would let them know after they all were done with breakfast.

He was pulled back into his focus on neutrinos and speculated that the Aliens were using them as well since the message had passed through the bubble and its construction with no discernible damage. He knew that neutrinos could readily pass through almost all ordinary matter. Top scientists had speculated about using them as a way of sending messages through the Earth or the Moon. Such an ability would greatly enhance the exploration of both bodies.

Since neutrinos had been discovered in the late seventies, he wondered why this capability had not been exploited and developed.

He would ask Erica to investigate to see if any progress in that field had been made. If there was an organization or group that had made significant progress, he might be able to accelerate the creation of the neutrino transmitter.

Pat had kept quiet as she watched Bram slowly and somewhat mechanically eat his breakfast. It was clear to her that he was deep in the development of something. She speculated, since he had invited Mallica who had been looking into how the Aliens were able to Fold their message that it had something to do with sending a response to the Aliens.

When she saw that everyone was through with breakfast, she asked Bram to let them know what he had laughed about.

Bram stopped and looked around the table.

He asked Mallica to give them an update on the progress she was making to determine what particle the Aliens were Folding to make their message.

Mallica took a sip of her coffee and then said that it was little, she thought it was smaller than an electron, but she was not sure what particle it happened to be or how it would be Folded. She went on to say that she had come to the end of her analysis and other than what she had just shared, she figured she had come out empty handed.

Bram nodded and said that she had just confirmed for him that he was on the right track and said that made her research useful and valuable.

He went on to explain that he had laughed about the fact that he was contemplating using common fertilizer to create the world's first Fold message transmitter out of material one step above sh-t.

This caused the whole table to burst into laughter.

Pat said that was probably all they all needed to know and that she would leave the details up to him.

Bram looked over to Mallica and told her that she was through with her assignment and that she should take time off with Orlando. He smiled and said that the price for such time off generosity was for Orlando to come up with a Tuesday morning ditty for the team to jog to on their way into work.

Orlando replied that he would have that done before lunch and he would stay until the Wednesday jog to lead them in singing the ditty.

Bram laughed and said that it was time to go to the site entertainment facility and play pool or ping pong and maybe get a dip in the pool before lunch.

Ron Mueller

Chapter 16: Leak

Bram was up and ready to begin work on constructing a neutrino generator. He went to the kitchen for his normal morning coffee before jogging to work.

He was surprised that Orlando and Mallica were at the kitchen table. He asked what was up.

Orlando smiled and said that he was going to lead the team in and get them into rhythm singing a ditty about the Aliens that he had promised to think up. He jokingly said that he had made it simple but was sure it would inspire Bram and speed his development of the Neutrino transmitter.

He then shared the ditty and said that he wanted the team to wake up all the Marines in the compound.

> Hurrah! Hurrah!
> An Alien's call.
> A red sun,
> Hot bun,
> No fun
> The message received, perceived.
> Bram's Aha!
> Can give them an answer?
> Hurrah! Hurrah!
> Frogs in hot water
> Bram's Aha
> Message transmitted.
> Were sure they'll get it.
> Hurrah! Hurrah!

Bram was surprised at its simplicity. Then he said it was time to go and wake up the Marines at the compound.

By the time they got to the hanger entrance, they had every Marine in the compound repeating the simple ditty.

Bram invited Mallica and Orlando to have breakfast with he and Pat.

Castro, Donna, Zoe, and Eric sat at the next table. They all complimented Orlando for keeping it simple.

They were all relaxed and chatting about what the next steps would be when what seemed to be a major earthquake hit and was followed by a huge explosion.

Bram was surprised when Lacy came on over the intercom and told everyone that a major attack on the compound was underway. She asked everyone to take cover but to stay in place.

He found himself under the table and realized that his bodyguards had pushed multiple turned over tables around them and had taken defensive positions.

He heard Orlando, comment to Castor that he would rather be fishing and that out on the water they had been able to return fire.

Lacy came back on the intercom and announced that Major Sharp and the Marine contingent had complete control of the compound, and the attackers were being taken out.

She said that her team had taken out the mortars located at the river's edge and had destroyed a personal carrier and a tank coming from the direction of the power plant. She said that the bubbles were in hot pursuit of several hundred retreating armed persons running for their vehicles and her team was showing no mercy.

It was clear that Lacy was using the bubble technology that seemed to be armed with missiles and other weaponry.

Orlando commented that Lacy and her team seemed to be swift and deadly and the only ones seeing any action. He wondered where she had got her weapons.

Bram commented that he had asked her to develop a Fold offense. He was surprised at the speed and the impact that her team was having.

Lacy came on again and let them know that all the escape vehicles were destroyed and that at least a third of the attackers were dead.

She went on to say that the person who had provided the funding for the attack was no longer around to fund another one and that the main leaders of the attack were also no longer in the picture.

Bram wondered where Lacy had gotten the authorization for such lethal action.

Major Sharp came on and announced that all the attackers were captured or dead. He went on to say that the hanger had suffered major damage and Wheel One was now in pieces after taking a direct hit in the mortar attack.

He announced that he and Lacy would hold a debriefing session at noon in the auditorium.

Bram asked Donna and Castor to go and find out if they could go to the hangar.

He suggested to Orlando and Mallica that they return to the housing area and let folks there know that none of the personnel at the compound had been hurt but no one should come to work until they got the OK from Major Sharp.

He asked Pat to go with him to his office and have a cup of tea. He was going to ask Linda to get the inside information from Lacy.

As they walked out of the Cafeteria, Bob and Thomas met them and said that they had received a message that the raid had been triggered by a message coming from inside the compound and they all were to go to Zuri's old office until Bram's office could be checked for explosives and cleared.

Bram invited Linda to come with them as he was getting ready to go to Zuri's old office.

Once they were all comfortable in what now was the Viewing Room. Bram asked Linda to see if Lacy could come and share the inside information.

He then asked if she could put in an order with the cafeteria for coffee, and other refreshments.

Once everyone was settled, he said that he would like them to participate in creating the response message to the Alien request for help.

He asked Pat to lead the effort.

Pat nodded and said that she no longer had a Wheel to command, and she needed to find a new skill that would keep her employed.

Bram knew that the destruction of Wheel One would have a sobering effect on Pat.

He had not told her, but he was sure that she was aware that he had been thinking of repurposing the materials of both Wheel One and Wheel Two since their original design was to have enabled a crew to stay out for extended periods of time and that no longer seemed necessary.

Pat had the group composing a reply message when Lacy entered.

The room went silent.

Lacy nodded and walked over to where Pat was standing.

She then looked over to Bram and said that her team had to wait until they were attacked before she had been authorized to act.

The authorization had been cleared to the very top of the military command and to the very top of the political hierarchy, the President.

Once the first mortar hit, her team took out all the mortars and the personnel at the mortar sites using their armed bubbles. They then turned toward the electrical power plant where a tank and personnel carrier backed by about three hundred armed fighters had been spotted. They eliminated the tank and the personnel carrier and then began to mow down the fighters.

She stopped for a moment. She went on to say that she and her team had discussed how they would respond if the site was ever attacked. They had decided that not only the attackers, but the backers of the attack would all be treated equally.

The local financial backer that had come to the area where the mortars were located had been killed. The remote financial backer in Seattle had a gas explosion at his home that killed him.

She stopped again and then said that the Fold organization had an offense that was second to none and it took no prisoners. She made the point that it was more difficult than defense because it required the setting of priorities and actions organized and planned in detail. It required discipline and the need to avoid distractions. It required a hard hand. She commented that the offense she had designed was lethal and meant to discourage future attempts.

She apologized for being a second off in the first part of the Fold's offensive action. By the time, the first mortar shell hit the hanger, all the mortars and the people using them had been eliminated. Her team had hesitated for only a fraction of a second and that hesitation had given the attackers just enough time to drop the first mortar into its barrel. They had nothing in place to stop that mortar round.

Bram thanked Lacy for having developed a defense that turned into offense at a moment's notice and that she had used what was available to her in a unique and deadly way.

He shook his head and commented that each time science made a technological leap forward, humans figured out how to use it as a weapon.

He commented that this time a seemingly sweet but deadly woman had developed the weapon.

Lacy nodded and replied that her mother had always advised her to make the most of what she had on hand. She looked at Bram, smiled and said that he had given her the most powerful hand that anyone could have to play, and she had made sure she was allowed to play it.

Pat asked where Lacy had obtained the weapons that were mounted on the bubbles.

Lacy said that General Tilson had connected her with a General in the army who had made all the latest small missiles, grenade launchers and small machine guns available and that her team had modified the bubbles that Remi had provided so that each could hold multiple weapons and carry the needed ammunition.

She volunteered to tour the team through the section of the Fruit Farm facility that was off limits to all but her team members.

She then excused herself and said that she needed to get back to her team and Major Sharp to assess the situation.

Bram thanked her for taking the time to get them in the know.

He then suggested they take a break, and then Pat should continue leading them through composing the response to the Alien message.

A knock on the door caused the break discussion to end immediately.

Zoe cautiously opened the door. Erica was standing in front of two armed Marines. She walked in and commented that it had taken orders from the General to allow her to come the compound.

She looked around and smiled and then said, "and what do I find but everyone chatting, having coffee and rolls and enjoying themselves."

She walked over and poured herself a coffee and took a jelly roll.

Pat commented that everyone in the room should take their seats, and they would get back to composing the reply to the Alien message. She pointed to Erica and asked if she was going to join in.

When it was closing in on noon, Bram knew that the reply was as done as it could be until the moment it could be sent. He thanked everyone for contributing and suggested that they see if the cafeteria was serving and that afterward they could go and listen to the details associated with the attack.

After lunch they all went to the auditorium. General Tilson was introduced by Linda who had been recruited to formally introduce him, Major Sharp, and Lacy.

A camera crew was at the top of the auditorium's sloping floor ready to record the presentation.

It was clear to him that the video would be used to update both the military brass and the political leaders. He knew that Lacy's performance would up the pressure to produce bubbles and use the Fold technology to improve the military capability of the country.

He resigned himself to the fact that he would have little influence over that process.

He was surprised to find out that the Marines guarding the compound had not fired a shot. The fire power had all come from the use of the bubbles by Lacy's team. Her team had killed almost one hundred of the attackers, destroyed ten mortars, one personnel carrier, one tank and more than thirty trucks and RV's.

Major Sharp commented that the Marines had close to two hundred persons being held as prisoners.

The General commented that some of those that had been killed were prominent local figures and one was known to have been financing the folks making the attack.

Bram asked what was driving the effort to stop the Fold program.

General Tilson replied that there was a political side and an economic one. It was similar to the demise of public transport via trains and busses as the auto industry pushed the individual automobile. In the case of the Fold technology, it was most likely many factors that involved transportation, military power, and current investment strategies.

He looked over to Lacy and asked what she had determined from her interaction with the many organizations she had contacted.

Lacy stood up and said that she had encountered economic fear, and she felt it by far was the biggest factor.

The folks she had engaged with feared that a technology change as dramatic as the Fold capability could cause a global economic collapse. Somehow a few very wealthy individuals had learned the basics of the Fold technology, and they were actively funding the efforts to delay or end it all together.

Bram asked how widespread this concern or fear was.

Lacy said that it was less than a handful of individuals, but these individuals had billions to spend on whatever concerned them.

Bram stopped asking questions but knew that he would be working to learn how he could counter those individuals that were willing to use their fortunes to hold back progress.

He was surprised also by those at the lower economic levels of society had enough concern or hate to give up their lives to support some individual's misguided belief. He thought about the carnage that Lacy had unleashed using the very technology that they thought they had a chance to stop.

The folks in opposition were unaware that the "ship had already sailed," or said another way, "the train had left the station." Bram knew that he had discovered a technology that would change many things around the world.

Bram returned to his office where Linda asked if her sister was mean enough for the role, he had promoted her to.

He nodded and said that she was as tough as the toughest member in the Stetson family, and she was in the right role, and she needed to be given a grander title and a raise.

He then asked that he not be interrupted for the next couple of hours.

The morning events had disrupted the work he had been focused on. He had turned his attention to developing the means of creating actual hardware that would enable the transmission of Fold based messages.

Bram envisioned several modifications that would allow him to control the transmission from the magnetron that created the Fold action.

The learnings from having translated the Alien Fold based message and how they had most likely been able to create it gave him fresh insight on how the magnetron could be physically manipulated to create Fold pulses.

He figured out that he had to synchronize the release of the neutrinos that would merge with the Fold pulses in such a fashion as to create a message the Aliens could read.

Remi wondered why Bram had asked him to come to his office. He stopped at Linda's desk and asked if she knew what the meeting was about. She said that Bram must have gotten a breakthrough of some kind because he had asked not to be disturbed.

He followed Linda into Bram's office.

Bram got up and pointed to the two lounge chairs and asked if Remi wanted tea, coffee, or a soft drink.

Remi replied he would go for a soft drink and walked over to the small refrigerator on the counter to see what kinds were available. He selected a citrus based drink. Then sat down. He was a little nervous since he had spent the morning with Bram, and nothing had been mentioned about meeting later.

Bram knew that he had created an apprehensive atmosphere. He had done it intentionally because he was going to ask Remi to change his current role. He was going to ask Remi to become the Fold Hardware Manufacturing Director.

He had laughed at himself as he sought to invent titles for different members of his team.

The title was of no importance to him but the fact that Remi had been a key part of getting the Fold hardware rapidly developed and constructed was important.

He asked if Remi was ready to be promoted.

Remi replied that he did not know of a role in the current organization that he would want to be promoted into.

Bram nodded and agreed that currently there was no role that suited Remi's superb capabilities, but that situation was about to change.

He then described the role that he had in mind. Remi was to lead a team that would produce hardware that would enable the manufacture of a magnetron that had variably controlled physical chambers, a neutrino generator that had controls that would synchronize with the magnetron pulses and the power systems that would support the two.

Bram went on to say that there were also physical production improvements that the Fold program needed for the continued improvement of the current Fold effort.

Remi would be responsible for selecting the members of his team. He stressed that Remi should select the folks that would contribute the most and that pay increases would be part of their participation.

Remi asked about Lori.

Bram replied that Lori would take on a bigger role in the Fruit Farm Production facility and that she was not in consideration for the role he was being offered.

Remi smiled and thanked him for the opportunity, and said he was anxious to get started.

Bram said that he should start by getting a facility designed and put in place next to the Fruit Farm Facility but in the short term he wanted to have him produce the first modified magnetron and neutrino generator in the current lab with the team that he would select.

He should also select a company that could produce the two pieces of hardware and if they worked out those companies could be absorbed or enhanced but the production should be done at the new Plant Production Facility.

Remi said he would see how fast his team could come up with what Bram was asking for.

He then said that he wanted Bram to be part of reviewing the design of the new facility.

Bram agreed that he would love to have input to the design of the new facility but that he needed to continue to focus on the design of the hardware so they would have a robust product.

Chapter 17: Inside Spy

⊘n the following morning, Linda let him know that Lacy and General Tilson had requested a meeting with him. They would come to his office at ten to discuss internal security at the Fold complex.

Bram asked if they had indicated anything more than that and got a "No." He then asked Linda to give him a five-minute warning and that he planned on working on the design of the hardware to generate a Fold signal.

It seemed that he had just explained his concept to Einstein and had taken a moment to take a sip of tea when Linda gave him the warning.

He put Einstein back into his kingdom and sat down and sipped his tea.

Linda knocked on the door and led the General and Lacy into the room.

Bram noted the look on the General's face and figured that they had come to deliver a message that they were not sure how he would respond to. He thought about the times he had railed against the security being put up around the compound and thought about how right it had been. He was just not use to the actions some bad people were willing to take.

Lacy began by saying they had two important and critical items to discuss with him. One was the fact that they were sure there was a spy inside the Fold organization and the second was a modification of Bram's Living arrangement.

The General went on to say that he would cover the changes that he was planning to take to increase the protection being provided to the Fold organization. He went on to share the fact that a Marine unit would be using the Fold technology to scan the area around the compound on a twenty-four by seven basis. This unit would be located remotely. They would take over as soon as Lacy set up the system and trained them.

Then he stopped for a moment and asked if he could have a cup of coffee.

Bram nodded and said that he needed one as well since he figured the next part of the discussion was going to focus on him. He asked what Lacy would like.

She replied, "black."

After Bram had served the coffee, he sat down and said that he was ready for the next part.

Lacy once again opened the conversation. She said that the General was insisting that the security around him needed to be beefed up.

Bram gave a small laugh and asked how much more security could possibly be added.

The General snorted and said that Bram was only on the first level of security and that he was only being moved one rung up the ladder.

He then said that he was going to address four areas where security would be increased.

One was at work.

A second area was at home.

A third area was the journey to work.

And the final area was in the area of rest and relaxation.

Bram smiled and said he wondered what moving up two levels of security would mean.

The General replied that he didn't want to know but it was much worse than the time Bram had spent in the desert. He then went on and said that he would cover each area in the order that he had stated them.

He looked around the office and said that the outside of the office would get a protective layer that would be able to withstand a small rocket. This would be a total encasement.

His bodyguards would be augmented. Two would be in the office and an additional two would be outside the door. He understood Bram needed his privacy and a bullet proof wall would be put up a few feet inside the door and the inside guards would be on the door side.

Bram looked at the space between his desk and the door and asked if his desk could be rotated so that it would face the windows.

Lacy replied that she would have Linda rearrange the office the way he desired.

The General then went on to say that his office would be guarded twenty-four seven and have an early morning bomb sweep before he was allowed to enter.

Lacy asked if Bram was OK with what was going to happen.

Bram shook his head and said that he was leaving security to those who knew something about security, and he would focus on doing something easy like Folding time and space.

He thought back about how he had railed against being put out in the desert for protection and how much his attitude had changed since then, after multiple attacks.

The General said he knew this was hard on Bram who he saw as a warm hearted but a naive liberal. He said he had a son just like him but not quite as smart.

The General then said the next part was about the modifications to the house.

A safe room was going to be added in the basement. Zoe's current bedroom located directly above would become his bedroom. He would be able to get directly to the safe room via a pole much like that of a fire fighter's pole but modified to have lowering and raising capabilities. He said that he would have preferred a full elevator but that would have wiped out the kitchen area whereas the proposed arrangement only took over the pantry area. The bedroom walls would receive an armored layer that would add additional protection.

The General stopped and walked over to the coffee pot and poured himself another cup. He turned and said that the next change would affect Bram's home office. It would be moved to the basement and would be totally encased in armor, but it would look exactly as the one he was currently in. The only inconvenience he could see was that getting to the study would require going down the stairs. Two people could use the safe room pole to go up to the bedroom.

The dining area would be expanded but the kitchen table space would be used to provide a kitchen worktable, and the kitchen rearranged so that the pantry area could be moved.

Lacy asked if Bram agreed to get the changes made.

Bram smiled and replied that he was sure that he was being informed about the changes that had already been decided upon.

Lacy nodded and said that she didn't see another way of protecting him unless they built a very large bubble and put it over his house and that would just make it a bigger target.

She was about to apologize when Bram put up his hand and reminded her that one did not apologize for doing the right thing.

The General then said that they were to the social part of the changes. He had suggested that coming to work should change to being brought to work in an armored vehicle, but Lacy had insisted that you would reject that proposal. She suggested several routes that could be used to jog to work each morning with the route being randomly chosen each morning but called in to the observation group that would ensure no one was in the area. And that the ride back to the house would be in an armored van that looked the same as the current armored van but fortified.

Bram thanked Lacy for having protected the one part that set his mood for the day. He had made that jog, rain, shine, or snow and felt it was a needed part of his existence.

The General added that he had listened carefully to Lacy. She had earned the respect of not only the Marine Corp but had received kudos from every group that had dealt with her.

He went on to say that he was almost through. The last part was that walks in the community would be given double security. He asked that for even impromptu walks that the observation group be notified. They would scan the area and monitor for any drones or missiles. In addition, the FBI protection would be augmented with four Marines.

For outings outside of the Fold area, the security would be beefed up in a similar manner. The details for them would be worked out at the time of the outing.

Lacy spoke up and said that she had suggested that any outing location should be guarded as appropriate. Everything was to be put into position ahead of time and anyone going there would be conventionally taken there but you and Pat should be delivered using Fold technology.

She asked him how he was reacting to what she and he General had decided needed to be done about his security.

Bram was silent for a moment. He was thinking through the changes and realized that the two of them had been very thorough about his safety.

He saw some continued weak security spots during his workday. Based on the attack, the additional Marine guards would seem like a normal addition.

He thanked both of them for having thought of almost everything, but he did have one request.

He waited a moment to create an anticipatory atmosphere. He wanted the room to lighten up.

He asked if Lacy could get a tailor to make a custom shirt with a target with a bullseye on the back of the shirt and he wanted a hat that hat a flat top and a bullseye target on it as well.

That caused the General to guffa and comment that he had just lost a twenty to Lacy who had bet that he would do something like he had done. He ceremoniously pulled out his wallet and handed Lacy a crisp twenty-dollar bill.

Lacy accepted the twenty and commented that she knew her boss and she knew that he would understand that the changes were needed.

Bram said that he was inviting them both to a Sunday breakfast so they could share all the changes in detail with the folks that lived with him and those that were close team players.

Both of them accepted and said that by the end of the week they hoped to be able to have all the changes documented and most would be in place.

The General added that the changes would not be reflected in the documents being stored in compound data bases but would be held back at headquarters. The old drawings would remain as they were.

Lacy then got serious and said that they were now to the part where Bram would be the key player. They needed to find out who the internal spy or spies were. She said that it was an area that had her stumped as how to proceed. She was going to closely monitor people around Bram wherever he was and then see if there was someone that stood out.

Bram said that he agreed with the monitoring.

He then added that she should look closely at the IT folks or folks that had access to the data bases. She should then look at the messages that had gone outside of the Fold firewall. They would be coded messages. He then said that she should see who had taken extra vacations or had purchased items that seemed to indicate spending more than would be expected from someone with their salary.

They should also investigate the bank accounts of the select few that would no doubt surface and also see about accounts that were larger than expected. He added that they might have outside accounts in other banks or offshore.

Lacy had been writing what he said down. She looked up and commented that she did not want to be hunted by him.

She said that she wondered if they could play a game of leaking information in the cafeteria to see where the leak went.

Bram said that was a good idea, but he should not be the person doing the leaking. It should be Pat and Linda talking at lunch, or she and Pat, or Erica, or Mallica. He added that he had only named women because he was betting on the spy being a male and naïve enough to think he was superior.

Lacy added that she also did not want to play poker with him.

The General wondered if any one of the Marines might be a spy.

Bram responded that there was little doubt that there were spies in the Marine Corp. They would leak the military aspects about the Fold compound. Given the most recent attack and the accuracy of the first mortar hit, he felt that would be the leak from a military mind and he should put his people on the list.

Lacy reinforced that by sharing the fact that the initial inspection of the targets for the mortars that were not fired had coordinates for the location of the second wheel, the lab area, the cafeteria, and his office. She commented that to her it certainly spoke of a military mind.

The General agreed and reiterated that he would have his people examine all those assigned to the Fold compound. He said he now felt certain that he had a spy in his command.

Lacy said that she had what she needed and that she would share her plan with him when she had it detailed. She planned to seek out the spy or spies and would include all personnel at the compound.

Bram thanked both of them for being thorough and for looking out for his wellbeing as well as for everyone at the Fold compound.

Lacy stopped and said she had almost forgotten to share an important announcement that she wanted to share with him first.

She smiled and said that she had accepted the proposal of marriage.

Bram congratulated her and then asked when she had found time for romance let alone snagging a husband.

Lacy said that on one of her many trips she had met him at a boring evening dinner hosted by John Morgan, NASA's director. Jeffery had introduced her to one of his organization's lawyers and financial advisor. His name is Raymond Daedlus. So, if I hyphenate my last name, my initials will be LSD.

Bram laughed and said that it was great news and having LSD around always brightened his day.

The General congratulated Lacy and then said it was time for him to get busy and get the people back at headquarters to check out the Marines assigned to him. He made the point that someone back at headquarters would contact her.

He would deliver the spy to her if there was one assigned to him.

Bram walked out with them to Linda's desk. The extra Marine guards were already in position. He asked Bob and Thomas who had the protection assignment for the day to come into his office.

Bob commented that the General had let them know about the additional added protection.

Bram shared the protection changes and that he had asked Lacy to breakfast on Sunday to explain in detail all of the structural changes to the house.

He then said that it was lunch time and that he was not sure how security was going to be managed but they should do the usual and let the Marine contingent do as they were ordered to do.

Bram Nielson Collection

Linda asked if he wanted Sunday's breakfast catered and that her family was eager to do it so they could all enjoy Lacy's good fortune. She shared that Lacy's partner to be, would be part of the breakfast and if they had dinner catered they would be there as well. She figured that lunch should be by the pool area and as relaxing as possible.

Bram said that he looked forward to a calm, relaxing Sunday where the Stetson family members pampered him. He asked if Lacy's partner to be had all the right clearances to attend.

Linda said she would make sure and let him know tomorrow.

The next morning Bram was surprised that Orlando was at the kitchen table having coffee.

Orlando let him know that the General had requested that he stay until the new protection protocol could be implemented and the internal spies apprehended.

Bram commented on his use of multiple spies.

Orlando replied that the General thought there was a Marine spy and Lacy thought there was as spy on the Fold civilian side.

He volunteered that he had enrolled all of the Marines that he trusted and had been with him long before there was a Fold effort to help find the Marine traitor. He said he had to get them to pledge that they would not injure or kill him but turn him over to him or to the General.

Bram thanked Orlando for staying and that he looked forward to his ditties.

Orlando said that he had a simple one for this morning's jog in. He commented that the jog would be on a new route and would be a little longer.

Bram put his cup into the sink and said it was time to get to work.

Pat had been listening to the exchange and also thanked Orlando. She commented that she had been worried about jogging into work, but she knew Bram used it to get ready to dive into the depths of his mind. Having alternate routes was important but having extra marine guards made it feel safe.

Orlando let her know that he had personally selected the additional Marines who he had been in battle with and who he trusted to have his back.

Ron Mueller

Chapter 18: Discovered

The increased security was noticeable to Bram. Two additional Marines were in front and two brought up the rear. The ditty singing seemed to have been augmented and it resounded across the terrain.

Bram now looked directly out of his office windows and had a great view of the river to his left and the Dalles power plant to his right. The distant snow-covered peak of Mt Adam's was at the center of his view. He thought the new office arrangement was better than the previous one.

The privacy bullet proof wall was installed and comfortable chairs where his two FBI bodyguards sat positioned facing the door.

He asked that they move the chairs to his side of the wall and face into the room. He felt uneasy having them in a position that would be deadly should a rocket grenade be used to blow in the door.

The bookcase and the refreshment area remained unchanged.

Given that he had no choice, he felt relieved that he liked the outcome.

The modification and security changes at the house was happening at a rapid pace. Work began when Bram left for work, and it stopped when he returned. The safe room was the first change to get put in. Then work went up through the house.

By the weekend, the two-person elevator from the basement to the bedroom was complete. The additional armor for the walls was next and was scheduled to be completed the following week. The remainder of the modification would take several more weeks.

The work was all being done by military personnel in a very disciplined manner focused on minimal living disruption.

Bram appreciated the attempt to minimize his personal life.

The office layout in the basement was almost a duplicate of the one on the first floor, but it was a little more spacious and it was built inside what could only be described as a huge vault.

He asked Pat to manage the basement office construction to meet her standards. She had more lights put in and made sure the ventilation was quiet.

Moving their books and drawings to the basement was done by a group of Marines that were supervised by Castor.

The location for the catered meals on Sunday was changed from the house to the community recreation center. The changes to the kitchen and dining areas were being done over the weekend and into the beginning of the following week.

Bram and everyone else in the house would take the following weeks meals at the main cafeteria while the kitchen and dining area was modified.

Bram asked his FBI body guards to be the reviewers and approvers of the kitchen area changes.

He focused his effort on developing the hardware that needed to be developed to create the ability to send Fold based messages.

By Sunday he felt that he and Remi were close to having a prototype that could be used to send a simple message. They were going to send a bubble to the far side of the moon and send it a message. It would then transmit it back using conventional technology.

Generating the message required the bulk of the power and the return signal was similar to the light that a mirror reflected and required just a fraction of the power.

He was aware that Lacy and the General had spent the week focused on identifying the spies. He planned to ask about their progress after Sunday's breakfast.

Linda had shielded Bram at work from the contractors by having him use the Viewing Room to get him away from the construction noise in his office.

Bram spent most of his time working with Remi in the Lab building the prototype Fold message transmitter. They came to the realization that they were creating a dramatically miniaturized version of the bubbles. These miniatures were being sent out in something similar to morse code.

It changed Bram's perception of folding the bubbles across the distances that they had done so far. It was like sending out one letter of the alphabet and then bringing it back. The Fold message transmitter was a machine gun version of Folding one bubble. The bubbles were the neutrinos, millions of times smaller, than a Fold bubble with humans or equipment, but in reality, it was just still a physical bubble that got Folded. When the machine gun was modulated to give it dit, dot and dash capability a rapid-fire Fold message could be created.

Designing the control system to enable creating a comprehensive Fold message using the Alien alphabet was a task that Bram was currently in the middle of.

He asked Erica to get the most powerful computer that was available as rapidly as possible. He stated that timing was critical, and that cost was secondary and of a much lower concern.

Meanwhile he had worked out a way to utilize a half a dozen top end desk top computers, but he needed something close to a supercomputer to have the control speed that would allow faster coding.

He and Remi had celebrated their success, at rapidly building the prototype, with a glass of wine. They were both looking forward to sharing their progress with everyone at the Sunday breakfast.

Lacy was having the opposite result. She had slogged through the records of all the folks working on the Fold project. She did a quick once over of all the records, but nothing popped up. There were no obvious spy standouts, and she had not expected there to be any, but the review got her oriented for the more detailed examination.

She then organized her small team of three people that she had personally scrutinized and vetted and assigned them to go into the details of each individual.

She had worked with Erica to arrange CIA and NEC support for her team as they delved into each individual being investigating. She asked Erica to stress the need for speed in finding the spy.

Personal phone use was a more difficult issue, and she learned that when she narrowed her spy list to just a few people. She asked the NEC if they would be able to get the phone logs and know what was being said.

She personally reviewed all the outgoing e-mail messages and noted the message recipients.

By the end of the week, she was down to three potential spy candidates, but she was not confident that any of the three was the spy.

She was frustrated and emotionally on a low as she left work for the weekend.

She shared her frustration with Linda, who said that she was sure that if she shared her progress on Sunday that someone would give her a nugget that would help her identify the spy.

During the same time, the General had each of the Marines assigned to the Fold project scrutinized by the specialists at the Pentagon. He concluded that the person that was identified had not been very smart about covering his tracks. It turned out his assignments had included being a guard at events where the two Wheels were located as well as being a gate guard and a perimeter guard.

The General thanked the Pentagon personnel for their quick response and asked them to trace all communications that the Marine had and who he had contacted. He said he was more interested to learn who else might be involved.

The General went into the weekend with the feeling of anticipation about who the Marine was working with. He was now sure that the direct hit of Wheel one was due to coordinates that the Marine had shared with someone on the outside. He expected to find another Marine, most likely higher in rank and somehow connected with the people that had attacked the Fold compound. He figured the next one up the ladder would not be the one that would have connections to the right civilian groups.

He was sure the Marine on the base was just the spotter and that someone higher up was a pure traitor.

Linda had observed each of the close team members and knew that the attack had affected all of them. Until the moment of the attack, she had felt that she was working in the most secure place possible. The ability for a major attack to be mounted against the heavily guarded compound surprised her.

She was surprised by everyone's unique response.

Bram seemed to brush it off and then dig deeper into the current technical problem.

Pat became more involved in the details of providing Bram security.

Lacy had enlisted her as she worked around the clock digging through people's personal lives trying to find the internal spy. And she knew that Lacy was very frustrated by not making any headway.

The General became invisible but when she saw him in the cafeteria it was clear to her that he had made progress.

The security changes for Bram's office became her primary focus and she pushed the architect and the contractors on getting the changes done rapidly. She had insisted that the work went on twenty-four seven so that Bram could settle into his office and concentrate on his project.

She was glad that Bram was spending his time in the Lab with Remi. It let her deal with the work in the office.

She went into the weekend looking forward to spending time with her parents as they catered the meals for the entire weekend. She had made that arrangement when Pat had shared the condition of the modifications that was going on at her home.

Bram was surprised when Rita Stetson greeted him for breakfast on Saturday morning and served him his normal two soft boiled eggs, sausage, toast, and a cup of coffee.

He recalled that Pat had mentioned it to him the previous evening, but he had not paid attention. He looked back into the kitchen and realized that it was all being rearranged and was not useable.

He asked about Ted and Rita said that he was out in the truck doing the cooking but planned to come in to say good morning and to see what Bram wanted for lunch and dinner.

Bram really did not have anything special in mind. He asked Pat what she had in mind.

Pat said that she wanted to keep the meals light and save herself for the meals the next day. She thought that at lunch a mixed salad with Salmon would be great and for dinner a small steak with mashed potatoes and steamed broccoli would be fine. She added that apple pie with ice cream would make a great desert.

Bram said he would take the same.

Orlando came in with Mallica and said that rumor had it that breakfast was free, and he had come to collect.

Bram chuckled and replied that the price had just doubled.

Orlando then said that Zuri had come home for the weekend and would be joining everyone on Sunday.

She wanted to show off her new wheelchair and had suggested they all take a walk after lunch.

Bram said that he was happy that she had come home and was looking forward to the walk. He asked Orlando about security for the walk.

Orlando replied that security was in place twenty-four seven and his guards would enjoy the walk as much as anyone. He made the point that sitting and waiting was the really boring part of a security detail.

Bram replied that he was used to having his security firing their weapons as the bad guys tried to get him.

Orlando continued the banter by saying that the battles only happened when the fish learned that he was fishing and notified the bad guys to take out the smart guy with the hook in the water.

Linda had come in with breakfast for Orlando and Mallica and burst out laughing as she took in the banter.

She added that they had it wrong and that the bad guys only attacked because they had not been invited to feast on the Stetson catered meal.

She continued by pointing at Bram and saying that she had witnessed him fighting the bad guys off to save the last piece of desert for himself.

Rita chuckled and added that now she knew why her two daughters had chosen to live at the compound versus staying at home. They had both caught the Bram flue and had lost their minds.

She went on to say that she hoped that Lacy's choice of someone to be her husband was resilient enough to withstand the whirlwind social scene that he was getting himself into.

Bram asked whether Ray had yet arrived.

Linda replied that he was arriving that afternoon. Lacy was meeting him at the airport. She said that the General had insisted that Lacy be taken to the airport in one of the armored vans and that four Marines would provide security. Two would go with her to meet Ray at the luggage area and would be in their parade uniforms but armed. Two would stay with the van and pick everyone up at curb side.

Bram nodded and said that he was pleased that the General had done that.

Orlando added that the General had issued a standing order that the people that he had listed would always have a security detail when leaving the Fold area.

He looked at Bram and said that the General would have assigned a tank to be part of that order for him but said that the highways in the area couldn't take the pounding. As it was Bram's protection was twice that of everyone else and it included a helicopter gunship overhead.

Bram said he would talk with the General about his protection. He said that so far all he needed were two top notch Marine's that knew how to shoot.

Orlando laughed and asked where he was keeping those two Marines.

Bram replied that one of them was mooching a free breakfast off of him and the other was likely sleeping while on guard duty outside the house.

Rita looked at Pat and asked if the back and forth ever stopped.

Pat replied that only when the two of them were not in the same room.

The highlight of the day was the walk with Zuri. It was clear to Pat that Zuri had already begun to grow socially and to have increased confidence in her own mobility.

Zuri put on a show of how she could manipulate her powered wheelchair and commented that it went faster than most bike riders.

She looked around and said that it was hard to see around Orlando and past all the Marine and other bodyguards. She said that she had been asked to interview two more Marine's that were being assigned to guard her.

Orlando agreed and said that the ones she was interviewing were so she would have time to tutor him and help him get his BS degree.

Zuri chuckled and said that he already had all the BS that he needed, anymore and he would earn a Master's in BS.

Bram agreed that there were too many guards, and he turned to show the back of his shirt that had a target with a red bullseye that said, "This is the Spot." He then took out the hat he had been carrying in his back pocket and put it on and bowed to Zuri so she could see the target on the Flat top.

Zuri broke down laughing. She said that now it was clear why so many guards were needed.

Bram enjoyed seeing Zuri with such a cheerful outlook.

He noticed that Linda had tears in her eyes and knew that she felt the same. Linda had been her nurse and had nurtured Zuri's intellect for more than a year and had constantly pushed to have Zuri evaluated to see if she was the genius that Linda had thought she was.

The walk ended at the recreation center, and everyone picked out what they wanted to do for the rest of the day.

Bram relaxed and watched as Orlando played ping pong with Zuri.

Mallica commented that seeing a macho Marine like Orlando be such a great companion to Zuri made her want to have kids that he could raise.

Bram asked when that would happen.

Mallica replied that it would happen as soon as he quit working her so hard.

Bram knew that Mallica had taken up learning how to write in the Alien language. It was a rather intense effort that he understood because she was constantly reviewing her progress with him. He in turn was learning the language with her. He figured that the two of them would be able to send back a reply that was written in Alienese.

He said that she better pick a different criteria because he was sure she would do her work so well that the reward would be to do even more of it.

The next morning, Zoe intercepted Bram as he was getting ready to go down to the recreation center for breakfast. She handed him a cup of coffee and let him know that they would go down to the recreation center for breakfast as soon as the bodyguard contingent was ready.

Pat gave Bram a good morning hug and asked what he was in a hurry about.

Bram replied that he had dreamed the solution of how to optimize the hardware and wanted to discuss it with Remi.

Pat chuckled and said that she was sure Remi was not going to be waiting for him at the recreation center.

Bram nodded and sat down at the table and waited for everyone to gather and be ready to go down to get breakfast. He decided that a chat with Ted about another fishing trip was what he would do until everyone arrived for breakfast.

He was looking forward to hear from both Lacy and the General on how their spy search was going.

He hoped that Erica had found the computer he wanted.

A few moments later he was being escorted to the Rec center by his small army.

Pat accepted her breakfast order and was slowly working her way through her three pancakes smothered in maple syrup with two over easy eggs on top.

She had been surprised that Bram had asked for the same but chose strawberry preserve to smother his pancakes with.

It was clear to her that he was controlling himself and that he was watching Lacy, the General and Erica.

She noted that Orlando was sitting on one side of Zuri and Linda was sitting on the other side. Mallica, Nuro and Jina were sitting on the other side of the table.

Lacy was sitting with Raymond, her husband to be. Luke and Cedric were at their table.

Rita and Marial were doing the serving and Ted was overseeing the cooking.

The General, Erica, Remi and Lori were sitting at a table that was almost in the center of the breakfast party.

Marcus and his family were at a table of their own.

The conversation was lively, and it was clear that it was not about work.

Linda had watched the breakfast activity and when it was clear that everyone was sipping their beverage, she said that Bram would like to have everyone take a moment to share how their week had gone.

She looked at Bram and asked him to take over.

Bram thanked her.

He looked over to Lacy's table and said that he was pleased to introduce Raymond Daedlus. A person of pure talent and intellect who Lacy said she had decided to wed in hopes that he would guide the Fold organization in solving the paradigmatic challenge in sending a reply to the Aliens.

He waited until the applause subsided and then he said that he was going to ask for updates from three persons but before calling on them he was going to give them the responses that he felt they should be sharing with the group.

He pointed to Erica and said. "Erica is going to share with us how she found and redirected a supercomputer to be delivered to the Fold project in the coming week. I can confidently say that because I am proof that nothing stops Erica when she is on a quest."

He then Pointed at the General and said, "The General has identified his man, but he is not satisfied with a foot soldier but is hunting the big cheese. He will keep the little guy on the hook until the big, mouthed bass strikes and then the General will reel them both in."

He then pointed to Lacy and said that she was struggling to find the person she was after. She was down to just two, but he suspected that neither of them was the person she sought. He said that because he knew the person who she was seeking. He knew who the spy was.

He then said that they should hear from each of the three in the reverse order that he had introduced them.

Lacy stood up and said that Bram should just tell her who the spy was because the two people that she currently had on the list did not seem to meet the criteria. One was financially draining all his savings to bailout his son from a gambling debt and the other had bought a pleasure yacht that turned into a hole to pour all his money into, and he was now on the verge of having it repossessed. She said that they were both going to get counseling, and they would either change their ways or they would lose their jobs. She looked at Bram and told him that she had no clue as to who the internal spy might be.

Bram thanked her for her update. He volunteered that he would like to get involved with the person who was trying to bail out his son and that he would see if he and Erica could be of help.

He then shared that his mind had been relentless at going through every meeting, every trip to the cafeteria, and every meeting in search of a recurring person who didn't seem out of place but who was always present in an inconspicuous way.

He was relieved when he finally found that person because it freed his mind from what had become cumbrous to manage and was eating too much of his time.

He said he would give her the name and she should check out that person's communication and finances. She might be able to tap into the General's connection and get help as well.

He just wanted to make sure that she did not send out her gunship bubble to take the spy out.

He said he would give her the name when the two of them got a private moment.

He then looked at the General and asked how close his guess had been.

The General smiled and said that he was indeed using the Marine spy as fish bait. There was no way for that person to get away but what he was after were the contacts that he expected to find up the chain of command. He shared that he was after a big catch and the bait would stay on the hook as long as he served a purpose.

He looked at Lacy and said he would be glad to help in checking out her bait fish and that they should see who that person was linked to.

Bram thanked the General and then looked at Erica and asked her to share the good news and let them know who she had alienated in repurposing their computer to the Fold program.

Erica stood up and said that Bram had hit the bull's eye. She had a team at NASA that had tried to stop her from the repurposing of their supercomputer. They had tried to use their connections to stop her but had found that her connections went higher than theirs.

She was sure she was the least popular person on their do not like list, but the computer would physically arrive during the following week and be installed at the Fold's computer center and would be ready the following week.

She said that she had learned long ago to support Bram or get out of his way. She had decided then to become his ice breaker and open the path he needed to be opened.

Bram thanked Erica and said that he was now on the hook to work out the kinks in his Fold Message transmitter system so he would be ready when the computer was ready.

He then shared that he and Remi were working kinks out of the hardware that would be controlled by the supercomputer. The goal was to make the hardware respond at the speed of a supercomputer.

They would then be able to compose the content of the messages and Fold them. He pointed out that to be able to achieve that speed the hardware had to be designed with no physically moving parts.

Pat said that breakfast was over, and she needed to enjoy her tea and just socialize. It was time to end the business part of breakfast and get on with the fun part.

Bram sat down and thanked her for stopping him from going any deeper into what he was doing.

Ron Mueller

<u>Chapter 19: Whisper</u>

When Bram came in, Lacy was chatting with Linda. He knew that she wanted to know who the civilian spy was and how he knew who it was. He asked for five minutes before they met.

He went in followed by Zoe and Eric. They sat down in the two chairs located behind the bullet proof shield and he took his seat in his desk that had been rotated ninety degrees and faced the windows. He invited them to help themselves to whatever snacks they would like as he poured himself a cup of coffee.

He had learned to accept his close in bodyguards and now he had two additional marine guards out by Linda's desk.

He had been surprised to learn that his office was ready. It had been re-arranged and painted. It smelled like a new office. He would have to tell the General that his construction crew had done a marvelous job.

He buzzed Linda and said he was ready for Lacy and Pat.

Pat had stayed with Lacy because Bram had asked her to. He said she would understand when he explained what he had in mind.

Pat helped herself to a cup of coffee and then sat down. She knew that Bram had identified the internal spy and that he had a plan on how to find out who external to the Fold compound they were sending their information to.

Lacy grabbed a bottle of water from the small frig and then sat down in the chair next to Pat. She then looked at Bram, as she twisted the cap off the bottle, and asked how he knew who the civilian spy was.

Bram said that he had gone through all the scenes of group gatherings for the last few months and had identified the individual in most of them or who might be within hearing range. He said that it was a picture search like 'Where is Waldo? Only the question was "Who is the spy? And who is her master."

Lacy said that she knew he had photographic memory, but she had not realized that he could play it back like a movie.

Bram chuckled and said that the memories did not reel out in a linear fashion, but it was more random, that is why it had taken him so long and each scene was triggered by something in the previous scene.

Zoe asked if he could count how many times, she had tweaked his nose.

He said that of course he could, and he smiled and said he was instead going to spend his time and focus on how he would get even with her.

He then nodded to Lacy and said that the spy was a woman. Her name was Cynthia Norris a member in the IT department.

Lacy said that she had reviewed her record and there was nothing on record to connect her. Her bank account seemed balanced with her pay and her meager spending. There did not seem to be any outside bank accounts nor were there many private messages.

Bram said that made her a perfect spy. He suggested that Lacy expand the check to the accounts of other family members and other close friends. He was sure that she could get help from the FBI or DEA.

He went on to suggest that they concentrate on finding out to whom she was sending information.

Lacy asked what he had in mind.

He looked at Pat and smiled and told Lacy that she and Pat were going to go to the cafeteria for lunch and share a secret that if it was true, would-be worth billions of dollars. It would be significant enough to cause their spy to contact the person she was sending information to.

Pat is going to tell you in a voice just loud enough for Cynthia to hear that the Fold process when run backwards will decrease the age of the person who is in the Fold vehicle and that I am in the process of calibrating it so that a person would spend a few moments going backward in time and when that person stepped out of the Fold vehicle, they would be years younger than when they entered it.

Lacy laughed and said that was a great idea. She then asked if by any chance it was close to being true.

Bram shook his head and said that so far time seemed to be a one direction occurrence. He was going to play with a negative Fold in the near future and if he found that time acted differently, she could be a guinea pig.

Lacy said that she could easily get a real pig for him to use before she went out.

Linda buzzed in to let them know that time was up, and Remi had arrived.

Bram looked at Pat and Lacy and said they should make the leak as real as they could.

As they walked out, Pat said that she thought they could enhance the lunch scene by having Erica participate. She led the way to Erica's office to share the plan with her. Pat asked her to come into the cafeteria on cue so that the leak could happen twice.

She would first tell Lacy about Bram's discovery and then Erica could enter, and Pat would share the breakthrough again.

Pat said that she normally had lunch at twelve sharp and that she would go in by herself and then Lacy would join her.

The hour hand on the walk clock seemed to be stuck but the hand finally clicked over to twelve. Pat left the lab and headed for the cafeteria.

After selecting a large salad and a large, iced tea, she sat down at her usual table.

A moment later Lacy walked in and walked over to her table and asked if she could join her.

As if by magic, Cynthia walked in a moment later, got her food and sat a table away.

Lacy asked if it was true about the discovery that Bram had made.

Pat replied that she was really excited about the fact that he had found a way to turn back time. He had sent out a mouse and it had returned back as a pink baby mouse.

She said he was in the process of calibrating how to turn back time in a controlled fashion.

Erica came over with her tray and joined them.

Lacy asked if she had heard about Bram's latest breakthrough.

Erica replied that she had heard it had something to do with time.

Pat replied that it indeed had to do with time. She then repeated the line about calibrating the process of reducing a person's age.

The rest of the lunch time was talking about the great dinner they all had enjoyed out at pool side.

When Cynthia left, Lacy said that she was going to get with her team who would be monitoring Cynthia's out going connections. The DEA was handling phone calls and text messages, and her team was monitoring the internet.

The internet connection was a surprise. It was a simple message to the Assistant Director of NASA! It said "breakthrough."

A few moments later a reply came through that said it was time for a progress review and Cynthia should come to NASA headquarters by Friday.

Lacy asked Linda to let Bram know that he had picked the right person and that she needed him to contact John Morgan, the director of NASA.

Bram asked Lacy to step into his office. Once he had learned who Cynthia was connected to, he said that he would make the call immediately and that she should plan to be at Cape Canaveral when the arrest was made and press the charge of spying.

John and he were well acquainted, and his call went through immediately. Bram made sure that John was alone and in his office. He then asked John to call on a secure line other than the one he normally used.

A few moments later John called back and said that he had gone several offices away to one of his security folks. He was alone and really curious about the desire to use a different line.

Bram explained about the information leaks at the Fold site and that one of the leaks went straight to the NASA Assistant Director. He said that the internal spy was a NASA junior employee who was coming with a message for the Assistant Director at his request and would be there for a Friday meeting.

He asked that a warrant be arranged that put the Assistant Director under arrest. He let John know that Lacy Stetson would be arriving the next day and would be there to assist in the arrest of the person traveling there from the Oregon Fold site.

John commented that he had heard about the attack on the compound and wondered if any of the NASA personnel had been involved in making that happen.

Bram replied that at the moment neither seemed to have a direct link to the attack but once they were in custody they would be questioned to see if there was some sort of indirect link.

John said he would be very surprised if his Assistant Director had links to an attack on the Fold site.

Bram replied that he would not be surprised because he was still looking for the source of the leak that had exposed the fact that the two wheels were in a hangar in the Seattle area and had almost caused a catastrophe that still haunted him.

John replied that he had not thought about that incident recently and if it were true then he had a major problem.

Bram replied that he had a major problem, and he should be looking at who would fill the Assistant Director role.

After Bram had hung up, he looked at Lacy and suggested that she take a little extra time in Florida. He suggested that maybe Jefferey, Raymond's boss would give him a few days off for him to join her.

Lacy smiled and said that she was going to call Jefferey and ask for that favor.

Remi had been sipping on a diet drink and had listened to the entire exchange as had Zoe and Eric.

He commented that life around Bram was better than being in a spy thriller movie that was full of gun battles, secret intrigues, unfounded love affairs and unforeseen twists. He said that around Bram all of it was real and not make believe and much more frightening.

Bram nodded and said that all he had ever wanted to do was to invent stuff and had never thought about how bad people around him would react to the good stuff he discovered and invented.

He looked at Remi and said that they needed to finish testing their current version of the Fold message transmitter and then get one designed to work with the supercomputer that Erica had reappropriated for them.

Zoe looked at Remi and said that Bram was able to move from being shot at, to shooting someone, to translating Alien and then working on the Fold equation all within a heartbeat.

She laughed and said he had even kept track of how many times she had tweaked his nose when he was in one of his deep trances.

Bram loved the exchange. It kept him from getting lost in his mind. He now needed to focus on how to modify the magnetron so that he could modulate it at the speed that the supercomputer operated.

He looked down at the picture of the Milky Way that was under the glass that covered his desk. It was his inspiration picture. He knew instinctively that he had to modulate the magnetron with a laser pulse that would hit a spiraled wall and generate different length pulses as it went along the spiral. Its curvature would be the curvature of a spiral galaxy. The different pulses generated by the laser bending as it moved to different points on the spiral could then be matched to the Alien alphabet.

He looked at Zoe and thanked her for having solved his problem and that he would go easy on the revenge that he figured out for her nose tweaking.

He then said that he was going to introduce them to Einstein with whom he always reviewed his finds and of whom he always asked for additional help in making improvements.

He walked to his bookcase and moved a set of books aside and got Einstein and brought him to his desk where he gave him a small piece of cookie.

He introduced each of them to Einstein and then shared his spiraled magnetron design concept with him.

He asked him what the spiral should be and then asked Remi to write down what Einstein agreed to.

He then asked Einstein if the spiral should be the Fibonacci sequence that starts with a zero, followed by a one, then by another one, and then by a series of steadily increasing numbers that followed the rule that each number is equal to the sum of the preceding two numbers.

He pointed at Einstein as his head nodded up and down and said that he had gotten positive confirmation.

He then asked if the laser should move one electron distance along the spiral to generate each unique magnetron pulse.

Once again Einstein seemed to nod in the affirmative.

He then asked if the laser power level should be increased to generate stronger pulses that could be differentiated from each other.

This time it was clear that Einstein was shaking his head in a negative response.

Bram stopped and thought for a minute and said that he agreed with him.

Then he asked if the laser beam frequency should be changed to enable additional signal generation.

Again, Einstein shook his head in the negative.

Bram then asked if the length of the spiral should be increased to make it possible to have all the signaling capability that might be required.

This time Einstein shook his head in the affirmative.

Bram looked at Remi and asked him if he had gotten it all down.

Remi nodded and said that it was hard for him to believe that Bram was using a mouse to make decisions about designs of the Fold Messaging system.

Bram chuckled and said that Einstein's batting average was one thousand and had been in the game from the earliest moment when the two met out on the desert on Einstein's boulder home.

Zoe asked how old that made Einstein.

Bram handed Einstein to her and asked her how old she though he was.

Zoe said that Einstein looked too young to have been around in the desert since that was more than four years ago.

Bram nodded and said that he had noticed the same thing about Einstein and the fact that Einstein seemed to be the same age as when the two first met on the boulder in the desert.

He said that he thought the Fold experience seemed to rejuvenate the animal that experienced the Fold. It did not necessarily turn back time, but it seemed to fix cell damage. So, his story about turning back time was not what the Fold process did but he was almost sure that it made the living entity experiencing it a healthier one.

Zoe looked at Eric and said that she now believed him when he had shared the fact that he had gone out feeling like he was coming down with a cold but when he got back, he felt great.

Bram nodded and said that he was going to set up a series of tests to verify that side effect of a Fold experience.

He then said that he wanted to keep Einstein's participation a secret. He said he did not want some mouser hunting Einstein down.

Zoe nodded and said that it would be hard to convince the FBI to assign mouse guards.

Remi said that if what he had written down that Einstein had agreed to worked, he would come in and stand guard of the genius mouse named after a genius.

Bram put Einstein back and said that it was about time that he took Einstein for a visit to his boulder in his desert home.

Linda called in and said that the supercomputer had arrived and was being set up in the computer lab.

He suggested they go to see what size a supercomputer was now days.

He was pleasantly surprised when Linh and Duong greeted them and led them to an area that was separated from all the other areas. They pointed to where technicians were connecting the computer to power and to the site internal internet.

The computer was about the size of Bram's office refrigerator. It was smaller than he had expected. Linh explained that they would be ready to program the computer that afternoon. She let him know that they would come to his office and connect his personal computer to the supercomputer so he would be able to operate it from wherever he happened to be.

Bram said that he would like Remi to also have access, and he wanted access in the short term to be limited to just the two of them. He also wanted to make sure that only his Fold translation program was allowed to run on the supercomputer.

Duong commented that made the job of getting the computer online rather easy. He pointed out that it could do much more.

Bram said that he understood that it could, but until he had mastered getting the Fold Message Transmitter operational and working smoothly, he did not want the computer doing anything else.

Remi asked what Bram expected him to do with his access.

Bram replied that the two of them were going to pretend to be Marconi and Tesla and send messages to each other. They would test the new Magnetron that they would have the machinists make that afternoon. They would power up the magnetron with their current power sources and use their current transmitters.

Once they were sure everything worked, they would have a transmission bubble created that could be positioned close to the Alien galaxy.

He wanted to be able to transmit the Fold message to the bubble and then have the bubble retransmit it to the Aliens.

He said that would ensure a two-level security shield for the location of the Earth.

Remi asked why Bram was thinking of the two-level security system.

Bram replied that he was just being cautious because the messages he would send out would continue to travel for millions of years through the Folded Space and there was no way to know what other civilization would receive the message. He wanted to make sure that Earth did not shout out, "Here we are come and get us."

He said that he wanted to quietly whisper, "Welcome we are friendly but fierce. We embrace intelligence and grace. We help those in need. May we all live in peace.'

Remi said, "Wow, I am working for the Fold Peace Whisperer."

Chapter 20: Money Connection

Bram suggested they try the supercomputer on how well it could break into very secure systems and not be detected.

Remi laughed and commented that he had just gotten the impression of a Saint and almost immediately he was working for a sinner willing to break security systems to evaluate his supercomputer.

Bram responded that Lacy was off to make sure that she arrested the Fold civilian spy that was going to meet with the person she was spying for. He wanted to check out that person, who was the NASA Assistant Director, to see if he had any growing offshore bank account and he wanted to check if he was communicating with any specific individual associated with the attack on the Fold compound. He figured they might as well put the supercomputer through its paces and see if they could use it to find out this kind of information.

Remi said that he didn't know how to write the code for a hacking routine that could break through the security systems that would yield such information.

Bram replied that he had obtained a basic hacking routines that would be on steroids when running on a supercomputer. He said that he hoped they would do.

They began by searching the cash inflows, on specific dates, of offshore banks. After an hour they hit paydirt. Shortly after, they had the assistant director's account detail, and it was clear that he was putting in a substantial sum every month. It seemed he was providing someone with a big account the information they were seeking.

Bram then had the computer track the source of the money transfer. It surprised him when the very company that had helped build Wheel's One and Two was the source. Someone was paying to get inside information about the Fold program.

Bram speculated that the Assistant Director was simply trying to make himself wealthy by sharing information about the Fold progress.

He would have Lacy find out who the person was that was paying the money and with whom they were interacting. He figured that that person might be the one connected with the attacks and was most likely also motivated by greed.

He then declared that he was satisfied with the supercomputer's capability, and it was time to program it to become a magnetron modulator that would enable a continuous signal generation.

He wanted it to be controlled by the person who was generating the message. This meant creating a storage buffer to hold the message in queue and then merge it with the magnetron signal to a transmit routine that controlled the position of the laser. The computer would then manipulate the laser that would shoot into the spiraled magnetron to generate the Fold based message.

Remi asked what he should do.

Bram said that he should call Linh and Duong into the computer room, and he would explain what code he wanted them to write that would do what he had just described.

Then they would go to the cafeteria for lunch and afterwards they would finalize the physical design of the magnetron and get it machined and have it and the laser synchronized. He projected that by the end of the week they would be very close to having a system that would work at the speed and the precision that would let them generate a reply to the Aliens.

Remi commented that now he understood Erica's comment that being around him was at times like standing calmly and watching a huge tsunami approaching and feeling the wind blow your hair straight back but not being able to run for cover.

Bram commented that she was exaggerating as he put in a call to Marcus and Mallica. He asked them to meet him the following morning at his office so he could bring them up to speed and get them prepared to generate the reply to the Aliens and to determine where in the universe the bubble relay transmitter would be located.

After dinner as he and Pat were sitting in their twin recliners, he asked her how she felt. He was thinking about the effect that a fold had on each living thing that experienced the Fold.

Pat replied that she felt great.

Bram asked her whether she had any chronic problems that had disappeared.

Pat looked at him and asked him what was up. What had he discovered about the Fold process? Did it actually make people younger?

Bram replied that the fact that Einstein had remained healthy and seemingly looked like he did when the two of them had met in the desert had made him realize that the Fold process did have a positive effect on a living animal. He thought it might be more along the lines of curing or fixing the problems that a body might have. If that was the case the Fold process would be almost as coveted as if it reversed aging.

Pat said that she did not have any chronic problems, so she was not a good sample of the Fold effect.

Bram said that they would have to set up a series of experiments to determine the longer-term effects on humans.

Pat suggested that they start out with some damaged fruit and vegetables and see what happened. She volunteered to set up that investigation.

She said they could utilize the cats and dogs that various people owned and then bring in some pigs that had some sort of specific problem.

Bram thanked her for volunteering.

Zoe, who had been quietly listening to the exchange said that she would volunteer to go after the pigs. She said that she had a scar on the back of her leg from a childhood bike accident that she would love to have removed.

Pat asked to see it.

Zoe pulled down her knee-high sock to show the scar.

Pat walked over and knelt and ran her hand down the back of Zoe's calf and said that there was no scar. She asked if it was on the other leg.

Zoe pulled the other sock down. She ran her hand down each leg.

Pat stood up and smiled. She commented that she had her answer even before she started the actual verification of the effect of experiencing a Fold. She would take the disappearance of Zoe's scar as the initial proof that experiencing a Fold was very beneficial.

Eric commented that he had thought the appearance of a healthy big toe toenail had occurred because of the medicine that he had been putting on it but now he felt that his Fold experience was the most likely reason.

Bram suggested that Pat start by interviewing everyone that had experienced a Fold to see if there were additional bits of evidence before going into a full-scale series of experiments.

Pat made some notes to remind her to look for the Fold effect in external physically visible markers. She then put down a series of questions.

How about internal organs?

How about the mind?

How about bone structure? This question popped up when she thought of Zuri.

Bram Nielson Collection

She decided to engage Amy to help her. She wondered who else might want to be a third person.

Bram looked at what Pat had written on her pad.

He said that if her investigation worked on bone structure, he would personally get involved to see that Zuri took as many Fold trips as possible.

He had been considering her to participate in a Fold wormhole journey. Such a journey currently was based on a series of sequential Folds, and it would be good to know how such a journey would affect Zuri before letting her take it.

Pat instinctively knew that her experiments would be verification experiments, and she planned to execute the experiments as rapidly as possible. She knew instinctively that Bram was already designing the experiment for Zuri. She wanted to get there before he leaped frogged her.

Bram commented that he promised to wait until Pat had tested her pig, but he warned her that he was already dying to see Zuri walking defect free.

Pat said that she would go as fast as bubbles could Fold and return. She cautioned them that they should keep the conversation in the room a secret until she had done the confirmation tests.

Bram smiled and said that his nose got tweaked but no secrets had ever leaked out of his office.

The next day he and Remi worked with the senior machinist to get the magnetron internals formed to the specifications they had determined were needed. The machinist commented that he did not have the equipment to produce the magnetron to the accuracy that Bram wanted. He knew a Navy machine shop in San Diego that could. He went on to say that it would need to be made of the finest and hardest steel available and the magnetron would need to be in a temperature-controlled environment in order to maintain the accuracy Bram was asking for.

Bram asked him to take charge and make it happen.

The machinist, whose name Bram found out was Henry Wilkins, said he would contact the San Diego shop and see if they could expedite getting it made.

Bram said that would be great and he asked that Erica be involved because she was one person that could get it expedited.

At lunch he asked Pat how her experiments were going.

She said that she had gone through many of them and would do the pig the next day. The pig had been delivered and she had used a scalpel to make a cut along its front left leg. She said she had named the pig Zoe since Zoe had claimed to have a scar on her leg.

She let him know that she had recruited Linda who had volunteered that she had a burn scar from the exhaust of a motorcycle.

Bram laughed and said that he wanted his support back unharmed even if she still had her scar.

Pat replied that so far, his Fold equation had not done any living thing in.

Bram asked if turning plants into ash counted as doing a living thing in because he had done that.

Erica came over with her lunch tray and joined them. She looked to Bram and said that he had thrown her into the briar patch when he had the machinist engage her in expediting getting the magnetron machined as a priority. She had agreed to go to San Diego and be there at eight Monday morning to pick up the first of the six magnetrons she had ordered.

Bram looked at her in surprise and said that he had only requested one.

Erica laughed and said that she was aware of that but the smart-alecky officer in charge of the machinists said that specifying the material to use, "as the best material" was too general and that meant that there were about six materials that fit that description. So, she told him to make one out of each of the materials and send them up.

He said that he could not provide the transportation that was suitable to keep the magnetrons in a stable condition.

She went to Henry Wilkins and asked him to make the environmentally stable containers to transport the magnetrons.

She said she had arranged for two drivers to take them down in a comfortable conversion van. The General insisted that a lead van and a tail van would provide protection.

Bram shook his head and said he apologized and that he had only gotten her involved because she had come through with the supercomputer. He said that he would design an experiment to test each magnetron to see if the material made a significant difference.

After lunch, Bram said he was going to his office to make a call. He asked Remi to set up their message transmitter and to use the behind the moon coordinate and set up the receiver/repeater bubble.

Bram called the General and explained the situation. He asked him to contact someone in the Chain of Command in the Navy that would straighten out the Lieutenant in charge of the machine shop.

He let him know that Erica would arrive in a reasonable time. He pointed out that the drive down would take more than one day.

He then suggested that the Lieutenant extend an apology to Erica for his rude behavior.

The General said that he was well acquainted with the Base Commander and Erica would get an apology and she would travel down at a reasonable speed.

Bram thanked him and then let Linda know that he would spend the rest of the day in the Lab with Remi. He asked when Remi's office at the new lab building would be ready.

Linda said that the office was going to be ready on the following Tuesday, but the entire lab would not be done until the following week.

He then asked to see her burn scar on her leg.

She gave a little laugh and asked if Pat had mentioned that she had volunteered to be a guinea pig.

Bram said that indeed she had and that he had warned her to bring her back alive.

Linda said that if Pat killed the pig, she would decline being next.

Bram said that would be a wise choice.

He then asked Linda to contact Erica and let her know that the trip to San Diego would begin at eight Monday morning and the drive down and back should be done at a leisurely pace and that she

Should expect an apology from the Lieutenant in charge of the machine shop.

He then left for the Lab to meet with Remi for the rest of the day and then he would go home for the weekend.

The lab was busy. Remi had set up at the far end in an effort to stay out of the way of the bubbles that were getting launched and retrieved, examined, and then launched again. He noted that Pat was turning the experiments around in record time and that she was taking copious notes but was wearing a smile the entire time. He figured success was in the air and hoped it would extend to the experiment that he and Bram were about to try.

He felt a degree of tension that he had not expected. He thought about the Magnetrons that were getting machined in San Diego and knew if the experiment that they were about to conduct failed those magnetrons would most likely be worthless.

He watched as Bram entered the lab. For a moment the entire lab seemed to freeze and then, almost in the blink of the eye, it snapped back into action.

Bram Nielson Collection

Bram was surprised at the bustle that was taking place in the Lab. He noted the people stop when he entered but Pat had them all back in action almost immediately.

She whispered that he scared people as she walked by.

Bram wondered why he would scare anyone. He walked over to where Remi had set up the computer with the message program. He asked if the bubble was ready.

Remi said everything was a go and the two bubble handlers were ready to be taken to the launch stand.

Bram said, "let's do it."

As the bubble was taken from the Lab, Remi asked what the first message would be.

Bram said that it was a saying that he had learned in his high school typing class that used all the letters of the Alphabet, "The quick brow fox jumped over the lazy dog's back."

Remi said that his professor had taught him that at coding school when he had complained about being a poor typist. He had practiced that until he could do it at sixty words per minute.

Bram stepped back from the computer and said Remi should Fold the repeater bubble into location and send the message five times and then see what they got back.

The launch as always was anticlimactic.

After a couple of minutes, Remi sent the message out five times.

A split second later,

The quick brow fox jumped over the lazy dogs back.

The quick brow fox jumped over the lazy dogs back.

The quick brow fox jumped over the lazy dogs back.

The quick brow fox jumped over the lazy dogs back.

The quick brow fox jumped over the lazy dogs back.

Appeared on the computer screen.

Remi pumped his fist and yelled out, "Yes!" Which caused everyone in the lab to stop.

Bram shouted out, "Success."

The lab resounded with the sound of applause.

Bram then typed a message in Alien and sent it out five times.

It too came back five times.

Remi asked what the message said, and Bram chuckled and replied that it was the same message in Alien that he had sent out.

It turned out that both he and Pat had been successful with their experiments and that evening as they sat in their twin recliners, they shared a glass of their favorite wine.

Ron Mueller

Chapter 21: Magnetron Romance

Saturday Bram got a call from Erica asking if she could be at Sunday breakfast at his place. He knew she wanted to know how he had been able to change the timing for her to go to San Diego. He assured her that she was welcome.

At breakfast on Sunday, Bram explained that he had asked the General to make a call to someone high enough in base hierarchy to take the Lieutenant in charge of the machine shop to the carpet for his rude behavior. He had no idea who the General knew or had contacted.

Erica said she got a call from the base commander, a Navy Admiral who evidently was an old friend of the General saying that she should take her time traveling down to his base and that she would be cordially greeted.

Not long after a Navy Captain that said he was the Lieutenant's superior called her and said he had the Lieutenant on the line.

The Lieutenant apologized for his rudeness and said that he was pleased to be able to produce the magnetrons she had requested. They would be ready when she arrived.

The Navy Captain had then invited her and her team to dinner at the base officer's club. He had also recommended an upscale hotel at which he could arrange a room at her request.

Bram said that was a great ending to a poor start with the San Diego base.

Erica agreed and thanked him for having taken action.

Pat commented that the cycle of events at the Flow compound had also gone from the very bottom to the very top. She shared that every one of her experiments was verifying the fact that a Fold experience was a positive event for both plants and vertebrates. She shared the fact that the pig that was delivered was in perfect shape and did not have a single scar. She had one of the techs cut the pig on the right front shoulder and another cut behind his snout. She would send the pig out on Monday morning and if he came back with no scar, then Linda would take the next trip out.

Bram said he was anticipating Monday's successes and once that was certain he would contact Elizabeth to arrange to have Zuri spend the next week making a series of Folds and they would see if the process would make a difference for her.

Orlando commented that if it did, he would be glad to lose his job.

Bram said that he could accompany Zuri on each of her Folds and maybe it would work on him, and he would be able make it through college and get a degree. He looked around the table and asked if they had ever met a Marine Sergeant smart enough to get a degree without some sort of help?

Orlando laughed and said that he hoped to get smart enough to compete with Bram and create a better Fold process.

Zoe said that she hoped that the Fold process would help her go from flat to having some round bumps.

Bram figured he would change the subject and asked who wanted to take a nostalgic trip back to the boulder where he had sat many a day as he worked to create the equation.

Amy had wondered why Pat had invited her for breakfast and Bram had just unveiled the reason. She said that she was definitely in.

Pat said she was in because she wanted to see that boulder and sit on it at five in the morning. Perhaps it would inspire her to help her decide what she should do next.

Orlando said that he was in. He wanted to see the desert that had somehow inspired Bram's non-linear mind create the Fold equation.

Erica said that she probably should go but she was not planning to make the trip. She commented that she was not the person she had been at that time, and she did not want to relive that part of her life.

Bram added that none of them was the person of that time and that the light of that time was now billions of miles away on its way across the universe.

On Monday morning, Orlando was in the lead as they jogged to work. He started to chant a ditty and soon had them all chanting along.

> *Fold, Fold, Fold*
> > *It's not about growing old.*
> > > *It's about being bold.*
> *Fold, Fold, Fold*
> > *Take a person from the chair.*
> *Fold, Fold, Fold*
> > *Give her legs, give arms, give her hair,*
> *Fold, Fold, Fold,*
> > *Lift her, Lift her.*
> *Let's be bold.*
> > *Lift her, Lift her.*
> *Let's be bold.*

Once again, the entire compound echoed the ditty as the other Marines joined the chant.

Linda greeted him at the door and said that she had tears in her eyes as she heard the ditty.

Bram said that he too was touched and hoped that by the end of the day they were arranging to get Zuri back to Dalles so they could see if the Fold process would do what Orlando had so eloquently expressed.

Pat asked Linda to come with her to the lab so she could get ready. She said that they would send the pig out and depending on the condition the of the wounds they might send him out again until the scars disappeared.

Then Linda would be next and once again how many of the Fold cycles she would experience would depend on the condition of her scar.

Bram redirected his desire to be there when Linda returned and instead went to the IT department. He wanted to see if Linh and Duong had been able to make progress in creating the Fold Transmission control software and the queue buffer that would hold the message until it was time to transmit it.

Linh commented that they had worked over the weekend to create their first draft that they wanted to debug the code that day. She asked whether he had been able to create the hardware for the laser that would activate the signal in the magnetron and create the Fold transmission beam.

Bram said that he and Remi would be working throughout the day to upscale the design that they had successfully tested. He expected to have that model online the next day. He then expected to have the magnetron connected and tested in another day.

He suggested that on Friday morning they would send out their rebound bubble to test the entire system.

At eight am sharp, the van to take Erica to San Diego stopped at the front door of the apartment building. She had a small suitcase that she had decided to take when she found out that the trip would take more than one day.

She noted that the van that she was riding in was in the middle of two other black vans. She felt like a dignitary on tour.

She got in behind the passenger seat.

Henry was sitting on the left reclining bucket seat.

She noted that there were two marines in uniform in the front two seats and there was one sitting behind her.

She asked them their names and wrote them down so she could remember them.

The Marine in the passenger seat was a sergeant and the one in charge of the other Marines who were all privates. He explained that they had been ordered to do as she requested. He said that each of them in the van only carried their side arms. He then said that the two other vans had four Marines in full battle gear, and they carried additional firearms for the three of them. They did not anticipate any action, but they were prepared for almost any attack.

He pointed to the cooler and the five boxes on top of the cooler and said that Chef D'Carluca had sent breakfast sandwiches, coffee, and juice. He had filled the cooler with a variety of drinks and a mix of fruit.

The Sergeant relayed a message from the General that wished her a good trip.

She thanked him and said that she was looking forward to their trip and that he should look ahead for a good place to have lunch.

She asked if they could make San Francisco and spend the night there and then get an early start for San Diego and plan to arrive there in the early afternoon.

When the leader replied that it would be easy to arrange, Erica asked that he let folks know. She commented that the Navy brass in San Diego should get their schedule.

She then suggested that he be the one to select the mealtimes, stops and that he arrange the hotel stays at top-of-the-line hotels. It would be on her budget.

She grinned as she realized that the overall site budget was still in Bram's name. She had decided to leave it that way because his name seemed to open the bank every time they needed money.

The music varied between country western, to current pop artists and to jazz.

She fell asleep and only came awake when the Marine in front quietly let her know that they were at the California state line, and it was time for lunch.

During lunch, the Marine clarified that dinner would be in San Francisco and if she wanted to continue, they could continue as long as she desired.

She said that it would be good to make Long Beach so that on the following day they would get to San Diego in the late morning. She suggested spending one night in San Diego and then the following day heading back to Dallas.

The Marine said they would arrange a hotel at Long Beach where they could all stay.

They ordered a takeout for dinner and arrived in at the hotel in Long Beach as the evening turned into a dark night.

The evening was uneventful, and they were on the road early the next morning.

The rest of the trip was one of dozing, sleeping, and dozing some more.

She learned more about Henry and his family than she wanted to know.

She came wide awake when close to noon the following day they arrived at the Coronado Naval Base.

The guard greeted them and said that the Admiral was expecting them. He stepped back from the van and made a call and then after a "Yes Sir," he directed the driver to the Officer's mess where the Admiral was waiting to meet them.

Erica had not been expecting such a high-level reception. She was in one of her practical pant suits and was glad that it included a jacket that made it look more formal.

The Marine up front doing the driving commented that he had never escorted anyone that got received by an Admiral.

Erica replied that she had not expected to be met by an Admiral either.

The Admiral was standing at the front of the Officer's Club and had two additional officers with him.

He came down the steps and held his hand out for Erica and then after guiding her up the steps, he introduced her to a rather handsome, somewhat young-looking Naval Captain. She was told that he was in command of the department that was the home of the machinist department. He then introduced the Lieutenant that was in charge of the machinist department. He commented that the two of them had talked with each other before and he hoped that all fences had been mended.

Erica smiled; she knew that the Lieutenant was in trouble. She replied that everything had worked out very well and she was pleased to have made the trip to pick up the magnetrons that the Lieutenant's machinists had skillfully made.

She said that the help of the Admiral's people were providing would help make world history and they all should enjoy the moment. She asked that their names be engraved on the six magnetrons.

She commented that she was sure they would all end up at the Smithsonian or some other comparable museum and their grandchildren would be pointing to the names and letting people know that their grandfathers had made them.

The Admiral then apologized and said that he had to attend to a video conference with his Navy bosses at the Pentagon, but he was leaving her in the care of Captain Sooner who was to make sure that she would get a great lunch and then he would ensure that everything was ready for her return trip.

The Admiral saluted her and then turned and walked off. The Lieutenant did the same thing after letting her know that his staff would have the magnetrons ready to go when she requested them.

Erica thanked him and then turned her attention to the Captain.

The Captain asked when she was planning to start her return journey.

Erica replied that after lunch she would like to take a quick tour of the base before going to pick up the magnetrons. She said that her Marine escorts deserved a good night's rest before starting back and that she was thinking to leave in the morning.

Captain Sooner said that a full tour would take the rest of the day. He suggested that he have his aid make reservations at the hotel of her choice and that they plan to have dinner at the Officers Club and then he would drop her of at the hotel.

Then in the morning she could pick up the Magnetrons and start the trip back to Dallas.

Erica thanked him and let him know that her team had already made the hotel reservations.

She said that she would enjoy spending the afternoon touring and that dinner at the club sounded great.

Captain Sooner had taken an immediate liking to Erica. She was very good-looking and had great self-confidence. He was pleased with the response she had given to the Admiral. It had probably saved the Lieutenant's career. He felt that he had met the woman he had been looking for and the fact that she had come to him seemed to be a sign.

On being introduced, Erica had felt an immediate attraction she had not previously experienced when meeting other men. She checked the Captain's hand for the sign of a wedding ring and was glad to see none but before she went too far, she would make sure he was single. She had not expected to be going on a date but it was clear to her that the Captain had made arrangements so they could be alone and get to know each other better.

Bram Nielson Collection

Henry had watched the interaction between the two and knew that he was going to be a third wheel. He enjoyed the tour of the base. The Captains historical information about the base was very interesting. He learned that it had been opened up as a US Destroyer Base in 1922.

Then it was expanded during World War Two when it was it became the US Repair Base. Then after the war it became the Naval Station San Diego in 1946. It became the Naval Base San Diego in 1990, and it now provided for nearly a third of the Navy's Pacific assets. The Coronado Naval Amphibious base was added in 1943 by dredging channel to increase its dept to allow larger ships to us it as a home base.

When it came time for dinner at the Officer's club, Henry said that he preferred going to the hotel and having a few beers with the Marines that were guarding them.

He was not surprised to hear the Captain volunteer to bring Erica to the hotel after dinner.

During the dinner, the Captain asked if Erica would like to relax and enjoy the piano bar and have a glass of wine or any drink that she would like. He said that if she was so inclined, he looked forward to a dance with her.

Erica was more than happy to be asked. She said that a glass of wine would be great.

The wine was great, and the dancing became somewhat romantic.

When they got to the Captain's car, Erica surprised herself by putting her hand behind the Captain's head and pulling him to her and giving him a kiss.

She was surprised by her action and not sure what to expect.

The fact that he responded by pulling her to him sealed the deal.

She felt a shiver run up her back and took in the moment. She knew that she was hooked.

When they got to the Hotel, she invited him up to her room for a night cap.

What followed was intimate and took her to a Shangri-La that she had never experienced.

The next morning, she sat on the bedside and relived the love making that the two had enjoyed. She hoped that it would blossom into a full romance. She was sure he was the one for her. Now she would see if he felt the same about her.

He had left early saying he would see her off but had a morning meeting he could not miss.

On the way to pick up the magnetrons she kept thinking about the great day, the evening dinner and the intimate love making she had enjoyed at the Coronado Naval base.

The Lieutenant met her van. He was now very accommodating, and the magnetrons were placed in the rear van.

He thanked her for having saved his butt.

Erica smiled and said that a very dear friend had told her that she should treat others as she wished to be treated. That simple adage had changed her life.

She said he should try it.

She was disappointed that the Captain was not there to see her off. She was just ready to get into the van when Captain Sooner's car pulled up alongside.

The Captain got out of the car and said that he was glad that he had not missed her departure and asked if in the very near future she would reciprocate and give him a tour of the Dallas site.

Erica resisted giving him a kiss but smiled and said that she would be very happy to give him the tour and that she would have the Fold Chef at the Dallas site prepare the meal of his choice and later they could enjoy a drink and have dessert at her apartment.

She then got into van and the Captain gave her a salute and said he would call her and let her know when he was planning to come up.

Ron Mueller

Chapter 22: Exploration Plan

Bram welcomed Erica back when she delivered the six magnetrons. He had each environmentally controlled box put into the six places in the lab that had been prepared for them.

He commented that rumor had it that she got the apology that she deserved from the Lieutenant that had given her a hard time. He then asked how the date with the Lieutenant's boss had turned out. He smiled and said that rumor also had it that this boss was planning to come to the Fold compound for a tour of the facility.

Erica's face turned red in anger at the thought that she was being spied on flared in her mind. She asked who had been spying on her and reporting it to him.

Bram chuckled and said that the rumor came from the very top of the military organization. It went from Admiral to General to him faster than she was able to travel back to Dallas.

He said that the General had the excuse that he wanted to update getting the magnetrons on site, but it became clear that what he really wanted to do was to talk about the Captain who had gone out with the most amazing woman that the Captain had ever met.

Bram then smiled and said that it seemed that the Captain was a favorite of the Admiral who asked him how things had gone and if the issue of how the magnetrons were handled had been resolved. The Admiral shared that the Captain was smitten by the charming woman that had come to pick up the magnetrons.

Erica lightened up and said that indeed she too had been smitten and she was looking forward to hosting the Captain when he came to visit.

She said that she never knew that the top brass gossiped.

Bram replied that they only gossiped about romance and never about military intel.

He complemented her on a successful trip and that he looked forward to meeting the Captain and hosting the two of them for a Sunday breakfast.

Erica then asked what he was going to do with six magnetrons.

Bram explained that he would set up all six for an extended trial to see if the material they were made of made any significant difference in the accuracy and reliability.

He shared the fact that the less precise magnetron that had been made at the Fold machine shop had functioned very well and he was going to verify if his very stretching specifications were needed.

He wondered if the expensive materials were actually required. He figured that would only be important if the magnetron ever went into mass production.

He jokingly asked if she wanted to become the Magnetron Guru or was, she through with magnetrons. He made the point that her first round with them had produced something better than gold.

Erica thanked him for offering but she replied that she was going to concentrate on her more boring role of managing the civilian side of the Fold site.

Bram excused himself and said he had to get to Marcus's office to review the Fold Wormhole exploration plan.

He felt like he had neglected the Fold Wormhole effort, but he knew that Marcus had been focused on it. He was confident that the review would verify that all was well in that area.

Marcus was nervous about the review. He had sent out more than one hundred scout bubbles to as many solar systems looking for a water world. Nothing promising had surfaced. There were countless galaxies and solar systems but finding a planet that was in the orbit that would allow it to be warm enough to have a surface of nothing, but water was a daunting task.

Once he found such a world, he would have to make sure that it was water in which life could exist and not so acid or base that it would dissolve objects that were in the water.

He wondered how he could improve his search algorithm.

Bram sensed Marcus's nervousness. He jokingly asked if Marcus had found a world to which Earth could send its prisoners.

Marcus caught the reference to how the British had managed both their political and criminal prisoners by sending them to Australia. He nodded and said that in fact he had found plenty such worlds, but ones covered in water seemed to be in short supply.

Bram's approach immediately put him at ease.

Bram asked which direction in the universe Marcus had been looking.

Marcus said that he had used a spherical pattern around the Alien's solar system.

Bram asked what the ratio of water worlds to desert to ice worlds might be.

Marcus shook his head and said he would have no clue.

Bram said he had no clue either, but he figured planets similar to Earth and the Aliens total water world that were located in an orbit that kept the planet warm enough for life to flourish were rare.

He suggested looking elsewhere in some other part of the universe.

He suggested Marcus reach out to the two lead agencies for astronomical research in the United States, NASA, the National Science Foundation NSF, the Department of Energy (DOE) and the Department of Defense (DOD) and check if there were potential water worlds that had been discovered or there were galaxies that were suspected to have water worlds.

At a minimum he should look in the opposite direction for water worlds.

Marcus agreed and said he would reach out to all of the organizations that had been suggested and he knew of several others that he would add to the list.

He said that he was sending out the scouts in mass to cut the search time.

Bram wished Marcus good luck in his search and said that finding a water world was the current priority and being able to let the Aliens know that a new home had been found would be the icing on the cake when Earth contacted them.

Mallica and her team had been focused on the return message to the Aliens and learning their language. She found that the four members with Asian heritage were extremely helpful as she tried to learn the Alien language. The nature of that language seemed to be very musical. The team decided to listen to the vocalization of Earth's whales to get a sense of how the Aliens might sound since they would be communicating under water.

A synthesizer was added, and the message was adjusted and sounded much different than when humans vocalized the alphabet.

In her review with Bram, she was going to ask if he could play music with his Fold Message transmitter. If he could she wanted to add music to the part of the message that provided the Aliens with the description of Earthlings. She thought of Music as a magnificent counter to the terrible side of Earth's social behavior.

Bram picked up immediately on Mallica's sense of accomplishment. He knew that she and her team had been eating, sleeping, and living with the Alien language.

Linh and Duong had practiced their Alien on him as they programed the supercomputer. They were even practicing making it sound closer to what a whale would sound.

When she asked if he could make a magnetron to send out the sound of music, he replied that he would need to set up an experiment on the supercomputer and see what it could do.

He suggested that she work with Linh and Duong to program a simple test. If the current magnetron design proved successful then they could program the piece of music that the team selected as part of the message.

If the current magnetron design failed, then he would work with her and her team to design one that would do so.

Mallica thanked him and said that her team would give it a try as soon as he allocated some time in his tests of the Fold message transmitter.

Bram let her know that he had the control program to debug and test. Then he had six magnetrons to test and analyze before he was in position to test the ability to transmit music. He pointed out that if it could transmit music, it would in actuality be equivalent to a Fold radio transmitter.

He jokingly asked if she wanted to send a picture of herself as well, if so, he would need to add testing the ability to transmit video.

Mallica laughed and said that she would send a picture of the Mona Lisa and The Last Supper by Leonardo da Vinci and superimpose the music of The Messiah by Handel.

She then asked when he would have the Fold ability to send pictures developed.

Bram shook his head and replied that she had just given him several years of work that she wanted to have in a few days and that he would get back to her about the timing.

Before he left her office, he complimented her on creating an excellent team that was really into getting the communication right.

He then said, "have a good day," in Alien and enjoyed the look of amazement on Mallica's face.

So far, he only knew a few phrases that he had learned from Pat who was part of Mallica's team.

He knew that Mallica had daily language lessons for the team and that Pat was as excited as the everyone else on the team about their progress.

Linda observed Bram coming down the hall, at least she observed the small army coming down the hall. There were two fully armed Marines in the lead, then Bob and Thomas were next and then two fully armed Marines behind him.

She knew that Bram had learned to ignore all of them by concentrating on the schedule that she worked up with him for each day.

She was prepared to review the rest of the week and then detail tomorrow. The two of them always planned two weeks out and then focused on the next day.

They had learned to only make plans for four solid hours of what Bram called work and to leave the rest of the time as white space to be used by the immediate occurrences on that day. This gave him a good work plan with the flexibility he needed to keep up with the various parts of the Fold program.

She reflected on how involved he had gotten her into the Fold effort and how little of the regular support stuff she did that most supports would have been doing. She now understood why Lacy had been such an enthusiast and supporter of both Bram and the Fold project. She knew that she had become just as passionate as her sister.

The whole Stetson family were Fold and Bram supporters. They had all grown closer together and their entire family conversations had broadened and expanded to topics that before they would never have even imagined.

Bram arrived at his office and was relieved to be going in and leaving his Marine guards at the door. He followed Linda in and walked over and got himself a cup of coffee. He offered it to Bob, and Thomas as Linda took a bottle of water from the frig.

He enjoyed planning ahead. He knew that it was the time now to do so.

He asked Linda to put down the development of sending voice and video via the Fold process as items in his to do list.

She commented that he had a long to do list that seemed to ensure her long term employment.

Bram agreed and suggested they put in vacations, parties, fishing trips and other activities on the to do list to ensure that work and play got an appropriate balance.

Erica was surprised when late in the afternoon she received a call from Captain Sooner. He asked if the coming Sunday was too soon to come for a visit of the Fold facility.

She responded that it would be contingent on him getting clearance for the Fold project and that she was not sure it would happen so quickly.

Captain Sooner said that he had asked his hierarchy that question and had received a go after the Admiral had checked with General Tilson.

Erica commented that the two men at the top seemed to know each other well. The Captain let her know that two had been classmates in the Academy.

She said she would be pleased to see him and that she would arrange accommodations at the Fold location.

She waited until close to the end of the workday before going to Bram's office to make sure about the weekend and the following weekend visit.

As the site leader it was her decision to make but she wanted to make sure that she did not encroach on the work that Bram was doing.

Linda knew that Erica had met Mr. Right and she wondered what she might want this late in the day.

Erica commented that she was there to see about getting an invite for a Sunday breakfast.

Linda buzzed Bram and announced Linda's arrival.

Bram wondered what was up and waited as Erica entered.

Erica smiled and said that she was coming in to give him the latest gossip that he could share when he went home. She then explained that her new flame had asked if he could come up on the weekend and she was checking on an invite to the Sunday morning breakfast.

Bram said that would be no problem but maybe she should consider spending the weekend at everyone's favorite mountain bed and breakfast. They could go hiking and enjoy river fishing.

Erica thanked him for the idea and said that she would see if she could get a room at the lodge. She was not sure about the fishing but as Mike at the lodge would most likely comment, she had already caught her big fish.

Bram smiled and said he was glad to see her lighten up. He was glad that she had gone to San Diego to get the magnetrons.

Erika nodded and agreed that at the moment she was on a high that she hoped would last.

Bram said that if she wanted when he met this Captain, he would make sure to check on his intentions.

Erica laughed and thanked him but said she figured she could handle the Captain. She went on to say that she was really happy that she had made the move from the politics of her East Coast role to the West Coast Fold environment. It was such a breath of fresh air and a time of personal growth. Meeting the Captain was more than icing on the cake, it was a shooting star that she wanted to ride for the rest of her life.

Bram smiled and added that the Fold community was a great place for a love affair.

He then added that he was speaking for himself. He had gone from a hectic East Coast environment, then she had sent him to an undisclosed place in the desert from which he had escaped to find love on the West Coast.

Erika replied that she had not sent him into the desert. She said that he should blame that on Jeffery and she pointed out that he had met his soul mate in Houston and not on the West Coast. But she agreed about the hectic East Coast and about the much more relaxed West Coast.

Linda gave Bram the ten-minute signal and Bram asked if Erica wanted a ride home to her apartment.

Erica accepted and followed Bram out to the van.

She commented on the small army that was assigned to protect him.

Bram nodded and said that the people that had attacked the site and had personally tried to kill him were responsible.

Pat had been listening to the conversation and added that life with Bram had the flavor of sweet and sour. Life with him was sweet but the attacks had been intense and added the sour.

Bram commented that even with the Fold counter offense being led by Lacy, he figured that when the world learned about the contact with the Aliens there would be additional attacks from enemies that at this moment, they had no idea existed.

Ron Mueller

Chapter 23: The Replies

That evening Pat said that the Alien reply team Mallica was leading was ready for a final review and let Bram know that it would be great for him to participate with the team the next afternoon.

He agreed and would let Mallica know in the morning.

Bram felt the competing pull of all the efforts he had initiated. He had the best leaders, leading several projects but they all wanted his periodic involvement that he knew he had to provide.

He had launched efforts in composing a reply to the Alien message and had put Mallica in charge.

Then, he had focused on his other efforts.

He had launched an effort to see if the Fold process resulted in the improvement of a person's health and put Pat in charge. He got updates almost every day from her.

Linda had shared the success of having her burn scar on her leg disappear after two-Fold round trips. She commented that the pig only needed one trip to heal his new scars but hers had been a very bad scar and now there was no sign of it ever happening.

He immediately asked if Zuri had been asked to come home and Linda let him know that it had been arranged.

He continued going down his list of teams that had been launched.

He had launched an effort to develop the Fold Message Transmitter and he and Remi were working on that together. That effort was at the stage where in the next couple of days they would know if they could use it to reply to the Aliens.

He had launched an effort to create a Fold Wormhole that allowed forward and reverse movement through the fabric of the space-time continuum. He was the primary actor, but Marcus was providing the direction and the Fold time dilation that would take a bubble to his distant targets that he had selected to explore for water worlds.

Most people would consider each a major effort. Each effort had been launched with very tight time targets that most would have thought was impossible to achieve.

Bram was making sure they were all on track.

Now it seemed that they were all coming to a head at the same time. He smiled as he thought that it was his fault for having picked such great leaders, who were making their efforts successful. They were making it happen.

The next morning, he had Linda contact Mallica to find out when she was scheduling the message review. He asked her to let Mallica know that he would attend.

He asked her to work with Pat to get him on the final review she was having. He said that he was especially interested in the next steps for the studying the health effects that the Fold had on plant and animals.

He then said that on Thursday afternoon he and Remi would share how the Fold Message transmitter worked, and they would demonstrate it by transmitting and receiving the message that Mallica's team had agreed on.

Then on Friday morning, he and Marcus would share the results of their Fold Wormhole experiments.

Linda asked who he would like to have in attendance for the Friday review.

He suggested that Jeffery, General Tilson, NASA's John Morgan, Elizabeth, Zuri, Lori, and Erica all be invited to participate in each session. He commented that he did not expect everyone to be able to make it and the invitation was to insure they had the opportunity if they desired to be involved.

Linda suggested that each review get videotaped and that she would arrange to have the videos professionally edited and then make them available to everyone that was part of the review or had been invited.

Bram agreed that would be a very good way to record and share the progress for each effort. He said he would like to put a forward on the recordings that recognized the exceptional work of the individuals and of all those involved in the Fold work.

Erica's Captain arrived early on Saturday. She had to meet him at the gate to get him into the compound. Then she took him on a walking tour of the Fold site.

She was not surprised about Gerald's reaction when he saw the USS Rainier, Wheel Two.

When she told him about the attack and the destruction of the USS Hood, Wheel One, he commented that The German Battleship Bismarck had sunk the British HMS Hood toward the end of WWII.

He was surprised when he learned of the response and the destruction of the attackers when Lacy used the Fold technology to route the attackers. He commented that the Fold technology would sunset all the ships that the US Navy had afloat.

Erica agreed and commented that the technology would change the world as much as the internet and the I-phone had done but it would be more drastic, and the transition that would have dramatic social and economic impact needed to go a bit slower to allow the physical structure of society to adapt.

The Captain agreed and said that he would need to look to his future to see what part he would play in empowering the Navy with the Fold technology.

Erica had chosen to end the tour of the Fold compound at the cafeteria. She had arranged with Chef D'Carluca to prepare a steak lunch with bleu cheese melted on top. She knew this was a favorite that Gerald had mentioned. She also knew that Bram had mentioned it was the best he had ever tasted.

Gerry, as he asked to be called, said that the cafeteria looked like a very large high-class restaurant and when he took a bite of the steak, he said that the food was better than the best restaurant that he had eaten in.

The Chef D'Carluca, who had been standing by to see what the reaction would be, thanked him and then looked at Erica and said that she had chosen well when she had chosen the Captain.

Gerry commented that so far the tour had exceeded anything that he had ever imagined. He said that his boss was told by the General to let me know to expect to be overwhelmed by what was going on and he said that what he had learned so far was more than overwhelming. It was mind altering.

Erica said that after lunch she was going to take him to the Viewing Room and bring him up to speed with all the projects that were going on in parallel and she commented that he would not be overwhelmed, he would literally enter a different world and realize that the Fold effort had opened up the Universe.

Before leaving the cafeteria, Erica went to Chef D'Carluca and placed an order for snacks to be brought to the Viewing Room.

Gerry asked about the snacks and how long they were going to be in the viewing room.

Erica said that it would be for at least four hours and that afterwards they would go to her apartment, and they would order dinner in.

Erica stopped the viewing after Bram's introduction and asked what he thought about it.

Gerry commented that Bram seemed like any ordinary guy that valued the people around him.

She shared how she had recruited him when NASA had identified the concepts that Bram was proposing as world changing. She took him through a brief history of how Bram single handedly changed the effort in which he was now the center. How he created the Fold technology. And how in a very short period established a program that had changed the personal lives of everyone currently working at the site.

She paused for a moment and then pointed out that, whether they knew it or not, he had changed the lives of everyone in the world.

She smiled and said that he had been a person who she at first thought naïve, then a person she thought wanted her job and then she realized he was a person who didn't want much for himself but enjoyed seeing others be happy and here she was one of his ardent supporters because he had made her happy.

Gerry looked at her and said that he was eager to meet this Bram Nielson, wonder man.

When the message from the Aliens was played and the review of the reply was played, Gerry asked whether Erica could serve him a double shot of whisky. He asked if it was all real and how long had the Fold team known about the existence of Aliens.

When Erica let him know that the team had known for two months and that they had all worked together for almost a month on learning what the message said.

She pointed out that it was Bram that had guided the team through the decoding of the message and that he had added Vietnamese and Chinese members to the team and their contribution had led to the breakthrough.

Gerry asked why Bram had selected them.

Erica shared that he had realized that the Alien alphabet seemed long and seemed to have a musical cadence. He learned that the Vietnamese had the longest alphabet in the world and the Chinese, Mandarin and Cantonese had the musical and visual elements. He felt that having such knowledge would make the difference and he had been right.

Gerry asked how he would know such a thing if he didn't know the Alien alphabet.

Erica laughed and said she really had no clue, and he should ask that of Bram at breakfast on the following day.

He looked surprised and asked about breakfast.

Erica let him know that the two of them were invited for breakfast at Bram's house. She told him that by the end of breakfast he would feel like he was part of the Fold team.

She then added that if he didn't, they would have to relook at their blossoming relationship.

Gerry's eyes widened and then said that he was now going to have a hard time sleeping with all the pressure he felt.

Erica smiled and said that she thought that might make the evening much more interesting.

Erica then took him through the review of the health effects of a Fold experience.

Gerry said that he needed to take a few Fold trips so that the pain in his back would disappear. He asked if the surprises would continue.

Erica said that indeed they would continue.

She then took him through the section on the Fold Message transmitter development.

Gerry thought for a minute and then asked how, if the Alien message was a Fold message had they been able to get it if Earth did not have a Fold receiver.

Erica said that like, the invention of rubber, and the invention of X-ray technology, luck had a lot to do with it. The message would never have reached the Earth for another few thousand years if ever. It had been captured by one of the scout bubbles sent out on a Fold reconnaissance and then later noticed during the analysis of the recording that had been captured.

Once Bram recognized that it seemed to be a message, he had to determine if it was recent and worth deciphering.

Once it had been deciphered, Bram decided that a Message Fold transmitter needed to be developed. The magnetrons that were produced in the shop in San Diego were part of that effort.

Gerry commented that it was hard to imagine all the efforts coming from one mind.

Erica replied that he would find it even harder when he met Bram, who appeared to be like any regular guy.

She then showed him the last clip on the Fold Wormhole effort.

Erica pointed out that Bram gave credit to everyone and individually praised their contribution. She commented that the sum of all their contributions would not have produced one breakthrough, but that Bram had listened to them and had provided the linkages that took their inputs and made breakthroughs with them.

Gerry thanked her for taking the time to show him the summary video of all the breakthroughs. Then he asked if there were any other surprises.

Erica said that yes there was one more that might happen if she could convince him to take a few extra days and go fishing with her.

"Wow, talk about a fork in the road," he commented and then asked why she was inviting him to go fishing.

She smiled and said that all lovers who had gone to this particular fishing location were now paired and that she figured they should give fishing a chance to do that for them.

Gerry took her in his arms and said that fishing sounded great to him and then kissed her.

Much later that night after he finally did fall asleep, he dreamt that a voice kept repeating that he should take the leap.

The next morning as they walked up to Bram's house, Gerry said that he felt a like an invader going to someone's home when he had never met anyone that lived there.

Erica chuckled and said that if she arrived without him she would be sent back to her apartment without breakfast. She said she was sure he would be well accepted, but he was going to have to endure a grilling like he had never experienced before.

Erica was correct. Bram was sitting at the dining room table. It was Eric's turn at the stove and Zoe's turn to serve. The conversation was about who was going to ask what of this "Captain" that Erica was bringing to breakfast.

Pat suggested that everyone take it easy and that a slow grilling was more effective than hitting him with a firehose of questions.

Zoe laughed and commented that the expert at making her catch had spoken and she would heed the advice.

Pat replied that she thought that everyone in the room had done well with their romances as well. She was pleased that Erica had found Mr. Right.

Linda and Lacy arrived before Erica and announced that she was right behind them, and everyone should get ready.

Bram stood up as Erica entered via the basement entrance and walked over to the "Captain" and let him know that everyone was eager to get to know him. He asked him what he preferred to be called.

He got the answer that the "Captain" preferred to be called Gerry by his friends, and he hoped that would be what everyone in the room called him.

Gerry added that Erica had blown him away showing him the summary that they had all appeared in, and she had given him a brief biography of each of them. He felt that they were all already friends. He went on to say that he was in awe of all of them.

Bram asked him for his breakfast order as he led him to the dining room table.

Gerry replied that he had been advised to try the pancakes smothered in maple syrup, two eggs on top, with sausage on the side.

Bram was quiet during breakfast and just listened to the questions and the answers that Gerry gave. He envisioned a championship tennis match and couldn't help but to keep score.

He finally smiled and told Gerry that he had just won the singles Fold community Grand Slam Q & A Championship and that he could now officially be deemed a friend.

Gerry beamed a smile and replied that Bram as the line coach had been silent and wondered what question he might have.

Bram chuckled and replied that he was silent because Erica had warned him not to ask him what his intentions toward her were.

Erica laughed and said that it was hard to keep Bram away from his initial inclinations.

Bram innocently replied that the Captain had asked, and he had just replied honestly.

Pat decided this was a good time to ask Erica if a fishing outing was in the works.

Erica smiled and said that she had rented the same room that Pat had used in the past and that the two of them were leaving that afternoon. She commented that the General had assigned two of his Marines to protection duty for them, so she had rented three rooms.

She added that Mike and Mary had asked whether there was any talk of Bram and the rest of his small army planning anything soon.

They said that they had reinforced the new door of the cave with a one-inch-thick steel plate that had fifty through the door bolts to keep it from being blown off and were now prepared for his next visit. They felt they were now able to host Bram again.

Pat said that she was ready for another fishing trip and that they should convince Bram to take time off to celebrate the tremendous achievements that had happened in the last couple of months.

Bram took a sip of his coffee and asked who wanted to go for another boring fishing trip to the Rushing River.

All hands went up. Zoe added that they needed to let Orlando know so that he and Castor would both be present for the next attack.

Bram agreed that Orlando should be invited but he commented that attacks didn't happen every time he went fishing.

Eric asked Bram to share a time when he had gone fishing when an attack had not occurred.

Bram nodded and was silent.

Little did he know that his fishing attack experience would be extended and intensified.

The Sunday morning breakfast came to a late end.

Late that afternoon, Erica and Gerry were greeted by Mike and Mary who commented that she was becoming as guarded as Bram.

Ron Mueller

Erica laughed and said that she had only two armed guards and one of them was the driver and only had to rent three rooms. Bram would come only when his small army could reserve the whole bed and breakfast lodge.

The next day's early morning fishing was great. They both caught some nice trout but had chosen to fish cast and release with no barbed hooks. The hike up the river was leisurely, the air was crisp, and the scenery kept them pointing and exclaiming at the wonderful interactions of the breaks in the forest, and parting of the trees that ran up the mountain side.

Mike and Mary interacted with them just enough to make it feel like they were with friends. Erica realized that this was how she felt with everyone she had met through Bram.

Then on the last day, after dinner, Gerry got down on his knee and asked whether she would hike with him for the rest of their lives.

Erica had not been expecting a proposal. She hesitated a minute and asked if he had a ring if she said yes.

Gerry held up a ring that he had woven from the tall saw grass that he had woven, and it had a gold nugget, that he had found in the river, intricately mounted to the woven band.

Tears welled up in Erika's eyes. She wondered when he had the time to make the ring.

She knew her answer and held out her hand and said that "Yes she would love to hike with him for a lifetime."

Gerry carefully slipped the ring on her finger and then stood and the two of them kissed.

Mike and Mary both raised their wine glasses and proposed a toast.

Chapter 24: Preparation

Bram had not expected Gerry to propose marriage during the fishing trip. When Erica told him about the proposal, he asked when the marriage would happen.

Her reply caught him by surprise when she said she had heard that somewhere in his past, he had become an ordained minister and was legally able to perform the marriage ceremony. So, she was thinking that they could plan another fishing trip, and he could make sure she landed the big one for life.

She smiled and said that from the journey from the desert to conferring Holy Matrimony was like a journey from the very depths to the very heights of heaven.

Bram nodded and said that so far it had been a great journey for both of them and it seemed that it would continue into the future. He said he was honored by her request and that they indeed should plan her fishing trip.

He pointed out that she had landed the big one on her own and he was just making it official for the Fold records.

Bram then asked about her engagement ring and how Gerry had been able to get one so quickly.

She smiled and opened up her purse and opened a ring case. She said that Gerry had found a gold nugget at the edge of the river and had seen it as a biblical sign. Since they were fishing, he decided to use a fishtail braid using the long river grass leaves growing on the riverbank above the spot where he had found the nugget. She pointed out the intricate way he had secured the nugget to the ring. She said that she had worn it home to her apartment but had put it into a ring case that she had for another ring. She said that the ring was a treasure that she would keep and show her children.

Bram examined the ring and asked how much the gold was worth.

Erica replied that it was worth her weight in gold and laughed and said it did not matter because it was priceless.

Bram asked what Gerry's degree was in and found out he had a degree in oceanography. He commented that it seemed that Gerry did indeed love the ocean. He asked whether he might be interested in a role on the Fold project in the near future.

When Erica asked in what capacity he would be hired, Bram said that as soon as they found a water world it would need to be analyzed and researched to make sure that it did not have intelligent life and that it was suitable as a new home for the Aliens.

He was already looking for someone to take the lead role. It might also be a role that would land the first human onto another planet.

Erica commented that it was a super opportunity. She would ask and see about his interest would be in such a role. She said that she knew at the moment, he was working through what he would do with his career. He had mentioned he did not want to be part of an old technology trying to hold on.

Bram told Erica to let him know and that now he had an appointment with Marcus in the viewing room where they were going to see about finding a water world. He pointed out that finding one was a million more times as difficult as finding a needle in a haystack.

Erica said she would let him know later about the timing of the fishing trip and the list of invitees. She commented that their close friends would be housed in the lodge, but she was not sure where else they could stay.

Bram said she should check with Pat because she had looked at several lodges in the area. He then got up and headed to the viewing room.

Marcus came rushing in just as Bram got the screens powered up.

He asked Marcus why he was rushing.

Marcus laughed and said he had been trying to beat him in.

Bram told him to relax and set up his computer so that he could lead the search for a water world.

He let Marcus know that he had asked Linda to order in the usual refreshment mix.

It arrived right on time as he finished speaking.

He suggested they get whatever they wanted before getting into the search.

Marcus said that he had picked three solar systems for them to review every morning for as long as it took for them to find a water world.

He said that he had also sent three bubbles into the Alien's solar system. He shared that he had positioned them behind a large moon, a small planet nearer the dying sun and one farther out than the orbit of the Alien planet. They would gather all the vital information about the Alien's planet and about the condition of the sun. He commented that he did not know when they would get around to analyze all the data the three bubbles would capture.

Bram commented that when they found a destination water world, he would assemble a team to do all the analysis.

Marcus said that sounded like a good plan. He commented that when they finally got into regular contact with the Aliens, there would be work for lots of people. He was sure that the political arm would want to reach in and take control.

Bram agreed and said he was going to push on Jeffrey to get into position to guide his old friend the President in the politics of dealing with the Aliens. He would suggest that they first focus on providing the aid that would transport the giant Aliens to another water world.

He said that they had the technology to build the size of enclosure that would be required to Fold them from their current world to their destination water world. However, the power needed for the Folds of such large bubbles would need to be generated somewhere in their solar system.

He said that he envisioned either using their sun as the source of energy or to use nuclear fusion to generate the power needed. He pointed out that either option would require several years to get into place.

Marcus nodded in agreement and said that dealing with the Aliens was going to be a big challenge.

Bram looked at the screen and said it was time to start scanning the three solar system Marcus had selected.

By lunch time they had verified that there were no water worlds in those specific solar systems. Marcus said that the surveillance scouts would return at twelve sharp and get processed and made ready for the following morning's survey of the next three solar systems.

Bram said he was meeting with Remi and Pat to plan an upcoming trip to the Alien solar system. He shared that the current plan was for he and Pat and Daryl, Pat's back up, to make the first excursion and then most likely Amy and Harold, Amy's backup would make the second Fold.

Marcus said that he planned to review the solar system selection and add an additional three to the list. He said that he planned to stay six solar systems ahead so that they would be able to keep searching in a continuous pattern.

Bram Nielson Collection

Bram said that sounded like a good plan, but he wanted to speed things up. He suggested that he use a hemispherical pattern in the sector of the universe that he had selected. If they did not find the water world in that portion of space, they should use a similar pattern aimed at a different sector in the universe.

He suggested that they figure out the characteristic metrics of what they were looking for and automate the data gathering so they could do more than a dozen planets a day.

They would only look more closely at those that met the required metrics that indicated a water world might be present.

Marcus said he liked the idea and would spend the afternoon developing the automation routine and get Remi to allocate some additional bubbles so that they could get that rolling.

He said that he had been as bored as Bram about searching in the manner that they had spent the morning doing.

Bram agreed and said that he was sure that he did not want to spend as much time as they had spent that morning unless there was a good prospect to look at.

Bram signaled that it was time to head for the cafeteria.

Mallica and Pat were sitting at their normal table.

Bram decided that a mixed salad would suffice. He had snacked and almost continuously fed Einstein during their look at the three solar systems. He felt he was on a sugar high.

Pat recognized the look on Bram's face and asked if he had figured out a better way to search for the water world.

Bram commented that once again she had signaled him that he should never play poker against her. She was too perceptive of a face and emotion reader.

He pointed to Marcus and said that Marcus had taken him through one of the most boring mornings that he had experienced for a long time.

Marcus gave out a long, ex-cu-u-u-use me, but who kept wanting to take a closer look.

Bram looked at Mallica and asked if Marcus had acted like that during his stay in the desert.

Mallica smiled and said that actually he had not because the two of them were so bored that both of them would have thought that looking at planets in distant galaxies would have been really exciting.

She said that at the moment that he had called to bring them to Dallas, they had been discussing if there was a cliff somewhere in the desert from which they could jump.

Bram bowed his head and said that he had been remiss, but that Pat had insisted that he deal with getting the two Wheels Fold from Seattle to Dallas before he was allowed to do anything else.

Pat said she had nothing to do with any decision making at that time and in fact she was afraid to talk to Bram. He seemed to be some sort of mad scientist that Amy had picked up each morning as he wandered through the desert.

Bram laughed and said that he really valued having such dear friends that thought so highly of him.

Pat let Bram know that she had spent the morning prepping Amy, Daryl, and Harold by reviewing all the work that had been done in preparation of replying to the Alien's call for help and in trying to find a new water world to which they could migrate.

She said that she had reserved the viewing room for their meeting.

Bram thanked her for setting up the meeting.

They all met in the Viewing Room and Pat took the lead to get the meeting started.

Bram shared the objectives of the meeting in the language of the Aliens.

He said he was ready to share a skeleton plan of a visit to the Alien planet's solar system and perhaps contact them. He was hoping to find a water world for them before they made contact.

The objective of the meeting was for them to think about such a Fold and to suggest activities or data gathering that should be included.

After that brief introduction he switched back to English and asked if there was anyone who had not understood what he had just said.

Daryl and Harold raised their hands and said that they didn't even recognize the language in which he spoke.

Bram suggest that they join Mallica's class on learning the Alien language. He told them to take a crash course because he was going to insist that the bubble pilots know the language.

It was clear to Bram that neither of the two would make the first two trips. He mentally put Pat and Amy in the bubbles with him for those Folds.

He then asked Pat to lead the group through a brainstorming session of what the first two visits should cover.

That evening he asked Pat about the two backup pilots and what they had been doing.

Pat replied that the two spent their day waiting for the next Fold.

Bram asked if they had shown any interest in any of the work that was going on.

Pat replied that they always spent the morning in one of the huddle rooms on their computers and then they left early in the afternoon and went to their apartments.

Bram nodded and said that he was sending them back to NASA and they could do whatever astronauts did there as they waited for a ride out to space.

Pat said that was not going to look good on their records and being sent back would mean an end to their astronaut careers.

Bram asked what she would suggest he do.

Pat thought for a moment then she said he should give them the feedback about his disappointment in their lack of initiative and put them on probation for a three-month period.

He should assign them to work for Marcus to find a water world and they were to attend Mallica's language class and pass her second level language test by the end of their probation.

Bram said he liked the part about them finding the water worlds. It would free he and Marcus to get on with other work. He agreed to what she suggested, and he added that they would be required to jog in to work each morning with him.

Pat said that the last was a good idea and might be key in changing their attitude.

Bram said that their current behavior was a surprise to him, and he wanted to get to know them better so that he would be ready for the end of their probation period.

Pat commented that the social fabric of the Fold community seemed to be bubbling and changing.

Bram replied that love was in the air and weddings being planned and now there were two people needing motivation. He commented that perhaps he had initiated too many major projects and people were losing connection with the required speed at which that work was happening.

Chapter 25: Water Worlds

𝒜 week later at breakfast, Castor commented that whatever Bram had told Daryl and Harold had changed their behavior and attitude. They had been known to the Marines as freeloaders but were now seen as two hustlers that seemed to have changed their ways.

He asked what Bram had done to change their ways.

Bram smiled and said he had threatened to have them inducted into the Marine core to learn discipline and how to do hard work.

That brought a laugh from both Castor and Donna.

Donna commented that she doubted they would get through boot camp if they did enlist.

She followed Bram out and was pleased to see the two astronauts waiting with the other Marines.

Later that morning, Bram met with Marcus and asked how the two were doing.

Marcus said that having them do the searching for a water world had changed how fast the search was progressing. He had now searched through more than a hundred solar systems and had identified just one potential planet, but it was really cold, and the ocean had a layer of ice that covered more than ninety percent of the planet.

He commented that the two only stopped their monitoring to attend Mallica's Alien language classes.

At lunch Bram asked Mallica how the two were doing in her language class.

Mallica said that they were whizzing through and had already passed the first level class where they learned the Alien alphabet and how to count to one hundred.

Pat smiled and said that he had put the fear of getting sent away into them.

She commented that the two had been picked as backup pilots because they were among the smartest and most experienced of the astronauts, so she was not surprised that they were doing well in both language classes and in looking for water worlds.

They had both talked with her and Amy and apologized for their lax behavior. They had expressed their desire to make up for their past behavior and were using all of their capabilities to slog through the immense amount of data they were going through in the hunt for a water world.

Bram said that he was glad to have made a positive impact on their behavior. He hoped they were actually getting into being part of the team in an enthusiastic way.

Marcus came in and joined the group for lunch. He had a huge smile on his face and in an excited voice he said that there seemed to be several water worlds in the last set of solar systems.

Daryl and Harold came in a moment later and shouted that they had found what they were searching for and pumped their fists up and down.

Bram pointed to a table next to where he was sitting and called out to them and congratulated them.

He then gave each of them a high five as they came to the table.

He asked them how it felt to find the needle in the Universe's haystack.

Both of them said they were still on a high from having found three water worlds in sequence after reviewing more than two hundred solar systems.

They pointed at Marcus and in Alien they together said, "Slave Driver."

Bram replied to them in Alien that they were invited to breakfast on Sunday.

He chuckled when the two of them looked at Mallica and asked what Bram had just said.

They then replied that they would love to be at Bram's famous breakfast gathering.

Bram asked since when has his breakfast become famous.

Mallica replied that it was Pat that had made it famous with her maple syrup smothered three pancakes with two over easy eggs on top and sausage on the side.

She pointed out that Bram had leveraged Pat's famous breakfast and used it to convince his guests that the Fold project was the best place to have a breakfast that was out of this world.

Bram asked Marcus to update him on the find and when they would go to those planets and get a direct view of the planets.

Marcus replied that would be based on when Bram decided to make the journey. He suggested that they do one-Fold to each of the Planets on separate days so that they could review all the data that they would gather.

Bram said that was a great idea and he wanted to add multiple Folds to the same Planet. He added that one of the Folds would employ the Fold Wormhole capability so that he could evaluate the ability to use it to get in close to the surface of the planet in question.

Marcus said he was going to refine the coordinate calculations and program three bubbles to Fold to co-ordinates of one thousand miles from the surface of the planet. Once they took that Fold, he would be able to make a more accurate calculation for the next Fold to the same planet.

Bram agreed that was a good plan and said that he had the seats for each bubble already decided.

He then said that he wanted to set up a remote laboratory where samples from each water world could be brought for analysis. The remote laboratory should be in the largest bubble that they were currently producing, and it would be located out near the Alien planet. He suggested that they get a team together to define the tests for the samples they gathered and then equip the bubble with totally automated systems to carry out the testing. The only thing that would come back to Earth was the information.

He said he envisioned them Folding, sending a small bubble near the surface of the water where it would take a sample of the water and the air and then seal itself so the samples would not get contaminated. The bubble would then Fold to its location in the Lab where it would have its own section that was isolated from the other three samples. The samples for analysis would be extracted via a specially designed syringe.

The data from the analysis would then be transmitted to the analysists located at the Dallas Fold compound.

He commented that he wanted the sampling and subsequent analysis to be kept a secret by a limited number of people.

He suggested that Marcus, Remi, and himself determine the minimum number of people that would need to know. Even the lab people that gave them the parameters to be measured should not know about the samples being taken of the water world.

Marcus asked why Bram was putting such a high level of security in place.

Bram replied that when the world found out about the Aliens the Fold project would be under political attack and the turmoil was going to be significant.

When the world found out about giving aid to the Aliens there would be a bigger backlash.

If they found out about the capability to get samples from other planets the Fold project would be overrun.

Bram Nielson Collection

He wanted to delay all information until the Aliens had the technology to move to the new planet. Then the turmoil and battles on Earth could go on and not endanger a species that was trying to survive the death of their star.

Marcus nodded and said, "top, top, super top secret." I got it and I agree. We have been attacked for a technology that only a few people are supposed to know about. The progress that we have made in the last few months makes the previous capability look like child's play. Even the top leaders still only know about that previous technology. There is no way they could imagine how far the Fold program has gone.

Bram said that when all the capabilities of the Fold program became public, they might want to be on a second Earth like world several light years away where they could hide and not be burned at the stake.

Marcus smiled and said that he had logged at least six worlds that were very much like earth and that they might want to set up another Bubble Lab so they could indeed make the escape that Bram had alluded to.

Bram nodded and said he was up for doing exactly that and they might as well at the same time as they set up the other Bubble labs.

That evening Pat asked why Bram had not shared who was going with him on the Folds.

He replied that he was going to make the final decision about who was on each Fold just before the Fold itself.

He let her know that she and Amy would be on the first and second Folds to each of the first two planets and that he would decide on having Daryl and Harold be backups on the two folds to the third planet.

Then she and Amy would be on the third Fold to each of the three planets.

Pat said she was surprised that he was giving she and Amy such a big piece of the Fold journeys.

Bram replied that the two of them were reaping the reward for the contribution that they had made and that their two backups were also getting rewarded for their more recent contributions.

By the weekend Bram had the lab bubble specifications defined, and he and Remi had selected the bubbles and had the construction under way.

Once defined, Bram took the list of the necessary lab equipment to Erica and asked her to procure it as soon as possible.

She asked about the rush and then put up her hand and said that she would get what he was asking for as rapidly as possible.

She asked if by any chance there would be a seat available on one of the exploration trips.

Bram smiled and said that only qualified pilots would be going out with him. He then told her to get with Pat and get herself qualified.

Erika thanked him and said she would.

She then said that she wanted to change the subject to Fishing. She said that she had reserved the required number of rooms and had arranged to have the wedding in the field on the other side of the Rushing River opposite from the lodge.

She had asked Linda to check on everyone's schedule and had gotten the green light for the dates.

Bram said that he was looking forward to going fishing and that he would make sure she landed her big fish.

He then asked if she had checked with her Gerry about his interest in leading the analysis and preparation of delivering aid to the Aliens.

Erica nodded and said that he was super excited about the opportunity and wondered what the timeline would be for starting.

Bram replied that it could be as soon as after the honeymoon. "And where in the world would the honeymoon take place," he asked?

Erica said that they were planning to go to Kuai for two weeks. They planned to hike, whale watch, surf and just hang out.

Bram commented that he loved her choice and said he was sure that it would be a honeymoon to remember.

Erica smiled and agreed.

Bram then said that he was going home to spend a weekend relaxing.

Erica nodded and said that his relaxing always worried her because it seemed that was when he came up with the next leapfrog Fold idea.

Bram replied that he would try to keep it to a little jump.

Bram left work knowing that he was going to think through each scenario that would take place in the near future whether he wanted to or not.

Pat commented that everything was happening at one time and asked what she could do to help.

Bram thought for a moment and said that she should make sure they went on their normal walks, took time to go to the recreation center, relax by the pool and have great meals. He said that she was right that he was going to run through every scenario whether he wanted to or not.

He shared that he would be working with Marcus and Remi to set up remote labs to analyze samples of each of the water worlds. He wanted to keep the fact that they could get that kind of information about planets millions of light years distance, a secret. He would appreciate her keeping an ear out to make sure it was indeed being kept secret.

He went on to say that there was going to be a lot happening that he was not going to share with the Fold community because if the information became public, the safety of the site and the members of the community would be jeopardized.

Pat nodded in agreement and said that so much of the Fold technology had advanced that what was known a month ago was now ancient history.

Bram asked whether she felt that Daryl and Harold could be trusted to keep everything a secret.

Pat replied that they would be as tight lipped as she or anyone else of their closest team members.

Bram then asked Zoe to have all the bodyguards meet with him in the study after they had dinner. He wanted to make sure that they understood the magnitude and critical importance of keeping what they knew away from their bosses.

Zoe asked what the content of their reports should be.

Bram replied that the content would be the truth about the support they were providing but there would be no mention of anything about the technology.

Eric commented that was very much like the current reports they were sending in, but it would be good to set up a standard report and then vary it a little so that each report sent in would seem fresh.

Bram agreed that what he did not want was to have the FBI leadership curious about what was going on at the site.

Zoe suggested that Bram have a discussion with the General and with their Marine bodyguards about secrecy. She said that they didn't necessarily know the details of the technical progress and capability, but they got the sense that progress was being made at a rapid pace.

Bram said that he would follow her advice and set up a meeting with the General and together they could get Castor and Donna to understand the need for secrecy so they could ensure their partner Marines would be tight mouthed.

The weekend was as deep as he had thought it would be. Pat was his anchor to the world of reality and made it possible for him to come to the surface and take in two beautiful days.

What was clear in his mind was that the capability to go to another Earth like world would be a great way to ensure that he could protect the community from the turmoil that would come at them in the near future when the world learned about what the Fold technology meant to the status of the current economic environment.

The money and political communities would want to gain control.

The religious communities would most likely be vengeful. He felt this to be especially the case when they found out that the Aliens were in appearance similar to whales.

He felt justified in having asked Marcus and Remi setup the bubble labs to include both the water worlds and the Earth like ones.

The future as always would be whatever it was meant to be, but he was going to make sure that whatever happened he and his Fold community would have the means of self-defense and would have the means to get out of harm's way.

He knew that in the very near future his preparation would be tested. He had no idea what the test would be, but his team would persist.

Ron Mueller

Chapter 26: Space Labs

℃y the end of the following week Bram, Marcus, and Remi had the two space bubbles that held four labs each complete minus all the test equipment that Bram had asked Erica to procure.

They had decided on a distant solar system to park them. Only they had the coordinates.

Bram scheduled the first Fold to each of the six worlds. He purposely excluded a Fold to the Alien planet since he did not know whether they had the ability to detect objects in their solar system.

The water worlds all looked acceptable. They gathered all the data possible from their remote locations and then returned to the Fold compound and downloaded their data for analysis.

Once they had the water world data downloaded, they did a Fold to each of Earth like planets and gathered the same data.

In total they made eight Folds in two days.

Bram looked at Pat and Amy and commented that they were looking much younger and that the Fold process seemed to be turning back the clock for them.

Pat laughed and said that she did feel better than ever but doubted the younger look.

She then commented that she had scheduled Zuri during the upcoming Christmas break to send her out multiple time on one day then rest for a day and then go through another cycle of Folds.

The rest day included spending time with the site psychologist to talk through her feelings about the change that would be happening.

She had arranged for Elizabeth, Linda, and Orlando to go out on the first three cycles. If the Fold process was repairing her body and more cycles were needed they would repeat the sequence.

She said that Nuro and Jina had expressed their concern about the potential repair process. They had talked with Zuri, and she had insisted that she be allowed to try. They said that they would pray for a miracle.

Bram smiled and said that all he wanted for Christmas was to see Zuri walking.

Amy said that such an event would be a miracle, and she was hopeful that it would happen.

Bram suggested that Pat have a structural diagram of a healthy girl her age put into the bubble computer that it could use as reference. He was not sure how the Fold process accomplished what it did, but he figured he would put that information in the same location as the Fold control system equations were located.

Pat highlighted a problem that Elizabeth had surfaced. If the process worked Zuri could not return to the current University that she was attending. If she were recognized the power of the Fold process would be at risk of being discovered and then there would be a full attack on the program.

Bram suggested that if the miracle happened, they try to get Zuri into one of the Ivy League schools or into Oxford.

Pat said that she would get Elizabeth to see about Oxford it was her alma mater, and she would have good connections there.

Bram said that the analysis of the data gathered so far would take place in the Viewing Room where Lori had arranged for two teams of analysts to share what they had learned from their initial review.

Zoe commented that the circle of people that knew about the worlds that had been discovered was growing. She was having the backgrounds of all the analysts checked again. She commented that they were among the most trusted lab members who had been with the project from its beginning.

Bram thanked her for her proactive actions. He agreed but said that he needed to get the analysis going. The actual physical of the physical samples would be used to confirm what they learned in the next few days.

If they had a water world that met the specifications that had been defined to support life then he would send the reply to the Aliens.

And then they would Fold to each of the water worlds and send down sampling bubbles to gather physical samples.

Daryl and Harold once again celebrated the fact that the analysis of all three water worlds confirmed that they met the criteria that had been established.

Bram reinforced the fact that they were great hunters and shared they would make the next Fold visits to each of the planets.

He smiled as the two nodded and quietly thanked him for the opportunity.

Erica had come in toward the end of the meeting. She said that she had good news and bad news.

Bram smiled and said for her to start with the bad news.

Erica replied that the bad news was the cost for the instrumentation was ridiculously high.

Bram smiled and replied that if that was the bad news then the good news was going to be great news.

Erica smiled and said that the General had sent three helicopters to fly to Seattle to pick up all the instrumentation and it would arrive the following morning.

Remi was the one that reacted in the fashion of pumping his fist in the air as Daryl and Harold had now made popular. He said that his team would have the Lab bubbles ready to go by the end of the week.

Bram said that once the Labs were on location, the necessary coordinates would be available so that the sample bubbles could be Folded into their clean sterile environments.

Immediately after that the next sets of Folds to the water world would occur.

The work on the lab bubbles consumed Bram for the next two weeks. Then Pat remined him that Erica's fishing trip was coming up on the weekend.

Bram replied that he was ready for the Rushing River. He scheduled the placement of the two labs on the following Wednesday and the revisit of the water worlds for the next day.

Success seemed to be in the air. The week ended in a rush, and everyone turned their attention to the wedding.

Erica was on the first of the helicopter flights to the Rushing River. She and the General flew in together with the Admiral. They were all staying at the lodge. Folks were staying at two other lodges in the area and would be transported there to Mike and Mary's lodge by the Marines.

After his arrival and getting situated in his and Pats room, Bram took the opportunity to sit on the veranda and chat with the General and the Admiral. Mike joined in and it was clear to Bram that the three were of the same vintage and liked sharing their "war" stories. He tuned out and envisioned each of the upcoming scenarios that would occur after Erica and Gerry tied the knot.

The Admiral touched his arm, and he came back to the surface. The Admiral commented that his favorite Captain had given him his resignation and was planning to take a role with the Fold organization and work for Bram. He said that it had surprised him since he had figured the Captain would spend his career in the Navy. He was on the list to be promoted. The Admiral asked what role could possibly pull the Captain away from the ocean.

Bram Nielson Collection

Bram thought for a moment, he smiled and then said that the role information was above the Admiral's pay grade, and he could not divulge it, but the Admiral could be assured that it involved the ocean.

The Admiral laughed and said that Bram would have made a great officer in the Navy.

Bram thanked him for the compliment and added that the General had already put in his bid to make him a Marine and he didn't want to offend either of them in any way.

Pat came out to the porch with Amy and Erica and joined the conversation. She commented that it was at this lodge that she had caught her big fish and that she was especially glad to see that Erica was making it a custom.

Amy added that she had learned that Lacy was planning to continue the custom.

Bram smiled and said that he was impressed with the actual fish Pat had caught and then later he had been confused by the fireworks and somehow ended up on her hook.

The General laughed and said that his two Marines, Orlando and Castor informed him that it was Bram that had been dishing out the fireworks.

Bram nodded and said that it was an accident and that he had his eyes closed the whole time.

Mike added that he had been there and couldn't get a shot in because Bram had rushed to point and wiped out all the attackers.

Castor had been standing on the porch with Donna as they stood guard. In a loud voice, he commented to her that Mike had correctly described the scene. He said that he and Orlando were too slow that day and Bram made them look like new recruits.

Bram looked over to Pat and asked if she wanted to take a walk up the river.

He watched as Castor and Donna took the lead, Bob, and Thomas took the rear.

He looked at the Admiral and commented that being alone meant alone with four other very close friends.

The General nodded and said he sympathized and added that there were as many Marines as wedding guests.

Erica thanked him for the precaution, but she doubted that it would be as exciting as what had just been described.

The following morning was the wedding breakfast that touted a breakfast special that Mike said was being called Pat's special. He added that there were also eggs to order and a variety of muffins and rolls.

The wedding was scheduled to begin at exactly noon and then an early reception meal at two.

Bram looked at Erica and knew that she had become the person she was meant to be. She was confident and she had become admired for her leadership style that focused on developing those working for her, she radiated happiness.

Erica looked over at him, smiled and gave him a thumbs up.

Later, a few minutes before twelve, he called on everyone to go to and assemble in the field across the river. He waited until everyone was at their seats and walked up to the platform that would serve as the altar.

He was about to start the wedding when Lacy stood up and shouted in a loud urgent voice, that they should all get into the Rushing River.

He knew immediately something was very wrong. He pointed to the river and said follow me. He grabbed Pat by the hand and pulled her with him.

He stopped at the edge of the river and looked out to a far mountain where a bright glint caught his eye. He shouted at Lacy and pointed to the far mountain.

She gave him a thumbs up.

He then jumped into the river and made sure the wedding area was clear.

Lacy shouted for everyone to get down into the water as deep as possible.

Bram had just pulled Pat to him and then pulled her under the last thing he saw was two bubbles firing and then an overhead explosion and what seemed like a fire storm drove him under as well.

He immediately stood up and looked over to see Lacy talking on her phone.

He heard her say that they should capture their attackers, if possible, but any resistance should be met with elimination.

He then shouted that he would complete the ceremony right where they were.

He went straight to does anyone object to this union and then declare Erica and Gerald husband and wife.

He pointed to the lodge and shouted that the way out of the river led straight to a warm shower.

Then Gerry, in full dress uniform, picked Erica up and carried her out of the river and into the lodge. The Admiral and General followed and then the rest of the wedding party got out and headed toward their rooms.

Mike shouted that the wedding lunch was still on and would be on schedule.

One of the Marines spoke briefly to Mike, who then turned to Bram and said he was going to bill him for another door to the cave. He smiled and said the steel plates that he had added were bent but they had saved the cave.

Bram laughed and said that if all the attackers had accomplished was to destroy his door, he was going to give Lacy the largest raise that she had ever received.

At lunch, Lacy announced that the attack had come from the mountain on the other side of the valley. She had sent six armed bubbles to that location and had surprised three men who tried to shoot the bubbles out of the air. The return fire had kill all three of the attackers and the General had sent out a unit to that location to secure the site.

Bram thanked her for the update then he said that her quick action had saved the day. He then jokingly said that he would send her the bill for the damage that the second rocket had done to Mike's cave and would have her budget pay for it.

Lacy knew immediately that Bram was pulling her leg since she was on his budget and waved her hand through the air and replied that she had saved his hide only to have hers nailed to the wall so she was going to see if the General would give her a place in the Marine Corp.

Bram laughed and said that she might also want to ask the Admiral to be a rear Admiral and see if she could double dip.

Then Gerry stood up and said that there would never be another wedding like this one. He had found inspiration and found his soul mate on the banks of the Rushing River. He figured being married in its waters was the highlight of his life.

Erica stood up beside him and said that she agreed and said that she had caught the big fish she was after in that same river.

Bram raised his glass of wine and said that he had a toast to the bride and groom. He wished them a lifetime of happiness, of prosperity and of good health and that they would come back to work as quickly as possible.

Everyone cheered.

A helicopter was waiting to fly them back to the Fold compound and then they would be driven to the airport to fly out to their Honeymoon in Kauai.

Pat suggested to Bram that they stay an extra day at the lodge and decompress. She felt that the day's events was more than had been expected.

Bram agreed and let everyone know that if they wanted to they could remain for an extra day as well.

The General and Admiral both left as scheduled. But before leaving he instructed the Marines to remain vigilant and make sure Bram was kept safe.

Lacy let Bram know that she was going back to the Fold compound to open an investigation into the attackers. She wanted to know how they had been able to find out where Bram was going to be and how they were able to get the rockets that had been used.

Bram thanked them and then watched two helicopters leave.

Mike suggested they go take a look at the doors to the cave and that afterwards they sit on the veranda and relax for the remainder of the day.

He suggested doing real fishing the next day.

Bram said that he was interested in the door that he had paid for and then afterwards the porch seemed like the place to be.

Ron Mueller

Chapter 27: Transformation

Bram returned to the Fold compound and went full throttle in getting the Space Fold Labs functional and ready to put in place. It took longer than he anticipated but he rationalized that the Fold project was pole vaulting technological heights and exploration that would make them triple gold medalists champions in the Olympics.

He knew that every team was functioning at top capacity and capability.

Erica reminded him several times that he was moving all the efforts, each of which were major efforts, faster than any similar project had ever moved.

Pat told him to ease up a bit and let him know that as soon as Christmas break occurred, she had arranged for Zuri to return so that she could begin cycling through a series of Folds.

Bram said that he had never experienced an emotionally trying feeling like the one he had when he thought about the transformation that Zuri might experience. He said that he thought it would be equally hard for Zuri and they should make sure she got the support that would help her during the transition of her body.

He asked about Zuri's admittance to Oxford.

Pat said that Elizabeth had received confirmation from her alma mater that Zuri was accepted into their program and that Orlando had also received confirmation that he could transfer in, but it was on a provisional basis that required him to keep above a three-point five grade point average. She said that Orlando had jumped up and down and then he had pushed Zuri around the campus shouting out.

Three-point five, Three point five
Tra, la, la
Not so hard
For the bard
Tra la le
Oh my, Oh my can this really be!
How can this be?
It's all downhill.
It's all downhill.
How can this be?
Tra, la, la
Tra la le
How can this be?

Bram laughed and said that he missed Orlando leading the way as they jogged in to work but he was pleased that he had been accepted to Oxford. He said that he agreed with Orlando that it was going to be a downhill run for him. He knew that Orlando was currently carrying a four-point average while still carrying out his responsibility to guard Zuri.

He asked Pat to schedule him on as many of the Fold cycles that he wanted to go on.

Pat said that she was sure that he would end up going on as many as Zuri. She said that she was not sure how he would take Zuri's physical transformation, but she was sure it would be positive and that he would help Zuri handle the transformation.

Bram agreed. He said that it would be good to have him at breakfast and describe the hoped-for transformation so that Orlando would have time to think about it and be prepared.

Pat said she would arrange for the breakfast.

Bram let her know that he was going to examine the space bubble that could hold an Alien. It was being built in the same hangar where Wheels one and two had been built. The bubbles were two hundred feet long and seventy-five feet wide. They were being equipped with water purifiers, aerators and chemical balancing units that would maintain the fluid at peak condition for the Aliens. He said that he was sure that it would hold two and maybe three.

He would have to make sure with the Aliens that such a bubble would be acceptable. In the long term he hoped to get the Aliens to make their own bubbles, but he was uncertain of their manufacturing capability.

The next day, Jose Estrada, the builder's project manager, met Bram at the airport. He greeted Zoe and Eric and then led the way to a waiting black van. On the way to the hanger, he thanked Bram for having asked for him to be the project manager of the giant bubble and asked about its design specifications.

Bram replied that currently he could not divulge that information but when he could, he would make sure to include Jose.

Jose said he would deliver the Bubble on time and at cost.

Bram thanked him and said that around Christmas, he planned to Fold the bubble to its destination and the hangar would be available for what he was thinking would be a second bubble order.

Jose said he looked forward to a second order.

There was a car entrance to the hangar that the van drove through. Bram got out and the size of the bubble towering over him and filling the hangar overwhelmed him. He had been expecting "Big" but what he now saw was "GIGANTIC."

He followed Jose as they walked outside of the bubble. The walk around it took about half an hour.

Jose stopped to show what at first appeared to be seamless joints but on a closer look you could see the intricated joint design that ensured the integrity of the joint.

Then they stepped into the bubble. What Jose called the tail end, was where all the equipment that would maintain the chemical and physical condition of the fluid that would be inside.

Jose pointed out tubes that ran the length of the bubble that had holes in them to ensure that the fluid condition was maintained throughout the bubble.

Several large viewing screens and computers were at the front of the bubble that Jose pointed out.

Bram asked how long the remainder of the commissioning of the bubble would take.

Jose commented that the deionized, distilled water would take almost a month to fill the vessel. Then the temperature and circulation control would be commissioned and finally the various chemical chamber functions would be tested. He said that in all it would take the remaining time before Christmas.

Bram said that the timing was perfect, and he appreciated the detailed testing that Jose had planned.

Bram looked at his phone and realized that it was near one in the afternoon. He then asked where they should go to have a late lunch.

Jose suggested his favorite Mexican restaurant. He said that the timing was perfect, and they would not have to wait to get a table.

After the lunch, Bram again thanked Jose and then went to the airport and caught the short flight back to Portland.

He was met by Castor and Donna who took point as they led the way to curbside. He noted that they had worn civilian clothes, and their weapons were in holsters beneath their suit jackets.

The black van was at the curb parked in front of a similar black van and behind another black van.

Castor opened the sliding door and Zoe and Eric got in back as Castor walked around and got into the driver's seat and Donna closed the side door and got into the passenger's seat.

Bram heard Castor instruct the drivers in the other two vans and then the ride to Dallas got under way. Bram was glad that it had only been a day trip and that he, Zoe, and Eric had been the only ones on that leg.

The following week was Thanksgiving.

Bram, Marcus, and Remi made several bubble Folds to check out the coordinates for the Fold space labs. The location they finally agreed on was one that had a phenomenal view of a bright multicolored spiral galaxy.

Since this was to be a secret location that only they knew about and that nothing would be written down, they each selected their back up person who would be given the coordinates in the event one of them died.

Bram said that once the relationship with the Aliens and the existence of potential expansion worlds for Earth's population became common knowledge the location would be made part of the Fold record.

Finally, Zuri's Christmas break began, and she arrived home.

Bram had invited her and her family to Sunday breakfast. He had also invited Orlando and Mallica as well.

Pat let him know that she had invited Linda and Lacy.

After breakfast Bram asked Pat to describe the effect that the Fold process seemed to have on living things.

Pat described the various tests she had conducted with plants, fish, rabbits, goats, and pigs of various sizes and how she had made sure the Fold effect was always a positive one.

She looked at Zuri and said that she was hoping that it would have a positive effect on her, but she said she was not sure how that would actually occur and what the changes would be.

Elizabeth asked Zuri if she wanted to see if it would help her.

Zuri gave a laugh and said if pigs almost the size of Orlando got healed, she figured she should try to see what it did for her.

Bram said that she would always have someone making the Fold with her and asked who she would like to accompany her.

Zuri looked around the room and said that anyone in the room was welcome but that on the first couple of Folds she would prefer Orlando, Elizabeth, and Linda.

She looked at her parents and said that once things seemed to be going well, the two of them should go with her. If things did not go well then, they could all cry together.

She looked at Bram and said that he would be welcome on every Fold as well.

Bram thanked her for including him but said that if the Fold process worked the way he anticipated, he would be crying most of the time and figured that the macho Marine could handle the situation better than he.

Orlando laughed and said he would most likely be the one crying. He joked that his role of being her guard was at stake.

Pat speculated that they would all be crying. She then suggested that the Fold process begin at nine the next morning.

Orlando was at breakfast Monday morning. He said he had a ditty to sing on the way to the compound.

> *Zuri's on the way*
> *On the way*
> *What a bright,*
> *A bright wonderful day.*

Ron Mueller

Zuri's transformation day
I say transformation,
*   You say transformation.*
Zuri's transformation day
*   On the way*
*   On the way*
What a day.

Bram took his breakfast plate and rinsed it off at the sink and said it was time to get it on the way and led the way out the door.

They all repeatedly sang the ditty as they jogged to the compound. As always, the entire contingent of Marine guards joined in.

Bram accompanied Pat to the bubble that would be repeatedly used. He asked where she was Folding to.

Pat said that she had worked with Marcus to determine the Fold coordinates and then they had made sure that it was a clean space environment by repeatedly Folding scout bubbles to ensure a safe location. She said that the coordinate was behind Neptune where they figured their activities would not be discovered and would not require too much power.

Bram complemented Pat on making safety the top priority.

Zuri was pushed in by Orlando and he helped put Zuri into the seat designed to hold her.

He got into the bubble.

Linda entered the bubble and took the seat on the other side of Zuri.

He nodded when Linda commented that she had held Zuri's hand for several years when things were looking bad and that she wanted to be holding her hand when things began to improve.

Bram remembered well, the look on Linda's face when he realized Zuri was a genius and he asked her to be on his team. Later when he wanted to promote Lacy, she had recommended her sister who she said was a super organizer and would make a great support for him.

Linda was indeed super organized, but she was also very intuitive about what his next request for her help would be and often delivered it immediately.

He felt that it was appropriate for her to be on Zuri's first transformation flight.

After each cycle, Pat and the site physician would examine Zuri, and the site phycologist would spend a few moments talking to her.

They both reported that some positive change was occurring, and that Zuri was handling it well.

Bram noted that the hands and feet were the first physical parts to show improvement. He saw immediately that Zuri's hands were no longer in a clutching position. Instead, she was wiggling her fingers and laughing.

Linda had a beaming smile and tears in her eyes.

Orlando was making a ditty about hands and feet.

Once Pat had listened to the two Doctors, she signaled for another Fold cycle.

Bram thought he had prepared himself, but he was amazed by the change that he was witnessing. By the sixth Fold cycle Zuri was able to stand on her own, but she was unsteady, and it was clear that she would need to learn to walk. Her arms seemed to be fully functional and her neck and back seemed to be straightening.

He had tears in his eyes as the day ended and Zuri asked to keep going.

Pat said that she felt the same way, but she said that the Fold cycle would be on hold for a day and then they would continue with another round of Folds.

Pat said the following day would be spent at the pool where Zuri would get some water therapy exercises so that she could train her rejuvenating body how it should function. It would be a day for Zuri to learn to move her legs and begin the process of learning to walk.

She said that she had arranged the therapy so that Zuri's body could adjust and so the subsequent Folds would then be able to make additional improvements.

Zuri nodded and thanked her. She said that she also needed time to let her mind absorb what was happening. She said she was afraid that she was dreaming.

She looked at her parents and asked how they were doing. She asked if they would be in the pool with her and then in the bubble on the following day.

Jina came over and gave Zuri a hug as did Nuro. Neither of them could speak but kept giving her hugs. Finally, Jina said that they were overwhelmed with the miracle they were witnessing.

Nuri looked over at Orlando and said he was fired as a wheelchair pusher, but she was hiring him to teach her to walk, jog and run.

His beaming smile and the tears running down his cheek were contrasts of emotion and he gave a thumbs up but was not able to say a word.

Bram commented to Pat that he had never seen Orlando at a loss for words until now, but he identified with his emotions.

By the end of the week Zuri was a transformed person. Her facial features had changed, and she resembled a young Jina but as Pat commented to Bram she had a radiant look that made her beautiful. She was now taller than her mother by at least two inches even though she was only twelve.

She took to the water and learned how to swim and said that her legs, arms, and shoulders all ached from what she was doing.

Orlando suggested that they design an exercise program to get her new body into shape. He promised to make her as tough as a Marine.

Zuri laughed and said she wanted to look more like Zoe, Pat, and Amy.

He smiled and said they were as tough as any Marine.

Everyone agreed that the physical change was a miracle.

On Christmas morning at the planned breakfast Zuri arrived with Orlando in the lead. He made a formal announcement that Princes Zuri had arrived.

Zuri walked in with Linda holding her left hand, Jina holding her right hand and Nuro bringing up the rear.

Zuri stepped forward, did a slow turn, bowed, and then walked slowly to each person and gave them a hug.

She came to Bram last and whispered in his ear that she was forever grateful that he had pulled her in when everyone else was ready to give her up.

Bram whispered back that she was the miracle that he had always prayed to witness. He said that now he knew why he had been given the vision to create the Fold process.

Later Bram had let Mallica know that he planned to send their reply back to the Aliens on the day after Christmas.

In the morning, he was surprised to see Mallica, Orlando and Zuri at breakfast. Zuri explained that she wanted to be part of delivering his second miracle to those distant beings.

Orlando said he was there to make sure they had a ditty to jog in with but that on this morning, the jog would be a slow walk so that Zuri could make it on her own.

He then shared the ditty.

Zuri's walking, give us room.
        Zuri's walking, sing this tune.
Zuri, Zuri has come home,
        Wham Bam, it's no scam,
        Wham Bram is the man.
Zuri's walking,
        Stop you gawking,
        She's just walking.
To a Bram miracle tune.

Bram led the way out and was surprised that every person that had a major role was standing and waiting to go in with him.

Pat said that she had invited them to go in and be part of the historic moment when the message went out.

Linda led them into the auditorium. She said that after the message was sent, Chef D'Carluca had his staff ready to serve breakfast in the auditorium and in the cafeteria.

She pointed to the camera crew at the back of the auditorium and said that everything would be taped.

Bram stood and looked out at the auditorium.

He thought for a moment and then asked Remi to join him. He asked if Remi remembered the preamble to the message that would be sent out.

Remi looked at Bram and then out at the audience. He said that the words he was about to say were from the lips of their very own Fold Peace Whisperer, Bram.

"Welcome we are friendly but fierce. We embrace intelligence, we embrace grace. We embrace every race. We help those in need. May we all live in peace."

Bram then asked Mallica to join them and share the message as it would sound to the Aliens.

She stepped forward and pointed over to Hoang who played the message slowly in Alien and she repeated it in English.

Bram then added that he was adding the fact that a water world had been located and that the initial exploratory vessel would be available to take their first alien explorers there.

He then looked over to Tran and gave the signal to send the message.

Bram was sure that there would be extreme surprise and wonderment on the Alien world

He looked forward to their response.

The End

Chapter 1 Return to the Desert

The Marine guards stationed at the desert compound had been notified to clear the helo pad and then standby for an early arrival of a group of people. The guards were on their desert rotation from the Fold compound located in Dallas, Oregon so they were familiar with the Fold technology, but they had never witnessed a Fold bubble departure or arrival. It was for them one of the more exciting mornings on guard duty.

Then the bubble appeared and hovered inches off the ground. They recognized two of their own, Castor and Donna as they got out of the bubble and took up the front position. Then a very beautiful young woman emerged who they had never seen before. She was followed by another of their own, Orlando.

Then they recognized the helo pilot that periodically flew one of their gunships back at the compound.

She was followed the person they knew as the genius and his partner.

The last two that got out they knew as two of the FBI bodyguards assigned to protect the genius.

They watched as the group walked away in the dark of the morning and headed out into the desert.

The night was pitch black. Millions of stars twinkled overhead that seemed to be behind a thin white veil covering the face of heaven. Bram couldn't see his hands in front of him. He took the lead up the almost invisible path. His feet knew the way through their body memory.

The bright shimmering star light made the surrounding grasses and sage brush appear alive as the light morning breeze caused them to waver and the limited number of leaves to rustle.

He was followed by Pat, Zuri, Amy and then the rest of the protection detail. Einstein was in his pocket.

He let everyone know that Pat, Zuri, and Amy were the only ones going to sit on the boulder that he had sat on during the development of the Fold equation. The four of them would watch the sunrise from the place where he had finally realized that he had made the breakthrough. A breakthrough that now he believed was guided by another hand.

He had thought of this outing as a way to bring Einstein for a visit to his home and to share with Zuri that instant of time that led to the miracle that she represented.

Somewhere, in one of the cracks in the boulder, was where Einstein had previously lived. Now at least five years old, Einstein would once again get to visit home.

Bram joked that Einstein had guided him in the quest to develop the Fold equation.

When they got to the boulder, Bram helped Pat, Zuri, and Amy up and then he sat down in his usual spot. He took Einstein from his pocket and placed him down beside him.

Einstein circled around once and then disappeared down the side of the rock. Pat asked if he would come back.

Bram said that he thought so but only when the sun broke over the horizon and its rays hit the boulder.

Zuri smiled and commented that she was honored to visit the place where Bram had sat and thought through the maze of equations that had transformed her from a very crippled person to a one with a normal body. It was, she said, a body about which she was still learning. She said that it was like a stranger returning to her home after an extreme remodeling and not recognizing most of what she saw. In her case everything about herself felt different and unknown.

Bram replied that her transformation was for him the grand reward, for his efforts here in the desert. He added it was a reward that would carry him through the rest of his life.

Pat gave Zuri a hug and said that her physical transformation was a positive reward for everyone working on the Fold project. They all believed that they had witnessed a miracle.

Amy added that she had first learned of the Fold capability sitting on the boulder and thought at the time that she had witnessed something that could never be exceeded. Then she had witnessed Zuri's transformation and knew that she had witnessed the real miracle of the Fold.

A thin bright line cut across the dark night horizon as the sun light broke over the mountains to the east and the star light seemed to wane. The line travel across the desert as if seeking the boulder. It worked its way like a thief in the night sulked up toward an open window. Its first streaks of light hit the boulder and slowly worked its way and worked upward like the thief climbing in the window. It seemed to slow as if trying to find its way, the way a mountain climber would look for hand holds as she made her way up the cliff.

Moments later Einstein came out and surprisingly another mouse followed him.

Pat commented that it seemed that Einstein had found a mate.

Bram nodded and put out two crumbs and said that he had probably lost his Fold confidant to a love affair. He said that Einstein deserved to have such an affair.

Einstein got up on his two hind legs and Bram lowered his hand. Einstein got into his palm and then the second mouse did as well. Einstein circled and lay down and the new mouse did as well.

Zuri commented that she could not believe what she was seeing.

Bram lowered his hand and both mice got out. Einstein then led the way down to the crack from which he had come and disappeared.

Bram commented that he would return in a couple of months to see if Einstein would return to greet him.

Small bubbles, holding tea, a sweet roll, and some cherries, appeared. There was one for every person in the group.

Bram said that they should enjoy the sunrise snack that Marcus had arranged and then take a walk in the desert.

Amy got up and as she went down the boulder said that she would be picking them up in a helicopter and bringing them back for a full lunch.

Bram left his cookie crumbs on the rock and then led the way out to the desert.

He was heading out one degree from true north. That was one degree more than the last time he had made such a walk. He knew that Amy would know where to take her helo. He was silent as he thought about what seemed like only yesterday but then all of the achievements that had taken place since that time seemed to be flashing through his mind.

He felt lucky to have made the discoveries that had so far kept getting better and better and it had reached a point that he was not sure where it would take him next.

Pat quietly asked if he was OK.

Bram smiled and replied that Einstein had been a good partner in his developmental surges. He gave Pat a hug and commented that giving Einstein a hug and getting a reply from him was always a short coming and that Pat would have to step up and take up the slack.

Zuri had been walking behind them and was thinking about the wonderful relationship the two had and her heart stopped when by chance she saw the rattlesnake. She stopped and quietly said that the two soapy people walking mindlessly ahead of her should pay attention and not tangle with the rattle snake they were about to walk into.

That caused everyone to stop. Both Bram and Pat looked to where Zuri pointed with her stick to where the snake was laying in the rays of the sun. It was still lethargic from the cold of the night.

Orlando said he would take care of the snake, but Bram stopped him and commented that the snake must just have moved into the sun's rays but had not yet been able to get warmed up. He said they were on its turf and should respect its territory.

He thanked Zuri for having been alert and then led the group around the snake.

He then related the story about having walked out from a center point and having recorded the terrain at one-degree increments until he had been able to match the topography he mapped in his mind and computer to a specific location in the United States.

He said that it had taken him a year and that today they were walking out along the three hundred and sixty first degree line.

Pat asked why the location had been so important to him.

He replied that it was a matter of principle. He was angry that sufficient security could be provided to so many important people, but he had to be treated like a criminal who was sent into isolated confinement. He was sure that it had to do with the fact that the folks had decided his ideas would be extremely powerful and they had wanted to ensure that the power it represented would not leak out of the country.

He pointed out that the leaks so far had come not from those associated most closely to the Fold project but from the very people worried about the leaks.

Zuri asked what he had done when he finally determined the location.

He replied that he had confronted Jeffrey and Erica and threatened to leak the desert location to the media. He made the point that the confrontation with the two was the beginning of the change that led to the social environment that they were now living in at the Fold compound.

He highlighted the fact that the confrontation had changed his relationship with Erica and subsequently changed her life.

Up until that time Erica wanted to be in control and thought that he wanted her role. She was upset because Jeffrey had given him the best apartment to live in. She believed that she was not being respected.

Pat commented that she had talked to Erica before coming back to the desert and had learned that for Erica the return to the desert would have been a return to a time that she now considered a dark time that she had successfully escaped and that she preferred leaving it in the desert.

Bram nodded and said that Erica was now living a different life with a new set of values and had found her soul mate and would most likely be happy for the rest of her life.

They had been walking for almost two hours when Zuri commented that she could not see the helicopter, but she heard it.

Bram pointed to a dark spot that seemed to be just above the ground that was fast approaching from the center point that was the compound buildings.

He commented that Amy had always flown her helicopter awfully close to the ground so she could pick him out as she passed over him.

He shared the fact that when he had some sort of place to hide he would do so on her first pass and then continue walking and wait until she realized that she had missed him and returned to pick him up.

It was a game of cat and mouse between the two of them the whole time they had been in the desert.

Pat shared that Amy had shared the fact that she knew that the two of them were always playing a cat and mouse game that she had learned to enjoy. It was, she said always the most fun part of her day.

Bram smiled and said that it was also a great way for him to start each day and that game had earned Amy the privilege of being the first person with whom he had shared the Fold breakthrough. He had taken her to the boulder and there he had introduced Einstein to her, and they had the same breakfast snack that they had just shared earlier.

Zuri commented that Bram had a desert experience that became the fabric that was still guiding the Fold program and one that she now personally embraced.

Bram smiled and commented that it was a very positive influence in his life and that the fabric of that life had been woven by his mother when as a young boy, she repeatedly told him that he had to treat others the way he wished to be treated. She had also said that if he embraced that one saying, his life would be rich whether he was a pauper, a wise man, or a genius.

He added that he tried to practice that philosophy even when he had the urge to kick some people in their derriere.

Pat laughed and said that most people would just say that they had the urge to kick some people in their butt.

Zuri asked what word she should use when she attended Oxford University.

Pat said that she thought Bum or arse depending on the social situation.

Bram laughed and said that they should get into the hilo and enjoy the ride back to the compound.

Amy landed her hilo in an open area and waved them onboard. She had Zuri sit in the front seat. Once everyone was in and had their safety harness on, she handed them each headsets.

They all got in and watched as Orlando led the rest of the group on foot back toward the compound. He had them singing a ditty and led off at a good jog.

Bram then told Zuri that she was about to experience a hair-raising flight that he had to endure every morning before working on the Fold equation and that she would learn why he finally had to make a breakthrough. He said that Amy had frightened him into being successful.

Amy laughed and then took off and flew out away from the desert compound. She flew just above the surface at a dizzying speed. She had arranged with Orlando to fly out long enough to let him get back to the compound.

Zuri shouted that she did want to live to enjoy going to Oxford.

Bram laughed and said that Amy would make sure that Zuri was so afraid to fail that she would graduate at the top of her class.

Amy took a sharp bank and headed back to the compound. She did a little up bob and then set the helo down at the center of the landing pad.

She looked over at Zuri and asked if she had enjoyed the ride.

Zuri nodded and said it had been much, much more exciting than the Wheel One flight to the back of the moon.

Bram added that the flight in from the desert had always been exciting for him and that he had made sure that Amy went to astronaut training in an attempt to train her to be a normal pilot. He now realized that it had not worked.

Amy said that flying a helo had been and still was one of the most enjoyable things that she did. She said that she had convinced the Marines back at the compound to let her fly one of their gunships on a regular basis. It had allowed her to keep up her flying skill during her time back at the Fold compound.

Bram said he would now worry about who was flying the protection helo when he jogged into work in the mornings.

Pat said that she had just thought of a good ditty for their next jog in

Who's that flying in the sky?
Who's that flying way down so low.
Is that someone that we know?
If its Amy then it's so.
Who's that flying in the sky
Is that someone that we know?
Yo, Ho, Yo, Ho
Look how low, Look how low.
Fly crazy, Ho, Ho, Ho.

Bram pointed to Orlando, Castor and Donna who were standing with Zoe and Eric at the side of the helo landing area. He commented that they had made good time getting back and he was sure that they would all have a great lunch before heading back to the Dallas Fold compound.

The return to the Fold compound via bubble was scheduled after their lunch.

Ron Mueller

Chapter 2: Alien Engagement

Sunday morning Bram rode the two-person elevator to his basement office. He made himself a cup of pour through coffee and sat down at his computer. He worked his entire equation with negative time to see if it would give him an insight to what might happen. What he learned was that his equation using negative time seemed to go in a circle or at least it became nonlinear and perhaps be a spiral. It seemed to defy definition or relation to one particular shape.

Pat, Zoe, and Eric came in and said they had been worried about where he had gone and that he had broken the protection protocol.

He nodded and said that it had never registered when he got on the elevator to come down to his office. He suggested they put in a camera and alarm so that when he did it again, they would immediately know.

Pat reminded him that they had agreed to go to the neighborhood recreation center for lunch where Melisa had gathered some of the younger children who they were going to play various games with.

Bram knew that his time thinking about negative space was over for the day.

He woke up on Monday ready to attack the day. On their five thirty in the morning jog into work, Castor took up the ditty that Pat had shared when they had gotten off the helo in the desert.

Who's that flying in the sky?
Who's that flying way down so low.
Is that someone that we know?
If its Amy then it's so.
Who's that flying in the sky
Is that someone that we know?
Yo, Ho, Yo, Ho
Look how low, Look how low.
Fly crazy, Ho, Ho, Ho.

Both he and Donna pointed to the helo overhead and Bram watched as it came down low to one side and wiggled and then went back up. He had not been able to see the pilot but figured it was Amy.

At that moment he was thinking about the response he was waiting for from the Aliens. It had been sent to them the day after Christmas. He figured that it would take them time to react to the message. The few days had passed, and he hoped a reply had been returned.

He, Marcus and Mallica were scheduled to check the location where they had originally intercepted the Alien's first message to see if a reply had been sent back.

Linda welcomed him back and reminded him about his meeting and asked about the rest of his day and when he wanted to update his two-week calendar.

Bram suggested that updating the calendar should take place in the late afternoon. He asked that she set up a meeting with Remi and check with Jose to see when he could take possession of the first giant bubble.

He then asked to get a meeting set up with Erica to discuss the building of another bubble and to check on any other financial issues.

Linda gave a small laugh and asked if this was just today's items or was it the two-week items.

Bram said he would be in his office to start the day and then he would meet with Marcus and Mallica.

Bob and Thomas took their chairs as Bram pressed the heat lever on the water pot.

Bram sat down at his desk and put his hand at the center of the Milky Way Spiral picture that was under the glass on his desk. He was thinking about the Wormhole equation and the negative space aspect of the reversing process. He was anxious to investigate what going into negative space would mean.

He fired up his laptop and reviewed the equation yet again. He had it burned into his mind and really did not need to see it but doing so let him imagine what might happen. It was like having a book in his hand that allowed him to feel the weight of the story. He was trying to envision the resulting shape of his negative equation.

Linda's call that he had ten minutes before his scheduled meeting with Marcus and Mallica brought him out of his speculation about the negative part of space. He realized that he had spent almost an hour deep in thought and that he had not made the tea that he had intended to make.

He looked over at Bob and Thomas and realized that the two of them had used the hot water to make themselves tea and had made him a cup as well, but it was still sitting at the refreshment center.

Unlike Zoe that was willing to pull him up from the depth, these two were not willing to take that chance.

He smiled and thanked them for the tea and said that it was time for them to go with him to his next meeting.

Marcus and Mallica were waiting outside of his office and suggested they go to the lab where the bubble that had been sent out to see if the Aliens had responded, had just been returned to its holding area. They had arranged for Remi to retrieve the computer recording. He had volunteered to review it on his computer.

Bram thanked them for getting everything ready. He hoped that there would be a response.

Remi greeted them and said that there was something on the computer, but he had resisted getting into it until they all arrived. He pointed to a large screen and said he would now open the folder with the message.

When the message came on the screen, Bram had an immediate smile on his face. The first line was in English, "Greetings, we on Swoosh are elated that intelligent beings have received our message and were able to respond to us using our language. We are extremely impressed. To be offered aid dried our eyes and caused us to surface and breach."

Then the messaged changed to the alien language and provided more information about themselves, their population numbers, and the number of species in their world. There was an explanation that they did not have physical structures as had been described existing on Earth. They were amazed that the human species lived on land and breathed air directly.

They added that the energy required to send the reply had exhausted their energy resource and it would take at least another journey around their star to rejuvenate it.

They then gave some data about the condition of their star.

Mallica commented the lack of power, and any significant structures had signaled her that rescuing the Aliens and transporting them to another water world had just gotten more complicated.

Marcus wondered how a species that could think deeply and develop a Fold message transmitter would not have developed the ability to build a large energy source.

On Earth, electricity, gas engines, and steam engines all existed in abundance. Often the power source had preceded the use it was eventually used for. He said it was hard for him to understand how the technology to send out the Fold message had been developed.

Bram agreed that it seemed inconceivable, but reality said that it had been done. He speculated about the whales and the dolphins and wondered if on Earth they had superior thoughts but were not able to develop the technology to communicate with humans.

Mallica then brought them back and asked about the response and pointed out that Earth would have to supply the short-term capability for the Aliens on Swoosh to begin to make the move to another water world.

Bram agreed. He pointed out that the first transport that would hold two maybe three of the Swooshians was ready for delivery. The three of them had to agree on the delivery coordinates and then make the Fold from the hangar in Seattle to the coordinate.

Marcus suggested a coordinate near the Alien water world that they had previously used since it would save time since he would not need to verify the spot did not have a field of debris.

Bram agreed and let Marcus know that the Fold would happen that afternoon. He had a meeting with Erica with the objective of her ordering a second bubble. He asked Marcus to call Jose at the building site to verify the coordinate of the bubbles center.

Then they would meet at three and Fold the bubble out to the coordinate near Swoosh.

Mallica asked whether they would respond to the reply from Swoosh.

Bram suggested that she get a message ready that asked the Aliens for the current chemistry on Swoosh and how soon the Swooshians would be ready to check out the new water worlds that met the parameters that were agreed on.

Mallica suggested they also ask how quickly the Swooshians were planning to make the transition to a new world.

Bram agreed and added that with the current Fold capacity it would take more than their lifetime to get just a small percentage of Swooshians to a new planet. He said they would need to figure out a way to set up a transport system that had higher capacity and one that did not rely on the Earth for the materials or the manufacturing of the bubbles.

He asked if she and Marcus might take that on as a project. They could recruit other folks, like Remi or anyone else that could add the knowledge they needed to set up a remote bubble production system.

Mallica said that a project like that would be exciting for her. She said that she was up for it and would get a group together to flesh out who needed to be on the team.

Bram thanked her and said that Marcus already had his hands full with determining where bubbles should Fold and making sure the Fold location was clear of debris. He expected that Marcus would be extremely critical in determining the coordinates for a bubble factory.

Marcus agreed and said he was excited about suggesting locations within the Swooshian solar system that might position the production facility near the materials needed to make the giant bubbles.

He then added that perhaps some even better locations would be in some other solar system near a planet that had the materials critical in making the bubbles.

He said that once he was given the ingredients from which the bubbles were made, the files with the data from the previously discovered planets could be examined and an optimum location could be selected. Perhaps the facility could be on the surface of such a planet but at a minimum it could be nearby, and materials mined and sent out to the production facility.

Bram said he had heard enough, and he was going back to his office and begin to work on his next project.

He was walking back to his office thinking about the negative realm of his equation when Erica intercepted him near the cafeteria.

She asked if Bram knew that it was lunch time.

He shook his head and said that it seemed that the time was flying.

Erica suggested that he follow her, and they would meet up with Pat for lunch.

Bram followed her into the cafeteria and waved at Pat who was sitting by herself at their usual table.

Erica had selected an Italian salad and was almost immediately on the way to the table.

Bram was not sure what he wanted. He looked over the offering and went for a slice of beef, asparagus, and a small, baked potato. He carried his tray out to the table and then decided that he wanted a lemonade to go with what he had selected.

Pat asked how his day was progressing.

Bram commented that he seemed to be constantly behind in what he had been planning to get accomplished.

Erica waited until Bram had finished and was sipping his lemonade and then asked him what their meeting was about and could they have it now.

Bram smiled and said that it was a short topic. He was having the current bubble moved out of the hangar in the afternoon and he was interested in getting another one on order.

Erica nodded, made a note on her phone, and then said it was done. She then said the order would be in by the end of day.

Bram thanked her and said that her meeting was one that had happened quickly and ahead of time. He said that when he got back into the office he would be able to focus on his next project.

He was leaving the cafeteria when he decided that where he needed to go was to the Lab and see if a bubble was available that he could use. His turn toward the Lab caught Castor and Donna by surprise and they hustled to get back in the lead and then asked where he was going.

Bram apologized and said that he had decided to see if a bubble that he could use was available.

Remi had left the cafeteria on Bram's heal and overheard the exchange. He said that he had several bubbles ready, but they would need the Fold coordinate programed in.

Bram replied that he was going to use the Neptune coordinates and that once they were programed in he was going out to try an experiment.

Remi asked about the experiment.

Bram shared that he was going to nibble at the impact that negative time had on the Fold reverse equation.

Remi asked why he did not send out the bubble on its own.

Bram said that he had done that previously and that there was nothing recorded on the visual or the coordinate calculator.

Remi shook his head and asked if there was a way to hook up a second bubble that could pull him back.

Bram said that he did not know how to program such a bubble and said that he felt that once he had a personal experience, he would be able to figure out how to navigate the negative space region.

Remi then suggested waiting until morning so that Bram would have an entire day.

Bram thought about it and said that the suggestion made sense, and they should plan to use the next day to do the initial exploration of the negative Fold space.

He spent the rest of the afternoon deciding what he wanted to learn in the negative Fold space.

That afternoon as they were riding back to the house, when Pat asked what he was planning for the next day, Bram shared that he was planning to venture into the negative Fold space.

He was surprised by the silence that followed.

He asked why there was no reaction.

Pat replied that she was thinking through what was bothering her and she would share her thoughts after dinner.

Bram found it hard to wait. Finally, after dinner he led the way down into his office and sat down on the two-person recliner. He was pleased that Pat sat down next to him and said that she was ready to share her concern and to ask him to do several things when he ventured into the negative Fold area.

She said that she was afraid that the scientific laws that were more or less absolute in their current reality would not hold in the negative Fold reality. She then asked how he thought time and space would function in the negative reality.

Bram admitted that he was not sure about anything in the negative Fold reality.

Pat asked whether he would consider waiting before Folding into the Negative.

Bram replied that he had considered that but there were no additional actions or developments that he could envision so he was planning to make the negative Fold to see if he could personally learn what was going on.

Pat then said that she wanted him to take enough food and water for a week with him.

She asked if he could use his body to gauge time. Or was there a way for him to separately keep track of time other than his computer.

She had no idea how he would be able to gauge distance and asked if he had an idea.

Bram thanked her for the food and time ideas and admitted that he was relatively clueless about everything that he might encounter.

He mentioned that her questions had triggered several ideas that he would act on in the morning.

Ron Mueller

Chapter 3: Gaia

Ƭhe next morning on the jog in, Zoe was the one that led them through a ditty.
Negative Fold
　　Negative Fold
Hold the phone.
　　Bram is clueless.
Loose screw to us
　　Clueless, Clueless
Negative Fold
　　Hold, Hold
　　　　Stop the Fold
Don't be foolish.
　　Don't be bold.
Negative Fold
　　Negative Fold

The entire compound resounded with the echo as the other Marines joining in.

Linda greeted him and commented that it seemed that the morning ditty might be a warning to which he should listen. She reminded him that this was the day that had been agreed on to Fold to the Swooshian world and that he would need to delay his negative Fold until the following day.

Bram thanked Linda for reminding him and agreed to do the negative Fold the next day. He asked her to work with Pat and arrange for a cooler of food to be added to the bubble that was being prepared for the negative fold.

Remi showed Bram a much larger bubble that had been modified to include a small latrine and a bed to sleep on.

When Bram asked about the modifications, Remi responded that Pat had made the request and he thought it had been from him, but he thought it was a great idea, so he made the modifications.

Bram said that the modifications were a good idea.

He then asked if Remi would come up with a common mechanical clock that could be digitized and add that to the modifications he was making.

Bram went to the printer and grabbed a good supply of paper, and he grabbed a mechanical pencil, a French curve, and a square from the drawing table.

He was now thinking through what his survival strategy should be. This had all been triggered by Pat and her concern.

He found the sensor that would sense the second hand on the mechanical clock and interfaced it with the computer program that was keeping track of time. He wanted to ensure that the time controlling his computer was the time that was flowing in the left to right direction. He wanted it to be distinctly his time not the negative Fold time and he felt the mechanical clock was a technology that was more resistant to negative time.

He then asked if the other bubbles that would go to the Alien planet of Swoosh were ready and if everyone on the list had checked in.

Remi assured him that the bubbles and everyone was ready for their noon launch. He commented that Marcus had estimated that their arrival would be sometime in the morning hours on Swoosh.

Bram smiled and said that he hoped that the Swooshians had the same wake-sleep cycle that humans had.

Gerry had been working on populating his team with a mix of experts. He had focused on the environmental and chemistry specialists. He wanted to be able to verify the suitability of the water worlds that had been identified as the potential new homes for the Swooshians.

He had also familiarized himself with the lab sampling bubbles that were to be used for the detailed analysis of the environment of each of the worlds. He was impressed with the capabilities and the equipment of the labs.

He wondered where Bram was getting the funding to cover the cost of the various projects that were underway. He had asked that of Erica and had been told that the money pipeline would remain full at least while the current President was in office.

He was pleased with each of the six members on the team. The analysts would stay at the compound. The team would take turns Folding to the water worlds.

He had a meeting with Bram to finalize the Folds to the four water worlds he and his team would analyze.

He had started to think of Bram as the Five Star Admiral of the Fold program. He would have to tell Admiral Becker, his sponsor that he had found that Five Star Admiral that they had always joked about.

Bram greeted Gerry and asked if he had been able to get his team organized and ready to go into action.

Gerry replied that he was impressed with the capabilities and the eagerness of all the applicants. He said he had focused on seeing how they got along with himself and with each other before making the final selection decision.

Bram said that he had worked hard at making sure any person that came onto the Fold team had the capability and had an inclusive attitude.

Gerry complimented Bram on being successful in his recruiting and that Erica had adopted the same approach.

He then noted that to date the Fold retention record stood at an unheard of one hundred percent.

Bram smiled and said that he figured it was the pool parties and the great food that was having that effect.

Gerry shared that all of the equipment in the four labs had been tested, the bubbles had been prepared and everything was a go.

Bram thanked him for being ready and that the noon departure was still on.

The Fold to the Swoosh system happened at noon sharp. The two bubbles Folded to the coordinates that Marcus had researched and had worked with Remi to make sure it was a clear location and that it would be near the planet so that they could get a water and atmosphere sample.

Bram asked Mallica to make first contact with the Swooshians.

She asked if he was sure that he didn't want to be first.

Bram smiled and said that her Swooshian accent was better than his or at least they would soon find out. He pointed out that she was by far the best at understanding the Swooshian language.

She got on the Fold transmitter and sent a message of greeting to the planet. She was not sure how to aim her transmission.

Bram had suggested that they hit the surface of the planet from pole to pole as it rotated so that it would not matter where it might be received. The first part of the message should clearly give the coordinate of their bubble so they could learn where the message was being received.

There was a delay of a response but then the Swooshians responded with a greeting that spoke of their amazement at the ability for their Earthling friends to be able to make the journey to their star system.

Bram then suggested they launch their underwater transmitter so they could speak to the Swooshians using a radio transmitter.

Mallica checked with the Swooshian she was in contact with and received an OK to the underwater transmitter. It was both a transmitter and it was capable of sending back a signal to the bubbles. Once it was in place Mallica tried out her skill at speaking Swooshian.

Bram was pleased with the response that they received that complemented Mallica at sounding very much like a Swooshian from the southern hemisphere.

He then asked in Swooshian what part of Swoosh he might be from.

He smiled when the reply said that his accent was a local one.

Pat then asked if they could take samples of the waters and the atmosphere so they could compare it to the waters and the atmosphere of the potential planets that had been found for the Swooshian population.

Bram smiled when the reply was that of course they could take the samples, and the question was if an exploratory Swooshian team might be able to learn more about the planets that had been discovered.

He shared the fact that a special analysis team was set up to analyze the Swooshian samples and then see if the samples from the other planets were within tolerance. Once a match was made, he suggested that the Swooshian explorers should take a trip to the planets and determine which would be the most desirable.

He asked if there was any concern that the bubble that would be their transport would only hold three Swooshians.

The Swooshian responded that they were amazed that a vessel large enough to hold three of them was available. They asked how the materials and the power to Fold such mass was available.

Bram replied that the exploratory Fold energy would be provided by an Earth energy relay feed, but that future Folds would need to utilize the energy of the Swooshian star. And materials to make more transport bubbles would need to be mined locally from the planets that were part of the Swooshian system.

The Swooshian that Bram was conversing with commented that those that were with him were amazed with the speed of response that they had received, and they were overwhelmed with the ease at which their new Earth friends spoke of mining the materials from planets in their star system.

They had been concerned about sending out a call for help in fear of finding unfriendly aliens that might take advantage of the Swooshian world.

Now they were ready to breach the surface in leaps of joy.

Bram replied that when they learned the violent history of Earth, fear would once again be part of their thinking.

He let them know that he was acting on his own to ensure that the Swooshian world would have its own capability to save themselves and would not be relying on Earth to make it happen.

The Earth society currently was ignorant of the technology that would save the Swoshians and when technology became known, Earth would experience a great upheaval.

Pat came on and said that the samples had been taken and the sample bubbles were now being analyzed.

Bram asked Marcus to share what would be the next steps to getting the Swooshians capable of being transported to the bubbles.

Marcus asked for specific coordinates where each Swooshian would be located, and he wanted the size and the weight of each Swooshian. He explained that when the time came these individuals would be Folded into the transport bubble and then the bubble would be Folded to the planet that they would explore.

He said that he would return in the near future to facilitate the Fold of Swooshians to the exploration bubble and that at that time the information he was asking for would need to be exact.

Bram shared that he expected that everything to make the Swooshians capable to explore their new world would be put in place.

He then gave the coordinates of the relay bubble where the Swooshians should send their messages and from where Earth would send their reply.

Mallica thanked the Swooshians for their welcome and said that she hoped that in the near future Earth would be ready to host them.

Bram then closed by wishing them all good swimming and that he looked forward to their next meeting.

On their return Lacy met them and asked to speak to Bram in private.

Bram was curious about what Lacy might have to share with him. She had been very effective in eliminating the physical attacks and had set up a surveillance system that provided another level of protection.

He was surprised at the topic that came up.

Lacy came in and said that she had learned that there was a bill in the Senate to put a watch dog committee in an overview and approval position of what was being done at the Fold facility.

Bram asked how long before that bill came to a vote and if there was any way to delay or defeat it.

Lacy said that she had contacted Jeffrey and asked him to see if he could delay it for as long as possible. It was not a question of defeating it because there are supporters on both sides of the aisle.

Bram asked Lacy to keep on top of it and to let him know how soon such a committee could be formed and put in place.

He had already decided to move the entire Fold operation to another location. A location that would be impossible for the committee to exercise oversight control. It would be on another world and in another star system.

He knew that time was the constraint in being able to make such a move.

Once Lacy left, Bram asked that Linda set up an immediate meeting with Erica and one with Marcus.

Erica went to Bram's office and wondered what he might want. She was thinking about his return from Swoosh and the meeting with the Swooshians and was anticipating something associated with the Fold.

Bram greeted Erica and brought her up to date with what was going on in the Senate.

He then asked her how quickly she could have prefabricated structures set up on the clear empty compound area. He wanted to build a small, prefabricated city with a dozen homes and several warehouses. He said that she should think of a miniature Fold community and get it all built.

He went on to also request a computer center and a multidisciplinary lab.

Erica smiled and asked if she had a week or a month to do what he was requesting.

Bram said that he was not sure but that she should talk to Lacy to get a feel for the timing. He was going to Fold all the structures to a location that only he would know.

Lacy smiled and said that he was becoming a real rebel, and she was pleased to be on his team. She said that when the time came, he should be sure to take her along.

Bram said that he would of course make sure she was on the list, but he was not sure of the timing.

As Lacy left the office, Marcus and Remi were waiting to enter. Lacy commented that they were about to get a surprise.

The two entered and Marcus asked what was up.

Bram updated them and shared what his plans were.

Remi gave a grunt and said that having an oversight committee would stall all their work and that moving the work to another location was indeed the answer but a challenging and time consuming one.

Bram asked Remi if he was willing to lead the analysis of the four Earth-like worlds that Marcus had found.

Remi said that he was honored to be asked and that he would send out sampling bubbles to each that day and have them analyzed by the end of the following day.

Bram looked at Marcus and said that as the prefab buildings got set up he would like to get them Folded to the world that he and Remi agreed was the most suitable. He asked that he and Marcus find the most suitable location to set up such a city.

Marcus asked what they would call the selected world.

Bram suggested Gaia.

Marcus replied that he liked the idea of using an ancient Greek deity as the source of the name.

Bram said that he was sure that Pat or someone else would want to have a naming contest. He said he was fine with another name as well. More important to him than the name was that it would be available for them to utilize on a time frame that made sense.

He asked the two of them to work with Pat and Amy in determining the layout for the new city they were about to establish.

He shared that not all the folks in the current organization would be able to be relocated to the new world and that they should think about if they personally wanted to relocate.

Marcus thanked him and said that he would discuss this at home. He was not sure how Myla would react. He said that Myla had been doing well in her recovery from the abuse she had suffered when she was a young girl, but he was not sure how she would take to the idea of moving to another world.

Remi commented that he was certain he would like to go but that he would be open to initially staying put.

Bram said that they would get together later to develop a transition plan. He personally would most likely be living in both worlds. He would need to keep up the appearance that the current site was fully functional.

Linda buzzed in and gave him his end of the day ten-minute warning.

Bram walked out to the van that would transport him home. He looked at the armored truck that had the lead position, his van that was in the middle and the armored truck that was behind it. He marveled at the small army of guards that protected his movement inside of a fenced in and guarded compound.

Bob commented that his job would keep him on guard duty as long as Bram was thought to be on Earth but when the time came he would like to be considered for the opportunity to go to another world.

Thomas said that he was with Bob on the request.

Bram replied that he would keep the request in mind, but he would not make any promises until the actual time came to make a choice.

He smiled and said that the choice might come much sooner than anyone might imagine.

On the way home Pat listened as Bram brought her up to speed on what had transpired. She asked how Bram planned to get a small city built on another world in time to avoid the oversight committee.

Bram replied that he was hoping that she would become a city planner and builder.

Pat replied that she would be glad to get involved and lead such an effort, but it would require folks that were real city planners. She said she was sure that Amy would also love to be involved. They had both talked about the fact that being called Captain no longer held much allure or meaning and they were both ready to sink their teeth into some meaningful project.

Bram suggested that she contact Erica who would be able to get the right resources. He said that Erica was onboard with his desire to establish this small city on another world.

Chapter 4: Negative Space

Bram had been pulled away from his exercise with the Fold equation to stay involved with communicating with the Swoshians now he was eager to get back to learning about the negative Fold space realm. On his arrival at the office, he asked Linda to have the cafeteria fill the order that Pat had given Chef D'Carluca for a weeks' worth of meals. He joked with her and said that the two of them could go on a picnic when he returned in the afternoon.

Linda replied that she felt like putting in more food so he would not go hungry and if he did return in the afternoon, she would invited extra people to the picnic.

Bram thanked her for her lack of confidence and said he was heading out to meet Remi and go over the bubble interior to make sure everything was ready.

Linda waited until Bram had left and then called in an additional cooler to be loaded with sandwiches and other items that kept well.

When he entered the Lab, everything went silent. Bram had gotten used to the reaction of the lab folks but this time the bustle did not restart. He took this as the fact that they all thought he was about to take a risk about which they were concerned.

He had sent out three scout bubbles that had never returned so he was concerned as well, but he figured that once he understood the problem with what happened to the three bubbles that had not returned, he would be able to solve the return problem.

He knew that Pat was super worried because she had not said a word about his Fold into the negative space since their discussion the evening before.

Chef D'Carluca arrived to personally deliver three coolers and to stock up the small refrigerator that Remi had installed in the bubble. He said nothing about the extra food that Linda had added or the same amount of food that he had added. He had also filled Pat's food order.

He figured that Bram had at least three weeks of food in the three coolers he put into the bubble.

Bram knew that the bubble was the largest that Remi had so far constructed, yet it seemed like a tight fit.

Remi explained that he had added extra battery power so that Bram could sparingly heat the interior. Remi then opened a locker and pointed to a space suit that had its own oxygen feed. He made the point that if the bubble was breached Bram should immediately get into his suit that would give him almost a days' worth of time.

Bram then knew that Remi was as worried as everyone else.

Marcus arrived and made sure that Bram had the most up to date coordinates of all of the solar systems they had so far explored and put others in as well. He said he had included the coordinates of every new world that they had found including Swoosh.

Bram hoped that all the worries being displayed would all be for naught. The overwhelming concern was having an effect on him, and he decided that it was time to Fold to his first negative coordinate.

He felt that this first negative coordinate which was for only a few centimeters would allow him to recover and backtrack if he felt that things had gone wrong.

Pat gave him a hug and in an unusual display she gave him a long kiss. She whispered that she had his back and that she would make sure he came back.

Bram thanked her and had to turn and enter the bubble so she would not see the tears that she had generated.

Bram took his seat and waved to all the folks that he knew would be watching. He smiled and said that they should talk to Linda about the picnic they would have when he returned.

He then pressed the button that triggered the first negative Fold.

The black void of space with countless stars appeared as streaks of light that made the screens look like a fourth of July starburst explosion display.

Bram knew immediately that negative space did not act in any way similar to the positive space in which his world existed.

The streaks of light stopped, and Bram knew that he was at the initial coordinates that he had programmed. He just had no idea where he was.

The area around him was an empty portion of space. Bram knew that the path of the solar system was along a spiral at the edge of the Milky way galaxy. The time to make one rotation was close to two hundred and twenty million years. So, the only logical thing that he could conclude was that time and distance did not stay synchronized as it did in positive space. He knew immediately that his problem was a significant one. If they indeed acted independently and he did not know how to manipulate time as he did distance, he was lost. It was like being dropped into an unknown forest in an unknown country on an unknown continent.

He knew he was in big trouble.

He felt that the initial miniscule distance he had programed should have him close to his own solar system.

He used his on-board telescope that was hooked to the screen and saw what looked like a solar system at the farthest distance that it reached. He figured out the coordinates and then entered them into the computer and pressed the Fold button.

The stars once again appeared to be streaks of light and then the bubble stopped.

Bram was out at the edge of the solar system. He noted that if it was the star that was his Sun then he must have traveled back in time. There were two planets that clearly were covered in water. One was in the position that Earth would orbit, and the other was in the position that Mars would orbit.

He determined the coordinate that would place him within the radius of the moon. It was then he noticed that there was no Moon!

He was then sure that it was a very young Earth, and it seemed to have more water than the Earth that was his home. He took note that there was only one huge continent surrounded by water. He could not see any living thing that was on a very wet continent that was barely above the water.

He determined the coordinate for the planet that he was sure was Mars. When he came out of his Fold, he was looking down at a world that was also covered in water. It, however, seemed to have plants or something green in the waters that were undulating as if dancing to a slow love musical of the sixties or a sad melody of one of the spaghetti westerns.

It was clear to Bram that life had first appeared on Mars. He wondered what happened that caused the planet to lose its water and become the bone-dry planet of his time.

Bram took a few moments to estimate where in time he might be. After a few moments of thinking about it he estimated that he was several billion years in the past.

He wondered how he would be able to return to his own time. He was certain that it would not be a linear path back and at the moment he was clueless on how to determine how to manipulate time.

Hunger interrupted his train of thought.

Bram Nielson Collection

He looked at his mechanical clock and realized it had been more than twenty-four hours since he had folded, and he had so far not eaten or had any sleep. He decided to have a sandwich and then try out the bed that was on the other side of the latrine.

He realized he had a major problem, and it was one that at the moment he had no clue how to solve. In fact, he realized that he did not understand what the problem was.

He took a wet towel bath as Pat had suggested. He realized that she had put in all the items that allowed him to take it. Afterwards he felt refreshed and ready to sleep.

When he awoke he checked to see if he was still at the coordinates at which he had stopped. He was surprised to find that he was not. This was something that he had not anticipated.

He checked to see how long he had slept and realized that he had been out for more than twelve hours. In that internal passage of time the exterior time in negative space must have changed much more dramatically.

He was no longer in the solar system!

He had no idea of the Bubbles coordinates.

He decided to try the coordinates to the first of four Earth like worlds he planned to visit. He wanted to visit each as quickly as possible and then visit the water worlds and end up at Swoosh as soon as possible.

He was hoping to get to a location that allowed him to Fold near to an Earth that was within a time that he would recognize.

Three Folds later with no signs of getting to the locations he had hoped, he was ready to try the Swoosh coordinates. The visit attempts to each of the previous worlds seemed to have happened at random times that he felt could be millions of or billions of years before the current Earth time.

He continued to feel ignorant of how time presented itself.

He realized that the realm of negative Fold had no linearity of time associated with it. Instead, it was more like a negative rhombicosidodecahedron (RCDH) with time randomly leaping from the edge of the negative time sphere to some other point on the spheres edge.

He knew that it would take him a significant amount of time and many experiments to see if he could learn to control movement in the negative Fold realm.

Time was a precious resource that he knew he was running out of as he ate yet another sandwich from the diminishing supply in the coolers. He had come to realize that Linda had indeed added more food to Pat's order. It seemed that everyone had added something that they thought he might need. He realized that he had many people worried about him. He decided he needed to begin rationing his food so that he would not starve to death.

He put in the Fold coordinates for Swoosh.

He realized these coordinates were closer in time than previous coordinates because Swooshes Star was into its early death throes. He had no clue how far from the actual time he was off. He decided to experiment with trying different Folds that were close to the one where he was.

After about a dozen such attempts and at least two of his normal Earth days he realized that he still had no clue how to find the right coordinates on his imaginary RCDH Archimedean sphere with more than sixty-two regular points on its surface. In fact, it might have thousands if the Folds were going to sub points of that surface.

He realized how totally lost he was and that getting back to Earth was going to take a miracle.

He decided to get another good night's sleep. When he woke up, he again tried to figure out how to get back to his time.

In the "morning" he found himself looking out at the Swooshian Star, but he knew immediately that he had gone farther back in time because the sun was in a state of good health.

He wrestled with the coordinate thinking about how to do so on the surface of a sphere where each segment represented a different time. After three Folds he learned to increment closer to the current Earth time. However, the sphere he seemed to be in currently encompassed the Swooshian system. It did not include the Earth, and he had no idea how to set the coordinates for the surface of the rhombicosidodecahedron surface that would encompass the Earth in the negative universe.

He was about to throw up his hands when the clicking on his radio receiver registered in his mind that it was morse code. He figured the only way for it to be possible was that it was being sent out via the Fold transmitter that he and Remi had just developed and it was the message that Remi had first sent out, "the quick brown fox jumped over the lazy dogs back." And then it was followed with a morse code in Swooshian that said, "follow the light, follow the blinking light, and at the very end it spelled out, I have your back, follow the blinking light."

Bram used the scope and at the extreme edge of the scope's range he saw the blinking light. He set the coordinates that he could determine that would get him closer to the blinking light.

The message coming in got stronger, but it took him another four Folds before the light became steady and then each subsequent Fold got him closer to the source. He realized that he had taken more than a dozen Folds before he felt that he was back to his own time.

But a scene from one of the movies that had a fighter pilot calling in as he approached a landing on an aircraft carrier that he was coming in hot was really appropriated. He was coming in blind and hot. He had no clue how to land his bubble.

He hoped the source was a few feet above the surface and approximately at the center of the bubble he was in.

He took out the last sandwich and took a bite and then hit the Fold button. He had hoped it would be his last Fold, but it took him three more times and he was chewing on the last bite of his last sandwich when the inside of the Hanger surrounded his bubble.

He then received instructions to put the coordinates that had just been sent to him into his computer and then do one more Fold. He recognized the determined voice Pat used when she was doing something she felt strongly about. It was not a request but an order that any Marine General would have followed.

He watched as the area around the bubble became surrounded by what seemed to be the entire Fold organization.

He was almost knocked over as Pat ran to him and jumped into his arms.

She asked him if he knew how long he had been gone.

Bram replied that he could only estimate that it had been much longer than he had anticipated and that even by rationing the food he had eaten it all.

Pat had tears in her eyes as she informed him that he had been gone for more than a month. Everyone had been concerned about him running out of food, but it seems that everyone had added extra out of concern.

Bram waved at everyone and said that they should plan to attend a celebration that Linda would arrange with all the extra food that he had come back with.

Linda laughed and asked if there was any food at all in the bubble.

Bram shook his head and said that he had eaten his last bite and had sipped his last bit of fluid which was a beer that he had found in the fridge.

He then asked how Pat had come up with a way to reach him. She said that it had been an idea that, Remi, Marcus, Mallica and she had come up with. Remi had suggested using morse code, she asked about sending out light via the Fold message magnetron, Marcus had provided more than a thousand coordinates of where to beam the signal and Mallica had added her part in Swooshian.

Bram complimented the four of them for having developed a beacon. He likened it to a light house beacon to warn ships about dangerous waters but in their case, they had developed a beacon to guide his ship into a safe harbor. He also pointed out that by beaming light, Pat had confirmed that the magnetrons would be able to transmit video.

He asked whether it was five in the morning or five in the evening.

Pat pointed to everyone in the hanger and said that they had all rushed to the hangar when word got out that you had returned. It has been a stressful time, but everyone continued to focus on their work and in your absence a phenomenal amount of work has been done.

She replied that it was five in the afternoon and that it was time to go home.

I am looking forward to sitting next to you on our dual recliner and listening to the tales that I am sure you have to share.

Linda asked if she could announce a day off and a picnic at the community center. She said that her parents were ready and eager to hold such an event. They said they would expect that they would get an invite to a Sunday breakfast where they could hear what he had learned.

Bram said he had no clue as to what day it was, but he suggested that they make the picnic on Saturday, and he would welcome the Stetson family for breakfast on Sunday.

Linda let him know that it was Thursday, and that Saturday would be perfect.

Pat guided Bram toward the side hangar door.

He realized that he was walking a pleasant gauntlet of friends welcoming him back. Every one of his close supporters were giving him praise for having come back safe and alive.

Once he was in the van, the convoy moved out and made its slow way toward his house. Zoe said that he looked like he had lost weight.

Bram replied that he had eaten as best he could, but Pat had just underestimated the amount of food he would need.

Eric commented that he was lucky that everyone added to the original order. He asked how the sixpack that he had put in the frig went down.

Bram chuckled and said that he had celebrated each time he got closer to the light and the last sip went with the last bite of food. He said that the beer was great.

Bob greeted them as they got out of the van and said that the Chateaubriand was just coming out of the oven, and everyone should go directly to the dinner table.

Bram thanked him and said that he was taking the elevator to his room and taking a quick shower, and he would be down in five.

It was a marvelously delicious dinner. It reminded him of the story of stone soup where all the people of the village contributed an ingredient so to a soldier who had volunteered to make a special stone soup. He put in the stone and the villagers kept giving him food items to add to it. In the end the soup had been fed to a hungry village that complemented the soldier for making such a delicious stone soup.

That triggered his memory about a Vietnamese story about a King who felt that he had not eaten well for a long time, and he put up part of his kingdom as a reward to the person who would feed him the best meal. All the famous chefs tried their hand and failed.

The King was out for a ride when a peasant said he was in the middle of preparing one of the best meals in the world. He invited the King to share it with him.

The peasant began by putting a water filled iron pot over the fire and added pieces of really tough meat. He suggested the two of them go for a walk while the meat cooked.

On returning from the walk, he added rice and stirred it in.

He sat and talked with the King about the tough life he had lived and the family that he had raised.

He kept checking the pot and as the day came to a close he said it was not quite ready. He offered the King his bed and took his place on the floor.

The next morning, he once again checked the pot and put in a head of chopped cabbage and cut carrots into chunks and added them.

He once again took the King for a walk. This time they walked along the canal, and the farmer threw in a baited line attached to the end of a bamboo pole and handed it to the King.

The King hooked and pulled in a rather nice sized fish. He commented that he had never been fishing before.

The farmer complimented the King on the prize fish he had caught and carried it back. He prepared it to put into the stew.

He then pointed out that it was rather late, and it would be better to wait until morning when everything would be cooked to perfection.

By the third day the King commented that he was really getting hungry.

The farmer dropped the fish into the stew and shortly he had a thick bowl of rice laced with soft sliced cabbage with the cooked fish the King had caught. He put the bowl of gruel in front of the King and suggested that he put the salty, fish sauce mixed with red pepper over the gruel.

The King took one bite of the steamy hot gruel and declared it the best food he could remember eating.

The peasant was granted his piece of land and became a close friend of the King.

Pat knew that Bram was off somewhere in his head and reminded him what he had agreed to during dessert.

Chapter 5 Political Driving Force

The dessert discussion led to a political discussion when Zoe asked what he was going to do about the oversight committee that the Senate had approved.

Bram looked over to Pat and asked how the city building on Gaia was going.

Pat shared that it was eighty percent in place. The power source was generated by wave water and would support a city at least three times the size of the present one that was near completion. She went on to say that the lab would be the most advanced one that the Fold organization would have.

Zoe asked who would be on the list to move there.

Bram replied that his bodyguards could make that choice, but he asked that they remain as his local bodyguards until the moment that he permanently made the transfer to Gaia.

Pat then smiled and said that she and Amy had run a contest to see what the planet's name should be. They took everyone on a visual tour of the planet that had been selected. She said that the visual tour was very beautiful and awe inspiring. The new world inspired a mirid of names and Mataia (Ma ta ee ah), meaning awesome, won the contest.

Bram shook his head and said that he wanted to see the video tour of Mataia so that he could get used to the name of the planet. He then asked what their star and solar system was called.

Pat replied that those names were still under consideration because they had spent the rest of the time looking for him and didn't have time to manage the next naming contest.

Bram thanked her for focusing on guiding him back and asked how she had figured out how to find him.

Pat smiled and said that intuition and luck had played the biggest part, but she credited Remi and Marcus for providing her the message and the coordinates to direct the beam too. She went on and explained that they had beamed twenty-four hours a day for more than a month during their search for him and that all of his bodyguards had participated in keeping the beam going.

Bram again thanked everyone and said it was good to be back.

He said that their work had provided him a way to try to see if he could explore negative Fold with bubbles that were equipped to look for and then follow the message beam back to a Fold point that would let them fold back to their launch location.

He figured that he would most likely lose a few bubbles before he figured out the exact way to enable the bubbles to return.

Zoe made the snide comment that he could go out a few more times personally to make sure his method worked.

Bram smiled and said he would need to look again at the folks that qualified to migrate to the Mataia. He said he felt like giving her a hug for once again being willing to virtually tweak his nose.

The next day at work, Erica came to his office and asked if he was willing to discuss how to handle the oversight committee that had been approved and was in the process of having members selected and approved by both political parties.

Bram said he was eager to discuss the strategy they should follow and how slowly they should educate the committee. He made the point that they had made so many breakthroughs that they needed to manage how to share those breakthroughs and who should be the face that shared them.

He said he had no interest in dealing with that committee after their initial on-boarding.

Erica agreed and said that she had no desire to be the face either.

She suggested that Jeffrey would make the best face. He had the political connections and had developed a close relationship with the current administration. She went on to share that John Morgan had recently told her that he was planning to retire and that he had been asked to be part of the oversight committee but had declined.

Bram asked if a message to the President suggesting that he designate Jeffrey as the next NASA director would help.

Erica said that it would make a significant difference since she had learned that there were two other qualified people on the short list. Neither of the two were familiar with the Fold effort.

Bram asked Erica to stay so they could immediately put together the message to the President.

Bram penned the message and ask Erica for her input.

He incorporated her suggestion of making the point that Jeffery had intimate knowledge of the Fold project and would make the best candidate that would bring a wealth of knowledge that he could use to educate the oversight committee.

Once the message was sent, Bram suggested they get an early lunch so he could get together with Remi and Marcus and plan out the continued exploration of negative Fold.

Pat joined them on an early lunch. She asked if the two of them wanted to take a quick tour of the city on Mataia.

Bram asked what the city name was going to be.

Pat smiled and asked Erica what the name was. Erica smiled and said that she had won the naming contest with the entry, Einstein City.

Bram gave a small laugh and said that the name was an excellent choice. He asked how long the tour would last.

Pat replied that they should spend a couple of hours but that a full tour would take closer to a full day. She went on to say that a day on Mataia was twenty-five hours long.

Bram suggested they take the short tour at the end of the day so he could get himself reoriented before the tour.

Remi smiled when Bram walked into the lab. He and Marcus had been discussing their success at having reached Bram and given him a beacon back.

Rem shouted out, "The quick brown fox who jumps through negative space is back."

The entire lab cheered and then clapped and shouted, "The Fox is back."

Bram smiled and thanked everyone and then sat down next to Marcus.

He more quietly thanked both Remi and Marcus for having spent the hours that they had in trying to get him back from negative space.

He then commented that in their current universe, time on the macro level always ran in one direction. It was always away from the time of the big bang. But on the micro level of electrons and quarks, time had no direction and could not be detected. He admitted that he had no clue as to why that was so, but it was so.

He then shared that in the negative space universe, time was present, but on a macro scale it had no orientation or direction. Its direction seemed to be random in nature. He was sure it was not random but followed a non-linear pattern.

He said that in trying to return, he had visited the Earth, but it was at the time when the single continent of Pangea existed. He then went out to Mars and discovered that at that time there was a sea that covered much of the planet, and it appeared as if there was plant life in the water.

He had traveled back in time!

That was something that was impossible in their universe where time always flowed forward.

Marcus asked how he had been able to position himself where he could receive the signal being sent out from their current universe.

Bram reminded them that Pat had put the bubble being used to send the transmission halfway into the negative Fold space and kept the other half in the positive Fold space.

He pointed out that what she had done was create a hole between the positive universe and the negative one. This let the signal being sent to originate from a single point in the negative universe.

He had been lucky to have folded to the distant galaxy home of the alien planet, Swoosh. He arrived there before their sun began to die. He then tried the coordinates of the dry worlds that had been found and then returned to Swoosh and this time it was near the time that the Swooshian's had sent out their call for help. It was close enough that a blinking light was at the far horizon of the on-board screen.

It was morse code blinking, "The quick brown fox jumped over the lazy dogs back," followed by, "I have your back."

It took me many tries to get close enough to that time in order to have the coordinate for the hangar to take effect.

I think you would put the entire return into the category of a miracle.

It is one that I know was supported by all but driven by the two of you and Pat.

Remi made the point that Pat was driving everyone to come up with any idea that might be of help. It was Mallica that suggested using Folded light to transmit the signal. He had suggested the fox message and Pat added "I have your back."

He pointed to Marcus and said that all Marcus had done was to give them thousands of coordinates to send the message to. In fact, the way he figured it Marcus had supplied several hundred thousand coordinates just to test the ability of the supercomputer system.

Bram asked which coordinate had worked.

Marcus replied that there was no way for them to know. He admitted to having set up a random coordinate generator to send out as many signals as the supercomputer could generate.

He smiled and suggested that Remi was just jealous that the random coordinate generator had worked.

Bram smiled and thanked the two again for having saved his butt.

He then asked if they would lead the effort in exploring the negative universe with bubbles. They would have to figure out how to send out bubbles and then retrieve them. After conquering that aspect, the negative Fold space could provide a look back in time.

He then threw out the possibility that they might be able to look to the future in the negative Fold universe. If they could, he doubted that they would be looking at the same world if they looked at Earth. He commented that if they could, then they could all get rich by playing the stock market.

Marcus smiled and said that Bram had a conniving part of his mind as well as the genius part. He said that he would enjoy exploring the negative Fold universe.

Remi said he would love to, but he had his hands full setting up his new lab, but he was really curious to see what the actual color of the dinosaurs' were.

Bram then brought up the oversight committee. He said that he was holding a meeting in two days to discuss how to bring that committee on board and what to share at what time. He said that he did not want them to learn about all their efforts at one time and there were several areas that he did not want to share until some distant future.

Remi smiled, looked at Marcus and added that Bram also had a shrewd section in his brain as well.

Bram smiled and said he was discovering totally unused space in the voids of his mind that the two of them were pointing out.

He looked at the clock and realized that it was time for the tour to Mataia that he was looking forward to.

He asked Marcus and Remi if they wanted a quick tour of the new city on Mataia.

They both said that they were eager as well as ready.

Bram led the three out to where Pat was awaiting them. She said that the three of them made for a full load. She said that Amy was staying behind to monitor the Fold and be there when they Folded back.

The coordinate for the arrival location was inside of what was designated the Arrival and Departure terminal.

Bram commented that the terminal had not been an item on his original list.

Erica shared the fact that Pat and Amy had made substantial improvements and had requested many items that had not been on his original list. She commented that they had practiced his bad habit of wanting it yesterday and had hounded her for every additional item.

Pat gave a small laugh and said that she had only gone after the critical things. The power generation system was one of those requests. She praised Erica for having found and delivered the water powered system and the resources that helped them install it.

Pat led the group around the housing complex that featured homes with spacious yards that had plantings. Every street was paved and had sidewalks.

Bram asked how she had managed to get the infrastructure in place.

Pat admitted that currently there was no water, no activated sewage system, and no electricity. The streets, sidewalks and light poles had all been Folded into position.

She pointed at Marcus and thanked him for his ability to exactly position every item.

Marcus said that he had only used the coordinates that she and Amy had provided and then adjusted them for the fact that both the Earth and Mataia were in orbit and spinning.

Bram commented that he was impressed with Marcus's mathematical ability.

Marcus replied that the supercomputer and the programing abilities of Linh and Duong had allowed him to write an initial algorithm that could be used over and over.

Pat led the group to a large building that had a sign designating it as Fold Work Center. It was another structure that Bram commented he had not specified.

Erica said that it was a building that had been folded from a location on Earth where it had been standing. It was actually a structure that was a couple of years old and had been purchased for a song. It had been scheduled to be demolished so that a housing complex could be built on the site. She had arranged for a building mover to set the entire structure up for moving. The building movers said they were not equipped to move any building as large as she was asking to move. She told them she was not asking them to move it but to set it up for a move.

She then worked with Marcus about the Fold to move it.

She gave the basement and footing information to Pat.

Pat said she had worked with a contractor to pour the footings and the basement walls above ground just outside of the Fruit Barn. She was told that they had never done anything like she was asking for, but they would do it.

She said that getting the hole dug was the hardest part. She confessed that she and Amy had learned how to automate a backhoe to dig a basement. They had repeatedly used it to dig basements for all the homes. Then it came time to do the big basement for the Work Center.

Then we automated a bulldozer and a bucket loader. We now possess a fleet of automated heavy equipment whose control programs we continually improve.

Pat added that they had learned the hard way that the shovel, spade, and hoe were still tools that they could not automate. They also automated a ground tamper and an electric generator to supply power.

Bram shook his head. He commented that he was amazed that they had found the time to do it all while he was wandering lost in time and space.

Pat commented that there was nothing else for her to do and both she and Amy figured that they would need new skills beyond being certified astronauts that were no longer needed as bubble pilots.

They felt they had achieved the status of city builders, and certified heavy duty equipment operators.

Remi walked into the lab and stopped. He commented that he was ready to stay. He asked who had specified the lab layout and all the test equipment.

Pat laughed and said that he had. She reminded him of the time he had shared what should be in the Lab and how it should be laid out. She waved her hand around the room and said he got what he had asked for. Or she corrected, that he had what she had heard and recorded.

Remi again said he was ready to stay.

Erica commented that Bram had paid a pretty penny for all the latest lab equipment.

Bram replied that it was a pretty penny well spent. He said he was impressed with everything that he had been shown so far.

Pat led them up to the top floor of the building. The view of the ocean in one direction and the view of the mountains in the other and then the long beach line in the two other directions made them all stop and take a deep breath.

Pat commented that she had made the entire floor plan open and that every desk had an amazing view in three-sixty.

Bram said he wanted to join Remi in staying.

Marcus spun around and said he had never been in an office that made him feel so invigorated and ready to stay at work.

Erica gave Pat a hug and said that she too was so impressed with what had been accomplished and she was ready for the next request.

Pat replied that in another month everything would be in place and the ability to stay would be real. And her next request would be the furnishings for all the homes and the offices.

Erica said that it would be no problem because Bram had a bottomless expense budget.

Bram nodded and said that they might as well live big and get the best of everything. He commented that he was sure both Amy and Pat would earn the title of genius interior decorators.

He walked over to Pat and gave her a hug. He commented that she had proved to be more versatile and effective than he could ever be.

He said that his Fold back was anticlimactic after seeing what she and Amy had done with their 'spare' time.

Bram walked over to Amy and thanked her for being the best desert pilot that he had ever known and that on Sunday he was having a special breakfast for all his personal pilots.

When they got back Linda reminded Bram that she had everything set up for a big lunch starting at high noon at the pool side club house.

She had gotten the two Marine bands and a guitar player to provide entertainment. She said it would be one of the best attended events that they had held. She knew that Jeffrey and his family would be in attendance and there might be others that were coming in.

Bram thanked her for the heads up.

After they got home, he said that he preferred a light snack and then he wanted to spend time in his office before getting to bed early.

He had missed sitting with Pat and was looking forward to sipping on a glass of sparkling water and having Pat laying against him and reading.

He commented that he enjoyed having a person of gigantic capability using him for a pillow.

Pat replied that she enjoyed leaning against a fearless though somewhat mindless genius who could solve the most difficult problems but could not recognize the danger and go mindlessly into an unknown environment.

Bram woke up early Saturday morning and after a quick shower he went down the two-person elevator to his office. He was deep into the mathematics of a rhombicosidodecahedron (RCDH) diagram when the office door opened, and his four bodyguards and Pat more or less burst into his office.

They said that they had worried about where he was but had listened to Pat who had assured them they would find him in the office with either a bubbly glass of sparkling water or a cup of tea.

Eric reminded Bram that he was to have two of his FBI body guards with him at all times.

Bram apologized and pointed to the two persons lift and suggested they put a Bram alarm on it because he had come down from his bedroom and he had immediately gotten into his negative Fold investigation and not thought for a moment about bodyguards.

He chuckled and asked them where they had been when he had needed them during his wandering in the proverbial negative Fold desert looking for the promised land.

Zoe shook her head asked if he wanted brunch.

Bram asked the time. Pat said that it was the same as the time shown on his computer. She smiled and said that he could believe his computer when he stayed in the positive world.

He pushed a button, and the large screen came on showing a screen full of equations and a series of mathematical symbols with scribbling. There was no computer time anywhere. He then asked again what time it might be.

Pat pointed to the wall clock and said that it was not the mechanical clock that he had relied on for more than a month, but it was showing real Earth time.

Bram smiled and said he had not looked up since he had glued his eyes to the rhombicosidodecahedron and started to break it down into a series of equations.

Zoe asked him to speak to them in English and not negative Foldeese and what was his answer to having brunch.

Bram shook his head and said that what he preferred was to shut down his computer and get the rhombicosidodecahedron out of his mind and walk down to the club house and see if Ted and company had any snacks and maybe he would ask Eric for a recommendation on what beer was the best to drink with a brat.

Bob commented that all four of them would be on duty during the picnic. He said they did not expect any attacks but that had been the case before every attack. He and Thomas had met with the General who had his observation team active, and they would be monitoring the area around the Fold compound looking for anything out of the ordinary.

Thomas commented that Bram's Marine bodyguards and every off-duty Marine would be present as well at the picnic. Their armament was stored in the back of the club house in a van.

Bram commented that he was surprised at the level of protection.

Pat said that Lacy had put out a warning that her network of listeners had picked up some discussion about eliminating Bram before he created a situation that would crash the financial market.

Bram smiled and said that they were too late, and he had already let the cows out of the barn. They should be happy to learn that the cows had tall grass to go through, so they were moving out slowly.

He stood up and said that he was now certain to need a beer or maybe two. He started for the door and Bob got out ahead of him and told him to follow him to the Club house.

When they stepped out of the house they were surprised to see Orlando standing next to Castor and Donna. Orlando was in a First Lieutenant Marine Officer's uniform.

Bram stopped and commented that he had never touched a Marine Lieutenants' Eagle Globe & Anchor Pin and slowly did so. He pointed at the Expert Rifle pin and commented that he had witnessed that expertise as it saved his life. He pointed at the Jump Parachute with wings and a machine gun across it and said that it would frighten anyone on the ground to watch Orlando coming down from the sky at them. He pointed to the Pistol expert pin and commented that he had witnessed Orlando shoot the fly off the top of his beer bottle and then take sip from the lips of that same beer bottle.

He smiled and then gave Orlando a hug and congratulated him on getting promoted.

Orlando gave a salute and said that he was promoted because of Bram's recommendation to the General that had suggested making him a Captain.

Bram smiled and said that he always did get confused by military ranks.

He then pointed to Castor and his new USMC Sergeant Major of the Marine Corps uniform and said that if he shot the next attacker before he the attacker could shoot one of them he would put in his recommendation to the General to the next rank.

Castor replied that he and Orlando had been together when they talked with the General who had made it clear that Bram had made his recommendation all the way up to the Chief's of Staff who had then called him to ask what Orlando, and he had done to received such a recommendation.

Zoe said that Bram valued being kept alive and protected and that he had a similar impact with his FBI bodyguards who each were promoted in place and had to turn down jobs at other locations so they could get him to keep sending in recommendations.

Orlando turned and said that it was time to get to the rec center. He said he would lead the way and make sure the bar got opened.

They were the first group to show up.

Bram walked over to Tom and after shaking hands asked if there might be a brat or two available.

Tom said that he had brats, sausages, sliced and barbequed brisket.

Bram asked for a brat and a sausage. He said that he was sure to have some brisket later.

Ron Mueller

Tom said that Rita had also prepared ribs, steak, and sirloin for the main course. He said that she kept asking what Bram might want the most.

Bram walked over to where Rita and her sister Marial were setting up the food tables. He gave them both a hug and then complemented them on the food they were preparing and that it looked and smelled delicious.

He promised that he was going to take at least a bite of everything.

Cedric had just put a dish of sweet potatoes down and came over and gave Bram a handshake. He commented that Bram had just made his wife and her sister very happy with his promise to try a little of everything.

The members of the community started to arrive.

The Marine Band set up and played classical background music.

One of the younger members of the community asked the band if they could play songs that would support the Harlem shake.

The Marine Band switched to the music that supported the Harlem Shake.

Bram was surprised by Zuri who gave him a hug, took his arm, and said that she would teach him the Shake.

Bram laughed and followed her to the dance floor. He did not wait but went into his version of the Harlem Shake.

When the music changed to "Teach me to Dugie," he did his version and again surprised Zuri who was laughing and shouting that she had found a closet dancer.

Then the DJ announce that the next song should be done in a Conga line and Bram decided that he would sit and watch. He saw that Orlando was in front and that Elizabeth was holding on to him. He was surprised to see Jina holding on to Elizabeth.

Bram saw that Pat and Amy were in the line, so he got up and broke in and got between them.

The dancing stopped when Ted announced that the food was served, and it was time to picnic.

Each table had a number on it and the food line went in the order of the table number.

Bram had selected the table whose number put him in the middle. He had made sure his bodyguards got one of the first tables.

Lacey and Linda had asked to sit at his table. Linh and Duong were also at his table and the last two were Orlando and Mallica.

Orlando commented that he had been asked to write a ditty about a mad scientist that was willing to risk his life by venturing into the unknown. He asked if anyone had any ideas about the wording.

Pat said she had a few words, but she could not share them in public.

Chapter 6 Negative Fold Scouts

The Sunday breakfast was fully attended. Bram was doing the cooking. He used extra blueberries and chocolate chips in the pancake mix and got great feedback on how great they tasted with Maple syrup and butter. The sausage patties on the side were consumed at a high rate.

Bram felt good about being able to serve the core of the people that had rescued him from the negative Fold world. He knew that he was the living example of what great teamwork could do.

He had worked with Pat to set up a video to share once breakfast ended. The lead in was a tour of Mataia, and Einstein City.

The Entire Stetson family, the Juma family, Marcus and his kids and a few other folks were in the dining area. If he had offered he could have filled the community center, but he wanted to share some information that he did not want to be widely know at this time.

Pat took over and said that unless someone had a better name, the city she was going to show was going to go by the name Einstein City. In time she said it would be the capital of Mataia, the planet that had been selected to house the Fold operation and its community. She shared that the solar system was at least two light years away and it had six planets. Mataia was the fifth planet out and the only one that appeared to be habitable, but she said that they knew very little about that system.

Pat and Amy had used a camera drone and had done an excellent job of mixing longer range shots that zoomed in and then gave close ups of many nature sights and also showed the details in Einstein City.

The tour impressed everyone, and Pat and Amy got tons of positive feedback and many questions about the plantings that were around the yards. Amy made the point that no Earth plants had been Folded to Mataia and that all plantings came from that planet. She stressed that up to this point plant life was the only life that had been found.

Pat made the point that everything Folded to Mataia had been sterilized in an attempt to keep from contaminating it. She said that she and Amy had installed an ultraviolet light gate that everyone went through when they arrived on Mataia and that those arriving walked across a rug saturated in disinfectant to prevent contaminating Mataia.

The presentation then transitioned to the Negative Fold realm. Bram shared how disoriented and how amazed he was that time seemed to be non-linear and that it did not flow in one direction as it did in the Universe that they lived in.

It instead seemed to randomly move based on the coordinates that a Fold was using. He commented that for him the mechanical clock keeping time in the bubble was the only thing that had let him know the actual time that had passed. It had allowed him to keep him from losing his cool. He admitted that the length of time that he had remained lost exceeded all of his expectations. He pointed at Pat, Linda, and Chef D'Carluca and said that the food they had all put into the bubble kept him from starving.

He then pointed to Marcus and said that all the coordinates that he had dutifully recorded provided a means of slowly getting closer to the time of his home universe. He had learned how to get back to his time, but he had also figured out that return by that route to his start time on Earth was beyond his lifetime.

He then pointed at Mallica and said that her use of transmitting light via the Messaging Fold Magnetron and Pat's ingenious use of well used phrases sent by old fashioned morse code provided the means to get back to the positive time universe. It became the beacon safety that he followed in via many more Folds than he had anticipated.

He looked around the dining area and said that they were all welcome when it came time to Fold to Mataia with him.

He said that such a move would only occur if it seemed they were losing control of the Fold program. He made the point that discovery of new capabilities had come so quickly and there was every possibility that new discoveries would continue, and he felt that oversight would most likely become very political and hinder progress.

He made the point that negative space, where time was random in its flow, might also lead to the ability to move forward in time and see the future. If such a thing existed it would be very troubling from a social-political point of view. It would be an ability that would make life as they knew it uncertain and more like a pool of quicksand.

He said that they and a handful of others would need to do a lot of exploring and development in order to understand all the breakthroughs on which they were working.

He pointed out that politics was now taking a first step into the Fold effort that so far had been a non-political effort. He made the point that there was no stopping it, but it was incumbent on them to manage it so that the power associated with the ability to Fold was somehow kept in balance and used for positive endeavors.

The next day, he Marcus and Remi met in Remi's new lab located by the Fruit Barn. They were setting up the lab to be where Marcus could launch and retrieve the scout bubbles that would be sent into the Negative Fold environment. The goal was to minimize the exposure of the effort but set it up for success.

Bram suggested they first use tethered bubbles that they could physically retract. He said that by repeatedly sending them out they might be able to map what was happening and how to control the bubbles.

He said that having the control bubble halfway into the Negative space area as they had done to rescue him and having that bubble held in place with three bubbles in normal space would provide the halfway bubble the stability needed to pull the negative space exploratory bubble physical back.

Together they designed and outfitted the control bubble and got the exploratory bubbles equipped. By the end of the week, they had the effort organized and ready.

Bram said that as soon as they learned how to control the exploratory bubbles he would step back, and Marcus could then determine how to explore the negative Fold arena. He asked that when Marcus learned how to direct the exploratory bubbles they all get together and figure out how to set up a control system that allowed the exploratory bubbles to move about on their own.

Pat and Amy had spent the week in continuing the development of Einstein city and Erica had delivered all the office furniture and artwork that could be hung to provide some break in the open office area.

Erica had made the point that the water treatment work had been a challenge since they were having the local contractors do the work normally done down in a hole in the ground out on a flat surface near the Fruit Barn building. After it was complete and the appropriate hole dug in Mataia, they would Fold the object into the hole.

She credited Pat and Amy with getting the exact coordinates needed at the moment of transfer and with Marcus's ability to hit those coordinates within a few millimeters.

She commented that she was impressed at his ability to hit a moving target more than two light years away so accurately.

Marcus had admitted that the movement of the solar system that Mataia was in and the movement of the planet itself had made identifying the exact coordinates a challenge. He shared that he and Mallica had come up with the equations that determined the transfer coordinates that the supercomputer generated just before the Fold. He said that so far it seemed to deliver the objects within plus or minus a half a centimeter.

Bram commented that such a feat was simply mind blowing since on Earth a tolerance that tight was seldom achieved in general construction.

Amy said that she and Pat were always amazed when their prefab objects popped into existence exactly where they needed them. Even after having moved several hundred large objects into position and doing several thousand smaller Folds they were still in awe that they could construct an entire city. They joked that the most work they had done was to program and automate several pieces of construction equipment to do the heavy work but had failed to automate the basic shovel.

Amy let out a pretend groan and bent over with her hand on her back. She said that Pat was forgetting all the pick, and the spade work they had so far endured during the city building.

Bram smiled and commented that he had wondered about Pat's six pack abs and her muscle-bound shoulders. He thought she had bulked up just for him.

He then complimented them and said that the capability that they had developed would be priceless in setting up the construction business for the transition it would face in the near future. He suggested they document their learning and be prepared in the future to train the construction community in the basics.

Pat commented that the city now had running water and an operating water treatment plant.

They had set up each home with geothermal HVAC systems that also generated the electricity for each home. The geothermal system also provided the lighting throughout Einstein City. This approach provided the margin of power needed to support the Fold process.

Many systems on Mataia were in place and the water powered generator was capable of topping off the electrical consumption needs. She pointed out that some of those needs would be for the additional manufacturing that they might not have anticipated.

Bram asked if there were any overhead services and learned that everything was either underground or in the case of the local internet it was broadcast to each house from the light poles in the neighborhood.

He asked Pat if she had their home picked out and furnished.

Pat let him know that the house was near the beach. It was furnished and his home office would impress him. She said that when everything was ready they could take a vacation to their new home.

Bram said that he would love to do that and that she should plan on the activities that they would engage in for their Mataia vacation.

Pat said that she wanted the two of them to pick out the locations they would visit on each day of their vacation.

Bram said that he would enjoy going through the video of the tour she had documented and pick out those locations.

Pat shared that she had requests from several folks about doing something similar. She asked if Bram had any reservations about such vacations.

Bram thought for a minute and suggested that she and Amy set up the protocol and that the folks that chose to take such vacations would adhere to a do not pick, disturb, or try to bring home artifacts of any kind.

Once back to the lab it became clear that the Folds into negative space was turning out to be a challenge. Even though tethered to the control bubble, the exploratory scout bubbles seemed to end up in random time periods and random locations.

Marcus had decided on a rapid mapping approach. He had determined the time it took for the bubbles to get to the end of their tether and had then pulled them back and reset them and then sent them out again.

The bubbles were going out at roughly five-minute intervals and Marcus was slowly plotting the pattern that they were making. He soon learned that the pattern was not random but followed the rhombicosidodecahedron surface that took on the size of where the Fold ended.

After making some forty Folds he realized that he was slowly forming multiple sixty-two-point rhombicosidodecahedrons that Bram had described.

Then he began to speculate on the coordinates of the next point based on the initial coordinates that the probe used. He hit a home run and knew that even on a tether, each Fold of the exploratory bubble took it to the next point on the surface of a rhombicosidodecahedron the size that was determine by the coordinates to where they had been sent.

This was amazing to him, and it also posed the next challenge and that was how the desired point on the rhombicosidodecahedron could be selected and a bubble sent to that specific point and then be brought back in a reasonable time frame by skipping the intermediate points.

Marcus asked Bram and Mallica to stop by to help him determine how to direct the bubbles.

Bram listened to Marcus and asked Mallica if she had any idea of how to proceed.

Mallica looked at Bram and said that she was ready to listen to whatever had just flashed through his mind.

Bram asked Marcus to pull up a diagram of a rhombicosidodecahedron. He then asked Marcus to put a small one on the left of the screen and a larger one on the right side of the screen.

He pointed to the small one and said that if they were to create a small launch rhombicosidodecahedron in their space and use each point as a launch point, he speculated that the exploratory bubble would go to the corresponding point on rhombicosidodecahedron in the negative space realm.

He went on to say that the size of the negative space rhombicosidodecahedron would depend on the amount of the time as measured in their space that the exploratory bubble traveled. Once it reached the comparable node it could be moved just as Marcus had learned to move the bubbles on his first round of sending them out.

The return when triggered should bring the exploratory bubble back to the point corresponding to the next point of the rhombicosidodecahedron in normal space that corresponded to the point on the negative space rhombicosidodecahedron.

Marcus nodded and said that it would take him almost a month to verify Bram's thesis, but he felt sure that he would verify what Bram had suggested.

Mallica said that she was going to work on a program that an exploratory bubble could use to then move around negative space in a controlled fashion and then return after it made its designated round.

Bram asked Marcus to look up the amount of time that had been set on his very first Fold into the negative space.

He asked that Marcus begin with that time. Bram said that once they verified that they could control the exploratory bubble, he wanted to return to that ancient past of Earth and see what animals were roaming on Pangea. He speculated that the dinosaurs where predominant during that time.

Marcus said that if they learned to control the exploratory bubbles he would certainly want to become a bubble explorer.

Mallica nodded and said that a host of folks would pay dearly to be able to take such a vacation trip.

Bram gave a laugh and said that the two of them could set up a business of taking folks on negative Fold vacations to ancient destinations.

He speculated that they might be able to take folks to see a gladiator battle at the famous Colosseum arena in Rome.

Marcus said that it had just struct him that the negative Fold realm would provide archeologists and other scientists a way to go to the origin of their particular field and learn firsthand the facts they were trying to verify.

Bram nodded and said that such capability would certainly be sought by countless individuals. It would be knowledge that needed to be shared at the end of all the changes that the current society would undergo.

He suggested that they needed to learn if they could only see the events or if they could enter and participate in such events. That would be one of the capabilities they would need to determine. He said that it was a particular frightening thought if they were able to enter into that fabric of time.

He speculated that initially they would only be able to look but he was sure that a way to enter into that fabric of time could be discovered. He thought about his own temptation and decided that the ability to enter the fabric of time would be the last place he would investigate, and he would make certain that those after him would need to really hunt to get to that capability.

Bram brought up the fact that the negative fold universe was one that they should all keep secret for their lifetimes. The upheaval of all the other breakthroughs would be all that the world could handle in the next several lifetimes.

Marcus, Mallica and Remi all agreed but Marcus said that he was personally going to see about the dinosaurs.

Bram said that every one of the primary participants of the Fold program would get a chance to learn firsthand about much of the ancient times.

Later when he shared the discussion with Pat she added that one of the biggest draws for her would be those moments mentioned in the bible.

That triggered the alarm bells in Bram's mind. He commented that the time of the human was especially worrisome. He pointed out that much of what everyone believed and that was a foundation of two thirds of the world's population might have many holes in the story they believed in.

Whatever they learned would need to be evaluated against creating a tear in the fabric of the current world social order. He pointed out that the changes that the Fold technology would create would be a dramatic strain on that social order and that adding a religious strain on the social system might be taking a jump into the abyss.

Pat said that she agreed and that she recognized that her eagerness was like a lemming rushing over the cliff in its eagerness to follow the ones in front of them.

Bram nodded and said that they were leading the millions that would follow, and they should relish what they were learning and then should carefully and slowly expose what they had learned to those that would follow them and those that would take their place.

Ron Mueller

<u>Chapter 7: Family Feud</u>

When Bram arrived to work on Friday morning, Remi was waiting and said he had to check with Bram to see if he had authorized anyone to take the exploratory bubble out.

Bram replied that of course he had not.

Remi said that the exploratory bubble was missing so either it was accidently Folded, or someone took it out.

Bram asked Linda to contact Marcus.

Moments later she said that she had no answer from Marcus and had not been able to leave a message because his phone was either off or out of range.

A feeling of concern went through Bram. He led the way back to Marcus's office. It was empty and it was clear that it had not been in use.

He then went back to the Lab where he and Remi had set up the negative Fold control computer. He refreshed the screen and pointed to the most recent coordinates. He said that he bet that those coordinates corresponded with Earth's location when there was only Pangea and that the early dinosaurs were roaming across its surface.

Bram activated the computer that he had used on his Fold into negative space and verified the coordinates of Earth close to that time. It was a close match.

Remi asked how they would get Marcus to return.

Bram replied that he was sure that Marcus would return on his own. He wondered aloud what might have caused him to take such a risk.

Remi shook his head and said only some extreme emotion would.

Bram led the way back to his office and asked Linda to contact Myla to see if she could find out what had upset Marcus.

Bram then led the way to the cafeteria. As he went past Linda's desk he mouthed where he was going.

He had been invited by Chef D'Carluca to taste a special cinnamon and cream Danish with which he was experimenting. Chef D'Carluca said that he would enter it into a cooking competition if he got a number of Fold personnel and Marines to say it was not only good but great.

He brought out two Danish that he had made that were still warm from the oven.

Bram savored the sweet of the warm cream and found the surprise of warm blueberry flavor as he bit into the piece that he had cut and was slowly chewing. It was indeed great.

He was about to compliment Chef D'Carluca on the magical creation that he had come up with when he saw Linda entering the cafeteria.

It was clear that she was not delivering good news.

He put up his hand and stopped her from saying anything. He cut a liberal piece of his Danish and pointed for her to sit down and try the most wonderful treat she would ever taste.

He took another bite for himself and then finished with a sip of the tea that had accompanied the Danish.

Linda finished her Danish and commented that it indeed was the most delicious Danish she had ever eaten.

Chef D'Carluca was beaming and said that he would fix all three of them whatever they wanted for lunch.

Bram said he would settle for a small steak smothered in melted blue cheese. Remi and Linda put in their orders.

When Chef D'Carluca left for the kitchen, Bram looked at Linda and said that she could now share the sad news that she had walked in with.

"Your right, but it really is sad news," I learned that Myla had decided to end their marriage. She felt as if Marcus was wed to his work versus her.

Linda said she had asked about the kids and learned that Myla wanted to leave them with Marcus. She wanted to start anew. Linda then shared that she had asked if Myla had told Marcus about leaving the kids with him and found out that she had not because he had left as soon as she had made her declaration that she was leaving.

Bram looked at Remi and said that he had just figured out how to get Marcus back home. They were going to let him know about the kids.

He thanked Linda and asked her to arrange a meeting with Myla at her home and that he would go there as soon as they had sent a message out to Marcus.

He then led the way to the lab and asked that the negative Fold interface bubble be put in position.

He then typed in the phrase, "Get good dinosaur pictures. The kids are yours and waiting for you. Follow the light back." He put the transmission into a do loop that would repeat the message over and over and then he went back to his office.

Remi had agreed to stay in the lab and wait for Marcus's return.

At lunch he asked Pat if she had time to go with him to Marcus's house and talk with Myla.

When Pat asked what was up, Bram explained the situation. He said that he felt that they should intervene and see if they could make the transition easier on Marcus.

Pat said that Amy could manage what the two of them were doing and that she would go with him.

Bram was silent as they took the short ride to Marcus's place.

Zoe and Eric had decided to be the ones to escort Bram.

Myla opened the door when Bram rang the bell. She stepped back and waved the four of them into the living room. She commented that it was like Bram to choose a face to face to find out what was happening.

She watched quietly as Zoe and Eric followed their normal routine of clearing the house.

Bram nodded and asked if the kids were in class. Once Myla verified that they were, he asked if her decision to leave was final.

Myla nodded and said that she had made the decision not so much about Marcus's work but more about the change that she had been experiencing as she attended her therapy sessions. She made the point that she felt as if she had arrived at many of her early life decisions based on her troubled past. She now wanted to experience the freedom she felt she had missed.

Bram commented that she was giving up lot to learn if that freedom, she was imagining, really existed.

Myla said she understood that and had discussed it in depth in therapy and had come to the decision she had made.

Her therapist had asked the same questions and given the same advice as he.

Bram then asked when she planned to leave.

Myla said that she was packed and ready to leave as soon as Marcus returned. She wanted to make sure the kids were safely in his care.

Bram asked whether he and Pat could have the kids for the afternoon until Marcus returned.

Myla asked from where Marcus would be returning.

Bram smiled and replied that was confidential, but Marcus would have real dinosaur pictures for the kids.

Myla shook her head and commented that Bram had just given her information that made her leaving easier and yes, the world in the Fold environment was one that held uncertainty and caused her anxiety.

She then said that he and Pat could have the kids for the afternoon or however long Marcus took to return.

She then thanked Bram for having helped in opening up the world for her. His support at just the right time had changed her and had given her new strength and would always be cherished.

Pat asked if she could arrange transportation.

Myla replied that Linda had called just before their arrival and had done so. Myla commented that Linda seemed to know exactly how this discussion would go.

When the honk of a horn interrupted the discussion, Myla stood and pointed to the three large suitcases that were in the corner of the living room.

She took one and asked if the two of them would push the other two to the door.

Zoe led the way to the door and stepped outside and joined Castor and Linda.

Once Myla was on the way, Pat suggested they go by the recreation facility, where school was held, and meet the kids there and bring them to the house.

Bram agreed and said that they should have a special dinner prepared and that he hoped Marcus would make it back by that time.

He contacted Remi and asked him to bring Marcus to dinner and that he was invited as well.

Remi commented that he did not want to get involved in the discussion with Marcus.

Bram reassured him that the discussion with Marcus would happen after dinner in the privacy of his home office.

Once they had Marcus Jr. and Mylan home, they got Zoe to take care of them. He watched as Zoe suggested they get any homework due the following day done and then she would watch a movie with them.

Bram discussed the evening meal with Thomas who had the cooking duty. He was pleased that it was to be sweet spareribs, green beans, and mashed potatoes. It was the type of dinner that could be held for some time and still be served hot and fresh when the time was right.

He hoped that Marcus was able to follow the light which presented a short cut past all the nodes that time would take him through in the normal return sequence. It turned out light in the negative Fold realm actually followed a very precise rhombicosidodecahedron node pattern whose size was based on the distance of the first fold. Following that pattern might take centuries and perhaps even thousands of years if the first Fold distance was as far out as Marcus had gone.

The parallel rhombicosidodecahedron in normal space that they had set up allowed the short cut that he had postulated, and that Marcus was to verify. He hoped that his theory had been right and that a quick Marcus return would verify the theory. He smiled when he thought about how he had underestimated the movement in the negative Fold realm and how Marcus was personally going to verify the concept of using a parallel rhombicosidodecahedrons in normal space to understand negative space.

Dinner had been ready for forty-five minutes when Remi called to say that Marcus had returned and had been apologizing for his weakness.

Bram suggested that Remi remind Marcus about apologizing about decisions that he had made and that the two of them get a ride to his house since dinner was about to get served.

Marcus's arrival pulled Marcus Jr. and Mylan away from a game they were playing with Zoe and Eric. He gave them a hug and then gave them each the dinosaur pictures that he had taken. The two kids took in the pictures and ask how he had gotten them and was the color of the dinosaurs the actual color?

Marcus spent a few moments sitting on the floor and talking to the two.

Bram declared that dinner was about to be served and everyone should fill their plates and then take their seats at the dinner table.

Pat guided the dinner conversation. She had the kids share how their day at school had gone and how they were doing in school.

When Mylan asked where her mother was, Pat said that Mylan would learn that from her father once they all got to their home.

Mylan nodded and a small tear ran down her face. It was clear she knew what was going on and that her mother had left.

Pat walked around the table and gave her a hug and whispered that she could come over at any time she felt like. She then gave Marcus Jr. a hug and made the same offer.

Bram complemented Thomas on the great desert.

Bob spoke up and said that desert had been his. It was a French version of Apple Strudel, but the Ice Cream was pure American.

Marcus Jr. said that it was the best desert that he had ever eaten.

Bram agreed. After a moment he asked Marcus to join him in his office. He led the way down the stairs to the basement where his office had been moved. He asked Zoe and Eric to wait outside of the office.

Zoe agreed but said that they would first check out the office.

Bram led the way in.

Marcus stood quietly. He had the urge to apologize for his actions but knew that Bram would just stop him. He knew that he had broken a key trust and wished he had not done so.

Bram began by saying he was sorry for the emotional pain that Marcus was experiencing. He went on to say that Myla had expressed the fact that she still loved him but that she needed to go out in the world to experience the freedom that she thought she had missed.

Marcus said that phrase, "the freedom she had missed," kept reverberating in his mind. He thought of their marriage as a relationship that was bound in love and warmth and held all the freedom that anyone would wish for.

Bram commented that Myla had said she was waiting to make sure he understood that she was entrusting the children to him because he was a great dad and that he would teach them the fundamentals of having a good life.

Bram then made the point that another unauthorized Fold journey would be his last. He reminded Marcus that it was strike two and there would be nothing in the Fold program after strike three.

He then suggested that they go back upstairs, and that Marcus take the kids home and explain what was happening. He suggested that Marcus send Myla a note letting her know that he would take care of the kids. Then he should take the kids on another weekend Fold vacation to where they could spend the time playing. He suggested a theme park and a beach.

Once upstairs, Marcus said thanks for the evening meal and then led the kids out the front door.

Bram and Pat watched as the three walked hand in hand toward their home.

Bram whispered to her that he wanted her to know that she provided him with the confidence to try anything. She was the bedrock on which he stood and the advice she had given him on how to handle the situation with Marcus had been dead on.

Chapter 8: A Fold Vacation

Pat turned to Bram and said that she was ready for the Fold vacation about which they had talked.

She shared the fact that Melisa had been traveling and locating Fold secure coordinates to be used to facilitate vacations. She had safe coordinates in most of Europe, the major parks in the US, Hawaii, and Alaska.

Melisa had asked if she should charge for the vacations and Pat said that she and Amy had suggested that there should be a charge that would pay for the cost of purchasing or renting vacation homes that had so far been contracted but the charge should be significantly less than that which tour groups charged for similar accommodations.

Bram suggested a meeting among the four of them and Erica to finalize how vacations were to be treated and get that approved. He said that Erica would manage getting the approval and once that was in hand the two of them would take a vacation through the northern arc of Europe and visit, Sweden, Norway, and Finland and then get warmed up with a stop in Rome.

Pat asked how long of a vacation he had in mind.

Bram replied that he figured a minimum of three weeks. He smiled as he said that a bubble-based approach meant that they would lose no time at airports so the time away would all be spent on enjoying the vacation.

The next day, the meeting was more of an articulation of the travel that Melisa and her husband had taken, as she went to each location and arranged for the housing, than a discussion of how to charge for the vacations. She explained that she had worked with local realtors to find a place at each location that she felt would work.

After either purchasing or signing a long-term lease, she worked with Marcus to determine the coordinates for the spot in one of the rooms that was designated the arrival-departure room. Marcus and she then tested each spot to ensure they had exact coordinates. She and Marcus had agreed to three tests to make certain that each location worked.

She smiled and said the bubble was empty for the first two tests but on the third test, someone from the team would transport in. She said that if they asked their closest co-workers they would learn that each had taken a one- or two-day mini vacation at the locations that were cleared to be used.

Once she had verified a location, she and her husband would take a weekend Fold there as they transitioned to the next location.

Bram looked around the room and asked who had already tried the bubble vacation.

Erica smiled and raised her hand and said that she had been to the Rome bubble location and had gone to the Fontana di Trevi threw in her penny to make a wish. She pointed to Pat and said that she had made her wish come true. She added that she had also toured the Roman Colosseum.

Bram shook his head and commented that the most work driven person on site had escaped to Rome and played while the rest of the team worked their heads off.

Erica responded that she was number six in the string of folks sneaking off to get away from the hard driving mad scientist in the room.

The exchange ended when Linda entered the room and let Bram know that it was time for his meeting with Remi.

Bram asked her where her bubble escape had been.

Linda smiled and commented that the cat must have gotten out and yes, she and Lacy had gone to Stockholm over a weekend.

Bram smiled and said that he was pleased that everyone had become willing to evaluate the accuracy of the coordinates and that no one had ended up inside of a wall or buried in the floor.

Erica replied that they all had confidence that Marcus would have the right coordinates.

Bram went out to the van and his small army left the compound on the way to Remi's new lab. They had been working on an innovative approach to the transport bubbles that would make them less expensive to fabricate.

Remi had discovered that a ten-foot tube made of the same material as the current bubbles would be half the price and could be of any desired length. He had worked with the fabricator and modified the tube into a U tube. Remi was pleased with the fact that he would have a flat surfaced floor to work with. He had designed a variety of tube lengths that featured two, four, six and twelve seat versions. The seats were paired, and each seat had its own control screen. Each pair of seats were independent from the others, but all could control the tube.

Bram complimented Remi for the design that he was implementing. He suggested that a refreshment center be located in the back and that each seat had access to a place to put snacks and a drink.

He asked how many tubes of each size Remi had on order and learned that Remi was waiting for the two of them to decide.

Bram said he thought three tubes of each length would be a good start. Later, if the program grew, more could be ordered.

He suggested having one tube that could hold several Swoshians.

Remi said that three of each size was what he had thought about as well and he had checked with Erica about such an order, and they had agreed to that number unless things changed during the meeting between them.

He said he would add the order for the largest one, but it would be for only one unit.

Bram agreed that was a good start. He said that he should contact Mallica to see if only one bubble for the Swooshian move was enough. He then asked if the bubble scout program was affected and learned that it was not and that scout bubbles were much smaller, and the cost of production was relatively low.

Remi commented that what was affected was the large bubbles that were being planned for the Alien transport. He commented that large enclosures made of two long J like extrusions mounted to a matching flat surface made making the very large vessels for the aliens much easier to make, assemble and to mount the interior equipment. The structure was much easier to work with than the bubble design.

When Bram asked about the assembly, he learned that it would be done in the same location as the first Swoshian bubble.

Remi then brought up the limitation that had surfaced was of getting the material to make the J and flat piece.

Bram suggested that the flat part could be of a different material and that the material from Mataia or one of the other discovered planets be directly Folded into a storage hangar at the producer's site.

Remi said that he would use each of the new tubes and make their first few trial runs, runs to transport the materials needed for construction of the next set of tubes. It would allow him to stress the vessels and not risk losing equipment or people.

Bram finally brought up the fact that he and Pat were going to take a rather long vacation and that he hoped that on his return the first new exploratory vessels were ready for trial.

Remi asked if they had decided on where they would go.

Bram replied that it would begin in Copenhagen then make a big circle through Norway, Finland, and Sweden and end back in Malmo, Sweden just across from Copenhagen. Then they would Fold to Rome and end the vacation there.

Remi wondered why they were going to Rome.

Bram smiled and replied that he was just trying to warm back up before returning to Dalles. He then added that Pat wanted to throw a coin into the Trevi fountain to wish for more vacations.

Remi nodded and said that he was with Pat on that.

Two days later he and Pat left for Copenhagen. Their Fold out was accompanied by their FBI bodyguards. Their bubble Folded into a large empty room of an apartment that turned out to be above a Sushi Bar.

Zoe and the rest of the bodyguards did a quick check of all the rooms. They then all walked slowly through the large corner apartment and admired both the design and the unique layout.

Zoe commented that the kitchen seemed designed for a chef. The pots were all hanging and arranged by size and function. The knives were on a magnetic strip below the hanging pans. A glass cabinet displayed a myriad of spices.

Eric opened the stainless-steel refrigerator and pointed to a note that said they should enjoy the variety of Danish cheeses and sausages, and it gave information about each cheese.

The cheeses:

Danbo – Often called "Denmark's national cheese" made of slightly sour cow's milk. (PGI status)

Esrom – "Trappist Style cheese. It has "Protected Geographical Indication (PGI)" meaning it can only be made in Denmark.

Tilsit Havarti – also known as Danish Tilsit has an intense flavor and aroma

Bla Kornblomst – "blue cornflower" it is luscious, rich, and velvety organic cow's milk cheese that melts in your mouth

Mycella – This blue-green veined cheese with a sweet and savory flavor smoky over tone is made on the tiny Danish island Bornholm in the Baltic Sea between Zealand and the southern coast of Sweden

Vesterhavsost – "North Sea Cheese," Produced from the milk of west Jutlandic cows and ventilated by sea air for at least thirty weeks.

Danish Sausages:

Garnatálg – This sausage comes from the Faroe Islands. Garnatálg is a specialty prepared with cured sheep intestines and sheep tallow. The combination is shaped into large, oval pieces which are then air-dried.

Rød pølse – Sausage made with pork meat lightly smoked over beech wood. Created in the 1920s by resourceful vendors who would color stale sausages with red dye and sell them at a slightly lower price.

Medisterpølse - Classic Danish pork sausages prepared with pork, lard, onions, and a variety of spices such as cloves, allspice, and pepper.

He commented that they would need to go out and buy a selection of Danish beers and wines so they could enjoy the cheese and sausage.

Bram commented that Carlsberg was the icon Danish beer.

Pat commented that grape wine was a very recent thing for Denmark and that it had just recently become legal to produce there. Before the law changed only the European countries designated as grape wine producers could legally make commercial grape wine. They, however, had a long history of making apple and cherry wine as well as wine with other fruits. She suggested getting a bottle of each of them as well as a grape wine.

Bram suggested they go out shopping and get the appropriate amount of beverages and any other food they wanted to stock up with. He then said that on their return from shopping they should try the Sushi Bar before they came back up to their apartment.

Once back and well into the meal they were all eating at the Sushi restaurant, a meal that they were calling dinner, they discussed what they would do for breakfast.

They asked the waitress to recommend a place where they could enjoy a traditional Danish breakfast. She recommend a restaurant where they would be able to partake of the traditional Øllebrød breakfast. She explained that it was a porridge or thick soup made of sourdough rye bread and beer and that had a slightly sour-sweet, caramelly taste. She commented that the restaurant she was recommending had some of the best breakfast coffee as well.

She said that after breakfast a walk to see the Little Mermaid would help to digest the wonderful and very filling breakfast.

Bram looked around the table and asked if everyone was up for a Danish breakfast. He said that afterwards he was planning a walk to see the Little Mermaid sitting near the entrance to the harbor.

Breakfast got a resounding yes vote and Bob said that he was really looking forward to the walk afterwards.

Bram had not mentioned that he had arranged for a van that would pick them up at the end of their morning walk to take them on a private tour to Copenhagen's most famous sites. He planned to have the driver meet them near the Little Mermaid statue.

Before Bram had left on vacation, General Tilson had approached him and suggested that he arrange for a Marine driver. He said he could have one at each desired location.

Bram had asked why the General was arranging for a driver and learned that the General was worried about his safety and that the van would be armored and the Marine a veteran of combat.

Bram had agreed and thanked him for thinking about it.

The General nodded and said he was just trying to protect the best assignment he had ever been given. He had let Bram know that he had made special arrangements for his drive from Oslo to Nordkjosbotn and that it would be the same driver as the one he would have in Copenhagen.

The Øllebrød breakfast turned out to be a big hit. Everyone kept umming and oohing and said that it was definitely a breakfast eating highlight though it was only a shadow of Pat's pancakes smothered in maple syrup.

Bram agreed and said that Melisa had arranged for a traditional lunch meal at a restaurant that he hoped would be as good.

Thomas asked what the lunch meal was called.

Bram said that he had Melisa write it down because it was a rather extensive menu that would certainly call for a really long walk.

He placed the handwritten menu on the table.

Zoe picked it up and read it.

Starter: a variety of Smørrebrød, which was buttered rye bread topped with any combination of meats, cheeses, and garnishes.

Main: Stegt flæsk med persillesovs, the "national dish of Denmark." It is a combination of crispy pork, potatoes, and parsley sauce.

Sides: Frikadeller, savory pork meatballs served with brown sauce, potatoes, and cabbage. Karbonader, breaded pork patties.

Desert: Rødgrød med fløde, a red berry pudding with whipped cream.

To drink: Your choice of beverage.

Zoe ended by licking her lips and said that she was already hungry, and she had just eaten one of the biggest breakfasts of her life.

Bram Nielson Collection

Bram agreed with Bob when he said he could hardly wait for lunch.

The walk from the restaurant took them through Langelinie park, a long narrow park along the harbor. The well-kept lawn seemed to call "sit your tush down for a moment and enjoy the feeling of my soft, thick coat."

The dark bluish green tree leaves provided shade as the sun rose slowly over the Swedish mountains rising above the building behind them. A warm breeze cooled by the cold water seemed to oscillate between being enjoyable and then chilling.

Bram pointed out that they would be Folding from their current apartment to one in Oslo that was about three hundred miles in the direction toward the eleven o'clock position from the Little Mermaid.

Pat held Bram's hand as they walked along the narrow part of the Park. She pointed ahead at the small statue of the Little Mermaid and commented that the bronze statue was just the right size and matched the vision she had of it.

Bram suggested that they continue the walk and go to the center of the park.

A very smartly dressed young man approached them and was stopped by Zoe and Eric.

He nodded and introduced himself as Marine Sergeant Matt Simple and said that a friend of theirs, Orlando had arranged for him to be the driver that would take them around Copenhagen and then he later would take them from Oslo up along the coast of Norway.

He pointed to where a black van was parked in the small circle a few hundred feet from where they were standing. He then said that Major General Lester Tilson had let Bram know that a driver would meet him at the statue of the Little Mermaid and that the General personally vouched for him.

Bram smiled and said he was looking forward to getting to know Matt better and to learn what he might have on Orlando.

Matt smiled and said that he had served with Orlando in combat and had some great stories about one of the bravest persons he knew.

Bram introduced Pat, Zoe, Eric, Bob, and Thomas.

Matt said that he had gotten reports on all of them and was impressed with all of them. He said that he had called Orlando and gotten his personal impression of all of them but the only thing he remembered at the moment was that he should not give Bram a weapon if he planned to shoot at anyone because Bram would wipe them out before he would have time to draw his own weapon.

Bram chuckled and replied that Orlando was known to often exaggerate a situation.

Matt nodded and said that he had learned about the first shoot out at the cave by the Rushing River and how Bram had rushed to the front. He knew Orlando like a brother, and he knew that Orlando loved to tell stories, but Orlando did not ever exaggerated about a battle.

Bram pointed at the Van and said that it was time for them to begin the driving tour of Copenhagen.

Matt said that the FBI had cleared the tour guide. He was known as one of the best guides in the region and he was sure they would all enjoy his narration as they toured the route that he had been given.

Bram liked the fact that the van had six buck seats in the back and had windows all around. He and Pat had the two middle ones. Bob and Thomas took the two front seats and Eric and Zoe the two back seats.

The view of the outside was clear, and the tour slowly headed towards their lunch destination.

Ron Mueller

Chapter 9: Scandinavian Food

&unch was the highlight that they all had expected. There was no doubt that it was going to be hard to beat the flavor and the general goodness that they all enjoyed. They all agreed that it beat out sightseeing and that they could sit all afternoon and pig out.

Their tour guide commented that they had just enjoyed the best of the best of Danish food. He said that he had a recommendation for dinner that would compete with lunch but in a different manner. He suggested they try a wild game and seafood mixed dinner. He said the restaurant was owned by a friend of his and was named "The Mermaid" so it should fit in with the tour well. They had started at the "Little Mermaid" and would end it at a place named after a sister.

He said they should lead with two pork spareribs tide together with soften dried plums and pieces of apple wedged between them and then roasted.

He then recommended Svinemörbrad which he described as open-faced sandwiches. He suggested slices of cold roast veal, whole fillet of sole, smoked salmon that would be served on well buttered rye bread and would be garnished with cucumber, scrambled egg, or some other variety of greens.

He went on to say that desert should be Æblekage which was an old-fashioned Apple Cake, or they could try Brombærsnitter, or Danish Blackberry Cakes.

Bram looked around and asked if they were all in agreement to try out the dinner that had just been described.

It was a unanimous yes vote.

The tour guide asked them to give him a moment to call his friend to make the arrangements and then they would take a short walk around the neighborhood so he could point out the unique architecture of the buildings and the time the structures were first built. He added that it would also give them a chance to walk off a few calories.

On the tour the guide asked about the security provided by the FBI and did they expect something to happen.

Bram smiled and said that the last time they had come to Copenhagen, a rude Dane had insulted Pat and this time she had insisted on protection.

The guide frowned and started to say, "But I understood this was your first time... and then he laughed and said, Oh I get it. I am not supposed to ask."

Bram nodded and the guide said he hoped that in the near future he would find out who his mystery tour members had been and why they needed protection.

They returned to the van and the driving tour continued.

They visited the Zoo, The National Aquarium, The National Gallery, The Amalienborg Palace, The Round Tower, The Rosenborg Castle, Christiansborg Palace, Kronborg Castle, a UNESCO World Heritage site, and finally ended at the Botanical Garden. It had been somewhat of a whirlwind and all of them were ready to sit down and relax.

They then drove a short distance to Nylavn street that bordered a boat channel and had a variety of boats tied along its sides. The guide friend's restaurant was next to a popular outdoor steak restaurant. Three tables had been set up outside of his smaller restaurant to seat them.

Their arrival had been timed so that the first course that consisted of the open-faced sandwiches were first. Both beer and wine were also immediately served. It was clear that they were getting special treatment.

The view of the canal was captivating. Tied off near the restaurant were very elegant boats with people sitting out on deck and enjoying a casual snack or dinner.

Every boat had a combination of sail and motor power to propel them and were very well kept and had small gardens of flowers planted at various locations on the boats.

The buildings on their side of the canal ranged in color from the grey of their restaurant to reds, blue, yellow or had their original unpainted brown bricks. The buildings across from them were similar in color and variety.

A constant stream of people strolled along the street.

The conversation at the table centered on the sites they had seen during the day and the guide continued to provide information and adding information during the discussions.

Matt asked about the timing of their travel and when they were planning to leave Copenhagen.

Bram asked Pat if she had enough of touring around Copenhagen.

Pat said that she was ready to go on to Oslo and do something similar there.

Bram took out his phone and opened the folder that had the information about Oslo. He said that they had a top floor of a building on Bankplassen way.

He shared this with Matt who had informed them that he was their driver in Oslo and then all the way up through Norway.

Their guide, whose name was Sten Møller let them know that he would also be their guide in Oslo. He said he had lived there for years and began doing guided tours there. He smiled and said that he would enjoy helping them pick out great restaurants to try the local Norwegian food and added that he had connections in Oslo.

Pat asked where they should plan to have breakfast in Oslo.

Sten volunteered that he knew a baker that made morning breakfast rolls and pastries for local restaurants and would most likely be glad to host them for a traditional Norwegian breakfast at his place. He pointed out that many of the very fine restaurants that were close to where they were staying did not open for an early breakfast.

He suggested they save the Café nearest to their place for an evening dinner and he would select a place for lunch that would fit with their tour.

Bram said that he liked the idea of relaxing and letting Sten make sure they got the best Norwegian meals.

Zoe asked if Matt would have a similar vehicle to tour them in Norway.

Matt replied that he was having his van shipped that evening to Oslo via a NATO transport vessel and it would be there for them to use the following day. He was going to ride with it to make sure.

He admitted that he had never had an experience quite like the one he was having and really wondered about who he was providing with a ride.

Bram smiled and replied that he was guarding a deviant from another galaxy who had invaded the Earth.

Matt laughed and said that he was ready to believe that it was something like that.

Pat chimed in and said that it was all about the ying and the yang of society. The two sides were always in a constant battle for control and at the end neither side really understood what the struggle was all about. However, it seemed that it was the little fish that always ended up on the hook and that the big fish never got on the line.

Bram shook his head and interjected and said that it was time to get to their apartment so that they would have time to finish their beer and wine and then catch their flight to Oslo. He recognized Pat's concern that had been triggered by Matt's comments.

That evening, Zoe commented that it was really hard to keep quiet about the Fold capability around Matt and Sten.

Bram Nielson Collection

Bram agreed and said that he was finding it hard as well but that they had to maintain tight security. He pointed out that he was going to have to insist that the folks going on these Fold vacations begin to use the word special flight as the description for how they traveled about.

Eric threw in that he was happy to be able to sit and enjoy his beer and snacks, be able to get a good night of sleep and then in the morning Fold to the coordinates of their Oslo location. He said that he hoped to continue to be impressed with Melisa's selection of places.

Bram agreed and said that he had instructed Melisa to determine what should be charged for each location but that it should be at least forty percent less than that of the top end hotels.

He commented that his bodyguards got a free ride and would actually earn income since they were on duty. He went on to say that after three beers or three glasses of wine they would have to declare themselves off duty and then the charges would quickly add up.

Zoe put on a sad face and asked if this was how he was going to get his revenge on her for her tweaking his nose.

Bram shook his head and said she was not even close, but she should make sure not to sleep too soundly when they returned to the Fold compound because she might wake up in negative space in a bubble with no food or water.

Pat sipped on her wine and said that the threats were getting a bit nasty and that she preferred they stick with deciding what they wanted to get out of their road trip through Norway.

Bram opened his notebook and showed the team the itinerary that Melisa had developed for them.

She had the ride beginning in Oslo, with a lunch in Donbas. The drive continued to Trondheim where they would stay for the night, and she had a set menu dinner reservation at the Trol restaurant that consisted of: Clam on the half shell, Trondheimssodd, Trondheim Soup, or Sodd, diced mutton meat balls, and a side of Norwegian flatbread. She suggested Stjørdalsøl beer and/or Karsk, coffee and moonshine.

She said they should set up breakfast when they registered at the Hotel Prinson.

She then suggested that they take plenty of snacks with them the next day and then go all the way to Grong where they could stop at the Garden Restaurant and do pizza or a wrap with ingredients of their choice.

They would then head to Fauske where they would have dinner and stay for the night.

Dinner would be at the Orlando Bar and Grill. She thought that would be appropriate because of their close friendship with their Marine friend Orlando. She recommended they keep the theme going and order the Orlando's House Steak, but it was their vacation, and they could choose to do as they pleased.

Their reservations for that night were at the Scandic Fauske Hotel. She suggested that breakfast be taken there and then they could drive on toward Bjerkaker where they could catch a late lunch and perhaps chose to spend the night.

But she had purchased a property up by Bardufoss out on highway Eighty-Six that had a large barn that could serve as a Fold site. She recommended trying to make it and then relaxing by taking a hike out into the forest.

Thomas said he was impressed with the suggested itinerary and that they Fold to their location in Oslo the following morning.

He added that a day or two in Oslo similar to their stay in Copenhagen would be enough and then they could relax, sit back, and enjoy the ride through the Norwegian countryside.

Bob added that he hoped that the food continued to be as good as they had enjoyed so far, and he suggested they add hikes at each of the stops they made so they would not balloon to double their size.

Pat agreed and asked that they all take some time and look at the cities and towns where they would stop and also the many parks and scenic areas they would pass and chose some key points of where to stop and hike.

She called up Google maps and began to follow highway six on which they would travel most of the time.

The discussion and the focus for the evening kept them all enthralled with what they were seeing. Zoe commented that she was really looking forward to the next leg of the vacation trip.

When they retired for the evening, Bram asked Pat how she was feeling about the vacation so far.

Pat replied that she was feeling very good, but she had the feeling that he had studied the trip much more thoroughly than she had anticipated and she was wondering what he might be holding back.

Bram shook his head. He said that he was holding back some information because he did not want to ruin the mood of wonder that he kept seeing from everyone as they discussed their experiences.

He admitted that General Tilson had some concern that the Marine spy knew about the vacation and that information might allow the big military fish he was trying to catch to take some sort of action. He was concerned that the long drive through Norway would provide some sort of opportunity for an attack.

The General had no specific intelligence, but he had taken every pre-emptive action he could take and was prepared to act immediately.

Bram added that as they drove along the highway, a US aircraft carrier would be sailing twelve miles off the coast with its fighter planes ready for takeoff. The General had been advised by his Admiral friend that the planes would always be less than five minutes away.

He then added that their driver Matt had been selected and assigned by the General. He was as much a war hero as Orlando and Castor.

Pat gave Bram a hug and said that he should tell the rest of the team so they could be as prepared as possible. She added that they were all professionals and did not need to be looked out for and it was their role to be on the lookout. She reminded Bram of having watched Zoe and Eric leap over the fence by the community pool in their skimpy swimsuits as they fired their weapons at the attackers. She pointed out that Bob and Thomas were immediately at his side providing additional support.

Bram nodded and agreed with Pat and said he would get them up to speed at breakfast the next day.

Not long after, they Folded to Oslo.

Zoe led the inspection of the apartment and then called out the "all Clear." Then she led the way around the apartment. They commented that the apartment was as luxurious and well-appointed as the one in Copenhagen.

Eric added that he was impressed with Malisa's eye to location and to her taste in the decor of the apartments.

They went out to do a brunch and were met by Matt as they exited the building.

Bram welcomed him and invited him to have brunch with them. Matt replied that it would be great to get something to eat.

Matt commented that their plane must have special clearance for them to beat him. He had sailed all night long and had arrived with his van just moments ago.

They went out to the recommended bakery and were greeted by the owner who let them know that Sten had called to let him know of their likely visit for breakfast.

He took them to a table that he said he had moved into the front for them. It had a large variety of muffins and sweet rolls and plates of cheeses and sliced meat.

He had everyone sit down and then brought two pots of coffee and a pitcher of cream to the table. He then made sure everyone had what they wanted and then left them to what he called his slice of heaven.

After everyone was well into eating and enjoying the cheeses and sausage, Bram asked Matt what he knew about the drive-up highway six.

Matt replied that he had no information other than that it was his job to drive and make sure everyone remained safe.

Bram shared the situation of what they might face in the drive through Norway.

Zoe took a sip of her coffee and said that the vacation had just taken on some spice, and they would be looking at the forest and mountains with a much sharper eye. She asked why Bram was sharing the information so close to the actual drive.

Bram admitted that Pat had convinced him that they all deserved to be as prepared as possible. He had hesitated because there was no actual evidence of any preplanned attack.

Eric gave a small laugh and commented that so far, they had never received any intelligence giving them a heads up before a specific attack.

Bram acknowledged that fact. He credited General Tilson with arranging both US Naval and Marine support.

Thomas suggested they all enjoy the sites they had discussed the night before but be prepared for the unplanned and for anything out of the ordinary.

Matt nodded and said that what he had just learned, explained to him the armament in the back of the van that he had been issued. He said he had been issued and qualified on a new smart laser guided grenade that had wings and a range of more than a half a mile. And he had been issued a weapon very similar to an AK 15, but the ammunition was smart ammunition that would bend toward a hot target.

Bram said that he was not surprised about the weaponry. He had been told by General Tilson that they were taking no chances and wanted to make sure that if there was an attack that he and the Admiral had the upper hand.

Matt looked around the table and said that he had no idea why Bram needed to be guarded, but he would do all he could to make sure they were kept out of harm's way.

Zoe pointed to Pat and said that they were just trying to keep Bram and Pat from getting into any major personal disagreements.

Matt smiled and replied that Orlando told him that Pat was known to be fearless and that she always had Bram's back. He would wait and see how Zoe handled the disagreements.

Pat said it was time to get in the mood for their day tour of Oslo and asked if their guide was somewhere where they could pick him up.

Matt said that he had Sten's address and phone number and would give him a heads up.

Once they picked up Sten, they all spent the rest of the day touring Oslo, and they had lunch and dinner at the places that had been recommended.

The day had been a long one but a very enjoyable one. Bram was relieved to have been wrong about sharing the fact that the General had given him some reason to expect trouble. He went to be hoping that the General was wrong to be concerned and that his folks assigned to protect him would relax and enjoy the vacation.

Ron Mueller

Chapter 10: Highway Six

The next morning, Matt met them outside of the Hotel and they began the rather long journey up highway six. They all agreed that their first stop was to get coffee and a morning snack.

It was clear to Bram that his bodyguards had resumed their guarding roles when they walked through the entire coffee shop before sitting down for their coffee. Even then one of them stood near the door in a relaxed position until replaced by one of the others.

He knew that the routine would continue wherever they stopped. This was what he had wanted to keep from happening, but he knew that given the past history of all the attacks they had experienced, the attack would occur when they least expected.

The drive-up highway six soon left civilization behind and nestled itself along the valleys that seemed to serve as passageways between the snowcapped mountains. Bram quietly took in the forest trees that seemed to form a gauntlet of various shades of green that had a soaring clear blue hood that seemed to have no end.

He thought that the sun's streaming rays seemed to be emitted from a glittering disco ball and belied the fact that somewhere ahead the black rays of hate might change that beauty into the vengeful rain cast on them by Od, the mad avenging Norse god. He likened it to the Ying and Yang of good and evil. He felt the presence of all the old warriors and mythical gods of the Vikings.

By lunch time the peaceful and relaxing ride had them at Donbas.

There they selected a tavern that Bram commented meant Musk Ox Tavern in Norwegian and that was offering Elgburger, that meant Elk Burger as their lunch special.

They all got a laugh out of the fact that it was a Musk Ox Tavern that had a special featuring Elk versus Musk Ox.

Zoe said that the restaurant owner must have gotten the idea by watching American Football where cows were recommending that folks eat more chicken.

The waitress suggested they try the Hubertus liqueur drink that was featured as a special to go with the meal. She explained that St. Hubertus was the patron of hunters, and that the bartender had a secret mix that people raved about because it was light and refreshing.

They all ordered it and later agreed that it had been a great drink recommendation.

After lunch, the drive continued to Trondheim. The plan was to stay there for the night. It was a pleasant drive with pine covered mountains on both sides.

They drove along the banks of several long lakes that made it look like the mountains and sky went up into the sky and also went deep down into the lake. They stopped at a high point and got out and stood and embraced the scene with their eyes and mind. They all stood in silence for a few moments absorbing the mesmeric beauty.

Zoe commented that it was hard to get back into the van and leave such splendor behind.

They arrived at just the right time at the Trol restaurant where the set menu featured clam on the half shell, Trondheimssodd, soup, or Sodd, diced mutton meat balls, and a side of Norwegian flatbread. They all ordered Stjørdalsøl beer with the meal and a Karsk, coffee and moonshine, with desert.

They agreed that the menu had been very different than they expected and the coffee with moonshine had ensured they would get a good night's sleep.

After the meal they agreed to a walk before checking in to the hotel.

They followed Melisa's suggestion and made breakfast reservations for eight in the morning.

The hotel desk clerk asked for them to select their breakfast items so the kitchen could have them ready for such an early breakfast time.

The next morning after a leisurely breakfast, they again followed Melisa's suggestion, stopped at a local grocery, and stocked up on snacks so they could last and have a late lunch when they got to Grong.

It was a long but enjoyable ride. The drinks and snacks were exactly what they needed.

In Grong they stopped and did pizza and then continued their drive to Fauske.

They arrived in Fauske and decided on dinner before checking in. The recommendation was to eat at the Orlando Bar and Grill. They all felt that it was appropriate because of their close friendship with Orlando. They decided that each of them would order a different item from the menu so they could get an overall impression of the place.

They got one order of Orlando's House Steak that, based on its size, they were sure was meant for a family of four, an order of ribs that was served on a large board and had onion rings heaped on it and a side salad, another similar order that had slices of beef, sweet potato fries and what seemed to be mac and cheese but with a different taste and one slab of ribs and fries made the final item.

A pitcher of golden Kroonenberg lager beer was ordered for the table.

The discussion focused on how good everything was and how enjoyable the ride had been so far.

They asked for a copy of the menu so they could send it back to Orlando as a souvenir.

After Dinner they checked in at the hotel and made their breakfast reservations.

The next morning after breakfast they piled in and headed toward Bjerkvik where they planned to have a late lunch and perhaps chose to spend the night.

They had agreed that their desired goal was to get to Bardufoss out on highway Eighty-Six that had a large barn that could serve as a Fold receive-transmit site.

Matt let them know that there would be a ferry ride from Bognes to a point were highway six continued in a valley on the other side of a range of mountains.

They got to Bognes, where they had to wait for the arrival of the ferry. They went into the coffee shop and had a coffee and an ice cream cone.

They were all outside walking along a path that led to the water when Pat pointed out the arrival of the ferry.

Matt led the way back to the van. He got the van in line leading to the ferry loading dock.

A truck cut in front of them, and Zoe commented about the rudeness of the driver of the truck. It seemed to strike a nerve.

The loader for the ferry signaled the truck to come onto the ferry first and positioned it up at the bow of the barge. He positioned cars around and behind the van.

The loader then positioned their van behind the truck. He seemed to be balancing the load so that the ferry would be level.

There was an announcement letting folks know how long the transit would be and that there were refreshments for sale on the enclosed viewing deck.

As soon as the van was in position and turned off, Zoe jumped out and signaled Thomas to follow her. She asked Eric to take Bram to the side behind the shielded part of the ferry.

She told Bob to stay and get ready for action.

Pat immediately had her radar at full power. She knew that Zoe was in the attack mode. She was not sure what had triggered Zoe, but she trusted Zoe's instincts.

Zoe followed the two men that had gotten out of the truck up to the viewing deck. She positioned Thomas on one side of the viewing deck, and she went to the other side. She was not sure what she was expecting but her senses were tingling. She moved in slowly toward the driver of the truck. He seemed pre-occupied as if waiting for something to happen.

The ferry pulled slowly away from the pier and then smoothly turned its bow in the direction they were going. The water was calm, and the ferry had only a gentle sway as it cut through the water. It was under way for about twenty minutes when there was a thunderous explosion. The nose of the ferry lifted up and then the nose seemed to take a dive down.

A horn started blaring and the boat seemed to stop and then the entire ferry trembled as the engines seemed to groan and begin a laborious pull backwards. The nose seemed to slowly come back up to the surface like a person who had fallen try to push themselves up.

Zoe called Eric and told him to push the truck off the ferry. At the same time, she pulled her gun and shot the driver of the truck in the head as he lifted his hand with a control pad in it. She took a quick step forward and deftly caught the control that was blinking in midair.

The bullet in the brain had shut down the signal to the finger about to push the button.

The controls in her hand was still active.

She heard Thomas shoot three times and knew that that the second person in the truck was dead. She kept her mind on the controller in her hand.

She felt the front of the boat rise higher and knew that the truck had been pushed over the edge.

She counted slowly to twenty and then pressed the button.

She had not been prepared for the size of the explosion and was thrown off her feet. She stood up and rushed to the window and saw the water that had been blown up into the air as if fell back down. She was surprised to see a ten-foot wave heading toward the ferry.

She called Eric and told him to get ready to withstand the wave.

The Captain had turned the ferry to a forty-five-degree angle as the wave caught up to it.

Eric pushed everyone behind the van. It seemed to be a reasonable place.

The water swept over the car deck and almost took Matt over the side. Bram reached out and pulled him back behind the van.

The front of the Ferry slowly rose out of the water and the ferry turned and the wave caught it on its side and pushed it along.

The Captain expertly guided the ferry, so that it turned and slid sidewards down the other side of the wave.

It was clear to Zoe that they were lucky to have someone at the helm that seemed to know how to handle the ferry.

Everyone in the viewing deck was flat on the floor. Zoe pulled out her badge and declared that she and Thomas were taking charge of the ferry.

She climbed up to where the captain was steering the ferry backwards toward shore and asked him whether he could make it to the other end of the journey.

He asked who she was, shook his head saying it didn't matter. He replied that he felt that he could but was heading in as close to shore as he dared just in case he had to off load the people. He then asked who she had shot with the gun she was holding.

Zoe holstered her weapon and said it was the driver of the truck bomb and his accomplice were both dead on the viewing deck. Everyone else was fine.

Out on the car deck, Matt had taken out his sophisticated rocket grenade launcher and was trying to get a sense of where the rocket that had hit the ferry had originated. He knew that he only had to get the approximate location and then the smart flying grenade would follow it's sensors to the target.

Bram reached into the back of the van and pulled out the weapon that looked like an AR 15 but was slightly different.

Matt pointed to the safety of the rifle.

Bram looked up just in time to see a low flying drone coming in just above the water surface. Without saying a word, he began to put out a stream of bullets in front of the drone in hopes that he would be able to put enough shrapnel in front of it to take it out.

Another explosion out to the front of the ferry almost knocked him down but he continued to fire at the incoming drone.

He saw the wave wash over the ferry and grabbed Matt and pulled him behind the van to keep him from being swept overboard.

The drone exploded a few hundred feet from the ferry and knocked both of them down. The van shook and one side of it was lifted by the force and the side panel could be heard crunching.

He recovered to see a second drone and was going to fire, but his weapon was empty. He felt Pat's hand on his shoulder as she handed him another cannister of bullets. He quickly removed the empty cannister and snapped in the full one. He then proceeded to fill the sky with lead.

Once again he was blown back into the van as the drone blew up.

Matt had repeatedly fired his flying grenades and was just getting back on his feet when three jets streaked in and lit up the mountain side with a series of rockets.

A mushroom cloud rose up from the area and for a few moments blocked out the sun.

The jets were followed by three Marine helicopters that could be seen coming in low and heading toward the point where the rockets had hit.

The ferry, now traveling backwards but staying afloat headed on to the landing dock. Once they were almost to the dock, the ferry captain turned the ferry and ran it full throttle up the ramp that was to the side of the off-loading dock.

He came on the loudspeaker and said that the authorities were on the way and that everyone would off load when cleared by them.

He announced that all refreshments were free.

He informed the passengers that when the vehicles were off loaded, they would be able to travel on after the authorities cleared them.

He then turned to Zoe and thanked her for having taken action against the attackers and then being generous enough to have paid for the refreshments. He was not sure how his boat would be repaired. It was his private ferry, but he said that having it up on the ramp was a miracle and he would worry about repair once he got over having survived.

Zoe followed the captain as he pointed out the damage at the front of the barge. He commented that the steel bulkhead with its doors closed had prevented the ferry from sinking

She gave him an address and suggested he get the repair done and send the bill and ask for reimbursement. She told him to refer to the Fold organization.

When the authorities arrived, they asked for Bram and then took them all aside and informed them that they had gotten clearance to go on from the very top of the Norwegian government. They were cleared to leave at any time. He suggested they get away from the scene in case there were more terrorists around.

Matt led them out to where the van was parked. He pointed to the passenger's side of the van and the place where Bram had been blown twice into it and commented that he thought that two Bram butt prints was the only damage the van had sustained. He shook his head and asked how Bram was feeling.

Bram suggested that Matt ask him the following day because he knew that he was still on an adrenalin high.

Matt asked Zoe how she had known that an attack was going to happen.

Zoe replied that she hadn't known but her senses had tingled, and she had acted.

Matt told her to let him know the next time that she felt that way.

They had been driving for about an hour when Matt commented that they were about to enter a tunnel that was almost a mile long.

They entered the brightly lit tunnel when Zoe sitting turned to look back at the entrance and saw a large truck come up from a side road and get behind them. She called out for Matt to floor it and go as fast as he could and if anything got in his way to go around it. She told him not to let anything stop him because she was sure it was a trap.

He floored it and took the van past the hundred mile per hour mark. He spotted a truck, ahead of them, taking up the middle of the road in front of him and knew he was in trouble.

He hesitated for a moment when he felt a foot press down on his gas pedal foot. Thomas yelled to make it fit.

He yelled for everyone to hold on as he passed the truck and both sides of the van scrapped. The metal siding ripping of the driver's side sounded like the crunching of a car crusher in a junk yard. The sparks seemed to engulf the van. Matt guided the van past the truck and kept the pedal flat to the floor as he tried to regain speed. The blue sky at the end of the tunnel seem to beckon but not get any closer. Matt kept muttering come on, come on.

Zoe looked back and saw the truck gaining on them. She climbed over her seat, used the cargo net to secure herself and opened the back door of the van. She began firing her weapon at the truck. She shot the radiator and the tires until she had emptied her weapon.

Eric handed her, his weapon when she emptied hers.

She kept on firing. She had the radiator steaming but the truck was still gaining.

Eric then handed her reloaded weapon back to her and she concentrated on the driver of the truck. The wind shiel of the truck shattered and she hit the driver at least three times.

Suddenly, the truck swerved and blocked the entire tunnel as it slid sidewards, still gaining on them, and then exploded.

The van seemed to get a push from behind like the next stage of a rocket launch as the explosion sent a shock wave out of the tunnel.

They were in the clear. Eric helped Zoe back across the back seat as Matt brought the van to a stop.

Matt got out of the van and looked over the damage that had been absorbed. He tried the crumpled and bent back doors and concluded they would not open. The force of the explosion had bent them, and they no longer were functional.

The rest of them got out and after looking at the collapsed rubble that had been the tunnel opening, they walked around the van.

The entire frame on the left side of the van was exposed. The metal bullet proof armor was still in place, but it looked like a picture from one of the science fiction Borg movies. The right side of the van had a flattened exterior, but it was still in place.

Matt commented that he was surprised that the bullet proof glass had withstood the various impacts.

He said that he checked off one miracle for having survived the ferry and now he checked off number two miracle, for having escaped the trap and having survived.

He thanked Thomas for having given his foot an offer it could not refuse.

Zoe asked if there were any more tunnels and if there were he should take the long way around.

He asked if anyone objected to driving straight through to Bardufoss to the farmhouse that was the final destination in Norway.

There were no objections.

Highway six had more tunnels but each time Matt took the old and slightly longer way around that took them along the coast.

He got no objections to taking the slightly longer ways along the coast.

They arrived to Bardufoss late in the afternoon and drove out to the farmhouse that Melisa had purchased.

They had not eaten since before getting on the ferry and were ready to go out before settling in for the night.

The restaurant that seemed to have the best menu was a Thai restaurant. They ordered sushi and egg rolls as starters then everyone ordered their choices off the menu.

Zoe was complimented for taking the lead in foiling the attacks that had occurred.

Bram commented that it was OK for her to tweak his nose in the future.

Zoe laughed and said that she had been so thrilled by all the adventure that Bram provided that tweaking his nose no longer interested her, but she wanted to go on vacation with him more often.

Matt said that he would warn other Marine's about getting assigned to escort the Bram group. He was going to report back to Orlando that he had just experienced more battle action acting as a driver than their unit had shared in Iraq.

Pat nodded and asked what they thought it was like living with Bram. She had yet to decide what a normal life with him might be. Anytime Bram took off from work, it always ended up with some short of fireworks. She commented that the last Fourth of July as they watched the fireworks she realized they were having a quiet night out.

Zoe added that she now swam in short shorts and wore a solid halter top just in case she had to jump any fences to save Bram.

Bram shook his head and said they were exaggerating and that there were quiet moments.

Eric nodded and said that there were many quiet moments if they could count the hours from ten at night until five in the morning as moments but otherwise, outings with him seemed to be times to make sure your weapon didn't jam.

Bob and Thomas both lifted their beers and said, "hear, hear."

Chapter 11: Finland

꩜n Helsinki, Melisa had purchased the entire sixth floor of a building in the center of the city. The apartment had one bedroom designated as the Fold arrival and departure room.

She had arranged for a day tour by private car. The tour guide was to meet them outside of the apartment building and would first take them to a restaurant of their choice.

The Fold in was flawless but a surprise awaited them.

Once again Zoe led the way for a sweep of the apartment before allowing Bram out of the Fold arrival-departure room. She called back that she had apprehended an intruder and was holding him in the living room and that Bram should come and verify who he was.

Bram knew that Zoe would never have called for him if there was any risk. He was, however, surprised by finding General Tilson with his hands up in the air but smiling.

The General smiled and said he had come to complain. He said that he was complaining about the fact that Bram and his FBI team had usurped the protective role of the young Marine with whom he had chatted this morning. This young Marine had complained that the action was usurped by Bram and his team, and that he felt that the protection that he was supposed to provide instead resulted in him getting saved by the person he was to protect. This Marine said he was especially impressed with a gun totting, sharp shooting young FBI lady that took out a bomb laden truck as she risked falling out the back of the van he was driving. He figured out later that she had just been trying to save herself by having the shock wave from the resulting exploding truck fling her back into the van and slam the van doors shut. Doors that this Marine said would need to be replaced.

He claims to have been the weakest link in the Bram Nielson army and was saved from being swept overboard into the cold sea where he was certain to have died. He said that a hand grabbed his uniform and literally lifted him up and put him down against the back of the van as a wave swept the car next to it into the sea. That hand was not the hand of god but at that instant it was certainly guided by the mighty one.

Bram smiled and replied that this young Marine that the General was describing was a student of Orlando and was demonstrating the story telling lessons he had learned from the great storyteller that had mentored him.

Bram emphasized that Sergeant Simple had the wrong rank and should be called Sergeant Major of the Marine Corps, SMMC, and also be made to wear the Marine great storyteller pin on his breast pocket and be recognized as a hard-core representative of the USMC.

He should also be commended with taking out the missile launch site that had scored a hit on the ferry and in driving like a mad man to get them out of the tunnel trap.

Bram said if the general didn't have a job for this Marine, he would make him an offer that would most likely be accepted.

The General gave a laugh and said that the young Marine indeed would be called Sergeant Major, and he would be in a role as an aid to a General that had caught the big cheese and who had turned down a DC assignment to stay with the Fold community.

Bram suggested they hear the rest of the story at dinner and rattled off twelve restaurants withing a ten-block radius. He made the point that the next big decision was to agree on which kind of cuisine they were interested in because the restaurants he had named featured Finish traditional to Vietnamese Phó and every cuisine in-between.

He suggested they avoid the Finish Traditional menu because he said that Melisa had arranged with the tour guide to take them to traditional restaurants during their day tour.

They decided to go with a restaurant that featured Italian cuisine.

They ordered several different items on the menu, and they agreed that they would share.

The final order consisted of Risotto Alla Milanese paired with Osso buco, a meat-based Lasagna, Spaghetti Alla Carbonara with guanciale, and two Neapolitan pizza variations as main dishes. They added Arancini, Sicilian rice balls, Eggplant Parmigiana, green beans, stuffed tomatoes, stuffed Artichokes, marinated mushrooms, and stuffed zucchini flowers as sides.

The waiter complimented them on the variety that had been ordered and said that soft Italian breadsticks would be out immediately with whatever drinks they ordered.

He let them know that there were three featured deserts that they might want to try: Lemon Ricotta Cake with Almonds, Tiramisu and Affogato, an Italian coffee-based desert.

Once the order was in, the General said that he had successfully identified the person that his Marine spy was informing. He was a recently retired Marine General that had been passed over and pushed out because of his behavior. He shared that he had personally recommended the ouster.

He described letting his small fish Marine take leave to go visit his family, but he was followed to Wyoming where the Marine General lived and seen going to his ranch.

The General shared that he had the NSA intercept the call from the ranch to a group in Norway, so I knew I had him.

I then assigned, Sergeant Simple to be the driver of a heavily bullet-proofed van that would carry you on the drive through Norway.

Had I known the fire power that was about to be used, I would have stopped the trip. It was a lesson that I will not forget. I underestimated the fire power that might be used.

I did arrange with my Navy Admiral friend to have an aircraft carrier doing an exercise along the coast and have them prepared to provide assistance if called for. I had a Marine Corps helicopter group assigned to the aircraft career.

When Sergeant Simple called for support and received both Navy and Marine support.

The Norwegian leadership at the very top were appraised, ahead of time, of the situation and agreed to clear the diplomatic way.

I learned from them about the attack in the tunnel when they informed me and shared that it was a miracle that the van had escaped. They let me know that the tunnel would be closed for at least six months.

He then shared that he had the Marine General being held in a Navy brig in San Diego. He planned to have all the nitty gritty detail of his traitorous actions exposed at his court martial. He was sure that at a minimum this General would get thirty years to life.

Zoe commented that she hoped it would be life. She said she wasn't vindictive, but she was amazed that a person that had spent his career in the military could end up so twisted in his mind that he was willing to support killing a person to settle a personal grievance.

General Tilson nodded, agreed, and said that in his mind execution would be more appropriate.

A second round of drinks were ordered as the meal was served.

Pat guided the discussion to the tour they planned to take on the following day.

Hours later the dinner ended with everyone sharing a little of each of the three desert specials.

During the walk back, the General said that he was Folding back to Dallas where it was now midnight. He planned to get things rolling and have Sergeant Simple promoted and transferred to be his aid.

The next morning, they went down and were greeted by the tour guide as they reached the street. She was a young lady that introduced herself as Anneli and her driver as Eetu. She gave a brief introduction of her qualifications and said that she had been giving tours for five years while she attended the University of Helsinki where she was about to graduate with a master's degree. She added that Eetu was also a student there.

She escorted them into the restaurant and helped them put in their breakfast order. She let them know that she had already had breakfast and would settle for a cup of coffee.

Bram asked what her degree was in.

Anneli said that her degree was in science and that she had focused on studying elementary particles, the development of the solar system, the stars, and galaxies. She said that the curriculum fulfilled the requirements for her degree. She felt that she had gotten an extensive understanding of these areas. She hoped to be able to land a job that would allow her to dig even deeper into one of these areas.

Bram asked how she was doing in her class.

She responded that she was trying hard, but she was coming out number three in her class and being out done by two very smart people. She said that she was in the last stage of her battle and planned to win.

Pat expected Bram to give the young lady his card but when he didn't, she knew that he was going to wait to see how she led the tour. She hoped that Anneli carried herself well during the tour.

Pat knew how it was to try and be on the top of the pecking order. She had fought very hard to earn the top spot on in her astronaut class. She had felt very lucky to have been supported by Amy who had been the number two in the class and who had a direct connection to Bram. It had been a total surprise to have risen from number three in the class and have taken the top spot. She understood the emotionally tough one had to be. She had lived the situation.

Pat knew that Bram had a keen ability to evaluate a person and know how they might fit into the Fold program. He was on the hunt for more brain power. So Pat was going to do everything possible to give Anneli the opportunity to show her ability.

Throughout the tour Pat asked questions about the history of a statue or the history of a building or an institution. She was pleased that Anneli would admit when she did not know an answer but replied that she would find out the answer before the end of the tour.

She watched to see if Bram had any reaction but knew he would not show any.

The first part of the tour ended when Anneli suggested they have lunch at a famous Finnish restaurant known for its traditional menu items. She said the food was superb and the view enchanting, but she warned that it was one of the more expensive restaurants in the city.

Zoe said she was all for it since the bill would be going to Bram.

Anneli called ahead to make the reservations and then shared that the restaurant wanted to let them know that the tip for a group their size was twenty percent.

This time Pat spoke up and said that she hoped the service and food lived up to Anneli's description.

They were greeted at the door and immediately made to feel as if they were important customers. They were offered a tour of both levels of the dining area. The place was crowded, and Pat commented that the aroma of food was making her hungry.

They were led to a table on the second level that had a splendid view of the harbor.

They discussed how to order. The waiter highlighted the available specials and said there were also set menus.

Pat had made sure to let Anneli know that she and Eetu were to join them for lunch. She immediately liked the way that Anneli at first said that she shouldn't, but it was so hard to say no. She said that she had always wanted eat there but had never been able to bring herself to spent that amount of money.

Pat gave a small laugh and said that it was on the budget, and she should enjoy herself.

Pat asked Bram what he was thinking about ordering.

He replied that he was going for the grilled scallops, rainbow trout roe, truffle, and the celery consommé.

Pat asked if they could share and said she would order the Pelmeni, mushrooms and the mushroom consommé.

Zoe was making a similar bargain with Eric and said that she was going for the pan-fried grouse, the goose liver, celery, and the hunter's sauce.

For desert they decided to order baked Alaska.

After all the lunch orders were in they discussed what type of wine they should order. They settled on ordering one bottle of Inniskillin Gold Vidal Ice wine that claimed to have a mouthwatering spicy apricot finish and a bottle of wine made from bilberry, a bottle of Artic bramble, and a bottle of white currant wine.

They ended up spending almost two hours for lunch as they each tried a little of everything.

Anneli said they should not worry about running out of time. She planned to make sure they got the full treatment and that she would end the tour outside of another great restaurant.

Anneli did a great job of taking them to a location getting them out for a quick walk around as she described the history of the area and then getting them to the next location. She kept up a swift pace but thoroughly described what they were seeing.

The evening arrived but because of the time of year, the night did not darken, and it seemed like only late afternoon.

Bob commented about feeling like it was early but said that his body told him it was time to eat again.

The menu once again had a great variety to choose from that was unique and delicious. They continued their adventure into the northern ice wines and unique deserts.

As the dinner came to a close, Bram finally handed Anneli his business card and suggested she send him her resume when it was time for her to graduate. He let her know that she would experience the universe like she had never imagined, and it would be much better than the two superb meals that she had just eaten.

Anneli commented that it sounded too good to be true, but she would definitely send her resume.

Bram's card had the word FOLD in red on a dark blue background and his snail mail address and his e-mail address of BramNielson37@gmail.com.

Anneli looked at the card and said that she liked its simplicity, and she would send her resume as soon as she got it written.

Pat hoped that she would and do it as early as possible. Pat knew it would be a once in a lifetime opportunity.

When they got back to the apartment, they decided to Fold to Stockholm so that they could have an early start the next day.

The apartment in Stockholm was similar in size to the others that they had used. It was on the top floor, and they later learned that it took up one quarter of the building it was in.

The arrival routine was followed, and they were soon moving into their rooms, showering, and heading for bed.

The next morning, they went out and walked the large square that was adjacent to the apartment. There were several restaurants, but none opened early except a Burger Shop. They decided to walk to a nearby bakery that featured a variety of sweet rolls, bread and a large selection of cheese and sausage.

Bram mentioned that they would have two large Swedish meals, and that Melisa had instructed their guide to take them to restaurants that served traditional Swedish Food.

Pat called the guide and let him know where to pick them up. The guide introduced herself as Elena and she introduced the driver as her partner Milind. She made the point that both of them were professional tour guides that had gone to a special school that focused on educating them in the history of Sweden and of Stockholm. She shared that the two of them took turns being in charge, but they were business partners.

She went on to say that the two had toured, a Melisa Etrius, who had set up the tour they were about to experience. She smiled and said that Melisa had been very specific about the tour being paced so that the main highlights of Stockholm would be visited and that the best restaurants enjoyed.

Elena then rattled off the land-oriented sites of the 13th-century Storkyrkan Cathedral, the Kungliga Slottet Royal Palace, and that the last place would be the Nobel Museum, which focuses on the Nobel Prize. She said that she would have a running commentary about all the historic buildings they would drive by, but she did not expect them to remember them but said that a video of the highlights of the entire tour was part of the package.

Then they would stop for a traditional lunch at a top restaurant that had a view of the bay.

Lunch would be a traditional Swedish lunch.

For the Main they would have the choice of,

Grilled Falukorv, a beef and pork sausage served with creamy macaroni,

Smörgåstårta, Sweden's number one meal where everything is put on bread, in layers, and serve it as a cake.

Korv, a Swedish Sausage Stroganoff with a bowl of steaming rice.

The table would be graced with a generous number of sides.

Julskinka ham
Wallenbergare – Veal Patties
Swedish Lingonberry Sauce
Raggmunk – Swedish Potato Pancakes
Hasselbackspotatis – Swedish Hasselback, spiral cut potatoes
Gubbröra – Egg And Anchovy Salad
Semla – Swedish Sweet Buns
Lussekatter – Saffron Buns

And then the desert selection would be.

Ostkaka – Swedish Cheesecake
Kladdkaka – Mud Cake
Prinsesstårta – Princess Cake

She stopped and asked if they had any questions.

Thomas asked what the possibility was to just go straight to the restaurant and begin eating because the choices seemed overwhelming.

Zoe asked if they could discuss the menu and see what they would do for lunch and still have room for a dinner in the evening.

Elena laughed and said that they would be having the evening meal after a ferry ride to Fjäderholmen and eat at their most well-known restaurant and be sitting right at the edge of the water.

There they would focus on

Gravlax Dill, which was cured Salmon, served with cold potato and even more dill.

Sill, pickled herring, and fried herring

Räkmacka, which was an open-faced shrimp sandwich with complimentary toppings that included lettuce, mayonnaise, egg, dill, and caviar

Kräftor, which was local crayfish that had been boiled and then served cold laying over an ice bed.

She suggested that it would be the time to enjoy the evening and drink great Swedish beer such as Norrlands Guld, Falcon pale lager, or Närke Kaggen Stormaktsporter that had a twelve percent alcohol level.

She pointed out that it was also a time to choose to try one of the many fruit wines or ciders.

Eric commented that he was joining Thomas in the request to skip the tour and just get to the restaurants.

Milind looked at Elena and commented that she was glad to be driving because it was clear to her they had a group that was going to be tough to impress with old buildings and walks inside of museums.

Bram joined in and commented that they should try working with such a group. He smiled, shook his head, and pointed at each of team and then said that it was time to tour.

The morning tour went smoothly and when lunch time arrived, they indeed enjoyed a delicious meal with a variety of tastes that were new to them.

They shared a variety of beers and wines, and the deserts topped off the meal.

Elena led them along the waterfront to where the Ferry was loading. She walked up to the gang plank and handed over the tickets and led them aboard.

They sat on the top deck where she handed out headsets and said that the ships tour guide would narrate the tour. They would first go along the center city side of the waterway and then they would turn and go close to the other side as they made their way to the island of Fjäderholmen. The journey was about ten miles out to the island. For much of the way Elena shared the history of Sweden and the Vikings.

Once on the Island, Elena led the way to the restaurant where a table had been set up and was waiting for them.

The waiter took their drink menu and shortly after the Hors d'oeuvre and the starters were brought out and they all got into the food as Elena described that food that was to be served.

Pat made sure that Elena and Milind were included in the meal.

They both thanked her for including them.

The sun was not in the sky, but the evening remained light and, on the ride back they enjoyed a darker view of the distant shoreline and as they approached the city, the lights seemed to sparkle.

The ride back to their apartment from the waterfront only took minutes. They thanked Elena and Milind for a great tour and said they would recommend them to their friends back in the states.

Pat handed each an envelope that held a generous tip before taking the elevator up to their apartment.

They spent a few moments checking what time it was in Dallas. Dallas was nine hours earlier than Stockholm. It was near ten in the evening, which they figured made it one in the afternoon in Dallas.

He and Pat had agreed to Fold to Rome at a later date. They both had enough of touring and were more interested in getting a good night's sleep in their own bed.

Bram suggested they all Fold back at midnight and arrive in Dallas in the afternoon. They would be able to have a late dinner and get a good night's sleep back in their own beds.

Zoe commented that she was looking forward to feeling safe in their armored home.

Ron Mueller

Chapter 12: Oversight

As the Fold back to Dallas materialized in the hanger, Bram saw that the General, and his new aid Matt and Linda were there to greet them.

The General greeted them, pointed to Matt's insignia, and said that his new aid should be addressed as Sergeant Major.

The team congratulated Matt and said that he deserved the promotion.

Matt thanked them and then commented that he could not believe what he was learning about the Fold program.

He said that he had spent a great amount of time talking to his buddy, now also a Sergeant Major but a guy that soon would hold the rank of an officer, about all the things that was going on in the Fold program. It all seemed to be surreal and seemed to be a story out of a science fiction book.

Bram smiled and said that he often felt the same way.

Linda greeted them and let Bram know that she had been fending off the leader of the Oversight committee who was insisting that the committee take a tour of the facility and get an understanding of the work that was going on. He wanted to examine the spending records and wanted to be shown where the money had been spent. She said that Jeffrey was on the committee as well and was the new head of the NASA organization. He had called her and shared that he was having a tough time with several committee members who seemed to think they knew a better way to manage the Fold program.

She let him know that Jeffrey was the first thing on his agenda on his first morning at work. She wanted to know what morning that would be.

Bram replied that he would be in on Monday and then he wanted to review all the work that had gone on with each of the team leaders before meeting with Jeffrey.

He also asked Linda to work with Zoe to verify that all the members on the Oversight committee had the proper level of clearance.

He then signaled for Castor to lead the way to the transport van.

Once they got to the house, they all gathered in his office, and he shared the fact that he was planning to move much of the work being done in Dallas to Einstein City on Mataia, but they would personally remain very visible during the workday in the Dallas facility.

The records he was going to give the committee would be extensive. It would be almost impossible for the committee to get anything useful from the records, but he hoped that they would spend their time trying to understand them.

He asked that his office get checked several times a day for listening devices, as well as video devices. He also wanted the perimeter of the office building checked for any parked vans or other vehicles that might house listening devices.

He made a point that he wanted the whole house checked and then he asked for a random check any time the house was unoccupied.

He said he was sure that an attempt would be made to compromise their communications. He asked that each member of the committee have their background scrutinized. He wanted to know every detail of what the members had ever done.

Zoe commented that the committee members had better be squeaky clean or they were toast. She was going to have a friend of hers check for anything that would disqualify the member.

361

Bram asked that she co-ordinate with Linda so that wires would not get crossed.

The next day, Pat invited Mallica, Remi, Melisa, and Marcus and his two kids to Sunday breakfast. She knew that Bram would take the opportunity to get back into the rhythm of his work. She figured that the breakfast would be a great way to allow him to do it.

Bram thanked her and said that he would prepare the morning meal.

Thomas heard the exchange and said that according to his calculations it was his turn to do the cooking, and he planned to do so.

Bram knew that was not the case and knew that it was his turn, but he appreciated Thomas's offer and thanked him.

The offer made Bram think about the role his bodyguards had played in the encounter in Norway. He went down to his office and documented what the four of them had done.

He asked the four to review what he had written.

Eric and Zoe both commented that he was making them all sound like heroes that had survived a perilous battle.

Bram replied that it indeed was a dangerous situation that the four of them handled exceptionally well.

He checked with both Bob and Thomas who each expressed a similar view that Bram was being very generous in his praise.

Bram then sent the document to their FBI boss first thanking him for assigning the cream of the cream to guard him and made the suggestion that the four get promoted and get financially rewarded.

Pat had come in and had caught the gist of what the report said. She commented that she wanted to be rewarded as well.

Bram gave a laugh and asked what she was currently getting paid. He said that her boss ought to at least double whatever that might be since she had to put up with him twenty-four, seven.

He did not know what her current salary was because Erica managed the personnel files of everyone in the Fold organization.

He sent a quick note to Erica suggesting that both Pat and Amy get raises to reward the work they had done in setting up Einstein City.

While he was at it he sent Jeffrey a note recommending a raise for Erica to reward her outstanding management of the Fold organization.

After making sure those who constantly had his back were rewarded, he felt good and suggested that they take a walk around the neighborhood.

He let Pat know that he was now into thinking about the beings from the Water World. He was wondering how they were doing. He said he was eager to hear from Mallica and Gerry who were leading the effort to get the Swoshians transitioning to a new Water World.

He then brought up the topic of the production of the additional vessels that the Swoshians would use to make the transition. He knew that Erika and Remi would be on top of that.

He wanted to catch up with Marcus on what he had found out about negative Fold space as well as the continued effort in the normal Fold space.

He gave a small laugh as he then highlighted the work that Remi was doing.

Then he looked at Pat and said that he wondered about Amy's progress in getting Einstein City completed and ready for use.

Pat smiled and said that she was sure Amy had made great progress, but the city would need tweaking and adjustment as they moved in and identified the things that had been missed.

She made the point that Bram had too many irons in the fire.

She highlighted additional irons; how Zuri and Orlando were doing in their studies, how Lacy was doing with her protection offense, and what Melisa's progress in setting up the around the world Fold vacation spots happened to be.

Bram agreed that there were many irons in the fire and that they needed to organize the work in such a fashion that the new oversight committee would not impede the progress that they were making.

Pat suggested that they use honey to distract the committee.

Bram asked what she had in mind.

Pat pointed out that the committee members would want to understand the Fold technology. Having them experience it would give Bram the opportunity to influence each of the members. She suggested that they do a survey of the committee members and determine what their favorite vacation spot in the world might be and then accompany them in the Fold weekend mini-vacation experience to that spot.

They needed to make sure that Melinda had vetted the desired location and set it up for a Fold vacation but other than that they could keep the members busy for quite a while as they all experienced a Fold vacation. She bet that afterwards the committee would be much more supportive of the work that was going on.

Bram agreed that Pat had hit on a terrific way to make the committee much easier to work with.

The breakfast was into full swing on Sunday morning when Erica and Gerry walked in. She looked around the table and saw that General Tilson and his new attaché Matt were also in attendance. After greeting everyone she looked at Bram and asked if it was a business meeting.

Bram nodded and said that he wanted to get ready for the coming week so that he would know how he would manage the oversight committee. He pointed out that he just wanted the top line of where everyone was and that the details could be held until the regular work week.

He looked over at Melisa and said he wanted to begin with understanding how the Fold tourist agency was doing.

Melissa said the Fold tourist agency was overwhelmed with the requests it had received. She had limited the weekend vacation departures from Friday afternoon until Saturday morning. She thanked Remi for making the dozen or so bubbles available.

She said that a bubble had gone out every ten minutes during the eight hours that she operated the weekend schedule. The feedback was off the charts and positive. She had made the charges seventy per cent of what a normal hotel reservations were. Food and entertainment were not included.

She said that the Fold could be automated but so far she had personally managed the Folds. She had wanted to ensure that no one got stuck in any of the locations. She said that everyone in the room had availed themselves of the vacation opportunity and that the best feedback she had received was that from Marcus Jr and Mylan who had made three weekend outings with Marcus.

Bram asked Mylan where they had gone. She said they had gone to Tokyo Japan, taken a bullet train to Mt Fuji, had visited the Imperial Palace and Shinjuku Gyoen National Garden. She said that they had eaten only traditional Japanese meals and loved them.

Marcus Jr. said that Australia had been great. It was like visiting the US, but the accent of the people there made it so much fun to talk to them when they met along the beach. He said that his favorite food had been the Lamingtons cake, which was a moist mouthwatering, butter sponge cake dipped in chocolate and coated with coconut.

Elizabeth commented that she loved Lamingtons cake and would bring one the next time they had a dinner at Bram's place.

Marcus volunteered that the New Zealand weekend had been his selection. There they went up the ten-thousand-foot Sky Tower and got a spectacular view across the city and the area around it as far as the eye could see.

He said that he had considered bungee jumping and sky diving but figured that with his luck the bungee cord would snap, and the sky dive parachute would fail to open and he smashing into the ground. So, he settled for a city bus tour and a walk on the beach.

He said that the truly unique experience was a meal of Hāngi the traditional Māori way of cooking, where food is cooked in a covered pit lined with hot stones and fire. There was an assortment of meat and vegetables wrapped in flax leaves and the food was amazingly tender and delicious.

He laughed and said that the other favorite was the Hokey pokey ice cream consisting of vanilla-flavored ice cream with small lumps of honeycomb toffee dispersed throughout it.

He added that the weekend mini vacations helped the three of them focus on getting their work done during the week so they could enjoy the weekend. It had been a great way to continue their bonding and getting over not having Myla around.

Erica volunteered that she and Gerry had visited three Islands, the Falklands, Palermo Sicily, and Cyprus. The beaches had been the focus of their stay in each, but they had enjoyed the local cuisine in both Sicily and Cyprus.

Lacy said that she and Ray had also taken advantage of doing weekend mini vacations. They had stayed in country and had gone to three National parks.

They had not camped out but had gone on day hikes and enjoyed the homes that Melisa had purchased. They had enjoyed the local foods that consisted mostly of steak or ribs fixed in very unique and delicious ways.

Mallica joined in and said she had Folded to the Orlando's apartment in Oxford three times and enjoyed weekends with he and Zuri. She said that they mostly ate, Italian, Chinese, and French cuisine but also cooked in.

She said that the weekend Fold cycle let her romance with Orlando stay fresh.

Linda then said that she too had taken advantage of the Fold mini vacation and had gone to Alaska, Cozumel, and Jamaica. She complemented Melisa in having discovered and set up the locations so that the arrival and departures were invisible to the local population.

General Tilson had been quietly observing the interaction of the people that he knew were closest to Bram. He was impressed with their dedication and their ability to independently make their own decisions and take action.

He spoke up and said he would share how he had used the bubble to help catch the big cheese he had been after. He said that he worked with Marcus, Remi, and Lacy.

He Folded to multiple locations that included Oxford where he had engaged Orlando and identified Matt as the person to provide the vacation protection for Bram and the rest of the team.

He had also visited the Admiral and personally gotten him to help in providing additional Navy support.

He admitted that he had underestimated and had been surprised by the ability of his adversary to mount multiple substantial attacks with the armament that had been used. He found it hard to envision that a military officer of his rank would to be willing to jeopardize the good of his country over a private game of revenge against him.

He then highlighted how impressed he was with the FBI body guards that took out two terrorists and prevented a truck bomb from being blown up on the ferry that had already been hit by a kamikaze drone.

He then related Matt's story about Bram shooting down two kamikaze drones while at the same time saving him from being washed overboard.

Bram spoke up and said that Matt had taken out the kamikaze launch site and later had driven like a mad man to save all of them from another truck bomb that had been positioned in a long underground tunnel as a barrier.

He recounted how Matt had propelled the van between the semitruck and the tunnel wall. He pointed out that because Matt had literally squeezed a size ten van through a size six car space they were all present to enjoy breakfast.

Matt said that he had not expected the van to make it through but an extra foot on top of his had not given him a choice and that afterward it was clear to him that the truck was going to be able to catch them, but Zoe willingly risked falling out of the back of the van to take out the driver of the truck. The truck crashed, exploded and he literally had to steer a van flying through the air. He was relieved to have watched the back doors of the van slam shut and Zoe climb back into her seat.

He said that he never expected to get the opportunity to learn why Bram and his team needed him to protect them but since he had arrived in the Dallas Fold compound, he had been exposed to so much new technology and wonder that he was finding it hard to absorb it all. He had no idea that such technology existed. He said that his ride back with the General had been so amazing that he still wondered if it all was real.

He smiled and said that the famous pancakes, smothered in Maple syrup helped him appreciate the taste of reality as it existed in the new environment that he was trying to absorb.

Bram acknowledged that Pat's famous pancakes always brought him to reality as well.

He then asked Amy how the work at Einstein City was going.

Amy replied that everything was ready.

She highlighted the fact that Remi was spending several hours each day making sure the lab facility was up and functioning.

She had recruited Linh and Duong to set up the computer systems and she reminded Bram of the old Electrician that had made sure the electrical wiring for the first bramlet Fold was done properly. She had recruited him to check out the electrical distribution grid and had made some adjustments based on his keen inspection skills. She said he had volunteered retire to Mataia and to run the electrical system.

Bram thanked her for her hard work.

Then he asked Lacy for her update.

Lacy commented that her work had almost become invisible to his adversaries, but her team had every one of them tied up in civil or criminal cases and having to use their resources to focus on themselves versus generously giving money to the troublemakers.

She commented that the bubble observation and protection function around the compound area was now being handled by a team that General Tilson had set up.

She shared that she had gotten her father to participate in identifying potential local small extreme antigovernment organizations and had been able to neutralize several of them.

Bram thanked her for her work and for tying up the finances of those funding the attacks.

He asked Marcus if he had anything to share.

Marcus nodded but suggested that they should meet during the week and get into the nitty gritty of what he had been doing. He said that he did not want to bore the entire group with double speak that he would most likely use and though it would be English it would be meaningless to them.

Bram nodded and said that indeed every time the two of them engaged in a meaningful, full conversation about negative Fold space they both walked away dazed. When they ventured to take actual negative Folds, they both ended up lost and needing rescue.

Pat suggested they enjoy a new underwater video that Amy had made on Mataia. It turned out that there were no creatures on land, but Amy had found a variety of underwater plants. She pointed out that Mataia was at a stage where life was just beginning.

Bram enjoyed the video and relaxed. Pat had set his mind at ease with how to manage the oversight committee and the team had provided him with assurance that he had the means to maneuver the oversight committee into a supportive role.

Ron Mueller

Chapter 13: Waterworld Migration

Monday morning when Bram got to the office, Linda let him know that her sister was in the office waiting for him and wanted a moment alone with him.

He asked Thomas and Bob to give him five before entering.

They both swept the office for bugs and then stepped out.

Bram walked in and asked Lacy what was up.

She said that she had left out a small detail during Sunday breakfast and she wanted to let him know what that was.

She said that she had taken out the three drones meant to hit the barge he was on. She took them out and eliminated the people at the drone launch area.

The truck she blew up must have been loaded with explosives because it sent up a mushroom cloud.

When the jets were coming in, she recalled her attack bubbles that she was personally controlling.

She said that this was the first time that anyone else knew of her actions. She had not wanted to share this during breakfast because she did not want to affect the recognition Matt had received for his actions.

She confirmed that his flying grenades hit exactly where they should have and had she not been there just seconds ahead of him, his attack would have been effective, and he deserved recognition for his actions.

Bram thanked her for waiting to share the information and commended her on her offense. He reaffirmed her decision to keep quiet. He said that he was pleased with her actions and would make sure she received recognition for the excellent work she was doing. He said that she should continue being super aggressive.

Lacy smiled and said that she would and that she had the best job and boss that she could possibly wish for and all the recognition she needed, he had just provided.

Linda called in that the ten minutes were over and almost simultaneously Bob and Thomas entered and said hello and sat down at their seats.

Lacy wished them a good day as she walked out.

Bram looked at the two and asked if they wanted a cup of tea.

Linda announced Marcus's arrival and Bram poured a cup of black coffee and put it across from him where Marcus could reach it.

It was clear to Bram that the weekend outings with his two kids had put Marcus into a positive emotional state and that was his old confident self.

Bram asked what he had learned about the Fibonacci sequence and the way negative Fold space worked.

Marcus shared that the first Fold in negative space did indeed follow the Fibonacci sequence as the bubble Folded out to the initial distance that the bubble had been programed to go. Then the movement at that time period was based on rhombicosidodecahedron points that were generated. The farther out in time that a bubble was programed to go, the larger the rhombicosidodecahedron and the number of nodes that the bubble needed to visit as it tried to return to its launch point.

So far, the only way he had been able to recover a bubble was to program in a routine for it to find the light that broadcast the message "Follow the light" sent out in old fashioned morse code using the laser light magnetron.

He had three bubbles that he figured would someday show up when they finally made it back along the nodes of the rhombicosidodecahedron. He was not sure what century that might be.

He had learned how to set the distance so that the time incremented in one-thousand-year increments. He was now trying to refine the process of being able to select any increment from a year to a billion years. He said that the big accomplishment had been to get a bubble to come back on schedule.

Bram complimented him on his accomplishment and asked when he thought people could safely travel in negative Fold space.

Marcus commented that to safely send people out they would have the same challenge in both the negative Fold space and the positive Fold space. That challenge was to make sure the Fold coordinates were clear of debris. He said that they needed a safety crew certifying that a given coordinate was free of debris. He likened it to Melisa's effort to secure an apartment or house where a bubble could Fold. Once a coordinate was cleared, he felt that Folds to that coordinate would be safe.

Bram said that Marcus had just identified a major barrier to rapid deployment of exploratory teams.

Marcus nodded and said that there would probably be more Bramlet One's as the exploration of space expanded.

Bram said that he wanted to strategically clear the coordinates associated with the needs of their small team.

He then suggested that the rooms that were being used by Melisa for the vacation Folds be emptied of any obstacles that might accidently be moved. He wanted the rooms to be cleared so there was no chance of an accident. It should happen before any more mini-vacation Folds took place.

Marcus agreed to contact Melisa and arrange for that to happen.

Bram said that Marcus should continue doing what he was doing and to enroll Daryl and Harold in verifying that the strategic locations were clear of debris. He asked Marcus to create a list of strategic locations for them to review by the end of the week.

His next meeting was with Mallica and Gerry who were engaged in enabling the Swoshian move to a new water world.

Mallica reiterated the fact that the u-tube design for the Swoshians transport bubbles had greatly accelerated the transfer process. The new vessels had a thirty per cent greater capacity and they were being produced at the rate of three a month at the same cost as one bubble. She had convinced Erica to order as many as could be produced in six months. She was not sure how many they would actually need but figured that the more the better.

Gerry commented that the Swoshians were aggressively moving their population and quickly seeding their new water world with the food supply that they would need. They were synchronizing the speed of their transition with the food supply of the new water world.

He said that it was "aquaforming" versus terraforming and commented that the Swoshian equivalent of environmental scientists were working feverishly to stay ahead of the push to transfer Swoshians.

He had worked closely with the environmental scientists that were helping Amy prepare Mataia to be self-sufficient using them to verify the concept of how to accelerate terra forming if speed were a key factor. He then extrapolated their answers to the Swooshian experience.

Both he and Mallica had reminded the Swooshian leadership that they had a considerable number of years to make the transition to their new water world.

Bram Nielson Collection

Bram said that it seemed that the two of them had everything in good shape. He asked how many Fold vessels were in use and how was the power to keep them active being generated.

Gerry shared that each Fold vessel had a huge battery that was recharged after each Fold by the light from the sun in each of the two systems. This eliminated the need for large power generation and allowed each vessel to make continuous scheduled trips.

He said that Remi had adapted many of his scout bubbles and other Fold vessels with the same battery design. This had freed up the Dallas power source for the long distant Folds.

Bram said that he was going to enjoy his meeting with Remi. They had been discussing what it would take to reach some of the more distant Fold targets that they had in mind. The amount of energy required had been one of the limiting factors. He figured that now with rechargeable batteries and with the additional available power they would be able to make some of those trips.

Linda buzzed in and let him know it was his ten-minute warning so he could make lunch.

Bram suggested that they all go and meet Pat for lunch and afterwards they would go on with their workday.

Chef D'Carluca greeted Bram and asked if there was anything special that he wanted for lunch.

Bram shook his head and said he was open to anything that he had in mind.

The Chef D'Carluca smiled and said that he had just finished trying a new pork barbeque rib recipe that was smothered with a special sauce. He was anxious to get someone to try it and let him know if it was as good as he thought it was.

Bram said he was looking forward to it and asked if there was enough for everyone.

Pat pointed to the rib on her plate and said that she thought one rib was enough for a meal. She took a bite and said they all should try one because it was delicious.

Bram sat down and told the Chef D'Carluca to bring the ribs on.

Remi came in just as the ribs were being served to Bram and asked if there was enough for him. He thanked the Chef for making plenty and sat down and dug in.

Bram asked if the two could meet after lunch and review what Remi was up to with the bubbles and the new U-tube Fold vehicle design.

Remi had a lot to share, including the fact that he had done little in the way of managing the lab and had turned over the lab back to Lori. He had been focused on the Fold spacecraft improvements.

He had also set up the lab at Einstein City and had tested all the equipment.

The last few weeks had cleared the way for the progress he felt that he had made.

He had Folded all the vehicles of the new design to Mataia so they would not be discoverable when the oversight committee toured the facility.

Bram spent a few moments at the end of lunch and encouraged Mallica and Gerry to set up a celebration meeting with the Swooshians. He wanted to celebrate the ability of the Swooshians to manage the move of their population without the help of anyone from Earth. He had been worried that support for helping the Swooshians would be a topic that would hurt the current US administration. He now could put that on the back burner of his worry about list.

He knew that the news of the existence of another intelligent species would be a political nightmare, and he decided to avoid all nightmares.

His meeting with Remi included Pat and Amy. Amy and Remi had continued to make considerable progress in getting Mataia able to sustain the initial population of Einstein City.

Bram had coached Pat and Amy on what Earth species to transfer to Mataia. He had made the point that they should strive to introduce the planet to life in such a fashion that they maintained an environmental balance. There was significant guess work in what plant and animal species they should introduce.

Amy shared that she had recruited Thomas's family who were farmers in Iowa. Thomas had shared that his family had decided to sell their farm because they could not compete with the big combines that had taken over the farmland around them.

Thomas said his family was eager to try farming on Mataia.

Amy had not told them about it being on another planet, but she had taken Thomas's father to Mataia, and they had scouted out the farmland on which he said he could supply Einstein City with all the corn, wheat, vegetables, chickens, turkeys, lamb, and beef. He said that he could also supply the milk and butter.

She had promised to provide him the funds to set up his farming operation.

She looked at Bram and asked if they had the money to do what she had promised.

Bram smiled and said she had the go ahead from him but should make sure it fit with the terra forming plans they were making.

He suggested that she engage Thomas and have him educated his parents and the rest of the family that would be making the transition about the fact they would be farming on a new planet.

Amy commented that she thought Thomas's dad would not be surprised because he had looked up at the sun and quoted, "we are not in Kansas are we?"

Bram said that he hoped all of the family cleared security and had no qualms about leaving Earth. He pointed out that with Fold capability they could all still go to family gatherings or take Fold vacations around the Earth.

Bram knew that it was going to take discipline and control to limit the rate of growth of the Mataia population. He felt comfortable in making sure that he and the Fold community, maintained control of their new home.

They would need to establish their own Mataian Constitution that would guide the social order.

He felt he was up to date on all the projects that were underway, and he felt ready to engage with the oversight community.

He was ending the day with a meeting with Erica and Jeffrey to discuss how to bring the oversite committee on board.

Just before the meeting Zoe shared the fact that the leader of the committee had voiced anti LGBT rhetoric during his last political election, but the fact was that he was married in name only and did not live with the woman who was on record as his wife but instead had an apartment that he shared with a man that had been with him for more than twenty years.

She said that he was most likely gay.

Bram thanked her for the information and said that he would make sure that fact either got the leader removed or was used to get him to be a supporter of the Fold effort.

Bram waited until Erica had come into his office and then he placed a video call to Jeffrey.

Jeffrey answered and commented that the meeting was timely because Senator Stately of Utah was insisting on going for a tour of the Fold facility.

Bram suggested that they engage the oversight committee over the next month and that they begin with a weekend outing to the location of the committee member's choice. It could be to anywhere in the world that a Fold facility had been established.

He said that he could send Jeffrey the list of over two hundred-Fold weekend vacation spots.

Bram Nielson Collection

He asked that Jeffrey have each member select a weekend date and a location to spend the weekend.

The idea was he and Pat to spend the weekend touring with the oversight committee member and at the end of the weekend that member would get a detailed tour of the Fold site in Dallas and be greeted by the Fold community at an evening dinner at the Fold community lodge.

Jeffrey commented that it sounded as if Bram was planning to bribe all the members and pull them into the work of the Fold community.

Bram repeated the adage that honey caught more flies than vinegar. He admitted that he had initially thought of providing the committee with sour vinegar to drink, but Pat had intervened.

Jeffrey said he was glad that it was coming out as a reward to be on the oversight committee. He said that he was putting in his request to take his family to the Kruger National Park in South Africa and go see the elephants, rhinos, and other wildlife. He added that it was one of the items on the family bucket list.

Bram said that his request would be fulfilled. He asked if Jeffrey needed either he or Pat to go along.

Jeffery replied that all he needed was to talk with Melisa, get the Fold location, and make arrangements for the safari.

He then asked Jeffrey to get the desired locations for the rest of the committee members so that those weekends could be scheduled.

Once all the Fold vacations had been taken and the initial tour of the Fold site had been done, Bram wanted to have the entire committee spend a week at the Fold site and get a handle on what was going on.

Jeffrey asked if the script was well oiled, and everyone knew their role.

Bram replied that his team had the best actors a director would want to direct in a fiction movie, and they were all eager to show their stuff.

Jeffrey said he was eager to see the play that Bram was directing and would give him feedback on how good or bad it might be.

Erica had been unusually quiet, but she commented that even he would be surprised at how detailed the play was and how long it would take for the committee to review all the progress reports. She said that her role was to feed the committee every report they might ask for and that she too was magical in her ability to paint a rainbow story.

Jeffrey smiled and commented that he planned to read a good book and let the rest of the committee review all the records that they would be given to review.

He asked that the science advisor, Charles Ford be presented with as much of the scientific information that could be shared. Charles was a great guy that was eager to keep the breakthroughs going.

Bram replied that he was looking forward to meeting Charles.

When the call ended, Bram asked Zoe to check Charles out and give him a report on his inclinations and scientific accomplishments.

Ron Mueller

Chapter 14: The Committee

A few days later Bram received the list of weekend locations that had been requested.

Senator Stately had requested three seats. He was planning to take his wife and his aid. He had requested a visit to Bangkok and asked that a tour be set up.

Senator Olivia Newton from Maine wanted to enjoy a weekend in Athens with her husband and two children who were still living at home.

Senator Bascom of West Virginia chose to do a weekend in Barcelona with his wife. He wanted to see the Basílica de la Sagrada Família designed by Antoni Gaudi, walk the length of Las Ramblas that stretched from a convent to the port and see the Gothic Quarter and visit the Cathedral of the Holy Cross and Saint Eulalia.

Bram concluded that the Senator had opened a tourist folder and listed it on the request.

And the Science advisor, Charles Ford wanted to go to Lima, Peru. He expressed his interest in touring the trendy bohemian district, Barranco, so he could take in its relaxed vibes. He also wanted to visit its many museums, see the colonial mansions and the vast ocean views. He asked to have a culinary tour of the restaurants that had international reputations.

Pat commented that the weekend outings would allow her to see places that she had not visited and were very diverse. She said that the detail that Senator Bascom and the science advisor had requested fit very well with what she thought she would enjoy.

Bram agreed they would have interesting weekend outings. He said that he did not plan to do any business on the trips. He wanted to spend time in making sure that everyone had an enjoyable time. He planned to focus on getting to understand the committee member.

He engaged Melisa and asked her to develop a full and very interesting tour at each location. He suggested using private tour guides that would provide a solid and educational tour.

He asked Linda to set up the Monday afternoon luncheons at the recreation center and have her family cater the event. The attendees should include everyone that was engaged in one of the projects. He suggested that she strategically seat each committee member with the Fold team players around them that was well versed on what the committee member was interested in.

Linda asked if it would be better to avoid having the multiple Monday afternoon luncheons and have only one where all the Oversight Committee members were present. They would then be able to exchange stories of their trips and bond with each other.

Bram thanked her for the suggestion and agreed they should have the luncheon when the entire committee would visit the site. He wondered about adding a Fishing outing at their favorite park.

Linda said that her family would be able to cater that event and suggested that the luncheon and fishing trip be merged. She commented that she would arrange to have the fishing boats. She laughed and said that the bullet holes in the boats had been repaired and they all looked brand new. She asked if the boats should come armed.

Bram said she should check with Lacy to see if there was any apparent threat on the horizon.

Bram then asked that she make all the detailed arrangements for the weekend mini vacations with the committee members.

Linda checked with each of the committee members to determine where they were to be picked up.

The pickup point for Senator Stately was to be Washington DC. Melisa gave Linda the address of the Apartment building on 24th Street NW where she had a long-term lease on the entire seventh floor corner of the building. She had just recently tested the coordinates and had cleared one room that was the bubble receive-transmit room.

The pickup point for Senator Newton and her family was to be in a house only a two-block walk from the Governor's house on Green Street. She told Linda that she was not sure where the senator lived but she figured the Senator would know where the Governor's house was located.

Linda learned that Senator Bascom wanted to also be picked up in Washington.

Science advisor, Charles Ford and his wife wanted to be picked up in Boston. Melisa let Linda know that she had secured the entire fourth floor of an apartment building on Prince Street.

Linda thanked her for the information and said that the information would be sent to each of the committee members.

She then contacted each of the committee members and agreed on the pickup time and date and asked about what they would like to see during their weekend vacation tour.

Once she had the dates for each of the committee members she arranged for Bram and Pat to arrive the morning of the day before. She worked with Pat to arrange the Friday tour and the dinner location.

Linda felt she had set a record in getting all committee travel arranged and also arranging Bram and Pat's outings.

She called Melisa and thanked her for making it possible to get everything done. Melisa said that after going to seventy-six different countries she had exhausted her personal desire to travel and was ready to just go fishing.

Linda sympathized with her and said she felt much the same way after getting everything arranged.

She let Melisa know that Bram was planning to host another fishing outing with all the committee members present.

Melisa gave a laugh and said that she had a new Kevlar jacket that she was going to wear on the event. She commented that Bram had yet to have a fishing event that didn't include a dramatic gun battle.

Linda agreed and said that her parents were catering the event and had commented about the same thing. They had approached Lacy about making sure she had her defense technology in place. Lacy said that it was not hers to command, but she was sure she could talk the General to be "at the ready."

Lacy commented that the Fold community had the top-level offense going and it was currently in action against all their detractors.

Her parents had let her know they would all be taking their weapons with them.

Bram was pleased with Linda's update and the fact that he and Pat would begin the cycle on the coming Friday. He thanked Linda for setting up the Friday tour to several of the out of the way places in the DC area that Pat had requested.

One major location was the National Arboretum to see the Corinthian columns that had been in the inaugural background of Andrew Jackson and Abraham Lincoln inaugurations in 1829 and 1861 as they stood outside of the Capitol building. At that time, the columns were still part of the Capital building. Now they were sitting by themselves in a stark, open field supporting nothing but air. The primary attraction of that site for him was that it looked down on the most stunning cherry blossoms display along the Tidal Basin during spring.

Pat had also requested a visit to the International Spy Museum to take in the tools of espionage. She commented that it claimed to have the largest collection of spy-related artifacts in the world.

The third request was to go to the National Bonsai Museum where she wanted to see a Bonsai tree that dated back to 1625 and had survived the Hiroshima bombing.

Linda said that she had arranged for a professional tour guide to take them on their tour and to show any other unique places that she had knowledge of if it fit the visit time frame.

She had left the choice of the lunch location up to the tour guide, but Linda specified she wanted it to be upscale. The dinner was to be at one of the top restaurants in Washington and was going to cost Bram one of his better nickels.

Linda let Bram know that she, Pat, and Zoe had spent time going over the menu of top restaurants at all the pickup and destination sites and had decided on which ones to try.

She then shared the evening meal menu for Washington DC.

Bram commented that he was looking forward to the Washington tour and the very interesting dinners.

He asked that she set up an informal introduction call with Senator Stately and to let the Senator know that his request was being fulfilled and give him the pickup address.

He suggested that Linda contact everyone else and let them know that their request would be fulfilled.

He asked if Pat and Zoe had already set up their before tours at all the pickup locations.

Linda said they were going to spend Thursday morning setting up the next three trips.

Bram nodded and said that was perfect and he said he knew he was in for a treat.

The next morning, he was ready to visually meet the Senator. He had asked Zoe and Eric to stay outside of the office so he would not have to explain the protection situation.

Linda placed the call, which was answered by the Senator's support. The two of them conversed and soon Bram was connected with the Senator.

The Senator took the lead, introduced himself, and voiced his interest in the Fold project and his concern about the finances.

Bram chose to ignore the bait and followed his script of greeting the Senator and making the offer to demonstrate the Fold capability by taking the Senator, his long-time partner and his wife to Bangkok and then completing the on boarding process at the Fold compound on Monday.

Bram had specifically made it a point of mentioning the long-term partner. He wanted to bring the Senator out of the closet. He was not going to let the Senator remain in the political closet that he was hiding in. He was not going to share top secret information with someone that was not confident enough to be open about his personal life.

The Senator changed his challenging tone. He must have sensed Bram's direct nature because he then focused on the Fold to Bangkok and asked if there were any issues with the request.

Bram replied that it was quiet acceptable, and two rooms had been secured at one of the top hotels at the center of the city. A top tourist guide would take them to the requested locations and would arrange the tour so that they would have lunch at one of the top restaurants.

The tour would end at the hotel early enough for all of them to refresh themselves and then they would be escorted to another world-class restaurant.

Bram let the Senator know that his support had been briefed about the restaurants and the meal selections.

He said that the arrangements at the Fold facility on Monday would go into all the details he was interested in.

He asked the Senator if he liked to fish.

The Senator replied that he had been an avid fisherman before getting elected and taking his seat in the Senate. He said that fishing sounded great.

Bram smiled and said that his fishing trips always resulted in everyone landing their share of fish. He did not mention that everyone also participated in a gunfight.

He let the Senator know that the entire Oversight committee was being scheduled in for an entire week and at the end there would be a celebration fishing picnic.

Bram reminded the Senator that the address for his Fold pickup had been given to this support and ended his end of the conversation by saying he was sure the Senator would find the weekend and his Monday visit to the Fold compound enlightening and that he would leave as a staunch supporter of the breakthroughs that would make the US the global leader that it was meant to be.

He asked the Senator if there were any questions about the upcoming visit.

It was clear that the Senator was on his heals, as he shook his head and said he would be at the pickup address at the appointed time.

After the call, Bram asked Linda to come into his office. Zoe and Eric accompanied her in and the four of them reviewed the interaction with the Senator. Linda shared her interaction with the Senator's support.

Zoe asked how Bram planned to introduce the FBI bodyguards.

Bram commented that they would all Fold together and tour together. He shared that he and Pat planned to Fold to DC on Friday and then they would all Fold to Bangkok as a group.

He asked Zoe to find out if the Senator's wife lived in Washington.

Zoe replied that she already had the background check feedback on the senator and knew that his wife lived back in Utah. She commented that she figured that her participation on such short notice was at best a fifty-fifty proposition.

He looked at Zoe and let her know that he knew that she was part of planning the Friday tour and dining and she should not pretend that she was unsure how he was planning to introduce her and Eric to the Senator. He commented that he had never kept her in the closet.

Zoe asked why he had asked to have the two of them wait outside during the discussion with the Senator.

Bram smiled and said that he was betting that the Senator was going to be surprised by what he was going to find out and that he wanted to overwhelm the Senator and convert him to being a Fold supporter.

He was using the FBI security as of the one surprises.

He was going to use Bramlet One and the lab environment as a second surprise.

He would use Wheel One and Amy as another surprise.

He was going to use the Fruit Farm production as a surprise.

He was going to use the fishing experience as another and final experience. During the picnic, the General would introduce the protection system and Lacy would introduce the Fold offense.

He figured the Senator, and the entire oversite team would leave as a supporters or the Fold Team would be leaving to Mataia.

He brought out the fact that the Senator faced an upcoming election. He was going to ask Lacy to help the Senator make it through the next election if he became a supporter of the Fold effort but if the Senator still insisted on trying to control the Fold project, he would ask Lacy to begin a negative ad campaign against the senator.

He made the point that the Fold project was too important to have a committee focused on obstruction.

Zoe smiled and said that she would never tweak his nose again.

Bram smiled and agreed that he was exposing one of his mean streaks.

The early Friday morning Fold was the first Fold using the new inverted U tube design. Remi escorted them out to the tube and spent a few moments getting everyone oriented. He pointed out that tube with six rows of two seats was the biggest model that had currently been produced.

He commented that the project would have versions all the way down to two rows of two.

Remi pointed out that every seat had the same controls but would only have control of the bubble if they engaged their computer and only one computer would be allowed to be in control.

Bram got in and commented on the comfortable seat and the spacious area around the seat.

Remi said he figured it was time to upgrade the Fold experience. He pointed out that the craft was powered by a rechargeable battery that converted sunlight into electricity. It could still be charged by plugging into an outlet but now it could travel anywhere in the universe and not run out of power.

Bram congratulated Remi on the improvements and then said he was ready to go to tour Washington.

On arrival, Bram looked around the receiving-departure room and noted that his request to clear everything out had been executed.

He stood by as Zoe and Eric cleared the apartment. He took a moment and asked Pat how she had come up with the unusual tour stopping points.

Pat chuckled and said that Zoe and Eric had both suggested what to see that would be different.

After they all took their suitcases to their rooms they took a quick tour of the apartment and Zoe commented that Melisa continued to get great apartments and appoint them exquisitely. She was glad that Bram had such a good budget.

Bram informed her that his budget had not put up a single penny and the Melisa had set up the weekend vacation program and any longer vacation as a money-making venture. She had set up the Fold Travel Agency LLC and had set up the books so she could legally manage the associated cash flow. He figured she would be one of the most affluent individuals in the Fold community.

He then followed Pat out of the building.

Pat was greeted by the tour guide that was a young woman that ran her own private tour company. The two and Zoe had met online and were chatting like old friends.

Bram liked the technology that connected people so quickly. He followed Pat into the Van. Zoe and Eric sat behind Stacy the guide. He noted that the driver was a youngish looking Black man that was introduced as Dikembe.

Stacey listed the order of the tour and said that she was pleased to do a tour that allowed her to go to a different venues than she normally toured.

At each location Bram took in sites and learned about stuff that he had not ever thought about but that filled in pieces of history that was interesting to him.

The columns removed from the white house and now standing out in a field made him wonder what else could become a tourist attraction.

The Spy museum was more interesting, and he enjoyed learning about a field that he had never pursued.

The length and the details of the tour proved to be about right.

Then they went to lunch and enjoyed a meal that rivaled the best they had recently eaten. The walk around the neighborhood that followed allowed Bram time to think about his meeting with the Senator.

The tour continued and the evening meal once again was of great delight.
Starters.
Jumbo Lump Crab Cake
Calamari Fritto Misto
A Clam Platter
Arugula & Fennel Salad
Main.
Surf n Turf, a Petite Filet and Lobster Tail
8 oz Center-Cut Filet topped with Crab & Shrimp sauce,
Lobster Béarnaise, Classic Oscar
Sides.
Wild Mushrooms, Fresh Asparagus, Broccoli Parmigiano,
Tuscan White Beans,
Creamed Spinach, Shrimp Risotto
Desert.
Strawberry Delicacy; strawberry panna cotta, makrut lime gelato,
honeycomb brittle

Bram commented that he was glad to share and glad that Zoe had an empty leg
to fill because just the starters were enough to fill him.

Stacey and Dikembe were both at the meal and they said that they had never
eaten at the restaurant because of the cost, and they had never eaten so well.

Pat said that she was going to have a bite of everything and share anything she
had ordered but her desert would be all hers.

Bram decided on following Pat's "a bite of everything" and at the end asked
her for a bite of her desert.

At the end, as he leisurely sipped on a hot tea, he realized that he was definitely
ready for a long walk.

Chapter 15: The Senator

Bram was up early. He went down to the kitchen to make pour over coffee. He was not surprised to find Zoe there ahead of him doing the pour over. Eric had set the table and had a variety of jam set out. He was standing at the toaster buttering the toast as it popped up.

Bram had grown to think of the Zoe as his younger sister and Eric as his brother-in-law. It was hard to think of them as fierce fighters who had repeatedly demonstrated the reason, they had been chosen to be his bodyguards.

Zoe was a petite woman that was lithe and athletic but somehow seemed too frail to have repeatedly demonstrated a world class athletic talent.

Eric was more rugged, but he too did not seem the type that would run toward gunmen who were shooting at him, but Bram had watched him do so.

Bram took a seat at the table and put some strawberry jam on one of the buttered toast. Zoe brought over a cup of coffee and asked how the night had been.

Bram joked about the fact that the pea under the mattress had kept him up most of the night.

Pat had come to the kitchen and commented that his snoring is what had kept her up all night.

Zoe joked that her hollow leg had emptied, and that hunger had awakened her early and she was ready to do it all again.

Bram asked Eric what his complaint might be.

Eric commented that his bed partner had kicked him all night as her leg emptied, and he was hoping that the bruises would not prevent him from wearing his shorts over the weekend.

Bram enjoyed their banter and fake complaints.

He was satisfied with three pieces of toast and was ready to make the transit to Bangkok.

He went to his room, packed his suitcase, and rolled it out into the living room.

They all sat down and wondered who would be standing on the other side of the door when the time came to make the Fold.

The Fold would occur roughly fifteen minutes later than the given schedule. Bram had arranged it so he would have a moment to greet the Senator and whoever was with him and then introduce Zoe and Eric.

The doorbell jangled right on time.

Bram walked to the door and opened it.

Senator Stately and his partner were standing at the door. Bram took note that there was no wife.

He brought the two into the living room and introduced everyone.

The Senator introduced his partner as David Conden, a lifelong friend.

He then asked about Alex and Eric.

Zoe stood up and replied that she and Eric were Bram's permanent bodyguards and were required to be on duty twenty-four seven. She explained that there were two more FBI bodyguards back at the compound and that they rotated their daily assignments.

The Senator commented that he had been unaware that the FBI had assigned bodyguards to Bram.

Eric gave him a brief description of the dozens of times that Bram had been attacked. He said that there was also a contingent of Marine guards that accompanied them whenever they were outdoors.

The Senator asked what the risk was of an attack on the weekend.

Bram replied that it was very low, but they would be cautious.

He then said it was time to load up and led the way to the room where the Fold tube would materialize.

He opened the door to an empty room.

He had the Senator stand outside the room and watch as the Fold unit materialized.

After a moment of silence, the Senator asked how such a thing was possible.

Bram commented that it was a matter of luck and advise from Einstein and led the way to the back of the unit and put his weekend bag into the bin located to the right of the entrance. He then stepped in and walked to his seat at the front. Pat followed and walked up the other aisle.

The Zoe had the Senator enter and go up the aisle toward Bram and David go in and up the aisle toward Pat.

Eric entered next and followed David.

Zoe entered put her things in the bin and closed it, closed the entrance door, and took her seat behind the Senator.

Bram gave a brief explanation of what they should expect. He asked that everyone put on their seat belts.

He then sat down and pressed the fold button.

Almost instantaneously they were in a similar room and Bram announced they were ready to disembark.

The Senator commented that he hadn't felt a thing.

Zoe opened the bin and the exit door. She and Eric got out and said that everyone should relax for a moment until they had cleared the apartment.

Moments later she announced that it was all clear and that they should disembark and see what a dramatically beautiful apartment Melisa had provided. She said she had no idea where they were in Thailand, but the view was stunning.

The apartment was the entire fifth floor that had four bedrooms a very large living room and a very well-equipped kitchen and an enclosed veranda. The air conditioning provided a very clean and refreshing environment.

Pat commented that Melisa had told her that the apartment looked out on the Chao Phraya river over to the Wat Arun Ratchawararam Ratchawaramahawihan area that had an ancient Buddhist temple, with an iconic, ornately tiled central spire as its main attraction.

Everyone agreed that the view from the top floor was stunning.

Bram took the Senator to one of the bedrooms and suggested that he and his partner consider enjoying the room. They could call and cancel the two rooms at the hotel. He pointed out that it would give them a much better chance of all of them getting better acquainted.

The Senator hesitated for a moment and seemed about to turn down the offer.

David nudged him and quietly said, "John, they know," let's take the room.

Bram knew that he had just witnessed a breakthrough moment.

The Senator nodded and said the room would be great.

Pat said that their guide was out in the van waiting for them. She reminded them that they had left the US at eight in the morning and that in Bangkok it was eight in the evening, and their tour would be to go to one of the upscale restaurants where they would all enjoy a local dinner.

Then for the next two days they would hit the spots the Senator had requested, and a few additional ones suggested by the guide.

They followed the young woman guide into the restaurant. A waiter led them to a private room that had a large round table with a Lazy Susan. They were all equally spaced around the table. The lazy Susan featured a wide assortment of Thai dishes and various sauces. The waiter pointed to each dish and gave the Thai name, and the guide gave the name in English. There was a bowl of Spicy Shrimp Soup, a bowl with Spicy Green Papaya Salad, a steel pan with Thai Stir-Fried Rice Noodles, another one with Fried Rice, another with Fried Basil and Pork and different version of noodles referred to as Guay Teow that meant Noodle Stir Fry. Then there was a bowl of chicken with Cashew Nuts, another with Green Chicken Curry, a platter of Thai Spring Rolls, a platter with Holy Basil Stir-Fry with Pork, a bowl of Mango and Sticky Rice, stir fried beef, a half of pineapple filled with fried rice, and an additional salad with strips of beef.

Once the waiter had described all the food, he asked if there was some additional dishes they might be interested in.

Bram laughed and said that if they ate half of what was on the table they would set a record for how much they could eat.

The waiter then took their drink orders. There was a choice of wine, beer, or nonalcoholic drinks. The group settled for a bottle of red Syrah and a bottle of Chenin Blanc.

The Lazy Susan seemed to be in constant motion as each person randomly selected a dish to try. If a particular dish ran low it was replaced with a full serving.

Pat commented that it was hard to keep track of how much she had eaten and whether she had tried every dish.

Zoe said that her approach was to try each dish in the order that it was on the Lazy Susan. Then she gave a groan as one of the waitresses rearranged the dishes as she brought out a new dish.

The Senator commented that he had given up hope and was just eating whatever stopped in front of him.

Their guide informed them that they could take anything they wanted back to their apartment.

Bram asked her if she would like any of the dishes and found out that she and her driver would love to have any of the dishes that were left on the table, and they did not want.

Pat told her to ask to have the remaining dishes put into carry out containers and that once they were in the van, all the dishes would be available to her.

She suggested they order several bottles of wine to take back to their apartment and an assortment of nuts and other small snacks.

Each of them carried out a bag with the leftovers and put them in the back of the van. No one was interested in taking any up to their apartment.

Pat thanked the tour guide and driver for having taken them out and verified that they would go out for a morning breakfast and then go on tour.

They all returned to the apartment and after getting the snacks served on trays and pouring the wine, they sat around talking about the great food they had just tasted.

Zoe asked David what he did while the Senator was in the senate and learned that he did research to help the Senator understand the issues associated with various bills and proposals. Later in the evening the two of them would discuss how the bill would impact their state or how they would trade their vote for support on bills important to their state.

Bram found that interesting and asked how often bargaining for support or for granting support took place.

The Senator commented that it was going on every moment of everyday and sometimes it was difficult to determine what was going on.

Ron Mueller

In the morning, the guide let them know that she was taking them to her cousins small restaurant. She said that they could eat anything for breakfast that they wanted but she had asked her cousin to make a small amount of several dishes. She said that one dish was a thick rice porridge known as Joke. Soft boiled eggs in a shot glass that was one of her favorites would also be available. Another dish was just rice and an egg omelet. A sausage, egg, and cheese biscuit would also be available. The Thai version of a donut made with a slightly sweet dough and deep fried with a fluffy inside and a crunchy outside would also be on the table. Sticky rice topped with custard and wrapped in a banana leaf, fried bananas, coconut gridle cakes would all be available to try.

And a wide variety of cut fruit such as mango, guava, papaya, pineapple, watermelon, rose-apple would be featured as well.

She said that they could have as much to eat as they desired and did not have to try everything. She said that lunch would be taken at the Floating Gardens and Dinner would be at a restaurant that her parents owned.

She asked if the arrangement was satisfactory and that if there were any objections she would make the desired changes.

Zoe spoke up and said that she liked the fact that they were connecting the tour with her relatives restaurants.

The Tour on Saturday was to the Greenville beach for an early morning walk or a casual seat with the view of the sea then they would drive across the city to the Taling Chan Floating Market where they would have lunch. During the drive to the floating market, they would pass a number of tourist spots that she would highlight and stop if there was interest to do so.

Pat said that sounded like a good plan.

The floating market had a wide variety of shopping that was pointed out by the guide. She had rented a boat that was taking them all along the various shops.

Bram was soon bored with the shopping portion, but he took in the lifestyles of the vendors in the various boats. He was personally not enthralled with the sights and was soon thinking about the Fold exploration he and Marcus had discussed.

He was relieved when lunch time arrived, and they got out of the boat and went into a sit-down restaurant. He was not really hungry and settled for a mixed salad and a soft drink. The local soft drink was on the sweet side and had a flavor that he thought was what mango and lime juice would taste like.

He was ready for the ride back to the apartment and a long hot shower before going out to the guide's family restaurant.

He was more interested in how the family restaurant would be managed and its hygiene. He had been negatively impressed with the noon time restaurant.

The Senator commented that the Floating Market was interesting but did not capture his interest. He said that so far the morning walk along the beach was the highlight of the day.

David seconded the opinion and said that the floating market had been his idea, but the beach was a much more enjoyable experience.

Zoe said that the fish that she had for lunch was great and was the highlight of the visit to the Floating Market.

The guide began to apologize but Bram stopped her and said that she should not take it personally. She was doing a great job and was fulfilling what had been requested. He said that he was looking forward to the evening dinner.

Once back in the apartment, Bram voiced the fact that he was a little overwhelmed with all the eating and not enough exercise. He took a shower and then spent the early part of the evening doing floor exercises.

Pat sensed that Bram was bored. She knew he was focused on influencing the Senator and turning him into a Fold program supporter, but it was something that Bram had no patience for.

She was going to see if she could move that process forward.

Bram was sitting in the living room relaxing while waiting to go out to dinner. He was pleased to have the Senator join him.

Bram engaged him and shared the fact that the Senator should be able to use his role as the leader of the oversight committee to expand the number of supporters that would vote for him.

The Senator agreed that it should help. He reminded Bram that he was running in a state that was extremely conservative and that deficit government spending was of great concern.

Bram pointed out that the Senator could position his role as strengthening the power of the US. He pointed out that the Senator could not directly divulge the details of the Fold capability, but he could insinuate that it would make the US the most powerful nation on Earth.

He then suggested that he should also take the opportunity to leverage his role to come out of the closet.

The Senator asked if Bram was joking.

Bram said he was not. He said that he would never support someone on the oversite committee who was willing to hide the love a person had for another just to satisfy a group of biased uninformed individuals.

He said that he would help the Senator win his next election if he was willing to come out of the closet. And he was prepared to make sure the Senator lost the election if he did not.

He made the point he could not share the details that made the Fold process work with someone who was not honest.

The Senator said that he was shocked at what Bram had just shared. He asked what made Bram think he could keep him from winning re-election.

Bram pointed out that the Senator had just told him how conservative his supporters were. How would they react if the lead up campaign adds highlighted the faggot in the closet.

The Senator commented that he had never met a person that was so direct and so clear.

He asked what the alternate ads would be.

Bram commented that it would show the Senator standing with the Senate building and the Statue of liberty in the background and him saying that Utah was the staunch supporter of the US being a world power.

He asked who Bram knew that would help him get re-elected.

Bram called Zoe in and asked her who the financial supporters of the Senator were. Zoe pulled out her phone and read off a dozen names and the amount each had donated to the Senator's re-election fund.

Bram asked her what would happen if the Senator went public with the fact that he was gay.

Zoe said that most donors would base their support on how the Senator could wield the power of leading the Fold oversight committee. She was certain that the Senator would win even though it might be by a tight margin. She commented that she had enough information on each of the donors to be able to influence their public response and to help them open their pocketbooks.

The Senator shook his head. He commented that he had never faced such a choice and would wait to respond after they were back at the Fold compound.

Bram said that would be appropriate and timely.

The remaining tour of Bangkok went smoothly and the tour of the temple directly across the river was a highlight.

They had scheduled the Fold back to Dallas to take place in the morning since that would be Sunday evening there and it would give them the evening to relax and prepare for busy Monday morning of touring the Fold site.

Bram had instructed Linda to give the Senator the vanilla tour, meaning that no detailed information would be shared. He was waiting for the Senator to share his decision of whether he was coming out of the closet.

The Senator commented that he had not expected the amount of work and progress that the organization had made.

Bram joked that it had all been made possible with little money being spent.

He commented that so far the Fold project had spent less than six hundred thousand dollars.

The Senator said that he was expecting a much larger number and was looking forward to seeing the books.

Bram wondered how the Senator would react if he learned about the Swooshians and the help that had been given that allowed them to move from one planet to another. That was information that Bram was going to withhold for as long as he thought necessary.

He knew that the technology would change the world economy and that learning about the Swooshians would shatter the belief that humans were the only sentient beings in the universe.

When they moved from one side of the Fold compound to the other, the Senator commented that it seemed that a small army was protecting Bram.

General Tilton was in the van with them and replied that going fishing with Bram had proved to be like going into battle. He shared the stories of past fishing expeditions and the role that Bram had played in each.

The Senator replied that the stories seemed a little exaggerated.

It was clear to Bram that the General was a little bit miffed with the Senator's attitude.

The senator was Folded back to the starting location when the evening came to a close.

Chapter 16: The Rest of the Committee

The team Folded into a home that was right on Willard's Beach where they were to meet Senator Olivia Newton and her family. This was a different location than the one that had originally been selected because it provided a better Friday experience.

Pat, Bob, and Thomas had talked through what to see in the Portland, Maine area and had decided on a sailing cruise in the afternoon and then an evening seafood meal at a top restaurant with a harbor view. The three of them had agreed that taking it easy was the way to take in a Friday night after a busy week.

They were all meeting for dinner at one of the top seafood restaurants and then they would return to Willard's beach and Fold to Athens which would put them there at roughly three in the morning.

They figured that they could get a quick nap in and then take a morning walk on the beach.

In Athens, the Fold was into a top floor apartment across from Kalamaki Beach.

When Pat commented that the apartment had enough space for all of them and suggested that they all stay in the same apartment. The senator welcomed the offer. She agreed that it would give them all more time to get to know each other and to enjoy the beach.

She made the comment that Senator Stately had ranted about the exorbitant expenditures that the Fold project had made and had convinced the committee that money was being wasted but after experiencing the Fold from Maine to Greece, she said it did not matter if the Fold project had spent billions of dollars. The technology would place the US in the lead in almost every technological field she could think of.

Bram smiled and said that he had spent a great deal of money, but he had not yet made it to a billion. He made the point that the most money spent to date had been to set up the Fold vacation spots around the globe and it was being managed as an investment with a three year pay back and no money had been from the Fold budget. The Fold to a location was free but the cost of the living quarters were part of the cost of the vacation package.

The Senator asked what she owed for her vacation.

Bram smiled and said that this first one was on him, but any future ones would be charged.

Pat sensed the ease with which they were all getting along and knew that Bram now had two for sure supporters on the committee, Senator Newton, and Jeffrey. She put Senator Stately in the maybe list.

The tour of Athens and the Greek ruins went as planned and the food was as good as always.

After the weekend and her tour of the Fold compound, Senator Newton was a little overwhelmed with the exploration already done by the Fold team and the ability of the team to produce its own equipment at such a low cost.

Just before leaving, the Senator again thanked the Fold team and pledged to support the efforts that were underway.

Senator Bascom of West Virginia chose to do a weekend in Barcelona with his wife.

Senator Bascom left West Virginia as a sceptic but after spending the weekend in Barcelona and enjoying the tour and dinners, he came around and was more supportive but voiced his one remaining concern about the open nature that decisions were made. He felt that it should be more structured and managed by the leaders.

Pat had hit it off with his wife and the two had spent their time walking together and talking. It was clear to Bram that Pat had had an inside track on influencing the Senator. He figured that the Senator would most likely come around to being a full supporter but at the moment he was on the maybe list.

The Science advisor, Charles Ford chose to go to Lima, Peru. He and his wife were very pleasant to be with and it was clear he was eager to understand how the Fold process was even possible. He kept asking if it was real.

Without exception every member asked it if the bodyguards were necessary. Pat explained that from the very beginning Bram had faced repeated attempts on his life. She shared that the attacks now numbered more than a dozen. She said that back at the Fold compound the number of bodyguards doubled in number because there was the FBI and the Marines both providing guards.

Bram, Pat, and their bodyguards made all the trips except the one with Jeffrey. He and Pat decided to surprise Jeffrey.

They Folded to Maputo, Mozambique to the eleventh-floor apartment that was the Fold location. They had dinner with he and his family before they were scheduled to Fold home.

Maputo was the closest Fold location to Kruger National Park and the location where they could all go out to dinner.

Pat asked Melisa to recommend a restaurant that seemed to offer one of the better menus.

Jeffrey was surprised by the impromptu dinner notice, but he and his family commented that it was nice to be engaged with friends.

Jeffery was also impressed with the fact that it seemed that Bram had turned the oversight committee to one that seemed like it was going to be supportive.

Linda had kept track of all the travel and had managed the scheduling of work that Bram was doing with Mallica, Marcus and Remi. She was surprised at the stamina that Bram displayed and the ease with which he managed the transition between the travel and then working with the various teams.

The week that the entire oversite committee was meeting at the Fold compound was a busy one. Linda had set up the main auditorium as the central meeting location for the committee and had scheduled a series of presentations and then mini tours that followed each presentation. She had designed the week so that it was a constant flow of information and then the showing of what the information had just described.

General Tilson gave the physical tour of the Fold Facility and explained how it was protected and that over time they had raised the level of protection to the point that it was as secure as the Fort Knox facility.

Melisa gave a tour of the housing area. She highlighted the recreation center, the ball fields, and the homes. Several people gave spontaneous testimonials about what a great place the Fold community was to raise their kids.

Erica took them through the Green House production area that was now in full production of the U-tube design Fold vehicles. The only Fold vehicle present was the one that had been used to transport the committee members in.

Remi gave them a tour of the new Lab facility and highlighted the research he was doing and had several test machines running just for show. He wasn't really running any experiments, but it appeared that his team was doing their research.

Marcus shared how he verified that a point in space was free of debris so that what happened to Bramlet Number one would not happen again. Bramlet One was the center piece and Marcus asked what had caught the attention of each of the Senators when they had Folded in and out of the Arrival-Departure rooms. He pointed to Bramlet One and said that the rooms were totally empty to ensure that those coming and going did not end up like poor Bramlet One.

Amy and Pat highlighted Wheel One that along with the destroyed Wheel Two had been the first vessels to take people out to the other side of the moon. They commented that the rapid progress that had been made had made both wheels obsolete and they added that the two of them had gone from being Fold pilots to unemployed.

Bram commented that how Fold affected the human body was a field of research that was now full time and would be on going for the near future.

Senator Newton asked if it had a negative effect on the body.

Pat responded that she had done extensive testing, and the Fold process seemed to fix the defects in the body. She commented that the Fold process had eliminated scars and burn marks on various members of the Fold team.

Committee Science Advisor Ford asked if it reduced hay fever symptoms. Pat smiled and said that she thought so, but she only had her personal experience to base that on and had not run any scientific research in that area. Ford said he thought it might because his normal hay fever seemed to have disappeared.

Mallica spoke up and commented that the Fold process would open opportunities that had yet to be recognized but it would certainly have a dramatic economic, social, environmental, and medical impact.

The Oversight Committee should plan on managing how each of those areas would be handled. They should also be considering the pace at which any of these opportunities were rolled out. If the timing was not well controlled global chaos would be the outcome.

Senator Stately nodded and commented that never in his dreams had he thought that the Fold technology would be as powerful as he now thought it would be. He commented that his initial approach had been petty and if Bram wanted to spend more money he was in full support.

Jeffrey spoke up and commented that the Fold effort had spent less than five hundred million dollars. He pointed to Bram and commented that they were looking at a penny pincher that was leveraging every dollar he had in his budget.

The most money that Bram had spent was on the housing for the personnel working on the Fold process and on building the facility that they had all now toured.

He laughed and joked that the extravagant spending was to take the committee fishing and have a picnic.

Linda stood up and commented that it was time to end the day's meetings and go and enjoy a fine dinner at the pool side facility.

She reminded everyone that the departure in the morning would be at five in the morning and that there would be a breakfast box for each person. The vans would take everyone to the boat pier where they would get assigned to one of the ten fishing boats that had been arranged to take them out.

Bram led the committee out of the auditorium and suggested they all walk to the poolside recreation facility.

Had anyone been looking it appeared that a small army was making its way on foot.

Suddenly Orlando started a chant.
> *Took the bite, took the fight*
> > *Took it from the Oversight.*
> *Nasty people's exoneration*
> > *Now in support of our great Nation.*
> *One, two, three, four.*
> > *Took the bite, took the fight.*
> *Took it from the Oversight.*
> > *Oversight, Oversight*
> *Just a bit short of being right.*

Soon they were all jogging, singing the jingle and laughing

Later Bram thanked Orlando for having come up with the ditty and said he had missed him and his ability to lighten the day.

The mood of the evening dinner had been raised significantly by the jog over. The committee members all commented that they had not expected such a warm welcome and they really liked the ditty that they had joined in singing.

Elizabeth nodded and said that in her lifetime she had never worked with a person who seemed to enrich and empower people the way that Bram did.

At various times during the dinner, a committee member would stop and thank Bram for having arranged the mini-weekend vacation that had been used to get them to understand the marvel of the Fold process.

He thanked them and commented that there was an unimaginable future for the technology and that they would all need to be very careful how the capability was communicated and deployed.

The dinner ended early, and Linda reminded everyone to get a good night of sleep. She said that if they were not use to Bram time, waking at five in the morning would be sleep shattering for almost everyone.

The next morning everyone managed to get to the vans on time and the hot cups of coffee were greatly appreciated.

Bram was personally wide awake and ready to go fishing. He now saw the oversight committee as a group that was going to be supportive. He was also hoping that the fireworks that Linda had planned would be the only fireworks of the day.

Ted met them at the park and led them all down to the pier. Linda assigned people to the boats and soon they were leaving the pier and gliding through the dark on a placid smooth lake.

The millions of stars overhead seemed to have twins shining back from the depths of the dark lake water. The only sound was the smooth purr of the boat motors that seemed to have embraced the night and were happily pushing their boat smoothly through the water.

Bram had his arm around Pat who seemed to be dosing. He looked over at Senator Stately and saw that David was leaning against him also dozing. The Senator nodded and gave Bram a thumbs up.

The sun was threatening to break over the far mountains when Tom cut his engine and let the boat glide forward on its own momentum. The other boats fanned out and stopped as well.

Bram noted that if he were looking from above the boats would look like a flock of geese in a V formation floating on the surface.

Tom shouted for everyone to wake up and throw their lines in.

Bram watched as the Senator took the back fishing chair and pointed for David to take the bow seat.

The boat was a little crowded. Zoe, Eric Pat, Tom, and he had to find a place from which to fish. The two spots on either side of the motor were perfect for Zoe and Pat.

He and Eric each fished off the sides in the middle of the boat. Tom had a small pole that he was using from the boat's driver seat.

Senator Newton and her husband were fishing out the sides of the boat and her husband and her two children were sitting in the main fishing chairs.

The fishing was as bountiful as Tom had promised and by the time the sun had hit its zenith, everyone had at least one nice catch.

Bram had put away his pole immediately after catching a nice bass. He then enjoyed watching everyone else as they talked to each other and displayed a fish they had pulled in.

He complimented Tom for taking them to a spot where everyone seemed to be lucky.

Tom chuckled and said that the fish could not resist the bait he had spit on.

Pat moaned and said she was now, for sure, going to give him her catch.

The Senator had just pulled in a huge fish and commented that he wanted a bottle of the spit.

Tom said that he would think about how much he would need to charge to make it worth his while.

He then called out that it was time to head back to the park for the picnic lunch.

Once they were back to the park, Linda informed Bram that the fireworks she had promised was going to take on a very different look than she had been imagining.

Linda said that when she had discussed this with Lacy, she had been reminded that the picnic was during the afternoon and regular fireworks were just not going to be very effective. She said that Lacy was going to put on a surprise demonstration with the fleet of protective bubbles.

Bram replied that he could hardly wait.

Not long after General Tilson introduced Lacy. He made an announcement that they were going to demonstrate how versatile and beautiful their fleet of protection bubbles could be. He asked everyone to look out to the center of the lake.

Clear bubbles with flashing lights that cycled between green, yellow, and red burst one at a time from the surface of the lake and rose rapidly into the air. As they rose the bubbles formed into V formation and fired tracer bullets that left a blue trail behind them. The bubbles swept into the sky, made a dive toward the park, and then rose and went straight into the air. They then made a long loop and disappeared into the water. Suddenly one at a time they shot up at the end of the pier and shot up into the sky.

They were so well synchronized that there appeared to be three parallel yellow, green, and red streaks rising into the air. As they reached their peak, a huge explosion sent out a rainbow-colored mushroom cloud. And suddenly all that could be seen was the trail of the rainbow colors slowly falling back to the surface of the lake. And then there was nothing!

Senator Newton's two kids, Marcus's two kids and Jeffrey's two led the cheering that rose up from everyone in the Park.

General Tilson was speaking on his phone letting the people that had programed and had controlled the attack bubbles know that they had outdone themselves. He held up his phone so those controlling the bubbles could hear the shouting and cheering.

Charles, the science advisor walked over to Lacy and complimented her on the choreography and synchronized dancing of the bubbles. He said he was amazed at the Fold versatility and flexibility. He said that he was ready to join them and learn how he could use his skills in the Fold program.

Senator Stately complemented the Fold community on their ability to embrace, entertain and envision the Oversight Committee. He said that he was returning to Washington a changed person who was going to work to ensure that the Fold program had a green light going forward.

Bram saw the sunlight being broken by something coming fast across the lake. He walked over to a marine who was holding a scoped rifle and asked to borrow it.

As soon as he saw what had caught his eye he ran toward the dock and began firing.

He could hear Lacy shouting for everyone to get down and the general shouting on his phone to get the attack drones online.

Bram kept firing hoping the lead he was putting in front of the incoming drone would have an effect.

Suddenly a huge explosion hurled him back and he lay on the ground hoping no one was hurt.

He rolled over to look to where the food table was still standing, and Marial was straightening it out.

He was shocked.

Lacy shouted that there were three more incoming drones but suddenly a swarm of attack bubbles appeared and quickly took them out and then flew on toward the far shore like a swarm of mad hornets.

Bram sat up as explosions across the lake sent small mushroom clouds into the air. Then a huge explosion sent a much larger one up.

The General was talking into his phone and asking why it had taken so long for the protective response and wanted to know who was asleep.

Bram stood up and handed the rifle back to the Marine who he had taken it from and thanked him. The Marine nodded and said he had more ammo anytime he needed to use his weapon.

Bram went over to the kids and asked if they were all right. They all gave him a hug and said they had a ditty.

> *Took the fight, Took the fight.*
> *Showed it to the Oversite.*
> *Shoot, Shoot*
> *Rat-tat-tat, Rat-tat-tat*
> *Blew it,. Blew it, out of the air.*
> *Took the fight, Took the fight.*
> *Showed it to the Oversite.*

Senator Stately looked at Bram and commented that he now believed everything that Bram had shared and that he planned to accept the challenge of coming out of the closet.

Bram asked who the committee had shared their schedule with and learned that all had shared it with their personal support staff.

The Senator gave a laugh and said that other than being blown on his butt the fishing and picnic was the most exciting thing he had done in his life, and he was now ready to eat.

He pointed at the General and said that he had gotten an earful of Marine language as the General tore someone a new one for being asleep at the switch.

The departure of the committee members at the end of the day was to be from the park. Ted's three catering vans had been positioned to form a U that would shield the Fold vessel from sight.

After a picnic that every committee member swore was the most exciting one, they had ever been invited to and featured the best food they had ever eaten, they got into the bubble and were returned to the Fold hangar where each got into a different bubble and were Folded home.

Bram Nielson Collection

Bram sat down at the picnic table and pushed Zoe into having the FBI trace the leak that had occurred.

Zoe commented that she had already launched the search, and she would let him know as soon as she learned where the leak led.

A few days later Zoe reported that one of Senator Stately's aids had obtained his schedule and had shared it with his office members.

One of the office members had sent the schedule to an opposition candidate in Utah that was planning to run against Senator Stately.

That candidate had shared the schedule with some of his supporters. It turned out that one of the supporters was a member of a far-right group that decided to eliminate the Fold leadership.

They had access to some older drones that could carry a significant amount of C4 and had decided to attack the picnic and eliminate the committee and as many Fold personnel as possible.

The first drone had almost succeeded. It was the one that Bram had shot down.

Bram shared this finding with Senator Stately and said that the Senator now had the ammunition to take out his political opposition.

The Senator replied by sending Bram the political advertisement that announced his run for re-election and clarified that he and his partner of more than twenty years were looking forward to keeping Utah well represented and being the leader of the group that would have oversight responsibility for one of the top scientific projects that would put the US in the technical and military lead globally.

He also included a blurb by his wife that also endorsed him as the right person for Utah as the right man, at the right time and in the right position. She constantly repeated, "Utah Senator Stately loves thee! And will make you great."

Bram was pleased with how the tone of the committee was now one of support versus one of control and adversity.

The detail of the leak highlighted how easy it was for the opposition to learn about what was going on in the Fold project and made him much more sensitive on what information should be shared.

He was pleased with the fact that the information about the water worlds, the new world and the negative Fold learning was still under wraps. He was going to reinforce keeping it all a secret for the foreseeable future.

Jeffrey and his wife let Bram know that they not only had a great weekend vacation and had enjoyed the surprise dinner with he and Pat, but they were now feeling that the role at NASA would be much easier than they had anticipated.

Bram smiled and said that it appeared that everyone was to have an easier time than they had expected.

Ron Mueller

Chapter 17: Election

Bram was not usually very attentive to the political scene. However, this midterm election was different.

Senator Stately had come out of the closet.

Bram had promised his support. He made sure that Lacy connected with all his financial supporters and made the case why they should make certain that the Senator won and remained the leader of the Fold oversight committee.

Jeffrey and his wife campaigned in Utah for the senator. It turned out that Jeffrey's wife was the one that was having the most positive effect. She had gotten together with the Senator's wife and together they had attended multiple rally's where they spoke of his upright character traits, honesty, and the power he yielded in the Senate.

The other factor was the three times daily political add that featured the Senator and commented that he was the right person, in the right role, at the right time and the smart people of Utah would be crazy to lose the influence, control and the financial benefits that the Senator gave the State of Utah.

Each ad began with "Land of the Pioneers, Utah Senator Stately loves thee!" and ended with the state motto of Stately supporting "Industry." One was the state tagline and the second was the state motto.

The senator won a resounding victory. He called Bram and thanked him for the help he had received for his campaign and said he was still trying to figure out why the Fruit Farm located in Dallas had run the overwhelmingly successful add campaign that his staff said had been one of the major reasons for his resounding victory.

Bram replied that he had promised the Senator a win and having the Fruit Farm do the ads was his way of delivering that promise.

The Senator thanked him and simply said David had commented that they both owed Bram one.

Senator Bascom of West Virginia seemed on a sure path to a humiliating loss. He had opposed the bill that would have provided a much-needed support for his poorer supporters, and he had voted for a bill that opposed abortions. A much more liberal candidate had a ten-point margin going into the election and came out the victor.

Senator Newton of Maine called Linda and left Bram a message saying that she was going to encourage the Massachusetts Senator to volunteer for the opening on the oversight committee. She said that the Senator, though from the other party was the type of person that would complement the committee. She suggested that if Bram was in agreement, Linda should find out where in the world the Senator would like to go for a weekend vacation. She was personally sure that she had the ability to get the support to seat the Massachusetts Senator.

Bram was pleased to have been given the heads up by Senator Newton.

The election turned out to be a good one for the President who was able to keep control of both the Senate and the House. It was also an election that allowed John Stately to assume the life that he had shunned because of politics.

Zoe looked into the Massachusetts Senator's background and found out that the Senator was a black woman whose grandparents had been brought over from Gabon. It turned out that her grandparents had been sold to the slave traders by a clan that was the enemy of the tribe her grandparents were part of. They had been told they would go to Brazil and be slaves there, but a storm took their ship off course, and they ended up coming to Virginia where they were auctioned off to a cotton farmer in Georgia.

Zoe found out that the Orungu clans at Cape Lopez organized a kingdom whose power rested on control of the slave trade through the harbor at the mouth of the Ogooué River. The Mpongwe clans of the estuary, who were already important traders, also profited from the slave trade, as did the Vili people of Loango, whose activities extended throughout southern Gabon.

She learned that only the Fang, who were migrating southward from Cameroon into the forests north of the Ogooué, refused to hold slaves or engage in warfare to obtain them.

She said that she had not realized that black people were selling other black people into slavery.

Zoe said that she had talked to the Senator who let her know that after the Civil War her grandparents had moved north and ended up in Massachusetts. They had chosen that state because at the end of the American Revolution, Massachusetts had more free black people than slaves, and by 1783, Massachusetts had abolished slavery. They had been aware that Boston was a destination point for the Underground railroad and had heard about Boston's tightly knit Black community that provided a place where they were welcome.

Later they had moved out to Worcester where they both had been able to find employment. Her parents had grown up there and had later moved back closer to Boston where they worked in one of the large hotels for most of their lives.

Zoe commented that she had looked up the Senator's name and found out that her first name Bonank meant, "finds wealth at home," and it seemed that the Senator acted that way. She was very tight with her family and publicly always highlighted what a great family she had.

Her parents had been born and raised free and they made sure she went to college. She had struggled at first but after two years in a junior college she had been able to make it into Boston University and had focused on getting a law degree.

Pat commented that it seemed that the Main Senator was reaching across the aisle to select another woman and a woman of color. She said that her respect for Main Senator Newton had gone up significantly.

Bram asked Linda to contact the Massachusetts Senator Etaing and learn where she would like to spend a weekend vacation.

He was not surprised to learn that Gabon was where the Senator wanted to visit.

He asked Melisa if she had a Fold location in Gabon and was pleased that there was one.

Melisa commented that Gabon was seen as the friendliest country in Africa. She had found a place in Libreville, the countries capital. The apartment was on the fifth floor of a building that was along the sea and had several restaurants within walking distance.

She said that she had a tour guide that had taken her to several locations and highlighted the Gabon historic past.

Zoe commented that the Senator had mentioned she wanted to visit the city of Ndjole that had been the place where her great grandparents had been born and raised during their early years.

Melisa looked that up and said that it was probably a couple hours' drive and then a few hours at the city and then the drive back. She said she would call the travel guide and get the details.

Bram asked her to verify the Fold delivery-departure point.

Melisa let him know that the delivery-departure point would be a few blocks from the waterfront below Bunker Hill where she had rented the entire seventh floor of a building. It had a great view of the USS Constitution, and several other ships anchored in the harbor.

Two days later Linda let Bram know that Senator Etaing had asked if her parents could be included on the trip to Gabon.

Bram replied that as long as they could get a secret clearance and signed a non-disclosure agreement it was OK with him.

Zoe let him know later in the day that Senator Etaing's father had an arrest record. He had been part of the marchers on the Edmund Pettus Bridge and had been arrested and convicted of being part of a riot.

Bram shook his head and asked if the FBI could clear up that situation and get the record expunged. He was convinced that the politicians in Alabama needed to get hot irons put under their rears so they would clear up the kind of mess they had created in the past.

A few days later he got a call from Senator Etaing who thanked him for having helped to clear her father's name. She said that she was impressed with his influence because she had been trying for years to do the same thing. She said that her mother wanted to have dinner with he and Pat when they got to Boston.

Bram said that he looked forward to it and would really enjoy eating at a restaurant that catered to the black community.

Later in the day Senator Etaing called him again and said that her mother had decided to host the dinner at her house because her friend that had a restaurant had closed it. The Senator wanted to know if that would be acceptable.

Bram said that it was, but he reminded the Senator that four FBI bodyguards would follow him while in Boston and two bodyguards when in Gabon and asked if her mother was ready to feed a small army.

The Senator laughed and said that dinners at her mother's house was always like eating with a small army. She said that she was sure that her younger sister and her husband and her younger brother and his wife and their two kids would all be there.

She suggested that Bram prepare himself for a house full of loud, laughing, crying, and singing people.

After the call Bram asked Zoe to check out all the family members. He commented that it all seemed normal, but he wanted to make sure.

Bram called Jeffrey and asked about Senator Etaing and whether he was in support of having her on the Oversight Committee.

Jeffrey replied that he was very enthusiastic as well as supportive. He added that the committee would be much more well-rounded, balanced, and enjoyable.

Bram then asked Linda to offer Senator Bascom condolences on his loss and to remind him of the sensitive nature of the information that he had acquired about the Fold program.

He was concerned that the Senator would try to use what he knew about Fold to try and raise a campaign war chest. He asked Zoe if she had any friends who might be willing to keep tabs on the Senator's actions and give them a heads up if there were any indications of improper information sharing.

Zoe replied that she had a woman friend that had family in West Virginia and based on her dislike of the Senator's stand on women she would love to keep tabs on him.

That evening, Bram had Zoe update the rest of the team on the upcoming Fold activity of getting Senator Etaing on board the Fold Oversight committee.

He then asked Pat to suggest what they should do during the day in Boston before going to dinner at the Etaing residence.

Pat suggested they get a walking tour guide but limit their walk to going to the USS Constitution Museum and then walking up to the Bunker Hill Monument and then having the tour guide take them to the Etaing residence.

Bram asked how everyone felt about that limited tour itinerary. Everyone agreed that it would fit into a Fold on Friday afternoon, give them a slice of history, and keep them focused on the dinner.

That next day Bram consulted with Marcus and asked him how the negative Fold calibration work was progressing.

Marcus commented that he had been able to get the calibration of the time by learning how each increment of distance affected time in the negative Fold realm. He had learned that for short increments linearity could be assumed but as the distance factor increased the linearity went out the door and he then could not figure out the relationship.

He suggested that Bram get involved so that they could figure out the relationship of time and distance and be able to control time.

He admitted that he had made multiple attempts at postulating a theory and then spent time trying to prove it, but all his theories were failures, and he was stumped.

He had asked for Mallica's help and she had proposed some interesting ideas, but they had not panned out. They together had again been stumped.

The two of them had gotten online with Zuri and the three of them had tried additional ideas but they all agreed that they needed help.

Bram agreed to focus on determining how to control time in negative Fold once he was back from his next Fold with the new Oversight Committee member.

The Fold to Boston was flawless and they arrived on time to go out and meet the tour guide who took them first to the USS Constitution Museum where she took them slowly through the museum and related the history of the USS Constitution and emphasized the fact that it was still a battleship that was on active duty.

They then drove back to the other side of the turnpike and then began the walk up toward the Bunker Hill Monument. On the walk up they passed several older buildings that the guide pointed out had been present during the Bunker Hill battle. She added that several of the owners had participated in the battle.

They reached the monument and got its history. She explained that the battle was actually misnamed because the majority of the action took place on Breed's Hill and that is where they were standing.

She pointed around the perimeter of the park and said that about one thousand colonial militiamen under Colonel William Prescott built earthen fortifications on top of Breed's Hill because it was closer to Boston.

She shared that it was during this battle that the Colonel knowing his men were short on ammunition is said to have shouted the words, which became famous, "Don't fire until you see the whites of their eyes!" She shared the fact that this was often disputed but seemed to have survived as where that saying had originated.

She went on to explain that Patriot gunfire cut down some 1,000 British troops, with more than two hundred killed and more than 800 wounded. More than one hundred Americans perished, and more than 300 others were wounded. She pointed out that because of sheer numbers the British defeated the Americans.

She underlined the fact that the Americans that survived, escaped, and avoided being captured by the British because Peter Salem, a Black soldier, shot and mortally wounded Major John Pitcairn, the British commanding officer who was leading the final charge up the hill.

Bram Nielson Collection

She highlighted the fact that Benjamin Pierce a father of the future U.S. President Franklin Pierce had fought in the battle.

She then explained that the first monument was a wooden pillar dedicated in 1794 to the memory of the most famous hero of the battle, Joseph Warren and was funded by the King Solomon's Lodge of Freemasons.

The larger battlefield was left largely undeveloped and unmarked until 1823, when an elite set of New Englanders that included Daniel Webster and Edward Everett, who were incorporated as the Bunker Hill Monument Association set out to build the current monument.

In 1825 one hundred thousand people gathered on Bunker Hill to watch the famous Frenchman, Lafayette lay the cornerstone and listen to a speech by Daniel Webster.

But fund-raising went slow, and construction lagged and by 1828, though most of the granite had been quarried, the funds to continue raising the monument were lacking.

The guide related that the Bunker Hill Monument was conceived as a way to express the gratitude of the American people for the sacrifices of the American soldiers who fought at the battle.

In 1830, believing that the lack of attention to the monument indicated a weakening of American patriotism, Sarah Josepha Hale began a campaign in her Ladies Magazine to raise funds from American women to complete the monument. In 1840, Sarah Hale organized a Ladies' Fair in Boston, where a number of women's organizations raised the final $30,000 to complete the work.

The monument was dedicated on June 17, 1843.

The guide made the point that it had taken almost fifty years before the current obelisk replaced the old wooden monument.

Bram commented that he had learned more about the battle for Boston than he could have imagined. He pointed out that they had used their afternoon well and that Pat had identified the perfect way to spend their time.

Pat thanked Bram for his kind words and pointed out that it was time to go to dinner at Senator Etaing's parents' home.

She led the way back down to the van.

As they arrived at the address of Senator Etaing's parent's home Bram made a comment about all the cars parked on the street and in their yard. He wondered just how many relatives and friends were going to be present.

The Senator came out to greet them.

Bram noted that she was more petite and slenderer than he had anticipated.

Zoe, Eric, Bob, and Thomas all got out first and fanned out among the cars and made sure all was clear before Zoe gave him the "all clear sign."

Bram then exited and held his hand for Pat to grab as she got out.

The Senator came over and gave Pat a hug and then turned to Bram and hesitated a moment until she was sure he was willing to get hugged.

Bram smiled and bent slightly so that the two could hug. He liked her already because he was a hugger.

The Senator asked them to call her Bonank or Bon and not Senator.

Bram introduced his FBI bodyguards.

The Senator greeted them and commented that he was one of the first persons she had interacted with, other than perhaps the President, who traveled with four bodyguards. She asked who he had offended to warrant such protection.

Bram nodded and shared the fact that he had been attacked about a dozen more times than the President and the four persons that she had just been introduced to had saved him every time. She was looking at decorated warriors of the highest degree.

The Senator said that they were going to get attacked by her family, but they were all friendly and meant no harm.

The Senator then led the way in and soon Bram was overwhelmed with smiling greeters welcoming all of them letting them know that they were going to enjoy the best dinner they had ever eaten.

The younger kids soon had Zoe and Eric down on their knees playing marbles with them.

The Senator's father led them to the living room where they could sit and talk.

He watched as Bob and Thomas scouted around the room and then assumed positions at each end.

The Senator's father commented that he wished he would have had their kind of protection when he had gone on the freedom marches. He said he still carried the scars that he and earned.

He thanked Bram for clearing his name and for agreeing to include he and his wife to the weekend mini vacation that Bonank had said they would take. He also said that he and his wife had signed the non-disclosure agreements and were both surprised that they had received secret clearances.

He asked how that had all been arranged when Bonank had been trying for years just to get his name cleared of the charge of being a criminal.

Bram smiled and replied that the wheels of justice sometimes just needed to be kicked in the butt and knowing where to kick was a specialty of one of his FBI bodyguards.

The Senator came in and sat down. She bent her head and said that her mother had pressed her to ask if her brother and sister might be able to be added to the trip.

Bram smiled and replied he was not sure and that he would check. He called Zoe over and asked her if such a request could be fulfilled.

Zoe asked Bram to step outside for a moment. As they went out to the front yard, Bob, Thomas, and Eric spread out among the cars.

Zoe said that she had checked out all the family members and they were all hard-working lawyers or doctors. If Bram agreed, she could get temporary clearances for the Senator's brother and sister. She said that she doubted that their spouses or children could go.

Bram nodded and said that they should get the temporary clearances and have the brother and sister sign them before boarding the Fold transfer vessel.

Zoe led the way back into the house and into the living room.

Bram noted that Pat was engaged in a conversation with the Senator's father and mother.

The senator looked up and beamed a large smile when Bram nodded his head up and down.

She then commented that she was hopelessly compromised as a member of the Oversite Committee, but she did not care. He had changed the lives of her family, and she owed him a lot.

Dinner featured three styles of barbeque chicken, a mac and cheese that had small chunks of ham in it, greens that had a unique vinaigrette dressing and a buttery smooth whipped mashed potato.

Bram tried some of each dish and was soon filled. He pushed his chair back slightly and said that he had eaten so much he had to push back from the table.

The Senator's mother brought in a peach cobbler and some small bowls and a bowl of vanilla ice cream. She dished up a bowl of the cobbler and gave it to Bram. She said she had used fresh peaches to make the cobbler and always left the skin on so that the cobbler got a deeper taste and often a pink hue.

Bram took a bite and commented that he hoped heaven would be as good.

Pat jokingly asked what made him think he would be going to heaven.

Bram replied that he figured she would make sure to put in a recommendation for him that would carry some weight.

The Senator's mother commented that anyone that had helped her family the way that he had would have her prayers and if she got there first she would make sure to put in a good word with St. Peter.

Bram thanked her and then looked around the table. He commented that he had eaten with a group of interesting folks, and he hoped that in the future they would be able to do it again.

He then said that it was time for he and his team to get back to their apartment and get a few hours of rest.

He suggested that those that were making the trip with Bonank get a few hours of rest as well because they would arrive early at their destination and then leave immediately on a long day of touring.

He reminded everyone that departure would be at midnight, and they should all gather at his apartment a few minutes prior to that time.

He then got up and like magic, his four FBI bodyguards got up thanked everyone for their friendliness and thanked Bonank's parents for their hospitality.

Pat gave Bonank's mother a hug and let her know that she would love to get the peach cobbler recipe.

Bram then turned and walked toward the front door following Bob and Thomas. He knew that Eric and Zoe would be bringing up the rear.

Ron Mueller

Chapter 18: Gabon

The tour to Gabon was somewhat was less exciting than Bram expected. The countryside was interesting but his recent journey through the Scandinavian scenery had seemed more enjoyable. Or maybe he thought he was getting used to having his life on the line while being attacked.

He decided to focus on getting to know the Senator and her family and listened to many of their family stories. He had overheard the Senator tell her mother that she might have to change parties because she was being treated with more respect by the folks in the opposition then she was being treated by her own party.

It reminded Bram that he did not care about a person's party affiliation. He focused on their behavior and what they did and if they acted with integrity.

He was personally opposed to giving special privileges to those with extreme wealth and power, but he also was not willing to personally spend his time trying to defeat a specific person who had other ideas about that situation. He figured that everyone should pay a fair share of the taxes it took to run the country.

He knew that his position in the Fold organization gave him access to monetary funds that he would not otherwise have but he had made sure that his personal income remained in the middle of the pack for scientists in the US.

The freedom to follow his mind into new areas of development and study was much more important than monetary wealth or power.

The weekend outing had given him time to think more about how time and distance interacted in the negative Fold universe. He wondered if the linkage to the past put the person making that linkage physically able to step into that past. If that were the case the people in the positive Fold environment would be able to travel back in time and physically interact with it.

For all he knew someone in his future may have had already done so. He was the discoverer of the link. He knew that it had been formulated in his mind and it had been done so through a tedious and very puzzling process. But eventually in the future others would gain control of the Fold process and would most likely discover the ability to go back in time and potentially alter it.

He wondered how he could set up a test that would unveil such actions.

He decided to run an experiment to see if his theory of being able to step out in the past was possible. He was personally afraid that it would be possible. It would mean that he had unleashed a power larger than any current weapon possessed by man.

He thought everyone should be very afraid of such a power.

On his return from Gabon, he gave Senator Etaing the tour of the Fold facility and then took her whole family fishing out on the Columbia river. The outing was almost as big as it had been for the entire Oversite committee team several months earlier.

Ted and his crew took them out where everyone caught fish and the shouting back and forth was boisterous and laughter filled.

It was clear to Bram that the Etaing's enjoyed each other, and they treated each other with love and respect.

After returning to the park and while they were enjoying the picnic every member of the family made it a point of stopping at his table and thanking him for the great time that they had experienced

Ron Mueller

Bram was touched by the Senator's mother when she said that she had never had such a great weekend and that the fishing outing showed her a man that had captured her heart and one who she was going to make sure her daughter remembered when tough decisions about the Fold program came up and had to be made.

The Senator sat down at his table and commented that it was going to be tough to be on the oversight committee because she was so overwhelmed and impressed with the work he was doing. She commented that she was equally impressed with the loyalty and support all his people had for him. She said that it spoke to her of a person who should get all the support he desired.

Bram thanked her and let her know that he was always more impressed with the way people acted and carried out their role based on the principles they held dear. It mattered not if the decisions were what he wanted but it mattered that they were made with fairness to all involved.

The Senator smiled, nodded, and replied that he just kept making her life harder.

Marcus was sitting at Bram's table and quietly commented that he had to put up with Bram and his fair attitude every day and he as well had to live Bram's motto of "treat others as you wish to be treated." He smiled and said that everyone in the organization could state Bram's motto and they all knew that the simple saying had a huge impact on the entire organization.

He ended by saying Bram was an example for them all.

The Senator thanked him for the comment and said that it would become her motto as well.

That afternoon she and her family all went to the airport. The Senator had let Bram know that she was flying back with the rest of the family, but she looked forward to her next opportunity to Fold to some exotic location.

The next day as Bram and Marcus began their meeting, Marcus commented about how much it meant to him to work with him on the Fold effort.

Bram thanked him and then said that they were going to try a simple experiment to see if travel to the past was possible. He said that he had Linda close and lock the viewing room. She had cleaned the white board of all writing and taken a picture of the board. This would serve as a time stamp.

He said that the two of them would enter the negative Fold universe and go back just one day and enter the viewing room using the coordinates of the bare floor that could hold their two-person Fold vehicle.

They would then write a message on the board and date it.

He asked Marcus what that message should be.

Marcus smiled and said that if it worked, instead of "Kilroy was here," they should write "Bram and Marcus were here" put a sticky note on the board that gave the time and date and imprinted by Linda with her notary stamp.

He suggested that they have Linda, Pat, Amy, and the bodyguards all go in first and ask them what they saw on the white board.

He added that if it was possible he might faint.

Bram commented that it would make everyone's life change and secrecy a thousand more times important.

They both walked to Linda's desk and asked her to witness the writing of the message and to put her notary stamp on it.

Linda asked if what was happening was connected with having locked the Viewing Room.

Bram smiled and said that her intuition and smarts was why he had selected her to support him. He asked her to call Pat and Amy and have them come to her desk. He then told her that the three of them and Zoe and Eric would open the viewing room and be the witnesses of what was on the white board.

Linda waved the note and said that if this ended up on that board she would most likely faint.

Bram nodded and said he might join her as well. Then led the way to where the Fold vehicles were located.

Bram asked Marcus to put the room's coordinates into the negative Fold program. He turned on the negative Fold return beacon that had become the key to being in the negative Fold realm. He then asked Marcus to initiate the Fold.

Marcus let out his breath and pointed to the blank white board that was next to the Fold vehicle. They both got out and Bram asked Marcus to put up their message.

Marcus wrote "Bram and Marcus were here" and stuck Linda's note at the end.

Bram decided to add a personal note. He wrote, "Take a deep breath, don't faint but our world had just changed dramatically."

He then said that it was time to follow the light and see how long it would take to return to their current time.

The return was almost instantaneous, and Bram let out the breath which he had held.

Marcus led the way back to Linda's desk.

He stopped at Linda's desk and thanked everyone for being willing to be a witness. He suggested they all take a deep breath and walk slowly to the viewing room.

Zoe did the opposite as she led the way and walked faster than normal to the Viewing Room.

Zoe broke the silence by saying that she had never been more nervous. She went on and stated that being practically nude in a gun battle had been nerve racking, but this situation was mind altering and it was one time where she thought she knew the feeling of fear.

Bram was aware that adrenaline was running high in everyone.

He asked Zoe to unlock it and then lead the way in.

It was clear to Bram, who was feeling anxious, that Marcus was very nervous.

He was very sure that the message would be on the white board.

Zoe fell to her knees in front of the board and reach up and took the notarized note down and read it.

Bram walked up to the seat he normally used and sat down. In spite of knowing, he still felt shaky.

Pat sat down next to him and put her hand on his. She quietly said that his break throughs just kept happening and this particular one was as Zoe had stated, mind altering. This one she was a little more personal in that it meant that the past might be able to be altered.

Bram nodded and squeezed her hand but had nothing to add.

Linda sat down in front of them. Zoe handed her the notarized note and asked if she had really signed and stamped it just twenty-five minutes earlier. Linda nodded and said that it was also recorded in her notary logbook.

Amy sat down on the other side of Bram and put her hand on his. She commented that maybe she should have left him in the desert when she had the chance. She pointed at the board and said that it would take more than a deep breath to ever take that picture of the message out of her mind.

Bram finally found his voice and spoke what was on his mind. He said that this moment was not to be recorded in any physical fashion and no one should share what they had been witness to.

He said that someday in the future things might change but for the foreseeable and maybe their lifetime, it had to be kept a secret. He commented that he had been worried about how the Fold technology would disrupt the world and now he was more than worried, he was somewhat terrified.

Zoe commented that if he was terrified she was petrified. She could not stop thinking about how the world around her could be altered without her knowing.

Bram commented that they might need to do more experiments to learn if they could tell when things had changed around them. He was curious if there was a way to know if a person would sense that change had occurred.

He replied that she was right about how she was thinking and that protecting him had taken on a new meaning. She and her partners were now protecting all of society. Their role had taken on a new greater and challenging scope and responsibility.

He chuckled and suggested they go and relax at a sport that they all knew how to handle and do something dull like fishing.

Eric smiled and said that going fishing with him had just taken on a new meaning as well. It usually resulted in a gun battle but that was small stuff as compared with the future being able to go back in time and join the gun battles.

Marcus had been quiet and finally commented that he had been thinking about how he should coach his kids. He was now not sure how the future would transpire. What guidance do you provide that you were confident would help them.

Bram emphasized his belief that the fundamental principles of truth, honesty, integrity and treating others as one wished to be treated remained the basis on how people should behave and that those fundamentals would be what allowed them all to live with this new capability and they would continue to hold the fabric of society together.

He made the point that his concern was about the fact that a sizable portion of society did not live by those unchanging values and principles and that portion posed a significant threat.

He then asked Amy, Marcus, and Linda if they were willing to be on a team that used the negative Fold realm to investigated the people that he would ask Lacy to name. Their objective was to identify any planned action against the Fold program.

Marcus commented that they were being asked to become time spies.

Bram nodded and said that like all spies they would remain unseen and covert.

The team left the Viewing Room a changed but still solidly aligned one and one that would follow Bram's guidance.

Bram once again made the rounds of all the projects and got caught up on what each had accomplished or any barriers they faced.

He realized that his perspective had changed. The knowledge that history could be altered had him thinking about how the Fold effort might be affected. He planned to be on the offense and keep from having to play defense against the unknown future.

Erica brought forward the first current issue. She shared that their production facility in Seattle was going to close unless they paid a holding fee to keep the space available to them.

Bram said that they should not pay any holding fee. He was not sure if they would ever wish to build the size of Fold transports that they had built for the Swoshians. He said they should take the chance that it would be far enough into the future that if they needed to, they would negotiate a new fee for the use of the facility.

He suggested that Erica work with Pat and Amy to look into determining the cost of building a basic but large enough structure on Mataia and use the money they would have used for extending the contract to make it happen.

Erica nodded and agreed that she would do so and most likely make it happen sooner versus later.

Thomas volunteered to move to Mataia and manage the construction of such a facility. Bob said if Thomas got to go, he wanted to go as well.

Bram thanked Erica and responded to Thomas and Bob that it would all depend on timing and the action taking place at the current Fold facility.

He then suggested they all go to lunch.

They were just minutes late, but their normal table was occupied by Marcus, Mallica, Pat, Amy, and Lacy. They took the next table and then went and got their lunch.

It was clear to Bram that the morning discovery that the negative Fold space could transport them back in time and they could physically interact in that time frame had them all envisioning different scenarios.

He personally knew that eventually he would be using it to protect the Fold program. He was not yet sure how he would do that, but he would do it legally and he would try not to negatively impact history in any major way.

The negative Fold universe was an area that needed careful study, and it needed safeguards that would keep people from making a mess of the flow of time. He would need to work on that safeguard but until he made that breakthrough, he would work hard to keep it a secret that only his team knew about.

Ron Mueller

<u>Chapter 19: A Fold in Time</u>

Bram had shared his concern about how easy it was to get into negative Fold space. Pat agreed with him that safeguards needed to be put in place. She suggested that the entire work that he had done with negative Fold somehow become invisible. She suggested that he purge all mention of the negative Fold work and that the information about it be put in a place where only he could access.

Bram thought about it and said that he would move everything to do with negative Fold space to Mataia. To work on negative Fold, one would need to be on Mataia and would need to reinitiate the placement of the control module that needed to be in position halfway into negative Fold space to gain access.

He said that he would only train one person to be capable to do such a thing.

Pat suggested Zoe for that role.

Bram asked her why it should be Zoe.

Pat responded that Zoe had become an ardent believer in his philosophy and her protection role would be very complementary to the effort and she would also need someone else's help to do anything in the Negative Fold realm.

He agreed but said that it still left too big of a door into that realm.

Then while working on a presentation, he was working on, he experienced being in a software loop.

A light went on.

He quickly programed a loop for the control of going into the negative Fold universe. He designed it so that if the step back into the negative Fold universe was attempted from Earth, the Fold vehicle would go to a jail-like cell on Mataia and then immediately return to its original coordinates. The person in the Fold vehicle would, in a fraction of a second, be back at the starting point of the Fold. If by chance they happened to figure out how to jam the loop, they would be in a jail cell on Mataia that would signal him in his time of that situation.

He decided to try it with Marcus without telling him about the loop.

After several loops, Marcus got out of the Fold vehicle and said that there was something wrong with the controls.

Bram then let him know about the do loop that he had programed into the control system.

He explained that they could disable the loop when they needed to but otherwise it stayed on twenty-four seven.

Bram made the point that only the two of them would know about the loop. He also highlighted the fact that the loop would be set up so that if someone tried to Fold into negative space, the loop software would count and report on how many times it had been attempted.

Marcus commented that he was now with Zoe about never playing poker against him. He would never trust any game since he now understood that he could be manipulated by someone in the negative Fold space.

Bram nodded and agreed that the knowledge about negative Fold had altered his thinking as well and had him thinking hard how to keep anyone from creating chaos in the flow of time. He said that for him the flow of time from its beginning out to infinity was now no longer as simple as he had once envisioned. He went on to ask the question, "has someone in the far future already reached back and altered the events that we are now experiencing?" He then asked, how long will my attempts to keep humans from going back in time stay in place?

Ron Mueller

When will some very smart person realize they are in a loop and break through the loop that I have programmed?

Marcus shook his head and agreed that it was only a matter of time before such a thing could happen. He pointed out that the technical changes that the Fold technology represented would significantly increase the technical capability of society and what usually followed was that the scientific side also made significant strides. That knowledge increase would mean that the person that would break through the loop would not have to be even closed to being a Bram. They would have the aid of new technology.

Mallica and Gerry came to his office and let him know that the Swooshian sun had accelerated its death throes and was expanding more rapidly than the Swooshian scientists had predicted. The evacuation was now happening at the fastest pace that was possible. Every Fold to the new water world was packed beyond its maximum capacity.

Gerry said that the Swooshians would make it off their current water world with time to spare and then they would focus on getting out all the species Folded to their new environment. The new water world would be ninety-nine percent the same as their previous world. It would have one percent new plants from their new water world that the Swooshian were making certain survived.

Mallica shared that Ohaan who she considered a Bram equivalent, had sent thanks from all the Swooshian leaders for the aid that they had received. They sent an invite for Bram to visit so he would see how they had populated the world that he had found for them. They shared that their celebration display would feature one thousand Swooshians rise from the water and jump through the air in a synchronized display.

He suggested that his Earth counterparts partake of their celebration drinks and food and watch the most extensive Swooshian display ever put on.

Bram asked what the Swooshian's ate.

Mallica said that Gerry had been the one that had gone deeply into understanding the Swooshian diet and asked him to describe it.

Gerry said that the Swooshian diet was remarkably similar to that of whales or other creatures in the top of the food chain on Earth. They ate a variety of sea creatures similar to krill, shrimp, and sea bass.

He said that the majority of their food was grown and managed in areas of the ocean where food for them was plentiful. The growing areas were strategically located so the Swooshian members could swim into the thick soup of krill or shrimp and get their fill and then go on. He compared it to a gas station where one could drive through, and the gas would be sucked in by the grill of a car.

The Swooshians ate about once a day, and a meal consisted of about six thousand pounds of the krill or shrimp-like creatures. The shrimp like creatures were similar in size to the very large Vietnamese shrimp. When they were consumed the tonnage eaten was the same, but it could be consumed more quickly and would be considered "fast food" and was often consumed when a Swooshian was in a hurry to do something else.

He said he had learned that there were Swooshians that had stopped eating the krill, shrimp and the sea bass like fish and now exclusively survived on plankton. He said that they consumed around twelve tons of plankton a day.

He commented that he was impressed with the way the Swooshians attended to growing their food and arranging eating areas so that their population could be distributed throughout their water world. He made the point that food was basically a part of the way the society was managed and there was no "payment" for eating.

He commented that Earth could learn a lot about how to manage the growing of food, so the world population had easy and equal access to the food they needed.

Bram suggested the Mallica set the visit up but that she include Daryl Narda and Harold Redat who had actually searched many solar systems and found the water world. He then rattled off a set of names that he felt had also contributed.

He then asked Linda to arrange a celebratory meal that could be put in the two transport bubbles. He wanted Chef D'Carluca to be one of the guests on the visit.

That day at lunch, Chef D'Carluca came to his table and asked if they could meet some time after lunch.

Bram suggested that they meet after lunch whenever the Chef was ready. He said that he usually had Linda give him a ten-minute warning to let him closed down any other work he was doing.

In actuality he had set that process up when Einstein was with him so that he had time to put him away. That thought made him think that it was time for him to go back to his boulder in the desert to see if Einstein was still kicking.

Amy asked him if she, Pat, and Remi could meet with him sometime in the afternoon.

Bram suggested they contact Linda and get her to set up the meeting time and the amount of time they wanted.

Linda stopped him as he returned to his office. She said that she had booked time with the Chef and the meeting would start in fifteen minutes. She let him know that she had scheduled time with Amy and her group for about two hours later in the afternoon.

Bram thanked her and let her know that she should include herself on the Swooshian trip.

A few moments later Chef D'Carluca entered and looked around Bram's office and gave a whistle. He commented that it was his first time to see the office and he was impressed. He pointed to Zoe and Eric and smiled and said that he had not realized that they sat in the office all the time. He commented that there was also a small army outside the door.

He went on and said that he was surprised that Bram did not have a food taster to make sure his food was not poisoned.

Bram smiled and said that he had instead chosen to have the best Chef in the world to ensure his food was the best and poison free.

Chef D'Carluca bent his head and thanked him for the compliment. He then asked if it was true that it was appropriate for him to make a variety of sea food dishes for the feast to be consumed during the Fold to a Water world where the Aliens were Whalelike creatures.

Bram said that it was indeed appropriate because the primary food of these Aliens were krill, shrimp, fish, and seaweed.

Bram let Chef D'Carluca know that he was going to be the narrator of a brief presentation of each dish that would to be presented to the Swooshians. He suggested that the Chef choose to make any dish he wished to but that he should have a picture of the dish and then a picture of each ingredient in that dish so he could present it to the Swooshians.

Chef D'Carluca shook his head and said that he was a little off balance. He commented that he had just learned about the Aliens, he was going to make his first Fold trip, was being asked to prepare a celebration dinner, and have pictures to present.

He said he needed guidance and help.

He said that he had planned a Fold trip to La Spezia, on the Ligurian Sea, for the coming weekend. He wanted to understand how a Fold worked so that he would feel comfortable with the Fold to another world.

Bram said that he should enjoy his weekend in La Spezia. He was sure that Melisa had him staying in a great place. Bram said that he wanted to hear all about it on his return because he and Pat had talked about going there.

He suggested that he give his request for help to Linda.

Linda called in her ten-minute warning.

The Chef got up and nodded and commented that Linda was indeed in charge of the work that went on in his office. He gave a salute to Linda as he went by her desk.

Remi led the way in and went to the fridge and took out a bottle of water and handed one to Pat and Amy.

Bram looked at the three and commented that they seemed to look serious.

Remi led the discussion. He commented that the three of them had been discussing how they might get Mataia ready to support the population at Einstein City and had decided that they needed guidance on how to approach terra forming their new world.

Amy added that they needed guidance on where to start and how to manage the timing and how to start with the most basic elements.

Pat then commented that she had contacted a group of scientists that were studying how to terra form Mars, and she had raised some basic questions about the process. She had been surprised by the knowledge of that group and was wondering if there might be great benefit for the Fold effort to engage with that group and work with them in how to terra form a new earth.

Bram looked at them and asked why they were in his office.

Remi smiled and said that they only wanted his money.

Bram asked how much they were planning to spend.

Pat said that they would most likely spend about a hundred thousand with the group of experts and then they would begin to spend somewhere between five hundred thousand to a million on gathering the various transformation plants, animals, and other transformation elements.

Bram nodded and said that as always money was not his concern. He was sure they would manage it wisely. He suggested they add Erica to their team and have her be the manager of the money and the three of them manage the terraforming.

Amy nodded and commented that the discussion had been easier than she had been expecting. She wondered if he had any concern about them making mistakes.

Bram nodded and said he was sure they would make mistakes as they made their move to a new world. He figured that they would manage the mistakes they made. He wished them a smooth terraforming experience.

He reminded them that they had talked about farming on Mataia and wondered how that fit in the terraforming plan they had in mind.

Pat said that they would keep that in mind when they got the guidance from the team they were engaging with.

He then asked Amy and Pat if they were interested in visiting a boulder in the desert.

Amy smiled and said that she had been curious about Einstein and what his family might look like.

Bram said that he planned to Fold there and watch the Saturday morning sunrise from the boulder.

Pat and Amy both said they were in. Remi asked if he might go as well. He had not been to this boulder but had often heard about it.

Bram said they would meet at their six-person Fold craft at five in the morning. He would work with Marcus to make sure the coordinates would put them at the foot of the boulder.

At four in the morning Zoe was in the kitchen making coffee when Donna and Castor came in. She asked them how they had found out about the Saturday morning outing.

Castor said that a certain partner of hers had let them know. He said that he and Donna had worked on a ditty for them to chant on the jog in.

He then shared the ditty.

Going to the desert
Going for the sunrise
But not alone.
Going back with a few
Going to the desert
We'll watch the sunrise.
But not alone.
Not alone
Have hope to bring a certain someone home.

Bram was surprised when he came down to the kitchen, but he had learned to accept the protective cover that was with him at all times.

He took Pat's hand and said it was time to go.

Linda and Castor led the way. Bob and Thomas followed them. Zoe and Eric brought up the rear.

Bram enjoyed the ditty and smiled as it was echoed across the grounds by the Marine guards.

Remi was standing at the six-person Fold vehicle when they arrived.

The Fold put them at the base of the boulder.

The black of the desert seemed formidable but the few steps from the Fold vehicle to the boulder was a way that Bram could do with his eyes closed. He led the group to the boulder and then climbed up and helped each of them up. He sat down in his usual spot. Pat was to his left and Amy and Remi were to his right.

They all sat in the dark that seemed to be a black comforter with millions of twinkling stars overhead providing the only light that allowed them to faintly see the rustling sage and tall grasses that surrounded them. A slight cool breeze put an edge to the morning, and they were all relieved to see the thin white line of the morning sun break along the horizon to the east.

Its slow steady approach was that of a black leopard moving stealthily in to capture its prey.

Bram watched as the sunlight slowly traveled toward them and then up the side of the boulder. It passed the opening from which Einstein had in the past always emerged. He wondered if Einstein was still around. He was just about to give up when Einstein appeared out of the hole on the side of the boulder.

Bram opened the small container that held an oatmeal raison cookie.

Einstein came up to Bram and stood on his hind legs.

Bram put his open hand down and Einstein climbed in and then circled once and then curled up as he lay down.

After a moment Einstein climbed down and scurried down the boulder. Moments later he reappeared and was followed by four other mice.

Bram put his hand down and one at a time each mouse climbed into his hand and curled up and then climbed out.

Bram put down some cookie crumbs and they all ate some.

Then Einstein guided two of the mice up into Bram's palm.

Bram held his hand still and the two curled up and lay quietly.

Einstein turned and he and the other mouse climbed down to the hole in the side of the boulder and disappeared.

Bram carefully put the two mice into his jacket pocket. He understood that Einstein had given two of his own because he did not want one to be lonely as he had been.

It brought tears to his eyes. A simple mouse had shown more compassion than he had shown in the past.

Remi finally broke the silence by saying that if he had not just witnessed what he had with his own eyes he would never have believed it. Now he really believed that Einstein had been the one that had guided and Ok'd Bram's ideas.

Bram had his hand in his jacket pocket and could feel the two mice. He nodded and said he hoped that his two new helpers were as smart as their father had been. He was sure he needed the continuing coaching, and he now needed twice the help.

On his return he excused himself. He and Pat went to his office and took the two mice out of his pocket. He noted that one mouse had a black mark above its left eye. He asked Pat to help him name the two mice.

She lifted the tail of each mouse. She smiled and said that the one with the black spot should be named Isaac and the other should be named Ada after two famous scientists. They could both help him with the mathematical problems he would face dealing with both the negative and the positive universe.

He and Pat walked out to where everyone was waiting. Bram said he planned to jog back to the house, and he had a ditty for them to chant.

> *Went to the desert.*
> *Got Isaac and Ada*
> *Help in dealing with the law.*
> *Went to the desert.*
> *Learned compassion.*
> *Returned with a life's lesson.*
> *Went to the desert.*
> *Learned that life is more.*
> *More Than work*
> *More Than Play*
> *More to life in everyway*
> *Went to the desert.*
> *Got a reward.*

Bram knew that he was set for the next phase of his work.

The End

Chapter 1: Growing Old, Growing Bold

Bram was going through his morning wake up preparation. He was standing in front of the mirror shaving and thinking about the "Negative Fold Universe." This was an accidental discovery made while he worked on what he now thought of as "The Positive Fold Universe" equation. He had been working on a way to move a Fold transport bubble in both the forward and reverse direction.

To go forward he had incremented time in each part of his Fold equation. He had done this by incrementing all the time components of the Fold equation in unison.

He discovered and had come to the realization that to go in reverse, he had to decrement time. This required one forward control program and a separate reverse control program.

Just as in an automobile both forward and reverse have different gearing. That was also true for the Fold equation. It took two separate programs that could not both be operating at the same time.

The oddity of the reverse equation was that once the Fold was back to its original start coordinate or zero start point, the equation kept going and operated on negative time. This is why he called it the Negative Fold Universe. He, however, had no understanding what the negative Fold equation represented.

The Earth that he had grown up on experienced time flowing from the point of the big bang that had created the universe out to infinity. He thought of it as flowing linearly from left to right.

He had not been able to determine how time was measured in the "Negative Fold Universe." He had now lost three bubble scouts and had no idea on how to retrieve them.

He was lost at how to maintain control of the bubbles entering the negative Fold zone.

He had come to the conclusion that he would need to personally go into the negative Fold realm to learn what was going on. He knew it was a risky thing to do but he felt that he would be able to figure out what was going on and make the adjustments that were needed to the negative Fold equation.

He had to try, and he had to do it alone.

This morning, he was carefully shaving and thinking about how he would handle the negative Fold universe and how to keep it invisible to the general population for the foreseeable future.

He suddenly stopped and stroked his hair back and realized that he had a streak of grey hair along the right side. He muttered a silent curse. Growing old was one of the few things that had not crossed his mind. He wondered how, when he was doing multiple Folds, he could possible develop grey hair. The Fold process had been proven to transform a person from a most deformed state to a perfect body and it had let him get grey hair!

Pat entered and approached the second sink and saw Bram looking at his hair. She had meant to mention the grey to him but had been distracted by recent events and had forgotten. She reached up and let her fingers slide along the grey. She commented that it gave him the distinguished look of a wise man.

Bram smiled and thanked her and said that age unfortunately did not equate with wisdom.

He quietly finished shaving and let her know that he would be down getting a cup of coffee and then he was eager to get to work so he could tackle the conundrum of both wanting access to but wanting to keep everyone away from the negative Fold universe.

Pat spent a moment thinking up a ditty that the team could chant on the way into the work area compound. She smiled as she thought about the praise she had received about her ability to come up with good ditties, from Orlando, who was the master of coming up with ditties. He was the root of her current talent.

She thought for a few moments and thought she had a good one for this morning,

> *He's got a Silver streak, no he's not a freak*
> *He's growing old but growing bold*
> *I'm not too sure, It's what I am told*
> *Silver streak, no he's not a freak*
> *Growing old but growing bold*
> *Knows his way, through more than Fold*
> *Silver streak, no he's not a freak*
> *Growing old but growing bold*
> *Hi, Ho. Hi, Ho.*
> *No not growing old, just growing bold.*
> *Not too sure, it's what I'm told.*

She went to the kitchen for her coffee and enjoyed a slice of buttered toast with strawberry jam. She took a moment, jotted down the ditty, and handed it to Zoe letting her know that she should give it to Castor and Donna.

Zoe read the ditty and said she would be right back. She hustled down the stairs to the basement exit door and stepped out and handed Donna the ditty and said that they should use it this morning. She then returned to the kitchen just as Bram was rinsing out his cup.

Bram announced that it was time to go and led the way down the stairs to the basement exit.

When Castor and Donna said that they had a fresh ditty and took everyone through the first round, Bram smiled, he knew immediately who had written it. He looked at Pat and commented that she was getting as good as Orlando at writing ditties.

Zoe commented that Pat was better because she was closer and was able to ditty the most intimate occasions.

Pat laughed and said that she would limit her ditties to visually obvious things. The intimate parts were for her alone.

When Bram got to his office, Linda commented that for some reason he looked much more distinguished than she had previously noticed.

Bram smiled and shook his head and said she was looking much better than normal as well and wondered what make up she was wearing.

Linda smiled and said she declared a truce and asked if they should start with setting up his two-week work schedule.

Bram replied that he wanted fifteen minutes and then they could set up the next two weeks.

He went in and started the pot for hot water.

He was followed in by his two FBI bodyguards, Zoe, and Eric.

Zoe asked if he was going to have tea or coffee. She would get the coffee ready if that was his choice.

Bram thanked her and chose coffee.

Bram Nielson Collection

He then went to the bookshelf and opened the little door leading to the two mice he had returned with from the desert where they had visited the rock where he had sat for more than a year during the development of his Fold equation.

He had gone there to visit Einstein his pet mouse who had been his advisor during the development of the Fold equation and whom he had returned to the boulder a few months before.

On this visit Einstein had given him two of his offspring that he had brought back the day before.

Pat had helped him name the two. One was Isaac, named after a famous scientist and the other, Ada, was named after another famous scientist. They both came out and got into his hand. Bram carried them to his desk and put them down at the center of the picture of the milky way. This picture was the size of his desk and was under the class covering. It was the picture that had captured his imagination when he was a young boy, and it had drawn him into the field that he was now pursuing.

He quietly told the two mice that he was going to ask for their help to set up the way to handle the negative universe the way that their father had helped him set up the Fold equation.

He smiled and pointed to them and said that they had both agreed by shaking their heads in the affirmative.

Zoe brought over his coffee and petted each of the mice with her finger and then put down some cookie crumbs.

Bram smiled and asked if she were trying to take his job or replace his relationship with his new advisors.

Zoe shook her head and said that she did not want a silver streak in her hair and that she would stick with dodging bullets and taking on the bad guys and he could go grey thinking about the Fold world.

Bram responded that he thought maybe the grey streak was a result of worrying about her tweaking his nose while he was deep in thought.

He then looked down to Isaac and Ada and told them that they now saw the stress he was constantly in because of this one bodyguard.

Eric brought over two more small cookie crumbs. He asked if the cookie was all that they got to eat.

Bram took Isaac and Ada back to the little door and they scurried in. He then opened the two doors below the main bookshelf and showed Eric the automated food and water set up that supplied the two mice with what they needed.

Isaac and Ada could be seen on the open side of the feeder taking a few nibbles.

He commented that the two had a fairly extensive tube system that also went outside where they could catch the morning sun.

He commented that there was even a transport tube that went to the Viewing Room and that it had been installed when the room was Zuri's office back when she needed the room for her wheelchair.

Eric said that he was impressed. He had wondered about Einstein and how he had lived while he was still with Bram.

Bram commented that he felt a little remorseful about having kept Einstein alone for so long. He said that Einstein had sent him a clear message by having him take two of his kids back with him.

He then smiled and said he hoped that the two were as smart as their father.

Zoe shook her head and said it was a little disconcerting to think that he was getting affirmation for his ideas from mice.

Bram smiled and said that he found the little creatures very critical to his thinking.

Linda knocked, entered, and said that his fifteen-minute reprieve was up, and it was time to work on his two-week work calendar.

Bram nodded and said that there was no escaping his responsibilities while she was around.

After spending almost an hour getting the next two weeks organized, Bram asked Linda to arrange for Marcus and Remi to meet with him. He suggested the ten o'clock open period on his calendar. He also asked her to see if Pat and Amy would be available for an afternoon trip to Mataia.

He asked Zoe and Eric if they needed to be with him on the Fold to Mataia.

Zoe commented that now that he had proven that he could get to the future it meant they could reach back into the past. This meant he needed more protection, not less.

Bram asked what she meant.

Zoe commented that unknown to any of them, he might have some enemy in the future that might take some sort of action against him. They should be ready for such an eventuality.

Bram nodded and then he smiled and said he agreed but he really felt that those in the future should love him and regard him as a scientific hero.

Zoe nodded and said that was exactly how everyone in their current time period should feel but it seemed that some of those that did not love him were willing to try to kill him.

Bram commented that they would need to rethink their current protection procedure and make sure they thought about an attack from some group from the future. He commented that they should put this discussion on the calendar and get General Tilson and Lacy in on the conversation.

Zoe suggested they do it sooner and not later because she had a bad feeling about the future.

Linda announce the arrival of Marcus and Remi, who walked in and welcomed him back from his trip to Gabon. Remi asked if they had ended up with a friendly new member on the Oversight Committee.

Bram commented that he felt great about the trip and about having an Oversight Committee that would be supportive overall of the Fold effort.

He then let them know that what he wanted to do now was to make the negative Fold capability invisible to the world for the foreseeable future. He wanted them to visit Mataia and determine what they needed to do to establish a center where everything about negative Fold would be located. He wanted to set up a work center that was harder to get in or out of than Fort Knox. He made the point that the negative Fold capability was worth more than all the wealth of their world and when that became known they would all be in danger.

He pointed out that it also was the ying and yang of the world of the good and the bad. He shared what Zoe had said about not everyone loving him. He did not understand why that was the case but as she had pointed out he was not allowed to go anywhere without someone attacking him. She had challenged him and asked him if he thought everyone in the future would love him.

Remi looked at Zoe and commented that he had seen her in action and that Bram should listen to her carefully.

Bram said that he had listened and was going to review all the protection systems and protocols that they had set up and add the threat from the future as a new complication.

He said that he would have Linda set up a session with General Tilson and Lacy for the following day. He said that they should all plan to attend and bring their attack from the future scenarios to share.

Marcus commented that he was going to ask his kids about an attack from the future and how it would be carried out. He said that he would make it a game and see what they would come up with.

Bram said that sounded like a great idea. He then added, "from the mouths of babes."

He then took the two into the objective of the meeting and that focused on setting up the negative Fold work area on Mataia.

Marcus and Remi both agreed and threw in their ideas about the design of the work center.

When it came time for lunch, he called it quits, and they went to the cafeteria.

Amy and Pat were sitting together when they spotted Bram coming in for lunch. Pat commented that his protectors were all acting as if danger were close at hand. Amy looked around the sparsely populated cafeteria and said that she did not see any threats.

Pat knew that Zoe had commented that the threat level had risen, but she had not volunteered any information but had commented that she would soon have Bram working on better protection.

Bram walked over to Pat and said that he was looking forward to going to Mataia after lunch and was that something that could possibly be made to happen. He was about to go and get his lunch when Chef D'Carluca brought out a dish that he said he was perfecting that he called Swooshian Spaghetti di Mare and that he wanted to have Bram be the first to try it and give him feedback.

He looked around the table and asked if anyone else wanted to be a judge of his latest creation.

Everyone raised a hand.

He smiled. He commented that he had been counting on Bram making everyone hungry. He said that he would have the plates sent out.

Zoe commented that she was glad that she was on duty and that she would have hated to have missed out on one of the Chef's latest creations.

She commented that one of the benefits of guarding Bram was that he had exciting fishing trips that always seemed to feature fireworks, exciting vacations that had missiles and semi's trying to blow them up and a Chef that loved to try new dishes out on him.

Castor said that he had to fight off other Marines in order to keep his current assignment when they had found out he got to feast on Chef D'Carluca's special dishes.

Bram laughed and said that other than dealing with explosions and dodging lead, their work was a piece of cake.

Chef D'Carluca's Swooshian Spaghetti di Mare was a truly delicious spaghetti made with baby clams, mussels, squid, and shrimp in a thick dark blue sauce. He explained that the blue color came diluted from squid ink.

Everyone complimented him and said that once again he was pushing the limits of extremely great flavor.

After lunch Castor and Linda led the way to the hanger where the six-person Fold vehicle was waiting.

The Fold into the Mataia Arrival Terminal was uneventful.

Bram described that he was looking to house the negative Fold effort as well as to house the vehicle or vehicles that would be limited to use in the negative Fold realm. He shared that he was planning on having a special vehicle that would hold ten with ten beds and a supply of food that would hold them for a month. He made the point that he was not planning any long forays into the negative Fold realm, but he was going to be prepared for any unplanned problem.

Pat looked at Amy and said that the empty hangar capable of holding Wheel One had plenty of space. She pointed out that a multilevel work center could be added. She said that the first level would be the Launch-Return site. They could equip that level with Sterile holding areas that would be isolated. The floor above it could hold a large lab. The third floor could be a large work center.

Amy commented that if the structure was located at the far end and the top two levels had windows to the external three sides they could make it feel very much like the work floor in the main Mataia Fold work building.

Bram asked Amy to walk off the area she was thinking about. After she had done this Bram asked to walk around the exterior of the hangar. He wanted to get a feel for the view, but he was also interested on how protection could be integrated into the building.

Once he had made the walk he asked Pat and Amy to join in on the meeting of Zoe, the General and Lacy to discuss how to make what they built as secure as his current office.

Amy thanked him and commented that she would take what she learned into consideration and have his office in the main Mataian building modified to have the same level of protection. She commented that protection had been overlooked when they built Einstein City and that she and Pat would take a cut at making sure they reviewed all the structures that Bram would frequent.

Bram thanked her and commented that every home and building should have a saferoom and they would need to experiment to see if they could set up a system that would prevent anyone from Folding into the safe rooms. He commented that making a Fold proof save room was going to be a challenge.

The next day during the meeting that focused on reviewing the safety protocol, Marcus said that his kids had come up with a variety of ideas that he would never have thought about.

One of their suggestions was to set up a laser screen around the perimeter of the room and test to see if Folding in was possible. They suggested that the laser screen should be similar to the screen on the porch screen door.

The second suggestion was to have a laser weapon that would sweep the room on a multilevel that was strong enough to cut someone into pieces.

He said another suggestion was to have a system that shot spikes up from the floor that were only inches apart.

The General laughed and asked what Marcus was feeding his kids.

Marcus said that he was always surprised by what his kids could come up with and that they were eating healthy meals.

Bram said that he would investigate each of their suggestions but the laser to cut people into pieces and shooting up spikes from the floor seemed to be out on the edge of what he had in mind.

He asked he General if he had any other better suggestions.

The General said, "touche" and then went on and suggested that they set up an armed bubble protection system on Mataia. He said he had two Marine's that needed to be promoted and who he did not want to lose. He could promote them and assign them to operate the protection bubble system on Mataia. They would still be housed on Earth, but they would always activate the bubble system on Mataia ahead of Bram and make sure the area was clear before his arrival.

Bram complemented the General and said that he thought that his suggestion should be implemented as soon as possible. He said that he would immediately begin to work on the laser screen suggestion that Marcus's children had made. He was thinking the screen should be a laser screen that as it sliced an object up would send each piece to separate random distances in negative space.

The General looked at Pat and asked what she was feeding Bram.

She smiled and said that Bram had the talent to take a simple idea and make it into a horror movie scene.

She then added that it was not what she was feeding him, but he was just seeing the side of Bram that she feared the most.

Amy joined in and commented that had she known about the Bram dark side she would have left him in the desert.

Bram stood up and bowed and said that he was ending the meeting on that note and planned to walk home slowly and absorb the painful feedback he had just received.

The General laughed and said he now knew how to quickly end meetings with him.

Ron Mueller

Chapter 2: Future Surprise

Bram began a head on attack to figure out how to gain control of the negative Fold universe. He knew that he needed to take an aggressive approach, and he needed to do it quickly before the Fold technology became known in his time. He read through several diverse fields dealing with the universe and reviewed competing theories. This led him to believe that the interaction of black matter, gravity, light, distance, and the expansion speed of the universe were all involved in creating the phenomena of a universe where time flowed both in a linear fashion from the big bang to infinity as well as the same universe where distance seemed to dictate the size of a rhombicosidodecahedron (RCID) where time was not measurable but inferred by the node sequence of the RCID. He was convinced that the greater the initial Fold distance the farther back in time the traveler would find themselves.

He personally had experienced that effect.

The way back from such a "time distance" was to jump from one RCID node to the next node in a given sequence for thousands, or perhaps millions of nodes. This in the linear universe he lived in would take an unmeasurable amount of time. He figured that most likely there was a way to choose what the next point on the RCID would be but currently he had no clue how to accomplish this.

As he reviewed the various papers that had been published on the measurement of distance across the universe and of the changing knowledge of how fast the universe was expanding the more convinced he was that the negative Fold environment was the result of the interactions happening similar to the interaction in his current time on the subatomic particle level. At that level, in the positive Fold world, it appeared that time did not exist. The negative Fold universe was a macro example of the same phenomena. Time did not exist in the negative Fold realm.

This was a concept that Bram found perplexing, but he figured that he would slowly work his way through until he understood the negative Fold universe. He likened it to the slow pace at which he had learned the Swooshian language.

He was convinced that what he had experienced in his first venture into the negative Fold universe was that distance had a similar attribute to time in his universe and he wondered if the measure of distance was linear from the big bang and followed the expansion speed of the universe.

The only thing that had saved him was the light that Pat had sent out with the old-fashioned Morse code that gave him a visual shortcut back to the time that he had entered the negative Fold realm. This meant that light was linear in the negative Fold realm and acted independently to both distance and time.

As he continued his studies it became apparent to him that the expansion of the Universe, the effects of gravity on light, the effects of gravity on matter and the fact that time did not exist, all interacted to produce a realm where reality was not the simple solid touch something and you knew it was real that was true in the positive Fold universe where time began with the big bang and existed as a constantly moving event.

He used the Bayesian inference statistical method and used all the elements he thought were pertinent to create a model of how nonexistent time affected where a negative Fold vehicle would end up. Once he had the model, he created a computer control program for one of the negative Fold bubbles.

He then needed to test how his Fold bubble moved in the negative Fold universe.

He engaged Marcus and together they began a series of trials and after several Fold trips they were able to recognize that the resulting location was based on the initial time settings in the Fold vessels control computer.

The time in the control settings seemed to interact with gravity and the black matter through which the Fold vessel traveled. Using his model, he reconstructed the gravity of the Universe throughout cosmic history in a computer model based on all the parameters including the positive Fold sections.

Bram realized that they were developing an equation that they could learn to manipulate not by brilliantly thinking through the model but by using plain old-fashioned trial and error experimentation. Each trial resulted in another increment of learning that allowed him to try yet another tweak of the model. This meant that he would be able to use his statistical model to continue tweaking the Fold equation and exploring the limits of traveling in the negative Fold realm.

Marcus commented that they were slow learners on how to handle how far the send journey would be and it was the light beacon that Pat had set up that allowed them to always retrieve the negative Fold vessel successfully.

Bram agreed and said that Pat had provided the practical tool that was going to allow them to slowly map the Negative Fold realm.

Both of them had been doing their work from their workspace in the new lab on Mataia as they waited for their new work area in the Mataia hangar to be built. Bram's bodyguards were with them at all times. Bram had made it a point that each day they Fold back to Earth for lunch.

It was Zoe that noticed that Bram's grey streak had disappeared, and she commented that she had figured out why Bram had suggested Folding back for lunch.

Bram chuckled because he had not noticed the change until Zoe joked about it. He put it down to the positive side effect of Folding. His team all had a list of ailments that they no longer suffered. He knew that his first mouse Einstein was living much longer than any mouse he knew about.

He speculated that somewhere in the future a huckster would be selling Fold trips with the claim that it would heal any ailment. As he thought about it he knew that more experimentation on that side effects of Folding was needed.

Pat had taken the lead in the ultimate transformation that took Zuri from her wheelchair through a phenomenal body transformation. Zuri was currently nearing the end of her time attending Oxford. She had moved universities from the one that accepted her in her wheelchair and had gone to Oxford where no one knew she had been wheelchair bound for all her life. She was a Fold miracle.

Zoe observed Bram thinking and figured he had come up with yet another project. She had learned to read the moments when Bram hit on a new thought. She had never told him that he would close his eyes and when he opened them, smile, and nod to himself.

Bram realized that his protection team was waiting for him to disembark the Fold vehicle. He had been lost in envisioning how therapeutic Folds should be managed. He would ask Pat to take the lead and organize that area.

Pat sat at the table with Amy. They were both looking forward to the usual team lunch. They had just completed the entire structure that would be the Negative Fold work building on Mataia. The entire structure had been built on a slab next to the Fruit Barn Production area on Earth. It would be Folded into location by the end of the week. They needed to work with Marcus so they could Fold it into the precise location at the end of the hangar.

She and Amy had already removed the section of the hanger on Mataia that would be filled by the new section they had just finished. The final finishing touches would be done by the workers that were currently finishing the interior of the building. She was pleased with the openness of the building's negative Fold work area. She knew that Bram would spend a great deal of time there and she wanted it to be a comfortable place with an outstanding view.

She was aware that Bram had developed a very sophisticated laser barrier system based on the suggestion of Mylan and Marcus Jr.

The grid to prevent any unsolicited Folds into the building would be implemented immediately after the building was moved into place. The shield was an amazing laser grid that would wrap around the entire building. Anything passing through it would be sliced into tiny pieces that were then randomly Folded into negative space. She knew that Bram had worked independently on the program and planned to locate the transmitter in a location only he knew about. It was his way of making it almost impossible for the future to interfere with the past.

She had the feeling that the transmitter would not be on Mataia but some undisclosed location and would have its own power system and would not need any attention.

She was aware that Bram had a Fold vehicle built that he was outfitting on his own. He let her know that no one would be allowed to see what was in it or to know where it was located. He said that it would also hold all the current knowledge of the Negative and the Positive Fold realms. He said that should he die, the information would be released a few centuries later.

She knew that he was trying to protect the entire human species as well as their Water World intelligent beings.

As Bram walked into the cafeteria, he looked over at where Pat and Amy were sitting and knew by their smiles that they had good news. He had been following the work they had been doing to get the Fold work center on Mataia built and knew they were close to completion. He had purposely stayed away from the area where they were having it built. Instead, he had focused his efforts on setting up the anti-intruder laser grid.

He had recruited Erica to obtain a series of laser transmitters that could be set up to create a fly screen pattern around the entire work center. The power required to operated it was substantial and he worked with Remi to build a Fold vessel that would be able to generate the power needed and be able to keep the shield activated from a remote location.

He sat down and took a few bites of the slice of rare top loin roast that he was dipping in a sauce that Chef D'Carluca had insisted he try. The sliced fried green tomatoes were his effort at making sure he had a vegetable on his plate.

He looked at Amy and asked if she had crashed one of the Hilos.

She shook her head and asked why he would ask such a question.

He smiled and said that he observed that she was fidgeting and closely watching him eat.

Pat said that the two of them were excited to be able to announce that the negative Fold structure would be Folded into place on the following day and then they would have the structure activated three days later. He would then be able to activate his anti-intruder laser grid.

Bram complimented them at the speed at which they were setting up the structure and getting it into place. He said that he had focused on a much simpler effort and was lagging behind the timing they were achieving. He said that he would have to put the shield grid back on the front burner so that he could immediately activate it when they had the building in place

He added that he wanted to prevent the future from putting in any monitoring or spying devices. He wanted a clean work area.

Pat commented that she figured that he would be far ahead of any action the future might take.

Bram shook his head and replied that he was hoping that speed would at least keep him in the lead.

Zoe felt a shiver run down her back. She spoke softly to Eric and said that they should be prepared. Eric knew immediately that Zoe had experienced one of her intuitive moments and was now in an activated high adrenaline state. It was the same when they were getting on the car ferry on the trip through Norway.

She had the premonition then and her swift actions had saved them. The two of them had discussed these feelings she got and how they had always been accurate.

He had no idea what had caused her to feel that way, but he had come to know that she was correct one hundred percent of the time.

Eric excused himself and said he would return shortly. He left and went to a locker outside of Bram's office where they kept their Kevlar jackets and high-power weapons. He took all the weapons and protective equipment for all four of them out to the Fold craft. He laid the gear out for each of them and then returned to the cafeteria. He got there as Bram was getting ready to return to Mataia.

As he and Zoe got ready to take the lead back to the Fold vehicle, he let Thomas and Bob know that he had moved all their gear to the Fold craft, and they needed to be ready for action.

He then let Castor and Donna know they should be ready for action and did they need to stop anywhere to get their gear.

Castor shook his head, patted his backpack, and said they never went anywhere without their tools. He said that they were at full readiness.

Bram sensed that the atmosphere had changed. He likened it to the dip in atmospheric pressure just before a storm. He observed that his bodyguards were silent. When they got to the craft to get in each of his FBI bodyguards put on their Kevlar jackets and positioned their weapons at their seats.

Zoe handed him his vest and asked him to put it on. He did as she asked. He had his own weapon under his seat. He took it out, placed it and the extra ammo clip within reach as he sat down in the Fold vessel. He asked Zoe what was up.

He was not surprised that she simply replied, "premonition." This was the same as her reply to Matt when he had asked how she knew the truck in the tunnel was a trap and a bomb.

Remi and Marcus were both with him and it was clear to him that they had not picked up on the change in atmosphere. They were talking about the huge difficulty of figuring out the coordinates to place a building on a planet going through space and how Marcus had worked with Pat and Amy to place it exactly plus or minus one half inch within the rectangle represented by those coordinates.

Bram asked them to remain to the back of the team when they got to Mataia.

Their arrival to the Mataian Arrival-Departure Terminal was normal. Amy insisted on checking the terminal before allowing the rest of the team to disembark.

Their walk from the terminal up to Remi's lab was a little slower and Bram was surrounded by his bodyguards but otherwise it was uneventful.

Bram wondered if Zoe's intuition was off.

When they got to the lab door, Zoe put her open hand up and her finger of her other hand to her pursed lips. She then started a loud conversation with herself as she approached the door. She opened it fast and dove in toward the left and Eric followed and dove to the right. Castor and Linda dove straight in and slid on their stomachs with their back packs in front of them.

At first the silence made Bram think that Zoe had overreacted but then the continuous roar coming through the door seemed to be that of several large gatling guns firing simultaneously, and the area sounded like a full war zone. Thomas and Bob had pushed him to the wall and were trying to shielding him.

He pushed past them with his gun drawn and entered, turned to the right, and immediately shot two armed persons who were attacking his bodyguards from the side. The bodyguards had their attention toward their front and had not seen the attackers.

Bram continued along the wall firing at the attacking fighters. Then he took down two more when he was able to shoot behind the shields they were holding. He ran toward the other side of the room as he changed to a new bullet clip. He then fired from the side and shot the remaining fighters.

Once the shields fell, the barrage from Zoe, Eric, Castor, and Donna took down the wounded fighters.

He was glad that he had supported Zoe's anticipation of trouble and had put on his Kevlar vest because he had felt the hits as he crossed the room during the fight. He had been hit several times and was sure he would later feel the pain but at the moment his adrenaline was serving its purpose.

He watched as Zoe walked up to two wounded attackers and shot them. The grim look on her face warned him not to say a word. She checked to make sure the other attackers were dead. She commented that only dead assassins would be sent back to the future.

He noted that Eric had gathered the attackers' weapons and was putting then into one of the steel chests. He wondered why and was about to ask when a loud explosion caused the chest to lose its shape and look more like a stainless-steel sausage.

He asked Eric how he had known that the weapons would blow up.

Eric replied that he hadn't known but that he and Zoe had discussed what to expect if the future came back to attack them. They had agreed that the weapons would most likely self-destruct, so that the past could not gain knowledge about the future weapons technology.

They had also discussed the fact that in a conflict the future would expect to win and would come in a group they felt would be sufficient to quickly overcome their adversaries.

Bram suggested they search for a Fold vessel.

Zoe commented that it was not in their time but would potentially Fold in to pick up the attackers. She asked that they all stay close to the wall while she walked around and checked out the lab. She got down and glanced along the floor and on top of the larger worktables.

She pointed to the four chairs at each of the four tables and said that the attackers had sat on the stools with their weapons at the ready and shields besides them. She went to the largest open lab area and said that the Fold craft from the future had sat down, and the attackers had all gotten out, then the craft had Folded away. She squatted down and pointed to one of the tiles that had some scuff marks on it and commented when they had the time, they would be able to match the scuff mark material to some of the boots on the attackers.

Bram asked Castor if he had any grenades with him. The lab was silent for a moment.

Then both Linda and Castor commented that they always carried several grenades with them.

Bram asked if they knew how to booby trap the bodies so that the future would receive a reply to their attack that they were probably not expecting.

He said that they as a team should not say another word about the attack so that the future would not know about the surprise they were about to get.

Zoe smiled and commented that how to behave was getting more complicated by the moment. She asked for everyone to help her get the bodies ready to take a trip to the future.

Bram watched as Castor placed his four grenades on four bodies and Donna did the same. It was clear to him that Castor had done it before in actual battle conditions and that Donna was watching Castor, so she placed and handled her grenades that same way.

Castor said that he would wire all of them together once they got them into their Fold vehicle. He would then attach the wire to the door. He explained the grenades would explode the moment the door was opened. He was not sure about the strength of the Fold vessel, but the open doorway would provide a way that he could launch a cloud of shrapnel. He looked around and asked if they had shrapnel that they could use.

Bram asked Remi what he had in the lab that they could gather to fill a container with, to put in the doorway.

Remi and Marcus went around opening drawers and cabinets and filling a trash can with a variety of metal lab tools and threw in glassware that broke. They carried back a large plastic trashcan full of the mix of glass and a variety of lab tools that included a set of knives and some tools that looked as if they belonged in a horror movie.

Zoe got everyone to stand against the wall while they waited for the Fold vessel from the future to appear.

Bram smiled when it Folded in. The vessel was still the same basic u-tube design that they were currently using. It made him wonder how close in the future his attackers were. He figured it might be close to his hundred-year Fold time capsule.

He watched as the team loaded the bodies and Castor and Linda worked together to wire all the grenades together.

He took a quick walk through the craft. He looked into the various packs and found several computer-looking devices. He did not recognize the brands but knew that the future was close enough that the technology was still recognizable. He handed the computers to Marcus and said they were souvenirs that he could study.

Marcus had been silent for the whole time, he said that he would love to fire them up and see what they would learn. He suggested that they should first figure out how to copy the memory. He said that they would most likely spend some time using the supercomputer to get past any passwords or whatever the lock to the computer would be.

Bram nodded and said they would all participate in breaking into the computers from the future.

Bram pointed to the forward single seat and said that it seemed to be the control or pilots seat. He noted what he took as the Fold button and suggested they put a weight over it that they could cause to fall and initiate the Fold back to the future.

Castor took a heavy piece of metal and put a set of folded paper matches to hold it up over the button. He said that they would have about thirty seconds after he lit the matches before the heavy piece of metal fell on the button.

Everyone got out and stood against the wall.

Castor lit the matches, closed the Fold craft's door got against the wall and when his count got to the word "thirty" the craft disappeared.

He said he would love to be able to see if their return gift caused the damage, he was hoping it would.

Bram commented that it might just be possible, but he still had some complicated analysis and experimenting that he would need to do. He let the team know that if it ever became possible to travel to the future, he would see about arranging such a Fold for all of them. He commented that until he was able to block the future, they should all standby for the attacks from the future versus the attacks during fishing.

Bram had overlooked that the attacks on the lake could just as well come from the future as well as from the current time.

Ron Mueller

<u>Chapter 3: Future Focus</u>

Bram had multiple areas in the negative Fold environment that he was eager to explore. The future had been at the bottom of his list. He felt he should leave the temptation of looking at what was to happen to mankind should be left untouched. However, the attack had catapulted it to the number one position, and he put every moment into understanding how to maneuver in this negative time realm.

He studied the elements in his positive Fold portion of his equation and thought about how he controlled the forward motion along the timeline. In doing so he realized that he had not adjusted the equation to account for the fact that time acted differently in the negative Fold realm. In fact, in that realm, he realized that he should replace most of the time variables in his equations with distance variables. He knew that he had to create a distance variable that he could calibrate based on how it acted in the negative Fold realm.

Bram made his first cycle of adjustments in the negative Fold equation and then used negative distance numbers. He decided on a way to test the adjusted equation.

He sent out a bubble with a specific value. Had it register where it was by snapping a picture of the galaxy and the solar system. He then had the bubble home in on the light beacon and return with the pictures. He then matched the pictures to the time that the galaxy matched the picture of the galaxy in the picture.

It took him more than a thousand negative Folds of the bubble before he, using the supercomputer was able to refine the negative Fold equations to enable his use of distance. This gave him the ability to move through the negative Fold realm in a controlled manner similar to the ability he had in the positive world he lived in.

He then asked Remi to work with him in testing the ability for them to reach into the future. He wanted to reach forward and determine who had initiated the attack on him and how had that individual known about Mataia.

Remi was eager to take part. He asked how they were going to prove that they could do that.

Bram said that he was going to deliver flowers to the future.

Remi asked again how they would prove that they had delivered flowers to the future.

Bram told him to take his picture when he left and then take it again when he returned.

He would take one at the point of delivery and then they could compare the result.

Bram said that he would deliver flowers to Linda fifteen minutes into the future. He would have her take a picture of he, the flowers standing before her and behind him he would have the Fold vessel with the mechanical clock facing the picture. Her phone would record the time that the picture was taken and anything the two of them said would also be recorded.

He would return and Remi would take his picture again. They would then slowly walk to her desk and ask Linda how she liked her flowers and how long it had been since he had given them to her.

She should be able to show them the pictures she had taken of him that gave the time of delivery and Remi would have a picture of the time he had left to deliver the flowers and the time of his return. The pictures would verify the ability to interact directly with the future.

Bram shook his head as he commented about the inherent danger of anyone being able to do so. It was a power that if used improperly would threaten the very fabric of mankind's existence.

He then said, "let's do it."

Bram stepped into the two-person negative Fold vehicle with the flowers.

On his return Remi took his picture. They then walked slowly up to Linda's desk.

Linda's eyes widened when she was asked when the flowers had been delivered. She instinctively knew that she was being used to prove one of Bram's theories. She commented that she felt like a guinea pig. She replied that he should know but she had a picture of his delivery.

Bram asked her to print the picture. It printed with a date and time on the bottom of the paper.

Bram showed the picture to Remi. The Fold craft was in the picture and the large clock in view in the craft and the time on the picture from the phone were fifteen minutes different with Linda's phone time fifteen minutes ahead of the one in the craft.

Bram then had Remi show the pictures he had taken that were fifteen minutes and thirteen minutes earlier than Linda's time.

Linda smiled and complemented Bram on having discovered yet another great capability of the Fold equation he had developed, and she would enjoy flower deliveries whenever he wanted to deliver them from the past. She said that she needed to sit down as she absorbed how old he seemed to be now that she had interact with his much younger self a few moments before.

Bram nodded and said that he felt that now the Stetson family would have to be defending him from two fronts. The current groups that kept attacking him when they went fishing and those in the future who would most likely be attacking in some other fashion.

He did not say anything about the attack that the future had already carried out. He figured that he had to remedy that situation quickly and quietly.

Bram invited Linda to lunch and the three of them walked toward the cafeteria.

Pat and Amy were both waiting for him and once again smiling.

He stopped and got a bottle of sparkling water and a pint of Black Raspberry and Chocolate chip ice cream. He took off the lid and after his first spoon full, he asked Amy what she was smiling about.

Amy said that after lunch she and Pat were going to put the new building into position on Mataia.

Bram complemented them on their fast work. He commented that he would be able to put in the screen shield as soon as they had it in place. He remined them that the building needed to have a one-foot void below it to accommodate the laser screen.

Pat said that the building had been poured with feet that were one foot high. When they put it down at the coordinates they had given to Marcus, the building would be his to protect.

Bram commented that he wanted all the buildings on Mataia to have the protective envelop that the new work center would have.

Pat nodded and commented that he had just given she and Amy an assignment that would be a challenge, but they would figure it out. She asked if the protection was necessary.

Bram nodded and said that they really had no choice. The future had already made the first move and most likely would continue until he could figure out how to neutralize that situation.

Pat used her spoon to take a taste of his ice cream and asked what he was celebrating.

Bram replied that they would all soon know but at the moment he could not share that information.

Linda said that she thought he was celebrating being nice to her and giving her flowers.

Bram nodded and said that Linda was right. The flower delivery had made him happy.

Remi said he was just happy to be able to enjoy a great lunch with a great group of people. This was his way to deflect any question that might come his way. He was trying to shield himself from being asked about what was up. He was terrible at making up deflecting stories.

Bram commented that as soon as the building was Folded into place, he would enclose it in the laser screen grid that Marcus's kids had suggested.

He looked at Marcus and said that on Sunday they should have breakfast so they could show the kids how their idea had been implemented and how it would protect all the buildings on Mataia.

Marcus said that would be great. He shared that he had not let the kids know that their suggestion had been turned into reality. He said that he was sure that the two of them would be celebrating for weeks to come because they had asked him if their ideas had been accepted.

Bram said that so far their screen laser idea was the only idea that he had figured out how to use. He had added a few twists so that the future would find it very hard to figure out about the screen and how it functioned.

He didn't say anything, but he figured that the future had found out about Mataia some one hundred years in the future. That was the time frame he had used to have his information bubble appear. He now planned to go back in time and change that to one thousand years. He wondered how he would recognize how his actions might have changed history.

He would have to determine some marker that he could reliably use to determine what had changed.

Remi led the way back to the hangar where two-Fold vehicles were sitting. One was loaded with a huge battery system and a computer system that controlled multiple laser transmitters and random transmit controllers that were situated around Mataia. The transmitters had multiple backups and would be able to sustain a laser intrusion protection envelope around every building on Mataia.

Remi pointed out that protective bubble systems and multiple backups and that the backups would be randomly located at coordinates that would also change randomly. He shared that the supercomputer predicted that the probability of someone finding and eliminating a protective bubble would be expressed by one divided by a number larger than one trillion.

Bram made the last adjustments to the control vehicle and then launched the control vehicle out to the coordinates he had determined was optimum for its purpose.

He asked Remi to prepare the second vehicle and position it at a random coordinate and now that he had brought up the fact that the laser bubbles had triple backup, they should add a third control vehicle.

He then had Remi Fold all the control bubbles into position. The bubbles would also control the random particle transmit signals of the very small particles that would result from any attempted entry.

They worked on it for the rest of the day and toward the very end of the day, Pat and Amy let them know that the building was in place and his to control.

Bram immediately activated the laser screen system and all the backup systems as well.

He thought about all the events that had transpired on one very long day.

He realized that he was beyond being exhausted, he was ready to collapse.

His trip home, laying down in his bed was a unanswered mystery when he got up. He went into the bathroom and automatically began brushing his teeth. Then he looked in the mirror and was just realizing that he had been hit multiple times during the gun battle when Pat walked in.

She looked over at him and just stared at the bruise marks on Bram's chest, his arm and left side. She counted at least ten bruises maybe more because some seemed to be double hits. She was shocked and asked what he had not told her about his morning on Mataia the day before.

Bram leaned in close and whispered that he feared the future was listening. They had sent back an assassination squad that the FBI team members with the help of the Marine team members had taken out.

Pat whispered back that evidently, he had taken an active part in the fight as well.

Bram nodded and replied that they had been outnumbered and needed his help. He had not realized how many times he had been hit until this morning.

He let her know that her quick work would allow him in the future to be enclosed in a protected work environment.

Pat asked if he was planning on an easy day.

Bram nodded and said that he wanted to spend the morning in his office and the afternoon at the rec center.

Pat gave him a gentle hug and said that she would shadow him. She said that she wanted to make sure the future did not reach out for him until he developed the defensive weapons with teeth that he needed.

Bram thanked her and let her know that his defensive weapons would all have extremely sharp teeth and a bite that would be lethal.

He spent the rest of the morning thinking through how he could protect the people around him from the future and how to still let the world benefit from the Fold capability.

He wished the oversight committee had supporters that would guide the deployment of the positive Fold capability. He was not confident that would happen in the current political environment of the world. He would see how that might happen.

What gave him more concern was how he would handle the ability that the negative Fold would give that same group of people to act against the past or conversely would allow those living in his time the ability to reach into the future to change what was to happen.

He decided he would ask his team to guide him in determining how to handle both matters.

He figured that he should take the rest of the day to recover and to relax at the rec center. After breakfast he and his entourage went down to the rec center.

He was stiff as a board and lost at ping-pong and at pool.

It was clear to Zoe that he was not his usual competitive self and did not have his smooth moves. She had seen Bram during the gun battle and figured that he had been hit. She walked up to him and asked how many times he had been hit.

Bram quietly replied that somewhere between six and twelve times.

Zoe's eyes went wide and said that he had not said one word about it and had worked for the rest of the day.

Bram said that he did not want the future to know that they had almost succeeded in their effort to kill him. If they realized that, they might immediately try a second time. He said he needed time to effectively neutralize the future.

Zoe said she was on the side of taking direct action against the future by attacking them and eliminate that threat.

Bram said that on Monday they would go to the future and deliver a message that would make it clear that acting against the past had an expensive bite to it.

Zoe smiled and said that his protection team members would all be ready to deliver the message.

Bram smiled and told her to ask Linda and Castor to bring plenty of C4 with them.

Pat watched Bram's quiet interchange with Zoe and noted her smile as she walked away. She knew that Bram had told her about his bruises and that he probably had told Zoe that he had a payback idea in mind. That was the only explanation to the smile on Zoe's face.

Pat saw her walk over to Eric and then the two then walk over to where Castor, Diane, Mike, and Bob were sitting and quietly enjoying their drinks. She watched the group talking and then they all did a fist victory pump in the air.

She figured the future was in for a surprise that the past would deliver in a spectacular display of force. She knew that Bram would reply with enough force that the future would not be able to ignore the message.

Bram walked over and said that he was ready to go back to the house and relax in his office, but he needed to have someone to sit with on the two-person couch and keep him warm.

Pat smiled and raised her fist and did a victory pump and said that she was ready for a good book.

She watched as the protection group responded in kind. She knew that she and the group were celebrating two very different scenarios, but both had to do with Bram as the center.

On the way to the house Bram asked Eric to have the team scan the house for listening devices or anything that might be out of the ordinary.

Castor said that he and Diane would check the outside area around the house as well.

Bram thanked him and said that for the next few days until they had set up the laser intrusion net around their work areas at their Earth Fold compound, they would need to be extra cautious.

He added that a rapid response to the future needed to occur so it would know that they were not safe just because they were in the future. Those in the future had to realize that they were vulnerable too.

Zoe had Bram wait outside until a sweep of the house could be made. After about twenty minutes she returned with several listening devices and two devices that appeared to be cameras. She asked Bram how he knew the house would be bugged.

Bram smiled and said that he had no idea but figured that such action could easily be taken by someone who was monitoring what the past was doing. He said they had spent enough time at the rec center for the planting of the devices to occur.

He held a descriptive finger in the air and loudly said that the future should take a hike.

Castor used a more descriptive action with an arm motion, a slap on his muscle and a Bafungo!

He handed Zoe several similar listening devices and cameras. He said he had called in a group of Marines to do a more thorough search around the outside of the house.

Bram said it was late and suggested they go in and enjoy the evening and then get ready for a great Sunday morning breakfast.

Ron Mueller

Chapter 4: Pomp and Circumstance

Sunday morning breakfast at the Bram home was known as the breakfast of surprises and the breakfast of friends. It was a breakfast that everyone liked to be invited to. Everyone knew that it was a time when Bram seemed to share many of his ideas or to highlight the people doing something doing some interesting work.

He worked hard at making each Sunday morning breakfast a highlight that those getting an invite celebrated. None of those being invited could be given the official or the national recognition that they deserved because the Fold program remained a super top-secret project. But he wanted those around him to feel valued, to be recognized and to see that their efforts were making a positive difference.

At work, on a daily basis, he made his rounds, and he made it a point to praise everyone for the work they were doing.

Sunday breakfast was a day when he could put a few of them on center stage and shine the spotlight on them.

This morning, he was going to highlight the fact that two of their young members had suggested the means that he had used to create the system that would provide intrusion protection from the future and also protect them from those in their own present time.

He would share the enhancements that he had added because of the suggestion Marcus's two children had made and then see if they had any other suggestions they might want to add.

He had spent Saturday afternoon using a scout bubble that he Folded to Mataia. He methodically took pictures of the new work center that Pat and Amy had Folded into place on the previous day. He was impressed at how the new building section seemed to have been constructed at the same time as the hanger. Once he had taken pictures from inside and outside of the hangar and had panned the landscape that would be viewed out of the third-floor work center windows, he was ready to demonstrate the protective screen that surrounded the building.

He had added the protective screen mere moments after the new section had been put into position. It was invisible to the eye, but it was fully operational.

He positioned his picture taking bubble scout high in the hangar and then Folded a second empty bubble to the coordinates in the center of the negative Fold lab area. His picture taking scout bubble captured the flash when the empty bubble hit the laser protective screen. The laser web was visible during the few seconds that the bubble was being destroyed by the laser screen and the small sections were sent to random coordinates in negative space.

He originally had the idea to visually simulate the laser screen but instead had decided to slow down the actual impact of the incoming bubble by a factor of ten thousand. The impact appeared as a slowly growing spot until it was the diameter of the sphere and then it slowly shrank back as the bubble passed its widest point then shrank to nothing at which time the laser field again became invisible.

He was intrigued by the tiny sparkles that appeared when the bubble shredded material that the shield Folded into negative space. It seemed that different Fold distances created different colors. The resulting sparkles made the sequence look similar to a fourth of July fireworks starburst that was occurring in slow motion.

He smiled as he looked at the result and knew that he had a unique video, and that the sparkling highlighted new information that needed to be studied. He knew who he would ask to study if the Fold color was associated with a negative Fold distance. He wondered if the light color spectrum could be used to map the negative Fold distances and be correlated to time.

Perhaps each node of the RCID decahedron had a color or color spectrum similar to a barcode. If so the RCID decahedron could then be mapped and perhaps it would allow a bubble to go directly to the desired node and bypass the rest of the nodes by sending it to a specific color bar code. This would then allow rapid negative Fold coordinates to be programed and the time that a cycle took could be managed using computer control.

This would result in the positive and negative Fold environments being controlled in the way that humans were used to using time as a control variable.

He made a final improvement to the video by adding music to the background and added a few comments to some of the video sections.

He let Pat know that he was excited about showing what he had accomplished.

Pat knew that Bram always enjoyed Sunday morning interactions with those he now considered their friends. The associations of the Fold community were numerous, and everyone was close. She had watched Bram develop almost every member in the community. He was relentless in encouraging individuals to be engaged with those around them in a positive way.

He did not push people to interact. He pushed people to learn from each other. He pushed them to recognize, accept and value differences. He pushed them all to respect each other and treat others as they wished to be treated.

She had talked with Amy about the fact that Bram enjoyed recognizing and rewarding those around them and that he was planning to award both Marcus Jr. and Mylan scholarships to any university they chose. He had shared the fact that the two had come up with the best defense against intrusions that might come from any time frame.

Amy smiled and said that she had close and deep experience with Bram's ability to inspire. He had inspired her to try to apply for a seat in the class of Astronaut training where the two of them had met, and he had also made sure that she got a seat. She commented that when Bram focused his mind on an objective he always achieved it.

She gave a small laugh and said that she had brought Pat back as her reward for him. She complemented Pat on having beat out a mouse named Einstein to be Bram's soul mate.

Pat laughed and joked that he should have left Amy flying hilo's in the desert.

The two took their coffee and joined Bram at the table and asked how he planned to engage his two special guests.

He replied that he was going to use the building that the two of them had just finished putting in place on Mataia and demonstrate an actual attempted intrusion.

Pat showed and voiced surprised because he had not given her any warning about an actual demonstration. She and Amy had turned over the building on Mataia to him late on Friday and now he was ready to demo his protective system. She asked when he had the found the time to prepare such a demonstration.

Bram confessed to having discussed it with Remi while at the rec center. He had asked Remi to provide him with two bubbles. When he came back to his office he had spent a couple of hours in the afternoon to try out the defense system.

Pat commented to Amy that living with Bram was to live in a double fast forward supercharged mode and there was no getting off the train because it made no stops.

Amy laughed and said that she should have warned Pat about the Bram train, but she wanted her to meet him first, after they had made it through their astronaut training. They had both recognized that the Bram train was the best opportunity they would ever get. She then said that she had witnessed Pat willingly get on the special cabin on the train and she should not complain about no getting off opportunities.

Zoe commented that fast forward seemed to keep all of his protection team on their toes and made each a day an exciting experience.

Castor commented that fast forward provided plenty of active weapon field experience.

Donna smiled, nodded, and added, "And some."

The doorbell rang and Zoe and Eric went to the door and checked who was ringing it.

Zoe opened the door to let Marcus, Marcus Jr and Mylan in. She saw that Remi was with them as were Linda, Lacy, and Ray. They all entered and Zoe led them to the kitchen to get their breakfast and drinks.

A few moments later Erica and Gerry, General Tilman and his attaché Matt were at the door. Once they were let in they went to the kitchen, got their breakfast, and sat down.

Amy commented to Pat that Erica was the top example of how Bram turned a lemon not into lemonade but into a sweet strawberry smoothie. She commented that Bram did not bring enemies close to his chest but instead made them friends who realized that life could have sunshine and happiness associated with it.

Pat replied that Bram considered Erica one of their best friends. And she made the point that the two of them knew how effective she had been at filling all their requests. She had become the lever and fulcrum that had made raising Einstein City from the ground up possible. She added that Bram's presentation after breakfast was only possible because Erica had been able to round up the required materials for the new Negative Fold Center at lighting speed.

Erica smiled raised her cup of tea and said that she had excellent hearing and agreed with everything that Pat had said.

Amy nodded raised her cup and silently mouthed a "thank you."

Bram had been quietly watching everyone. He had also overheard most of Pat's and Amy's verbal exchange and liked the way the two of them had complimented Erica.

He announced that this was a special breakfast and that he had designated it "The Young Geniuses" breakfast.

He pointed at Mylan, and Marcus Jr and said that they were what made this breakfast special.

He was a little surprised when the room went silent. He then said they should all enjoy what he was going to share and suggested everyone refill their drinks and asked that the donuts and sweet rolls that Ted had delivered be put out on the table.

Thomas brought them out on three platters. He and Bob strategically placed them so everyone could reach them.

When the room was again settled, and everyone had what they wanted Bram turned on the large viewing screen. The low background music of pomp and circumstance provided the introduction. He had added all the names of those present and had highlighted the contributions each had made.

He had made the golden yellow contribution writing scroll slowly up the screen and back over stars and galaxies in the dark background. It was a ploy used by many movies to highlight the central theme of a movie.

He momentarily stopped that video and congratulated everyone for their great work and asked for a round of applause. It seemed that the Marines did not know how to clap but every one of them shouted out "Hurrah" multiple times during the applause.

Bram smiled and pumped his fist in the air and closed with a "Hurrah."

He then thanked Marcus Jr. and Mylan for providing the answer of how to protect everyone from those who lived in any time and who wanted to break into their facilities and homes. He let them know that their laser idea was the only protection suggestion that had so far been implemented.

He then reactivated the video that took everyone on a tour of the new Negative Fold Facility.

He complimented Amy, Pat, Marcus, and Erica for having set a record pace in getting the facility built, the offices and work areas be beautifully appointed, and the building placed in the ware house in a manner that it seemed to have been part of the original construction.

Then he took them on a brief external tour that highlighted the view of the mountains, and the sea.

The tour entered the building and highlighted the dining room and break areas and the storage, refrigeration and the kitchen that had been designed by Chef D'Carluca.

It then went up to the second floor to the Fold Lab, the computer center, a machine shop, and the work area.

Remi commented that Pat and Amy had delivered his dream lab.

When the tour entered the third-floor office and work area everyone commented that they wanted to work there. The camera slowly panned the room and showed the finished interior, the furniture, and the artwork. Everyone made a comment about the view and the striking layout and about the appointment of the work area that had been done.

Pat pointed at Erica and said that the appointment was totally her doing. She added that the view was Mataia, and it was Amy that had insisted on having surrounding glass walls as the design of that floor.

Bram pointed to Erica and thanked her for the great furniture and pictures that she had selected and delivered in record time.

He then pointed to Amy and Pat and complimented them on their ability to build and place the beautiful three-story building with an awesome view in less than a month. He commented that the two of them could make a fortune in building homes back on Earth.

He looked at them with a sad look and commented that they had a whole Fold community of buildings that required an upgrade.

He stopped the video and let Amy, Pat and Erica know that he had requested Jeffrey to award a bonus to each of them for their exceptional contributions.

Amy thanked him and commented that she was once again glad that she had picked him up in the desert.

Erica said that she had made a personally right decision in accepting the role of managing the Dalles based Fold organization, and she planned to live her wonderful life with her trophy husband and travel the world spending her bonus money.

Pat thanked him and said she just wanted to be able to sit on their couch and read books while leaning against him and she planned to give her bonus to whatever charity Linda recommended.

Amy said, "Wow, I can't look like a cheap skate so now I will have to do the same with my award."

Erica shook her head and said that she was not sure what the award amount would be, but she planned to keep enough for at least a couple of vacations, but she would join both Pat and Amy in channeling the award to the organization that Linda recommended.

Linda smile and thanked them for being generous and said that she would work with the three of them and together they could determine which organization they wanted to enrich.

Bram had waited quietly during the exchange. He then he said that everyone was doing great work and all deserved recognition and that he would take the opportunity to see that no one felt left out.

He then said that one suggestion made by the two youngest folks at the table, Mylan, and Marcus Jr. was the only one that had resulted in the creation of a Fold defense system for all the Fold community homes and work buildings.

He then again showed the negative Fold facility. He said that it was currently shielded by a laser grid with holes that were the same size as the holes found on most normal screen doors.

Bram asked the two if what he was describing was what they had suggested.

Mylan nodded and said that it was exactly what she and Marcus Jr. had talked about.

Bram then said that he had added a couple of special features. He pointed out that the lasers were powerful enough to slice up almost all objects that might try to penetrate it. He said that he had used an actual empty bubble that Remi had provided and set its destination Fold coordinates to the center of the lab.

On the video, a small bubble came slowly into view. Bram explained that he had slowed down the picture by a factor of ten thousand, so they were watching everything in extremely slow motion.

The bubble encountered the laser screen and the small laser squares appeared as a circle of sparkling lights that slowly shot fire of different colors into the air.

The sparkling circle first grew in size and then slowly began to shrink. Finally, the sparkling stopped, and the building looked like any other building. There was no indication of anything unusual about the building.

He then shared that the enhancement that he had added sent each tiny fragments of the object interacting with the laser screen randomly out into the negative Fold universe. Each piece created a sparkle of a different color.

He looked at Marcus and said the sparklers were the result of his children's idea and that it was going to be his job to figure out what the sparkling lights meant.

The picture went black and then after a quiet moment and a drum roll, "Pomp and Circumstance" came more loudly through the speakers. As it played he announced that for suggesting the laser screen protective shield idea he had set up the Mylan and Marcus Jr. scholarship fund that would pay the expenses to any college they chose, and they would each immediately get a five-thousand-dollar gift from the Fold program.

Mylan smiled, said thank you, and then she said that she would put half of the five thousand in her savings account, but she said she wanted to spend the other half on all the weekend vacations that she could get her dad to take.

Marcus Jr. said he would do the same.

Marcus smiled and said that he was very proud of his two kids, and he would plan on taking every weekend Fold vacation that he could schedule. He thanked Bram for the scholarships and said that he saw sparkling lights in his future.

Bram then shared that he was naming the protective screen the "MyMar Shredding Screen (MMSS)" after them and that a screen would soon encompass all of their living and work areas as well as all the vacation homes and apartments on both worlds.

He then challenged Mylan and Marcus Jr. to play a ping-pong game against the current doubles champions and he wanted to play each of them in a game of snooker.

Pat knew that Bram was the best ping-pong player as well as the best snooker player. She was sure he had asked Zoe and Eric, who were the doubles champions, to play Mylan and Marcus Jr. because his bruises were affecting him, and snooker was a game that he knew how to loose when he chose to.

Linda volunteered to call her parents and ask them to cater an afternoon grill out at the recreation center.

Bram agreed and said that the grill out would begin at the time that the first brats were on the grill.

He said breakfast was over, but everyone should stay as long as they wanted and enjoy donuts and drinks until it was time to go to the grill out.

He excused himself and said that he was going to his office to relax before having to face the competition he expected to face on the snooker table.

He was feeling the effect of all the bullet hits he had taken and just wanted to sit down on his recliner and let his body chill.

Later, when Linda called and let Pat know that her father had just thrown the brats on the grill she and the rest went down to the recreation center.

Word about the grill out had circulated and the number of people that began to show up seemed to be skyrocketing. It appeared that everyone was going to show up.

Bram let Ted know that everyone was welcome to take part and enjoy the food. Ted nodded and put some additional brats and dogs on the grill. He called out to Rita to bring some more ribs.

Bram watched as Mylan and Marcus Jr. played a game of ping-pong with Zoe and Eric. She and Eric let Mylan and Marcus Jr run up the score then Zoe demonstrated her skill with a series of trick shots that closed the margin but when she was within a couple of points she began to miss. Mylan and Marcus Jr. got to eleven exactly two points ahead and won the game.

Linda brought two plates with a barbequed rib and a prepared hot dog loaded in what she called a Chicago dog and asked the two what they wanted to drink with their late lunch.

Bram was sitting at the table with the two and asked if either of them had ever played snooker.

Marcus Jr. said that neither of them had ever played.

Bram then suggested that he would teach them how to play instead of making it a contest.

Mylan said that would be great since she had wondered what the larger table was all about.

He then shared a bit of Snooker history and made the point that it was a more sophisticated and skill-based game than pool. He pointed at the Snooker table and then pointed at the Pool table and asked if they could see how much larger the Snooker table was. He said that Snooker was much more difficult than pool because there were many more shots, many more strategies and many more positions as compared to the game of pool.

He explained that the game was invented in Jabalpur India by a British army officer, Sir Neville Chamberlin. At that time, the word "snooker" was a well-established derogatory term used to describe inexperienced or first-year military personnel and somehow it was the name given to the game.

Bram then put on a demonstration of the different shots that could be made and he had Mylan and Marcus Jr. try a few. In a few moments it became clear that Mylan had enough of snooker, but Marcus Jr. seemed to like the game.

Bram Nielson Collection

Bram commented that Jabalpur, India was just about 100 miles from Agra where the Taj Mahal was located. He let the two know that Melisa had established a vacation apartment in Agra that was available for a Fold weekend vacation.

He suggested that Mylan visit the Taj and see the Red Fort and they could then all drive down to Jabalpur and visit the museum that had one of the original snooker tables on display.

Pat commented that she was not sure that Marcus's two would want to do that weekend vacation, but Bram's story had convinced her that she wanted to spend a weekend at Agra.

Mylan asked if maybe the five of them could go together on the next available weekend.

Bram asked Marcus whether that would be acceptable and that reminded him that there would also be bodyguards coming along.

Marcus agreed that it would make it a great Fold weekend.

Ron Mueller

Chapter 5: Forward Payment Plan

The impromptu grill out was the medicine that Bram had needed. The next morning, his bruised chest, the bruises on his left arm and left side were still tender but the yellowish, blue, and purple made the bruises on his body look worse than they had at first. He wondered how long it would take before they disappeared.

Pat wondered how Bram was feeling but she figured his work would keep him from focusing in on what she knew had to be painful bruises. She lightly touched his bruises and then told him that he looked like a person that had been beat up by the mafia for not paying off his gambling debt.

Bram smiled and said that she had the right metaphor and that he did owe somebody payment and he was going to pay it back.

The jog in to work actually helped him by loosening up the ab and arm muscles. He asked his bodyguards to accompany him to the viewing room.

They were greeted by Marcus and Remi.

He asked everyone to sit down so they could spend the early morning planning how to repay the future for trying to kill them.

Zoe smiled and said that they were only trying to kill him, and his bodyguards were just seen as collateral damage.

Bram asked that the Viewing room get checked for any listening and visual recording devices.

A few moments later Zoe declared it clear.

Bram explained that he wanted to demonstrate to the leaders of the group from the future that had attacked them that they too were vulnerable. He planned to totally demolish their office or work center. He hoped to be able to take the building down but to do it at night with the building empty. He had no desire to hurt any incidental people that had chosen to work all night.

Bram then said that he was going to write on the white board and once they had a plan agreed to he would wipe it clean. He said that from now on information would need to be doubly protected.

He then listed what he thought they would need to do and asked the team to identify any misses.

He said that they would need to send out a series of scout bubbles to identify the time in the future that would be the point of their forward payment.

Marcus suggested that they use all thirty of their scout bubbles and position them five years apart. That way they could check one hundred fifty years in a few seconds. Then the gathered data could be processed in their supercomputer and by lunch time they should have the exact year in the future that they desired.

Remi pointed out that Earth was a loud planet that broadcast information out into space. The bubbles could be kept behind the moon and get all the information that the team needed. They would be there only a few seconds and would most likely never be sensed.

Bram had been writing down the logical order of what they needed. He said that once they found the year they were after, they would need to locate the headquarters of the group that attacked them.

Zoe asked how Bram planned to determine what the start time in the future where they should start the search.

Bram said that the computers carried by their attackers that he had in his possession had manufacture dates on them. He suggested that Marcus start at that date with the first scout bubble and then move forward in his suggested five-year increments.

Zoe said they should be able to identify the exact year and location by scanning the news for a report of an explosion that happened when they sent back the booby-trapped Fold vehicle with the dead bodies of the attackers. She figured that it would be reported as a gas leak or a lab explosion. The location would allow them to then get drawings from the county computer records and they then would know the design of the building.

Remi said that once again this could be done by using a scout bubble as the relay station for the transaction between their supercomputer and the one at the county records office that held the building plans.

Castor said that while they were getting all the information together, he would contact a friend who had been in his unit that had gone into the business of demolishing buildings. He would get a quick lesson on what they should consider.

Bram suggested that once they had the building drawing, Castor share the drawing with his friend and ask him to recommend the optimum way to bring it straight down. He asked Castor to offer his friend payment for the information.

He looked at Marcus and said that once they had picked the year, he wanted to arrive at the building at midnight on a moonless night. He asked Marcus to determine the coordinates that would put their Fold transport inside the basement of the building.

Remi suggested that they verify the coordinates in the basement with a scout bubble and if it was on target and the area clear they would Fold in.

Bram suggested that after the verification they take a two-person Fold vehicle in first and make sure the larger one would fit. He did not want to Fold in with a load of C4 and accidentally be part of a huge explosion in the basement.

After rigging the building, they would Fold out to the coordinates of the home of the leader of the group that had attacked them and leave him a calling card.

Eric asked what the calling card would be.

Bram said that they would leave an unarmed chunk of C4 and a piece of chocolate in the kitchen with the message, "the past can be sweet" or it can be aggressive and much meaner" and that the past had the means to retaliate. The C4 would be placed in front of a family picture. The message would make the point that the building had been a warning but any future attempt to hurt someone in the past would result in a response that would sow mayhem into his personal world, and anyone associated with him.

Diane asked if he worried about starting a time war.

Bram replied that it had already started. His next step was to go back in time and change the time of Folding all the information about the Fold program from a one-hundred-year reappearance time frame which was where they were going, to a one-thousand-year time frame. He would Fold to that future to verify that it was a better time frame and if it was not he would go out farther in time.

Eric suggested that they needed to set up the study of the future and determine how they could influence the development of a society based on good versus the current one of conflict for power. He pointed to the fact that there might be bad people one thousand years or even ten thousand years in the future that might take the same action. He suggested that the Fold information be put on a long journey and that Bram figure out how to pass along the information of where the Fold information was located.

Bram said that Eric had a very good idea, and they would need to work fast before the Fold process became exposed in their time and became an issue that made the conflict worse. He had no idea how to move human nature from the desire for power and dominance to one of peace and love.

He said that he would need to rethink how to ensure that the Fold discovery moved into a peaceful future.

He said he would need to think about the best way to protect humanity from itself.

Marcus picked coordinates that started their search and sent the thirty scouts out on five-year increments. He commented that without their supercomputer and the program he had just written it would be impossible to identify the coordinates of a location from behind the moon. He hoped that his bubbles were remaining invisible and that in the five seconds each spent in their future time frame they went undetected or if detected became observations that had no explanation.

Zoe, Eric, Thomas, and Bob were doing rapid analysis of the returned data.

Diane and Castor had contacted the friend and were becoming proficient in the process of bringing a building down. Castor offered to pay his friend for consulting with them and setting up a building for demolition.

His friend suggested they share the building drawing, and he would do a quick analysis and suggest the layout for the explosives.

Then not much later in the morning the returned data gave them the point in time and the location of the build that they felt was the one they were looking for.

Zoe commented that the building was in the downtown area of Seattle not too far away from the space needle.

Bram was surprised that the location was in Seattle on Roosevelt Rd. He commented that the enemy seemed to be close enough to Dallas that the whole affair might be connected.

Bram got the supercomputer to break into the future internet and find the computer with the county building records. The building they planned to bring down was a ten-story building. This was larger than Bram had anticipated. He hoped that it was not too large.

He looked at the clock and realized that the team had spent the morning but were now ready to get the building drawings into the hands of Castor's building demolition friend.

Castor and Diane connected with their building demolition friend and shared the building drawings. He looked over the building and commented that the building was what he called light construction and would easily be brought down. The support beams would need to have explosive charges put on each column and on each floor. Then the explosions would start at the bottom and in close synchronization, each floor above would be set off about three seconds apart. The building should fall down onto its footings and the only thing that might not come straight down would be the dust. It would follow the prevailing winds.

Bram and the team had been listening and when the call ended, he commented that they were on track to a late afternoon Fold to the future with their Forward Payment.

He suggested they all go to lunch and that afterward they prepare their C4 charges, while the basement of the target building got checked out. He commented that Marcus and Remi had come up with a scheme to check the basement out using the scout bubbles put into a formation taking up the same space as their team Fold transport.

During lunch, Pat, Amy, and Lacy were sitting together when the team entered. Pat commented that things must have been progressing well because the folks walking towards them were smiling and talking to each other with open enthusiasm.

Pat asked Bram if the future had been visited.

Bram shook his head and said that after lunch the team needed to prepare the gifts they were going to deliver to the future.

Amy asked if they could be of help.

Bram thought for a minute. He quickly calculated the fact that the team would need to prepare close to one hundred blocks of C4 to be placed on each column in the building.

He counted heads and realized that each person that was currently involved would have to safely prepare ten blocks of C4. He thought that would be a challenge.

He replied that they actually needed to recruit a couple more folks and suggested that Linda and Mallica join them as well.

He said that they would work in pairs and Castor and Dianne would supervise them.

Remi commented that they would be working in his Lab, and they could engage all the lab folks and Lori.

Bram nodded and said that would make it make it feasible to get the preparation work done quickly. Each pair would only need to prepare two or three blocks of C4.

Castor shook his head negatively and said he did not want to be in the same room with a bunch of amateurs handling C4. He suggested that they check with the General and ask him to have a group of experienced Marines prepare the C4. He figured it would be routine for the Marines and it would certainly keep Bram and everyone else safe.

Meanwhile, he said that he would take the team through a practice of the placing and wiring of the C4. He commented they would each need to practice several times and that they needed to do it fast enough so that they would not get caught in the building. He said that placing the C4 was going to be dangerous, and they needed to take their practice very seriously.

Bram smiled and said that he wanted to hug Castor but then the two of them would need to listen to a ditty accusing them of some unsavory behavior. He suggested they contact Matt to get the help in preparing the C4.

Castor opened his eyes wide and asked if Bram meant Marine Chief Master Sergeant Matt.

Bram smiled and said of course that was what he meant.

Bram looked over to Pat and Amy and said that he thanked them for their offer of help, but he felt much better having Castor engage seasoned Marines to work with the C4.

Amy nodded and said that she felt much better as well.

Bram asked Castor for the best place for them to practice applying the C4 explosives.

Castor suggested they use the beams in the hangar and practice taping on blocks of wood about the size of the explosives.

Zoe said that she liked the adjustment that had been made. She added that she was eager to deliver the forward payment but wanted to survive and savor their success.

After lunch, Bram had just passed his exercise of tapping the C4 to a beam when Marcus and Remi came in smiling and shaking their heads as they came back into the hangar.

Marcus said that they had sent a scout bubble into the basement that had returned with a broom handle sticking into the bubble. He and Remi had parked that bubble next to Bramlet One where it looked like a little brother. The big brother had a boulder sticking out of the side and the little brother had a broom handle sticking through as if it had been trying to get to the computer.

Marcus went on to say that the scout had served its purpose and located a space that looked like it was meant to hold a truck or store pallets. He and Remi had then sent in the scout bubbles in the shape of their large transport bubble and verified that there was plenty of room to spare. They had agreed to send in a scout bubble a few seconds before the team Folded in with the larger team transport bubble to make sure the space remained empty.

Bram thanked them and said that losing one scout bubble was worth making sure that they did not end up with any object sticking into their bodies.

Castor thanked them and then told them it was their turn to qualify to hang and wire the explosives.

It seemed to Bram that somewhere, someone was coordinating their actions because as they finished practicing, the Marines that had prepared the C4 carried in ten boxes. They opened one box and displayed the C4 with connecting wires neatly rolled up and attached to each block.

One of the Marines explained that the wires were long enough to connect to the next explosive block, and he picked up one wire roll and said that it was attached to the explosive closest to the stairwell that led down to the next lower level and long enough to get connected to the wire from that floor and the wire below was long enough to reach the next floor down.

This would go on until the last attached wire was taken down into the basement and connected to the battery power that would be activated to blow the building.

Two marines carried in another box and when they lifted the lid it had six lead acid batteries that were connected together to form the power supply, and two terminals where the wires running down into the basement would be attached.

They pointed to an enclosed relay that had a motor attached to it. They said that the motor was set up to turn when it received a command that would be sent to the control box from the Fold transport. The signal to activate the explosives required two buttons to be held down at the same time.

Bram nodded and thanked them for making the teams mission possible.

Castor led the way, and all the boxes were loaded into the transport bubble.

Bram asked Marcus when they had to Fold to be at their destination in the dark of night.

Marcus smiled and replied that it could happen any time Bram desired because they controlled when they would arrived in the future no matter what time they left from the present.

Bram nodded and said he was having a hard time getting use to manipulating time. He said he had grown up with it always flowing into the future and now he had become the object that could flow.

Remi said that it was hard for all of them to keep from being totally lost.

Bram asked that they do one more thing before the Pay Forward Fold. He wanted to identify the leader of the group who had attacked them and learn where he lived and some personal details about his family.

Marcus said that he had the name and address and could send some scout bubbles to get detailed information.

Bram suggested that they do it immediately so they could complete their mission before the end of the workday.

Marcus smiled again and said that he could make their Fold back a few minutes after they Folded forward, and when they returned they could go home early.

Bram smiled and said that they should wait until they learned how long they would be in the future. He pointed out that no matter what the clock would say their bodies would log in the real time.

Castor came over and said that everything was ready. He had taken the opportunity to put weapons on the Fold transport for everyone.

Bram thanked him and asked that he see if everyone could get a Kevlar jacket to wear.

He then asked Marcus to get his spy bubbles launched and find out about the leader's family. He commented that he wanted their message to have a very personal touch to it.

Marcus looked up the information about the leader of the organization that was housed in the building and learned that he lived in Laurelhurst which was a very high scale Seattle community.

Their person of interest had been married for twenty-seven years and had a daughter that had just graduated from the University of Washington. He also had a son that was a lineman on the college football team and another son that was still in high school.

Bram asked Marcus to get a picture of each of the kids at some highlight moment. He wanted one of the family at the daughter's graduation, one as their son was playing in a football game, one of the youngest son walking into his high school and a final picture of the family in their backyard.

Marcus nodded and said he would have the request filled in about forty-five minutes.

Bram asked Castor to organize the team and talk them through the timing and sequence of placing of the explosives several times. He said he wanted the practice to be in the hangar.

Castor assigned Zoe and Eric to the tenth floor. Bob and Thomas to the next floor down. Marcus and Remi to the eighth floor. He and Linda to the seventh floor.

He then said that after Zoe and Eric finished on the tenth floor, they would do the sixth Floor, Bob, and Thomas the fifth floor, Marcus, and Remi the fourth floor and he and Linda would do the third floor.

Then he and Linda would go to the top and check all the connections and come down and check each floor. While they were doing that, Zoe and Eric would do the second floor, Bob, and Thomas the first floor and Marcus and Remi would do the basement.

Bram asked if Castor had forgotten anyone.

Castor smiled and said that Bram would stay in the basement and set up the explosion control center and test it and make sure it was responding to the control computer. Then when Marcus and Remi were through with the basement and all the wires were together, Bram would hook them to the terminal. Bram had to make sure that the kill switch remained open, and the isolating piece of plastic remained between the contacts.

Bram's job then was to keep everyone away from the box.

Bram nodded and repeated what he was supposed to do.

Zoe commented that she was sure everyone else would be as far away from the box as possible and they would be eager to get in the bubble and get out.

Marcus walked over to the printer and when he came back to the table that they were all standing around, he spread out the pictures that Bram had asked for.

Bram looked at the family name and said that it was the name of one of the leaders that had attacked the compound a few months ago in their current time and who had been killed when Lacy unleashed her attack bubbles.

He called Lacy and asked her to verify the name.

Lacy commented that she was surprised and wondered if this future relative had staged the attack because of the family connection. She commented that it would make it the longest family feud in history.

Bram smiled and said that it was not a family feud, and it was certainly nothing like the Hatfields and McCoys feud. This was perhaps a family obsession and a weird desire to get even.

He wondered how this person would have learned about the Fold connection with the past.

He said that he would potentially use the family feud reference in his message to the future.

Castor asked if it was time.

Bram nodded and replied that they go for it.

Ron Mueller

Chapter 6: Forward Payment

*C*astor smiled and commented that Orlando claimed that Bram was more of a Marine than anyone thought. He then suggested that the team be called the BTR or the "Bram Time Raiders" who were "Swift, Timely and Deadly" and they should make sure that the enemy in the future knew that they should "Make Peace or Die."

He then loudly said Oorah, let's go do it.

Bram smiled as he realized that Castor had just uttered a series of Marine jargon. He let out a loud "Hurrah!" and led the way to the team's Fold craft

Zoe, Eric, Bob, and Thomas all let out a loud, "Hurrah" and followed.

After first verifying that their target coordinate was still clear by Folding an observation bubble there, they made the forward Fold.

The Fold delivered them to the empty spot in the basement of the building. They all let out their breath.

Marcus then quietly said, "no broom sticks on my side,"

Zoe asked everyone to remain in the bubble while her team swept the building to ensure that there were no people in it. She asked Bob and Thomas to go to the top and work their way down. She said that she would start at the entry of the building and that she was expecting that there would be at least two-night watchmen. She said that they would bring anyone they found into the basement.

Castor and Linda began unloading the C4 boxes and taking them to the elevators. He said as soon as Bob and Thomas cleared the tenth floor he and Linda would start delivering the C4 boxes to each of the floors. He said they would open the boxes and distribute the C4 to each position where they would be attached.

Donna suggested that all the C4 get attached in their position first and then the wires get connected.

They both then said, "Let's do it" and began to move the boxes to the elevator entrance.

There were two elevators.

Bob and Thomas got on one and pressed ten and went off to the top floor.

Zoe and Eric took the second elevator and got off on the first floor. She pressed the basement button so it would go back to where she knew Donna and Castor were ready to load the C4 boxes.

Zoe stealthily located the two-night watchmen that turned out to be where she expected. They were just around the corner from the elevators and were surprised when Zoe came casually around the corner. She had a smile on her face and politely said good evening and said she was in to inspect the quality of the monitoring system. She continued to walk behind the desk. Once she was in place she pulled out her weapon and asked the two not to touch anything and to step out and away from the desk area.

Eric quickly pulled their hands in front and crossed their wrists over each other, and zip tied them.

They then guided them to the stairs leading down to the basement.

They took them over to where Bram was getting the control box prepared.

Eric asked the nightwatchmen if anyone was in the building. The two claimed that the building was empty.

Zoe asked Bram whether she should shoot them now or later.

Bram replied that they should be hand cuffed to one of the support poles and he would talk with them as he did his part of preparing their forward payment. He suggested they get to the top floor and do their part.

He then turned to the two handcuffed watchmen and pointed to his own weapon and said that they should relax and at the appropriate time they would be released and would be able leave unharmed. He added, "try to escape and I shoot both of you."

He then focused on setting up the control box so he could test it and get it ready for the wires that would be brought to him.

He asked how long the two had worked as the nightwatchmen for the building and learned that one had been in his role for ten years. He said that he normally was there during the day but one of the normal night watchmen had called in sick and he had volunteered for the night shift.

Bram casually asked what they thought of the top brass and was surprised at the disenchanted responses and the negative opinions that the guards expressed.

The older guard commented that he had stayed on because the pay and benefits were very good, but the brass deserved a kick in the butt. He described them as arrogant towards and disrespectful of the working guy. He was not sure exactly what the company did, but it seemed like they milked the stock market but produced nothing.

Bram listened and felt better about his Pay Forward package.

He asked if the two would be able to find another job.

They both commented that the job market currently was not good. They said it would be tough to get another job in the current job market.

Bram asked if the dollar was still the currency being used.

The guards both said yes and that it was the strongest currency in the world.

Bram stopped and took out his wallet and put a hundred-dollar bill in each of their pockets. Before doing so he asked if they recognized the money. One of the guards commented that the bills were crisp but looked really old.

Bram nodded and then suggested they go to the bank and check if the bill was more valuable as a collector's item. They might be able to offer it to a numismatist because the bills were at least one-hundred years old. He suggested that they say they found the two bills on the shore at Gas Works Park to keep people from flocking around the remains of the building and in an attempt to find more money.

Both of the Guards nodded and said that that story was a good one and the park needed more people to visit it.

Bram finished setting up everything and then prepared the Fold craft for departure.

He reassured the guards that he liked them, and they would soon be released. Once out they should get well away from the building because a few minutes after they were set loose, the building would come crashing down.

If asked they should let their big boss know that the building had been demolished as a warning to him that he should not try to kill folks that had done them no harm and that any attempt to get even would prove to be fatal.

The older of the two guards asked Bram who he was. Bram replied that he was who the owners had tried and failed to kill and that they were receiving a warning not to mess with him. He said if they did not heed the warning they would be surprised by the next step since he took no prisoners and left all who opposed him dead.

As he finished his discussion, Marcus and Remi came down the steps into the basement pulling two wires.

They then went around the basement positioning the last of the C4.

A moment later, Zoe and Eric brought down a second set. They were followed by Bob and Thomas.

Bram Nielson Collection

When Marcus and Remi brought their wires over, Bram checked to make sure the safety plastic was in place and the switch to the batteries was open.

He then carefully hooked all the wires up as he had been instructed to do.

Bram suggested that they take the two-night guards out and escort them well away from the building.

He asked the nightwatchmen if they had any problem just walking away and not looking back until they heard the explosion.

They both shook their heads and said they would do as they had been asked to do.

Zoe looked at Bram and said, "Boss you're getting soft in your old age. A few years ago, either you or I would have shot them between the eyes. Are you sure you want to let them go? They've seen our faces and can identify us."

Bram liked the drama that Zoe was adding.

He replied that he liked the two and they did not have to die just because they worked for people that were arrogant pricks.

As he finished talking Castor and Diane came to the basement and said that the building was ready.

Castor added just the right words. He asked whether he should shoot the two guards, so they did not have to have to be buried alive.

Zoe shook her head and commented that the boss had gone soft and was releasing the two.

She let the two loose and led them to the exit and took them across the street. She instructed them to walk away and not look back. She waited until they were a block away and then she and Eric double timed it back to the basement.

A soon as they were in the craft, Bram Folded out and once they were several thousand feet away, he sent the signal to blow the building.

At first, he thought they had failed, he put his hand on the plastic shield that had been on the contacts to make sure he had not forgotten to remove it.

Then the building seemed to be slowly deflating and starting in the basement each layer came to rest on the one below. It seemed that the building was deflating in slow motion. It was an amazing sight. What was even more impressive was the lack of any dust and debris.

The explosions were softly muffled sounds the created ten muffled explosions that seemed to signal the next level to slowly lower itself down.

When the last layer settled the pile of rubble was an almost perfect thirty-foot-high square.

Bram took the next step and Folded to the time at which they had originally arrived and to the coordinates of the leader's home.

The night was pitch black.

The coordinates put them in the open area in the family room.

The house was dark.

Marcus had been able to get the control settings for the light and motion sensors. They were able to quietly exit the transport bubble.

Bram put out the pictures that they had obtained of the family. He arranged the pictures in collage fashion on the kitchen table. He figured that once he imploded the building a call would soon bring the leader down into the kitchen where he would find the collage.

Bram wrote "don't mess with the past' on the refrigerator door with a large black marker.

Each of the pictures had a date on it and a note warning that it was personal, and any additional attacks would be answered in a fashion that would be very personal and devastating to the family.

Marcus said that he had placed the observation modules that were invisible to the eye but powerful enough to reach the very small relay bubble they would leave in the upper atmosphere. A more powerful and larger relay bubble was positioned on the surface of the moon and would constantly shift in time so that it would be almost impossible to find.

Bram checked the reception on his computer and said that it was time to Fold back to their time. They would be able to see the future from the Viewing room at their Fold work complex.

They Folded back at the end of their normal workday time.

Physically they were exhausted because they had been working nonstop for at least twenty hours.

Bram declared the next day was a work holiday for all of them and said they should all plan on sleeping in, but he would host brunch at ten.

He made sure that the feed from the future was available on his computer and then joined Pat for a ride home.

Pat gave him hug and asked how long he had been gone.

Bram shared that the team had been gone for more than a day but had decided to return on the same day that they had left so that no one in the present time would worry about them.

Pat shook her head and said that this new ability to do what she thought of as time travel was another complexity that the Fold capability had brought to their lives.

Bram nodded and said that the future for all of them was going to require a higher degree of disciplined thinking and a strong adherence to the principle of not trying to change the past to achieve the desired outcome in the future.

He added that inevitably there would be those that would try to alter the past and he had to come up with a way to prevent that from happening. He said that he planned to keep the ability of being able to go forward in time a secret. He shared that he had thought of changing the time frame of when to share all of the Fold capability out to one thousand years in the future but had been advised against it by Eric who asked, "what made him think that the aggressive culture on Earth that had for more than ten thousand years had been a continuous series of battles and wars, would change in the next one thousand years?"

Pat said that she agreed with Eric and pointed out the fact that sharing the capability at any time did not make a significant difference. If the bad guys in the future got that information they could travel in either direction and they would wreak havoc.

Bram thought about that for a minute and asked if Pat had any idea how to maintain the integrity of time.

Pat replied that Coke was an example of successfully keeping a secret to protect their brand. Bram had a brand called Fold. He had to keep the secret and pass it on to his successor.

She added that Bram needed to establish a Fold team that would be tasked with ensuring that the use of the Fold capability was used only for good. She suggested it be called the Fold Protection Team.

Bram replied that he had considered something along those lines, but the amount of Fold information seemed daunting. He then said that he would not release of the information into the future. He shared the fact that now that he had experienced traveling to the future to counter a threat because he had released the information, he agreed with her that they should revert to keeping it all close to a select team and keep it a secret. He commented that the teams name should carry some sort of powerful message.

Pat said that keeping it secret would probably be better. She also recommended that he choose the latest technology to store all the information on and put that information in a secret location and just pass on the secret location to members on the team.

He said that he would put the secret into a Fold bubble and the secret would be the coordinates of where the bubble was located and how the Fold bubble would go from coordinate to coordinate over time.

Bram asked her to remind him to set up that system the next day.

Once home and after a long hot shower, Bram fell asleep as soon as his head hit the pillow.

He woke up at nine the next day and when he got to the kitchen, Pat gave him a hug and kiss and a cup of coffee.

Bram sat at the table and slowly sipped on the coffee. He saw that Pat was getting the pancake batter ready and had bacon and sausage sizzling in the frying pan.

Zoe entered the kitchen and went straight for the coffee and joined Bram at the table. A few moments later Eric, Bob, and Thomas entered and sat down at the table with their coffee.

Pat asked what each of them wanted.

They all replied that they were after her famous pancakes with maple syrup.

She was placing the pancakes on the table when Castor and Donna arrived and joined them at the table.

Marcus entered and quietly sat down and said that he had left the kids down at the rec center where they were playing a game of snooker and being watched by Melisa.

Remi entered and sat down.

Pat poured Marcus and Remi a cup of coffee and put a plate of pancakes with some sausages in front of them.

The two of them thanked her and prepared their pancakes with butter slices before pouring the maple syrup over them

Bram turned on the large screen and connected the feed from the future.

The kitchen in the future with the messages came into view. A few moments later, their nemesis entered as he talked on the phone. He stopped short when he saw the photos on the table. Each time he picked up a photo he would look around the room. He turned and saw the writing on the refrigerator and again looked around as if expecting to see someone.

He finally picked up the message and shook his head in the negative.

He tapped his phone, and a large screen in the family room came up that showed the collapsed building that the team had imploded. A newscaster was commenting that the two-night watchmen had reported that they had been escorted out of the building and then when they were a block away the building had come down as if it had decided to take a rest.

The newscaster asked about the people that had escorted them out. The older of the night watchmen commented that he thought they were associated with the mafia because the leaders underlings had asked about killing the two of them, but the leader had said not to do that. The younger night watchman commented that he was surprised that the leader was seen as the lead killer by the underlings because he had treated them well and with respect.

They both added that the team was very professional, efficient, and seemed to operate more like a group of Marines on a combat mission than mafia killers.

Castor let out a "Hurrah" that Donna repeated. He laughed and said that he was proud of the team giving the night watchmen the impression they were dealing with a Marine team. He was equally proud that Marines one hundred years in the future still had an impeccable reputation of being organized and proficient.

Zoe groaned and commented that she did not feel like a Marine at the moment but more like a tired old lady.

Bram quietly uttered "Yut" and complimented them for having brought the building down in a manner that looked like it was gently laying down to rest. He pointed out that very little dust had been generated.

Marcus commented that their Marine building demolition expert deserved much of the credit for their successful mission.

Bram agreed and asked Castor if his friend was married and had kids.

Castor replied that his friend was married to his high school sweetheart and had a boy that was eight and a girl that was seven.

Bram said that he would ask Linda to set up a scholarship fund for the two kids and that he was personally putting in an initial twenty-five thousand dollars into the fund. He looked around the table and suggested that they all owed Castor's friend big time.

Zoe said that she would put in ten thousand. Eric, Bob, and Thomas said they would match her.

Pat said that she would match Bram.

Castor shook his head and commented that his friend was going to be overwhelmed with their generosity and that he and Donna must be getting paid a lot less than they all were, but he was going to put in five thousand.

Dianne looked around the table and said that she would short her wedding dowry and match Castor.

Bram thanked them and said that he was going to recommend that all his bodyguards get some sort of reward from their employers but that he would personally pay the expenses for two, Fold weekend vacations for each of them.

Suddenly he stopped as a shiver went down his back.

He looked at Zoe and said he had a premonition and that he felt cold all over.

He dialed up Linda and quietly told her that he wanted her to smile, and then nod in the affirmative and hang up the phone, pick up her purse and walk out of the building and come over to the house. She was to act as natural as possible.

He hung up and asked Castor and Donna to double time and meet Linda but when they met her act as if it was a planned meeting and walk back with her to the house. If they were attacked, they should shoot first.

He looked at Zoe and asked her to sweep the house for bugs.

He asked Remi to get a Fold craft ready to Fold into the living room of their adversary in the future.

He asked Marcus to prepare to Fold someone into their new work center on Mataia.

He put up his hand when Marcus was about to say something and said, "I know." He then asked if Marcus if he could do it.

Marcus nodded and said he could do it.

Bram then said that the code word to make the Fold happen was written on the sticky note he had just given him. The sticky note was only to be read once the Fold to the future had occurred. He said that the coordinate for the person to be Folded would be three feet in front of where he stood.

Then he simply said "go" and everyone went into action.

Zoe returned and said that the house was clean.

A few moments later Remi returned to the dining room and said that the turkey was ready and should make a great lunch.

Then, Castor, Donna, and Linda came into the room.

Bram thanked everyone for their quick action and played back the scene in the future of their adversary in the kitchen. He asked them all to closely observe the person.

This time he kept observing the actions that occurred after the adversary had looked at the building going down. As they watched it was obvious that he dialed a number and said that the past had sent "them" a message and asked how "they" should respond. He argued that he did not think it would be a good idea. He listened some more and then said well if you insist, you're the boss.

Bram then went back and froze the scene the moment that the phone was pressed to dial a phone number.

He asked Marcus to record the number that was transmitted so they could trace it to its owner.

Marcus nodded and Folded a monitoring bubble into the future and captured the transmission. He then retrieved the bubble and sent the transmission to the supercomputer and a moment later he had the phone number and had located its owner in the future.

They were all surprised when they learned that the phone number was that of the director of NASA!

Bram shook his head in disbelief. He commented that it was hard to believe but it did make some weird sort of sense. If the future NASA director was learning the Fold secret, he might decide that eliminating those in the past that knew it, would then put him in control and he could use it to his advantage without worrying about it being in someone else's control.

He commented that they had found an evil Jeffrey as a Director of NASA.

He asked Marcus to determine the coordinates for the director and be prepared to Fold him to the same location that he had asked for the first Fold. The two Folds were to occur one after the other.

Marcus replied that he understood and would comply.

Bram led the way to the basement where their Fold craft was waiting. He got in and everyone took their places. The Fold put them exactly where they had been before. They then Folded their craft out of the living room.

They were in position as their adversary ended his call to the person he had referred to as "the Boss."

Bram Folded in, got out and walked quickly to within three feet of his adversary. He took in the look of surprise on the adversaries face and uttered the word "Payment."

Bram was just beginning to wonder if Marcus had acted when the adversary disappeared.

Bram walked to the kitchen, picked up all the pictures and the C4 but left the chocolate. He then erased the message on the refrigerator. He looked around to make sure that they had left no noticeable trace of their presence. He picked up the phone that his adversary had dropped and brought it back with him.

Castor simply said, "shoot first, ask questions later."

Bram got into the Fold craft.

A Fold later, Bram exited the Fold craft and led the way back to the dining area.

He asked Pat how long they had been gone.

Pat replied that if they had maintained the integrity of the forward flow of time they had been gone for fifteen minutes.

Bram checked the activity of the work area Fold barrier on Mataia and verified that two unauthorized entry attempts had been repelled.

They all sat in the Viewing Room and viewed the future, and they watched and listened as the wife of the target was asking the kids if they knew where their father happened to be.

Bram quietly said, "randomly everywhere."

He heard her say something about how nice he was to leave her the chocolate but wondered why he had left so early.

The scene made Bram wonder if the world would mature and how long it would take before a more gentle and tolerant society would create a world where treating others as one wished to be treated became the norm.

He looked around the room and thought about what each person would need to handle the emotional strain properly and effectively that he was sure they were all experiencing.

None of them had been trained or conditioned for the battles they had recently faced. In fact, as he thought back at all the attacks they had faced and come out unscathed he thought it was a miracle that he and they were still sane and functioning harmoniously.

He asked Linda to schedule some therapy sessions that would be both group and individually oriented with the Fold phycologist, Dr. Windal. He personally called Dr. Windal and asked her to work with Linda to set up some therapy sessions.

She responded by reminding him that he should call her Serena and that she would do so if he agreed to be one of her patients.

Bram knew that he had avoided sitting with her and discussing his emotions but this time he also knew he needed to talk about what had transpired and get it off his chest.

He knew that his decision of using the intrusion protection lasers to eliminate the two future adversaries had taken them all to their emotional limit. He was the one that had decided on that approach, and he felt responsible to find a way to reduce the strain on everyone.

He turned his mind back and focused on the next priority. His next actions needed to be a return to his past to prevent himself from sending out the time capsule with the information. It made him wonder about all the stories of the effect of a person meeting himself in the past. He would need to think through how to stop himself from taking an action that he already had taken.

Chapter 7: Future History

Bram sat in the viewing room waiting for the team members to gather and sit down. He was thinking through what his next step needed to be and how he might handle the situation.

He gazed at the phone from the future that he held in his hand. It was very similar to the ones that were currently available, but it was clear to him that as he examined it that it was a solid chunk of some sort of plastic. It clearly had a front and a back but both sides seemed to function the same. It was a trophy permanently associated with one of his more radical actions against the instigator of the attack from the future.

The three computers on table in front of him were taken from the attackers that had been killed when they attacked the team on Mataia. That was another incident that had left all of them psychologically marked.

Finding out more about that group was on the long list of to-do's. He hoped that there was not a follow up action required to prevent a similar attack.

Both events had a very negative connotation, and he wondered if the Fold program effort was worth enduring such attacks and then living with the forceful response to those attacks that he had so far been a part of. He corrected his thought and added, "that he was responsible for."

The information on the exteriors of the computer had provided the time marker in the future that had allowed them to find the time and the identity of those responsible for the attacks.

He and Marcus had not yet had the time to extracted the information in the memories of the computers. He was anxious to get into the computers and learn if there was any technical information that would be meaningful and useful.

He had put the extraction work to the back burner so that the immediate threat to them could be focused on.

He felt that the phone would allow him to identify potential future threats that might be associated with the two leaders who had been responsible, and he planned to follow up on them and their contacts next. But that could also wait until he had removed the Fold information that he had sent out to the future.

He knew that none of the attacks or the response of the Fold team would have been necessary had he not sent out the information to one hundred years into the future. It was a hard lesson to learn and to accept. It hurt.

He knew that he had to move quickly to eliminate his own action of sending out the module with the Fold information. That meant an immediate trip to his past. He was uncertain how he should manage getting himself to not send out the information bubble.

How did one change the actions that had already been taken?

After thinking through several approaches, he decided to ask his team to help him out. He was sure that one of them would be able to come up with a way that he at the moment was not thinking of.

Once he had NOT sent out the information, he could be more confident that he had the time to set up a way to keep the Fold process details secret. He had come to the conclusion that he would need to slowly erase the Fold knowledge from the project records. He would needed to slowly dumb down the oversight committee and over time see if he could make the Fold project appear to be a failure.

He would need to study the hundred year out future in more detail to ensure that he had indeed removed all the Fold information from that time and then keep checking the close future to ensure that the Fold secret was being kept.

The far future, at least one thousand years out, needed to be examined to see if somewhere in time the competitive and combative nature of humans had decreased and a more peaceful society, which could handle the power that the Fold process unleashed, had emerged. He hoped to find a society engaged in the peaceful exploration of the universe.

As soon as he had that thought he thought of all the current combative situations currently in progress and he knew that he might find something similar even one-thousand years in the future.

The thought of space exploration made him think he should look in at the Swooshians and see how they had progressed over the same period of time. He was sure they would most likely have maintained their very inclusive and balanced society. They were the most stable beings that he knew.

He wondered if other species that might exist in the universe had been discovered in the future or communication from them had been intercepted. He knew that the Fold technology and a lot of luck had been responsible for them discovering the Swooshians.

He added the search for other intelligences to the Fold team's, "to do list." They would need to determine how to strategically execute such a search.

Once everyone was seated in the Viewing room he pointed at the trophies that they had accumulated from the future. He commented that they would examine each thoroughly but first he had to take the next step by himself and stop himself from sending the information to the future. He said that he was going to do this alone but was not sure of the best way to keep himself from sending out the bubble.

He shared he was not sure that meeting himself in the past would work. He said that maybe he had read too many science fiction stories that always highlighted a startling and shocking end to that occurrence.

Zoe suggested he destroy the bubble as soon as he deployed it.

Bram said that suggestion posed the same problem as telling himself not to send it, how would he know to destroy it?

Pat commented that maybe he did not need to meet with himself but needed some indirect way that would keep him from sending the information out.

She wondered if perhaps he would react to a message asking him not to send the information out.

Bram asked who could possibly get him to accept a message to not to send the Fold information out.

Pat took out a small perfume bottle and sprayed the mist on a red sticky pad. She wrote a message on it and handed it to him. She had written the current date on it and the words "Pat asks that you do not sent the Fold information to the future."

Bram read the message, he smelled the perfume and nodded. He smiled as he thought about the fact that Pat had saved him from himself several times. This approach was as imaginative as her use of a light flashing in morse code to give him a beacon home when he was lost in the negative Fold universe.

He heard her telling him to put the sticky note on the bubble just before his past self-arrived to put all the Fold information into the bubble.

Bram gave her a kiss on the cheek and said that she had just sent a shiver down his back and that he was going to see if she could reach back in time to correct his mistake. He commented that she had reached into the future to save him from one of his previous huge mistakes. He said that he was now going to trust her to keep him from making a huge mistake in the past.

He held up the sticky and said that he was going to work with Marcus and Remi to arrange his trip back.

The three of them went to the lab where Marcus figured out the coordinates of the desired spot in the lab during the time when Bram was to send out the Fold information bubble. Remi positioned the bubble at in current time in the spot it needed to be in the past time. Marcus then figured out the coordinates for both the bubble that would take Bram back and the viewing bubble that would allow all of them to see what transpired in the lab a few months ago.

He had to make sure the relay bubble that would send back the video would move about on the moon in millisecond folds so it would not be discovered.

Marcus did a quick run through with the observation system and then declared everything ready.

Bram noted that Marcus had become very proficient at determining the correct coordinates for almost any time and location that was requested of him. He planned to review what tools Marcus had created to facilitate such speed and accuracy.

They all went back to the Viewing room, and they all got a view of the past and the bubble that would send out the video to the future.

Bram got a hug from Pat, and she whispered to him that his past self would respond to her message.

He held up the red sticky for everyone to see and said "Hurrah" let "Pat save me from myself" and walked out of the viewing room. He and his small army of protectors proceeded to the lab with Remi.

Once there, Bram got into the bubble, waved, and made sure they were all in synch and then Folded into the Lab in the past. Remi had positioned the bubble in the current lab in the exact spot that it needed to be in the past lab.

Bram got out, walked around the table, and put the sticky note on the bubble that was sitting on the stainless-steel table where Remi in the future had been standing.

He saw a tape dispenser on the table and decided to tape the message to the bubble as a precaution to prevent it from falling off.

He walked back to the bubble and then Folded back to his own time. When he got out, he asked Remi how long he had been gone and learned that he had taken less than a minute. He and Remi and all his protectors walked back to the viewing room.

The chatter in the room ended as they walked in.

He walked in and sat at his chair. He commented that he was feeling a little weird and wondered whether he would actually respond to the message.

Pat reached over and held his hand.

The tiny monitoring camera bubble caught his arrival in the bubble. He stepped out and walked to the Fold information bubble and put the sticky note on it. As he turned he saw the tape dispenser on the table and took a piece and taped the sticky note to the bubble. The camera then showed him getting back into the bubble, Fold out and disappear just before his past self walked in.

His past self-put his computer on the table. He stopped after opening his computer when he looked up at the bubble and saw the red sticky note taped to it. He walked slowly around the table, and slowly reached for the sticky note. He carefully pulled it off and read it as he folded the scotch tape against the back of the sticky note.

As he read the message he was holding he looked up over his shoulder as if he expected to see a camera. The past Bram stopped and shook his head slowly and then read the note again. He brought the note up to his nose.

Bram now, sitting in the viewing, room knew that a tiny camera too small to be seen had indeed been where he, in the past, had looked. He then also remembered the smell of Pat's perfume in the past.

He watched as, he in the past, pointed his thumb in the air, kissed the note and carefully put the red sticky into his wallet. He, his past self, folded his computer shut and then stepped to the bubble and pulled out the computer that was in the bubble and then he Folded the empty bubble to its coordinates.

He shook his head and mouthed, "I love you too," in the past, and then waved his hand into the air as he walked out of the lab.

Everyone in the viewing room let out a cheer.

Pat smiled and gave him a kiss. Then said she was now waiting to be given the red or was it now a pink slip.

Bram commented that he was now wondering when he would be finding the slip in his wallet.

Pat said that it had been there since the time he had walked out of the lab.

He took the wallet out of his pocket and opened it. He shook his head as he pulled out a well-worn red sticky note that was now more pink than red and whose wear spoke of being in the wallet for a long period of time. He handed it to Pat and thanked her and said he was giving her the pink slip.

He looked around and asked if they all still remembered the Fold to the Future.

Zoe replied that the Fold to the Future was clear as a bell. She stopped, frowned, and pointed at him and in a quivering voice slowly asked who he was.

The room went silent. After a long moment, she laughed and said she was just kidding. She had just walked with him out to the lab and back.

Bram laughed shook his finger at her and then asked all of them to pay attention to anything that they seemed to have forgotten. He said that he had no idea how what he had just done might affect what they had done. He said that the pink slip in his wallet had not been there when he went to the lab and into the past to put it in place. He could not remember having it until a moment ago when he had opened his wallet and pulled it out.

Pat smiled and added of that if anyone had forgotten something, it would be a challenge to know what changed.

Bram then said that he wanted to check what had happened in the future.

He asked Marcus to capture the empty fold vessel when it materialized at the coordinate in the future.

Marcus nodded and after a moment commented that maybe that should have been the way they prevented the future from getting the information instead of having him use his intuition to accept the note from Pat.

Bram complemented Marcus on being a great Monday morning quarter back and that he agreed with him. He looked around and asked if he should go back and retrieve the red slip before his past persona arrived at the lab to find the sticky note and then return to the present to implement Marcus's suggestion.

Zoe pointed to Castro and told him he had permission to shoot anyone who agreed to that suggestion.

Bram put up his hands, commented he was not moving. He said that his experience had cemented the fact that they needed to protect the world from the technology that he had developed. He shook his head and said that he wished he had not opened up Pandora's Fold box.

Zoe commented that he should not blame Pandora. He had opened a different box that in the future should be called Bram's Fold Box. She added that his box was more dangerous than Pandora's box.

Bram asked Zoe, Eric, Bob, Thomas, and Remi to work with Marcus to check out the future to see if their Pay Forward actions had in any way changed.

He said that he was going to take trips about a thousand years up stream. He wanted to look but not interact with anyone. He was planning to look at the condition of the Earth, the Swooshian water world, and Mataia.

Bram Nielson Collection

He asked Daryl and Harold the finders of the Water worlds, Mallica and Gerry the two that had facilitated the Swooshian Migration, Pat, Amy, and Erica, who had established Einstein city on Mataia if they were interested in making the Fold journeys with him.

Pat said that both she and Amy would absolutely love to see Mataia a thousand years in the future. She said that she personally wondered how much of their original work would still be in existence. She thought they had done a very good job of establishing Einstein City and they both had hoped it would last a thousand years.

Amy added that the trip would be a reward of her lifetime and that she hoped Einstein City would not look like Modern Rome with its historic ruins at its center. She wondered if after all the years whether any of them would be personally remembered.

Erica was all smiles. She thanked Bram for including her. She wondered if any of the original paintings that she had paid a pretty penny for had survive into the future.

Mallica agreed that seeing the condition of the water world would also be a dream come true for her. She wondered if the Swoshians had ever become under water structure builders. She wondered if they might have come up with the ability to create robots that could do work for them.

Gerry agreed with her and said that it was going to be a dream come true for him. He had so far been hard at work providing the Swooshians with the technology that would allow them to become builders of their world.

Daryl, and Harold the finders of the water worlds put their fists in the air and said that "their prayers had been answered."

Everyone agreed that their upcoming Fold journey was an extraordinary opportunity.

Bram added that it would be a reward for him as well. He commented that he wondered what of the Fold technology had traveled forward during that period. He said that at the minimum it would help to calibrate the actions that he was planning to take or should be taken and then learn the effect it would have in the future.

Bram said that after they took their journeys they would gather at his house and be served the meal of their choice. He wanted to spend quality time in discussing what they all had learned.

He asked Linda to take the meal orders and ask Chef D'Carluca if he could fulfill the order. He suggested that everyone in the viewing room plan to attend, and that Linda could decide who else should be there.

Linda recorded the orders and said that she would evaluate where to have the dinner based on how many people would attend. She said that her family would work with Chef D'Carluca and handle the setup and provide extra food if the gathering was large.

Bram asked if everyone was ready to begin their Fold journey to the future. There was a resounding shout of, "let's do it."

He then stood up and said they would Fold to the three destinations.

Bram asked those going with him to decide the order of the Folds that they wanted to make.

Pat suggested they visit the future Earth first to see how it fared and how society had evolved. This she thought would provide the basis on how to manage their current knowledge in their current time.

Amy suggested that they visit Mataia next to see how the world that they had established had progressed and grown. She thought it would be a good way for them to evaluate the work each of them were doing and would be doing in their lifetime.

Erica agreed with Amy and added that she hoped that Pat and Amy would be remembered.

Mallica and the Water world group agreed with the order. Then she said they were very interested on how the Swoshians had progressed, but they were just as interested in the first two visits.

Bram agreed with them that all three visits would be very enlightening. He reinforced Amy by stating that what they were about to learn would most likely affect what they would do for the rest of their lifetimes.

He said that he wanted to bring back a broad swath of information that they could study in their attempt to have the Fold capabilities contribute to the betterment of all the worlds over their lifetime and beyond.

Mallica commented that every day, every week, every month, the Fold technology was opening up a new world to all of them. Now their new ability to travel forward and backward in time would give them the ability to learn from both their past and their future. They could balance this knowledge to methodically prepare their race to grow and progress.

Amy commented that such knowledge could easily be misused or even when good intensions were at work, they could make big mistakes. They would need to become very disciplined and thorough in what they did.

Pat suggested that on their return they should all participate in a process to establish the guidelines of how to use the power that the Fold unleashed.

Bram said that he would get them together as soon as they returned.

He suggested that Zoe and those going with her verify the hundred year out impact that would happen when no Fold information went out. They should do additional Folds forward in time to verify that the Fold information had indeed been erased.

He said that the thousand-year Fold would start early the next morning at eight sharp.

<u>Chapter 8: The Close Future</u>

Zoe, Eric, Bob, Thomas, Remi, and Marcus went to the hangar and got into the Fold bubble. Marcus entered the Fold coordinates to take them to a point in time where the empty bubble that Bram had sent from the lab in the past should appear.

He had worked feverishly to determine when and where the bubble would appear. He wanted to retrieve it as soon as it appeared.

Zoe commented that they should be able to watch themselves arrive on their Pay Forward Fold. She commented that this ability seemed to counter everything she had ever heard about time travel to or from the future.

Remi added that it was something that he had not done much thinking about in the past so the whole topic made his head reel.

Marcus pointed to the screen where a small blip had appeared. He Folded over to it and had a robot arm grasp the small bubble and put it into the cargo bin. He then Folded to the far side of the solar system to be out of sight before Folding forward in time to check whether the Pay Forward Fold had occurred as they all remembered it.

Zoe commented that remaining undetected was tricky. She wondered if there were human outposts on the Moon, Mars and on some of the moons of Jupiter.

Eric said that there must be. They were one hundred years into the future. He expected there to be a significant human colony on Mars and a supporting launch terminal on the Moon.

Remi suggested that they fold observation bubbles to check out Eric's suppositions.

Marcus agreed and said they had enough bubbles to do so, and it fit into the scope of their Fold mission.

He spent a few moments working on his computer and said that he was deploying the observation bubbles to check out Mars, the Moon, Europa, and Enceladus the two moons of Jupiter thought to have the possibility of life below their thick layers of ice.

Marcus shared the fact that the planetary rotation of Mars was very close to that of the rotation time for Earth though its rotation around the sun was almost twice as long as the Earth's.

He let the team know that he had programed the observation bubble to skip in time around the circumference of Mars in one second Fold hops to get a picture that they could later study to see what had happened on Mars in one hundred years. He said that he was going to do the same observation on the Moon, on Earth, as well as the two moons of Jupiter.

He commented that they needed to come up with a routine to do the analysis and let their supercomputer do the initial scan and reduce the number of pictures to a manageable one.

Bob commented that he had been wondering what he might do once his bodyguard duties came to an end. He said that he had no desire for more of the same guard duty and there seemed to be little else that interested him at the Bureau. Thomas said that he too was looking for something that would capture his interest. He had thought to go into farming on Mataia with his father, but farming had never been an activity that drew him

Studying future history seemed intriguing. He had enjoyed studying Earth's past history and now he had the ability to study future history as it was made. He commented that he would request to be on the analysis team.

Marcus commented that he had found his calling. Bram had given him the job of a lifetime as the person that figured out the coordinates that a craft was to Fold to. That challenge had him constantly developing programs that would determine positions of objects that they were going to Fold.

The math, computer modeling and trips such as the one they were on provided a continuous, challenging and an interesting environment.

He said that Pat's and Amy's establishment of Einstein City and all of its associated elements had been a huge undertaking and had been a challenge that he enjoyed as well.

He laughed and said that Melisa's work in setting up the weekend Fold vacation spots had tested his ability to identify coordinates in buildings that were randomly scattered around the world.

He asked if anyone had thought about determining and maintaining the coordinates for a room that was rotating with the velocity based on its location on the surface of the earth. He said that every vacation Fold had to be recalculated before every Fold, based on the time and date of departure and again for the time and date of return. The whole vacation program if all the vacation spots were triggered at once would crash the supercomputer they had. He had created a safeguard program that spaced the Folds at a minimum one second intervals.

Zoe asked if they should be thinking about getting a second supercomputer.

Marcus replied that he and Bram agreed that they should not only have a second one but establish several on Mataia. Those super computers would focus primarily on the Negative Fold effort.

Zoe looked over to Eric and asked him if he had any interest in studying the history of the future.

Eric shook his head and said he would enjoy working with Marcus on figuring out how to place a Folded object in a very specific coordinate.

Marcus smiled and said that he could use the help.

Zoe commented that she had mixed feelings of what to focus on, but her future was not going be in the FBI. She commented that Bram was going to need protection for most of his lifetime and she was sure the Bureau would decide to stop the protection detail at any time. Her choice would depend on the politics of the day and whether protecting Bram was still a need.

Eric commented that protecting Bram would always be feasible as long as they could at the same time be doing other work.

Bob and Thomas agreed and added that such a mix would allow them to grow intellectually and broaden their skills while still keeping their bullet magnet functional and safe.

Zoe agreed that they could continue to provide the protection and grow intellectually.

Marcus said that his observation bubble was approaching the point in time that the Pay Forward Mission had arrived and that he would capture the entire sequence of what had transpired.

As they watched the building implode, Zoe commented that it seemed to be a job done by a group of professionals and not by a group of amateurs doing it for the first time.

Thomas pointed out that they had been following the directions of a leading building demolition expert and they were more like trained monkeys doing what they had been taught.

Zoe agreed but said it still was a rewarding sight to watch the building gently settle down.

Marcus pointed to two individuals dressed in what looked like police clothes that walked up to the corner of the street and stood there looking at the building and then turned away and left. He asked if they were the guards that had been escorted out of the building.

Eric replied that those were the two. He commented that they had speculated that the team was either a Marine squad or members of the mafia. He laughed and said that the comparison was a ying-yang one.

Marcus then Folded to the home of the person that had sent the attack group back to their time to kill Bram. He folded a tiny observation camera bubble into the family room where they watched the scene unfold. The initial placing of the family pictures and Bram writing the message on the refrigerator. It ended with Bram returning and signaling the Fold of the perpetrator and the NASA director to the coordinates inside the new facility on Mataia.

Marcus commented that he was still working with his therapist on the impact that it had on him when he Folded those individuals to the Lab coordinates knowing that they were going to be shredded into less than one eighth inch body pieces that would be randomly spread throughout the negative Fold realm.

He said he had not been prepared to be the person who, as in the movies showing the execution of the bad guy, pushed the switch to electrocute the person in the chair. He knew it was Bram's call, but it was his emotions.

He said that Bram was the judge, but he was not the guy pushing the switch.

Marcus shared the fact that Bram had put a block on the video so that the Fold of the two persons from the Future to the Lab could never be shown in slow motion. At Fold speed all that is visible is a brief flash. He commented that Bram had slowed the video of the bubble hitting the screen that he had shown everyone, by ten thousand times.

Zoe agreed that the emotions triggered by recent events had affected her as well and added that she too, besides attending the group therapy that they all were attending together, had several additional one on one sessions with the therapist to talk through the feelings that haunted her.

She added that her actions after the gun battle at the Mataia lab had been appropriate but counter to Bram's more loving motto of treat others as you wish to be treated. She shared that she had summarily executed several survivors from the future.

Regardless of how she felt, Bob said he supported her actions and that she had done the right thing.

Thomas pointed to the screen and asked if Marcus could focus in at what appeared to be a blinking light.

Marcus moved the tiny observation bubble to where the barely visible light was located in the ceiling, and they were able to make out that it was some sort of observation camera.

The only reason Thomas had been able to see it was that their bubble was located higher in the vaulted ceiling, and they were looking down at the observation camera from above.

Zoe asked if Marcus could determine where the signal went.

Marcus said that he thought there was a unit in the attic. He sent the observation bubble into the attic, and they were able to see the unit that was blinking as it transmitted the picture.

Zoe asked if they could figure out where the information was being sent.

Marcus interrogated the transmit unit and found the address it was sending the message to. He tried that address and after several iterations he said that it was going to a NASA location that was very near to the coordinates that he had used to pull the NASA director into the past into the laser barrier on Mataia.

He sent an observation bubble to the coordinates and discovered they were in a computer room. He was able to pinpoint which of the many computers in the room was the one that the signal was going to.

Zoe asked whether they could fold the entire computer back to their time.

Marcus said the computers were only as big as his countertop oven and he could Fold every computer located in the room back if she desired.

Zoe shook her head and said they should limit it to only the one associated with the person being observed. She then suggested they search the house for other observation cameras or listening devices and Fold those back to their time as well.

She pointed out that they would need to study who had accessed the computer to determine if there were any other individuals who had looked at the video.

Marcus suggested they move slowly forward one month at a time and see if there was any mention of their Pay Forward visit.

Marcus placed one very tiny camera/listening device at the home and then found what they determined was the NASA directors meeting room and put a unit there.

Their final monitoring was of the National News.

Then Marcus put them on a daily forward Fold journey for a month. That journey only lasted an hour in their time. They ended up with a tremendous amount of recorded audio and video that would need to be reviewed.

Marcus asked if everyone was ready to Fold back to their time and then asked how long should they have been gone.

Zoe suggested they return at the end of the workday on which they left.

Marcus nodded and said that they would arrive in the hangar at four-forty-five.

When they Folded into the hangar, Remi suggested they take their trophies from the future and place them in the large stainless-steel drawer of the now famous worktable. He suggested that they gather there in the morning and plan on how they were going to study what they had come back with.

Zoe said that she could immediately think of the categories of investigation.

She wrote them on the white board by the table.

Review
1. Specific viewing content
2. General computer content
3. Computer software capabilities
4. Computer hardware design
5. Observations sensor design and capabilities.

Eric said that he was ready to go home and prepare dinner. He wondered when Bram and his group would be back.

No sooner had he uttered the words than Bram walked in.

Bram walked in as Eric finished his question and answered that his team was back and had a wealth of information that they would be spending the next few days processing.

Pat and the team had been right behind Bram, and she suggested that all go home and discuss their trips over dinner.

She introduced the person standing next to her as Marial and that they would all be able to meet her over dinner.

Chapter 9: One Thousand Years

Once everyone got into the Fold vessel, Bram initiated their first agreed Fold to one thousand year into Earth's future. They first Folded out very close to Neptune so they could determine where they could Fold to and not be seen. It became immediately clear that there was no place in the solar system where they could easily remain and not be found.

Bram immediately put them into a series of mini-Folds that lasted only a few seconds. This gave them enough time at each Fold coordinate to gather significant information about the condition of their Solar system and the condition on Earth. They were also able to intercept and capture the news feed at each Fold node.

Amy commented that Bram would have made a great combat helicopter pilot because he knew how to weave and dodge.

Pat said that one crazy helicopter pilot in the group was enough.

Amy counter that she was not a crazy pilot just an enthusiastic one and crazy was how enthusiastic pilots flew.

Mallica said the two of them had spent too much time together getting Einstein City built.

She looked at Bram and asked him if he was ready to take the two affected women to see what their handiwork had evolved to in a thousand years.

Bram nodded and said he had gathered enough Earth material that they would tie up one supercomputer trying to analyze it all.

He was ready to see what Mataia had transitioned to be.

Daryl commented that when he and Harold had found Mataia and Marcus had summarily put it into the not interested pile of other worlds they had found, they had been disappointed. He was now really interested in what had become of their planet. He was pleased that it had come out of the pile and had been selected as a second place where humans could migrate.

Harold added that he wondered how many people now existed on Earth and on Mataia.

Bram replied that he and Marcus had select Mataia and rescued it from the proverbial pile when he was looking for a way to protect humans from themselves. He planned to move his entire Fold operation to Mataia. At this point he was planning to first move the negative Fold work there.

Bram had no sooner Folded into Mataian space when he received a message asking him to identify himself. He was surprised but pleased that the Mataians were so much more awake than those on Earth had been.

Bram responded with I and my companions are from your past. I am Bram Eric Nielson, the developer of both the positive and Negative Fold equations.

Silence from the challenging end was the response. Then there was the sound of cheering. The challenger came back on and said that they had arrived at the exact time that had been on record for a thousand years. They asked if Pat and Amy were really on the craft.

Then they said that the Terminal they had designed was still in use and it was ready to receive them and celebrate them as celebrities that were beloved by the almost one billion people on Mataia.

The speaker said they were in for a surprise.

Bram smiled and asked if everyone was willing to step into the future and learn too much about what they had done with their lives in the past.

Pat smiled and replied that she was personally very interested. She knew that it was dangerous to know too much about ones future but just as he had survived his ventures into the unknown Fold world she would survive and grow in a positive fashion, no matter what.

Amy said ditto.

Mallica said, 'let's do it."

Bram Folded to the Arrival Terminal coordinates.

The crowd in the terminal was cheering and a formal band was playing.

Bram got out first and was met by a person holding a microphone. Bram turned and as each person exited, he introduced them.

Pat and Amy got cheers and a resounding welcome that took a few moments to settle down. Then Mallica exited and the cheering was her name being repeated over and over. When Bram introduced Daryl and Harold as the two that had first found Mataia the cheers again went up.

Erica was the last to exit and for some reason the crowd went quiet. Then the cheers rose as they repeated, the art queen was real, the art queen was real."

Erica shook her head and quietly said that she must have done something that she was just learning about.

Bram chuckled and replied that she had just been told about her new career on Mataia.

He then introduced himself as the perpetrator that had caused the ripple in time that was still expanding across the Universe

The roar and the noise went through the ceiling.

He was greeted by a host of people that introduced themselves and were eager to get him to walk out of the terminal.

As he walked with them out toward the hangar that housed the work center, he saw the huge statue of himself standing with his left arm around Pat and his right arm pointing to the sky. Pat's left arm was pointing at Einstein City. Amy was standing in the arms of a person, and she was pointing at Einstein City as well.

Marcus, Mallica, Linda, Lacy, Daryl, Harold, and Gerry with his arm around Erica were around the base all pointing to Bram.

Bram asked if he could have a picture of the statue.

The person who had identified herself as the current leader of Mataia replied that they had prepared a complete history of Mataia and its development over time that would be part of the gifts that had been prepared in advance of his arrival. The fact that he had arrived exactly as predicted had righted what had become a question about the reality of what they thought they knew.

She asked that she be called Marial and said that her family name was also Nielson and smiled. She then let Bram know that she was a student of his and had spent many hours studying Mataian History and had also studied most of his work but understood very little about it.

She asked how he was preventing the future from going into the past.

Bram looked at her and said that her features favored Pat and that perhaps the curiosity gene that he possessed had traveled a thousand years into the future ahead of him and was now in her possession.

He smiled and thanked her for the question and truthfully replied that he had no clue because he had yet to do that, but he would send her the answer once he developed the block. He admitted to having the thought and would implement it to prevent people from trying to alter the past to satisfy some desire in the future.

She smiled and said that he would be very successful in the block that he had created. It had been in place and impregnable for the past one thousand years. She was aware of dozens of teams who had put their minds using the information on record to see if they could find the secret.

She turned to Pat and asked what it was like to live with a person who seemed to think universe changing thoughts.

Pat smiled and commented that it was a pleasant challenge and that she never competed with Bram in the technical realm but often had to rescue him in the social and political realm or to save him from himself and the risks he was willing to take in his endeavor to explore the Universes he had opened with a technology that was both a boon and a perhaps fatal one to all intelligent beings.

Their host smiled and said that Pat was helping put a sense of life and reality into a history that had over a thousand years grown into mythology. She admitted that though she had wished it were all true she had until the very moment of the call been ready for disappointment.

She asked how long they could stay.

Bram smiled and said they were capable of staying any length of time they desired but they were actually on their normal daily work cycle and were visiting the future to get calibrated on their desire to do the right thing in their time. He said that seeing Mataia doing well put the icing on the cake for him. Meeting her lit a thousand candles that warmed his heart.

He then asked about the contact that Mataia had with Earth.

Marial replied that they had chosen to keep that contact at arm's reach. They were constantly and secretly recruiting desirable people from Earth, but they had kept Mataia a secret. As far as she was aware, Earth did not know that Mataia existed.

Bram nodded. He shared the fact that he had kept Mataia a secret in his time because there had been multiple attacks on him from people in his own time and he had kept his work a secret and blocked the future because of an attempt on his life that had come from the future Earth.

Marial shook her head and said that such details had not come forward in history. She said that she felt better about Mataia not having made closer contact with Earth. She then pointed out that he had not given Mataia the secret of his work. She asked why that was the case.

Bram replied that at that time he had no way of knowing how well he had recruited those that ended up on Mataia and that he felt obliged to protect humanity from their base instinct of wanting to control others.

Marial nodded and said that she hoped that what he learned about the current Mataian Society would allow him to at least give them the ability to Fold in their current time.

She said that as the current leader she had continued to follow his teachings.

Amy smiled and said that she should continue to fly her plane as she was doing until someday in the future more people followed Bram's favorite saying of, "treat others as you wish to be treated."

The crowd let out a thundering cheer as Amy's words were heard.

Marial smiled and said that those words were the opening words of the Mataian Constitution.

Bram said that was the best thing that he had heard so far. He asked how the Mataian society was doing.

Marial said that it was a challenge to live by those words when disagreements arose, but those words were constantly being referred to and it always helped. The population on Mataia was a constant point of discussion because when they looked at the Earth with its twelve billion people.

The people on Mataia then asked if they were under populated. Many of them pointed out that Mataia was the same size as Earth. She was on the side that felt the Mataia did not need a huge population. She felt that it needed just enough of a population to be truly self-sufficient.

She pointed out that their diversity of wild animal species was well beyond what was now left in the wild on Earth which had almost no wild space left. Making Mataia the planet that harbored all species in a natural balance was her objective.

Mataia had become the place of survival for a series of animals that had gone extinct on Earth. She commented that the great majority of the Mataian population supported the view that very slow, controlled population growth was the right approach.

Bram complemented the Mataian society for its well thought out approach to keeping Mataia a paradise.

Marial commented that a celebration dinner had been prepared for them and asked them to follow her.

He said that he was looking forward to the Mataian dishes that had been prepared for their arrival and that after enjoying them he and his team were planning to leave.

Marial replied that she hoped to convince him otherwise, but they should now focus on the banquet that had been prepared.

She said there was one dish attributed to a Chef D'Carluca called Blue Swooshian Spaghetti de Mar that had always raised the question of what a Swooshian happened to be. She had looked through all the historic papers she could find, and it was never referenced.

Amy laughed and asked Bram if she could divulge that secret. He said no she could not, but Mallica and her team could.

Mallica smiled and said that it was an honor to be able to reveal a thousand-year-old secret.

She paused and the entire listening crowd went silent.

Mallica said that Bram had made contact with an intelligent Alien community that referred to themselves as Swooshians. She then explained that the Swooshians were intelligent beings on a water world. She made the point that Bram had created a team that had facilitated the migration of the Swooshians from the system where their star was dying, to a water world where they were now located.

The listening Mataian public remained silent.

Marial asked if that population followed Bram's rule or the first line of the Mataian current constitution.

Mallica said that humans had a lot to learn from the gentle Swoshians. These were beings of extremely high intelligence as well as being as big as a blue whale. When last she had contact with them they had the same reverence for Bram as was being displayed by the Mataians.

She commented that the Mataian constitution was first written in her time, and it started with the same words that still existed in the current Mataian constitution.

A cheer again went up from the crowd.

Bram said that his team was going the planet of Swoosh next and there was one empty seat on their Fold bubble and if Marial wanted to she could accompany them and while there investigate whether it was time to establish a link between Mataia and Swoosh.

He suggested such a relationship should be one that provided both societies a chance to grow.

He made the point that the Mataian constitution pointed to a social norm that would want all intelligent beings to positively influence each other.

He made the point that social power was the potential for social influence and Mataia would have a positive approach to positive influence and power.

He was certain that they would find a water world that would benefit from Mataian influence and that the Mataian society would benefit from the Swoshian influence.

He felt that it would lead to positive change in both societies. He offered up the fact that when two societies interacted with the simple opening saying of the Mataian constitution a breakthrough of friendship and knowledge growth would be the outcome.

A cheer went up from the crowd and they chanted, "treat others as you wish to be treated."

Marial replied that she was eager to go with him to the Swooshian water world.

Bram smiled and said they should eat first and then travel toward a fresh future.

The crowd around the lunch table that was on a raised platform were all loudly enthusiastic. There was a human chain of uniformed men and women that was keeping them away from the platform.

Bram asked if they were police.

Marial replied that they did not have police as she had learned about from her studies of Earth, but they had a large organization that was deployed for crowd control or for storm relief if it was required. They were not armed and relied on their ability to work together as a team when they were being used as they were at the moment to control a large crowd. They would also take immediate action if the crowd tried to move forward in mass.

Pat took Bram's hand and guided him slowly around the table so that each person at the table had a chance to shake his hand and say a few words. It turned out that she and Amy were as sought out as was Bram. She got the gist that the two were given much of the credit for having established the foundation of the Mataian society.

Marial pointed to the seat at the head of the table and the two seats to each side and said that Bram should take his seat at the head of the table, Pat should sit to his left and Amy should sit to his right. She said that her seat was next to Pat's who she hoped was her great, great, great, great, great, grandmother. She laughed and said that she had no clue how many generations had passed but the person she was sitting down next to looked young enough to be her sister.

The crowd let out a roar as she finished and chanted, "Sister, Sister, Sister," over and over.

Bram looked at Mallica and commented that he heard the influence of Orlando coming up from the chanting that the crowd practiced.

He smiled and said that perhaps he did see some grey in Pat's hair and got a little kick in the shin.

When the main dish, Blue Swoshian Spaghetti de Mar was brought to the table Bram stood and walked over and took a picture of the large serving bowl it was in.

The caterers put a helping on his plate, and he took another picture. He knew that Chef D'Carluca would be absolutely astounded when he found out that his recipe had survived for a thousand years.

He was also going to share this fact with the Swoshians when they Folded to Swoosh.

His first bite told him that the name had survived but the original actually prepare by the Chef of his day had a deeper flavor but what was being served was very good.

He was now eager to get to Swoosh and then back to his own time to share a gold nugget that he had not expected to find.

He used his time at the table to ask about the location of the various cities on Mataia. He asked about a desert island and what lived on that.

Marial replied that the island was a mystery that had puzzled the Mataians for centuries. It was the only place where mice existed and thrived.

She then said that the information he was asking about was in the information that was included in the records module she was providing. She commented that the module would have the history, the current technology, the current political situation and all the issues that provided a challenge to Mataian society all included.

As Bram finished his desert and put down his spoon, Marial stood and announced that she was going to spent the next few hours with Bram and visit a water world that presented an opportunity for Mataia to have a relationship with another intelligent species. She looked at Bram and asked if he had any parting words.

Bram stood and said he was extremely proud of the Mataians, and the Mataian Constitution was a treasure that warmed his heart. He pointed at his team and said that he would not speak directly for them, but he wanted to complement them for having contributed to the creation of a society like the one currently on Mataia.

Now that he was aware of the situation on Mataia, he would likely return in the near future to this time because the people were so friendly, and food was so marvelous.

He then said that his Fold craft awaited them and that he would bring Marial back with knowledge that would take the Mataians through a knowledge growth spurt that they should all enjoy.

The crowd roar kept up as Bram, Pat and Marial led the way back to the Arrival-Departure terminal.

Once everyone was seated he let them know that they were Folding.

In the blink of an eye, they were looking down at a blue green planet that was all water. Bram pointed at a large structure that was rising above the water.

He said that the Swooshians had figured out how to build a transmitter tower that allowed them to create a more powerful Fold system.

As Bram finished making his statement, a call came into their vessel asking for the Fold vessel to identify its self.

Bram asked Mallica to give the reply in Swooshian. He let everyone know that what they would hear what would be said in English by the translation AP that they had developed for this situation.

Mallica smiled and nodded. She put on her mouthpiece so she could mimic the Swooshian gurgle that accompanied Swooshian speech. She said that it was none other than Bram and his team making a visit from the past.

Bram was not surprised by the silence, but he added in Swooshian that he hoped all was well and that he had not interrupted anyone's meal. Bram knew that this was a traditional polite saying.

Finally, a Swooshian came on and replied that legend had it that one day, Bram would visit and that he had just turned legend into a reality that far exceeded the highest breach that any Swooshian could make.

He asked if the first speaker that spoke perfect Swooshian might be the very famous Mallica Evenston and whether by any chance was Gerald "Gerry" Sooner present. There was momentary pause, and the speaker continued and inquired whether Daryl Narda and Harold Redat were also on this particular visit.

Bram replied in his best Swooshian that the team that had facilitated the Swooshian migration was indeed with him, and they sent their greetings and hoped that the krill were numerous, and the water was the perfect temperature.

The Swooshian with whom they were conversing replied that he was the fifth Swoshian in a long line from that migration date and he was proud that the tales of "Bram the Great" had been passed on from one generation to each of the following generations.

He stated that the tales include everyone that he just asked about and that they also included others like Patricia Fleming that was with you many times, may she be well.

Bram Nielson Collection

Pat smiled and replied in Swooshian that she was indeed well and sitting with her partner and she had brought a person that was a family member that was from the time they were now in. She then introduced Marial as the leader of Mataia a planet similar to Earth that was interested in establishing a working relationship with Swoosh.

She handed Marial a microphone and let her know that her words would be translated and sent down to Swoosh in Swooshian.

Marial sent down her greetings of "may all be well with all of your kind." We on Mataia live by the saying, "treat others as you wish to be treated." I am hoping that Mataia and Swoosh may become close and be able to link our two worlds in friendship and in a pleasant interchange of learning.

The Swooshian Leader replied that the words, "treat others as you wish to be treated" was a saying that Bram had used with his Swoshian ancestor, and it was still in use on Swoosh to this day.

Bram was not surprised when the Swoshian asked why Marial had waited so long to visit.

He spoke up and said that he back in his own time had blocked the future from accessing the Fold technology. He said that he had not wanted the Earth to become too powerful and misuse the Fold technology. He had also kept the existence of the Swoshians as secret to protect them.

He had asked Marial to visit, at this time, with him because he felt that it was time that a bridge should be built between Swoosh and Mataia.

The Swoshian replied that Swoosh would welcome an interaction with anyone that Bram approved of. They trusted his judgement.

Bram thanked the Swoshian for his compliment by saying that the krill that he had just swallowed was the best tasting in the Swoshian world.

The Swooshian thanked Mallica and Gerry for making sure they had the best tasting krill.

Bram then asked if the Swooshian was a descendant of Ohaan or Anon.

There was a loud gurgle and then the speaker replied that he was Ohaan the fifth.

Bram smiled and asked if he could breach as far out of the water as Ohaan the first. That in essence was asking if he was as smart and knew as much.

Ohaan replied that as hard as he tried he could not breach that high.

Bram said that he hoped to have many more visits with Ohaan, but his time was running short, but he had an interesting story to share.

He let Ohaan know that this was the first time that his team had made the leap so far into the future. The goal was to assess if the three societies with which they were familiar with had progressed and reached a time when they could interact peacefully with each other.

He said that sadly Earth had not made the desired progress but Mataia, a planet that had been discovered at the same time that the current Swoosh planet had been discovered had made significant social progress and deserved to make contact with Swoosh.

He shared that back in his time the keeper of the Earth Krill had developed a dish he labeled Blue Swoshian Spaghetti de Mar. It was recognized as the most delicious batch of Krill that anyone could possibly raise.

On this current visit to Mataia, he had been welcomed and they had served him a batch of Krill called Blue Swoshian Spaghetti de Mar. The skillful way to raise such a batch had survived for five Swooshian generations.

Ohaan gurgled and said that any society that would keep such a skill alive for five generations was a society that Swoosh should engage and learn from.

Marial replied that any society that inspired a person to herd the Krill so skillfully was one that Mataia looked forward to learn from and to share the best tasting Krill with.

Ohaan replied that Marial was making him hungry, and he looked forward to having additional conversations. He asked if Mataia had Fold communication capabilities.

Marial replied that area of the sea was currently empty of Krill, but she would see if she could guide a batch in.

Ohaan said he understood and added that she was sitting with the best Krill guide that had ever lived and he wished her good swimming.

Bram wished Ohaan good swimming and said that it was time to get to the feeding field. He then hit the Fold button.

Chapter 10: Mataian Empowerment

Marial looked out of the Fold craft at the inside of the Arrival-Departure hall and thanked Bram for returning her home.

Bram smiled and said that she was not home but on Mataia at the very beginning of its development. He said that he had made the decision to let her visit the origin of the myth and to return to her time with the technology that would allow Mataia to interact with the Swoshians and to have the capability to make excursions around the Mataian and Swoshian solar systems. He said that he would keep a lock in place that would prevent Earth getting to Mataia.

He said that he would supply her with a working Fold message transmitter that would allow interaction with the Swoshians. He made the point that the Swoshians had developed the Fold message transmitter as a means to send out a beacon asking for help.

He and his team had intercepted the message and had back engineered the Fold message transmitter so that they could send a reply. He pointed out that the message transmitter that they developed was more powerful than the original Swoshian one because the Swoshians lacked the capacity to create the power needed.

He pointed out the Swoshians never developed the capability to build the Fold vessels because of their lack of capability to generate the power they needed.

One of the team members that she would meet, Marcus Smith who he would introduce to her later, led a team that found the water world needed by the Swooshians. He pointed to Daryl and Harold and said that they were the ones that had searched hundreds of systems to locate the water world and in doing so they also discovered Mataia.

The Fold team built the Fold transports that the Swooshians used to depart from their dying world to the one where they currently live.

Marial shook her head and said that being around him and his team had inspired her to return and urge Mataia to take a leap forward in both technology and in exploring the Universe. She was amazed at what she was learning. She said that most of what he was sharing had been lost over time. Some of it was thought to have been myth.

Bram said that he would be pleased to help Mataia of her time flourish and become the Fold powerhouse that they could become. He had brought her back to the beginning of the Mataia journey as a first step in empowering Mataia of her time.

They were all walking toward the Negative Fold hangar when a Fold vessel materialized in front of them, and Zoe and the rest of the bodyguard team jumped out and surrounded them.

Zoe approached him and asked what was going down.

Marial had taken a step back to where Mallica was standing.

Bram smiled and said that he was running a test to see if his bodyguard team was paying attention and was ready to do their job.

Castor replied that Marines were always ready but being ready did not matter. What mattered, "was to win the battle when you got there."

Bram nodded and replied, "Hurrah."

Marial asked quietly if every outing ended in such excitement.

Zoe heard the remark and smiled. She replied that it only happened when Bram wanted to test his protection team. She stopped and realized she was speaking to someone other than Pat and stared. She then asked if she was Pat's one thousand years in the future granddaughter.

Marial said that the people around Bram amazed her.

She nodded and said that she was Marial Lyn Nielson of the Mataian year one thousand. She shared the fact that Bram had arrived at Mataia of her time on the day that the story of his legend had predicted. Long ago a message had been mysteriously received that from all investigation was determined to have come from an earlier Mataia. That message had become a myth that continued to grow and become more and more important to the people of Mataia.

She said that when Bram messaged Mataia of his arrival, he set off a celebration that she was sure would continue for many days to come. The fact that the other legendary Mataian figures accompanied him made the event even more exciting.

Zoe said that she was disappointed that she had missed being there, but she and her team had been busy cleaning up a rather dangerous situation in the future and had returned with rather good news that the future Earth no longer knew of the Fold technology.

Bram let her know that she would be able to make the next Fold trip to the future Mataia with him.

Zoe asked if it was Ok to share in front of Marial.

Bram nodded and said that the secrets that she might share would be about a thousand years old when Marial was back in her own time, and she would be free to share them as she pleased.

Zoe said that when Bram and his team folded to Mataia, she had Remi Folded the equipment they had brought back from Earth's future into the Lab here on Mataia.

Bram explained to Marial that the attack from the future had come from Earth one hundred years ahead. He explained that he had Folded the information of the Fold technology into that time frame thinking that it was far enough out that the world would have matured. He said that it was one of his major mistakes. He and his team had acted against the future after a major attempt to have him killed. Then he had gone back in time and corrected his mistake. He commented that Pat had been the person who had guided him in correcting that mistake.

The trip to one thousand years into the future was his follow up to see if there was somewhere in the Future where the breakthrough that the Fold technology represented could be openly shared.

He looked at Marial and said that what he was doing was taking that first step with her and what he had to share was what Zoe had referred to as Pandora's box on steroids.

Marial replied that she was familiar with Pandora's box and wondered what the Fold technology could possibly have that would be worse.

Bram replied that it gave a power that allowed all of history and time to be manipulated and potentially changed. It could be used to do immeasurable good or unbelievable harm.

Bram pointed to the building on the other end of the hanger. Once he was close enough, he threw the stone he had carried in with him at the building.

There was a brief flicker as the stone reached the laser barrier.

Marial chuckled and said that in her time that barrier was part of the mythology of the facility, she commented that it must have stopped working hundreds of years earlier and though she searched for a way to prove or disprove that myth she could not find out how it might have been powered.

Bram Nielson Collection

Bram shared the fact that the laser that she had just observed was powered by multiple Fold bubbles around Mataia. The bubbles were battery operated and had their batteries recharged by Mataia's sun. He said that the barrier had probably died when the bubble batteries powering the lasers died. He figured that with no maintenance the battery life was probably about one hundred years.

Marial said that she had spent many hours enjoying the view from the third floor of the building ahead of them. She complimented Pat and Amy on the amazing buildings and houses they had built. She asked how they had been able to make such beautiful structures on Mataia.

Pat commented that all of the original construction of Einstein City and the Hangar had been built on Earth and Folded into position.

Marial asked if she had heard it right and that all of the initial buildings in Einstein City had been built on Earth. Earth was many millions of miles away.

Bram nodded and replied that was one of the awesome capabilities that the Fold technology represented.

Marial pointed out that the Fold capabilities that Mataia currently possessed was limited to Folds within the Mataian planet. The Fold Scientist were besides themselves because they could not figure out how to make it happen otherwise.

Bram nodded and said that the current Fold limitation was one that he was currently thinking of so that it would provide Mataia society a way to easily move about on the planet but keep it from being used beyond that.

Marial said that his approach had been successful at having kept the Fold secret a true secret and the Fold capability limited to travel on and around Mataia only.

She asked about the approach he had taken on Earth.

He pointed out that in his time Earth had eight billion bickering people and, in her time, it was up to twelve billion bickering people. He said that it was hard to imagine the economic and cultural upheaval that the Fold technology represented for the Earth at either time period. He had chosen to lock them out entirely.

He made the point that the change for Mataia in her time would still be a risk, but it would be a manageable one.

He then asked if she thought she wanted to try to incorporate the Fold technology. He said if she did not he could check out Mataia some five hundred years earlier.

Marial looked at Pat and asked if Bram was always so accommodating.

Pat replied that Bram worked at Bram speed and on Bram decision making and both were very fast.

Marial replied that she would guide Mataia through the change and do it in a fashion were everyone would benefit. She commented that Mataians would rise to the occasion and leverage this new capability to improve not only Mataia but to learn about the universe around them. She envisioned a Mataian race to the stars and to the far reaches of the Universe.

Bram nodded and said that was his belief and why he had decided to make the offer of slowly releasing the Fold capability to her time.

He asked Zoe to get Marcus and Remi to Fold to Mataia. He said he wanted to introduce the two to Marial and he was going to ask Remi to prepare one of the larger Fold vessels for Marial to take with her when she returned to the future Mataia.

He wanted Marcus to work with Pat to prepare a Fold Message Transmitter and the associated peripherals to be transported to Mataia so Marial would be able to communicate with the Swoshians.

Marial asked how long the preparation would take.

Bram replied that it would take about one Earth day, but it would not matter. She would return late in the afternoon of the day they had left the celebration.

Bram then suggested they all Fold to Earth and enjoy some of Chef D'Carluca's Swooshian Spaghetti de Mar. It would allow her to compare the taste of the dish as prepared by the legendary Chef and the one they had enjoyed in her time.

She could also take in how beautiful and scenic the Earth was and rest up before returning.

Marial shook her head and said she was beginning to understand the complexity of managing the Fold capability. She said that she was still thinking of time as being linear and not something that might be manipulated at will.

Bram nodded and said that she was seeing only the tip of the iceberg.

Marial said that she was not familiar with that saying or what an iceberg might be.

Pat asked if Marial was familiar with ice cubes.

Marial said that yes but only in a glass.

Pat asked how high out of the water an ice cube floated and how much of the ice cube was below the water.

Marial said that she understood that most of the ice was below the water, but she still was not sure what an iceberg was.

Pat replied that berg in ancient Earth meant mountain.

She then described areas where giant pieces of ice would break from mountain high accumulations of ice, fall into the ocean, and then float with only the very tip out of the water. These large chunks were referred to as icebergs. And only a small portion of the iceberg was above the water.

Marial smiled and said that she now understood the comment. She said that Mataia did not have icebergs.

Bram said it was time to get back into their Fold transport and they would all Fold to Earth. Once they got there he would arrange to have Chef D'Carluca prepare his Swoshian Spaghetti de Mar for their dinner.

He was sure the Chef would be thrilled to know how long into the future his creation had traveled, and he would especially appreciate the pictures of his creation in the future.

Once they were in the hangar on Earth, Bram called Linda and asked her to ask Chef D'Carluca to prepare his Swoshian special.

Pat asked when they had returned.

Bram smiled and said that they were back for lunch on the same day that they had left but their bodies knew that they had been gone for more than twelve hours. He said that after lunch they should all go home and get some rest.

Marial commented that she was totally disoriented and wondered how they were all handling such a confusing situation.

Bram replied that they were still learning how to manage their time and really had not mastered handling time at all. They were all as disoriented as she was.

Marial said that it seemed that every passing moment she gained a greater appreciation for the complexity of managing the Fold technology.

Pat led the way to the cafeteria and the group arranged the tables, so the bodyguards were seated around the periphery of the group.

Marial asked about the arrangement and Pat pointed out that the bodyguards were in place to prevent any attack on Bram.

Marial said it was still hard for her to accept such attacks.

Chef D'Carluca came out of the kitchen followed by a line of servers who proceeded to set the tables and to offer everyone the choice of starters.

Bram introduced Marial, their guest from one thousand years in the future. Marial stood up and asked if she could take a picture with him.

Chef D'Carluca beamed and replied that he was always rewarded when a beautiful woman chose to have a picture taken with him.

Bram Nielson Collection

Bram explained that his name and his recipe for Blue Swoshian Spaghetti de Mar was still being prepared one thousand years in the future. He explained that it had been served in the future to the team as part of a welcome celebration and he had the pictures to prove it.

Chef D'Carluca ask if could sit down for a moment to look at the pictures. It was clear he had tears in his eyes. He asked the team how the meal had tasted.

Bram said that it was good, but he was sure that the one that would be served in the cafeteria for lunch would be better.

Chef D'Carluca looked at Marial and said that he wanted to hear her assessment once she tasted it coming from his kitchen. He looked at her and said that she seemed so familiar and then turned and went to the kitchen.

Marial sat down and said that there were no Chef's in her time because everything had been automated. She was going to have the picture of her standing next to the Chef put in the art museum in Einstein City. She said the picture of her with the Chef was a gem in an already very rewarding visit.

The Chef followed one of his helpers who was pushing a cart with a huge bowl that held his Blue Swoshian Spaghetti de Mar. He took an elegant plate that had a seashore scene as the boarder and was finished on the edge with a gold band. He said that the plate had been his great, great grandmothers and had not been used since he had come to the US. He made filling it a production. Once he had it arranged and garnished the way he wanted it, he placed in front of Marial.

He then signaled his helpers to serve the rest of those sitting at the tables.

Pat noted the fact the Chef had always focused on Bram but this time his focus was on Marial. He followed her every bite.

Marial had closed her eyes and was slowly eating the spaghetti and had forked in a clam. When she opened her eyes she stood up and gave Chef D'Carluca a hug and said that she had never eaten food that had taken her to heaven and beyond.

Pat took a bite and agreed that it was superb, and she noted how much better it was as compared to the one in the future.

She heard the Chef agreeing to send a serving with Marial when she returned to the future.

At the end of the meal Bram stood up and thanked Chef D'Carluca for one of the best meals he had ever eaten.

He then said it was time to go home and get some sleep. He stood up to lead the way out of the cafeteria. His protection team surrounded him and took the lead. Once out at the van convoy they got Bram and his team into the center van.

Marial chuckled and said that she wished she could take one of the vans and display it in the Antiquity Museum. She asked why it took so many people to take them home.

Bram explained that the lead vehicle was a Marine corps armored truck capable of taking out a tank or an attack helicopter.

The van they were in could take the direct hits of a rocket propelled grenade.

The truck that came behind was a duplicate of the one in front.

This was the way that he got home every day. The way in to work had the same configuration but he normally jogged in and there were attack bubbles that monitored the entire area around the compound. He finished by saying that he had been attacked at least three time at the compound.

Marial said she was surprised that there was such a concerted effort to try to kill him. She then said that she had never seen a tank, nor an armored truck, nor a rocket propelled grenade. These were only mentioned in a few documents, but little was known about such things.

Bram smiled and said that the times he was attacked outside of the compound was something like ten times higher than the attacks in the compound.

Marial shook her head and said that maybe he needed a bigger army.

They arrived at the house and the van drove into the basement.

Pat led the way up the stairs into the kitchen.

Marial stopped and looked around and said, "Oh my." She pointed at the microwave and said that it was the same model that was displayed in the Antiquity museum.

She went on to say microwaves were no longer used. They were replaced with molecular activators that heated anything that was put in a space similar in size to the microwave.

She pointed at the stove and commented that gas was not used because cooking had been mostly replaced with the Meal Generator that delivered the desired dinner heated to the ideal temperature. The meal whether meat or vegetable were all mineral based. No plants or animals were killed on Mataia of her time.

She said that the kitchen was no longer a place to prepare meals but a place to pick up the meal of your choice that was delivered by the Meal Generator.

Thomas smiled and said it was time for him to move to the future, but he wondered if he would miss the Steak with blue cheese on it.

Marial smiled and said that meal was one of her favorites and when he came for a visit she would make sure he got to try the totally synthetic version.

She then commented that the Blue Swoshian Spaghetti de Mar they had eaten on Mataia had been prepared by several Meal Generators. She went on to say that she was taking the serving of the one that she had just eaten so she could get the Meal Generator adjusted to match the flavor she had just experienced.

Bram suggested they all call it a day and get to sleep early and then go into work

Marial asked what they did to fall asleep.

Pat replied that she just lay down and closed her eyes.

Marial asked why they didn't use sleep inducers.

Zoe replied she had an idea what a sleep inducer was but if Marial had any problems falling asleep she should just count sheep. She asked Marial whether she had ever used a manual shower.

Marial said that maybe Zoe could give her a quick lesson on how to properly use the bathroom and the bedroom. She was sure that she needed help. She did not know what a shower was but figured that it had to do with cleaning one's body.

Zoe smiled and said that Marial would have to reciprocate when she visited the future.

Chapter 11: A Walk-Through Fold History

The next morning the team was sitting at the table and having a cup of coffee as they waited for Marial to come down. When she cleared the stairs, she shook her head and said that she had counted nine thousand sheep before falling asleep. She said she missed her sleep solution.

Zoe commented that such dependence on a drug was not good and that in this current time it was called being hooked.

Bram suggested that Marial let nature do its job. Then he said that it was time to jog into work.

She thanked Pat for the change of clothes and asked if she could take them back to the future with her.

Pat said they were hers to keep.

Marial smiled and said that once back in the future she would give them back to Pat's statue in the museum.

Pat handed Marial a pair of new running shoes that had a Velcro strap. She had noticed that Marial was wearing shoes that had no laces.

Marial commented that Velcro was still in use in her time.

The team purposely chose a slow jog.

Then Donna launched a Ditty, and the team began to sing.

> Soft but willing. So soft but willing
> Counted sheep but couldn't sleep.
> Brand new shoes are on her feet.
> Counted sheep but couldn't sleep
> Brand new shoes, are on her feet
> Feet, Feet, catch the beat
> Running, Running, Running
> Look at her, Just look at her. Look at her.
> A future heart, and she is smart.
> Brand new shoes, couldn't sleep,
> Pay attention catch the beat.
> Repeat!

As they jogged towards the work center the entire Marine guard contingent joined in.

Bram was pleased to hear Marial join in and chant the ditty and see the smile she had on her face.

He led the team directly to the cafeteria and ordered his breakfast then sat down at the table. Pat guided Marial through the breakfast line and then sat down next to Bram.

Marial asked what the chant was called and asked who had created it.

Castor and Donna raised their hands and said that it was called a ditty. They shared the fact that that Marines were always thinking one up and then jogging to its rhythm. They complemented her for having kept up and said that she had passed the test when she joined in repeating the chant.

Marial said that she planned to write a book about her experience, and she would add the ditty to it.

Bram asked if Marial was willing to get a thorough understanding of the history of the Fold break through.

Marial asked how she would get that breakthrough history.

Bram smiled and said that he would take her on a trip through time but in the comfort of the Fold Viewing Room. He would follow the timeline from when he was first recruited by NASA, through the breakthrough and bring her up to the current time. He looked around and asked that everyone participate. He assured her that she would personally understand the growth that each of them had experienced and the reason for the teams dedication to the technology.

He looked around and added that none of them including himself had ever taken this journey so they would all enjoy accompanying her.

He asked Marcus whether he could calculate the coordinates to specific locations in the past and use his miniature camera bubbles to capture those specific moments in time.

Marcus replied that he could do it, but he would not be able to do it in a smooth seamless manner because the position of the Earth would affect the exact coordinates that he would need to determine.

Bram replied that he would narrate and having a moment between historic locations would work very well.

Marial put her hand on her heart and said that she was experiencing a wonderful dream and wanted to make sure she was not still sleeping.

Pat said that the shoes on her feet were real.

Bram smiled and chanted,

"You have brand new shoes upon on your feet,
You'll get a story that can't be beat."

Donna and Castor repeated the chant three times.

Marial laughed and answered with a chant in reply.

"I have new shoes upon my feet,
Willing, Willing, Oh I'm so enthralled and willing,
To get the story that can't be beat."

Bram said that he was going to lead a tour that would enthrall the group, including himself.

Erica shook her head and said that she had been on the upcoming tour and had directly experienced a great deal of it. It had dramatically changed her life. She said she did not want to miss Bram's version of it.

Bram commented that all of their lives were dramatically changed. He smiled and said that he had changed from a person resenting being personally isolated to a person whose life had become so threatened that he had accepted the FBI and the Marine Corps providing him a small army to protect him. He commented he had traded the isolation in the desert to an isolation from society outside of the Fold community.

Castor agreed but said in the trade Bram had stepped up. He added that Bram had three hundred full time Marines on site and about another one hundred observer Marines that flew the protection bubbles. He said that Bram was now one of the most protected individuals in any world.

Bram suggested they move to the Viewing Room while he and Marcus worked on determining the coordinates.

He ask Pat, Amy, and Erica to work with Linda to invite the team members that were not with them at the moment. He said that those that were located remotely would be able to view the journey later on the video that he and Linda would prepare.

Marcus said that he would link into the supercomputer so he could manipulate the viewing bubbles. He asked Remi to give him control of at least three of the tiny camera bubbles.

Bram Nielson Collection

The tiny Fold bubbles were sent back in time and went down along the street outside of Bram's apartment. The viewers watched as a young and extremely professional looking businesswoman exited a black Mercedes limousine. It was a younger version of Erica walking confidently into the building and up the stairs to the door of the apartment on the fifth floor.

Her knock on the apartment door was answered by Bram, whose appearance looked a little disheveled as if he had been running his hand through his hair.

The smile on Erica's face seemed to be painted on and not at all genuine.

Erica, sitting to the back of the Viewing room laughed and said that she looked like the wicket witch of the East with too much make up on.

The current Bram giving the flash back presentation commented that he had found her a little overwhelming, but she had given him a plane ticket and said that all expenses would be paid. He had been so happy to have the US government showing some interest in his rough theories about the ability to Fold time and space that he had put up with a person he felt was rather pushy.

Erica added that as she looked at her old self it was hard for her to recognize and remember the person of that time.

Bram commented that they had all grown significantly since that time. He said as he looked at how he interacted with Erica at that time, he was surprised that she had given him the airplane ticket to get him to the meeting where he met a team who he felt had little knowledge about his theory.

The next scene on the screen was Bram arriving in Washington. Two men in black suites and dark sunglasses guided him to a black van whisked him away to the Pentagon. They then led him to a meeting room where a group of people were gathered to listen to him describe his theory.

Once Bram was in the room and seated, Jeffery Mikelson introduced himself and then went around the table introducing the "team" that Bram was to join.

Those in the Viewing room listened as Elizabeth Miller introduced herself as a Moral Theorist. The younger Bram of the past stood up and walked to her, shook her hand and the two hugged.

He froze the video and shared with those in the Fold Viewing room that she was a person who he had admired and followed for many years. He said that she was one of the persons whose theories on fairness had inspired him and her presence had impressed him enough that she had made him decide to stay in what he took as a fake meeting.

He re-activated the video and they all watched as he shook hands with her, and she pulled him in for a hug. The little drone captured her whisper saying that, "the team is fake, and it has been set up for you, but the desire of the government for him to pursue his theories was real. Bram had smiled at her and nodded his head.

In the Viewing Room, Elizabeth let out a little groan and commented that the little Fold bubble had too good of a microphone.

Bram laughed and said that her whisper had caused him to hesitate to refuse a role on the team, but that hesitation was meaningless because Jeffery gave him an offer he could not refuse.

He commented that her presence had been what captured his interest on being on the "Team" and made him feel less like he had been shanghaied.

He added that the other people in the room were of top talent, but they didn't seem to know each other and seemed to only know what he had written at a superficial level.

Bram shared that Jeffery was very direct and made him a top salary offer. He was told that he was getting the best possible deal but the choice about joining was not an option.

Bram stopped the presentation and said that they should all take a short break as he organized the next part where he was out in the desert.

Erica commented that the offer that Bram received was forty percent higher than her salary at that time.

A few moments later when Bram saw that everyone was back in their seats and ready, he turned on the screen. The view he was presenting was from high above the desert and looked down past a very large boulder to the building at the center of a large fenced in compound that had razor wire at the top.

A shiny red helicopter glistened as it sat at the center of its landing pad.

The sun rays reflected off the black photovoltaic panels on the building roof that provided most of the power to the site. A ten-foot-wide cleared area outside of the fence went completely around the compound.

Bram guided the small viewing bubble around the area to show the fact that the desert was very dry but there was an abundance of plant and animal life.

He then took them all into the building and his living accommodations. As the apartment interior came into view. Bram commented that the spacious and well-appointed interior had immediately impressed him. He commented that the deck was large enough to practice his Tae Kwon Do and Aikido.

He had added the early morning hikes into the desert to his exercise routine.

That is where he met his mouse confident and counselor who he named Einstein.

Marial interrupted and asked if Einstein City was named after a mouse and not the famous scientist of that same name.

Pat replied that she had run a contest to determine both the name Mataia and the name of the first city. Einstein was Zoe's entry for the cities name.

Next Bram guided the viewing bubble in close to the large boulder and commented that it was the place where he had spent many a morning waiting for the sun to rise and then spent time sharing his thoughts with Einstein.

The screen went dark, and Bram commented that what they were seeing was what greeted him when he arrived at the boulder a few minutes before sunrise.

The folks in the View room could just make out someone arriving to the rock, climbing up, and sitting down.

The sun outlining mountains, out to the right of the boulder, seemed to be cutting the mountains away from the dark of the night sky. The battle of light against the black of night caused the desert to take on a mystical appearance.

Then everyone watching seemed to suck in their breath as the bright line of sunlight slowly unveiled the desert as if it were a bride getting her veil lifted and getting ready to kiss her new husband.

It seemed as if a line of light was slowly advancing toward the boulder and waking all that it touched. Then the line of light reached the boulder and like a mountain climber slowly making his way up the face of a cliff, the sun slowly traveled to the point where it began to illuminate Bram. And then as if by magic a little mouse popped out of a hole in the crack of the boulder and scurried up to sit next to him.

Everyone in the Viewing room heard Bram say, "Hello my good friend, I hope you had a good evening. Here are a few sugary crumbs so that you will be willing to listen to my current theories and questions that you need to help me on."

Then after a lengthy discussion on how he might link the various theories postulated by people much smarter than he, they watched Einstein go back into the hole in the boulder.

The screen then went into a super-fast forward like mode and the boulder scene and the walk out into the desert repeated itself multiple times.

Bram laughed as he watched the scene and commented that he had never seen the desert in such detail so fast and that the only thing he recognized was the red streak made by Amy flying her helicopter because that red streak was pretty much what his experience had been in riding with her.

Amy commented that she loved him too and that he had told her that the helicopter ride was the highlight of his day.

Bram smiled and replied that for the whole time in the desert he never started a workday feeling down because his heartbeat was always at its peak from the ride back with Amy.

The next scene showed he and Elizabeth, Marcus and Mallika walking down the hallway and entering the meeting room.

He stopped the video and explained that he had skipped a year of meetings and that the meeting they were going to witness was a key meeting where the Fold effort changed.

Bram restarted the meeting, and the camera zoomed in on Erica's face.

From her seat in the Viewing Room, she asked who the witch happened to be.

Bram gave a chuckle and replied that he had no clue and that he had heard a rumor that a house had fallen on that person.

Erica shook her head and said that the rumor was not true. She said that her world had been blown up during that meeting when she realized that Bram was not interested in having power or in her role and that instead he recommended that she get promoted to a much better role. It was a moment that had changed her life.

The scene continued and the Bram in the meeting indeed recommended Erica for a better role. He recommended that Elizabeth lead the technical and scientific team.

There was total silence in the Viewing Room.

Bram again zoomed in on Erica's face to show the look of surprise and he turned it to show Jeffrey's face who also had a look of surprise.

In the Viewing Room, Elizabeth commented that it had become clear to her during that meeting that Bram did not need support of any of his team in the technical realm that he was working in. He was quite independent and engaged the rest of the team in philosophical discussions but seldom in the science he was engaged in.

Erica spoke up and said that she at that time had been upset that Jeffrey had given Bram the best apartment. She privately thought that it should have been hers. The person she was at that time figured she deserved it. Instead, she had been assigned a one bedroom on the second floor. Jeffrey told had her that she would only be there part-time and did not need anything more.

She commented that Bram had told them both that unless they quit playing games he was going to let the rest of the world know where he was located, and they should come and pick him up.

She shared that both she and Jeffrey were amazed that Bram had figured out exactly where he was.

Bram commented to the folks in the Viewing Room that he thought that both Jeffrey and Erica had expected him to want a bigger project role.

What he had wanted was to have control of his own time and activities and he did not want to feel like a prisoner being held in captivity. He commented that he had used the location exposure threat to emphasize that he was changing how he was to be managed.

He added that things did change after that meeting.

He said that he had one more scene before leaving the desert. Two figures could barely be seen walking along what must have been a path but in the dark it was not visible.

The taller person climbed up and helped the more petite person get up on the rock. They both sat down and once again the line of sunlight came quickly across the desert and climbed the face of the boulder.

Einstein came up the rock, climbed into Bram's hand, and curled up and then got out. Bram could be seen breaking up a cookie crumb. The camera zoomed in on Amy's face that clearly showed surprise.

Two bubbles could be seen floating between them. Bram moved his hand under the bubble to show that it was floating and stationary in the air. Then he pulled the bubble a short ways away and let go and it returned to its original location. Amy did something similar and then could be heard asking how such thing was possible.

Bram at that time answered that he had no clue but if he figured it out he would let her know.

The Bram sitting on the boulder told Amy to enjoy her breakfast fruit that was in the bubble. He had encapsulated an apple, a bunches of grapes in each clear plastic bubble.

He told her that she was the first to witness the breakthrough he had been working on.

Amy let those in the Viewing Room know that it was at that moment that she knew she was looking at a true genius. But not just any genius, he was one that seemed to care about those around him and look out for them. He was a person who took the greatest breakthrough that could possibly be made as a moment to share with a lowly helicopter pilot. She added that it was Bram that got her a seat on the very next astronaut class.

She said that he had never gotten back to her with the answer as to what made the bubbles float. She ask if he had ever figured that out.

Bram said that he had not yet figured it out.

He stopped the presentation and said that it was close to lunch time, and they would all go to lunch together and then return to finish the tour.

He stood up said that he wanted to say a few words before lunch. He shared that getting Amy into the astronaut class had taken a little maneuvering, but it must have been ordained because Amy introduced him to Pat and Marial was evidence that the introduction had successfully led to a long line of family.

He was pleased that Marial had agreed to listen to her family history.

Marial said that she had a curiosity question. Was the boulder still in the desert?

Bram said as far as he knew it was still there.

All Marial did was to nod and thanked him for the answer.

Bram then gave a brief description of what would transpire in the afternoon and asked if he needed to make any adjustments.

Castor spoke up and said that he wanted to get a Bram's eye view of each of the firefights he had participated in. He wanted those in the Viewing Room to recognize the fact that Bram had not only discovered totally new universes but was a battle tested hero in his own right.

During lunch Marial was very animated as she discussed what she had learned about the Fold discovery and the fact that her current time had no clue about the power of the Fold. It was described in their history, but they had no experience with it and had misinterpreted it as just a part of the mythology associated with Mataian history.

She said that she knew that on her return much of the Mataian history would need rewriting.

After lunch and once back in the Viewing room, Bram went quickly through the meeting with the US President and the demonstration of the Fold during that meeting.

Marial commented that she had never held that formal of a meeting with so many armed guards and apparent pollical aids. She complemented Bram on an outstanding demonstration of the Fold capability. She was impressed with the fact that he had been able to use candy to convince the US President and also amazed that Folding such small objects had used so much energy.

Bram commented that at the beginning he did not yet understand the power required to move an object. At the next location he was taking them to he would demonstrate his cluelessness, and he would recruit two people to rescue him.

He then went to an overhead view of an isolated warehouse in the middle of a forest. He kept the fast forward going and they all watched as the large electrical substation blew up three times.

The bubble entered the warehouse and showed several large blocks of steel. He explained that the explosions of the substations had been associated with the fact that he had tried to Fold the larger blocks. He shared that the power company refused to rebuild the substation after the third explosion. He knew that he needed to determine how much additional power he needed.

He pointed to Mallica and Marcus and gave them the credit for determining the power he would need for the largest block. He had no idea where he could possibly find the amount of power to achieve the Fold of the largest block.

He added that he was so engrossed in getting enough power and continuing his development that he left both Mallica and Marcus stuck behind out in the desert.

He pointed to Erica and gave her credit for searching the area and finding their current site at Dallas. The Fold project took over the entire supply of electricity generated by the Dallas water generators.

He said then made a mistake of having the steel blocks transported by truck versus trying to fold them to the new site. He said he would highlight why that was a mistake later in the presentation.

Bram then explained that he was going to fast forward the bubble views and they would watch the construction of Wheel One and Wheel Two.

Elizabeth spoke up and let Marial know that Wheel One had the name USS Hood and Wheel Two was the USS Rainer and that Pat was the pilot of Wheel One and Amy was the Pilot of Wheel two and she had been the Captain of one ship and Bram the Captain of the Hood.

Marial thanked her for the explanation and shared the fact that those details had been lost in a thousand years of history.

Amy commented that she and Pat had been overwhelmed at being given the opportunity to be pilots of such an advanced craft. They had wondered how Bram had been able to obtain such prize assignments for two raw recruits.

Zoe gave a small laugh and said that we have all learned that Bram's management style is act fast and ask for forgiveness if any objection arises otherwise maintain a rapid forward attack.

Bram nodded and commented that he always selected talented people that he could count on. He said that speed had its advantage but in a moment they would all witness the risk that speed sometimes carried.

The fast forward of the construction of the bubbles was fascinating to Bram. He appreciated the effort that Jose Estrada the construction manager put in to insure everything was constructed with safety and construction integrity in the forefront.

Bram paused the presentation for a moment and said that since Marial was present, he was going to Segway to the scene where he knew Pat was going to be his soul mate. The bubble then took a arial view of the Atlantic ocean and came down to the interior of a very nice restaurant.

The view then took the perspective that Bram would have as two very good-looking women entered.

One was the young Amy; her dark hair framed a calm and serene face. She looked very different in her dark black outfit with a low cleavage than the other times when he had seen her in military garb.

The second woman was Pat. He commented that she had immediately caught his attention as he took in her long curly red hair, freckles, and green eyes.

Bram had the bubble pan the room as all the people followed the two women to his table.

Bram commented that he felt an immediate attraction for Pat. He took note that she was as direct and confident in herself as was Amy. The two were a contrast in looks and in mannerisms but both were stunning in their appearance

They all listened as Amy describe her training routine. She shared that Pat had finished first in the class and she had finished third. He congratulated them on their achievement and said that it qualified each of them to command one of the two, Fold, modules.

Bram paused the presentation and said he was going forward to the very first Fold of the Wheels. He commented that Folds were because of a riot outside the construction hangar that threatened to expose the top-secret Fold program.

Bram then had the viewing bubble looking down at a huge crowd that was demonstrating along the fence line demanding to see what was being built in the large hanger. He said that several years later they would solve the mystery of how the crowd had learned about the Wheels. They would link the leak to a Fold IT specialist who was having an affair with the NASA assistant Director. She would be discovered only after Wheel One had been destroyed by a missile fired by a small attacking group while it was tied down in the Dallas hangar.

Marial spoke up and commented that she had never attended any presentation that feature so many heart stopping scenes.

Bram restarted the video and reoriented everyone again and said that they were now looking at the empty Dallas hanger. He then showed the large screens that had been put in place to be the Wheel Control Center at the Dallas site.

The two, Fold Wheels were shown on the left side of the screen where they were still located in the hangar near Seattle and the screen was blank on the right side that showed the empty Dallas hangar.

Bram's back was visible as he gave Pat the instruction to Fold. Then the view was of Bram's face as the lights blinked and there was a delay of the Wheel One appearing on the right. It was clear that the blood had drained from his face and then the lights blinked again and Wheel One appeared in the Dallas hangar.

The bubble was centered on his white face, as the loud cheering from the hangar made it difficult to hear him informing Elizabeth that there would be a delay of the Fold of Wheel two.

The view changed to Bram walking up to one of the older substation transformers that had overheated but had tripped offline and had saved itself from blowing up. He was heard telling the person with him to get as many blowers as he had available and cool all the older transformers.

Bram stopped the presentation and commented that they had witnessed one of the perils of moving too fast. He had almost lost Pat on that first Fold. They had witnessed a scene that went through his mind every time he was about to make a Fold decision. He added that it was a scene that often went through his mind when he and Pat sat comfortably on their two-person recliner.

He said a prayer every time.

Pat spoke up and said that everyone on the Wheel teams had talked about failure and dying and had been prepared not to make it but had agreed that they were willing to be the first and to take a risk of losing their lives.

Elizabeth added that all of the people on both Wheels had agreed that they would take the chance, "no matter what." She said that it was very personal for her. Bram had made her dream of going to space a reality for a woman old enough to be his grandmother and she would go into negative space anytime he asked her to.

Bram said that he was going to go through much of the rest of the history in fast forward. He said that he would focus on a few highlights of all the attacks that he and those around him had experienced.

He commented that the first scenes of Fishing on the Rushing River was to set the foundation for the series of attack experiences that were to follow.

It caught the scene on the veranda of Amy thanking him for all he had done for her and his wishing her the best in her new romance.

Amy interrupted and said that up until that moment she had been concerned about sharing her feelings for Jose because she was not sure how Bram would react. She pointed out that Bram seemed to know exactly how to make that concern evaporate.

Then the scene changed and seemed to frame Pat with her red hair, light green blouse, trim dark green shorts, knee-high socks, and black booted long legs.

Bram froze the scene and then smiled and commented that it was not the beautiful woman that stood out so obviously that had caught his eye and impressed him, but it was the chest to ground length of the largest fish he had ever seen that had caught his attention and the fact that someone as petite as Pat was able to hold it up off the ground.

He smiled and commented that it was the scene that always flashed through his mind when he saw Pat.

He then reactivated the camera, and they all watched him come down the steps to help Pat carry the fish to the side, kitchen door. There they could all overhear Mike greet them and help put the fish on a wood block table. He congratulated Pat on catching one of the largest fish he had recently seen coming from the Rushing River.

Bram said that was a great fishing trip and one that resolved the direction of several love affairs.

He then said that they were now entering into a series of different attacks and then the aftereffects.

The next scene was of Zoe and Eric jumping over the recreation perimeter fence in their skimpy swimsuits as they were firing their weapons. The camera turned and caught Bram delivering a killing blow to one of the attackers as all four of his bodyguards shot and killed the remaining shooters.

Bram guided the bubble to the Recreation center and zoomed in on the two people that had been shot. He commented that his mind had unconsciously pushed him to action because he had realized that Pat was the next person to be targeted but after the three shooters had been killed the situation caused him to lose track of what he was doing.

He had forgotten why he had attacked the shooter that he had killed.

The bubble then zoomed in on Pat sitting against the back of the recreation center shaking and crying.

Pat spoke up and Bram paused the bubble camera.

She commented that the realization that she was the next target had a huge negative mental effect. She had gone to counseling after that, and it was slowly helping but she was afraid that she was going to lose her role as the pilot of Wheel One. That worry only made it worse.

Bram added that at the time he was confident that she would recover but decided to ask her to go fishing at Rushing river where they had experienced such a great atmosphere the first time.

The next scene was of the area along the Rushing River and the Bed and Breakfast. Then the camera framed Pat in almost the same pose as they had seen her a few moments before. It framed her red hair, light green blouse, trim dark green shorts, knee-high socks and black booted long legs and she was holding a very large fish.

Bram commented that he had convinced her to go fishing in hopes that once again experiencing a quiet time would help her recover.

He then said he would take everyone through a fast version of what happened.

Pat asked that he take their first kiss in slow motion.

This caused everyone in the room to say, "very slow motion."

He took them through going to the cave to avoid the threat of potential attackers.

When time came to go to sleep, the scene showed Bram getting into the top bunk. He slowed the video.

Pat said that this was the first time she had seen what had made her heart, beat feverishly. She said this was a clip that she would put on an endless do loop.

The explosion of the door and being thrown from the bed triggered the fast forward action and the next scene was of Bram seemingly ignoring the risk and rushing out firing his long gun and shooting the attackers.

Elizabeth made the comment that fools rush in while the rest of us run the other way. She added that what Pat had experienced on that fishing trip had made her one of the strongest persons on the Fold team.

Pat spoke up and said that it had nothing to do with fishing but everything to do with her first kiss of the person she had been afraid to approach until the very moment of that attack.

Castor let out a 'Hurrah!" and everyone in the room replied.

Bram then let the following series of attacks all play out at high speed. The noise and scenes of attacks filled the viewing room for fifteen minutes.

Marial was the first to say something. She commented that it was a miracle that she existed. No one on Mataia's history had experienced or knew anything about what her ancestors had lived through. She gave Pat a hug and said that she felt that she was hugging the bravest person in the world.

Zoe spoke up and said that perhaps now Marial could appreciate why a small army was guarding Bram. She then added that the reason Bram had gone to the future was to see if there was any hope of sharing the information that would empower humanity with the ability to visit throughout the universe and throughout time.

Eric then added that learning about the Mataian society a thousand years into the future would make the decision to move permanently to Mataia much more desirable for everyone involved. They would know that they were giving Earth a chance to change but it would be up to them to create the society that embraced the saying, "treat others the way you wish to be treated."

Bram said that he was now going to share views of all the locations on Earth where Melisa had secured Fold vacation homes so that Marial could appreciate Earth's beauty and then on her return she could share this with all those in her time. It would connect them with Earth without taking a chance at exposing Mataia.

He said that Mataian's that were cleared would be able to travel to Mataia's past to visit their own history and from this time take Earth vacations.

Chapter 12: Fold Invisibility

Marial thanked Pat and Bram for their hospitality and told them it had been a wonderful visit and one that had personally warmed her heart but one that would also empower the people of Mataia to grow and to become the people that the two of them had always desired them to be. She suggested they go forward in Time and see if that were true and if not they should return to her time and correct the situation.

She thanked Bram for providing her with a large twelve-person transport vessel and the Fold Transmitter so Mataia could communicate with the Swooshians. She was sure that the video of all the scenic points on Earth would be a huge hit with the Mataians. It would help to lessen the desire of one small group to communicate with the Earth of her time. She was sure that his invite for the Mataians to visit their past and to then be able to visit the Earth of his time would go a long way in reducing the interest of the future Mataians wanting to make contact with the Earth of their time.

She commented that the new coverage of the multiple armed conflicts on Earth would most likely be even more effective at reducing that groups desire to make contact. She shared that Mataia had none of the weapons that were used on Earth.

Bram commented that he had provided three small bubbles programed to return to the current time and ask for any help if it should be needed.

She now knew a tremendous amount more about the history of Mataia and the fact that there was also fierce deadly opposition that he and his team had to overcome to protect the Fold capability. She now understood that Mataia had been established to ensure that the Fold capability would only be used for good.

He commented that he had much work to do to protect not only Mataia but to keep Earth from attaining the Fold technology. He was planning to simulate a fatal flaw of the Fold technology and slowly remove all information of Fold capability from Earth records.

Zoe spoke up and said that the conversation had just let her know that she wanted to take on removing the Fold information from the records on Earth. She smiled, thanked Marial for being a part of giving her what she knew would be a lifelong career.

Marial gave a chuckle and said that seeing Zoe jumping a fence in almost no clothing and firing a weapon at the same time would always be embedded in her mind. She said that she envied both her great body and the fierce protective aura that she had displayed in action.

She added that it comforted her to know Zoe would be erasing the Fold information from the Earth records. She added that she must have been successful because in her time Earth did not have that capability. She wished Zoe a long and enjoyable career.

After a round of hugs, Marial went to the twelve-person vessel and was just about to close the hatch when Chef D'Carluca came rushing to the Fold vessel with a container that he said was a batch of Blue Swoshian Spaghetti de Mar.

He received a hug from Marial who invited him to visit and teach those in the future to learn once again to cook.

Chef D'Carluca said that he would be honored to be given that opportunity.

Marial entered the Fold vehicle, the hatch closed and suddenly the hangar was empty.

The Chef shook his head and said that he needed to get out of his kitchen more often.

Bram thanked him for thinking of providing a very personal touch to Marial's departure. Bram suggested that he set up an online Chef class and get both current students and those in the far future to participate. Then when he was ready to test the capabilities of his students, they would discuss a Fold into the future for him.

Chef D'Carluca sauntered out of the hangar with a huge smile on his face.

Bram commented that the Chef's interaction had catalyzed some of the ideas floating around in his mind. He realized that he could do something similar with the future. He wondered what it would have been like if the actual human Einstein would have had such an opportunity. Then he shook his head and knew that it might have accelerated the destruction of the Earth. He personally would have to be very selective about his interactions with the future. The future Mataia provided an opportunity, but he would need to contain his enthusiasm.

He decided that his first responsibility was to put in the Fold blocks to prevent the future from visiting the past or from going very far into their future.

He and his team would continue to be Fold explorers, historians and developers knowing that sometime in the far future their knowledge would empower the Mataian people of that time.

Knowing that he and Pat had a descent in the far future made him realize that there was an immediate action that he desired to take.

He knew that one of the first things he wanted to do was to formally ask Pat for her hand. She had unasked given it to him, and he knew they would be together until the end of their time, but he felt that he would like to formally let those around him know that he and Pat were true soulmates.

He decided that he would ask her at the Sunday breakfast. He spent a moment inviting folks to the breakfast.

He then thought about holding the wedding at the Rushing River Lodge in what he hoped would be a less exciting wedding than Erica had experienced. He felt that he needed to make sure that there were offspring that would eventually lead to Marial being born.

He gave Pat a hug and said that it was time to go home and get ready for an exciting Sunday breakfast.

She asked what would make it an exciting breakfast. He pointed at Zoe and said that she was cooking, and that the Chef had given her a new recipe for the pancakes.

Pat laughed and said that she would have to stay in the kitchen and see how Zoe made mixing and cooking pancake dough exciting.

They all were leisurely walking back to their house when suddenly several missiles hit and exploded as they hit the laser shield that Bram had put up around their house.

In what seemed an instant the entire compound was on alert and Bram and Pat were pulled into the armored carrier and the entire group was surrounded by Marines armed with a variety of light and heavy armament.

Bram wondered from which time the missiles had come. He looked at Zoe and asked if the one-hundred-year future had been cleared.

Zoe replied that they had brought back a computer that was being used to monitor their original perpetrators home. They had not been able to find who might have had access to that computer. That computer was currently sitting in the same lab table that he had visited on his trip to the past.

Bram commented that once the immediate threat was over, they would need to figure out who in that time frame had access and if they had arranged the missile strike.

The armored truck was too large to drive into the basement entrance, so Bram and Pat were hustled into the basement under full guard and escorted into the saferoom.

Bob and Thomas joined them and shared that whatever just happened it felt like a huge earthquake and all the cupboards in the kitchen had opened and much of what was inside had fallen out. They saw all the Marines and asked Castor what was up.

Castor replied he had no clue other than that the house had been hit by at least four missiles and had survived, so they should thank Bram for having put up and activated his laser protective shield and they should be glad that it had worked as well as it had. He said that they had missed the most beautiful display of sparklers that he had ever witnessed.

Donna shook her head and added that from her position on her butt she thought the world was coming to an end.

Bram went into his office and then put in a quick call to the General and asked him to follow up with his monitoring group to see if they could back track where the missiles had originated.

The General replied that the monitoring team had tracked the incoming but had not been able to intercept the missiles. They were already zooming in toward the source that seemed to be in a remote part of the forest. He said that it was definitely some local group that had somehow been provided with some very sophisticated field missiles.

Bram then called Lacy and asked her to check if any of the people she was following had moved any large sums of money to a new location and if they had, what country was that money moved to. He let her know that he was looking for a sum of money large enough to pay for several field launched missiles with war heads on them. However, the money was probably transferred in a series of small sums in an attempt stay under the radar.

Lacy asked if the request was connected with the earthquake that had just occurred.

Bram let her know that the earthquake was due to four missiles hitting his house.

He let her know that she and Linda were invited to breakfast.

Pat handed him a cup of coffee and asked when he had put up the laser barrier.

He said that he had put it in almost at the same time as the one that he had put around the building in Mataia. The one at the house did not go underground and it was open around all the entrance areas and ended just about head level. He had meant to mention it, but the recent activities had distracted him.

He commented that he wanted to put the barriers up for all the buildings at the compound, but it would need someone to manage getting it into place and then to monitor it. He said that one of the drawbacks was that birds were vulnerable, and he had wanted to see if there was a way to modify the screen. He thought maybe he could make the shield less deadly for slow moving creatures like birds.

Pat said that she would make sure that everyone was aware of the shield.

Zoe said that she would work with the General and Lacy to establish a process to put the shield in place for all buildings. She said that she needed more to do than guard a guy who seemed to guard himself. She said that the shield had just saved two of her partners and they all owed him for having put the shield in place.

Bram thanked her and said he appreciated her stepping up.

Bob and Thomas said that they owed Bram and that he wouldn't have to wash dishes for the rest of the year.

Bram laughed and asked if one year of dish washing was all their lives were worth. He shook his head and said they did not need to do anything extra. They were willing to put themselves in harm's way for him and that meant more to him than their concern to repay him for what had been an almost unconscious action on his part.

What he needed was to keep ahead of the people who were willing to go to such lengths to try to stop him. He said that they were trying to stop knowledge about the world around them and that there was no way for them to do so even if they succeeded in doing him in.

Bram spent the evening sitting on the two-person sofa with Pat at his side. They listened to some classical guitar by Andrés Segovia, and he went through his mind thinking how he would erase Fold information from the records so that it would become non-existent on Earth.

The one step he was sure about was that he would immediately move all Fold work to Mataia. The work at the compound would be some supportive work but the fundamentals and all computer records would be moved to Mataia.

He would need to outfit the Fold building on Mataia with additional super computers and the labs with additional equipment.

Then the hard part of selecting the key personnel who were willing to leave Earth for good would need to get underway.

Bram was up early for Sunday breakfast. He had been pleased to learn that Zuri, Orlando, and Elizabeth were all going to be attending breakfast. This meant that everyone who he had envisioned being present when he proposed to Pat would be there.

He had worked with Erica to obtain a top-quality Ruby in a gold setting, for the engagement ring. She had made the deal, and they had figured out how to use the Fold technology to whisk it from Rio de Janeiro to Dallas.

She had commented that he had made it possible to wait to the last moment and still come through with an engagement ring at the very last moment.

Zoe wasn't sure what was up, but she had been around Bram long enough that she knew that he was going to do something where he wanted everyone close to him present.

Bram had anxiously waited for everyone to finish breakfast. He then put on the love theme from the Godfather.

Everyone stopped and looked his way.

Once he had all of their attention, Bram got down on one knee and asked Pat if she would spend the rest of her life with him.

Pat smiled and said that she would spend every moment possible with him for the rest of her life.

A cheer went up from everyone present as he slipped a large ruby ring on her finger.

Pat held it up for everyone to see.

She said that Bram listened very well and that she had described this ring to him many times. She laughed and said maybe she should have described matching jewelry.

Erica smiled as she handed Pat a jewelry box and said that it was her gift to celebrate the proposal that she felt she was responsible for, since she was the person who had recruited Bram.

She opened it to show everyone a necklace with a dangling ruby and matching emerald earrings.

Orlando stood up and said that he had a composed a quick ditty for them all to chant.

Pat, more beautiful than a flower
Pat the woman with true power.
Has Bram down upon his knees.
Has a sparkler larger than most bumble bees.
What matters more,
She has Bram down on one knees.
Pat, more beautiful than a flower
Has Bram down upon his knees.
Knees, Bees, Flowers
Pat, Bram, knees, the birds, and bees.

Pat thanked Erica for the earrings and then she looked at Orlando and commented that he, as always, had added meaning to her day.

Pat sat down and then began to cry. She had thought of this day but had not been prepared for the way it was all taking place.

Bram thanked everyone for their good wishes and said that they would all be invited to a fishing trip at the Rushing River lodge.

That brought out a series of comments about having an explosively exciting wedding that would either take place in the river or in a cave.

Bram laughed and said that he did not plan to copy Erica and have a wedding in the river but planned to have a leisurely one in the Lodge.

Orlando suggested that he put a laser shield around the cave and have the wedding there.

Ron Mueller

Chapter 13: The Listener

The festive atmosphere of the Morning breakfast persisted throughout the day. Sunday afternoon the entire team gathered in the recreation center were they celebrated Bram's proposal to Pat. Everyone in the Fold community had long recognized Pat's intense love for Bram. Her intense, ingenious, and unrelenting pursuit to save him from the negative Fold realm had captured everyone's veneration. They came to think of Pat as the ultimate and intense problem solver. She had enrolled everyone around her and had gained the admiration of everyone.

They lauded Bram's public humble display and the fact that the ruby engagement ring was what Pat had said that she had always dreamt of.

Pat was surrounded by those admiring her ring, necklace, and earrings.

Bram called Mike at the Rushing River lodge and asked if he was willing to hold a wedding in his lodge.

Mike let out a whoopee, and complemented Bram on catching the prize fish and yes, he would be honored for the wedding to be at the lodge.

Mallica had overheard Bram and asked about the possibility of making it a double wedding.

Pat had just got away from the throng of well-wishers and overheard Mallica. She gave Mallica a hug and said that it would be great to have a double wedding.

Mallica smiled and said that she had planned to share her engagement at breakfast but had decided that she did not want to compete with Bram. She laughed and said she was too afraid to be sent back to the desert where he had imprisoned her for almost a year.

Bram smiled and said that since she had picked his favorite Marine, he would make an exception. He then gave her a hug and congratulated her.

Linda asked what was coming down and when she found out she asked whether three weddings would be too many.

Pat asked who in the world had Linda gotten on his knee.

Linda gave a laugh and said that he was a long-time friend, Rafael Evender, who had stood by her when she was having a hard time dealing with Zuri's wheelchair bound and ignored situation.

She said that they had all met him in the attack. She said that when Bram was walking out one of the peers shooting. Rafael was walking out on the other doing the same thing.

Linda went on to point out that Pat had backed up Bram and her mother had backed up Rafael because she was covering Zuri.

She said that her mother and father were not yet aware of Rafael's proposal. She commented that they loved him, so there would be no issues, but she just had not yet been able to have the right time to share it.

Pat asked if the following Sunday breakfast would be soon enough to make it public. They could get Chef D'Carluca to cater an afternoon banquet at the recreation center afterwards.

She asked if it was OK to also give Mallica a chance to make her engagement public at the same time.

Linda replied that it would not only be OK, but it would be great.

That evening as Pat sat next to Bram on their recliner, she said she sensed that during the afternoon he had gone from being very upbeat to seemingly concerned about something. She asked if it was about his proposal to her.

Bram pulled her to him and gave her a kiss and replied that she was his anchor, and he was making sure she would always be with him to keep him safe.

He shook his head and said that it was the fact that Zoe had returned from the future with a computer, which had been hooked to a tiny camera in the home of the person who had attacked him from the future, was what was bothering him.

Both Zoe and he had assumed that the assistant NASA leader was the one doing the monitoring. He and Zoe had discussed this during the afternoon and had concluded that it seemed unlikely. They had agreed that such an assumption about the future was most likely worse than the old saying about assumptions.

Zoe had been quietly sitting and listening. She held up several devices that she said she had found when they had come up from the recreation center. She made the point that they were new plants, and they were from the future. It confirmed the fact that there was at least one additional perpetrator and maybe more.

Bram commented that he had been successful in sending an empty information bubble and that those in the future were now working off what they had been able to lift from the original bubble that had made it through before. The team needed to make sure they erased all information that might have been copied to another computer and it would most likely be a major undertaking.

Eric commented that they needed to write an application that they could plant in the computer systems of the future that would slowly erase any information about the Fold. He wondered if Linh and Duong might be able to write and install such an App.

Bram said that he had no doubt that they could. He said he felt like calling them immediately. They had been at the rec center during the afternoon.

Zoe said that she had already dialed the number. She put the phone in speaker mode and they all listened as she explained to Linh that they had a major software problem and would like to discuss it with her immediately. She asked if she and Duong could come over.

Linh replied that they were walking over immediately.

Zoe hung up and said that they had done exactly what she had hoped by not asking what was up.

Zoe then made another call and got Remi on the phone and asked him to bring the equipment in the lab table's large drawer over to the house.

Remi simply said, "see you in a sec" and hung up.

Bram shook his head and said that he was putting Zoe in charge of cleansing future and present computer systems of references to Fold. Her goal would be to eliminate all references to Fold that existed on Earth at any time.

Linh and Duong arrived a few minutes later and after entering asked if it was safe to ask questions.

Pat led them into the office. She offered them a choice of any beverage they desired. She said that they were waiting for Remi before explaining the reason for asking them to come over.

Remi's sec was more like five minutes but they all knew that he had most likely rushed from his apartment and gone to the lab and then had turned around and lugged the future computer system and the listening, camera unit back.

A van entered the basement and Remi unloaded the equipment from the future. He commented that he had brought a power supply system so they could activate everything.

Bram thanked him and complemented him on his resourcefulness.

After Bram explained the problem, Remi, Linh, and Duong spent the next half-hour activating the computer and monitoring system. Once it was powered up Remi stepped back and told them it was all theirs.

Bram asked that they check the system to see if a third person might have accessed the computer.

It only took them a few moments to get into the code by tying in the supercomputer to scan the two units. They then verified that there indeed was a third person.

Bram recommended that they get a good night's sleep and then early the next morning they would journey back into the future to repay the person or persons for their attack.

He sent a text message to Marcus, Castor, Donna that said that he would see them early.

The General called and asked what they were doing to make the future mad enough to try to rocket the house a second time. He let them know that the bubble offense team had taken out four incoming drones and then taken out the launch site.

He commented that the future was improving their tactics, but they had not yet grasped the full capability of his offense team.

Bram replied that he appreciated the update, and the rising sun would bring a bright new day.

The General grunted and replied that the sun always rose, and he would see him bright and early at work.

The next morning on the jog into work two large explosions at the perimeter of the site was enough to stop the jogging and Bram and the team made the rest of their journey inside an armored vehicle.

The General and Matt met them as they entered the building and walked with them to the hangar. On the way he commented that the future must be very afraid of what might happen and must have activated everything they could muster to attack and try to kill Bram.

Bram commented that they had the right to be afraid. He and his team were going into that future and would personally put an end to the attacks.

The General asked if there was enough room to send a few extra Marines.

Bram commented that if the Marines didn't mind sitting on the floor he would appreciate having about a dozen of them. He stipulated that Castor and Diane should be in control of the Marines.

The General nodded and said that he would make sure that all his Marines had the latest weaponry. He commented that Bram should make sure that Castor and Diane knew exactly what was expected.

Bram looked over at Castor and Diane and asked if they had yet thought of a good ditty to describe the General's orders.

Pat spoke up and said that she had a ditty for the team.

> Sitting on the Floor.
>> Armed, and ready for a war.
> The Generals dozen plus eight more.
>> All to guard Bram's life once more.
> The future has no clue about the hornets from the past.
>> That bring a burning deadly sting.
> A Sting delivered by the best.
>> No more the future will attack.
> The Generals dozen plus eight more.
>> Armed and ready to go to war.

Bram smiled and commented that Pat was beginning to rival Orlando in her ability to quickly gin up a ditty.

He then asked the General to assign the dozen so they could all make the Fold into the future.

He asked if Remi was alright to standby with Marcus.

He intended to repeat the elimination of the person or persons in the future in the same manner as before. He would stand three feet in front of the person to be Folded. This time the termination coordinates would be his house in the compound.

Marcus commented that he could handle it.

Remi responded that he intended to be there no matter what and the two of them could later bemoan the fact that they were the ones that pulled the final switch to the execution chamber.

Bram asked if he could activate the switch himself.

Linh said that she could quickly put a line in the Fold command that Bram would be able to activate.

Bram asked her to do it.

Marcus thanked Bram. He said that it was a relief.

Bram nodded. He said that it was hard, but he also knew that the cycle had to be broken to prevent the situation from getting worse. He was sure the future would have more deadly weapons than their current time and he had to prevent them from getting used.

He said that he needed Marcus to figure out the coordinate of the individual in the future and enter it into the computer and he would do the rest. He then suggested that Marcus and Remi monitor the screen around the house and verify the execution.

The General agreed and said that his men would be able to handle almost any situation if it came down to a firefight, but it would be much better if the situation could be managed the way Bram planned.

When the dozen Marines arrived, Bram asked everyone to get into the transport vessel so they could Fold into the future. He commented that the first Fold would be into the Computer room that held the monitoring computer. They would get there one day before Zoe and company arrived to remove the computer that was receiving the information from the monitoring cameras and audio from the home of their first attacker

The objective was for Linh and Duong to find out who had access to the computer.

The two had become familiar with the program since it was the same computer that Zoe would remove and bring back with her to Earth in the past. They were able to quickly learn that the person who also had the ability to access the computer was none other than the NASA director.

Bram shook his head. He looked at Zoe and asked who she thought the director would be sharing the information with.

Zoe said she had no clue. She looked at Linh and asked if there was a way for them to tap into the phone system and see who the Director might be calling.

Bram asked that before they searched out the human connection, Linh and Duong should install the application that would seek and erase any mention of the Fold information.

A few moments later Duong said that the app was like a trojan horse app that would slowly get into all computer systems that connected with each other.

Bram then asked that they see who the Director was sharing information with.

Linh commented that they were lucky to be on the inside of what seemed to be a very secure computer firewall. She commented that being inside allowed her to scan the entire personnel call record. She commented that the director seemed to have lately often been calling two numbers.

One was a person in Miami, and one was a person in Seattle. The calls to the person in Seattle corresponded within a day of an attack on the Dallas Fold compound in their time. It appeared that the call to the person in Miami happened a day before the calls to Seattle.

Bram asked if the person in Miami was the one with the money, and the person in Seattle the one who was reaching back into the past to buy the attacks on the compound.

Linh commented that would appear to be a good way to explain the relationship, but she had no way to confirm any money transactions.

Bram said that they would eliminate all three, but he wanted to see if they could determine who the person in Seattle was communicating with in their time.

Linh suggested they get into the computer being used in Seattle.

Bram asked if there was a way to tell how the Fold removal App was working.

Duong replied that it was sixty percent distributed across the computer systems and that in another hour all systems would have the App functioning.

Bram asked the date and times that the last call to Miami and to the Seattle area had been made.

Once he had those times, he said it was time to arrange to listen to each of the calls.

Linh quickly listed those times.

Bram said that they would plant listening devices in all three locations and then listen each time a call was made.

Bram noted that they had been gone for four hours and suggested they Fold back to their time and have lunch brought to the Viewing Room and from there they would monitor the calls and the messages while they ate lunch.

Amy, Pat, Linda, Marcus, Remi, and the General were all in the cafeteria getting ready for lunch when Bram entered and let them know that he would like to take lunch in the Viewing Room so they could listen in to the future as some calls were made in that time.

Bram had arranged to have three screens displaying the feed from the future. The NASA directors office was on the center screen. The screen showing the Miami office stood out about three feet on the right side of the NASA screen and the Seattle connection did the same on the left.

The first discussion was between the NASA director and the Miami connection. The discussion was how hard it was to eliminate their target in the past and that a powerful rocket attack on the home of their target would be the most likely to succeed.

Then a few moments later the Miami connection called the Seattle connection and said the money was deposited in the account and the countermeasure they had agreed on should be executed.

Bram commented they had just listened in to the arrangement for the first attack that they had already experience.

He then said that they were monitoring the Seattle connection to see how the attack had been carried out.

Linh and Duong were monitoring the phone and computer systems in the future, and they spotted a Fold signal leaving the Seattle area and being received in present Seattle at one of the largest missile manufactures in the area.

They said that they had the number of that person, and that person was the person who had the authority to release weapons to specific buyers.

Bram asked if Linh could check that persons financial standing.

A short time later, Linh said that she had been able to determine that this person was sending large sums of money to an offshore account in small amounts that ended up being a quite large sum when all the small sums were added together.

She wondered why this person was still working since he had accumulated at least one hundred million dollars in his offshore account.

Bram commented that it was greed and the fact that it seemed to be a safe activity. The person did not fire the rockets but simply made them available to the radicals that were ever so happy to launch what they thought would be an attack that they would be able to walk away from.

Duong informed them that the App to remove all information about the Fold was now in all computers in the future.

Bram said that the goal now was for all the hardware that had been involved in handling the information get removed from the Future.

Zoe said that she and a few Marines could get that job done in the afternoon and they could then concentrate on slowly cleansing the current time of all Fold information.

Bram nodded and said that they all would then carry on the development of the Fold technology in their facilities on Mataia.

Elimination of the people would not be necessary once they no longer had access to the fold technology.

Chapter 14: Mataia Establishment

The sun on Mataia was just coming over the horizon as Bram sat at his desk. He noted that it had a darker yellow cast and seemed to loom larger in the sky then the sun on Earth. The few clouds in the sky looked very much like those on Earth but seemed lighter and fluffier on this specific day. The gentle waves of the ocean ran along the beach as if they were chasing something down along the shoreline that they could not catch up to. It held Bram's attention as he thought about what his next moves on Earth needed to be.

The actions they had taken to erase the Fold knowledge in Earth's future must have been successful. The people who had perpetrated the attacks had been eliminated and the Earth one hundred years in the future no longer had any information about the Fold process.

The attacks on him and his team in their current time seemed to have ceased but he feared some sort of residual effects that might have already been agreed to but were currently dormant might be activated.

As far as the FBI was concerned, Zoe, Eric, Bob, and Thomas were still providing protection for him. The four in fact were but each now had an additional future role that they were developing.

Zoe and Eric were working together to slowly erase the Fold knowledge from Earth's current internet and computer systems. It was an effort that would take them quite a long time.

They had enrolled Linh and Duong to work with them. Together they had written programs that were imbedded into the internet to seek and erase information that dealt with the Fold process. The trick was that they had to not only handle the internet, but they were checking every computer when it logged into the internet for any reference to Fold. One quirk they ran into was that the word fold often appeared in sewing instructions, cooking classes and origami videos or instructions. They had programed in a content checker to shield their program from such references.

Thomas had decided to study future history to understand Earth's social and economic situation over time. Bram and he had come up with qualitative data guidelines to evaluate text, video, photographs, or audio recordings to evaluate Earth's progress toward becoming a more inclusive and peaceful society.

Thomas commented that he really was into the qualitative research that had him studying the future in-depth by using grounded theory or thematic analysis. He shared that by studying things in their natural settings he was stretching himself to interpret phenomena in terms that the social environment gave meaning to them. He commented that some of the social changes just a few years into the future was making him feel like an old man.

Bob had chosen to study Mataia's future in a similar fashion and then provide Bram with the information of how his current decisions were affecting the future. This was a service that Bram came to rely on so that he could adjust his thinking or modify his actions so that he delivered improvements.

Linda and Lacy had agreed to work together to study the ancient history of Earth and had agreed to staying at least twenty thousand years in the past. This was Bram's attempt at keeping them away from getting involved in what was and wasn't true about the more recent human history from the time of the Bible to the current moment.

Lacy had most of the current antagonists of the Fold program tied up in court and making sure that they had little time to focus on disrupting the Fold program. She said that her participation with Linda would not affect her ability to continue her Fold offense against their more aggressive distractors.

The opposing party won the Presidential Election and got control of the Senate. The oversight committee was disbanded as part of the reorganizing of the various committees.

Bram was pleased with the change and let the team know that it was time to accelerate making the Fold effort invisible.

Senator Olivia Newton contacted Bram and asked if there was a role she could play in the Fold organization. She shared that it seemed that the Fold organization was fading from the political scene, and no one had come forward for more money to continue its funding. She asked directly if Bram was working to make the information disappear from the record.

Bram inquired if the Senator was willing to leave her current residence and move to Dalles, Oregon. He let her know that if she joined the Fold effort she would be a good person to help set up a governmental based Fold organization. He wanted it kept simple and said that she would have great insight on the workings of the business of governing.

The Senator agreed that it was an opportune time for her since she had not run for re-election and was currently looking for a new career. Bram let her know that she had a great role to play that he would share with her if she could visit him in Dalles. Once she understood the role he hoped that she would be so excited that she would immediately accept.

Her response was that she had no doubt that she would be surprised and would most likely be very excited about going on a new adventure, but she insisted that he address her as Olivia and drop the Senator from their discussion. She verified that she could immediately fly out and they could discuss the opportunity in person.

Bram said that he was looking forward to meeting with her and asked her to contact Linda with her travel information.

In a conversation between them, Jeffrey asked to be included when it came time to pull the plug and disappear. Bram asked why Jeffrey thought the Fold effort would disappear. Jeffrey commented that his IT staff had let him know that he needed to ask for a new set of Fold information because theirs had been somehow erased. He figured that Bram had begun to purge Fold information.

Bram assured Jeffrey that he and his family were all welcome to continue to be included in the Fold family.

Jeffrey thanked him and then said that when the oversight committee had been disbanded, Charles Ford, the science advisor, had requested to get more involved in the Fold effort.

Bram asked Jeffrey to describe how Charles could contribute to the Fold effort. He personally had a positive feeling about Charles, but he wanted to get another perspective.

The discussion with Jeffrey got him to engage Erica. He asked her to vet all the potential persons that might be asked to move to Mataia.

Erica reacted in a very positive way. She made the comment that she had found the very best person to discover the Fold process, and she would make sure that those going to Mataia were those people that like herself had become true believers in treating others as they wished to be treated.

Bram thanked her and asked her how married life was working out.

Erica smiled and said that she and Gerry were no different than he and Pat and they were looking forward to his wedding at the Rushing River. She hoped that the wedding would be a little less exciting than hers had been. She said that she and Gerry were still recovering from getting wed by a crazy practicing layman in the middle of a freezing river.

Bram laughed and said it was the only way he could think of getting her, Gerry, and everyone else out of the ice-cold river and into a warm place to recover. He said it was one of the coolest weddings he had presided over. He agreed that he was also hoping that his wedding would be less exciting and held in the warm interior of the Inn.

When Bram asked Marcus about the move to Mataia, the reply had been that he was looking forward to the move, but he wanted to make sure that the school system there was set up before making the move.

His comment cause Bram to think about two people that he wanted involved in such an effort. The two people were Elizabeth and Melisa.

He was certain that Elizabeth would organize a great education system.

He wanted Melisa to continue to organize the activities that had brought the Fold community together. He also wanted to continue to maintain the Fold vacation system on Earth that she had developed and to set up a similar one on Mataia that would allow for well managed vacations to be available on what he considered their new home planet.

Amy and Pat had followed through on preparing every building on Mataia and on Earth for the laser shield that Bram had developed.

Bram had continued the development of the laser shield to the point that he had created a laser shielded vehicle. This represented a major breakthrough because it meant that he was now able to shield the Fold transports and any Marine vehicle.

Pat, Linda, Mallica, and Lacy were all spending a great deal of time arranging the wedding event.

Bram stayed away from the specific details that they were getting into, but he had a few things of his own that he was going to arrange. He called Mike and Mary and asked if he could come up and discuss making the four weddings as safe as possible.

Mike commented that his new doors at the cave were doubled armored with half inch steel plates and ready for any attack by Bram's well-wishers.

Bram was planning in putting a safety shield around the Inn and perhaps at the entrance of the cave. He was also going to try out his mobile shield by shielding the three vans that were taking him to the Inn. This would provide a field test of his mobile laser shield.

He installed the laser shield on each of the vans and let Castor and Linda know about them and asked them to warn the rest of the Marines to wait on his all-clear signal before exiting their vans.

He left the following morning with his small army and went up to the Inn.

Mike and Mary met them in the parking lot. They commented that they had several current guests, but they had made all the arrangements for the upcoming weddings. They had been in contact with the neighboring Inn's and had coordinated with them. Mary smiled and shared that the fact that their Inn was drawing so much business to the area had their neighboring Inn's asking how much money they were spending on advertising the business.

Bram said that for as long as he was working on his projects in the Dallas area, they had his business as often as he could take the time off.

Mike added, "and be able to afford to pay for all the repairs the place went through at each of his stays." He commented that the steel plates on both sides of the cave door had cost close to a thousand dollars.

Bram nodded and said that protecting the cave and the Inn was what he had come up to discuss. He picked up three large stones. He then asked Castor to get everyone to stand away from the three vans.

Once they were clear Bram activated the laser shield.

He told Mike and Mary that he had just invented a way to provide protection to an object. He then threw one of the large stones at the first van. A small multicolored flash appeared as the stone reached the van. He threw the next two stones at each of the other vans. Each time there was a multicolored flash.

Mike commented that Bram had just shown him a protective screen like he had seen in the movies only this was the real thing. Mary commented that she liked the flash of color.

Bram then threw a small pebble at the first van, and it produced a small sparkle. He said that the screens were very effective, but they were also very dangerous. Ones like that on the vans were dangerous to any one unknowingly reaching for the door handle.

Bram paused to shut down the screens and called out that the screens were deactivated.

Bram then said that he wanted to put the screen around the Inn and activate it during the weddings.

After the weddings, he would elevate the screen so it was held above the first floor and could be dropped into place if there was a serious attack.

Mike and Mary both commented that after the last wedding excitement they would welcome the protective screen. Mike added that he did not think the cave needed it. He was getting use to building ever stronger doors.

Bram said that he would make sure that the Inn's protective laser screen had very visible markings to keep everyone away from it.

Mike asked if Bram was expecting an attack.

Bram replied that he had been attacked several times since the wedding in the river and that this time he was trying to stay ahead of his attackers.

Mike laughed and said that the last wedding indeed had a chilling touch to it in more ways than one. He was OK with the plan to provide the Laser shield, but he wanted to make sure that there was no way that a guest could accidently walk into the shield from either side. He suggested that Bram erect two chain link fences about two feet apart that would go all the way around the periphery of the lodge and that the shield be between the fences. In that way the shield could stay in place for the entire time that the wedding and reception was going on. Afterward, the shield could be turned off and the fence removed.

Bram thanked him for suggesting the fence and said that he would send a crew out to put it up and asked that Mike let them know where he wanted the two fences.

Once they got back underway on the return trip to the Fold site, Donna and Castor began to chant a ditty they had come up with. They had their radio connection with the other two vans and instantly everyone was singing the ditty.

Got to see a laser show.
Bram threw rocks and made them glow.
We didn't know it could be so.
Sparklers, Sparklers, what a show.
Those coming at us just don't know.
It is, it is, it is so.
Shoot, shoot, shoot at us and see the show.
Shoot at us and get to know.
That laser screens are on the go.
If we shoot back, there is a sting.
The deadly part of a laser show.

Bram chuckled and said that he was surrounded by raggers that loved to chant.

Bram Nielson Collection

Bram enjoyed the camaraderie of everyone in the three vans.

They were driving along the two-lane highway on their way back to the compound, when a semi coming from the opposite direction moved from its lane in a maneuver intended sideswipe them and push the vans down into the steep almost cliff like ravine at the side of the highway.

There was a continuous brilliant streaking flash as the side of the truck making the side swipe attempt was vaporized. The three vans only experienced a slight sideward pressure as if they were being hit by a strong wind.

The truck lost almost two feet of its tractor and trailer. It slid down the highway on its side for more than one hundred feet and looked like a relic out of the junk yard. It came to a stop with the vaporized side down on the surface of the highway.

Bram quickly turned off the protection shield and yelled that it was safe to get out.

The Marines ran out and surrounded the truck and then pulled the driver from the cab. The driver had lost most of his left arm. It was not bleeding but cleanly cauterized and looked like it had been removed by an skilled surgeon. It was clear that the driver was in a great deal of pain and one of the Marines administered some pain killer. They put the driver in the back of the third van and covered him with a blanket.

Castor asked that three Marines stay at the accident scene until a Marine back up unit could be sent out to retrieve the Semi. He said that they were going to continue back to the compound.

He left orders that the semi was to be kept in the possession of the Marine corps.

When they got back into the van, Castor put in a call to have a team come out and get the semi back to the compound. He made the point that the semi was the property of the Marine corps.

Bram reactivated the laser protective screens of the three vans and then listened to Donna once again lead the ditty.

The attack had provided the best field test of his portable protective screen that he could have thought off. It had prevented a death ride for all of them down the steep mountain side ravine.

Castor reaffirmed his thoughts when he said that the screen had worked so well that the impact of the semi felt more like being hit by a stiff gust of wind from the side. He said that he was still seeing sparklers that the screen made from the two feet of the semi that it had vaporized. He said that it was an unbelievable experience and one that would be with him for a long time to come.

Bram nodded and said that before the truck had tried to side swipe them, he had no idea exactly how the protective screen would act but it essentially absorbed the energy generated by the impact and turned it into a continuous stream of material being randomly scattered in the negative Fold environment.

He complemented Castor on making sure that the semi got brought back to the compound. He asked that the semi be put in the hangar vaporized side up so that it would be easier to examine.

General Tilman was standing in the hangar when the three vans drove in. He saluted the Marines getting out of the van's and congratulated them on a job well done.

Several Marine EMT's took the driver of the semi and said that they were taking him to the hospital where he would be kept under guard. They commented that they had never seen a severed arm in quiet the condition as the drivers left arm. It was the cleanest amputation that they had ever witnessed

The General requested a demonstration of the new protective screen capability that Bram had developed for vehicles.

Bram nodded and commented that his newly developed mobile protective shield had gotten tested before he had been ready, but the result was all that he could have hoped for.

He asked everyone to step away from the three vans.

One of the marines brought him three stones from outside of the hangar.

Bram threw a stone at each of the vans and three colored flashes occurred.

The General asked if it was the same technology that was being used at the house.

Bram said that it was but with the difference being in how the protective envelope traveled with each van. Bram went over to the vans but before reaching out to the van he threw a nickel at it and then picked the nickel up and opened the back of the van to show a small box at the corner of the van. He said that it was the coordinate locator that was monitored by the bubbles that generated the laser beam.

One of the break throughs was the greatly reduced size of the bubbles as well as the increase in laser power. He commented that each vehicle took four bubbles to maintain the screen. He used a laser pointer to point to approximately where the bubbles were at the moment. He then opened his computer and commented that the energy used when the shield protected them from the semi had drained the batteries on the bubbles to less than twenty percent. So, the semi attack had actually been a close call.

General Tilman shook his head and said that the military world would love to have the Fold technology.

Bram nodded and said that was one of the things he was really trying to prevent. He felt that the immense power that the Fold capability represented was like the atom and the hydrogen bomb being used together.

The General agreed and said that it was not ready to handle such power.

Chapter 15: Wedding Shield

Bram and Pat began to spend at least fifty percent of their time on Mataia. She commented that it really helped her to get their home outfitted so it would be in live in condition. She added that the walks on the beach were also quite enjoyable.

The laser barrier had influenced who resided in each house on Mataia. For the first time Pat and Bram were alone together in their own home. It was just the two of them.

The houses on each side and the one directly in back was where their four FBI protectors resided. Mallica had one of the back homes and Erica had the other behind them. The three houses across the street had Linda, Elizbeth, and Lacy living in them.

This put Bram and her in the center of all the homes.

She said that each of their friends had chosen the homes specifically to surround him to ensure they were ready to help if necessary.

Bram replied that he hoped Mataia would be a sanctuary for all of them and that the attacks on Earth would cease now that they had eliminated the future and would soon neutralize Earth in their current time.

She asked if he were ready to get a brief tour of the honeymoon location that she had selected. She took him to a mountain valley that was v shaped with the ocean at the wide part of the V and high mountains on each side and a water stream that meandered leisurely down its center. There were no trees on Mataia, but the blend of grasses and tiny plant like flowers created a stunning view. She said that each day for their weeklong honeymoon, she would like to walk the beach in the early morning and then hike around the valley during the day.

Then at in the evening they would return to their home and enjoy the evening by having dinner that was prepared by Chef D'Carluca and delivered via their Fold technology. She said that all they had to do was to agree on the dinner menu because the Chef had already agreed to do it as his wedding gift.

Bram said that it sounded like a very romantic honeymoon that he was eagerly looking forward to. He commented that being able to return each evening to their comfortable home and have a Chef prepare their meal put a very positive spin on the entire affair.

Pat said that it really did and shared that Linda, Lacy and Mallica were doing something similar, and they all had agreed that on their last honeymoon day they would all dine together at the Mataia Work Center Dining Hall and the rest of their friends would join them. It would be a casual affair that everyone could enjoy.

It would be the first trip out for Chef D'Carluca, and he planned to use the facility on Mataia and prepare a special that he was in the process of inventing. He said that he was thinking of calling it Mataian Delight.

Pat said that she had convince him to let the team have a contest to name the main course after they had all tried it and a prize would be awarded to the winner and to the Chef who had prepared it.

Bram asked how their honeymoon locations would be named.

Pat replied that the honeymooners would get to name them. There would be no prizes, but they would have the joy of having named a specific location on Mataia. Pat added that she and Amy had decided that later the honeymooners would also have the privilege of deciding on the terra forming that would take place in their honeymoon locations.

The day before the wedding Bram took inventory of the various projects and the situation each was in. It became clear that everyone had been working feverishly to get as much done as possible before the wedding.

Each of the projects were hitting their goals with the exception of Lacy's offense team.

Lacy made the point that battling individuals that seemed to command billions of dollars was a monumental task. She called them spoiled fish because they just plain smelled rotten. What frustrated her was that they were very proficient at providing bribes that repeatedly got them off with such a low penalty that it did not matter to them. She had won almost every case but had lost the battle because the penalties were insignificant. She made the comment that having kept them in court as long as she had was the only significant achievement of that effort.

Bram replied that if Lacy traced any attack back to one of her spoiled fish he would be sending that fish as sparklers into the negative realm.

Lacy smiled and commented that he had grown very sharp teeth in dealing with the future.

Bram nodded and replied that he had decided to reduce the risk that those around him faced because of such thoughtless individuals.

Mike called him to let him know that the two fences around the Inn had been erected and was ready for use. Mike said he liked the fact that it had only one entrance gate area that had locks for both the interior and exterior fences.

He said that he and Mary were celebrating their living in a fenced in neighborhood.

Bram replied that he was happy to hear that they approved of the fence. He let Mike know that he would be up to test the laser shield. When he got off the phone, he thought of using the Fold transport but decided against it. He trusted the two to keep such a secret, but it was an exposure that he felt was not warranted. He asked Linda to arrange for a trip up.

Linda said that it would be no problem but suggested that he not create another piece of scrap the size of a semi because there was not much room left in the hangar.

Bram replied that if he did create another piece of scrap he would need to recycle Wheel Two to make room.

Linda frowned and said she was just kidding and that Wheel Two rated to at least be a historic museum piece.

The next day he and Pat both got into the van.

Zoe commented that she was glad that it was her and Eric's turn to guard him during the day. She said that she wanted to see the compound that had been created for the wedding event. And in case of another attack on the vans she wanted to see the shields in action.

She asked when he was going to create a personal laser shield.

Bram smiled and said that he was not sure if he were capable of programing the lasers to create a dynamic shield that moved exactly like the human in it and if it could react fast enough for unanticipated movements.

He ask if Zoe wanted to be the model for the creation of such a program. If she was the model he would call their nose tweaking stand off a draw.

Zoe replied that he was being a little extreme for just a little nose tweaking and that he should use a pig to create the model.

Bram replied that the punishment should fit the crime and using an innocent pig would be inhumane.

The arrival at the lodge brought tit for tat to a close.

Bram had modified the laser shield for the vans so when a door or window was opened, the shield would shut down.

Bram asked Castor to keep all the Marines with the vans and that he lock and guard the outer gate and that Donna lock and guard the inner gate.

Bram led everyone else to the inside of the compound.

He greeted Mike and Mary and thanked them for being willing to go to this extreme.

Pat looked up at the smoking chimney. It was the first time that she had seen it in use. She asked if Mike had an experiment underway.

He smiled and said he wondered if the air inside the shield was able to enter and leave through the shield.

Bram looked at the amount of smoke and said that he had not thought about smoke, but he had been trying to figure out how to keep small animals and birds from getting fried.

He said that Mike's experiment might help him in solving that problem.

He then asked Donna to lock the inner gate and Castor to lock the outer gate and that they both take one step back.

He then energized the laser shield. The red light went on. It was meant to show that the shield was active. It was accompanied by three loud blares.

He and everyone else turned to look at the smoke rising from the chimney.

Pat commented that there seemed to be a few random sparks but most of the smoke made it through the screen.

Mike asked if the fact that some smoke particles interacted with the screen if there might be dust or other things in the air that might be reacting with the screen.

Bram replied that the experiment had given him new insight to the laser screen's interaction with the environment that it was in.

He picked up a stone and threw it up in the air. The stone hit the screen and was vaporized. He asked Donna to do the same along the wall.

He commented that he would have to set up a statistical experiment to learn more about the shields properties.

Castor said he wanted to throw some rocks too.

Bram chuckled and said that all the Marines were welcome to go around the screen and throw stones at the shield. He figured that it was an easy way to test that the shield was complete.

He asked that they check that the red warning lights on the corners were also activated.

Castor let out a "Hurrah" and gave the order to throw rocks.

Bram asked if Mike and Mary minded if they all had a picnic lunch on the veranda. He said that the two of them could try out Chef D'Carluca's version of the Vietnamese sandwich, bánh mì, that had ingredients similar to that of a submarine like sandwich.

Pat explained that the ones they had brought with them was made with the Chef's own crusty bread rolls smeared with pate and mayo, Asian ham as the main protein, pickled vegetables, green onion, cilantro, some fresh chilies as additional garnish. The seasoning was packed separately and was to be drizzled on with a spoon just before eating the sandwich.

Mary said that a picnic sounded great.

Bram deactivated the shield and asked everyone get on the porch.

Castor had the food coolers carried to the porch.

Bram then had Castor lock the outer gate from the inside and do the same with the inner gate.

He then reactivated the screen.

Castor assigned several of the Marines to bring chairs out to the porch and one per cooler to hand out the bánh mì. He made it clear to start with Mary and Mike and then Pat and Bram.

Pat shared that the Chef had packed extra sandwiches because he said that Marines were always extra hungry.

Castor let out a quiet "Hurrah" and said that his first bite of the bánh mì had convinced him that he would have at least two.

Mike said that he would need to learn how to make the sandwich. He would see if the Chef would teach him when he was up for the wedding.

Bram suggested that he get the lessons directly from the Chef who had started making teaching videos that he featured online. He would ask the chef to create a video on how to make his bánh mì. He added that he knew that the Chef had used only fresh ingredients for his bánh mì creation.

The porch scene went quiet as everyone enjoyed their lunch.

When it was clear to Bram that the picnic was over he asked how many sandwiches were left.

Castor looked into the coolers and retrieved six sandwiches.

Pat asked Mary if she would like to have the six.

Mary said that she and Mike would love to have them. They would enjoy them in the next few days.

Mike commented that the sandwiches might be gone sooner than a few days.

Bram then deactivated the shield and green lights came on over the fence gate and at the corners of the fence. He then asked Castor to open each of the gates.

When Castor opened the first gate a physical arm was pulled up as the gate opened and then it fell away from the gate and swung through the space between the fences.

Castor said that he loved that feature, but he still threw a nickel through the gate area before stepping through.

He looked at Bram and said he had learned that trick from a crazy smart scientist.

Bram smiled and replied that it was always smart to be safe versus sorry especially when sorry was to be scattered randomly into negative space.

Mary and Mike waved from the porch and yelled that they would see them all in a week.

On his return he asked Linda to set up a meeting with General Tilman and she should include Castor and Donna in the meeting.

Bram let Linda know that he wanted to find out if the General planned to have a contingent of Marines attend the wedding.

An hour before the end of the workday, Linda escorted the four in.

Bram greeted the General, Matt his aide, Castor, and Donna who followed them in. He let them know that he wanted to understand how his Marine friends were going to protect him and how many would attend the wedding.

He asked Castor and Donna to update the General and Matt about the laser shield. He listened as each of them shared a feature of the enclosure and the invisible laser shield.

He then asked the General what his plans were.

The General said that he was planning on deploying one hundred of his Marines to the wedding.

They would set up camp across the river, but they would be on duty around the lodge twenty-four seven. He also planned to have his attack bubbles on line twenty-four seven.

Bram said that sounded like a good deployment strategy. He then said that he would make sure that all the Marines enjoyed the dinner that would be served at the wedding reception. And just before the wedding they should all gather on the inside of the laser shield where Donna and Castor would manage them.

He asked Castor and Donna to stay a moment at the end of the meeting.

He took out the control for the shield. It looked like a simplified television controller. It was labeled lodge shield. Both buttons were covered. The activate button had a special release cover that needed to be pressed twice to allow it to open. Once the activate button was pressed the cover closed. The cover for the deactivate button could then be flipped open and the deactivate button was available.

Bram showed them a series of similar controllers and said that they would eventually be given to each homeowner, but they had one more feature that during the day that automatically lifted the protective shield up seven feet off the ground to prevent anyone from accidentally walking into the shield.

Castor asked if the two of them could accidentally activate the shield at the lodge.

Bram said that the question was a good one. He said that they would need to be within twenty feet of the fence to be able to activate the shield.

Donna said that made sleeping at night possible. She was deathly afraid of the laser shield and what responsibility of its control implied.

Bram nodded and said he agreed and that he, Remi, and Marcus had worked hard to come up with a way to minimize the risk of mistakes being made by anyone who had access to the controllers. In fact, the risk of someone making a mistake had made them question the activation of the shields for the community.

He said that, currently on Earth, only the shields for his house, for his office, the Viewing Room and now the Rushing River lodge were ever to be activated. Currently he controlled all of them, but he was passing the control of the Rushing river lodge to the two of them. He said that if they accepted he would inform the General.

Castor held the controller up and said that Bram should tell the General that the two them would handle it and say that "they had it."

Bram smiled and said, "hurrah."

Both Castor and Donna replied with a "Oorah" and saluted.

Bram invited them to dinner at this house and suggested they all get a good walk home to help get ready for a dinner that Zoe and Eric were preparing.

Bob and Thomas, who had been silent for the entire time asked if the shield was deactivated so they could safely get out of the building.

Bram nodded and led the way out.

Ron Mueller

Chapter 16: Until Death Do Us Part

Bram had declared the Friday before the wedding a holiday for everyone involved in the wedding party.

Pat had asked all of the wedding party to dinner and had asked Chef D'Carluca to cater the meal but four weddings at once meant that the dinner became quite large and after some discussion, she agreed to have the Stetson family cater the dinner and let the Chef focus on the wedding preparation at the Rushing River Lodge.

The dinner gathering was moved to the recreation center and the Stetsons agreed to cater it.

At dinner Pat asked each of the members involved in the wedding to introduce who they had selected to be part of the Wedding.

Linda said that she had asked Linh and Duong to be the brides Maid and Best man. She shared that Duong had agreed to step in to be best man because Rafael's best friend had spent six months in jail for having gotten into a bar fight and did not get cleared by the FBI because he was currently engaged in a civil trial. She thanked Duong for being willing to stand in.

Pat said she was sorry to hear about the problem with the friend, but she agreed that Duong was a great stand in.

Lacy said that she had asked LeAnn a long-time friend to be her bridesmaid and had her stand up and say a few words.

Raymond stood up and said that his long-time friend Navy Lieutenant Lee Upton would his best man. He had Lee stand up and say a few words.

Mallica said that she had asked Donna to be the brides Maid and Orlando had asked Castor to be the best man.

Donna and Raymond both stood up, bowed, and then sang out a ditty.

Marines are best at everything
Love their weapons, Love to sing
  Love almost everything
  We are brothers, sisters, we are friends
  Now were starting a new trend,
  Guarding weddings, Guarding Weddings
  A new thing, A very new thing
  But Marines are the best at everything

Bram and Pat both stood and chanted the ditty and waved to everyone to stand and do the same.

Orlando reminded everyone that all the Marines that would be present during the wedding would be in their dress uniform. Their weapons would be at the ready and within reach, but the intent was to compliment the event and not distract from it.

Bram then let them know that Amy would be the Bridesmaid and that he had asked Marcus to be his best man and Remi to be a second.

They had all agreed that Marcus's two kids would be ring bearers for all of them.

Pat added that Zuri would be a bridesmaid to all, and she would walk in with the flower girl.

She added that the color for the brides maids dresses was a dark forest green. The groomsmen would all wear matching dark green tuxedo's with light green hankies. She added that everyone would have a white corsage or bouquet.

She then added that Elizabeth and her current heart throb, Dr Wilkins, Rita, Ted, Marial, and Cedric had all agreed to their roles as mother and father to them all.

Zoe asked Bram if he had put up the laser barrier around the lodge because of premonition.

Bram replied that it had been a premonition but now felt that it was more of a certainty that an attack would occur. He said that the semi-truck attempt at running the vans off the highway was a clear indication that someone was once again providing funding and arms to the local extremists.

The dinner ended with everyone enjoying some dancing and using the recreation center facilities.

Very early on Friday morning a large contingent of Marines escorted the wedding party to the lodge. They would spend Saturday morning transporting a large number of the Fold community to the lodges in the area.

Melisa set up the Fold Recreation center so that the rest of the community would be able to attend remotely.

Bram had thanked her for volunteering to set up the remote viewing. He had also arranged that the wedding reception dinner would be served there as well.

General Tilman had arranged for the Marines to provide additional fire power to set up camp during Friday and then take up positions inside the Fold compound. The contingent protecting the wedding would be assigned around the Rushing River lodge periphery.

Bram requested that the Marines all gather inside the laser shield during the wedding and observe the ceremony via several large screens set up on the veranda. They would then be served the same meal as those inside the lodge.

The order for getting meals had been randomly assigned and the Marines were included in that random scheme. There would be three serving tables to ensure the meals were rapidly made available.

He thanked the General for ensuring that the Marine band was part of the one hundred and that group would get special treatment so that they could enjoy the food and then play the background music and then get everyone to dance.

Bram reminded everyone that the wedding event and reception was going to be a continuous process.

Saturday morning after a light breakfast, the wedding party practiced for the wedding ceremony. The Fold Marine Chaplin guided them all through the ceremony. It was to be a nondenominational ceremony.

The processional was from the side entrance to the dining hall. Elizabeth was the officiant and had a short welcome to everyone present or watching. She would then introduce each couple that was getting married.

She then planned to address all four couples and give them the same message of their marital responsibilities.

There would be no readings. It would flow straight to exchanging vows. The four couples had agreed on one vow that they would all say together.

"I am your soul mate and will support you for our lifetime. I will treat you as I wish to be treated. We will have each other's back. The simple gold band that I place on your finger symbolizes the circle of life that we will share."

Then the Chaplain would say a simple prayer and wish them prosperity and a continually growing bond.

The recessional would be a short walk the length of the lodges gathering room and then each couple and wedding party would go to their table where their meals would be served.

Then the food serving lines would be activated and everyone would help themselves to the same meal that the wedding party was enjoying.

Bram commented that he liked the simplicity of the ceremony.

Mary and Mike commented that they liked the fact that Chef D'Carluca was the one that had prepared the enormous amount of food that would be served, and that Stetson Catering was providing the personnel to serve the food.

After the practice, Pat said they had a short time before the actual ceremony began and they should all take a break and then get dressed.

Orlando commented that Castor was getting very proficient at leading the Marines assigned to the wedding protection detail.

He had gotten them all into the compound early and had put the laser shield up. He led the way out to the veranda where General Tilman was welcoming the Marines to the wedding. The General threw a nickel at the screen where it flashed out of existence. He commented that they were all safe and under the guard of one Bram Nielson who on this day would formally wed his soul mate that all of them knew as Pat. He smiled and said that Pat had become as good as "Lieutenant" Orlando Gutieres at coming up with ditties. He held up a piece of paper and said he had one that she had written for her wedding day.

He handed the ditty to Orlando and asked him to lead the troops through it several times.

Orlando stepped forward and like an Orchestra leader led the Marines through the ditty. They were loud enough that everyone at the wedding not only heard it but joined in on chanting it.

> It's Bram's wedding on this day.
>> Hey, Hey, It's his wedding, let out a loud hurray.
> Won't let threats get in the way.
>> Plans to marry a girl named Pat
> She's the girl that's got his back.
>> We ask who out there stands in his way.
> "Lieutenant" Orlando Gutieres says.
>> It's his marriage day today.
>> He stands at ready, to pass the test.
> Linda and now more than her best friend
> Rafael will wed as well along with the rest.
>> Those objecting are no fun, they better run
> For Bram has planted a surprise.
>> And there will be no compromise.
> Cause General Tilman wants some fun.
>> No compromise, but a surprise.
> Run, Run, Run, Cause the General wants his fun.

Bram gave Pat a hug and said that he really liked her ditty.

The Chaplin called the wedding to order and the Marine band played the bridal chorus."

The flower girl and the ring bearer led the way. The rings were handed to the Chaplin, so he could give them to each couple during the ceremony. All the rings were the same plain gold band but made to fit the fingers of each couple.

The four brides were escorted in by four Marines in their dress uniform and led to the altar that had been set up at the end of the large common area.

The four grooms all had broad smiles on their faces and took the hands of their brides when the Marines lifted it to them.

The Chaplin wed each couple and had just uttered the words asking if there was anyone that objected to the marriages when four successive explosions rock the Inn and literally knocked everyone off their feet.

The General could be heard giving orders to seize the perpetrators of the attack.

He then turned to Bram and asked if there was a way to let his Marines out.

Bram shook his head and asked the Chaplin to finish the wedding and that the attack had been by those who objected to the wedding, but they did not count.

The Chaplin smiled and declared the four as husbands and wives and they should kiss to seal the deal.

After a long kiss, Bram turned to the guests and said that it was time to eat, dance and party.

He walked over to General Tilden and asked if they were going to have some live attackers to question and find out where they were getting their weapons.

The General said that he had eyes on their prize. He had instructed his Fold bubble offense team to follow each truck that had served as the drone launch pads and he had three helicopters following behind but staying out of sight.

He planned to bring all the people in the trucks to the Fold compound and interrogate them. He figured they were the triggers that had launched the very sophisticated drones, but he wanted the person or persons above them. He was determined to hand those names to Bram and together they would find the people with the money.

He commented that Bram seemed to have a way to make those folks disappear.

Bram asked that when the General had those that had been the fingers on the trigger he would like to get involved in interrogating them.

He smiled and said that he would hold them in their cells until his honeymoon was over.

Bram then went to his wedding table and enjoyed the Chef's wedding day special.

Pat announced that there was a contest to name the wedding day special created by the Chef D'Carluca and that all guests could enter and that the prize would be a thousand-dollar shopping spree at the store that the winner chose. The prize to the Chef was that his creation would be entered in the contest of his choice, and she would cover all expenses associated with him attending such an event.

There was a cheer from those physically at the wedding and a similar one at the Fold recreation center.

Bram took Pat's hand and led her out to the dance floor area for the first dance.

The Marine band played a cha-cha and he and Pat put on a show.

Orlando immediately threw out a ditty as he led Mallica out to the dance floor.

Not only smart. Finds a beautiful woman right at the start.
Takes her out for lifelong romance.
Not only smart but knows his part
Dance, Dance, Dance.
Romance, Romance, Oh! Sweet Romance.
Not only smart, A beautiful woman from the start.

Bram laughed and asked if Orlando was making ditties about himself.

A few moments later Zuri came to his table and asked Bram to dance with her.

Bram obliged and they went on the dance floor and danced a tango. It was clear to him that Zuri had been taking dance lessons and she saved him a couple of times when he faltered, and she put on a solo display and then returned to him.

They then danced a waltz and Bram bowed out as one of the young Marines tapped on his shoulder and asked for the dance.

Pat congratulated Bram on having kept up with their miracle young woman.

Bram nodded and replied that it was hard not to cry as he watched the very beautiful Zuri out on the dance floor. He commented it was hard to recall her condition when they first met when she was wheelchair bound.

Pat put her hand on Bram's and said that she too was still in awe at the transformation that the Fold process had on Zuri. She said that she, Elizabeth, and Zuri's mother had spent many hours talking about the miracle transformation. They all agreed that no matter what other amazing things the Fold process would expose, none would ever match the transformation of Zuri from a deformed body to one that was healthy and beautiful.

Bram nodded in agreement.

The General came to their table and complemented Bram and Pat on their dancing and noted that Zuri was attracting all the young single men. He pointed to the young Marine that was dancing with her at the moment and said that the two had now been dancing with each other for at least a half dozen dances and it appeared he had a Marine that was captivated and maybe a Zuri who was as well.

He then said that he had the three drivers of the trucks and three accomplices that were passengers in the trucks. They had spotted a dark green pickup standing in the forest and had followed it back to Seattle. There the green pickup went to a parking lot and two people got out and went to their vehicles. The bubbles were able to follow each to their homes. He had a local Marine contingent on the way to take them into custody and whisk them to the Fold compound. He said this stretched the legal limits, but he did not want to get any outside law enforcement involved.

They would have nine people and their computers and phones and would figure out who they were in contact with. The General commented that he would let the men sit in their cells and wait to interrogate them until after Bram returned from the honeymoon. He added that Lacy would also be back from her honeymoon and would be able to follow through on any financial connections.

Bram thanked the general and said that when he returned they would pursue the matter right to the financial backer and then they could decide what to do.

Pat signaled the other brides, and they all grabbed their new husbands hands and said that it was time to leave the reception.

Bram collapsed the laser screen and Castor, and Donna opened the gate.

This time Donna was the one to throw a nickel past the gate.

Pat walked to the second black van and got in after Zoe and Eric got in the back. There were four vans to transport the wedding party back to the compound.

Bram had prepared two twelve-person Fold transports. Both would Fold to Mataia for the honeymoon.

Ron Mueller

Chapter 17: Ether Trail

All the honeymoons were on Mataia. Each was a separate event and took place at the locations selected by each couple. They had all chosen to use their homes in Einstein City as the place to stay at night but to spend each day at their honeymoon destinations.

The honeymoon came to a close at the catered dinner prepared by Chef D'Carluca who had Folded to Mataia.

It turned out that the Chef had come up with a totally vegetarian dish that he had prepared from the plants that he had gathered around Mataia. The spices and a few of the ingredients were from Earth but he named the dish Mataian Lover's Delight. This time he said that he was in the right place and that the dish was a delight to prepare.

Pat complimented him on the ingredients, the wonderful taste of everything. She told him that he had surpassed himself in his inventiveness.

Chef D'Carluca smiled and said that she had provided him with his dream kitchen, and he was going to relish preparing meals on Mataia. He asked if Mataia was going to remain without the animals that provided the meats that he used in many of his dishes.

Pat replied that she and Amy were in the process of terraforming Mataia, but it would be years before Mataia would be providing many of the ingredients that he used. However, he would be able to Fold all the ingredients that he currently used from Earth.

The dinner conversation focused on the wonderful honeymoon experience each of them had. Each couple had taken video pictures and shared the location where they had spent each day of their vacation.

Lacy and Linda and their husbands had spent two nights camping in their honeymoon locations and the rest of the time they had also returned to their houses in what they were all referring to as the "Einstein City" suburbs. They commented that they were going to have to develop star maps and name the different constellations that they had observed.

Bram replied that doing so could be a lifetime naming contest that he was sure his new wife would be willing to organize.

Mallica said that she already had three constellations named. Two of them would be the Castor-Orlando Twins because the two seemed to be guarding a third constellation that she thought should be named the Bram Boiling constellation. She then showed the three constellations on the large screen.

Everyone laughed and said that she had hit the nail on the head. They all agreed that she had named the first three constellations and had won the first contest.

Pat said that she could have two servings of the dessert.

Mallica laughed and said that she was expecting a much larger reward for being the first winner and was going to take three servings.

The next morning, they all got in the same Fold transport and Folded back to Earth.

The General, Marcus, Remi, Lori, and Erica were all in the hangar to greet them. After all the hugging and greetings, the General suggested they meet and discuss how to proceed with the men that they were holding.

Lacy suggested they use the Viewing Room to organize the interrogation process.

Bram agreed and asked that Remi and Marcus join them because they might be able to use the control they had in their ability to view events both in the past and future. He said they could check the truthfulness of the answers that their captives gave to questions that were asked.

Marcus commented that Bram was adding a new twist to the use of the negative Fold environment.

Bram nodded and said that one of the jobs they had was to think through how to set the guidelines of how the negative Fold capabilities should be used but for the moment he was making the call.

General Tilman said that he could think of a dozen ways that the military would want to use that capability. He commented that he did not think that the world was ready for that capability to be in any military hands.

Bram agreed and said his fears were how the military, political and financial organizations would each use the Fold capability. It was beyond what he could imagine.

Lacy suggested they focus on interrogating their attackers. She said she would be pleased to be part of the team that set the guidelines for negative Fold capabilities but at the moment she wanted to nail the perpetrators that had tried to disrupt her wedding.

Bram asked Marcus to get setup to calculate negative Fold coordinates and Remi to Fold observation bubbles.

He asked the General how he wanted to proceed with the interrogation.

The General responded that there was an interrogation room at the holding area that they could use. He thought that Matt should do the questioning. He said that the three of them could be in the observation room and could feed Matt the questions. He commented that their captives had not been exposed to anyone, but their Marine guards and they were to the point where if they were going to talk they would do so with just a little pressure.

Bram asked Lacy how that sounded.

Lacy suggested they make sure that Marcus and Remi were prepared to also send observation bubbles out to locations where the big shots might be located. She finished by saying that she would have preferred a Russian style approach of beating the answers out of their captives.

Bram hugged her and said he understood her resentment but that his mother always said that "you can catch more flies with honey than with vinegar."

Both Remi and Marcus said that deploying the bubbles would be no problem.

Bram noted that a Marine was sitting at some equipment and was adjusting the screen in the room and talking to Matt to get the volume set. He commented that the interrogation room was a little daunting in its emptiness and the observation room seemed to be set up to be relaxing.

The General agreed and said that Matt had on the Marine field uniform to make him seem a little more dangerous. His holster held a fake weapon, and it was intended to be seen by the person being questioned so they would feel intimidated.

Bram nodded and said that now they needed to give Matt a good set of questions.

The General took out a sheet of paper with a set of questions on it.

The first question was to ask the person how they preferred to be addressed.

The subsequent questions on the list were:

What is your age?
What sports in High School did you play?
Who had hired you?
Had they launched the drone?

How much were they being paid?
Who was putting up the money?
Where had they picked up the drones?
Who had armed the drones?
How was the launch timing determined?
How were the target coordinates determined?

Bram said that the set of questions seemed adequate. He asked Matt if the questions were in the order that he thought was about right.

Matt responded that they seemed to be. He asked if Marcus and Remi would be able to verify the answers in real time?

Marcus answered and said that Matt should give him a signal when a question was important enough to check out and he would give Matt a heads up about the verification launch and then give him what had been learned. He suggested that Matt go slowly through the questions and fill in with conversation when he wanted verification to a question to take up time to allow the search.

Matt said that he would be a sympathetic homeboy and pretend that he had a similar background to the person being questioned and then spin many of the tales that his teacher, Orlando had used on him.

Bram suggested that Matt remove his Marine insignias so he would look less elite while still looking dangerous.

Matt nodded and took off all the pins and shoulder insignias.

Bram said that they should get started and they should go in reverse order of importance of the individuals, passenger seat persons first and drivers second.

Then they should question those who had been in the pickup truck last but also passengers first. In the pickup truck they should begin with the passenger in the back seat then move to the passenger in the front passenger seat and finally the driver.

Lacy said that when a person being questioned seemed to have some sort of extra knowledge she might throw in a question that popped into her mind.

Matt said that he would be ready for any side questions that might pop up.

Bram was impressed with Matt's easy and seemingly friendly questioning approach. The persons that had been in the passenger seats were not very useful in getting information. It was clear to him that they had been more or less clueless helpers who had been attracted by what they saw as easy money.

They were done quickly, and it was time to deal with the drivers.

The tone changed when the questioning of the drivers began.

The first one looked around and asked where the other interrogator was. He took a lunge at Matt who stepped in and stomped on the lungers foot and then physical put him in the chair and shackled his hands to the table.

The driver threatened to sue Matt.

Matt laughed and asked if he understood where he happened to be and if he wanted to live long enough to grow old.

The attitude changed.

But other than having been attracted by the money and willingly deliver the missiles and then drive away with the empty heavy-duty flatbed trailers they were not very useful in learning who was doing the ordering and preparation.

They did learn the pickup point location where each of them had been recruited and would be able to dig deeper at a later time.

They had learned from the delivery drivers that the drones had come ready to fire and all the drivers needed to do was to position the trucks and call in that they were in position. The rest was handled remotely.

Bram then asked Matt to go very slowly with the three that had been in the pickup.

Matt went slowly and methodically in the final session of the three in the pickup truck. It was clear that the three were not answering in a truthful manner. They were not revealing any useful information.

Bram suggested that they take a break and figure a way to get more information from the three.

During the break Marcus suggested that they show the three some pictures of their families at key events like they did for the attacker in the future. He wondered if it would have the same effect on the three and get them to open up.

Bram supported that idea and asked Marcus to get the information as quickly as possible.

Marcus suggested they reconvene after lunch. He figured that by then he would have all the materials.

Bram invited Matt and the General to take a walk around the compound and noodle the approach they would take during the afternoon.

He shared with them that in dealing with the attacker from the future they had taken pictures of his family members at key moments and then put them on the kitchen table. The pictures had triggered the attacker to call the person he was working with.

He shared that after lunch Marcus would have key pictures of each of the men in the pickup at some key event in the past and pictures of wives and children that they would share with the three drivers and then ask them the same questions again.

The General asked how difficult it was to get such pictures.

Bram said that Marcus seemed to have developed a lot of expertise at getting the pictures, but he was not sure how difficult finding information on the men in the pickup would be.

After lunch Marcus came into the cafeteria with a folder. He said that he had mixed news and thought they should meet and discuss what he had found.

Bram suggested returning to the interrogation observation room and Marcus could share what he had.

Marcus said that he had three different results, and each seemed to provide a different amount of leverage.

He said that the guy who had tried to attack Matt had warrants out for his arrest in three states. Two of the warrants would mean misdemeanor charges but one state had a warrant out for an assault and battery that would mean at least ten years in prison.

He commented that the assault warrant seemed like the best leverage, but this guy had also stonewalled answering questions in previous arrest interviews. He was a veteran liar and troublemaker. He had driven the pickup. He suggested that he preferred turning him over to the state issuing the warrant that would lead to the ten-year prison sentence unless they needed his information.

The front seat passenger in the pickup truck was a friend of the driver and had been in multiple bar fights at a local bar that they often frequented. He added that he was a family man but one who drank too much and gambled. He was rather in a deep financial hole to the bar owner.

He had accepted the job as a payoff of his debt. He believed that he would be clear and away from the grips of the gambling ring but in fact the Boss had commented that they had a sheep in their fold. So, it would be a surprise to that man that he had been duped into believing he would be free from his past mistake.

The youngest of the three, seemed to be an ordinary guy. His car and the grocery cart with the food he had purchased were reported to the local police. One of the checkout clerks remembered checking him out. He and his daughter were joking about the cereal they were buying. The clerk said that the two seemed to be relaxed and enjoying themselves.

Marcus commented that the two seemed to have been abducted in the parking lot.

Marcus said he had figured out how to find her and had verified that the daughter was alive. He had deployed an observation bubble to the site where she was being held and had a bubble standing by with Donna and Castor ready to Fold into the room where the girl was being held. He looked at the General and Matt and said that it would be their call.

The General commented that he wanted to send additional Marines in to take the whole building and asked if Marcus knew how many people were in the building.

Marcus said that the place was a drug house used as a laboratory to synthesize drugs.

The girl was being held in one of the ingredient storage rooms. The two people guarding her were in the hallway outside of the room. She was sitting quietly looking through a book.

He pointed out that they would be able to Fold in and out without disturbing the two in the hallway.

He suggested they inform the police department and let them take care of the rest of the drug house. He made the point that the Marines did not need to be exposed to the drugs.

Matt spoke up and said that he thought Marcus should get the girl out as soon as possible and bring her to the compound. He would use her to get whatever information that her father knew.

Marcus figured that they would be able to get two of the three to provide whatever information that they had.

Matt said that he felt they should begin with deploying Castor and Donna and then bring the girl's father into the interrogation room.

He said that he would get that person to talk.

Bram agreed and said that Donna and Castor should bring the daughter to the detention center and have the doctor check her over. He also suggested that they give her the meal of her choice and get her to feel safe.

The General got on his phone and talked with both Donna and Castor. He told them to get the girl out and if possible to do it like ghosts. He chuckled and said that he knew that the Ghosts were Army, but he wanted the two to be ghosts in action not Ghosts with a capital G.

Bram heard Castor reply and say they would have her out safely in five.

The General replied that they had thirty seconds and hung up.

Bram smiled and complemented the General for having given the Army some recognition.

The General grunted and said that he just had a weak moment, but he was over it.

Matt was surprised when less than a minute later the General answered his phone.

The General put his phone in speaker mode.

They all listened as Donna explained that they had Folded back to the hangar because they had made the call that the girl should be taken to the doctor, be given a shower as well as something to eat.

She said the girl was the same size as one of the girls in the community and she had asked Melisa to bring over a plain but fresh outfit.

Castor said that they would then bring her over to the detention center.

The General smiled but in gruff voice said he would have to talk to both of them later about stretching his orders.

Once he hung up he looked around and said that he wanted to give the two a hug but thought it might be inappropriate and ruin his image as being tough.

Matt shook his head and said that the General's toughness index was pretty low, and he should just go ahead with the hug. Matt smiled and added that of course if he did do the hugging the whole compound would learn about it via a Castor or Donna ditty.

Bram looked at Marcus and asked how he would react if he were the person being questioned and it was his daughter that had been kidnapped.

Marcus immediately answered that unless he got to hug his daughter, he would refuse to answer any questions.

Bram nodded and said he thought as much. He suggested a delay in doing the questioning until Donna and Castor brought her over to the detention center.

He called Pat and asked if she could join Donna and Castor at the Doctor's office. He explained the situation. He had his phone on speaker mode as Pat answered that she and Amy were walking there as they talked. They would stop at the gift shop and get a couple of things.

The General complemented Bram in activating the tough love section of the Marine Corps.

Bram smiled and said that he was using a phrase that he had learned from his mother about using honey and he had the Marine version of honey on the way.

About a half hour later Castor came into the viewing booth and said that he had come in for his chewing out but before that started he wanted to report that a beautiful young girl surrounded by a flock of women were in the meeting room across the hallway.

The General smiled and complimented Castor on doing his job exceedingly well.

Castor snapped to attention, saluted, and replied, "Bamcis." He then said, "follow me."

Bram was the first to follow. He was not surprised to see Pat on one side and Amy on the other side of the young girl. They were carrying on a conversation with her. Melisa and Donna were sitting across the table from them and were also chatting with the young girl.

The room went quiet as the General came in. He looked around and then at Bram and commented that he thought it was his job to explain to him what was going on.

Bram asked that girl her name.

She smiled and said that she was Orianna.

Bram asked if she knew her name meant morning sun.

Orianna stopped for a moment, blinked her eyes, and said that her mother had told her that all the time and added that she missed her mother.

Bram nodded and said that it was hard to lose a mother, but she seemed to have a good dad.

Orianna said that he was the best and she asked if Bram knew where he was.

Bram replied that he did and that she would soon be able to give him a hug.

He turned to Matt and asked if he were ready.

Matt nodded and turned and led the way out of the meeting room.

Marcus commented that he felt that they should somehow figure out how to get this guy away from the drug gang and to a place of safety.

Bram said that he agreed but they would wait to see how he cooperated before deciding how to help him.

They were all in the viewing room when Orianna's father was led in.

Matt began by asking for his name.

The young father answered that he was Ethan Alexander and was thirty-four years old.

Matt turned on the screen and showed the shot of Ethan's daughter in the drug house.

Ethan muttered a curse and asked how Matt had gotten that shot.

Matt replied that he could not share that information. He then showed the shot of everyone in the nearby waiting room.

Ethan asked if it was real.

Matt replied that it was and asked if Ethan was assured of safety for he and his daughter, would he be willing to help them find out who was behind the attack using the cruise missiles.

Matt said that he wanted to give his daughter a hug first to make sure it was all real. Then he wanted to know how Matt could provide them safety. After that he would be an open book and share the little that he knew.

Marcus commented that he had spent his time going back through Ethan's history and found that he was a very reputable person before they had kidnapped he and his daughter. If Ethan shared times and locations, they would be able to get the details and then follow the ether trail to the source giving the order.

Bram asked what skill Ethan possessed.

Marcus replied that he was involved in the sale of defibrillators and a line of pap machines manufactured by a leading manufacturer.

Bram put in a quick call to Melisa and asked her if she could use a person with sales skills. He was not surprised to learn that she would take as many people as he would provide.

He let Matt know that they would offer a job in the Fold compound to Ethan if he volunteered to help.

Matt nodded.

He told Ethan that he was having his daughter brought to him for a hug, then it would be time for Ethan to share what he knew.

He ended by saying that those in power had also authorized him to offer Ethan employment in their secure compound if he participated in earnest to capture the perpetrators of the attack.

Ethan nodded and said he would love to participate in taking out that had kidnapped he and his daughter.

The door to the interrogation room opened and Orianna rushed into his arms.

In a whisper, Bram suggested they all relax for a few minutes and then let Ethan know that at the end of the interrogation, he and Orianna would be taken to an apartment where they would spend the night and that on the following day Orianna would be looked after while he returned to work with them on tracking down the bad guy.

Matt nodded and commented that he was happy to see Orianna safely in her father's arms.

Ethan continued to hug Orianna as he looked at the glass behind Matt and said thank you. He went on to say that he was all theirs. He owed them his daughter's and his life because he would not have survived losing both her mother and her.

Matt stood up and said that interrogation was over and that Ethan and Orianna would be taken to an apartment for the night and dinner could be ordered in to the apartment. There would be a guard on watch but just to provide security. He would be picked up on the following morning after Orianna was taken to school.

Bram suggested that they split the remaining interrogation up. He would work with Ethan in the office area Viewing Room on the following morning and get him to share his information there.

Marcus would stay in the interrogation viewing room and work with both Matt and he in parallel.

He said it would be easy for him to be versatile with time if Marcus needed to help Matt make progress.

He said that he had a good feeling about Ethan. He asked Melisa to be with them in the Viewing room and chat with them in a sort of informal interview.

Matt chuckled and accused Bram of picking the sweet apple and leaving both a spoiled one and a sour one for him to cook with.

Bram wished him good luck and that he was available for any consultation Matt might want. He reminded Matt that he had pulled him back from drowning in the sea but that he still expected him to cook on his own.

Matt let out a "Hurrah" and said that he was ready to cook.

The General let out a "Hurrah" and said he was ready to be the fry cook and singe the remaining butts that refused to cooperate.

Bram replied with a "Hurrah" and said, "lets attack."

Chapter 18: The Good and the Bad

The next morning, Bram had Ethan and Orianna brought to his house. Pat greeted them and asked if Orianna would enjoy some pancakes smothered in butter with Maple syrup for breakfast.

The breakfast was rather quiet, and Bram preferred it that way. He had invited Melisa to join in and then walk with him into work.

After breakfast he led the walk to the office Viewing Room. He listened as Melisa chatted with Ethan as she did a walking interview.

He was not surprised to hear Ethan ask if Melisa was the good cop establishing his profile. He said he was OK with it but said he had not prepared for her subtle approach.

Melisa replied that she was checking him out to see where he might fit in the organization when Bram gave her the word.

Ethan asked her if it was Bram that ran the place.

Melisa replied that there was an official program manager, but Bram was the person who guided them all.

Ethan and Orianna were holding hands as they walked, and he bent down, and he asked what she thought of everyone so far.

Orianna squeezed his hand and replied that everyone had been super nice. She thought that Mom would approve of everyone. She looked around and commented that there were a lot of people walking with them and there was a helicopter flying over them. She asked why they were all around them.

Bram looked over his shoulder and said they were afraid that he would trip and fall. They were there to pick up the pieces and put him back together.

Orianna laughed and said that he didn't act or look like a humpty dumpty.

They arrived at the entrance to the office area and Bram led the way to the Viewing Room and it was time to see how helpful Ethan might be.

Linda had followed them, and she asked what she could do.

Bram asked her to order in refreshments and then show Donna and Orianna to a huddle room where they could enjoy playing a game or reading. He asked Castor to remain in the Viewing Room. He asked Zoe and Eric to go with Orianna and see if she knew any games they could all play. He knew that Bob and Thomas would remain, and he asked them to sit with Ethan.

Ethan said he played competitive chess, but he was not going to challenge Bram to any game because he hated loosing.

Bram smiled and replied that he knew every chess move but he had a much bigger and more complicate board that he now played on where staying alive was the reward.

He asked whether Ethan was ready.

Ethan nodded and was starting to apologize about not knowing much.

Bram stopped him and asked him to only answer questions. He then asked the location of where he had been approached by the drug dealer.

Ethan said he was coming out of the grocery store when he and Orianna were stopped at gun point and told to get into an old decrepit van.

Bram asked for the date, time, and location of the grocery store.

Ethan had the date and location then he stopped to think about the time. He said that it was after picking up Orianna from school, so he figured that it had to be around three forty-five or so. He was going to ask a question, but Bram again put up his had to stop him.

A moment later Marcus said he had it and the scene came on the screen.

Ethan began to utter a curse but stopped. His eyes seemed glued to the scene as it unfolded.

Bram asked if the scene was how Ethan remembered it. He then asked, "do you know where they took you?"

Ethan shook his head and said that they put a hood over both of their heads. He said when the hood came off he was standing in a room looking at a person that he figured was the leader of this gang, but Orianna was nowhere in sight.

Bram spoke to Marcus for a moment and then the screen showed Ethan standing with his wrist zip tied behind his back standing in front of a rather well dressed and handsome drug dealer who was leaning back in a very large business desk chair. He was wearing sunglasses and smiling. He stood up and came around the desk and patted Ethan on the cheek and then asked if Ethan wanted his daughter back alive or in little pieces.

Ethan ask what he possible could have that was valuable but yes he wanted his daughter back alive.

Bram panned the room and took in three other people. He got clear shots of their faces and then asked Ethan if he knew any of their names.

Ethan shook his head and said he didn't even know the bastard that was the boss.

Bram replied that he was not the boss of much. He ran a meth lab and a few drug pushers. The bigger fish simply collected a percentage of the take.

They all listened as the drug dealer said that the boss had received a call from his boss in Miami and told him to find a patsy at random and coerce that patsy to push a button when he was instructed to do so. For doing so whoever was with him at the time of pickup would be allowed to live.

Bram asked if that was how Ethan remembered it.

Ethan nodded but it was clear he was speechless.

Bram said that later everything would become clear, but Ethan should hang in and continue to answer questions.

After they left, the leader dialed the phone. Bram asked if Marcus had the number and who it belonged to.

While they were waiting they listened to the conversation and learned that Orianna was to be kept alive as a potential bargaining chip, but she was on the chopping block if it became clear that she would not be needed. The boss on the phone went on to say that her dad was dead meat walking.

Ethan shook his head and commented that his arrest had saved his life.

Bram nodded and said that there were a couple of more scenes he wanted him to see.

Ethan had a hood put over his head and led out the back and put into a van. They followed the van to a warehouse area where Ethan was taken out of the van and the zip tie cut off. He was told to count to twenty and then take off his hood. He would be picked up by someone driving a dark green pickup truck.

Ethan took off his hood as the large dark green shiny pickup truck entered the parking lot and drove over to him. Two men got out of the truck and walked toward him. They asked if he was expecting to be picked up.

Ethan responded that he was.

The driver handed him a small black controller that had a red cover over a button.

The driver held up a similar one and so did the second person. He said that they were all being held hostage and unless they pressed the button when they were told to do so they or someone they loved would be killed.

Bram asked Marcus if Matt was seeing the three in the parking lot.

Marcus replied that Matt had been waiting until he had some sort of information that would give him an idea of how to continue the interrogation.

Matt came on and said that he saw the two.

Bram suggested that they follow the truck back in time to the point where the driver first got in to begin the journey to see if they could pinpoint the moment when he got enrolled.

Marcus did a great job doing a series of Folds back in small enough increments that it looked like they were following the truck as it drove backward. The truck backed into the Turtle Bar and Grill, the driver, and the passenger both got out and walked backward past the bar and to a room located at the end of the bar. Marcus took several large steps in time to the point where the two were escorted in and faced the person sitting at the desk.

They then listened as the two were told that their hefty bar bills would be erased, and they would get an additional ten thousand dollars for simply pushing a button.

The driver asked what the buttons activated and was told not to ask and once the buttons were pushed the controllers were to be trashed.

Bram asked Marcus to go back to when the Bar owner got the call and when the controllers were delivered.

A few moments later Marcus came back on and on the screen they could see and listen in on the call. The bar owner was talking to a person in Miami and replying yes sir, yes sir I can find the right guys. They heard the Miami boss saying that each of the two would get one hundred thousand dollars and the Bar owner saying he could definitely get the right guys at that level of compensation.

Bram asked Matt whether that might give him some leverage with the two. He pointed out that the questioning might not be needed since Marcus had the phone number and would soon have the location.

The Miami connection was the in the same building as the one they had gotten from the drug dealer, but it was a second person in Miami. Bram speculated they were sharing the risk but most likely there would be one major money trail.

Lacy spoke up and said that both of the persons on the Miami end were on her list. They both took money from her main suspect and did dirty jobs, such as bribing folks or threatening them. She said that they needed to take one more step and intercept the request to the two.

Marcus said he was ahead of them and had followed one of them to a meeting in a limo that took place in a parking lot.

Bram and everyone in the Viewing Room watched as Marcus took a tiny camera bubble through a gap in the limo driver's side window and was able to get a clear shot of the back seat area. They watched as the controllers were handed over with the explanation of how they should be handled.

Bram asked Marcus to find the coordinates of the person in the back seat in current time.

He let Marcus know that he was ending his meeting and was then going to the lab.

Once he was off the phone with Marcus, he asked Ethan if he wanted to work as a travel agent in Melisa's travel agency.

Ethan asked if the work was in the protected compound.

Bram replied that it was and if he were interested in the job he should give her a call and volunteer to work for her. Bram said that the two of them would discuss the compensation.

Ethan replied that the pay was not as important as knowing that Orianna would be safe. He would only need enough to buy food and pay the rent.

Bram smiled and said that he should also consider being able to save money so that Orianna would be able to go to college.

He then asked Castor to get Ethan and Orianna a ride to their apartment.

He asked Matt to turn the driver of the pickup over to a Texas ranger since that person had an outstanding warrant for manslaughter. He should turn over the second person over to the Montana Highway patrol who was looking for him for causing an accident with a bus were multiple people were injured.

Lacy asked about the billionaire that they had exposed.

Bram said that he would personally handle that situation.

He asked her to handle the drug pusher, the Portland bar owner, and the Miami connection.

Lacy said that she had enough information and would work with Marcus on any loose ends and together they would have all of them sitting in some penitentiary.

Bram left the viewing room and went to the lab where he met Remi.

Remi pointed to the bubble and asked if he needed any help.

Bram pointed to Zoe and Eric and said that the two of them were deadly enough on their own.

Castor commented that he was miffed that he and Donna were being left behind.

Bram smiled and replied that he would be back in a second and they could continue the tit for tat.

He Folded to the coordinates provided by Marcus

He heard Marcus quietly state that he had his back and that he had the billionaires coordinate and Bram only had to Fold him.

Bram Folded into the coordinate of the billionaires office.

The billionaire was standing at the window looking out at the ocean.

Bram walked up, tapped him on the shoulder and when the billionaire turned to face him and he looked him in the eyes, pressed the Fold button and the billionaire vanished.

He had followed his Aikido instructors adage to act first and talk after. Once he had pressed the Fold button he got back into the transport and Folded back to the lab. There on the large screen they all witnessed a small multicolor flare as the billionaire's body met the laser protection screen of the house.

He turned to Zoe and Eric and asked if the Fold had been exciting.

Zoe looked at Castor and said if he thought Bram was fast at the trigger in battle he was even faster when he was Folding someone into the activated laser shield. He was so fast that he said goodbye to the billionaire after he had Folded him.

Bram said that it was time to go home and enjoy dinner and he would concentrate on how they would disappear all the Fold information from Earth.

The End

Chapter 1: Transition Plans

As the saying goes, all good things must come to an end. It was clear to Bram that it was time to end the presence of the Fold effort on Earth. He had mixed feelings about the ability of everyone making the transition to another planet, in another solar system in another galaxy. Mataia, the destination planet was equivalent to what earth would have been before more than plant life had begun. It was less stressed and had less tectonic plate activity but otherwise it had a similar proportion of water to land mass and the atmosphere was almost a duplicate of what the Earth had.

The ability to Fold between Earth and Mataia had made the transition a reality.

Bram met Eric, Jeffrey, and Elizabeth to discuss the transition of the Fold effort to Mataia. The four of them developed an initial transition plan that was as flexible as possible.

Bram pointed out that it would take several years to fade out the Fold project from Earth in a manner that it would draw no attention. The Fold program had never become public but there were influential individuals who had been aware of it. He pointed out that Olivia Newton a member of the now dissolved Senate Oversight Committee was coming out to meet with him in a desire to be part of the Fold project. He added that he hoped that Jeffrey and she would work together to establish the Mataian government.

Jeffrey smiled and replied that he would love that assignment from his new boss.

Bram shook his head and replied that his head would remain in the world of science in an effort to move the Fold capability forward.

He then asked Erica whether she would lead the move of the Fold project from Earth to Mataia.

Erica nodded and said that she was pleased to be the one to help get Mataia going. She felt that it would be a high point of her work life.

Bram said that his objective was to leave Earth in such a fashion that no one would know they were gone.

Elizabeth spoke up and asked what an old lady like her could possibly do to help make it all happen.

Bram said that she should think about setting up the education system on Mataia. She would need to recruit top talent to be the teachers and instructors of a system that began at the lowest grade and went through to where PhDs were graduating.

Elizabeth asked if there were school buildings on Mataia.

Bram smiled and said that she should get together with Amy and Pat to lay out the buildings and then work with Erica to figure out how to outfit the school system. He added that her question highlighted the monumental undertaking that the move to Mataia represented.

He said that he had done a little thinking on the details but was certain that there would be several areas that he felt would be challenges.

One was the logistical arrangements that were necessary to support a functioning Einstein City. Supplies from Earth would need to be constantly Folded in. He felt that they needed a facility separate from the current Arrival Terminal to accommodate the arrival of the logistical materials.

He went on to point out that there most likely were additional facilities that they had not thought about that would need to be built and then transported to Mataia. He was planning on having Amy and Pat be the two who would lead that effort.

The second challenge would be to vet the personnel that would make permanent moves to Mataia. Their selection needed to be carefully considered. They should be vetted as to their love for the work they were currently doing in the Fold project and to seeing a future for themselves in living on Mataia in the long term. He added that for all their lifetimes return to Earth would be possible but at some point, that would become a rare occurrence.

Erica suggested that she spend time with each of the other team members and develop the details of a transition plan. She pointed out that sometime in the future the Fold facility at Dallas would need to be slowly erased. She did not think folding the existing buildings to Mataia would be practical nor desirable because Amy and Pat had improved the way homes and other structures were built for Mataia. However, she pointed out that the homes at the site could be Folded to various countries to establish very nice communities for people needing homes. She thought that the industrial buildings could be relocated to a strategic location where they could continue to be used as part of the logistical material handling facility for things going out to Mataia.

Bram thanked Erica for taking the lead in that area.

He said he wanted to work with Elizabeth and Jeffrey on selecting the personnel that would be emigrating to Mataia.

He added that he also wanted to work with Melisa and Marcus to set up vacation spots on Mataia as well as a way to maintain the Earth vacation spots. He said that he felt that the transition would be much less stressful on everyone if their leisure time could be spent on both planets. In that way, leaving Earth would not be so dramatic.

Jeffrey asked whether the members of the Stetson family were in line to move to Mataia.

Bram shared that he had talked with Lacy and Linda and the two definitely were eager to be included. The rest of the Stetson family were on the fence. They were quite willing to aid in the transition, but they felt that they were going to remain on Earth. Linda had let him know that her brother Luke was eager to set up the transport manufacturing center on Mataia or do whatever was needed. He thought that his future was going to be there.

Bram later met with Pat and Amy to discuss what they thought the transition needed to include.

Amy pointed out that it would take years to slowly change the Mataian environment to at least make it able support life like Earth.

Amy pointed out that they needed to keep everything in balance and that the transition should move slowly forward over their lifetime and perhaps beyond, in short it would take time.

Bram said that he would love to take part in some of the Mataian transformation details of moving as time permitted but they would all be very busy for as far into the future that he could see, and they should continue to default, to taking it slowly and Fold plants and animals to Mataia in a controlled and well managed manner. He added that he was counting on the two of them setting up a team that would manage and oversee that effort.

He then met with Marcus to discuss the transition to work on Mataia.

Bram Nielson Collection

Marcus said that he was eager to make the move and would plan to work there each day. He needed to get his home there organized. He pointed out that he was taking mini vacations with Mylan and Marcus Jr. on almost all the upcoming weekends for the next several months. He had been outfitting his house on Mataia and had taken one mini vacation there with the two and they were now enthused about the move. The two had really enjoyed the beach that they had gone to and the hike in several of the valleys.

Bram reminded Marcus that there was a naming contest for all locations on Mataia and as well as for naming the stars visible from the planet's surface. He suggested getting the two into those contests as a way to enthuse them about their move. He also made the point that they could move into their new home and still attend classes in Dallas or on weekends do mini vacations on Earth.

Marcus smiled and said that the discussion had solved his concern about their safety at his current home at the Fold housing complex. He would be making the move as soon as possible.

Bram shared that he and Pat had started to live on Mataia and Folding to work in the Morning and that his FBI bodyguards were doing the same. He was hoping all of the inner circle would soon be doing something similar.

He pointed out that doing so had already surfaced several life activities that were not significant but that needed to be addressed as they transitioned.

Marcus asked for an example.

Bram said that setting up the materials and supply chain logistics was the area that had been exposed when they had to take up a supply of toilet paper and paper towels. That simple need had clarified the fact that there were no trees to supply the fiber to make paper. So, both those items needed a replacement or a long-term logistical plan.

Marcus laughed and said that they would certainly have to solve many such weighty and critical problems.

Bram's next meeting was with Mallica in person and Orlando on screen. They discussed getting Mallica focused on working with him on exploring both the positive and the negative Fold environment. He shared that she and Marcus would be central to that effort.

He asked Orlando if he were willing to establish a way to keep order on Mataia.

Orlando commented that he thought he would enjoy such a role.

Bram challenged him to do it in a way that would require no weapons and would fundamentally be based on the philosophy of treating others the way he wished to be treated. He challenged Orlando to make the way to keep order a friendly embrace.

Orlando laughed and asked if he should wear a Santa Clause outfit.

Bram shook his head and said that he wanted Orlando to be the Marine that he was and to see if he could set up a system that would make Zuri proud.

Orlando nodded and in a more serious tone said that he now understood how serious Bram was.

Orlando smiled and said he understood perfectly what Bram expected.

Bram suggested that he enroll Castor and Donna in that effort.

Bram realized that Mallica had tears in her eyes and asked what was up.

Mallica shook her head and commented that she had just thought through all the things that had transpired since hanging on out in the desert compound where they had all started. She was glad that Elizabeth had convinced her to stay on.

Bram nodded and thanked her for staying. He felt bad about that time but felt great about everything that she had contributed. He added that she was a big part of the success of the Fold effort and Orlando was a big part of having kept him alive. They were both more than just his good friends, they were now more like family.

His final discussion for the day was with Remi and Lori.

Remi commented that he was eager to make the move to Mataia and to get his lab functional there. He said he and Lori had reviewed the people in the lab and agreed that they had a group of very hard-working people who were eager to be a part of the continuing Fold effort. The research and analysis of the Mataian environment and any samples that would be gathered from somewhere in the universe would be something they would never be able to experience in any other work environment.

Lori added that she had met with each of their current staff members, and everyone had said they definitely wanted to stay with the Fold effort.

Bram asked the two to work with Pat and Amy to make sure that housing would be available, and that the logistics group be kept appraised of the number making the move.

He commented that the pace of transition was going to be limited by how quickly they could establish a place for everyone to live and to adjust the quantity of materials logistics to support Mataia and to obtain equipment to handle and store the materials.

He said that he would need to make sure that Erika had a handle on world building at a fast forward mode.

That evening he discussed the situation with Pat as they sat on their two person recliners.

Zoe and Eric were having a cup of tea in one set of easy chairs and Bob and Thomas in the other set. In the past only two of the four had been in the office at the same time lately the four had often sat in at one time.

Zoe commented that the four of them had discussed the mountain of effort that faced them all for the move and had decided that they should figure out how to jump in to help and in the short term do whatever was needed during the initial transition.

Bram thanked them and said that they should get with Erica, Amy and Pat and see where the help was needed. He said that he was sure they would be taken up on their offer to help.

Zoe commented that she was excited about the move, but she also wanted everyone to remember that the role of the four was first as the bodyguard for their loveable and zany mad Fold scientist.

Bram said that he hoped that in the near future, they would think of each other only as very good friends.

The next morning Bram asked Linda to see if Ray could join in on the meeting that he was planning to have with Olivia Newton in the afternoon.

Linda smiled and asked if Bram was going to make Lacy's new husband an offer he could not refuse.

Bram smiled and asked if Ray had any legal and organizational skills.

Linda replied that she had no clue how good he might be, but he had impressed her sister enough to marry him and that spoke highly about his character.

Bram said that Lacy's acceptance was good enough for him and yes, he would make him an offer that he hoped was a big enough net to pull him in.

Linda asked if it was OK to share with Lacy that Ray would be in the meeting with Olivia Newton.

Bram said it would be fine, but he did not know exactly what the offer was going to be.

Linda said that any offer would be acceptable, and that Ray had been worried about not being able to get on the Fold staff.

Linda then asked what he might have in mind for Rafael.

Bram asked Linda to give him several suggestions about where Rafael would be most interested in working. Then she could set up a meeting with him so that he could get to know him better. He commented that he had spent time with him before and after the wedding, but they had not discussed work.

Linda smiled and said the Evenders, and the Tailors would be the Stetson replacement on Mataia.

Bram thanked her and said that he wondered when fishing on Mataia would be as good as the Stetsons had shown them in Dallas.

He asked Linda to let him know when Olivia arrived and to make sure there were overnight accommodations ready as well.

Bram then went into his office after Zoe and Eric had declared it clear. He went straight to the bookshelf and opened the tiny door and took Isaac and Ada into his hand and carried them over to his desk.

He asked them whether he should move the boulder in the desert to Mataia and laughed when both of the mice nodded their heads up and down.

Zoe came over and asked whether they should make sure that their father, Einstein, also made the trip. She pointed to them as they bobbed their heads up and down.

Eric asked whether there was a desert-like area on Mataia.

They all looked at each other and said that they could not remember seeing a desert in any of the videos they had seen. Zoe said she would follow up and go searching for the right place to move the boulder.

Bram said that Marial had mentioned that one of the many unexplained artifacts was a large boulder located on one of the few desert islands on Mataia. There seemed to be no explanation of how it had gotten there nor why the island was the only place where mice were the dominant species. He suggested that Zoe look for that island.

Linda buzzed in and said that Olivia would be at his office in fifteen minutes, and she had Ray standing by.

Bram picked up Isaac and Ada and carried them back to the bookcase and closed it after the two went in.

Linda knocked and brought Olivia in.

Bram greeted her and made the point of recognizing Zoe and Eric as part of the meeting. He had Olivia sit next to him at the table and with Ray on the screen across from them.

After introducing Olivia, Bram stated that the objective of the meeting was to establish the leaders of the group that would write the constitution for a new world government.

Ron Mueller

Chapter 2: Mataia Constitution

His statement was met with silence. It was clear to him that he had surprised everyone in the room.

He looked at Olivia and then over to the screen at Ray and asked if there were any questions.

Olivia asked where he was planning to set up his government. Ray asked if it would be on Earth.

Bram said he was asking them to write the constitution for a world government, for the world of Mataia. It would be the planet that everyone associated with the Fold effort would move to.

Once again Bram was met with silence. He asked Linda to que up the Mataia video.

He then explained what the two were about to see was something that only his inner circle had seen before. They would see a world that had been named Mataia.

The tour of Mataia began and for the next hour they watched the presentation. Both Olivia and Ray would periodically comment on the splendor and the beauty that was shown. At the end, Bram said that they had taken a quick tour around a new world. It was a world located several light years away in a solar system similar to Earth's solar system. This new world would be home to those who were willing to leave Earth and live there.

Bram then turned on the tour of Einstein, City and declared that it was the first city on the planet and was already being used by about twenty of the Fold personnel, including himself. It needs many small items to make it a fully independent functioning city and it would take time to make that happen.

After the brief arial tour Bram stopped and suggested they all get a cup of tea, coffee or other refreshments and then continue the meeting.

While they were getting coffee Olivia asked if what she had just seen was real. She had been blown away when they had gone on the Fold Vacation in Greece but to be shown a full city on another planet seemed to be impossible. How had he achieved it in such a short period of time and how had the buildings been built in such short order? She said she saw no construction equipment or ongoing construction. She commented that it seems so polished and perfect that it was hard to believe.

Bram sat down at the table and nodded and said that he had his team of super people to thank. They had accomplished what she had seen in record breaking time. He went on to share that everything that she had seen was built on Earth and Folded into place on Mataia.

Ray mentioned that Lacy had told him that he would be blown away by what he was going to learn in the meeting.

He knew she had been dying for him to learn more about the Fold effort. She said that he would learn it from Bram or not at all. He asked what he personally had to do to be an integral part of the Fold effort and that he wanted to be as passionate as Lacy was about it.

Bram asked Olivia if she was ready to commit to the Fold effort.

Olivia nodded and said that she had some family-oriented questions before jumping in, but she did want to jump in. She wanted to make sure about the short- and long-term education of her children. She also wanted to know what her husband could do. Finally, she wanted to know how the transition would be handled. How would the family stay connected with friends and other family members?

Bram liked her questions. He made a point that he was working on Mataia during the morning and finishing the day at his office on Earth. Other than having to keep the Fold technology invisible it was in fact no different than commuting to work in the morning and going home in the afternoon.

He said that how one handled the day and how the transition would be handled would need to be tailored to each individual. She would only need to set up an isolated location where she and family could be picked up and then return via Fold. She and family could design the transition as it fit their needs. The only difficulty would be making sure everything was kept secret.

Olivia shook her head and commented that it was hard to grasp the flexibility that was available in going to and returning from a place several light years away. She had not envisioned the Fold capability to the extent that she was now getting exposure to.

She asked why Bram was isolating the Fold capability from the rest of the Earth's population.

Bram shook his head and asked her to think about the impact to the current social, economic, and military situations that she knew about. If she came to a different conclusion and had the means to manage making the Fold capability part of Earth's current situation, he would like to hear about it.

Olivia thought for a moment and said that she did not have a clue how that would be possible.

Bram said that he had come to that conclusion, but he had also asked those on his team the same question and they did not have an answer either.

He shared the fact that the Fold effort had suffered many physical attacks that included military action, rocket attacks from both the current time and had suffered attacks from the future as well.

He pointed out that Fold was a capability that had yet to be fully understood and it was a threat to a reality that everyone had come to believe was fixed but was in fact malleable.

Olivia asked how he was going to manage that from Mataia.

Bram replied that Fold was being disappeared on Earth and he was working on how to put barriers in place that would help contain how Fold got utilized on either planet. He admitted that he was not sure how it would all get done and whether he would be successful. He commented that he had no clue if the attempt to contain and control the Fold capability would be successful.

Olivia said she had one final question and that was how long the transition would take.

Bram replied that it would most likely be longer than any of them would live and that their children or grandchildren would be the ones that would live in a completely independent Mataia.

Olivia said she like the tenor of his answers. She said that she would definitely embrace the effort. She would do her best at creating a government that would last through future generations and would produce a society that focused on embracing and honoring each other.

Bram smiled and said that he looked forward to her leadership and in being part of setting up the Mataian government.

Bram Nielson Collection

Zoe had expected that Bram would convince both Olivia and Ray to be part of the effort. She had previously had her friend in the FBI do extensive checks on both of them and had been please to find out that they had no blemishes other than some speeding tickets.

She had learned that both of Olivia's kids, though very good in school, were heavy party drinkers. She felt that this would be a risk to the Fold effort.

Ray was the one with the speeding tickets, with the most recent being in the last month.

She spoke up and asked if they could openly discuss a few issues that were personal and involved other family members.

Bram let Ray and Olivia know that he had asked Zoe to dig into both of their personal and family backgrounds. He followed up by saying that he wanted to make this a positive move and not a punitive one.

He suggested that they tackle Ray's issue first and then after that ask him to sign off. They would then address the issue associated with Olivia.

Ray put up his hands and said he was guilty. He shared that he received the official notice of his speeding ticket in the mail just that morning.

Bram nodded and said that he needed to pay off the previous two as well as the one that he had just received. He should figure out how to control his lead foot or risk losing his new job at writing the Mataian constitution and figure out how to live remotely from his wife.

Ray said he would take care of his problem immediately and become a casual driver.

Bram thanked him and said that Erica Wilson would be in touch with him to arrange his transition into the Fold program.

After Ray signed off, Bram looked at Olivia and said that her problem was family oriented, and it was about her two children.

He commented that he had acted just as they were now acting and that it was a growing up phase thing. He wanted to let her know about it so they could figure out how to change the actions that put them at risk.

Olivia had her hands on the table, and they were trembling. She asked if they were into drugs.

Bram said that they were not into drugs, but they and their friends were into drinking too much at the parties they were throwing. This was the issue that they had to address.

He asked where the two were thinking about majoring at in college and what career they were interested in.

Olivia said that she had asked them and had been disappointed that neither had expressed a passion for any particular field and they were more or less at a loss to what they wanted to do.

Bram commented that he had talked with them during the weekend Fold vacation, and it seemed they were very smart.

Olivia replied that both of them got very good grades and were in the top five percent of their class.

Bram asked if perhaps they could get them more seriously focused in an area that would be fruitful for the Fold effort.

Eric spoke up and said that Dennison had expressed his interest in the FBI or in law enforcement. He could be on the team that designed the support and aid force on Mataia.

Zoe said that she had spent time with Angela and had learned that she wanted to design clothes. She might be enticed by setting up a fashion design shop on Mataia that at first imported luxury brands from Earth.

Bram smiled and looked at Olivia and said that it seemed they had two volunteers to engage her children and give them a vision of the future that might help get them to stop their heavy drinking at parties.

Olivia said she would love the help but how would they connect them in a natural way?

Zoe suggested that they use the fact of her new job would require them to move to a new location as a way to get them to come out to Dallas for a visit. While they are visiting, they could stay in the new home that you would be living in. They could meet a couple of the older members kids in the Fold community who are getting ready to go to college. They could be touring the work projects that are underway.

And then Zoe laughed and said that they could go fishing with Bram and be in some really live action.

Olivia laughed and said that it sounded like a good plan, but she wanted them to wear Kevlar vests when they went fishing.

Bram said that he would plan several fishing trips before they went out to make sure his fishing trips had entered a peaceful time frame.

He then declared the day over and that they would all go home and enjoy whatever dinner Bob and Thomas had prepared.

As they walked out, Linda stopped Bram and told him that Lacy had called her up and said that she thanked him for figuring out how to get lead foot Ray to slow down. He had called her and had said that he had paid all his speeding tickets and had ordered a throttle limiter that would prevent him from going more than five miles over the speed limit.

Bram laughed and asked Linda to tell Lacy that he hoped that it would work.

Olivia said hello to Pat as they walked to the van waiting for them. She thanked Bram for inviting her to join them for dinner. She asked what was on the menu.

Bram smiled and said that unless Zoe and Eric knew then it would be a surprise to all of them. Bob and Thomas were doing the cooking, and they always picked a recipe that they wanted to try out and rounded out the main course with salad and some vegetables.

Olivia said that she thought that was a great way to end the day.

Bram agreed and said that all of them, himself included had developed a broad set of meals they liked to prepare. He admitted that he probably had the narrowest set of meals that he periodically prepared, and he mostly did breakfasts and lunches. His meals were weekend ones where he had enough time to cook.

Pat said that Bram had improved over time, but Zoe and Eric were the ones that seemed to come up with the most interesting menu's and that she was just ahead of Bram in meal recipe preparation but not by much.

Zoe said that it was an unfair comparison. She and Eric got the opportunity to search out and cook recipes every other day. They had also gotten recipe help from the Stetson catering group who sent over recipes they thought would be of interest. All she and Eric had to do was to cut down on the ingredient amounts because the recipes were generally for a large number of people. She laughed and said that properly reducing the spicing often led to hilarious results.

Bram agreed that what the two put on the table had to be treated with a good amount of respect. He remembered two times when the spices were overwhelming and one time that he had to ask for the soy sauce and hot pepper. But some of their good meals could rival those of Chef D'Carluca.

Their van drove into the basement. Bram said that he was going to stop a moment in the office and then come up for dinner.

Pat escorted Olivia up the stairs.

Zoe sensed that Bram planned to share something that was on his mind. She and Eric did a thorough sweep of the office. There were no listening or other devices.

They signaled for Bram to enter. His Marine guards waved and backed the van out of the basement.

Bram walked in and sat at the front edge of his desk. He asked how the four of them were taking the move to Mataia and if there was something that he could do to make the transition smooth for them.

Eric replied first and said that he and Zoe had discussed this in length with each other and they had also engaged with Bob and Thomas.

They all agreed that they wanted to take the transition slowly. They would continue to maintain their current protection cycle until they got notice that the assignment was ending. This would allow them to use their FBI contacts to vet people and to check out suspects until the very end.

Zoe added that after that time they would use their knowledge about the system and the help of Linh and Duong to tap into the various systems when they needed to get the information to vet someone.

Bram said that he agreed with waiting until they got the notice that the bodyguard assignment was over.

He said that he would like to be informed when the more clandestine effort was needed. He was sure that they could pull off such efforts, but he wanted to make sure that when such an effort was needed that all the resources would be aligned to the effort.

Zoe nodded and said that the four had discussed exactly the point that Bram had just made.

Bram thanked them and said that they should complement Bob and Thomas for their great support for the expanding work of the Fold program.

Zoe said that there were two complexities that had surfaced during their discussions on the transition to Mataia.

She said that both Bob's and Thomas's remote love affairs had reached a new level, and they were wondering how to handle them.

Bram asked what the barriers to making their romances work might be.

Zoe replied that both of them wanted to have weekends off so they could pursue their romances. They were wondering if they might be able to use two of the smaller Fold vehicles so they could spend weekends with their girlfriends.

Bram replied that they should contact Melisa and arrange for that to happen. They should also ask to stay in the facility where the Fold would deliver them.

He asked where the girl friends live and learned that one had a position as a Bank branch manager in Philadelphia and the other ran a small leather goods boutique in San Diego.

Bram asked if Zoe had vetted the two.

Zoe replied that both Bob and Thomas had asked her to do that early in their romances.

Bram said that he gave them a green light and wished them well. He then pointed to the door and said that it was time to see what was for dinner.

Ron Mueller

Chapter 3: Erasure

The next day in the office, Bram was explaining to Isaac and Ada that there were several critical things to do in parallel. He asked them whether he was going to figure out how to contain the Fold knowledge on Mataia and if the team would be able to learn how to manage that knowledge.

Both of them seemed to nod in the affirmative to each question.

Zoe smiled and commented that she was beginning to believe the mice really understood the questions that Bram asked them.

She gave the two a small crumb of cookie and asked them if she should focus on erasing the Fold knowledge from Earth and if she should erase the political knowledge first. She gave a small laugh when the two seemed to nod in agreement to each question.

Bram asked if the move to Mataia should be done slowly and be paced at the speed of the Fold knowledge erasure.

He received a supportive nod.

He then asked if the boulder in the desert should be Folded to Mataia and again got a positive nod.

His final question was if any other animals should get Folded to Mataia any time soon and got a negative shake from both of them.

Then he asked if their parents should be included in the Fold to Mataia and got a positive nod.

Bram looked over to Zoe and Eric and asked if they had any more questions to ask of their two extremely intelligent mice.

They both held out their hands like paws and shook their heads back and forth negatively.

Bram laughed and then returned Isaac and Ada to their bookshelf home and sat down at his desk.

He commented that he needed to spend the next several days figuring out how to set up the Fold fences to keep the knowledge contained. He needed the knowledge to become a secret that only the Fold team knew. He added that he had to hide the equation details and how the equations worked from everyone including the team. He shared that he would record the essential equation details in the stored record but not share it with any living person. He commented that Marcus, Mallica and Zuri were the only three that had a current in-depth understanding, but they did not have access to all the changes he had made.

He asked Zoe and Eric what they thought of the approach he was taking.

They both agreed with what he was considering. They shared that they had discussed the topic of how to contain the knowledge and agreed that somehow limiting who knew the details was the only approach they could think of.

Bram had shared this approach with Pat and had gotten similar feedback.

He had also shared it with Elizabeth to test and evaluate whether it was ethical for him to set himself up as the only person who controlled such knowledge.

She had responded that the only thing he would need to control was his own desire to change the future history of the Earth. She then added that her statement also applied to the past history of the Earth.

In their discussion she brought up the fact that Mataia and Swoosh should be included in the concern of meddling by anyone in current time.

He smiled and asked whether having empowered the Mataians one thousand years in the future qualified as meddling.

Elizbeth smiled and said that it did, and she was sure that he had not created a ripple in time but most likely had created a tsunami going out into the future.

Bram nodded in agreement and asked Elizabeth to lead a team in establishing the guiding principles of how the Fold knowledge should be handled. He said that he already knew the temptations and had already created several ripples in time by eliminating the people who had attacked the team on Mataia and the additional two people that he Folded into the laser protective screen. He was sure that he would create more ripples, but he wanted to be guided by what the team thought would keep such ripples small and contained in a manageable way.

Linda interrupted his thinking to let him know that the meeting in the Viewing room would begin in ten minutes.

He thanked her and turned his focus to the topic of setting up the Fold Erasure Strategy.

He, in discussion with, Erica had agreed on a two-step approach to developing the strategy. He, Mallica, Marcus, and her would work together to outline the strategy. Then they would hold another meeting with the entire team and finalize the strategy.

This was the first meeting of the four of them and he had asked Erica to lead the meeting.

Once they had their strategy agreed to, they would all participate in the creation of an action plan with the entire team. Each action in the plan would have a team leader, clear measurable objectives and the timing that was to be achieved for that objective.

He was the last to enter and he noted that a cup of coffee and a bottle of sparkling water was set at his table. He looked at the clock and noticed that he was a few minutes late. He took his seat.

Erica stood and stated that they were most likely attending the first of several meetings. They were to establish the move of the Fold knowledge and the people supporting the Fold program to Mataia. She stated that they should consider the strategy they came up with as a draft strategy open for additional input from the entire team. She shared that she hoped they could get their draft to be ninety percent complete, but they should be open to modifications and improvements.

She suggested that part of their effort should also be to develop a draft execution plan based on the strategy they came up with.

Zoe asked whether she and Eric could participate in this current meeting.

Erica nodded and said that Zoe was leading the effort to erase the Fold knowledge from all the computer systems in the world and certainly should have input.

Bram spoke up and said that the transition to Mataia was something new to all of them and doing it in a fashion that preserved the camaraderie that they had established was of great importance to him. He shared that they would most probably miss some items, but he was also sure that they would be small and manageable problems.

Erica led the team through three days of strategy development. She suggested a one-day break and said that they would then spend about the same amount of time developing the draft execution plan before assembling the entire team.

Bram commented that they were making great strides, and he would work with Linda to set up several days with the rest of the team. He suggested they include Linh and Duong in the development of the detailed execution plans because he was sure that the digital world would be on the critical execution path.

Zoe reinforced Bram's suggestion by sharing that the two were on three of the current execution teams and they had recruited an additional group of IT specialists to help them with all the systems and computer languages involved.

Bram reiterated that there would be three areas they should think about as they develop their execution plans.

One area was to erase the Fold knowledge from the Earth.

The second area was to establish the Mataian, government, society, and environment.

The third was the physical transition to Mataia that included erasing the current physical Fold community from Dallas and perhaps their work center as well.

Mallica added that the timing of each was going to be critical. Every move needed to be thought out carefully so that the disappearance of the Fold program and the disappearance of its physical existence went unnoticed.

Marcus commented that perhaps they should ask Thomas who was already getting into monitoring the future of the Earth to periodically check on the gradual disappearance of Fold as a way to ensure that mistakes were not propagating into the future.

Bram said he was not against it, but they should review how they would monitor that situation to make sure that the monitoring did not end up being intrusive and noticed.

The draft strategy work and the draft execution plan were completed in two weeks. This was much longer than they all thought it would take but they had spent the quality time required to make their initial work as good as they could.

Erica worked with Linda and had her set up the meeting with the entire team for the week after they had completed the draft work.

She suggested that they use the auditorium where they would be able to use the huddle rooms for small teamwork when they broke up into work groups.

Linda said she would set up the refreshments at the back of the stage and have lunch catered in.

Bram had created a rendering of what he thought the community grounds that were currently in use for the Fold program should appear to a visitor in the near future or in about ten years. His rendering had the orchard refreshed but the old barn gone. The current housing area was shown as a maple and oak mixed forest with a green area that had a small lake on the downhill area where the current swimming pool was located and featured a soccer-baseball field combination about where his house was currently located.

Erica commented that it looked great but where was the old barn and where was the apartment building? She understood that they were already in the process of Folding the houses out, but she had not thought about the larger structures.

Bram suggested that the location of where to Fold the structures other than the houses needed to be evaluated. The Fold location could be to either planet. Where to locate them on that planet was also a question.

Erica nodded and said she was demonstrating why the strategy, and a detailed execution plan was going to be critical.

Bram nodded in agreement and added that determining when to tackle the physical environment was going to be critical. He added that the transition speed when they did tackle the change of the Fold property was going to be another key consideration. They had to do it in a way that did not cause widespread interest or make the news.

Zoe brought that erasing the rather widespread Fold knowledge was going to be the bottleneck of the execution plan. She shared that she had already run into difficulties dealing with the technical side of eliminating the information. She highlighted that Linh and Duong had learned that almost every major computer system had multiple backup programs that needed to be addressed and set up so they would load a backup copy that had Fold erased from it. These backups needed to all be erased at the same time so they would not put the erasure effort into a do loop.

She then highlighted that eliminating the knowledge of people would most likely be more difficult. It would be great if all of them could end up on Mataia, but she knew a few that she personally thought should not be part of that migration.

Bram said that taking her input into the evaluation of the time required to make the transition was going to be critical and perhaps it would be a timeline that would actually be more manageable.

He added that selecting the people with meaningful knowledge would be difficult and the team would need to develop ethical guidelines for not only evaluating and convincing them to make the move to Mataia but also in how to deal with those who had no interest in doing so.

Erica thanked Zoe for speaking up and agreed that on the one hand she had surfaced some key barriers, and she had also provided a sense that the timeline was going to be longer than anyone had expected.

Bram asked Mallica what was on her mind.

Mallica replied that she felt that no matter how successful Zoe was in the effort to erase Fold from the Earth someone was going to remember, and they would write an expose.

She suggested the team instead become good Fold photographers. They should call what Zoe was currently doing the Fold aperture. She was reducing the amount of light and dimming the picture. They should set up the picture shutter speed to provide the least amount of Fold light possible. And finally, they should ensure they had a very low Fold exposure sensitivity so that what was exposed would be of little value.

She said that the Fold exposure should share very disappointing information to satisfy the person or persons digging for the Fold information so they would end their searching.

She suggested that the team write the expose. Tell the story the way they would want it to be told and then plan on the exposure event sometime in the future.

Bram smiled and said that maybe he had left her out in the desert too long and the desert heat had affected her. She had caught his disease of looking into the future and figuring out how to manipulate it.

He thanked her for the reality that she had just exposed and asked if she was willing to be the leader of the team that wrote the expose.

Mallica replied that she needed a master spinner of storytelling fiction and asked whether he would agree to participate in the fabrication of a good fairy tale.

Bram chuckled and agreed that the whole Fold effort seemed like a fairy tale fabrication, but he pointed out that they had all experienced its awesome power. They had seen the miracle of seeing a wheelchair bound young lady be transformed into one that could dance the tango and cha-cha-cha.

He commented that once they were all on Mataia they should figure out how that awesome power could be put to use in the positive fashion they all desired.

Chapter 4: Eastern Breeze

The final strategies for each segment, of what turned out to be a very detailed transition strategy, took several weeks. Bram complemented the team on creating a great set of strategies but even more important he complemented them on having turned the strategies into very detailed and measurable action plans.

He pointed out that the critical path to the transition was the area of eliminating the Fold exposure and information from all systems on Earth, that Zoe was leading.

He thanked Pat and Amy for joining Zoe's team while they waited to start implementing the transformation of the plant and animal life on Mataia. The critical path layout clearly highlighted that the Mataia transformation effort was going to take the longest and its timing was affected by the need to evaluate the resulting impact of transplanting first the sea life and then with land plant and animal life transfers.

Each evaluation period would take several years to complete. This meant that it was the most flexible and of course the longest action plan.

Pat and Amy said that they were setting up their transplant team in a fashion that would allow each area to run almost by itself. They said being on Zoe's team would fill in their days in a meaningful way.

Bram then reviewed Mallica' and Gerry's detailed action plan that dealt with the current and the far future of the Swoshian society. He reviewed what they were doing during each time frame. They pointed out that they were learning from the Swoshians in current time and then they were making sure that the future had not lost any of the critical elements that made the Swoshians such a great race.

Bram asked what they expected to learn from the Swoshians in current time and was pleased to learn that the two were focused on how Mataia should handle the way that food, medicine, and education would be provided to the Mataian society at no cost.

Mallica pointed out that the Swoshians had no need for money.

Gerry shared the fact that medical care was often required but it was administered as a normal part of the society.

They both commented that what they really liked was that education was considered a lifelong pleasure that was a part of daily life.

They both suggested that the people that would be the first Mataians be required to learn about the key elements of the Swooshian culture. They added that Chef D'Carluca had asked to be a part of their team. He had said he was fascinated with how they handled their food distribution and wanted to make sure that Mataia applied their methods. He wanted to organize on land what the Swoshians did in the sea.

The continuing and substantial analytical needs during the transition to Mataia and also associated with any exploration turned out to be another area that became very clear. Remi had led the development of a very clear and detailed plan and had worked with Lori to estimate the number of additional technicians that would be needed.

Once he had made his contribution, he stepped off the analysis team and joined forces with Luke Stetson to develop the plans that would establish a new manufacturing organization that would begin their efforts on Mataia with the development and production of the Fold transport bubbles. He would lead the development side of the effort and Luke would be in charge of the logistics and manufacturing side.

Luke pointed out that the manufacturing side would focus on small volume manufacturing so it could easily and continuously add the items that should be manufactured locally versus being brought in from Earth.

He added that he anticipated that Mataia would for generations to come be importing many items from Earth. He added that multiple logistical Folding locations need to be established on Earth and kept secret. This they felt was going to be a major challenge.

They had suggested that the current Fold hangar and all the work areas should be Folded to Mataia. It would become the Development and Manufacturing center.

Bram suggested that they would need to begin small and use the current hangar on Mataia and then when it came time to Fold the current Dallas based hangar, they could position it at the location that made the most sense.

Einstein City Planning and expansion was another area to be a surprise for Bram. Pat and Amy were the key leaders but Matt had requested to be part of that effort and made the suggestion that they needed to embrace the far future and begin with that end in mind and should plan the cities of the future so they would be located in the geographically right places. He suggested that the City Planning team become the Mataian City Location and Planning team. Bram complimented Matt on his expansive vision and jokingly said that he was glad that he had kept him from being swept off the ferry during their Norwegian adventure. Bram suggested that they cheat on the locations, visit Marial, and learn where the cities were located and if they were all successful.

Erica had listened as Bram reviewed and complimented each of the teams. She then pointed at him and said that she was going to complain about the fact that he had used all of them to do the dirty work of giving input to hiding the greatest secret in the world. She asked if he had enough information to figure out how to hide the Fold secret and close the lid on the Fold Box.

Bram put his Strategy and the action plan that he had developed into action. His strategy was simple. Work alone in isolation and make Fold invisible but easily accessible. His action plan was to put the Fold information on a journey that only he would know about. When he was doing his work there would be no bodyguards present.

He thanked everyone for having contributed their ideas and said that he would use many of them, but they would never know how he had used their input.

Pat had listened to Bram as he went over the various ideas on how to make the Fold information inaccessible. She knew that something that Marcus had suggested had crystallized an idea for Bram. She had been very curious about what Marcus had suggested and reviewed the video of the brainstorming session to see if she could tell how Bram had reacted to Marcus's suggestion.

She could not tell by any facial expression, but she realized that Marcus had only made one suggestion about sending the Fold Box on a long-distance journey in both the negative Fold and the positive Fold RCID's.

From that input she knew that the Fold information would be traveling a multimillion-year journey as it made its way methodically node to node, skipping between the RCID's in both the positive and the negative Fold realms. She had no clue how that would be set up, but she was sure Bram would accomplish that goal.

Bram Nielson Collection

Bram had been watching Pat and knew that she had most likely figured out the general concept that he would implement. He smiled as he thought about her ability to figure out some of the most complicated problems. She had used that capability to save him when he had foolishly and ignorantly gone into the negative Fold realm trying to figure out what it was. He decided that she would be the one person with whom he would review his final solution.

Lacy had left the stage and was up at the other end of the auditorium. It was clear to everyone on the stage that something strange was happening.

Bram asked everyone to continue wrapping up, but they should be ready to do what might be asked by Lacy for them to do.

The call had Lacy talking to herself. Her team had uncovered the fact that the North Koreans had a submarine on the way to the west coast and their intension was to eliminate the Dallas Fold site.

She remained at the other end of the stadium but waved to Bram indicating that the stage get cleared.

Bram knew that something very troublesome was occurring. He asked Linda to clear the auditorium and then get ready to do whatever Lacy told them to do.

He got off the stage and walked slowly toward Lacy. He watched her give some sort of command and telling whoever was at the other end to do it immediately.

He then knew she was talking to the General and telling him get the attack bubbles into position. She told the General that she had no idea where to send the attack bubbles, but they needed to intercept the sub out at sea and eliminate it.

He knew exactly what he had to do. He was going to break the rule that he had expressed concern about using the negative Fold arena to alter history.

He waited until Lacy was ready to share what the problem was. He listened as she explained that her network had picked up chatter that North Korea had somehow learned about the Fold effort and had its one missile launching sub on its way to eliminate the Dallas site.

He then told her to take the necessary actions in the current time, but he was going to Fold back in time and eliminate the threat. He asked her how much time he had.

Lacy replied that she had no clue but figured that he had less than an hour in real time.

He then asked where the sub was located when it was not at sea.

Lacey called into her team and in a few moments was able to give him the location.

Bram called Marcus, Remi and the General.

He asked Marcus to get the coordinates in the past for the submarine.

He asked Remi for a Fold vessel to be ready to be used under water and have an exit chamber on it.

He asked the General for a diver that would be able to place an explosive to a hull of a sub that was under water.

Marcus replied that he would have it in a few moments and would meet him at the Fold vessel.

Remi asked if a bubble attached to the outside of the lager Fold vessel to serve as an exit would be acceptable.

Bram said that what Remi was proposing would be acceptable.

The General called back and let him know that he had two Marine divers with the required skill on the way.

Bram thanked him and let Lacy know that he was on the way back in time to eliminate the threat, but she should continue doing what she needed to do in current time.

Lacy nodded and turned up her fist with the thumb up.

Bram waved his small army of protectors on and led the way to the hangar.

Pat joined him just outside of the auditorium and took his hand as they continued to walk. She commented that he seemed to have become the Fold marauder. She asked who was going with him.

The entire protection team shouted that they were going along.

Bram hoped that Remi had prepared the twelve-person Fold craft because he figured he had no time to argue with his protection team.

Remi had just finished showing the two Marine divers how to use the bubble attached to the twelve-person Fold vessel.

He looked up as Bram approached and asked if his protection team was going.

Bram nodded. He watched as Marcus exited the Fold vessel and the two Marines practiced going in and out.

Castor asked the two Marines if they were ready and got a "yes Sergeant Major." He turned to Bram and asked if he was ready to go.

Bram turned to Marcus and asked if he was ready to go.

Marcus nodded and said that he and Remi would be standing by and communicating with him in the past negative Fold realm and providing him any seek and find help that he might need. He said that he had found the moment that the sub was leaving port. He added that the Fold vessel that Bram was taking had six scout bubbles that could go underwater. He would provide continuous coordinates and depth for the sub. Bram would need to select the location that made the most sense to incapacitate the sub.

Marcus asked if the crew would survive.

Bram thanked Marcus. He understood how hard it was for Marcus to think about the crew losing their lives.

His reply to his last question was that the leaders of the crew would get every opportunity to save themselves. They would have to choose to surface or die. He said that the sub would be sunk at sea, but the crew would have the opportunity to get off.

Marcus thanked Bram and said that he would sleep much better knowing that no matter what the outcome the decision was going to be made by those most affected.

Bram got into the Fold vessel and Folded to the time and coordinates that Marcus had provided. He took in the port below and then Folded under water out at sea. He reviewed the pictures he had taken and verified that the sub seemed to just be casting off.

He sent up a scout bubble that skipped in millisecond skips in time alongside of the sub at the water line. This made the bubble virtually invisible but allowed Bram to follow the sub. When the sub submerged, he set the bubbled down on the hull.

He then asked Marcus to locate the tracking bubble out in the middle of Pacific.

A few moments later Marcus replied with the coordinates for the sub in the Middle of the pacific.

Bram noted that it was roughly a day and a half into the future and made the Fold to where the sub was located.

He placed the Fold transport on top of the sub's forward deck and asked the two Marines to go out and place the explosives on the forward planes at the point the planes attached to the hull of the sub.

He then watched as the two worked together to first set up their safety lines and then move the two boxes of explosives into place. He knew he was watching two extremely talented divers as they handled the swift water flowing past them while carefully moving their explosives into position.

It took them only ten minutest to have their explosives in place.

They returned and got back into the bubble. They simply said, "It's all yours," and sat down.

Bram thanked them. He then activated his radio transmitter set on the subs interior communication frequency and announced that the sub was going to be sunk. The bombs had been set on the forward control planes and would be detonated in ten minutes.

The choice of whether the crew would live, or die was up to the captain of the ship.

He waited until he got a reply. It was in clear English which relieved him because he was not sure if his English to North Korean translation was accurate.

The person replying asked how Bram could possibly sink his sub when there were no vessels within radar range.

Bram replied that it was very possible since he was sitting on the Sub's front deck and had just placed the explosives on the forward planes.

Bram then said that the conversation was over and that he would wait until the sub surfaced to blow the planes off and sink the sub. This would give the Captain a chance to radio for rescue and save his crew.

There was a momentary silence. Then the Captain came back on and said that he was bringing the sub up.

Bram waited until the water was breaking over the bubble and then Folded to a high point in the sky.

He wished the Captain and crew well and told them that they had ten minutes to abandon the sub.

He watched as part of the subs crew was getting into large life rafts, but he noted that some divers had been sent over the side.

He sent two observation bubbles down two where the divers were and used them to hit them on the side of their heads and then knock their goggles off.

He watched the two shouting up to their Captain.

He decided to hit the Captain on the side of the head with one of the observation bubbles. He knew that it would be a significant blow.

The Captain looked around trying to figure out what had happened. He shook his head and shouted to the two divers who swam to one of the rafts that were now joining together.

When the Captain stepped off the sub, Bram triggered the explosives and watched as most of the forward section of the sub pulverized and fell into the sea.

He then watched as the rest of the sub seemed to follow in slow motion but within a minute it was gone.

Castor complimented the two Marine divers for having done a great job.

Bram added that they were invited for Sunday breakfast so that he could show the video of them in action and then the sub sinking.

He added that he was going to do several Folds over their current location so they could make sure the crew got rescued.

Donna began cheering when they watched a US Navy destroyer racing at top speed and zeroing in to rescue the subs crew.

Bram called back to Marcus and asked him to find the news reel that highlighted the rescue of the North Korean crew.

Marcus replied that Bram's action had a surprising impact on what was transpiring off the coast of Oregon.

He explained that the US Navy had intercepted an unknown submarine and was about to drop depth charges when the sub disappeared. He commented that the Navy said that they did not know where the sub had gone but it was no longer in US water and could not be located.

Bram asked Marcus to tell the General to tell his Admiral friend that the sub that had threatened the US coast was sunk out in the middle of the Pacific.

Zoe looked around at those in the Fold vehicle and commented that she would never get use to how time and the actions taken during each moment of time could be so easily manipulated. She said that it was enough to give her nightmares.

Bram added that it was the stuff of science fiction, magic, stardust mixed with the horrors that might be perpetrated by those without scruples.

Chapter 5: Erasure Failure

The General had a band to greet them on their return. He shared that their actions had adverted a major political confrontation between North Korea and the US. He went on to say that their timing had been unbelievably well-timed and then he added that they had presented the Navy brass with a mystery of how a sub declared by the North Koreans to have been lost at sea could possibly have been spotted off the coast of Oregon. He laughed and said his Admiral friend, Dennis in San Diego had called and asked what kind of shenanigans the Fold team was up to.

He complimented his two divers for job done well done.

He laughed when they replied that it was the only way they had figured out to get an invite to a breakfast at Bram's house.

He gave them a salute and suggested they ask for the Pat Nielson breakfast special.

Marcus spoke up and thanked Bram for having made sure the sailors on the sub got rescued. He added that he had followed the reporting about the US Navy rescue and had found out that the rescue had been blacked out in the subsequent time period. He wondered if actions that might cause too big of a ripple in time were self-limiting. He had feared a time tsunami, but the ripple was hard to find.

Bram replied that Marcus should quit identifying investigations that they would have to follow up on. He, however, put it on his list of things to look into. He was curious how big the Time ripples he had so far created happened to be.

Pat walked across the hangar with the two Marine divers and got their names and ranks. She had a reason for doing so. She was planning to put their names on their pancakes for their Sunday morning breakfast. She had talked with these Marines before. She made it a point of being personal and friendly with all the people involved the Fold effort.

Lacy came running across the hangar and gave Bram a hug.

She had tears in her eyes.

She said that she had her team out with their observation bubbles right at the sub when the lids to the sub's rocket launchers opened and a missile began to rise slowly out of one of the tubes. Then the sub and missile disappeared. Her observation bubble was left looking at a spot where, for one moment, it seemed the sub was going to succeed and then it was gone.

Bram hugged her back and said that she should bring her footage of what she had just described and share it at breakfast on Sunday. He said she would be showing everyone the second miracle that the Fold capability had delivered.

Lacy nodded and said that she gave the credit for those miracles to the person she could give a hug to and get reinspired to continue what she was doing.

Pat gave Lacy a hug and said that she agreed with her perspective, and it was his personal humility for his immense capability and brilliant mind that made her not only love him but made her use all her capability in supporting him.

Bram shook his head and said that it was Friday, and it was time to call it a day. He was looking for a quiet evening sitting with his favorite couch buddy and focusing his mind on the warmth she radiated. He took Pat's hand and led the way to the van that would take them home.

The shiver that had run down his back when Lacy had shared what had happened once again made him realize how close he had come to losing his soul mate. He wanted to make sure that such a close call would not happen again. He had to accelerate Zoe's erasure of the Fold knowledge from the current time frame. He also wanted to accelerate the move of the Fold effort to Mataia where he had much better defenses in place and where the Earth attackers could not attack him or the people around him.

General Tilton asked his marines to walk with him. He complimented them and said that they had made him proud. He asked Donna to describe what she had been able to observe from inside the Fold bubble.

She sensed the General wanted an evaluation of the two Marines and replied that she was impressed with the speed with which her two Marine brothers had executed the placement of the explosives.

Castor spoke up and added that not only were they fast but when Bram triggered the explosion the entire front end of the sub was vaporized, and the sub went down like a rock.

The General chuckled and shared the fact that his admiral friend had already called him to ask how the Fold program could possibly make a sub that was being intercepted by a US destroyer that approaching it at full speed simply disappear.

He thanked all of them for providing him with crowing rights over his admiral friend's Navy.

Linda and Marcus had been walking behind the Admiral and the four Marines around him and they had heard the entire exchange.

Marcus simply asked the Marine divers where they had been when they sunk the sub.

One of them answered they had been in the middle of the Pacific.

The General said it would be hard to tell his friend, the Admiral, that the sub had never made it across the ocean.

The General stopped and looked at Marcus and asked him how that was even possible.

Marcus smiled and said that he should make sure to be at the Sunday breakfast when his two Marine divers were going to be in the spotlight.

The General looked at Matt, his aid, and said that now he should understand why retirement was looking so attractive.

Marcus smiled and commented that he understood that the General was looking at being involved in setting up the Mataian self-help organization that would ensure that crowds remained in control. It didn't sound much like retirement to him.

The General nodded and said what frighten him most was that he would actually have to work again the way he had done as a young man.

Linda said goodnight and said she would see them all at the Sunday morning breakfast. She said that she was just as intrigued how it had all happened. She added that the Fold capability twisted her mind into a pretzel.

She had no idea how Bram and Marcus had pulled off saving all of their lives, but she was extremely happy that they had.

Zoe had waited until after Breakfast on Saturday to ask Bram how the North Korean's attempt to eliminate the Dallas, Fold site would affect her effort to eliminate the Fold information from all sources on the Earth. She was bothered by the fact that information about Fold had somehow reached one of the most radical regimes in the world.

Bram replied that he felt that her efforts were critical and that they would have to make sure that the Fold elimination virus that her team was putting in place needed to be able to get into all the various computer systems in the world. He asked if she would mind having him work with her team to review their current trojan horse virus and see if he could add any ideas of how to make it more potent.

Zoe smiled and replied that she couldn't wish for more than that. She added that Linh and Duong had recruited at least six additional IT personnel to help in searching for Fold information and in placing the Fold information erase virus, but the task was immense.

Bram agreed with her on the size of the task. He pointed out that once her team had done their first cycle of elimination, they would need to improve their search engine and repeatedly keep checking all the various networks. He commented that the information might hibernate in someone's personal computer or thumb drive and then resurface sometime in the future. He suggested she add an alarm feature that would alarm and notify her any time Fold information resurfaced.

Pat had listened to the discussion and thought it was time to put work behind them. She suggested that they all go to the recreation center to relax. They could all play some pool and ping-pong, and someone might even be able to play snooker with Bram.

Bram said he was up for it but wanted to finish putting his Sunday morning presentation together. He said that he had all the video footage taken during the trip, and he had received the footage that Lacy's observation bubbles had captured of the sub off the Oregon coast. He commented that it was a fascinating twist of distance and time. He chuckled and said that it would twist everyone's mind.

Pat nodded and said that she was going to prepare the pancake dough for Sunday's breakfast. She then added that the names of the two Marines were Gary Tatum and Art Baratta, and they were both Marine Corporals.

Bram thanked Pat for letting him know. He then said that he expected the General to promote both of them to Sergeant on Sunday.

Pat said that gave her an idea for their pancakes.

Bram knew that the two were going to get a unique surprise. He suggested including both Castor and Donna who were sure to get promoted as well and thought they would both get promoted to Master Sergeants.

Pat asked how Bram would be so sure of what the General would do.

Bram smiled and said that was the last thing that he had asked the General to do before leaving the work center to come home and he had gotten his agreement.

Pat looked over to Zoe and told her that it was her job to get Bram to the recreation center for lunch and walked out of the office and went up to the kitchen.

Bram saw that Zoe and Eric were both sitting down with a bottle of water and were engaged in a discussion. He focused on getting the video ready for the next day.

He was surprised when Zoe stood before him and asked if he was ready for a game of ping-pong.

Her timing was perfect he had just finished his video. He closed his laptop and stood up and told her to lead the way.

Mallica had been talking with Pat at the recreation center when she saw Bram walk in. She had been worried about the situation on Swoosh and had asked Pat for her advice about sharing it with Bram when he came to the rec center.

Pat had suggested that Mallica approach him with a beer and a brat and share what she was concerned about.

She took Pat's advice and met Bram with the beer, and brat.

Bram thanked her and sat down at one of the tables. He knew something was concerning Mallica enough to cause her to approach him in the way she had done.

Mallica waited until Bram took a sip of his beer before sharing her concern.

She then shared the fact that the shrimp-like creatures that was the main meal for the Swooshians were dying at an alarming rate. If they could not figure out how to reverse the trend the Swooshians faced starvation.

Bram took a long sip of his beer and remained silent for a moment as he thought about the problem.

He then smiled and said that she must have missed his exchange with Ohaan the fifth when they had visited Swoosh. He suggested that she go back to that exchange and realize that she had solved the problem.

Then he suggested that they send a care package of each type of shrimp on Earth and see how they flourished on Swoosh. Then they could select the ones that did well and that were palatable to the Swooshians. They could send a continuous stream of the selected shrimp to Swoosh until the Swooshians were able to grow their own supply.

Mallica smiled and thanked him for confirming but also broadening her initial idea. She had already decided on sending some shrimp for them to try growing. She liked the idea of sending a sample of each type of shrimp to see which ones did well. She would then let the Swooshians decide how many varieties they wanted.

She asked if that is what she had done to solve the Swooshian food problem.

Bram said that he was not going to answer and asked Mallica whether she was up for a game of pool.

She laughed and replied that one critical win was satisfactory and now she could face the loss at the pool table bravely.

She commented that she was now eager to review the interchange that had gone on during their visit to Swoosh because she realized that the Swooshians had survived at least one thousand years into the future.

Bram added that it was nice to know that you had succeeded even before you had done the work.

Mallica nodded and accepted that she had just lost another game of pool to Bram.

Chapter 6: Fold Erasure

Bram was prepared and anticipating another interesting and captivating Sunday morning breakfast.

He was going to orchestrate a time Fold story that was sure to twist everyone's minds. He knew that it had twisted his mind, and he was still thinking through how two separate events could be happening to a missile launching submarine at the same moment of time. It highlighted the complexities of playing with the flow of time.

He was now certain that fooling with time was fooling with everyone's lifeline, and he had no clue how that ripple in time would affect an individual.

At the same time, he was in the middle of the Pacific sinking the submarine, it was off the coast of Oregon ready to launch missiles to destroy the Dallas site. Lacy had her observation Fold bubbles and had the submarine in sight but was in shock because she was watching the missile leaving its tube and beginning to rise and then there was nothing.

He again wondered how that could be.

Pat had made special pancakes for all the Marines that had accompanied him on the Fold to sink the sub. She had made one pancake for each that had their name and their new Marine Corps rank. The Names were elegantly written in red Edwardian Script. She had made the pancakes and frozen them so they could be warmed to be added on the top of a pancake stack that would be served.

Zoe had worked with her and added the Marine corps insignia. The insignia was a twisted rope golden circle, then a black background that had the words in gold, United States at the top of the black circle and Marine Corps at the bottom of the circle. Four golden stars were on each side between the two. Then the Eagle, The Globe and the Anchor were set on the red center that had two thin gold lines enclosing it.

Bram commented on the amazing beauty of the Marine corps insignia. He said that he doubted the pancakes would be eaten. He was sure all of the Marines in question would ask for it to be frozen.

He took a picture of each Pancake and added the pictures to his presentations. He was sure that they would be a highlight to his presentation.

He joked with Zoe that she had earned four nose tweaks for doing such great artwork on the pancakes.

Zoe replied that she instead wanted him to help her tweak the noses of their adversaries and help her eradicate the Fold information from all the systems on Earth.

Bram replied that he would spend all the time she asked from him. She was leading one of the most critical tasks that would allow him to guide the Fold program to a continuing and successful effort.

Zoe was pulled back to her role of protecting him when the doorbell rang. Bob and Thomas were the two that answered the door, but Zoe and Eric were the ones that stood between Bram and the entrance area.

Bram as always, was amazed at the willingness with which his bodyguards always stepped in toward the potential threat.

He was delighted that once the door opened a steady stream of arrivals came in.

Bram noted that the newlyweds, Lacy, Ray, Linda, and Rafael all came in together.

He was impressed by the fact that the General, Castor, Donna, Gary, and Art were all wearing their formal parade uniforms as they came in. Each gave him a salute before sitting down at the table.

He was pleased that Melisa was one of the persons that was attending.

Pat purposely saved serving their Marine Corps guests until last. Then she announced that on this Sunday morning the Marines got special treatment. She then led out, Amy, Zoe, Eric, Bob, and Thomas who each carried out a plate of pancakes. The special decorated pancake was on top, and she had worked with Marcus to have a camera bubble hovering at the top of the room so she could show the plates as they were placed in front of each of the Marine guests.

The Generals top pancake had a large Marine Corp symbol that covered most of it. Then each of the other Marines were served their plates and every one of them commented that there must be a mistake because it addressed them at the next rank up.

The General stood up and thanked Pat for having provided him the moment. He then turned and asked Donna and Castor to stand. He congratulated them on their very good work and their willingness to put their bodies at risk every day. He then gave them their new insignia and a metal. He saluted them and then asked Corporals Gary Tatum and Art Baratta to stand. He complemented them on the exemplary work they had done in sinking the missile launching sub and presented them with their Sergeants insignia and the same metal he had given to the other two.

He saluted them and said that they had made him proud. He then said it was time to enjoy breakfast.

When he sat down, he looked at his pancake and asked if he could save it.

Pat replied that yes, he could but as she showed each of the pancakes on the big screen, she said that the picture that was worth a thousand words had been taken but the picture worth ten times that would happen when it showed each of them eating those pancakes.

Donna and Castor uttered a loud "Hurrah" and poured their maple syrup over the pancakes and took their first bite.

Everyone at the table repeated, "Hurrah" and began to wolf down the pancakes.

Melisa said that she could get the insignia sewed on and that by noon they could have their pictures taken with their new ranks on their uniform. She made a couple of calls, and a few moments later there was a knock on the door. The "community seamstress," one of the wives of a Fold employee had come over to get the Marine jackets.

Once breakfast was over, Bram turned on the video. The lead in was a full version of the Marine Battle Hymn and then it faded into the background and the view of a missile launching submarine came on the screen. It left the harbor and then it slowly sank below the surface.

The view then switched to an underwater view of the sub that lasted for a few moments before the Fold craft appeared on the sub. It was in front of the subs conning tower. The flow of the water was emphasized by the stream passing across the front of the Fold vessel. The bubble attached to the side of the Fold vessel held the two fully dressed divers and the two boxes of explosives.

When the first diver exited, it became clear that he was fighting the flow of water as he hooked his safety line to the front of the bubble. The two divers pulled out the first box of explosives and carefully maneuvered it to the point where they were just in front of the port diving plane. One of the divers lowered himself and stood on the diving planes leading edge. He was leaning forward as he fought the flow of water. The second diver slowly lowered the box down to him. Once the box was in place, the diver flipped two wings out from the edges of the box, and they snapped onto the hull.

Bram stopped the video and asked "Sergeants Tatum and Baratta" if they had anything to add to what had been shown.

Gary Tatum commented that he had been the one to go down on the port fin and that "Sergeant Baratta" was the person to go down on the starboard fin. He then commented that their training had included simulating how to sink a sub, but the real thing was a lot tougher to do than the practice.

He admitted that when they got back to land, they had all sat around drinking beer talking about what everyone had seen on the screen. Now that he was seeing it for himself, he was ready to take part in drinking another round of beers to celebrate their survival.

Bram praised both of them and added that when he watched them from the safety of the Fold bubble, he felt lightheaded. He said that he could feel the water trying to rip each of them from the sub exterior.

He then turned on the video and watched the second box of explosives being place.

Then the scene changed to a picture of the same sub as the cover of one of the missile tubes slowly opened. Then the scene was of a US Navy destroyer plowing through the sea and a crew preparing to launch depth charges. It flashed back to a missile slowly rising.

Then the scene switched back to the sub with the bombs on the diving plane. They all listened as Bram explained to the submarine captain that his submarine was going to be sunk and that he had ten minutes to get his crew off the sub and into their survival rafts. The scene then took in the set of rafts as they moved away from the sub and suddenly the explosion roared, and the front of the sub disappeared. The remainder of the sub seemed to quietly back itself down into the ocean.

The screen then split, and two US Navy ships were shown. The background music softly played Anchors Aweigh. One ship was approaching the rafts holding the sub crew. The other ship was clearly in a search and destroy pattern looking for a submarine that had vanished. An underwater view of nothing closed the scene.

The music switched to the Marine Battle hymn. Bram commented that how both ships could have existed at the same time was a Fold mystery that he could not explain. He added that Lacy had captured the part of the video that took place off the Oregon coast and asked her to add a few words.

Lacy was shaking her head in disbelief. She said that the video clearly showed what she had seen but it could not convey the unbelievable fear that had gone through her when the missile tube opened, and a missile began to rise. She shared that she had awakened for three nights screaming, NO! NO! NO! and wept in Raymond's arms. She said that she had attended several sessions with Dr. Windal and was finally over most of that trauma.

Bram shook his head and apologized that by being the target of people trying to kill him, the entire community was at risk. He added that he was using all of his resources to reduce that risk.

He then said that erasing all the Fold information from Earth was the only way that he knew to address the risk. Zoe was leading that effort, and he was joining her to see how to accelerate the erasure.

General Tilson stood up and thanked Bram for having provided him a reason to retire from the Marine Corp and to make the transition to Mataia. He asked how he could help expedite the Fold information erasure.

Bram smiled and said that the General should delay his official retirement until the final Fold to Mataia was planned. He was welcome to be part of the Erasure team but his presence as the Marine Officer in charge of the Fold facilities was critical and he was needed in that role until the last moment.

The General nodded and said that he understood besides, he had to synchronize his retirement with his long time Admiral friend that would be going to Mataia with him. Meanwhile he would use the video to tease his friend on the fact that the Navy had provided much entertainment in their cluelessness.

Bram shook his head and said that he was not going to be involved in that exchange.

Pat stood and suggested that they end breakfast, take a break and they could all go to the recreation center in the afternoon and end the day relaxing and discussing what they had seen at breakfast.

Bram thanked everyone and said he was heading for his office.

Half the table emptied as he and his bodyguards left. Zoe and Eric led the way, and they all went down into the basement. Zoe and Eric checked the office and cleared it for Bram to enter.

Bram asked Zoe if she wanted to spend a little time to noodle how to proceed at a faster pace of erasure.

Zoe nodded her head and said that living their sub sinking experience again really made her want to work twenty-four seven until the erasure was done and she could move on to contributing new substance to the Fold effort in a positive concrete way.

Bram displayed his Excel spreadsheet on the large screen and typed in, "Rapid Earth Fold Resource Erasure Strategy Hammer, (REFRESH). There were seven columns with each of the words in one column.

He then said that they had to make a list of actions or ideas under each column.

He gave an example for rapid multiple people, parallel actions.

Then he did the same for every column. When he got to Hammer, he listed Zoe, Eric, Duong, and Linh.

He then made a bad joke about how refreshing getting the task of erasing would be.

Zoe laughed and said she was going to go back to tweaking his nose.

Bram smiled and replied that he was glad that his bad jokes were at least understood and that the point he was trying to make was that utilizing all their resources they could get the initial erasure task implemented in less than a month and the longer-term validation put in place to operate on an automatic routine that would last for a lifetime but would only take a few hours each year to maintain.

Zoe came over and gave Bram a hug and said that she could now go down to the recreation center and be able to relax and enjoy herself. She felt like a weigh had been lifted off her chest.

Bram said that she should never do what depressed her and to always look at how to make what you had to do as enjoyable as possible.

Zoe replied that she normally did just what he was suggesting but she had already been warned about tweaking his nose and erasing stuff from computer systems had turned out not to be fun. She went on to say that figuring out how to automate that work to the point that it would only take a few hours a year sounded like fun, and she had two folks on the team who could make it happen.

Bram suggested they take one run through the seven columns and then hustle down to the recreation center and enjoy the rest of the day as Pat had suggested.

Chapter 7: Past History

Bram played a couple of games of pool and one game of ping-pong. Then he overheard Lacy, Linda, Amy, and Pat talking about how they should approach studying past history.

The twenty-thousand-year boundary eliminated many of the topics that were of interest to all of them, but they had come to the realization that there was more than five million years of human history that would take their entire lives to study and share. They were talking about the twenty-five major segments that they had decided would guide their efforts. They were sure that they needed to make their team large enough to have all twenty-five segments investigated at the same time. Even after that split it was still clear to them that their work would take them a lifetime.

Bram asked about the specific time frame split.

Pat took out her phone and displayed a list of time frames that took them back five million years. She pointed out that was the time when the ancestors of humans were just making their appearance. She added that they were following a part of a timeline that was published online that had highlighted events that occurred at various periods. Their small team had decided to focus on all twenty-five periods because it would provide a tremendous amount of information to the Mataian society. She then said that their team of three should grow to be at least two hundred and fifty individuals on twenty-five teams.

She then added that there were several other ways to look at the history of the Earth,

The formation periods where the oceans and the crust of the Earth developed.

The tectonic plate movements and watching mountains grow.

The weather cycle and pole position and pole shift.

Understanding of the creatures of the past and the associate evolution processes

She asked if he got the gist that her team could put triple the number of people she had mentioned to work for a lifetime.

She smiled and said that they also thought a supercomputer should be made available to them.

Bram gave out slow, low whistle. He said that he was impressed with their approach and was pleased that they were looking to populate the effort with a substantial number of people. That last fact alone made her request for a supercomputer reasonable. He suggested the team also determine where the team would work and that perhaps they needed a large work center of their own.

Pat thanked Bram and said she was going to talk to Erica about a supercomputer and that she and the team would think through about a separate Earth History Center. She then said that the team had recommended that initially they work from home and once every twenty-five days they would meet in the large meeting room in the Mataian Work Center and work together. She said that each team could also schedule work sessions on their own that would be based on their need to do so.

If they decided to populate more efforts the team might need to rethink how they managed all the people.

Bram said he like what they were doing and to have Erica clear the people that they selected to work with them. The people they selected should be brought on board to the move to Mataia and be willing to do so.

Amy spoke up and said that she had asked the question of Erica about the number of people moving to Mataia and she said that currently there were three thousand folks working at the Fold compound.

They had ten times that many people involved in some support capacity. Erica said that it would take about fifty thousand folks to have Einstein City functioning on its own.

Bram walked over to where Erica was sitting with Gerry and sat down. He lifted his glass of beer and complimented her on the good work she was doing to get Einstein City up and running. He asked her if they were financially well enough off to make the move.

Erica smiled and replied that he knew they were financially well off because he was the one funneling money into their bank accounts. She said that he was doing well and that the finances would not be an issue. She pointed out that finding enough people that met his criteria would be the challenge.

Bram asked if they should speed up the timeline in getting people to begin living on Mataia.

She suggested that all the current Fold personnel and their families begin spending fifty percent or more of their time on Mataia. She would work with the current facilities maintenance folks to do the same. This would ensure that everyone had time to adjust to a slightly different set of homes and facilities.

Bram lifted his beer and said that she should make it happen. He added that Pat, Amy, and their team would be asking her for a supercomputer, and he was in support of their request.

Gerry commented that he really enjoyed being on Mataia and that he had Folded a small sailboat to Mataia and had enjoyed the relative calm sea off the coast of Einstein City. When he did so he immediately realized that there should be a rule against any use of engines out on the Mataian seas. He had already written down a set of rules and he wondered how they would be enforced.

Bram smiled and said that his Admiral sponsor was planning to retire to Mataia. Gerry should get in contact with him and set up a rules of the sea team.

Gerry shook his head and asked how Bram knew about the Admiral's retirement location.

Bram smiled and said not to worry about the tight relationship that he had with his supporter. The information he had was via a certain General who was planning to retire to Mataia and was going to help set up the Mataian organization to maintain social calm and distribute help when needed.

Gerry nodded and gave a small laugh. He said that the Admiral had shared with him that he and the General planned to retire to the same location. He, however, had not told him about the location. He asked how a Marine Corps General had gotten the role of setting up an organization with the goal of maintaining social calm and distributing help.

Bram replied that he had asked him to do it.

Gerry again shook his head and asked why Bram thought that a Marine General would be able to set up an organization that would establish such a warm social order.

Bram smiled and replied because he demonstrated that he could be lifelong friends with a Navy Admiral.

Gerry laughed and said that it was a logic he had not thought about, but he was sure Bram had somehow connected everything together and that it would work.

Bram asked if having a visual tour of the last five million years of human history would be of interest for a Sunday morning breakfast.

This time both Gerry and Erica asked how he had gone from talking about the retirement of an Admiral and a General to a tour of human history.

Bram Nielson Collection

Bram thought for a moment and then replied that he had an earlier discussion with the General about announcing his retirement at the next breakfast. He then talked with Amy and Pat about their plans for their study of Earth' past. Then as he was talking to the two of them the idea of sharing retirement announcements and updating folks on what the history team was doing merged.

He then asked if they should invite the Admiral to come up and announce the location where he planned to live after retirement.

Gerry replied that he would love to invite the General for the Sunday breakfast. Gerry asked why breakfast had become the meal when Bram made all his spectacular announcements.

Bram smiled and said that breakfast allowed it to be a simple meal that had some great food, and it did not need catering.

He thanked them for letting him talk business with them.

He headed to where Marcus, Remi and Marcus's kids were sitting.

He got hugs from both of the kids and then asked what they had been doing all week. He listened as they talked about their time in school and the fact that they were both on a basketball team at the school.

Pat had been sipping on her ginger ale watching Bram making his rounds. It was clear to her that he was following some thread in his mind, and she would later listen to him as they sat together, and he shared what he was thinking.

Zuri's comment about Bram's nonlinear mind came to her and she smiled. Nonlinear, inventive, and always with people's wellbeing at the forefront.

She wondered what he was thinking as he talked with Marcus' kids.

She knew that since their trip one thousand years into the future and meeting Marial their distant granddaughter he had become much more interested in speeding up the move to Mataia.

Bram noticed Pat watching him and smiled. He decided that his information fishing trip should end, and he would see if she would play a game of ping pong with him.

Linda was sitting with Rafael at a table next to where Pat was sitting. She commented to Rafael that she had just watched Bram load up on ideas that would lead to additional work for her and for everyone on the team.

Rafael replied that Bram had demonstrated to him that he was capable of almost anything, but he was sure giving Linda more work was not his direct intent. She was just caught in his friendly fire and not involved in what he now knew about Bram's deadly fire with both bullets and Fold executions.

Linda nodded and said that he had made sure she got out of the way on the last interaction with the antagonist in the future. Bram had never mentioned what had happened to that antagonist but had asked her to get him put on Dr. Windal's schedule. She wished she could get a look into Dr. Windal's mind. She had to know more about each of the team issues and problems than anyone.

Bram stopped at Linda's table and asked her to contact Elizabeth and set up a meeting to discuss the School on Mataia.

Linda smiled and said that she would be pleased to do so and to schedule all the other work he had just now been rounding up.

Bram lifted his now empty mug and replied that he was sure she would be the one organizing everything. He lifted his empty mug and said he would fill the mug, and he was sure she would fill his schedule.

He then wished both of them a good afternoon and went to sit with Pat, Amy, and Jose.

Amy asked whether he had been flying his helicopter close to the ground so he could see all the plants and animals.

Bram smiled and said that he was not that talented and instead was more like a bumble bee that bounced from flower to flower hoping to find an open bloom with some nectar in it.

Pat asked to see all the pollen pellets clinging to his hind legs. She said that she doubted they would be pellets but would be more likely to be pollen baskets or giant corbiculae.

Bram replied that he was just being social. He had not gone out intentionally seeking anything in particular, but he always listened to the ideas people had.

He then asked if he could get a brief overview of each to the twenty-five time periods that they had defined.

Pat gave a little moan and said that would cost him a glass of Moscato and then she would share what she had.

Amy asked if he would bring back two glasses so she could join in.

Bram asked Jose what he would like.

Jose stood up and said that he would go to the bar with him.

On the way Jose asked how soon he should be planning to have bubble production established on Mataia.

Bram did not hesitate to say that he could start immediately to move production of whatever he could to Mataia and to continue to add to the things that got produced on Mataia. The only thing that should be kept in mind was that there should be no short cuts that would pollute Mataia. The practice would be to continue to import all goods that they could not be produce cleanly.

Jose smiled and replied that he sounded a lot like Amy and Pat on making sure he didn't bring pollution along with the manufacturing effort. He said that it would be a challenge that he was going to make sure he accomplished.

Bram said he should hear it from every person that would live on Mataia.

Pat and Amy thanked Bram for the wine. Pat asked if she and Amy were next in his gathering of pollen.

Bram smiled and took a sip of his wine. He nodded and asked if they would share how they were approaching the study of the history of Earth.

Amy replied that the team that they were leading had decided that their current interest was on the history of humankind and that other teams should be formed for the other periods and other topics. They had chosen to focus on the last five million years and had up to this point chosen to accept the splits of time that they had found that was currently in use.

She said that she was going to share the information that they had gleaned from the online information and later they would develop a more detailed investigative plan to work from.

The **first period** was 5.5 to 4.5 million of years in the past. It was when the very first erect beings were believed to have been living. In this time period Mammoths, polar bears and brown bears were present. We figure that these animals indicate that many other smaller animals were also present but that will be left for some other team to study.

The **second period** is from 4.5 to 3.5 million of years in the past. It is the time of Australopithecus a bipedal great ape. It is known that zebras were present so again there had to be a variety of other animals.

The **third period** is from 3.5 to 2.8 million of years ago. Our distant relatives had developed stone tools. It was also the time that those that were to be called human lost their fur. Cats, condors, raccoons, armadillos, opossums, the giant sloth, and hummingbirds are known to have been in existence and moving around in North America. This is the time when Lucy existed in what is now Ethiopia. She has been credited to be the mother of everyone else. We don't believe this a true fact but finding her energized an entire generation of anthropologists.

The **fourth period** is from 2.8 to 2.2 million of years ago. Megalodon becomes extinct. More tools were found in Africa, China, and India. It is the start of an ice age.

The **fifth period** is from 2.2 to 1.8 million of years ago. It is when homo erectus is said to first appear.

The **sixth period** is from 1.8 to 1.4 million of years ago. One of the first up right beings, Australopithecine goes extinct. Homo erectus begins to migrate out of Africa and is found in Europe and a true hand ax exists.

The **seventh period** is from 1.4 to 1.1 million of years ago. One line of early humans dies out and another evolves. We figure this time period had as much activity as most of them but there has been less evidence found for this time period. We plan to be through in looking at this time period and bring our knowledge of the time up to the same level as all the other time periods.

The **eighth period** is from 1.1 million to 900 thousand of years ago. Humans cross the seas to Indonesia. Cooking fires are thought to have existed. Human stone tools and footprints are found in England.

The **ninth period** is from 900 to 700 thousand of years ago. Early humans are found in northern China. There is evidence of use the of fire. Branches of the human species are found in the Philippines, Indonesia, Sub Sahara Africa.

The **tenth period** 700 to 550 thousand of years ago. Homo Antecessor and Heidelbergensis are in existence. Indication that cannibalism was occurring.

The **eleventh period** 550 to 450 thousand of years ago. Spear stone points found in Africa. Etchings on a seashell in Java. The oldest known spear is found in England. Homo Heidelbergensis exists across Germany, France, and Greece.

The **twelfth period** 450 to 350 thousand of years ago. It is the early first appearance of the Neanderthal. First believed homicide case is found. Hominin footprints in Spain.

The **thirteenth period** 350 to 280 thousand of years ago. Middle stone age tools and long distant trading is documented. Evidence of fire used to pretreat stone for making blades.

The **fourteenth period** 280 to 220 thousand of years ago. Woman bearing traits between Homo Erectus, and Homo Sapiens is found in Korea. Evidence of deliberate entombing of the dead is found. Stone tools are found in Mexico.

The **fifteenth period** 220 to 180 thousand of years ago. Homo Sapiens in Greece and Palestine.

The **sixteenth period** 180 to 140 thousand of years ago. Neanderthals build circular piles of stalagmites. They wear clothes by this time. Sea fish and other marine food enters the diet. Mitochondrial Eve from whom all living humans are said to descent. Amy pointed out that this was of particular interest for them to investigate.

The **seventeen period** 140 to 110 thousand of years ago. Crete artifacts indicate that seafaring had begun. Evidence of humans in Victoria, Australia. Spear point made from whale tooth is documented. Numerous indications of improvement to tools and the higher use of symbols and paint to decorate items and walls.

The **eighteenth period** 110 to 90 thousand of years ago. Homo Erectus goes out of existence. Shells with holes found indicating that they were used to make jewelry. Evidence of Paint being made in a cave on the Southern Cape coastline.

The **nineteenth period** 90 to 70 thousand of years ago. Homo Sapiens in Arabia. Shell beads are found in Morocco. Evidence of use of insecticide and glue in Sibudu cave in South Africa. Arrowhead like projectile points possibly poisoned arrows discovered.

The **twentieth period** 70 to 55 thousand of years ago. Start of one-thousand-year ice age most likely due to super volcano eruption. Evidence of aboriginal Australian culture and humans at Australian Northern territory. The Cave art in Spain is discovered. Neanderthals build circular post structure near Poitiers France and also reenter Britain.

The **twenty first period** 55 to 45 thousand of years ago. Denisovans use sewing needle and thread. Remains of string found in France. Depiction of warty pigs in cave drawing.

The **twenty-second period** 45 to 35 thousand of years ago. Homo Sapiens in Bulgaria. First painted story. Needles and sewing documented. Tools made from animal bones, hematite, and other stones. It appears that shoes are being worn as indicated by foot bones. Tuna is being eaten which indicates deep sea fishing. Dyed Flax fibers found in Georgia eastern Europe. Neanderthal disappears.

The **twenty third period** 35 to 28 thousand years ago. Ostrich egg beads being traded over a long distance. Surgical Amputation in Borneo. Humanoids are in Ireland. Oats are ground into floor. Evidence of human presence in Japan. Stone mortar and pestle used to grind fern and cattail. Aboriginal Australians make first settlements at Sydney, Perth and Melbourne and they apparently do first cremations. Rock paintings in India. First known ceramic documented. First ovens found.

The **twenty fourth** period 28 to 22 thousand years ago. Twisted rope, harpoons, boomerang, and saws are being used. Woven cloth makes an appearance. Ivory sculpture indicates art continues to be made. Natural fiber used to make baby carriers, clothes, bags, baskets, and nets. Carving of a face found. Huts are being built of rocks and Mammoth bones. First apparent permanent settlement. Cave Bear thought to be extinct. Humans living in Alaska, and Yukon.

The **twenty fifth period** 22 to 18 thousand years ago. Early humans known to live in Canberra, Australia. Tally stick indicates understanding of how to use the primary number sequence. Human footprints at White Sand Natural Park in New Mexico. Stone tools use evidence at Toca da Tira Peia, Brazil. The making of traditional Inuit clothing. The remains of mud huts at Ohalo, by the Sea of Galilee. Artifacts found on Cactus Hill at Virginia, USA.

Pat asked if everyone was still awake and said that there would be a quiz on what they had just been taught.

She went on to say that Bram should not worry about employing all the personnel at the site. He had just listened to Amy share a brief focus on the human history. Their team had commented that the heavens, the solar system, Earth's land mass, the creatures in the ocean, land, and skies all needed to be studied and documented.

She suggested that what Bram needed was a team to identify and launch teams to do all the learning and studying.

Bram nodded and said he would take her up on the suggestion. He then said the important question was should he get another glass of wine or some other drink.

Chapter 8: Future History

Bram looked across the rec center and spotted Bob and Thomas sitting with Zoe and Eric. He figured he might as well finish his round of querying folks about what they were up to. He was interested in how Bob was approaching the effort of studying Future history. He had high interest in learning how seeing things in the future compared to looking at history in the past. His highest interest was how his actions would play out in the near future and how he could learn to change, modify, or improve how he made decisions on the work he was doing or contemplating. He wondered how choosing one priority over another would affect the near future.

Marcus had been making progress in identifying the various nodes on the rhombicosidodecahedron (RCID). He had made the discovery that the RCID expanded to match initial distance the Fold vessel was sent out but luckily the first early nodes on the RCID remained the same and they learned that the new nodes once defined by their color spectrum remained the same.

The two of them had come to the conclusion that the RCID that was generated from their current Earth launch point was actually one entity that achieved its size by the distance chosen at the very beginning.

They had discussed the strategy of space exploration by setting the initial distance to the maximum and then jumping to a desired location by choosing the node that was closest to the point of interest and then going to the next desired Fold using the specific color spectrum of that node. They speculated that they could send out numerous exploratory Fold bubbles and explore a huge portion of the Universe. They agreed that for Earth they would stick with the Milky Way Galaxy. However, they speculated that to find other intelligent beings they would need to send several search bubbles out on a RCID that encompassed more of the universe and encompassed Galaxies that were many light years away.

Then when they got to Mataia they would need to set up a new interface between the positive and the negative Fold realms and establish the RCID that had its focal point near Mataia. This meant they would have another view of the Universe and would most likely be looking at a totally different set of Galaxies. They both believed that having two RCID focal points doubled their chances of finding other intelligent beings.

Bram was also interested in guiding Bob in his forward look to see how the action that he and Marcus took affected the future.

By having visited the future he had learned that with none of the initial actions he was planning but not yet taken had not provided the forward flow Fold of benefits to the future. He had been very successful in locking the knowledge up but the condition out one thousand years was not as advanced as he hoped it would be.

The other concern he had was that a change during his lifetime would have a negative impact on Marial's time in the Mataian year 1000.

One of the tasks he would ask Bob to perform was to check the future after every action that he took in the present.

Once he understood the ripples in time he was creating, he desired to control them so remained a reasonable size that the future could comfortably surf.

He was pulled back to the present when Zoe asked if he was going to join their world or was, he going to stay in his mind and ignore them?

Bram shook his head and apologized and explained that he had envision how Bob and Thomas were going to contribute to the transition of the negative and positive Fold interface being moved to a Mataian focal point.

Bob took a sip of his beer and asked Thomas if he had any clue what Bram was talking about.

Thomas shook his head and said he must have been asleep when Bram explained that concept.

Bram asked what they knew about studying the future.

Both of them said that they had been Folding bubbles to the future and slowly learning to control how to get to the time they were interested in. They both complemented Marcus on being willing to help them set the controls so that they got their viewing bubbles close to the time they were targeting. They had learned how to time skip their observation bubbles to avoid being discovered.

Bram said that it was time to accelerate their learning.

Bob asked whether both he and Thomas would be able to close on their long-term, long-distance love affairs before they devoted their hearts to their future Fold History studies and learned how to navigate that from their new Mataian home world.

Bram smiled and lifted the glass of beer that Zoe had brought him and said that he was glad to hear that they were getting serious about their life and asked when he would be getting an invitation.

Zoe spoke up and said that both Bob and Thomas wanted a Rushing River wedding, and they wanted to ask the most famous river preacher to reside.

Bram laughed and said that as long as he did not have to stand in the river, he would be honored to perform the wedding. He asked when he should be planning to perform the weddings.

Bob said that he was going to propose on the coming weekend and had already scheduled his Fold to his hometown of Philadelphia.

Thomas said that he was doing the same thing at the same time, and he was proposing to the girl next door. However, his next door lived a good two miles away and they had gone to a one room schoolhouse that was located almost exactly halfway between their two farms and later they had ridden the same school bus to a consolidate junior high and high school that was about five miles away.

He shared the fact than neither his parents nor hers had been financially in a position to handle the cost of college, so they had both attended a small community college and each of them went to separate Universities. He had worked his way through the University of Iowa, and she had done the same at the University of Illinois.

They had continued to reunite at Thanksgiving and Christmas, but they had also dated other people.

They had reconnected when they graduated. Thomas said that he had been hired by the FBI and she had gone to work as a finance manager with a large manufacturing company. He said that he had refreshed that connection by using the Fold weekend vacations to do so.

Bob asked if Bram had found where to press Thomas's talk button and that he had never been around him when he talked so much.

Bram asked Bob how he had reached the marital stage point.

Bob said that he had met his future wife at the agency. She was an office manager that managed a team of secretaries or that were now called support personnel. Like Thomas he had used the Fold weekend vacations to develop closer ties.

Bram smiled and said that it seemed that the two of them had changed roles for the afternoon, but he was very pleased that the weekend Fold vacations had made it possible for them to reach the "I do" decision point.

He asked them to make sure all their intended guest got FBI clearances.

He asked Thomas whether his wife to be family might be interested in farming on Mataia. He then suggested that if so both his father and his wife's father should be linked to Amy and Pat who were in charge of the Mataian transformation.

He suggested that they call and arrange a good time for the wedding with Mike and Marry at the Rushing River.

Zoe said that she would be glad to handle those arrangement when she and Eric went fishing on the following weekend.

Bram said that he planned to engage a couple of other folks and then he would signal them when it was time to head for the house.

He put down his full beer glass and told Zoe that she should have given him the same iced tea with lemon that she was drinking.

She smiled and said that she was just trying to put a new curve into his non-linear mind.

He smiled and said that she would need to be better at figuring out how to affect his spiraling nonlinear mind.

He then headed to where Remi was sitting.

He engaged him and asked if he was having a secret affair that he wanted to share.

Remi laughed and asked how many beers Bram had consumed.

Bram replied that it had nothing to do with beer, but he had recently learned that Linda had arranged a date for him. He had also heard that Melisa had done the same and that Jina had done something similar.

He commented that indeed Remi seemed to have become the center of their attention. Remi said that he appreciated them introducing him to some very nice women. He had enjoyed the outings. He smiled and said that he had found the person of interest on the other side of the fence in the apple orchard. He had watcher her picking apples and had used an observation bubble to get a closer view. Then he had a gate installed in the fence and went out and asked her if she would pick an apple for him. He said that her smile and the apple she gave him had convinced him that he wanted to know her better.

He had asked Zoe to check her out to ensure she had a clear background before he got more involved and was pleased that she could get a secret clearance.

Bram congratulated Remi in finding his apple in the apple orchard.

He then asked Remi his thoughts of how they could leverage Future history to make sure that the Fold effort would continue to make improvements on the human condition.

Remi thought for a minute and responded that there would be two views of future history. The Mataian centered rhombicosidodecahedron would view the universe from a different perspective than the rhombicosidodecahedron that was Earth centered. They would be able to see the past and the future from two different perspective. He suggested that once they began to understand those two different perspectives they might desire to establish another rhombicosidodecahedron that was Swoshian centered. He wondered what they would learn from the past and the Future of Mataia and Swoosh. What they would learn from the Earth centered rhombicosidodecahedron was already presenting the Fold organization with a challenge that would absorb most of the current available resources.

He then added that on Mataia they could use forward history to evaluate decisions made in current time and might allow making changes in current time to adjust what was happening in the near future. He commented that he had no idea how being able to quickly evaluate the choices made in current time and then adjusting them by what was learned would turn out.

Bram commented that for a simple lab scientist Remi had developed into a Fold whisperer. He asked if he wanted to be a Fold change guide and advisor.

Remi replied that the changes that Bram was planning to make to protect the people around him looked to him like an experiment. He went on to say that every experiment he conducted began with defining how the experiment would be verified and the technique of verification. The verification for both experiment success and its failure always resulted in new learning. The new learning often led to additional improvements or modifications.

He commented that doing it at Bram speed would be challenging but it would also be invigorating. He had engaged Marcus and Mallica to improve his understanding of the Fold theory. He hoped that he could be the lead in verifying the actions that Bram took managing Fold.

Bram asked what resources Remi would need to do what he had so eloquently described.

Remi replied that he would love to have a small group of evaluators and suggested Marcus, Mallica, Pat, and Amy. He said that having one senior IT and four Lab technicians to support the actual gathering and evaluation of future data would make things run smoothly.

Having someone other than himself looking forward evaluating his actions solved one of his concerns. Having someone like Remi doing it reassured him that changes would be thoroughly evaluated. Having the evaluation pass through a team consisting of Marcus, Mallica, Pat and Amy reassured him that true open thinkers were using their judgement. He thought of Elizabeth and decided to add her name to the list. He valued her viewpoint on social matters.

He asked Remi about having Elizabeth join the change evaluation team.

Remi replied that he would love to have her on the team.

Bram asked that Remi get the Evaluation team launched immediately.

He shared that the Fold information was being erased from the records on Earth and would be transferred to three super computers on Mataia. At the moment only one supercomputer was available, but Erica was working on getting the other two installed.

He suggested that Remi work with Pat and Amy to arrange the work area where the Fold Evaluation Team would meet and do their work. He should immediately establish the team and get organize because they were a month late already.

Remi laughed and commented that he was going to ask Pat for a ditty on how fast her partner moved and the fact that there was a trail of supporters that could not catch up. He then thanked Bram for giving him an opportunity that he was sure would keep him engaged and growing for the rest of his life.

Bram smiled and said that he thought the ditty would be available a few moments after he asked Pat. He commented that what Remi was calling a growth opportunity was critically important to him and would most likely remain critically important for the foreseeable future.

Chapter 9: Sealed

Pat's warmth seemed to flow into him as the two of them sat on their two-person recliner. He was thinking about how to contain the Flow information and ensure that it was used for good. He thought about Zoe's comment that he had opened up something much worse than Pandora's box. He thought about the Greek mythology that told of how Zeus had punished Prometheus for stealing fire from the heavens and giving it to the common people of Earth. The punishment was that the wife to Prometheus's brother Epimetheus, overcome with curiosity, opened a jar left to her husband. When she opened the jar she released the curses of sickness, death, and many other evils into the world. That incident became known as, Pandora opening the box of good and evil.

A shiver ran down his back when he recalled Zoe commenting that the Fold container held a much worse set of curses. Those were not exactly her words, but he was feeling the dramatic impact, both positive and negative that it had so far released.

He thought about the two marriages that he had made and the two-Fold wives he had embraced.

When the veil of his positive Fold wife was lifted, he was greeted with warm radiance and beauty and knew that he had a lifetime of warmth and comfort ahead.

When the vail of the negative Fold wife was lifted he knew that he had a tumultuous life ahead. It would not be boring. It would be challenging. It would require his constant attention.

He shook his head as he envisioned the Ying and Yang of two very different powers that he had unleashed.

Then it struct him that he had a polygamous mind that had many more mental wives than just two.

His thoughts were interrupted, and Zoe surprised him by asking if he was thinking about the Fold Box and how to get all the Fold curses back in it.

He wondered what made her ask.

Zoe commented that she had been talking with Thomas and Remi and had put two and two together.

He complemented her on her keen sleuthing and replied that she had hit the nail on the head.

Zoe said that she had been thinking about it as well and had concluded that erasing the information on Earth was a huge accomplishment that seemed to accomplish much of what he was concerned about. His management of that capability on Mataia was now the challenge and agreeing to set up Remi's Fold Evaluation team was a monumental step forward. She said that she wanted to rephrase her comment about the Fold Box. Fold should not be in the box, and they should not be gods. Self-determination within the net of "treat others as you wish to be treated" should be nourished by the actions taken using the Fold methodology.

Pat had quietly listened to the exchange. Once there was a break, she spoke up and suggested that Zoe should consider taking her place on Remi's team. She and Amy were duplicates in how they currently thought about Fold whereas Zoe would add a truly different perspective. She pointed out that she and Amy talked every day so she would be able know if there was something that she wanted to be involved in.

Zoe thought for a moment and then thanked Pat and asked Bram if he agreed to the two of them changing seats.

Bram said that he supported the move. He smiled and said that Pat got an earful of his thoughts and ideas every day and probably should get a break of having to evaluate his Fold actions. He just needed her to save him from himself from time to time.

Pat got up and poured herself another cup of tea. She looked over to Eric and asked what he thought of the discussion.

He said that he agreed with all of it, and he was saving himself to discuss where in the three-Fold rhombicosidodecahedron (RCID)s to send the Fold scouts and what they would be looking for.

Pat returned to her seat and asked when had a third RCID been decided on.

Bram replied that he had discussed this with both Bob and Thomas. He did not recall who had suggested establishing the third RCID, but they had agreed that one with a Swooshian focal point should be considered. That would provide the ability to triangulate a huge portion of the Universe giving them a new way to measure special distances, the speeds of galaxy movement and other objects, and the overall size of the Universe.

Pat commented that the current set of people employed in the Fold project was not going to be enough to be involved in the Fold effort and to be involved in populating and maintaining Einstein City. He needed to accelerate getting people to Mataia and in bringing new people on board so they could be vetted.

Bram agreed and would make sure to give Erica a heads up on accelerating the Fold program hiring and the Fold movement of people to Mataia.

He asked whether she and Amy were ready to handle the influx.

Pat commented that they had set up the production of houses on Earth so that once a month six new houses were Folded to and set up on Mataia. They had also worked with Remi and with Marcus to set up Fold stations that would allow a person to Fold to anywhere in the city or to other parts of the Fold housing area. They had decided to keep all Fold locations outdoors so that buildings could be modified and not affect the Fold stations.

Bram said that even with the regular weekly update meetings happening, he was learning about the Fold stations as they talked.

Pat smiled and said that all the teams he was setting up were all trying to match his pace. However, he had set up so many teams that the week-to-week sharing sessions would always surface another surprise. She had come to the conclusion that it would be great since they would not have boring meetings, and the Fold effort would continue to be fun.

Bram gave her a hug and looked over to Zoe and Eric and commented that his four bodyguards were stepping up and surrounding him with their help. He went on to say that from the General on down, every Marine were eager to make the move to Mataia. Instead of the hesitancy that he thought he would face, he was faced with not moving fast enough with the transition to Mataia.

He said that Erica had recruited several of the Marine support staff to help in managing the transition and had said that she was still shorthanded.

He looked at Zoe and asked how her bottleneck at removing the Fold data from Earth was coming.

Zoe shook her head and said she was not talking until the next day when they met to do the review. She asked who was ready for a late snack of grapes and strawberries before going up for a long hot shower and getting a good night's sleep.

Pat took the lead and said that she loved the idea of a snack but wanted to add a scoop of vanilla ice cream to go with the strawberries,

Bram shook his head and said that he would just refresh his tea and watch. He added that a late snack would only fuel his wandering mind, and he would spend the night flying through either the negative or positive Fold universe and wake up exhausted.

Pat and Zoe sat and quietly talked to each other and chuckled. They were secretly penning a ditty for the following morning.

Bram knew that the two were up to something, but he was more focused on the three RCID's and what the objectives he should consider for each and did not try to figure out what they were up to.

As usual, the next morning Pat was one of the first down to the kitchen. It was not long before Zoe joined her. The two sat down with their coffee and wrote down the ditty that they had created.

> Bram is fast, but so are we.
> We have time to drink our tea.
> He creates so many teams.
> Then complains of work in reams.
> He gets himself so far behind.
> That at night he's an easy find.
> Lap top up he's working hard.
> Struggling to be the Fold's true bard.
> Writer of equations, founder of nations
> But has worries and trepidations.
> Worries about what's in the box.
> Not to worry it's not a fox.
> Bram is fast, but so are we.
> We have time to drink our tea.

When Bram came into the kitchen, Zoe went out to where she knew Donna and Castor would be and handed them the ditty.

The two of them nodded as they read it and said they would start as soon as they started the jog.

Bram was oblivious to everyone around him. He was deep into how to manage the three RCID's but then the ditty registered, and he had to smile. He knew what Pat and Zoe had been up to. He smiled and joined in on chanting the ditty as they jogged. It was clear to him that everyone on the Jog had been waiting for him to join because the volume of the group then increased dramatically.

He smiled as all the Marines on duty joined in and the entire compound reverberated with the ditty.

Linda smiled and asked if he wanted some tea before they set up the next two-week work plan.

Bram smiled because she never made him any tea or coffee so he knew she had heard the ditty and was pulling his leg.

He shook his head and said he had to get his lap top up.

Linda smiled and said he had his fifteen minutes of peace and then she would be in.

Bram walked over to the bookshelf and opened the small door and held his hand open so Isaac and Ada could get onto it. He then carried them over to his desk and they got out of his hand. He put down a few crumbs of a sugar cookie and then proceeded to tell them about the desire to utilize and manage three RCID nodes. He looked over to Zoe and Eric and asked them to pay attention. He then asked Isaac and Ada if he should utilize all three RCID nodes in both the positive and negative Fold realms.

Isaac and Ada both seemed to shake their heads in the affirmative.

He then asked them if there should be three teams assigned and each team handle each Fold realm.

The two mice once again nodded in agreement.

He then asked if he should be an active member on the teams.

The two mice seemed to shake their heads and indicate a no.

He then asked if the teams should evaluate the effect of his decisions.

The two mice shook their heads in the affirmative.

He thanked the mice and was going to put them back when Zoe stopped him as she put down an oatmeal cookie crumb.

Zoe said that their sage advice and direction deserved an extra treat. She then put down her hand and the two mice got on board, and she carried them back to the bookshelf and let them get off and scurry into their abode.

Bram congratulated her on being accepted by the mice.

Linda walked in and said it was time for the two-week work plan.

Bram dutifully followed Linda's planning process. He called it Linda's, but they had worked together and polished the planning process to the point that they got it done in less than a half hour.

This morning, he was going to meet with the team that would be involved in managing the three RCID systems. The Earth system had been exercised for the past several months and they had learned a ton from having use it. It provided the framework for the other two.

The two new RCID's were going to be very different from the Earth centered RCID. They were dealing with two planets that they had very little knowledge about. In fact, Bram put what they knew about the planets close to a zero.

The very first thing they had to do was to establish the node points for each one.

Zoe led the way into the Viewing Room.

Bram looked around the room and thanked everyone for being there. He highlighted three objectives.

One was to charter the three RCID Fold teams. Another was to agree on the Strategy and Objectives for each RCID Fold. And the third objective was to charter and kickoff the Fold Change Evaluation Team.

They would lay out each team's draft work plan and then have each team separately develop the schedule they would follow. Before leaving the meeting each team would have their next steps identified and scheduled.

Each of the those in the room asked a series of clarifying questions that took more time than Bram had expected.

He was conscious that he had been thinking in a very detailed way about the four efforts. He recognized the fact that he would need to be involved with all of the teams early on so that they would be on the right path and not be wandering around.

He asked each team to work with Linda to schedule his time so that he could attend at least their first three meetings. He promised that he would then get out of their way. He was pleased that all the participants seemed to be pleased that he was going to spend time with them.

Zoe, Remi, Bob, and Thomas, all thanked him for being willing to help them launch their projects. They unanimously agreed that they were overwhelmed as they thought about the span of each of their projects. It was, they all agreed, a lifetime span.

Bram nodded and agreed that managing the Fold effort would be a lifetime endeavor for all of them.

Pat stood up and invited anyone interested to the Mataian Transformation team review that would take place in the Viewing Room at nine the following morning. The team would review its strategy and current execution plan. The team was interested in getting input as well as starting the education process for everyone that would be moving to Mataia.

Bram thanked her for reminding all of them and asked that those planning to attend should let Linda know.

Ron Mueller

Chapter 10: Mataian Transformation

*T*hat evening as Pat leaned against Bram quietly reading, she wondered if the conservative approach that she and Amy were taking in the biological transformation of Mataia should be done more quickly. The two of them had spent quite some time interacting with specialist on Earth. They had concluded that it would not happen in their lifetime. Now she was wondering if they had been too conservative. She closed her book and put her hand on Bram's chest and asked if he had a moment that he could listen to her doubts about how she and Amy were approaching the Mataian transformation.

The request brought Bram immediately into the present. Pat normally quietly read and periodically got up to refresh her drink, but she seldom disturbed him. He said that of course he could listen.

Pat shared the basic Mataia transformation timeline and asked if it was too slow.

Bram said he had no clue. He was sure that Pat and Amy would be close to the required timing. Pat was the methodical, thorough person that would insist on thorough results testing while Amy had the tenacity and the aggressive approach that had made her a top helicopter pilot able to skim the desert floor and scare the devil out of him. He figured the two would reach a balance that would most likely be close to what it would take.

He decided to reinforce the current timing and suggest that they use Bob on their team to verify the progress of their plan was close to what they had predicted and if not, they could make adjustments. The forward look would allow them to modify the timing that they had agreed to.

Pat nodded and said that she would make sure that they engaged Bob and had him move slowly forward along the timeline. She asked how they could make corrections if things were not working out.

Bram shook his head and said that she, Amy, and their team would need to work through each specific issue and determine what the appropriate action would be. He added that he had no clue what they would face but he was quite willing to get involved when they determined he might be able to help.

Pat patted him on the chest and thanked him. She got up and asked if he wanted anything to drink or eat.

Bram asked for a bottle of sparkling water. He watched Pat as she walked over to the snack bar. He realized if the most confident person he knew was having doubts about her upcoming role on Mataia then most likely every person would be having similar doubts. He realized he had sensed some of the doubt surfacing in almost all the team members. He looked over to Zoe and realized that she was watching him. He realized that she had shared a similar doubt about the erasure of the Fold information on Earth.

He decided to say something out loud that applied to all of them.

He said that he had his own doubts about how things would turn out and he was sure he would make numerous mistakes. However, they should all use their thousand-year trip to the future and remember what they had found. The learning for him was that they might be able to do better but everyone in the future had survived.

They should also spend more time to evaluate what they had learned and see if they could think of actions, they should take in their current time to make things better in the future.

Zoe nodded and added that as she thought about the condition of the Earth, she would like to adjust her erasure plans to include some sort of education and development that would make what they found on Earth at the thousand-year point more appealing and an Earth that had become kinder.

Bram nodded and replied that he agreed with her, and she and her team should take on the challenge to have Earth as ready as Mataia was at the thousand-year point.

Zoe shook her head and said she would set her goal at the height that he suggested but would be very pleased if on their next excursion to the one-thousand-year mark her team had hit fifty per cent of their goal.

Pat had been listening and added that she now felt better knowing that she was among a group of folks that had similar doubts but were charging ahead.

Bram asked Eric about his reaction to the discussion. Eric said that he was on a challenging assignment working with Marcus, but it had less of a social or environmental impact. He would be willing to work with any of the teams if he could be of help, but he was less affected emotionally than the leaders that would be molding the social and environmental changes that they were in charge of.

Bram suggested they put on a Straus soundtrack and relax so they could get a good night's sleep.

He listened to the music and in his mind, he worked on a ditty that he would ask Castor and Donna to chant as they went in to work.

> Doubters, Doubters, a team of many Doubters.
>> If I challenge their feelings, they will call me a jerk,
> Doubters, Doubters, a team of many Doubters.
>> Planning social, sea and mountain transformations.
> Doubters, Doubters, setting up the Mataian population.
>> What could possibly go wrong,
>>> What could they possibly know?
>>>> About how to make the Future Flow
> Doubters, Doubters guiding change,
>> Change aimed at making them all grow.
> Doubters, Doubters will work hard to make it so.
>> I am a doubter, you are a doubter, we all make it go.
> Doubters, Doubters, embrace each other we will make it so.

The next morning, he was the one that handed the ditty note to Donna.

Pat and Zoe caught on immediately, laughed, and then chanted the ditty with enthusiasm.

When they went through the compound and the other Marines joined in, Pat felt like a weight had lifted from her mind.

Later as they got ready to enter the Visual Meeting Room Pat gave Bram a hug and thanked him for the ditty.

Bram was pleased that he had a positive effect on her and now that he was clear about the issue, he would ask Linda to set up a meeting to address the issue of doubt. He would ask Dr. Windal to attend and give them all her view of what doubt represented.

Pat and Amy more or less enthralled all those listening to their strategy and plans of transforming Mataia. There was great interaction. Everyone seemed enthusiastic about what the Transformation team was planning. There was great interest in the timing as well as the order of the transformation.

Amy's explanation about a truly bottom-up approach where she said that they were going from the bottom of the ocean and working themselves up to the sky gave everyone in the room the gist of how the transformation would proceed.

Both Amy and Pat repeatedly responded to various questions that required lengthy explanations that they were not prepared to go to that level of detail, but they would keep everyone informed on a weekly basis about the details.

As the session drew to a close, Bram stood up and thanked Amy and Pat for being the first to share their Strategies, Work plans at a high level and the general flow of the Mataian transformation.

He then shared that he had asked Linda to set up a session where they would discuss the issue of doubt and concern about the actions, they would each be leading or be involved with. He said that he would share many of his own concerns and get Dr. Wendall's take on how to handle his doubts.

That afternoon Linda informed Bram that his couch session with Dr. Wendall was the following day at one.

Bram was surprised at how quickly Dr. Windal was able to respond. He asked Linda to arrange to have Dr. Windal's chair and the chair she used with her patients located in the middle of the viewing room. He said that he would think about his top doubts and share those with her.

Linda let him know that Dr. Windal was really excited about hearing of your doubts. She shared that you had never discussed your doubts with her and now you were going to do so in public.

Bram put a call into Dr. Windal and asked if she had time to discuss the session they would do in public. He could not miss the eagerness as she let him know she was available and would love to discuss the session with him.

She said she would immediately walk over to his office and hung up.

Bram looked at the phone in his hand and as he placed it on the desk, he saw the grin on Zoe's face. He asked her what the grin was about.

She said that after he volunteered to share his doubts, the fact that he had doubts spread like wildfire. Linda had been rejecting plea after plea from people wanting to be in the session.

Bram shook his head. He thought for a moment and then called Linda and asked to record his session with Dr. Windal.

Linda brought Dr. Windal in and before she left, she let Bram know his request to record the session would be met.

Bram asked Dr. Windal if she wanted some refreshments. He was using the same entrance question that she always used with him.

He was pleased that she immediately caught on and asked if he was taking on her role.

He shook his head and then said that he would like to walk through the analysis that she was going to lead on the following afternoon.

Dr. Windal asked if it was to be a real analysis or a staged one.

Bram shared that it would be a little of staging and a lot of real analysis. He shared that it would be recorded and be made available to everyone in the Fold program.

Dr. Windal looked around the office and muttered a quiet "Wow."

Bram said that he would share some real doubts and concerns. What he wanted was for the session to be an educational one that highlighted how doubt could be a catalyst that could lead to doing great work. He also wanted to distinguish between Identity Doubt, where a person doubted their abilities, character or personality, and Idea Doubt when there was some doubt about an idea that was going to be implemented.

He *emphasized* that he wanted the team to focus on how to handle Idea doubt. He wanted to emphasize how doubt makes one explore, listen, and reinvent what was done. He added that it also led a person to risk more.

He wanted to highlight that handling doubt was a tough ask. He said that everyone should embrace doubt and make themselves capable of handling the uncertainty of the future.

He wanted doubt to be what inspired everyone to work harder and hone their skills to increase their self-confidence. Though it does take time, you can overcome your doubts.

And when one feels doubt no matter what, they should take a smaller step.

Dr. Windal looked to where Zoe and Eric were sitting and asked if he was going to share the doubts now that he would with her on the following day and was, he fine doing it with two other people in the room?

Bram nodded and said he was fine. He made the point that his bodyguards had saved him multiple times. He then said that he was going to use an example in the past and his top two in the current time.

She asked if she could record his doubts so she could think on how to weave in the educational points he had highlighted. She added that she was supper excited about what he planned to do. The session would apply to everyone including herself.

Bram agreed to her recording their meeting.

He said that his first doubt would be out in the desert and the ritual he went through at five in the morning. He walked out to a large boulder thought to have been pushed there by the ice age glacier. He would sit on top of it in the dark waiting for the sun to rise.

Once the sun's rays reached the boulder a little mouse that I named Einstein came up and sat beside me. He earned the name because he would answer questions that relieved my doubts. He provided the release of many of my concerns, and he was always right.

Bram clarified that doubts at the time was whether his idea of merging the various theories developed by several genius minds that he felt were superior to his.

He stopped and walked over to the bookshelf and brought out Isaac and Ida. He put them on the desk and introduced them to her. He said that these two were the offspring of Einstein. They were now the ones that listened to his doubts.

Dr. Windal asked if she could touch them and after his nod, she stroked each one and asked where they had received their degrees in psychology.

Bram smiled and said that one did not need to be a psychologist to help someone get over doubt. It could be a pet, it could be a friend, it could be a mental self-exercise, and it could be a talk to a psychologist. He then smiled and said that he would ask the two if they had a degree from the Desert College of Phycology.

Dr. Windal said that she didn't need to see the degrees. She agreed that managing doubt really depended on each individual. She then asked what the second doubt he was going to share.

It was a doubt about what Zoe was doing in erasing the Fold technology from the records and systems on Earth. This was as big as his first doubt, and it was happening in the present.

Zoe got up and walked over to the desk. She petted the two mice and then walked around the desk and gave Bram a hug. She looked over at Dr. Windal and said that knowing that Bram had doubts about the Fold information erasure, already helped her deal with hers.

Dr. Windal smiled and said that she was beginning to understand why her clientele seemed to be from outside the circle closest to Bram.

Dr. Windal shook her head and said that the erasure of the Fold information was the first she had heard about it. It surprised her and she said that she was going to have to process that to be ready by the following day.

She then said she had some trepidation about asking about his third doubt.

Bram stood up and walked to the window and looked out. He then turned and said that the third doubt was about his ability to manage, control and leverage the Fold technology out into the future. He had already experienced messing that up several times. He was not sure and had many doubts about his and the team's ability to take the actions in current time that would be most beneficial in the future.

The room went silent. Dr. Windal bent toward the desk and stroked the two mice. Zoe gave her a cookie crump and said she should give it to the mice and then ask them the question that was in her mind.

Dr. Windal smiled and asked the mice if she was capable of running the analysis session in the way Bram had envisioned.

Zoe pointed to both Isaac and Ada bobbing their heads up and down.

Dr. Windal laughed and said that the two had just erased her doubt about their capabilities. She said that she had come over expecting a dry discussion and had never dreamt of a session where mice were analysts and Bram would share such significant doubts.

She said that she felt that she had just been called up to from the farm team to be on the professional first team.

Bram commented that she had always been on the professional team and that it was her time to hit a homerun. He would pitch the doubts, and she would hit each of them out of the park and they would all win the game.

Dr. Windal stood up and said she was going to spend what little time she had practicing in the batting cage, so that she would have a chance to hit the homeruns.

Bram watched her leave. He picked up Isaac and Ada and carried them back to their home.

Zoe asked him why he was exposing himself to the broader team to so much of what he was doing.

Bram said that only the folks in the room would be hearing the doubts and countermeasures for the doubts. The video would be used selectively with other key individuals. He felt that it would be a useful tool to bring other folks along the journey and make them more relaxed about what they were being asked to do.

He then said that he felt they should accelerate the move to Mataia. He needed to have his inner team move almost immediately and they should have no doubts about their transition to a very different way of life.

He added that it would be a good time to prepare the FBI for the departure of his four bodyguards. He wanted to orchestrate the situation so that their bosses closed down his protective duty. He thought maybe someone like Jeffrey, or ex-senator Newton from Maine could effectively plant the suggestion back at FBI headquarters. Once that happened, he wanted them to be more or less full time on Mataia.

Zoe looked at Eric and asked if he was ready. He smiled and said that he loved the house on Mataia. He laughed and added that he would only be cooking meals for the two of them.

Linda gave Bram his ten-minute warning that it was time to go home.

Ron Mueller

Chapter 11: Doubt Analysis

Pat lay against Bram and took in his easy breathing as they sat on their dual recliners. She was nervous for him, but he seemed perfectly calm. She had never expected him to talk openly about having doubts. He was the bedrock of the Fold program. He had made all the Fold breakthroughs. The entire team had made improvements and additional breakthroughs, but they were all built on his initial work.

She asked him what had made him decide to expose some of his doubts.

He smiled and said she was why he was doing it. She had inspired him. She had openly admitted to having doubts about the effort to transform the Mataian world. He recognized that he had always had doubts about some of his actions, but he had simply plowed ahead. She had saved him from himself by rescuing him from the negative Fold realm. He wanted to save the team from the stress that doubt caried with it.

Zoe spoke up and said that the meeting with Dr. Wilkins when he shared the doubts that he was about to make public about the correctness of erasing all Fold information from Earth immediately lifted the stress that she had unconsciously built up as she did that work. She had almost jumped with joy when he had mentioned his own doubt.

Bram smiled and said that he never realized that on a daily basis he had used Einstein and now Isaac and Ada to release the stress generated by doubt. He said that it was a mystery how a small mouse first found and befriended him and had helped him get over the stress of what seemed like a hopeless circular effort in absurdity. His relationship with Einstein had slowly evolved and now he realized that it had a calming effect.

He had never thought about how the ditties they chanted as they jogged into work helped address the doubt about what he was doing.

He shared that the first Fold of the two wheels had taken him up into the Mount Everest of doubt and he had almost given up doing any farther development on Fold.

Then all the attacks began to put up mountains of doubt about his ability to guide the Fold effort and not lose the people around him.

He then gave Pat a hug and said that doubt was his friend in that it made him think through each of his actions multiple times and his work through multiple failures until he felt that he could deliver a successful, safe product.

Pat gave Bram a hug and said that he might have doubts, but she could not think of anyone that had more fight and bravery. He had inspired all of them with his willingness to run in towards the battle and gun fire, while the rest of them either froze or ran the other way. She said that she agreed with Orlando when he claimed that Bram was a Marine in heart and action.

Bram thanked both Pat and Zoe for erasing any doubt that he had about holding the session with Dr. Windal with everyone watching.

He asked Eric to turn up the volume so he could close his eyes and listen to Nat King Cole.

Eric got up and turned up the volume. He then quietly said that being around Bram seemed to have a magic effect on him. He always got energized. He commented how lucky they had been to have been selected by the FBI leadership to guard him.

Zoe commented that all four of them were assigned to the duty because the FBI leaders did not want to send in their best to protect someone so far down on the food chain.

Bram smiled but remained silent. He thought about the fact that he had almost refused to accept the four bodyguards and now they were an integral part of the Fold effort and would take on some very important roles in the very near future. Roles, that he thought would put them several steps higher and in more influential roles than their bosses held.

He had just received a message from Jeffrey that President Natorly that had supported them through both of his terms had contacted him and asked if there was a role to play in the Fold organization. The president had commented that he wanted more than the three candy kisses that had convinced him that the Fold effort would change the world.

Bram had immediately envisioned the president working with ex-senator Newton to establish the Mataian government. He also knew that the more people that knew about the Fold capability and moved to Matai, the easier it would be to erase the Fold knowledge from Earth.

The next morning on their jog in Donna and Castor took up a ditty.

> Doubt is good, Doubt is fine.
> Well, managed it tastes like wine.
> No one is free, we all have doubts,
> Is a good fight where we win most bouts.
> We redo when we lose, redo, redo till we win.
> We work hard to give it the right spin.
> Hard work, good thinking, and a pinch of luck
> Keeps the effort from running amuck.
> Doubt is good, Doubt is fine.
> Well, managed it tastes like wine.
> Bram is going to share his doubts.
> Bram has doubts what about?
> No, he cannot, No, he cannot, have any doubts
> Oh! My but yes, he does.
> He makes our doubts into sweet wine.

This time Bram couldn't figure out who had written the ditty, but he enjoyed it and sang along as they jogged into work. He asked later and found out that Zoe, Eric, and Pat had collaborated on it.

Linda teased him by greeting him and letting him know that she had no doubt that he would do fine.

Bram smiled and replied that he had no doubt that that they would all shout when they found out what he was about.

He then asked if she had enough and that they should both just head for the Viewing Room and get the sessions started.

Linda nodded and said that she had worked with the film crew. They had set up two cameras so they could switch between viewing him from the front and then viewing Dr. Windal from the front. They had let her know that the front view would always be on the person speaking.

Bram nodded and got a bottle of water from the back of the room and then sat down on the chair across from Dr. Windal.

He could tell that she was very nervous. He smiled and asked if she had a good night's sleep and if she had any doubt about the good outcome of the inquisition he was about to face.

Dr. Windal smiled and thanked him for getting her on the road to overcoming her doubts about doing a therapy session in public and having it filmed so it could be shown to others.

She then caught the rhythm and began with a lengthy period where she highlighted the various forms of doubt and then focused it to the purpose of the session. The session would focus on idea or decision doubt. She defined idea doubt as doubt about the goodness of an idea. The reason for that doubt was often due to the lack of clarity of what the meaning of good actually might mean. She then went on to and pointed out the fact that idea doubt often lead into a series of decision doubts as the idea was transformed into actual actions.

She then made the point that within decision doubt there was the doubt before the decision that often delayed a decision. Then there was the doubt after the decision that caused extra verification work to prove that it was at least an acceptable decision.

She said that she had heard that Bram's decision making both before and after was the rapid fire of a machine gun. She smiled and went on to say that his idea and decision-making train had no delays, no stops, just forward movement.

She then asked Bram to share one of his doubts.

Bram hesitated for a moment and then shared that many of his doubts were experienced in the desert where he had worked to develop his Fold equation. He took his doubts out early in the morning to a large boulder where a friendly and wise mouse who he named Einstein would join him at sunrise.

He would ask Einstein questions that surrounded the doubt that he carried out to the rock each morning. Einstein would listen and shake his head in the positive to show agreement and in the negative when he did not agree. He earned his name Einstein by providing guidance to the creation of a successful Fold equation. He helped me overcome my doubt that I would ever be successful, and each day gave me the inspiration to try again. I tried again and again for the better part of a year.

Dr. Windal shook her head and said that having a mouse be a psychologist was a first for her, but Einstein had indeed played that role. Bram had spilled out his doubts and Einstein helped him keep on going by relieving the tension and pressure of the doubt.

Bram nodded and said that he had never thought of Einstein as a psychologist, but he had thought of him as a friend. So, can friends act in the place of a psychologist he asked?

Dr. Windal replied that friends that listen to an idea and how one was dealing with implementing that idea without judging but with encouragement helped to reduce doubt.

Bram looked around the room and thanked all his friends for helping him overcome his doubts.

Dr. Windal asked him to share his second doubt.

He said that his second doubt was whether having Zoe erase the Fold information from all the systems on Earth was an appropriate action. This doubt was as big as his first doubt, and it was a doubt that was happening in the present.

Zoe interrupted and said that knowing that Bram had doubts helped her deal positively with her doubts.

Dr. Windal nodded and commented that Idea doubt was often overcome by knowing others had similar doubts. The caution when that occurred was to keep the work going forward and not stop because of mutual doubt about an idea. Improvement to the idea should be pursued but then action taken. The result of the action should be evaluated.

She asked Bram to detail some of the doubt he had with erasing the information for the record of Earth.

Bram replied that he had weighed the danger of having the Fold capability spread around the Earth and had concluded that it would turn the Earth into chaos. His doubt was about the rightness of acting like a judge that denied bail to an accused person because they seemed to him to be a flight risk when there was no real reason to believe so.

Dr. Windal noted that the world seemed to be constantly ricocheting from one major man-made catastrophe to another. It had seen two major world wars, and a continuous run of battles from Vietnam, Korea, Iraq, to Afghanistan. She asked the question if Fold could possibly add more chaos than was already happening.

Bram asked Zoe if she had an opinion about the level of chaos that Fold might unleash.

Zoe nodded and replied that everyone knew the story of Pandora's Box and the pestilence and disease she unleashed when she opened up a box her husband was safe keeping for the gods. She looked around and then said that the Fold box that Bram had opened had unleashed a power into the world ten time worse than anything that came out of Pandora's box. The Bram Fold box could end both history as they knew it and any future that they might be imaging. There was no fixed event in time. It was all fluid and malleable. There was no event in the future that was fixed. Time might not exist and only distance might mean anything. She finished that Fold was non-linear and mind twisting.

Giving this power to the various totalitarian governments invited them to create a chaos that would have no end.

Bram agreed that his doubt was trumped by the risk of the chaos the Fold knowledge would mean.

Dr. Windal commented that she was out of her league. She was not equipped to give guidance on a topic that was so deep, so random and seemingly so nonlinear. It was becoming clear to her that progress was not progressing smoothly from one stage to the next in a logical way. It seemed capable of making sudden changes and to develop in multiple directions at the same time.

Bram nodded and made the point that it was impossible to operate in the Fold environment with only linear thinking. He made the point that until Fold had become a reality there were only five non-linear relationships in mathematics: Quadratic, Cubic, Exponential, Logarithmic and Cosine relationships.

The Fold realm had introduced the sixth nonlinear relationship: the rhombicosidodecahedron (RCID) relationship. This Fold RCID relationship had the most complex existence possible because it varied in size as a factor of distance. Time was a variable and it flowed with distance.

Dr. Windal shook her head and said that she had heard what Bram had said and could verify it was shared in English, but she had understood maybe five percent.

She then said she was afraid to ask for his third doubt, but she would do so.

Bram said that the third doubt was about his ability to manage, control and leverage the Fold technology out into the future. He had already experience messing that up several times. He was not sure the actions they had carried out were appropriate given what they had all learned since then. He had many doubts about his and the team's ability to take the actions in current time that would be most beneficial to those in the future.

Dr. Windal smiled and asked if there was any one in the room without Idea Doubt.

Pat and Amy stood up and replied that they were continually reviewing their Mataian transformation and discussing the steps they were taking. It was their way of addressing the doubts they had. They did not want to mimic Earth's current situation but wanted to slowly bring Mataia into a natural balance as Earth might have been some time in the past. Their doubts were about the order of establishing a supportive environment and still keep Mataia pristine.

Mallica and Gerry stood up and commented that their doubts was on the ability to evaluate the conditions on Swoosh and take the corrective actions soon enough to ensure the Swoshians environment reached a balance that might be different from their previous world but ensured their survival. They had faced one such event when the krill from the original Swoshian world began a rapid die off. They introduced a variety of Earth krill and shrimp with some doubt that it would work.

Mallica said that Bram had relieved them of their current doubt by reminding them that the leader one thousand years in the future had thanked them for having saved the Swooshians by introducing the best krill mix in the Swooshian world. They said that knowing that their actions would all be on the positive side had almost eliminated their doubts about their current work.

Dr. Windal looked around and nodded her head. She commented that she was impressed with how they managed their doubts and now understood much better why so few of them came to her office. She laughed and said that she did not have two smart mice to help her eliminate doubt and stress and such close friends to also help.

Bram replied that her work was essential for the team. The current group sessions and for the individual sessions were paying off. He valued her skill with providing the support those sessions required. He thanked her for her willingness to hold the session with him in front of everyone.

He then addressed the team and thanked them for speaking up and sharing their examples. He would continue to ask them to help him resolve his doubts and they now knew about his other two confidents that resided with him in his office. He then looked over to where his FBI bodyguards were sitting and added that he was not talking about them but about Ada and Isaac.

He waited until the clapping died down and then said that it was time to go and celebrate the lunch which Linda had scheduled for them and Chef D'Carluca had prepared.

Ron Mueller

Chapter 12: Mataian Move

Bram stroked Ada and Isaac as they nibbled on the crumbs and as he listened to Erica update him on the moves to Mataia. He had asked her team to accelerate the moves, and she was following up with an update and had indicated that to accelerate she would need additional help.

Erica was describing how she had organized the moves and who she was working with. She let him know that Pat and Amy were the ones that were determining the locations for the additional homes on Mataia. She shared the fact that she was pleased to learn that the two were working with a city planning group on Earth and with the crew that would maintain the infrastructure on Mataia. This reassured her that the additional homes would have the same treatment that all previous homes had experienced.

The interior home decor was being provided by a very happy team which commented that they were enjoying the best business year ever. It was the same team that had worked with her on the initial homes.

She finished by saying that at the current rate they were transitioning everything seemed synchronized.

She then shared that Melissa was determine the location where the current homes in the Fold community that were to stay on Earth would be Folded to and working with Marcus and the same city planning group that was working with Amy and Pat. She added that the sequence of moving people to Mataia was determined by who lived on the edge of the current Earth Fold community. She was trying to keep the elimination of the Fold community shielded from the public until the last moment. They had left all the empty homes around the very edge in the community. The next layer of homes was being folded to the locations determined by Melisa. The moves of the homes were followed by landscaping where the home had been.

She brought up the fact that she was working with Luke Stetson and Remi to move the bubble manufacturing to the current hangar on Mataia. The bottle neck was in arranging the manufacturing material logistics and coordinating that with the movement of the people working in the manufacturing.

She commented that the people able to work from home had a lower priority to the new homes than the priority of the people that had hands on type of work. She praised all those involved for understanding and accepting how she was determining the Fold move priorities.

She then shared that General Tilman, and the Marines were in this second priority group that were not needed in the same capacity on Mataia. He had his in-house personnel management team working with all the other teams to determine where to place all three hundred Marines that wanted to remain as a part of the Fold effort. A great deal of time was spent on matching a Marine's discharge date, their interests and qualifications and the help various teams had identified that they needed. She complimented the General and his staff for communicating their detailed plans and listing the key skills of their Marines. This was a great help to the Fold teams that were all looking for additional people.

She then brought up the fact that Elizabeth had asked about recruiting and including a set of medical specialists in a move to Mataia.

Bram responded that they should consider clearing Dr. Windal but recruiting additional medical specialists should wait until later.

He suggested that the initial focus should be to set up a suitably sized hospital and then begin the recruiting and the vetting of specific medical personnel. Until Mataia had a local facility, she should arrange to have a medical bubble available to transport anyone needing immediate medical attention back to Earth.

Erica asked if Bram was willing to discuss this directly with Elizabeth and Dr. Windal and felt relief when he agreed. She agreed one hundred percent with him, but she sensed that Elizabeth was expecting the go ahead and did not want to be the one who pricked the bubble.

She then brought up the Stetson family. She highlighted that they wanted to maintain their presence in both worlds.

Bram responded that it was fine with him and asked her to clarify the issue.

Erica commented that she had no issue with their request, but she was just verifying with him that such an arrangement would be acceptable. She pointed out that this might increase the number of Folds between Mataia and the Earth.

Bram said that they should worry about that when they were running short on Fold bubbles or were having difficulty achieving the goal of maintaining a zero increase in the weight of Mataia.

He pointed out that the Mataian Transformation team had a goal of zero additional weight add to what Mataia began with. He said at the moment he had no clue how they were proposing to achieve that goal. He asked Erica if she wanted to attend the meeting, he was having with that team to better understand how they proposed achieving such a feat.

Erica asked when and where was the meeting being held.

Bram replied it was in the viewing room that afternoon.

Pat and Amy had brainstormed how they could protect the environment from all the people that would be living on Mataia. They and the other team members had set a goal that the move of people to Mataia would be managed in a fashion that there would be zero pollution and zero added weight to the planet.

One of the team members asked how would they achieve that goal when they moved whales to Mataia.

No one had an immediate answer.

Pat suggested that they stay away from speculation and focus on the actual problems they currently faced. Each additional home weighted in on the average of at five hundred fifty tons. She pointed out that it meant the building of a house, the infrastructure to support the house and the people themselves.

The new hospital would weigh in almost one hundred times more than that. She went on to list the fire station and additional manufacturing and suddenly it became a monumental issue.

Amy suggested that they use Mataian material to make each house. She suggested they develop the home building capability as soon as possible so that the additional homes could be constructed on Mataia from Mataian materials.

The team quickly pointed out that the material gathering infrastructure to achieve such capability was not available on Mataia.

Pat then suggested that they use one of the other dry worlds as a way to achieve their zero-weight gain goal. They would Fold the excess soil from the construction of homes and buildings to that world.

This was immediately agreed to. A sub team was set up to oversee the way the material was transferred to the chosen dry world. The goal was to enrich that world and not condemn it to be just a dumping site. They had all agreed that they were cheating and pushing their problem to another planet.

The next improvement that the team suggested was that all the human waste would be processed and then sent to Earth to enrich the garden products that were to be produced on several Mexican farms that were being established.

One of the team members highlighted that once again they did not have the facilities on Mataia to do waste processing. She pointed out that the waste could be sent to Earth and the water that was Mataian could be sent back.

Amy suggested that they should see if the water should be sent back or if that additional weight loss would cover the gain in other areas. She suggested that a couple of members work on that problem and let the rest of the team know what they had determined.

The team arrived at the goal that each home would be energy independent. Each home would generate all the power it needed. This was feasible but it required redesign of the current way homes were built but could be immediately applied to all new homes and the existing ones would be slowly retrofitted.

The team then extended this concept to all buildings and processes that would operate on Mataia. This eliminated all power and sewer systems.

Then the challenge was extended to making each home free of any water piping. The suggestion was that each home have a large Fold water bubble that would sit on the top of the home and would provide the water and the water pressure for distribution through the house. Empty Fold water bubbles would automatically Fold to the refill site. Full Fold water bubbles would arrive at each house when the empty water bubble Folded away.

They then decided that the kitchen would be totally electrically operated. They discussed the option of delivering preordered meals via meal Fold bubbles. They agreed that Fold in food service would be part of the service that would be available.

Pat led the team through a planning exercise that identified that learning how to terra form the third dry planet was the bottleneck. It was clear that it represented the solution to keeping the weight of Mataia what it had been when they first discovered it. However, they did not want to ruin another planet.

She was pleased that the team had made a group of significant decisions. She was also pleased that the choices they had made would make it possible for them to meet Bram's request to speed up the move of the Fold personnel to Mataia.

The only thing they needed was to expand the team to handle the additional workload.

Bram entered the meeting room right on time. He immediately sensed that the team had made progress that they were eager to share.

He sat down.

Amy took the center of the floor and said that Bram could move as fast as he desired. She said that the team had leaped across the barriers facing them and were zooming along at ground level height and they had blasted their way through to a solution that met the needs for speed and for environmental maintenance.

Bram smiled and asked if she had been at the controls.

Pat joined Amy and slowly point around to the members of the transformation team and said that each and every one of them deserved recognition for identifying both barriers and the solutions to overcome the barriers.

She then shared the way they would maintain the pristine environment of Mataia and at the same time continue to expand Einstein City.

Amy then said that there would be no electrical, water, or gas lines as part of the Mataian infrastructure.

"Each house and building on Mataia will be totally independent," Pat added.

Amy added that any imbalance of weight would be handled by moving any increase in weight to the third dry world. She went on to say that the team to manage the third dry world transformation was identified and needed staffing.

Pat then shared that the handling of waste from each home would be folded to Earth where it would be processed and used on the food raising farms. She said that eventually this capability needed to reside on Mataia but until that was feasible the initial approach would be implemented.

Bram commented that he was impressed with the speed and the depth of their approach. He was eager to see them implement their plan.

Erica said she agreed with Bram, and she was prepared to respond to their requests for the resources and qualified people they needed.

Bram asked that as soon as possible he would like to view the third dry world. He suggested using a camera Fold bubble to do a tour of the third world. He asked if Pat was going to have a naming contest and give the third planet a name.

Pat smiled and replied that they had already had the contest. Before revealing the name, she wanted to know how bad Bram wanted to know the name by the size of the prize he was willing to award.

Bram responded that he would award the same prize that had been awarded for the naming of Mataia.

Pat shook her head and said that inflation should be factored in, that the prize should be at least twenty percent higher.

Bram chuckled and looked around and commented that the team had picked the right person to bargain with him. He raised his hands and said he was in agreement with the increase in the size of the prize.

Pat smiled and said that the winning name was Terimund which was a smore name smashed together from two Portuguese words.

Bram said he liked the name and complimented the team in naming a planet. He asked whether the plans included doing more than moving excess weight from Mataia to Terimund.

Pat replied they had not discussed this in any detail since they knew so little about the Terimund. She added that they would first do a thorough analysis of Terimund's environment.

Bram said that he was interested in knowing if Terimund should be considered as another world that they might populate.

Pat and Amy both nodded and then agreed that they would follow through with a thorough evaluation of Terimund but that would require them to properly staff that team. At the time they did not have the people to properly set up that effort.

Bram commented that they should be able to rapidly get the people they needed because the General had his staff processing the Marines wanting to be part of the Fold effort on Mataia.

Erica said that she would be glad to facilitate getting the people they needed.

Bram smiled and said that he had no doubts about the Mataian Transformation team achieving their goals.

Amy returned the smile and slowly moved her arm to bring in the whole team and said that she had been super impressed at how well and how fast the team had developed their challenging but doable plan.

She thanked Bram for having reviewed their plans.

Pat then stood up and said that it was time to name the winners of the prize. She shared that one person was from Mexico and the other from Portugal and that the two had collaborated on the name. She handed them a large cardboard check for Fifteen Thousand dollars. She then added that she and Amy were gifting them with a hundred dollar each to spend however they wished.

Amy then declared the meeting over.

Bram walked around and chatted with each of the team members. He then cornered Pat and Amy and congratulated them on setting him up.

Amy smiled and asked what made him think such a thing.

Bram Nielson Collection

Bram chuckled and pointed to the large cardboard check that they came in with that had already been made out and signed for fifteen thousand dollars. All they had to do was orchestrate his agreement. He added that they had done it very well.

Amy nodded and said that it was all Pat's doing.

Bram gave them both a hug and said that he had enjoyed their pranking him.

Ron Mueller

Chapter 13: Mataian Living

The move of people to Mataia became a constant but slow stream. Bram was impressed by the homes being built for the new arrivals. Pat and Amy managed to build new homes that were totally self-sufficient. From where he was now spending every night, going to the main work center was an easy jog in and going to the Fold work center in the hangar was a longer jog but one that he chose to do most of the time. He had a bubble at his disposal to go anywhere he desired but chose to move around on foot whenever possible. He monitored the number of people that had moved to Mataia, but he stayed away from the actual details.

Zoe had relented on how intense his protection needed to be but insisted that during work hours he would always have two bodyguards. She insisted that he have the full contingent of bodyguards when working on Earth.

Most people that had moved to Mataia were living there full time and were very pleased with their experience. He and several of the team members worked on Earth part time. He was maintaining his Earth presence until the time all of Fold information would disappear. This would be a hat trick timed to coincide with the work that Zoe was doing to erase Fold information. And the fading memories of those outside of the Fold family. A third consideration was to erase the Fold site without making local or national news.

Pat had set up a contest to see who could guess the date closest to when the three consecutive actions would happen. She shared the history of what a hat trick meant and named the contest, New Hat for Mataia. The prize was a hat that had Mataian Hat Trick Winner written across the front and had a five thousand dollar check inside. The contest allowed everyone to select the date, but Pat made the point that the contest was set up so there would be only one winner.

Erica had continued working with Melisa to move houses out of the Earth Fold site and had let him know that it was time to think about closing down the Earth Fold facility.

He asked if everything was coordinated with all the folks managing the move.

Erica said that she was working with the General to finalize the movement of the Marines that had been assigned to the Fold site.

When Bram called the General, he learned that all of the Marines had been processed and when Bram gave the word, they were all free to Fold to Mataia. He said he was pleased that all of the Marines that had been at the Fold site had been eager to make the move

He thanked Bram for letting him know that visits and vacations to Earth would be available because this had been the one concern of some of the Marines. Visiting their families and continuing the personal relationships they had with friends and sweethearts was the one thing that had been a barrier.

He had contacted Melisa and learned how taking the Fold weekend vacations were managed and had let his Marines know.

He praised Pat and Amy for providing the video tour of Mataia and showing the homes that were available to choose from. When he and the Marine guards and the support personnel took a tour, they had all raised their hands when he asked who wanted to move to Mataia. He added that it was the best opportunity for every one of his Marines. He included himself in the comment and added that it allowed him to remain relevant.

Bram thanked the General for the information and asked him to work with Erica to coordinate the moves and to work with the project team leaders to get the ex-Marines on the teams that fit their interests.

Marcus, Mallica and Remi had been working on establishing the hangar Fold Work Center. They had recruited several of the IT folks that worked for Linh and Duong to set up the three new super computers. One supercomputer was designated to be used only by Bram.

Another supercomputer would be used by the teams studying the histories of Mataia, Earth, Swoosh, and the additional dry planet.

Another supercomputer would be used for those studying the past for managing the Transformation of Mataia.

Bram had let the team studying forward history know that they should expect to welcome another team studying the future of Terimund. He then introduced Castor as the Leader for that team. He said that Castor had resigned from the Marines after a heroic career and would move permanently when the final move to Mataia occurred. He then asked Castor to say a few words.

Castor stood up and quietly said that he would not accept the role.

The room fell silent. Then with a broad smile he went on to say, "Unless Bram agrees to preside over my marriage at the Rushing River Inn."

A cheer went up in the room and everyone clapped.

Bram gave Castor a handshake and said that he would be honored to preside. He then asked if they knew who that lucky woman happened to be.

Castor replied that it was a long-ago high school sweetheart that he had left when he became a Marine. He had reconnected with her when he went on one of the weekend Fold vacations to Green Bay, Wisconsin and the two of them had accidently run into each other. She was still single and the two of them reignited their romance. He had Zoe have the FBI clear her as soon he got back from that first reconnect. He had then been seeing her every weekend possible.

Bram smiled and commented that he did not know that Melisa had established a Fold location in Green Bay, but he was pleased that she had and that for whatever reason Castor would go to Green Bay he was pleased with the outcome.

Castor shook his head and replied that you go to Green Bay to watch a great football team play. He laughed and asked Bram if he had ever gone to a football game before.

Bram shook his head and replied that he had never gone to any sports game and had never watched one all the way through.

The room started a chant of, "Bram has got to see a game, Bram has got to see a game."

Bram put up his hand and asked when the next game was going to be on television. He would ask Melisa to set up the event when the recreation center was Folded to Mataia.

Donna stood up and asked if it could be a double wedding. She said that she had just accepted the proposal of the most handsome Marine attached to the Fold effort and would love to have Bram preside over her wedding as well.

Bram smiled and commented that the move to Mataia was triggering a spate of weddings. He asked who that handsome and lucky Marine might be.

Donna smiled and said that he was the one Bram had saved from being washed into the sea and saved for her.

Bram looked over to where Matt was sitting with the General and commented that his choice of soulmates repaid the debt for being saved but he did not want to hear any future complaints about his romance.

Matt replied that it had been hard to hide their romance. It had started right after he got recruited to be the General's Aid. It was not an allowed romance within the ranks, but he discovered that they could not be apart and had kept it under wraps until Donna's announcement in this meeting.

The General smiled and said that Matt was fired and then congratulated him on selecting among the best for his, "beautiful Marine."

Bram was pleased that his close friends were all finding happiness. It was clear that the Fold technology rivaled the internet technology and maybe surpassed it in the sense that it opened a person-to-person interface versus a virtual one.

Pat brought up the issue of waste management. She said that it had become the bottleneck to finalizing the move to Mataia. She said that the clean waste, the soil from digging basements for the homes was on track and easily managed since it was being folded to Terimund. She said that they were currently keeping all the soil in one location so that it could be handled by the oncoming Terimund Future team that Castor would be leading. She revealed that setting up the waste processing that would be used on the farms was the bottleneck. The purchase of the farms in Mexico, Canada, Argentina, and Vietnam were getting executed and set up in a timely manner by Melisa who was doing a superb job. The issue was in setting up waste processing facilities. It turned out that close investigation of the required permitting in each of the countries required too much exposure as to where the waste originated.

She said that they had found a sugar mill on the Island of Maui that already had a waste processing license that Melisa was in the process of purchasing. Once the purchase was complete, they would not only own a sugar processing plant but a large amount of land to grow sugar cane.

They could easily put the Fold terminal there and improve the waste processing system that already existed. The waste would not need any additional Folding since it could be used in the sugar cane fields.

Bram said that sounded like a good solution but suggested they look far enough forward so that the balance being used on the Island matched the quantity of materials they were taking from it. If there was an excess of material going in, then they should consider Folding the excess to the farm locations in an even dispersal manner.

Olivia, Jeffrey, and ex-President Samuel Natorly were sitting together in the corner of the room. Jeffrey stood up and said that the three of them had finished drafting the proposed Mataian Constitution and were prepared to review it and have improvement work sessions.

The clapping in the room was loud and continued for some time.

Bram raise his hand to quiet everyone. He pointed out that the clapping indicated how important having a constitution was to everyone. He asked that they work with Linda to set up a constitution finalization event.

The General asked to work with the Constitution Team before the event to make sure the work that he was leading in setting up a crowd management and relief organization would be addressed as part of the constitution.

He thought it might influence the wording that they might have used in the constitution. He added that he thought that the leadership traits of the Marine Corp, Bearing, Courage, Decisiveness, Dependability, Endurance, Enthusiasm, Initiative, Integrity, Judgment, Justice, Knowledge, Loyalty, Tact, and Unselfishness should also be used during the constitution finalization event. He suggested that bearing should be considered when thinking about how the wording in the constitution would affect the future.

Unselfishness could be thought about in how the constitution described shared responsibility. Dependability should be thought about when considering all the various scenarios that would be faced in the future. Constitutional endurance should be considered when choosing the wording that was used. Justice for everyone should be a fundamental consideration. Integrity should be the goal that the constitution espoused.

Olivia replied that she was sure her two partners on the team would love to sit down with the General and see how his concepts could be woven into the work they had done.

The General put up his hand and said that General should be dropped, and Les or Lester used to address him. He went on to say he would set up a time with them to share his thinking.

Bram smiled and commented that "Lester" was sure to influence the constitution team. He said that his only input was that the constitution should state that people should treat others as they wished to be treated.

Lacy had enjoyed the discussion that had seemed to flow naturally from one key topic to the next. She asked if Mataia would be doing any search for additional intelligent beings. This was an area that greatly interested her, and it was an area that so far, she had heard little about.

Bram replied that she had touched on one of his continuing interests but that current events had prevented him from pursuing it. He suggested that Lacy set up a team to search for intelligent life and set up a Fold beacon system that sent out a query looking for that intelligence.

Lacy nodded and said she accepted the challenge.

Bram asked if there was any other information or actions that needed to be taken.

Zuri, who was currently in England, commented that she had been busy writing lyrics for an album she was planning to record called Mataian Melodies. She said that she was planning to reside on Mataia to complete her album, would enjoy getting suggestions from anyone and would like help to merge her songs with the right melodies.

She said that the meetings discussion had added several lyrics to her list, and she was eager to engage everyone that was interested.

She shared that she would receive her diploma at the end of the current semester and would then be ready to Fold to Mataia.

Everyone in the room clapped.

He dabbed the tears he had in his eyes. Bram knew that the Fold miracle, genius child, had been transformed not only in body but she was leveraging her mind and fulfilling the opportunities that had opened before her. He complimented her on her graduation and on pulling Orlando along with her.

He later found out that Zuri had graduated number one in her class and that Orlando had graduated number five. He made a point of having that shared with everyone.

Chapter 14 Leveraging Fold

Bram was pleased with the way the transition was proceeding. Everyone seemed willing to adjust to a different way of life from what they had experienced on Earth. Their homes were not only comfortable and somewhat on the luxurious end of the spectrum, but they were arranged so that each neighborhood had a central green area that included a tennis court, and swimming pool. He noted that Amy and Pat were laying out a series of communities that supported an outdoor lifestyle.

He was surprised when Pat let him know that their home would be moved to a location that was almost exactly between the main office building and the hangar where the Fold Work Center was located. It would also be improved. She said that the move was in conjunction with having each housing area having the same arrangement. She said the area that they were currently living at would be redone to have the same layout as all the other areas.

She went on to share that their home would have some modifications made that would make it totally self-sufficient and it would eliminate all the early work that they had done when they were thinking about underground services. She and Amy were leveraging the Fold technology.

She likened the novel approach to the green thinking on Earth that was focused on taking everything back to its natural low energy footprint. On Mataia it was not making unnecessary footprints.

Bram asked how far it was to the waterfront. Pat smiled and assured him that she had that in mind when she arranged the move. The view from their living room window would have the beach in front of them and the mountains out to each side. She was having the living room enlarged and new windows put on each side. In the back of the room would be an open dining area with the kitchen behind it. She said that it would really be a great enhancement.

Bram asked about the other homes and learned that those living in each of them were doing similar upgrades and were excited about the new location.

Bram let Pat know that he liked what she was doing.

The first meeting of the week was with Marcus and Remi. Marcus shared that he had hired one of the female Marine guards to take care of the kids. He was pleased with how she got along with the Marcus Jr. and Mylan.

He said he was also pleased with the new educational facility and how quickly Elizabeth had gotten the school up and running. He was also pleased with the large campus that surrounded the school. It seemed to be a park big enough for several schools.

Bram let Marcus know that Elizabeth had shared her vision of establishing several sites for continued learning. She wanted to place the sites around Mataia so that students could get away from parents and learn to be on their own.

He suggested that she should pick the location and have the schools established. Once she had that done she could see how to staff the schools and universities. He had let her know that he was very supportive of making the Mataian society a very well-educated society.

Remi asked if Elizabeth's vision included schools of medicine.

Bram nodded and said that Dr. Sewal was working closely with her and was the one focused on establishing the medical practices and facilities on Mataia. He had agreed to get that done before recruiting other doctors and physician. He said that this was the approach he and the two of them had reached. It was a slower approach than the two of them had at first argued for, but it was one that he felt kept the horse before the cart and it allowed time to vet the people that Dr. Sewal had in mind.

Linda called into the office and let Bram know that Mallica and Gerry were standing at her desk and wanted to share an idea that they wanted his opinion on.

Bram asked Remi and Marcus if they wanted to hear what the two were thinking about doing or if they would rather go about their workday.

Marcus said that he would go to work on setting up the coordinates of all the building moves that Pat and Amy were throwing his way. He added that Elizabeth had started doing the same with school buildings she was having Folded in from Earth.

Remi said that his effort was having a slow start, and he was interested in what Mallica and Gerry were up to.

Bram let Linda know to send the two in.

Mallica headed to the service bar and grabbed two bottles of water and handed one to Gerry.

She then asked Gerry to share the idea that he had.

Gerry corrected her and said it was their idea. He then said that he wanted to provide the Swoshians underwater robots that they could command to build things for them. He described a robot that could extrude plastic shapes, or one that could assemble a structure or maybe one that could herd the krill. He said that he was not sure what the exact robot mix should be, but he suggested they work with the Swoshians to see what they wanted to do.

Bram smiled and reminded them that their work and apparently his supporting decision had been on exhibit on their Swooshian visit one thousand years into the future. It was the communication tower that rose a good thousand feet into the air above Swoosh's ocean surface. Additionally, they should have spotted the various Swooshian Fold bubbles that were recording the Fold bubble they were in. He said that the recording Fold Bubbles had a distinct Swooshing shape that looked much like a sea lionfish with a center camera where the mouth would be located and lights where the eyes would be. He said that he had the scenes captured and stored on the recordings he had for that trip. They should look at the scenes. He admitted that at the time he had not seen what he was describing but he had reviewed the video multiple times since their return.

Both Mallica and Gerry said they would love a copy of what had been captured on that trip.

Bram looked down at his computer and a moment later said that the information was sent to them. He suggested that they move slowly and make sure the Swooshians were leading the way because the capability they were proposing would be a significant step up in what the Swooshians would be able to do. It could throw off the balanced way of living that they had enjoyed for centuries.

Mallica said that they would make sure to ask the Swooshians to thoroughly think through each change idea.

Bram smiled and congratulated them on their upcoming good work.

Gerry shook his head and said that he would never get use to how knowing the future affected what he was choosing to do in the present.

Bram voiced his support to the fact that he did not think there was a way to get used to it.

Linda called in and asked if she could come in and work with him to lay out his two-week calendar.

Remi got up and said that now it was time for him to get to work on his own stuff and that he had no desire to listen to Linda load Bram up for the next two weeks.

That statement made Bram think about the calendar and how time was being kept on Mataia. He knew that a day was slightly longer than on Earth and the year was about the same. However, he needed to have the Mataian time and calendar reviewed and made Mataian.

Linda began by saying that almost every team was asking for his review. She wondered if there was a better way to handle his time.

Bram nodded and said that he would like to get Erica back into the project management role and let her review the progress of various teams and filter what he should be involved in.

He empathized with the lack of confidence that the teams were experiencing. He suggested that each team also set up a regular session with Dr. Windal to share their doubts and concerns. He did not think the work would get easier, but the team members needed to develop a way to check their progress that reinforced what they were doing or thinking about doing.

Linda asked him how she should handle the requests coming to her.

Bram suggested that they agree to a request filtering approach using at least the four kinds of filtering.

A request that had a clear objective and goal that needed his input.
She would ask:
- When the project was ending.
- For the meeting objective.
- For the critical time element associated with it.
- If the request could be delayed for a short period.
- If an open time on his two-week agenda fit their need.
- If the review was on an effort about to be done.

Linda said that what he was suggesting was very similar to her approach. She liked the fact that he had clarified what she would say to the requester based on their needs.

Bram reinforced his confidence that she could handle all the requests. He added that he wanted to shield himself from too many of the important but smaller details that he hoped the team leaders would handle. He had learned that encouraging the leaders to make the decisions in most situations was the best choice. They were closer to the action.

Linda said that she had adjusted the next set of meetings based on the new criteria and would get them on his calendar when she got back to her desk.

Bram suggested she do that after lunch and the two of them should go to the cafeteria in the Main Work Center and enjoy lunch with Pat, Amy, and any of the rest of the team that might be there.

Linda said that she would love to do that. She confessed that she had not gone there for lunch since she had moved to Mataia because the staff that Chef D'Carluca had put in the Fold Work Center cafeteria put a mean menu out almost every day. She wondered if the Main Cafeteria fared any better.

Bram confessed that his experience was the other way around, he ate very often in the Main Cafeteria because Pat worked out of the Main Mataia Work center. He would have to ask the two to alternate lunch sites so he could enjoy both cafeterias. He went on to say that he enjoyed his breakfasts at the Fold Work Center Cafeteria and knew all the kitchen personnel. A few of them had been Marine guards at the compound on Earth.

Linda commented that it was a little strange to be working with and around all the Marines now turned Mataian civilians. She said that they seemed so young and made her feel a little old.

Bram chuckled and simply replied that he was a member of the old age club.

When they arrived at the Main Cafeteria Pat and Amy were sitting and discussing the latest home placements and central park completions.

Pat commented that Bram had been surprised at their action to relocate the initial homes that they had put in place first. She had convinced him that making all the homes similar in capability was important in the long run. He had supported the move and then had complimented the two of them for making the homes self-sufficient.

Amy asked how he liked the new location, view, and the closeness to the ocean.

Pat replied that the location and the proximity of the ocean had drawn praise from Bram. He said that now his jog into work was just right, his closeness to the ocean was just right and his house was just right. He had joked that all was as right as right could be.

Bram took in the discussion going on between Pat and Amy and figured it was about his attitude to the house move that they had made.

He went through the line and selected a slice of baked ham, a mixed salad and a tall lemonade and carried it to the table.

Pat asked if he had forgotten the mashed potatoes.

Bram shook his head and said that the morning jogs into work had warned him to get in better shape.

Amy teased him by saying she had noticed how slow he was pacing himself.

Bram replied that he had not seen any helicopters passing over head.

Amy replied that she missed her red helo. She enjoyed zooming around in a Fold bubble, but it was hard to generate the thrill of skimming the surface of the ground and hearing the purr of her helo.

Bram said that she had just reminded him of sitting on the boulder with Einstein and that he was going to visit him after lunch and see how the boulder fit on Mouse Island out in the Mataian sea.

Pat asked if she and Amy might go along.

Bram said that he would love their company. He said that after lunch he was going to round up Ada and Isaac and take them along.

Amy asked how he liked the tunnel arrangement her team had added for the two mice that ran completely around the eves of the building and the home they had in the bookshelf in his office.

Bram complemented her on providing the two mice with a spacious home. It was clear to him that the two spent a great deal of time roaming around their tunnel.

He said that the favorite feature for him was the air blast cleaning system that kept the tunnels clean. He complemented Amy on the pigging system that also periodically did a thorough scrubbing of the tunnel system.

Pat and Amy returned to his office with him and once he had Isaac and Ada in hand, he led the way to the transport area. Pat grabbed a cookie to take with them and then they all got into the bubble and Folded to a spot high over Mouse Island. The island was about ten miles in circumference but was more egg shaped than round. It was in fact a desert island.

Pat commented that the island represented an action that went against the protocol they were following everywhere else. Since the island was far away from all of the rest of Mataia's mainland, they had folded everything that had been around the boulder when it was on Earth to the island. It was in fact a small piece of the Earth on Mataia.

Bram smiled and said that he would ask Einstein what he thought about the move. He then Folded to the back of the boulder and they all climbed out and got on the rock.

He let Isaac and Ada loose and they scurried down into the crack on the boulder.

Bram Nielson Collection

A few moments later Einstein came out on the rock and was followed by his mate followed by Isaac and Ada. One small additional mouse followed as well.

Pat broke off a piece of the cookie and put it on the boulder.

Einstein took a couple of sniffs then a small bite.

Bram asked whether Mataia was an acceptable home and smiled when Einstein seemed to indicate that it was.

He then asked if there was enough food on the island. This time Einstein shook his head to indicate that there was not enough food.

Bram looked around and wondered what might be missing. He noted that Amy and Pat seemed to be doing the same thing.

He asked how often it rained on the island, were there any birds or any flying insects that might not have made it. He suggested to Amy and Pat that in the short term they put a self-filling feeder near the boulder and make sure there was both fresh water and food available. In the long term as they repopulated the Mataian environment they could study the desert more and determine what might have been missed and then determine if the missing elements could be Folded to the island.

Pat and Amy looked at each other and said that the one place they had thought they had nailed by Folding what they thought was the entire environment was showing them the complexity they faced in populating Mataia with the plant and animal life from Earth.

They both agreed that they were glad that they came along with Bram to visit Einstein.

Einstein pushed the little mouse into Bram's hand when he lowered it for Isaac and Ada.

Bram smiled and told Einstein that he would be eating better by the end of the day and that his new little one would flourish in Ada's and Isaac's kingdom. He let Einstein know that on the next visit to Ada's and Isaac's home he would get a tour of the Mataian mouse kingdom.

Ron Mueller

Chapter 15 Alien Discovery

The next morning, Bram was having a conversation with Zoe about her work when suddenly Linda came in and simply said "incoming, I couldn't stop her. Zoe drew the gun she still carried and stepped between him and the door.

Bram was surprised!

Lacy was surprised. She stopped and raised her hands in the air. She was breathing hard as she stood very still.

Zoe put her gun into the holster and asked what was so important that she would rush unannounced into the office.

Lacy then said that she had intercepted an alien message. She said that she had received an entire string that resembled the message that they had received from the Swoshians.

Bram smiled as he remembered Zuri's challenge about whether the Swooshian message was fresh or ancient.

He asked whether it was a fresh or an ancient message.

Lacy's eyes opened and asked how she could tell.

Bram asked whether it was a Fold message.

Lacy shook her head and said she was not sure. The message had come to her exploratory bubble, and it had relayed the message to her monitoring computer, but she was not sure whether it had passed through it.

Bram asked if she was able to use his computer and locate the bubble that had received the message.

Lacy said that she could. She spent a few moments and then had the bubble's coordinate.

Bram asked if she had a second bubble that could be used.

Bram called Marcus and asked for his help to send a bubble back a few hours in time so that he could determine if a message that Lacy had intercepted was a Fold message and fresh or not a Fold message and an ancient message.

Once Marcus received the exact time that the message was received and the coordinates for the bubble that had received it, he verified that it was the same a few hours earlier. He then set up the second bubble's coordinates so that it would be directly behind the bubble that had received the message.

The second bubble was in place when the message arrived, but it did not receive it.

Bram shook his head and said he was disappointed but remained hopeful that those sending the message might still be alive and exist. Decoding the message was now the important next step.

He saw the disappointment set in on Lacy's face.

He said that he had hoped it was fresh, but it was not. He went on to point out that it might be millions and even billions of years old.

He complimented Lacy on having intercepted the message and let her know that it was a great achievement even if it was old. He asked her to work with Marcus and determine the source of the message so they could know its origins and how long ago the message had been sent.

He said he would ask Mallica to work with her to set up a team to decipher the message. It was an ancient message but nonetheless it was very important for them to decipher it.

Lacy began to apologize about having rushed in unannounced and then immediately stopped. She realized that Bram had praised her for her efforts and that he never looked for an apology. She switched what she had started to say and instead complimented Zoe for the action that she had taken to protect Bram.

Zoe smiled and complimented Lacy on her quick thinking.

Bram said that he was going to the cafeteria for a snack and take a moment to think through the rest of his day. He asked if they wanted to join him.

Zoe quickly said she was in.

Lacy asked whether they could noodle on how to move forward on the translating the message.

Bram said that was exactly what he had in mind. He put in a call to Marcus and Mallica and invited them.

On the way out he asked Linda to join them.

The cafeteria was empty, but the line staff was immediately asking what they might provide.

Bram asked for a cup of strawberries, a stick of mozzarella cheese and half of an avocado.

Zoe asked for a banana with chunky peanut butter.

Linda asked for fresh apple slices that had cream cheese on them.

Lacy shook her head and commented that she needed to come with them more often for snacks. She said that she would copy Bram's request so that the other half of the avocado would not lay around and turn black.

Mallica and Marcus walked in shortly after and joined them.

Mallica congratulated Lacy on her messaged intercept.

Bram went right to the point and asked Mallica to reassemble the team that had deciphered the Swooshian message and work with Lacy to set up a deciphering meeting.

He went on to say that even though this was an old message he wanted the deciphering to be a priority for everyone involved. He asked Linda to set up a series of meetings and to make sure he was included

He asked Marcus to work with Lacy to locate the source of the message and then to send some observation bubbles to examine the source, but he did not want the source to know they were being observed.

The snack break had taken a little longer than expected and the cafeteria line was being set up for lunch when they left.

Bram asked Linda to work with Lacy to share the find with the rest of the Folks on Mataia. He wanted a positive uplifting message that would capture the interest of everyone.

Bram went into the office and opened up the small door leading to Isaac's, Ada's, and Einstein Jr.'s kingdom. A few moments after he opened the door the three came out and climbed into his hand. He had installed a call system that was at a frequency that only the mice could hear to get them to come out of their vast tunnel system.

He carried them to his desk and put them down on the glass.

Zoe brought over some cookie crumbs and put them down by the mice and let them know that it was time to answer some key questions.

Bram looked down on the new picture the was beneath the glass. It no longer was the spiral of the Milky Way galaxy, but it was the Spiral galaxy in which Mataia was located. The stars in the background were not as familiar as those that he had come to know from his time on Earth, but they were astounding and beautiful.

He smiled at Zoe's comments and then asked the mice the first question.

Was deciphering the Alien message as important as he was making it?

All three mice seemed to answer at the same time and shake their heads in the affirmative.

Bram thanked them for their answer.

He then asked if having Mallica lead the deciphering team was the right choice?

Again, he got three affirmative head shakes.

He asked whether his decision to visit the source of the message was appropriate.

For a third time he got affirmative head shakes.

He then asked if he should ask Zoe to quit carrying her weapon?

This time all three mice shook their heads in the negative.

Zoe complimented the three for being such smart mice as she put her hand down and let them climb into it.

She carried them over to the little door where the three got out and scurried into the tunnel.

Bram asked how she knew that he was done asking questions.

Zoe said that it was obvious that he had moved on to non-critical questions.

Bram smiled and agreed.

He was now thinking about a dual path of dealing with the knowledge that another Alien race existed.

He wanted to know the message and he wanted to get a firsthand look at the origin of the message.

He called Marcus and asked how long he figured it would take to pinpoint the location of the message source.

Marcus replied that he might know as soon as the day after. He had bubbles that were rapidly making their way toward the source. They were leap frogging their way almost a light year at a time. It was clear to him that the alien location was a very long way away.

After talking with Marcus, he walked down to Remi's lab. He asked Remi to set up a bubble for twelve to go to the alien home when Marcus located it.

Remi asked if he was one of the twelve going.

Bram went down the list of people he was considering. There would be at least eight counting Remi. He replied that Remi was one of the top people on the list.

Remi asked how long they would be out on this Fold.

Bram replied that he expected that it would be a full work cycle.

Remi said that the upcoming Fold would let him evaluate his new model that had a bathroom facility at the back of the enclosure. He had designed it specifically for longer Fold times.

He added that he had installed new vibrating seats, and the floor of the aisle could be turned on to act like a tread mill. The seats were in the middle but were separated by a ten-inch space that had pull up tables and refrigerated and heated chambers to hold snacks and meals.

Bram complimented Remi and asked him where it had been built.

Remi replied in the Mataia production facility that was now running.

Bram said it was great to know that Mataia now had production capability.

Remi commented that perhaps he should qualify his statement to say that the assembly was done on Mataia, but the extrusion of the shell was still being done on Earth. They had yet to develop a pollution free extrusion process.

He pointed out that it would take a long time to begin producing extrusions on Mataia. The ban on digging and using minerals from Mataia was another limitation. He had talked with Pat and Amy and had been instructed to look on Terimund for the materials. They had warned him that even there they expected to maintain the environment as clean as possible.

Bram reinforced the position that Pat and Amy had communicated.

Remi replied that he also supported them and had no problem maintaining the current approach.

That evening as he and Pat sat together, he shared his plan of visiting the alien planet as soon as the day after tomorrow.

Pat voiced her surprise. She asked if he had already invited the folks that would go with him.

He said that he had not. He wanted her to go, and he would have Linda send out the invites to Amy, Mallica, Marcus, Remi, Zoe and Eric, and Lacy. He asked Pat if there were any additional folks of which she was thinking.

Pat thought for a moment and asked about Linh and Duong.

Bram said that he would decide on the final names when Marcus shared what he had found. He expected to have initial information about the Alien planet before they departed. That information would help him decide on the final list of passengers.

Linda greeted him the next morning and asked if his work agenda needed to be changed.

Bram let her know that he wanted to have a meeting with Mallica and Lacy. He said that he wanted to make sure that they understood how important understanding the message was.

He then wanted to meet with Linh, Duong, Wang, and Zhang and get them to be thinking about how they had contributed to breaking the Swooshian message and that he wanted them on the effort to decode the recent message from another alien civilization.

Finally, he wanted time to go see the new Fold vessel that Luke and Remi had designed and built.

Linda said that she would let him know when each meeting was to take place.

Bram walked into his office behind Zoe and Eric followed him in.

The primary change of his new office versus the one on Earth was that both Zoe and Eric had desks locate on each side of the entrance door. There was a wall that blocked direct entry and the person entering had to turn left, take a few steps before entering into the room.

Zoe occupied the desk to the left and Eric had a desk on the right side.

This morning as they entered, Zoe quickly made a search of the office before sitting down at her desk. She had mimicked Bram's idea of a glass top with a picture below it. She had chosen a picture of the Mataian valley where she and Eric had honeymooned.

Eric had done something similar, but he had a picture of Zoe and himself on the beach where they had honeymooned.

Bram was pleased with the layout of the office. It was spacious and well appointed. Most of his books had been replaced by objects that he had gathered in his Fold travels. Each object had its history written on a white card that Linda had written in calligraphy. The small door to the Mouse Kingdom was an elaborate little door that Remi had presented to him. The intricate carving on the door made it a masterpiece.

It seemed he had just gotten in looking at the work that Bob, who was looking into the near future and reporting on when Linda said she was ready to share his schedule changes.

He clicked on the calendar symbol and saw the times and location for the meetings.

Linda commented that the order was based on the availability of the people he was seeking to meet with.

The order was not important to him, and he said that the times were fine.

He noted that the first meeting was with Jungfeng Wang his Cantonese speaking person he wanted on Mallica's team.

He made a quick call to Mallica and shared his intension of speaking with at least one of her team members and asked if she wanted to participate.

Mallica said that indeed she did and would join him. She asked where the first meeting was to be.

Bram said that it was at the main Mataian Work Center in about ten minutes.

Mallica chuckled and thanked him for giving her plenty of time to get ready.

Bram replied that he had learned the time one minute before her.

The Fold over to the Main Work Center made the timing possible.

Mallica commented that the ability to almost instantaneously call a meeting to take place anywhere on Mataia or on Earth made a huge difference in the ability to hold an impromptu meeting like the one they were going to.

Zoe added that it allowed meetings to be scheduled at Bram speed.

Bram knocked on Jungfeng's door and entered when he heard the come-on in.

He shook hands with Jungfeng and asked how he and his family were doing.

Jungfeng asked everyone to help themselves to drinks while he got a couple of more chairs. Eric went with him, and they returned with four chairs.

He then replied that his family was doing well. He thanked Bram for being patient with him about the move to Mataia. The fact that he could Fold back to Earth to spend time with his family had been all he needed to know. He was in love with his work and could not think about working anywhere else. He shared that he was having his longtime girlfriend checked out by the FBI.

He looked over to Zoe and thanked her for making the check happen.

Zoe nodded and said that she was personally always enthused by helping someone with their love affairs.

Jungfeng shared that the current situation was that his potential bride was in China, and it was very hard to get her cleared. He had personally taken it on himself to hire a Chinese friend who was more or less a detective to run a check as well.

Bram let him know that he hoped she would be cleared so she could join him on Mataia.

Bram asked Mallica to explain why they were meeting.

Mallica did an excellent job in briefly describing the situation and how she and Lacy planned to proceed. She shared that they were going to use their Swooshian experience to guide them on this decryption process.

Jungfeng said that he was super excited about being part of her and Lacy's team. He was fascinated that they had been able to find another alien civilization so quickly.

Bram agreed and said that it was the ability to Fold the scout bubbles to multiple location that seemed to have accelerated that situation.

He then invited Jungfeng to join him on a trip to the Alien home world.

Jungfeng immediately gave an exuberant yes.

The meeting just before lunch with Haoyu Wang the Mandarin speaker was almost a duplicate to the meeting with Jungfeng.

Bram suggested they eat lunch at the Main Work Center cafeteria and say hello to Chef D'Carluca.

Pat and Amy joined them in the cafeteria.

They were not surprised when Chef D'Carluca came to their table and offered to serve whatever Bram desired.

Bram smiled and replied that he saw that the main course was spaghetti alla vongole which was one of his favorites. He said that a serving of the spaghetti and an espresso after would make a great lunch.

Chef D'Carluca smiled and asked everyone else what they wanted. After he had their orders, he walked briskly to the kitchen area where they could hear him giving his team instructions.

Bram brought Amy and Pat up to speed and let them know that a Fold out of the Alien planet was planned for the following day.

After a great lunch they all returned to the Fold Work Center where both Linh and Duong met them in his office.

They were excited to be part of the decoding effort and were thrilled when they were invited to be part of the group that was Folding to the Alien planet.

Bram went down the list of the people that he had currently in the Fold vessel and realized he was up to ten people. He had room for two more but was not sure who the two seats should hold.

Chapter 16: Alien Planet

The next morning as he was preparing to go down to the Fold launch area, he got a call from Lester, who he still thought of as The General who asked if there was room for, he and Admiral Becker on the Fold vessel.

Bram said the two were welcome, but he had just heard from Marcus that everyone would be asked to participate in managing the thirty small bubbles that would sweep across the planet and get a complete visual and environmental survey of the planet.

The General said that he and Dennis would do their part.

Bram said that the two had about ten minutes to hop on board and that they had the last two seats in the back.

Bram grabbed his laptop and said it was time to go to the launch area and led the way out.

Zoe led the way and Eric was right behind him.

When they arrived at the launch area, Marcus said that Pat was already on board and that Bram should go down the right-hand aisle and sit next to her. He then called out all those sitting on the left-hand seats and followed by calling out the names in order for the right-hand seats.

Once everyone was on board, he asked them to power up their laptops and download the aps that he had sent each of them.

He then told them that each of them would be managing three observation bubbles that would make many small Folds around the Alien planet making visual recordings and taking air samples. He let them know that the bubbles were very sophisticated and would capture images in multiple frequencies so they would have a very thorough understanding of the planet.

He said that their role would be to set the elevation coordinates that he called out. It would require typing in some numbers each time he decided that the bubbles should be at a lower or higher altitude.

He then said they were going to practice three times to make sure everyone had their role in hand and mastered.

A few minutes later he said they were ready, and Bram should Fold to the coordinate that had just been sent to him.

Bram pressed the button and said Fold.

They were several thousands of miles away from the planet. It at first seemed to have no life present. From their distance the planet presented itself as a black planet that had three oceans that looked grey.

After a few moments of observation Bram suggested they get a closer set of coordinates, and he asked Marcus to make the Fold.

The next view was a thirty-thousand-foot view of desolation. From this vantage it was clear that the land was suffering from a major devastation and was mostly black with random patches of green and brown areas. There appeared to be rivers, but they appeared as grey flowing water that entered a less grey sea. There were scattered clouds that displayed a range of colors.

Everyone was silent. Marcus spoke up and said that he was launching the video bubbles and gave the high coordinates with which they should begin.

Their vessel began to make a series of Folds that kept up with the bubbles. The devastation was total but when they arrived at the coast it appeared that there was some sort of life that was struggling to survive.

Marcus stopped the Fold progress and sent his three bubbles down to get a closer look.

What they saw was a rude awakening.

There was a group of what resembled walking cats cutting pieces from a grey skinned sea animal that looked somewhat like a spoon billed platypus. The group they were observing were having to fight off a flock of what appeared to be parrot-like birds that had huge claws.

Some sort of animal that looked somewhat like a ground hog but had more of a canine mouth was sitting patiently for the periodic chunk of meat that was thrown their way.

Marcus had the bubbles scan across the horizon, and it seemed that there was some sort of village up away from the sea.

Bram suggested they continue with the scan of the world and then they would address the situation of the beings they had just observed.

The rest of the day the conversations were minimal and subdued.

The General made the comment that the Earth was a candidate for the destruction they were witnessing.

No one replied.

They absorbed the eight hours silently.

Bram had seen some areas that looked like there might be ruins of those that had once populated the land.

They were all silent as they returned and got out in the Mataia Fold landing area.

Bram suggested they all call it a day and that he would host a breakfast in the cafeteria the following morning for all of them and they could talk about what they had seen.

He then went to his office. On the way in he asked Linda to work with Marcus to set up a meeting that everyone on Mataia was to attend. They should attend in person whenever possible and that the auditoriums, Recreation Center, and the cafeteria were all places where they should gather.

Linda said she would see that everything was coordinated. Then she asked how bad was, what they had found?

Bram shook his head and said that it was impossible to describe in words and the scenes they would all see would shock them.

Once they got home Pat asked what Bram was going to do about the situation.

He replied that he was not sure, but he was going to find out how something like it could possibly happen.

He then texted Marcus that he would like to focus on the survivors of whatever holocaust had occurred. He said that after they had absorbed the horrendous situation that they found the Alien life in, he wanted to Fold back in time to just before it had all happened.

Pat said that it probably happened by accident. She said that at least she hoped so.

Bram asked her to say more.

She replied that it most likely happened when someone accidentally spilled their coffee on the keyboard of the computer controlling a nuclear missile and it got launched. Then the oppositions responded, and the response triggered the remaining rockets to be launched.

Bram nodded and agreed about it being an accident, but he did not think it was a nuclear war because the environmental stuff he saw did not indicate radio activity. He wondered about whether some other weapon powerful enough to create the destruction that they had witnessed had been developed.

He thought the fact that the planet was slow to recover had to do with the type of weapon that was used. It seemed to have turned everything into a powder or dust.

Pat asked if he planned to go back in time and see how it had all happened.

Bram replied that, yes, he was planning to do so and to record how it had happened. He felt that understanding that might possibly help them understand the situation on Earth and maybe they could take some sort of action that would save it.

Pat asked how he would intervene on Earth.

He replied that the team would need to be creative in how it influenced the key players that might be able to have influence taking a step back from the brink.

He hoped the doomsday clock could be set back a few minutes every year as they moved into the future. He said that the objective of the team would be to identify the little things that would help Earth take those baby steps back from the brink.

Pat asked what will happen at if baby steps back didn't happen.

Bram asked if she had been with him on the thousand-year trip.

Pat nodded and said that they must have been good enough that the Earth did survive to that time. She said that she would be interested in seeing what could be done for the Alien survivors.

Bram suggested that they see if they could determine what the makeup of the animal that was being harvested was and make food similar to it. He said as they got better information, they might be able to provide a more nutritious mix of food.

Pat said that she and Amy would most likely step forward and lead such an effort.

Bram asked if they could handle another project.

Pat said that she would see what they might face once they reviewed the footage that Marcus was editing.

The next morning Bram stopped at Linda's desk and asked if she had heard from Marcus.

She said that he was the first person to talk to her.

Bram asked her to contact Marcus and see where he stood with organizing the material that they had collected.

Linda called him shortly after and said that Marcus was in the viewing room and asked if Bram could join him.

Bram walked over to the new viewing room that they had on Mataia. He liked the layout, which was more spacious than the one they had back on Earth.

He and Erica had agreed that their work building and hangar on Earth would remain in its current location until sometime in the future when they were sure Folding it to some other location would not be noticed.

He walked in and immediately knew that Marcus had been at it all night.

He asked how he might help.

Marcus commented that he had used all the power of the supercomputer and finally had one massive video file that showed all of the Alien planet.

He estimated that there might be about a million Aliens still living. It appeared that at least ninety percent of them lived along the coasts of three oceans that like on Earth were between the land from the upper part of the planet to the southern part.

He said that it would take a great deal of study to get to all the details. He asked what Bram wanted to highlight to the Mataian population.

Bram asked if there were any ruins anywhere on the planet.

Marcus said that surprisingly there were only a few. He was not sure what had caused the destruction, but it seemed that there were only a few locations that had any large structures. He wondered if their population had moved off the planet's surface.

Bram said that was a possibility. He asked to see the ruins before they began to make the video they would show.

He stopped the display at one of the more visible ruins. He asked Marcus what he was looking at.

Marcus said that he was not sure. It was nothing that he had seen before.

Bram said that he thought it was a space elevator anchor point. He pointed to the anchor point and the remains of what appeared to be a container that might have been a space elevator laying on the ground. There seemed to be a pile of rubble around the anchor point that Bram said could have been a building that had crumbled.

Marcus said that he could see it now.

Bram asked how many similar ruins Marcus had seen.

Marcus said that he had lost count but there were quite a few.

Bram said that they would need to send exploratory bubbles to take a closer look at the ruins. If most of the people were living in space on city platforms there should be a few platform wreckages somewhere on the planet.

Marcus said that it would be a large project to study the planet.

Bram agreed and said that at the moment he was not sure who that might be and who was available to be on that team.

Marcus suggested they focus on the video that Bram wanted to share with the Mataian crowd.

Bram said that he wanted to start with the solar system and point out the various planets in that system and then zero in on the fourth planet. He asked if there were any other habitable planets in the system.

Marcus said that he was not sure, but he could immediately send out ten observation bubbles to the other nine planets of that system.

Bram told him to do it, and he would get Mallica to help him put together the video.

Marcus left the Viewing Center and went to the lab.

Remi saw Marcus come in and said that he looked terrible.

Marcus replied that it had been a long night, and it had not ended yet.

He asked for help so that he could send out nine observation bubbles.

Remi said he would get each one ready, and that Marcus should give them their coordinates.

It only took them a half an hour before the bubbles went out.

They then decided to go to the viewing room together.

Bram and Mallica had worked smoothly and had pieced together what they thought would be a very interesting video. Bram had left gaps in the lead in where he figured he would highlight the other planets in the system.

Marcus said that in about fifteen minutes the observation bubbles would be returning and would have video of all the planets.

Bram asked that Marcus and Remi scan the third and fifth planed and look for the ruins of space anchors.

Almost immediately Marcus let out a whoop and said he had one on the fifth planet. He and Marcus scoured the fourth planet and a few minutes later they said they had an anchor.

Bram asked for the video and then he inserted it into the spots that he had saved for them.

Marcus asked if there was time for them to review the video.

Bram said there was, and he wanted them to add music to the video.

Mallica said she had a piece and was adding it as they talked.

Bram Nielson Collection

Bram went slowly through the video and added his take on what had happened. He described three planets that were the home of the Aliens. These Aliens lived on giant platform cities anchored to the surface with huge cables attached to a ground anchor that must have reached down toward the core of the planet.

He pointed out that three planets in the system were in the habitable zone and each had a series of cities in the sky. There must have been a fierce battle among them, and all the cities were blasted out of the sky. He knew a few of the Aliens survived on the fourth planet. At this point he did not know if there were any aliens on the other two planets.

The video then went in closer, and it first displayed the space anchor and what could be a space elevator. It then went to the coast and showed the aliens harvesting meat from an apparently large sea animal that had washed up on the beach. The grey and black seemed to make the video a black and white one but it was in color. The color of the environment was a monotone grey that covered everything.

The video approached a collection of shelters that were about three football fields from the sea and showed a group of adult looking Aliens and few much smaller ones that seemed to be young aliens. It was clear from the video and the actions of the people eating what looked like blubber that they were very hungry.

Bram then observed the passing scenery on a tour of the coast they were on. He saw similar shelters some of which appeared to be abandoned. He pointed out that so far, they only had time to view the beach they were all looking at but there were thousands of miles to study.

He ended by saying that it would take a substantial amount of effort for a team that he would charter in the near future, but he first needed to review the current staffing assignments and then charter the team.

Ron Mueller

Chapter 17 Initial Plans

⟊efore Bram walked into the main Mataian Work Center Auditorium. Linda let him know that there was almost one hundred percent attendance. The finding of another alien civilization was of great interest to everyone.

Bram thanked her and said that unlike the discovery of the Swooshian where they met a very intelligent society of other sentient beings, this alien connection was going to weigh heavy. It was an extremely sad situation.

Bram walked up to the stage where Lacy, Marcus, Mallica, and Remi were sitting. He had kept the group on stage small. He wanted those in attendance and the viewers to focus on the video.

He quickly introduced the four and thanked them for their arduous work to get the video ready so quickly.

He warned everyone that it was a sobering video.

The video screen went white then black and Vivaldi's concerto in A minor played for ten seconds before the first scenes of the Alien solar system came on.

Bram's voice was dubbed over the music that continued playing. He explained that there were three planets that seemed to have been populated. He explained that they had only visited the fourth planet. The picture zoomed in, and the dead dark grey surface of the land filled the large screen. The scene then went to a coastline where the incoming waves were not blue as on Mataia but a distasteful grey that spoke of some sort of pollutant similar to the ash from a wood fire. It was camara panned across the ocean that was almost the same color as the land.

The music and Bram's sobering flat voice had the viewers in the auditorium very quiet. The silence was deafening.

Bram raised his voice and said they were looking at, "the remains of an advanced alien civilization that had destroyed itself."

He was silent as the scene did a close up of the Aliens and the work, they were doing to harvest the fat and meat from the dead beached animal that looked somewhat like a huge platypus but with the skin of a shark.

Then the scene changed. The video panned out to show huts visible from the beach. It then zoomed in to the area around the huts and very hungry people roasting the meat over an open fire. It was clear how hungry they were by their gaunt appearance, and they were eating some of the fat directly. Several of the smaller aliens that Bram said were probably children were being given food by those closest to the fire.

The video took a quick tour around the planet and focused in on several space anchors. Bram explained that the only structures that had been found on the planet were the anchors. He said he believed the Aliens had moved off the three planets and were living on platform cities in the sky.

He ended by saying that the war they had fought had reduced them to somewhere around a million people on the fourth planet. He stated that there might be additional survivors on the other two planets and the team that would be formed to study the alien worlds would first see if there were additional survivors.

He then announced that the study of the Alien planets, providing food for the survivors and potentially rejuvenating the planets would be the work of a team that he would form in the coming days.

He let the audience know that separately he was immediately setting up a small team to provide food for those they had discovered.

There was a polite clapping, but it was clear that those in the audience had been emotionally affected by what Bram had shared.

The next morning Linda said that she had received more than a dozen calls from people volunteering to feed the Aliens.

Bram went into the office and looked over the list. He selected two former Marines. One had been a cook, and one had been in logistics. He let Linda know to ask them to come in for a quick interview.

He had no sooner hung up when he received a call from General Tilson and Admiral Becker who were in the General's office at the Main Work Center.

They wanted to volunteer to lead the Alien project. They said that they were the most qualified two people to evaluate what had happened.

Having them volunteer was what Bram needed. He felt the two were underutilized and would do an excellent job in analyzing what had transpired. He would guide them in the use of negative Fold capability to actually see what had transpired. He knew that their military history would allow them to understand what and how such an apocalyptic event had happened.

He asked to meet with them to set up a team charter, agree on the strategy, and get a work plan established.

He let them know about the two former Marine personnel that he was putting in place to immediately feed the Aliens and asked them to consider the two for the Alien research team.

The General asked for their names. He commented that Bram had chosen two good people.

A short time later Linda announced the arrival of the two people that he was going to assign to feed the Aliens.

Bram welcomed them in. The two looked over at Eric and Zoe, then at him. He explained that the two were his bodyguards that refused to quit.

He then asked if they wanted anything to drink or to snack on. He asked each of them to share their background and what made them volunteer to take the lead in feeding the Aliens.

The female ex-Marine began by stating that she was Gwen Southerly who had been on a logistics assignment in the Marines. She shared that she was emotionally affected by seeing the aliens struggling to survive. She said she had grown up in a very poor family and had often, just before the day that her parents got paid, only ate peanut butter on day old bread. She had never been as hungry as the aliens she had seen but she knew how it had felt to her when she was young. She felt that her logistics experience in the Marines and her personal background should qualify her for the task of making sure the aliens got fed.

He thanked her for sharing her personal experience.

He asked the second volunteer to share his reason for volunteering.

"I am Will Faterly. I grew up in Wisconsin to a middle-class family. I had a great childhood and then in High School I was a first-string football player, and I wrestled as well. I joined the Marines, went to culinary school, and became a certified cook. I am currently working for Chef D'Carluca and taking the Chef's training classes he is giving. I am planning to become a chef in a couple of years. I figure that feeding the aliens will give me a deeper perspective of what a Chef should be considering as he develops new dishes.

He finished by saying that his background uniquely qualified him to be on the team that fed the Aliens.

Bram thanked them both and let them know that they both had the job, and he was recommending them to be on the longer-term team that would study the Aliens.

He asked them if they had any questions.

Gwen asked if the leader for the Alien Study Team had been selected.

Bram smiled and said that there would be two people sharing the lead role. One would be General Tilman, and the other would-be Admiral Decker

Will let out a quiet whistle. He commented that he would have to work up his courage to work directly with the General.

Bram suggested that he approach the assignment as an equal. They were all on new ground and no one had any pre-knowledge.

He suggested they get with Marcus to understand how many care packages needed to be organized and positioned. He went on to say that they should also work with Marcus on sending the care packages to the coordinates that he provided. And that they should also work with Pat and Amy to determine what the care package should contain.

He asked the two to act proactively to know how much, how often, what kind of food and to where food should be folded. He said they should work within their team to see if there were survivors on the other two worlds that might need food as well.

Gwen looked at Will and said that they had their hands full.

Bram agreed and said they should spend their next couple of hours putting together a plan and then review it with Marcus, Pat, and Amy by late afternoon and have food going out by the end of the workday.

They both stood up and gave him a salute.

Bram smiled and loudly said, "Hurrah."

Once the two had left the office, Zoe commented that it seemed hard for the Marines to transition to a less structured life.

Bram said while he agreed with her, he felt that the instilled Marine discipline would serve them well.

Shortly after the two left, Linda called Bram to let him know that the General and the Admiral were both standing at her desk asking to meet with him.

Bram replied that he was not ready for a serious meeting with them, and he was planning to go to the cafeteria for a morning snack. They were welcome to do the same and then afterwards they could get into the serious work.

Linda replied that she would let them know.

Bram stood up and signaled Zoe and Eric to lead the way.

After returning to Bram's office, Lester, and Dennis, as the two asked to be called, shared their initial Charter, their strategy, and their plans.

Bram was pleased that the two had already taken a big step in organizing the Alien Study Team. He complimented them on the great start. He then suggested they determine when the war had occurred and if recent enough, they should seek any survivors that remembered the war. He also suggested that one of the initial actions was to locate all the survivors and make sure they had food. He asked them to remain as invisible as possible until they were ready to engage the survivors. Bram then asked them to lead the deciphering of the Alien message and to learn their language.

Lester smiled and commented that Bram had just doubled their work, and they would need to go through another cycle of integrated planning.

Bram nodded and responded that studying the aliens was a lifetime project. He was interested in how they had destroyed their civilization, but he was just as interested in guiding the survivors back to a state where they were growing and flourishing.

Dennis commented that he and the General had zoomed in too close to the battle events and needed to take a step back and look at the bigger and longer-term situation.

Bram volunteered to teach them how to use the ability in the Negative Fold area to go back in time and view the events that led up to the doomsday battle. Those learnings would be valuable for all of them, and it might affect how the team dealing with Earth should be influencing politics and impacting the economic side.

Lester thanked Bram for his input and said that the two of them would get back to him after they organized their team.

Bram asked the two to accept the two Marines, that he had just sent off to get the feeding of the Aliens organized.

The General said that Bram had select well and that they were on the Alien Analysis Team.

Bram suggested that they try for the following week to get a trip back in time to view the Alien civilization before it destroyed itself.

Dennis stood up and said he was pumped and ready to go and that the meeting had given him the same feeling as when he had graduated from the academy.

Bram smiled and said that he was constantly getting reenergized by the work going on around him. He commented that he had once worried about running out of challenging things to do but now he was worried he would never be able to accomplish all the things he could see needed doing.

The General let out a "Hurrah," and everyone in the room echoed it back.

After the two left the office. Zoe commented that everyone she talked to seemed to have the same viewpoint about the fact that the atmosphere on Mataia was a positive one of discovery, growth, and personal enjoyment in what they were doing.

Bram responded that it was great to hear that what he had hoped for was being experienced by those around him.

That evening as he and Pat were sitting with each other on their dual recliners, he asked her about her experience on Mataia.

She smiled and replied that it felt like a comfortable, safe place and that the people were into following the new Mataian Constitution that began with, "Treat others the way you wish to be treated."

She reminded him that they now knew those words had been put into the constitution in their time and that it was still in the constitution one thousand years in the future.

Bram nodded and agreed that it was great to know. He said that he was going to spend a significant amount of time with the General and Admiral to learn what happened to the Alien civilization.

He asked that she and Amy spend some time with that team and see if their terraforming knowledge might be applied to the three Alien planets. He hoped that with their knowledge and utilizing the negative Fold capability they would be able to re-establish the three planets.

He suggested they train team members in actually carrying out the re-establishment role because he saw it as a big and long-term effort.

Pat agreed and added that she and Amy had their hands full adding Earth life to Mataia. She said she wondered if they should also consider adding life from Swoosh and now from the Alien worlds.

Bram suggested they get done with their current effort before expanding it to looking at other life forms.

Pat said that she agreed that it was too early to expand their Mataia transforming work.

The next day Bram spent some time with Marcus and Eric to organize their involvement in the study of the Alien worlds. He wanted to get them ready for a significant amount of work in determining specific coordinates on and around the Alien world.

Marcus suggested they set up some algorithms that asked for the time, the location, and the altitude that someone wanted to put a specific bubble.

Bram thought that would be a good idea but pointed out that the two needed to consider training the users of the algorithms. There were no experts on any of the teams and the new team would most likely have the lowest capability as they began their efforts.

Eric spoke up and said that he would enjoy writing that algorithm and presenting it as an App that could be on a person's computer or phone. He wondered what other teams could use some Apps that might simplify what they were doing and improve overall efficiency and effectiveness.

Bram said that Eric had a good idea, but he should focus on the Alien team before doing any work for other teams.

Bram then asked Marcus to determine the coordinates for a series of Folds back in time to a coordinate that put a bubble close enough to the three planets to get pictures with good resolution of the surface of each of the three planets. He said that he wanted to be able to see the plant life, the cities anchored to the surface of each planet and if possible, views of the oceans. Later he wanted to send bubbles into the oceans to get a sense of what the sea life might be like.

Marcus volunteered that he had bubbles that would go back in time and collect samples and perhaps capture fish and animals for transport to the future.

Bram replied that the Alien Analysis Team would most likely take him up on that capability. He on the other hand wanted to take the General and the Admiral for a firsthand look at the earlier situation.

Marcus said he would have a series of coordinates available by the next day.

Bram thanked him and said he was off to meet with Mallica and her team trying to break the Alien code and learn the language.

He listened to Mallica bring him up to date about her team's effort.

After a few moments, he stopped her and said that they were missing a key piece that would significantly accelerate their effort.

He suggested that her team take a trip back in time and visit the alien planets and learn their alphabet and the language firsthand. Maybe they should find a school and send in some tiny observation bubbles into a classroom and learn the alphabet, the language and the form of writing that might be in use.

He pointed out that the information they surfaced needed to be shared with the new team that had been established and was being led by the General and the Admiral.

Mallica replied that things were, as always, moving at Bram speed. She said that she and the team would immediately accept his approach, and they would coordinate with the new team.

Bram thanked her and said that once again he needed to get home and relax so that he could keep up with all the good work that was being done by all the teams.

Ron Mueller

Chapter 18: The Way it Was

Marcus sent the miniature recording bubbles back in time to the coordinates of the three Alien planets.

Bram had decided to give everyone the opportunity to view the three Alien planets before the destruction. He had arranged with the IT folks to make the videos for the three planets show up on screen side by side and accessible on the computer as well as on the viewing screens that were in most offices.

The recording bubbles were being folded so they would go around the planet. Marcus had determined the height of the ground anchored cities and had set the recording bubbles so they would pass about a thousand feet above them.

Bram was impressed with the control precision and asked Marcus how he had been able to do so.

Marcus confessed that Eric had figured out how to get the supercomputer to be constantly adjusting the height as time passed. He said he was glad that Eric had chosen to work with him otherwise he would still be trying to figure out how to control the viewing bubbles.

Bram looked over at Eric and commented that he was too smart to be an FBI bodyguard.

Eric smiled and replied he was glad to have gotten the right bodyguarding assignment.

The three planets came into view on the screen and the Viewing Room went silent. Each of the planets had a different appearance as the bubbles approached.

The third planet seemed like one large desert with a few oasis-like spots distributed randomly around. It was what one would call a desert world.

The fourth planet had three dark blue oceans that split the land in almost three equal continents that ran from one pole to the other. The three continents were covered by lush forests and wide green valleys. Unlike Earth there were no large mountains but only some large hills.

The fifth planet was a cold planet that had two continents separated by what appeared to be frozen water.

All three planets had cities in the sky. The cities were all located towards the top sides of the planets. All the cities were covered by some sort of clear material that formed a bubble over the structures inside. It seemed that the Aliens built each of the cities to be the same size. There were only twelve cities on the third and fifth planet. On the fourth planet there were in excess of one hundred cities. It was clear that the Aliens were spreading their civilization out and utilizing the two planets that were nearest them.

Bram asked if they could get one of the recording Fold bubbles to go into one of the city enclosures.

Eric said he thought he could do it but wanted a moment to check the calculation of the coordinates he needed to use.

Then the center screen displayed the inside of one of the anchored cities. It displayed a city not unlike New York that was made up of many high-rise buildings. It was clear there were no vehicles, and that transportation was by moving walkways that moved at different rates. There were green areas evenly distributed around the city. The city had roughly a five-mile diameter. Eric commented that he had given the computer an estimate of how many beings would live on each floor of the high rise building and had gotten an estimate for the number of people in the city as thirty-five million. That meant that the initial estimate for the number of Aliens on the planet was roughly three and a half billion people.

Bram asked for a close up of a statue that caught his eye. The bubble went up to it and they were able to see that it was a statue of planets circling a star. The names of the planets were engrave on each of them.

They were not able to understand the names, but they got the lettering associated with the star and the planets in that system.

Bram looked over to Mallica and said that as soon as she learned the Alien alphabet he would like to know the names of the star and the planets in that system.

Mallica replied that she had already scheduled her visit to the Alien school and would very soon be able to give him what he was asking for.

Marcus said that the quick tour was over and that he would work with the Generals and the Admirals of the Alien Study team to schedule similar future update videos.

Bram smiled and thanked Marcus and went on to say that there was only one General and one Admiral leading a team to study the Aliens. He asked the two to share their thoughts and to make any other comments or request they might want to make.

General Tilman stood and said that he was finding it hard to get anyone to call him Lester or Les and he didn't mind being referred to as the General, but he hoped that over time he would earn at least the name Les.

He then added that he and his longtime friend Admiral Becker, who would like to be called Dennis or Denny, felt privileged to lead the team to study and understand the Aliens and what had occurred. He looked over and asked "Denny" whether he had more to add.

The Admiral stood up and said like his friend Les, he wanted to be called by his given name, Dennis. He went on to say that they had only been at it for a day, and it was very early on a journey that the two of them figured would take most of the rest of their lives. He said that the tour they had just taken had solidified his desire to help all three planets recover to where they had been before the Aliens destroyed their beautiful planets. He shared that the footage that they had seen of the survivors was the priority and with Bram's push they already had two Marine volunteers preparing food packages that would go out to the alien survivors. The team was in need of at least twelve talented players. He asked for anyone interested to step forward, they were all wanted. But anyone coming forward only stood a chance of getting on if they referred to him as Dennis or Denny and to his friend as Lester or Less.

The last statement earned him a round of clapping as he sat down.

Bram thanked "Lester and Dennis" for stepping forward to lead the Alien Research and Restoration Team or the "ARRT." He smiled and said that he expected that team to paint a masterpiece that would make everyone on Mataia smile.

He was not expecting a Mona Lisa but a restored green landscape with the Aliens enjoying an outing that was framed by a blue sea.

Lester stood up and said that he would need to get a painter on his team so he could satisfy the Fold dreamer.

Bram smiled and said that yes it seemed like a dream at the moment, but he was certain that just as they had figured out how to move the Swooshians to a new water world they would put the Aliens on a path to a bright future.

He looked over at Lacy and said that she needed to wait a few months before discovering any more Alien messages because at the moment she had given them all the work they could handle.

He then said it was time to get back to work.

Pat stood up and quietly said that it was lunch time, and they should get to the cafeteria before it was packed.

Bram followed Pat and Amy who were leading the way to the main cafeteria. He was not as familiar with the way as when he was at the Fold Work Center. He knew that Chef D'Carluca would be doing something special, so he decided to quickly get the main course from the serving line and go sit down.

It was not long after that Chef D'Carluca came to the table and said that he had a most delicious treat he wanted Bram to try.

He had one of his helpers roll out a cart with a covered dish. He lifted the lid and pointed to an all-white frosted cake. He explained that it was a pineapple-banana spice cake with cream cheese frosting. He thought it was one of his better creations and would like to get the opinion of those willing to try it.

Bram took note that by the time the cake had been shared, there was nothing left.

Everyone commented on how good it tasted.

Chef D'Carluca smiled and commented that nothing was too good for everyone on Mataia.

Bram thanked him for giving him a treat and invited him to come to the kitchen in the Fold building where he could prepare his next delicious meal or desert.

Chef D'Carluca asked if the new Chef in the Fold Center building was preparing delicious food.

Bram reassured him that the new Chef was excellent and that he had only praise for the meals he prepared.

That evening as they were sitting together, Pat asked what Bram was planning with their departure from Earth.

Bram thought for a moment. Then he said he was not sure. Thomas was doing the forward history study and doing an excellent job, but he needed someone like her to assess the direction that Earth's politics and the world situation was going.

He needed forward looking eyes that could follow the thread back from the future to the present so that they could take action before a perilous fork in the road was taken.

He complemented her on the ability to do that evaluation very well.

Pat asked why he was complementing her.

He smiled and said it was because they both knew that Earth had survived out to at least a thousand years into the future. All she had to do now was identify those forks in the road.

Pat smiled and said that she would turn her focus from the past to the future.

The next day when he came in, he asked Linda to set up a meeting with Erica so he could get caught up on the departure of the Fold effort from Earth.

Erica came in a few moments later and said that she had been so busy with the Alien find that she had kept away and focused on what she needed to do.

She said that the site was down to only the homes that were visible from the highway. The other homes had been Folded to sites in Mexico and Argentina. She said that she had some very large trees planted where his house had been, and a beautiful lake made where the pool and apartment building had been.

The hill leading to the compound was now a series of trees of various sizes. The remaining few houses and the work center would be Folded out when the decision to disappear was made.

She added that she had all the trees, and any plants required to finish the park on the property. She made the point that the General had kept a skeleton crew of Marines working on transforming the Fold property into a park.

She then shared the fact that Ted was facilitating getting the property ready to present to the Dallas city. He had a lawyer friend working the title paperwork transfer.

She ended by asking how much longer the Fold facility would need to stay in place.

Bram said he was not sure. He said that Zoe was the one in charge of erasing the Fold information from any records, but she like himself had been pulled over to focus on the Aliens. The other element was the memory of any folks that knew about the Fold program and the Fold site.

He had checked with Senator Stately of Utah, who had agreed to come to Mataia once his term in the Senate ended. The Senator had said that he and David agreed that leaving Utah would be great.

He let her know that Senator Bascom of West Virginia had committed suicide shortly after losing his reelection run.

Charles Ford the science advisor that had been on the Senate Fold oversight committee would Fold up at the same time Jeffrey and his family did.

He said he talked to Senator Etaing about coming to Mataia and when he shared the fact the entire Fold program and information would disappear, she smiled and looked at him with her head to one side and said she was already forgetting who he happened to be.

So, the few people that might have known a little about the Fold program might still be around but if they were to talk about it there would be no record anywhere and they would be left wondering what had happened.

Erica asked if she should eliminate the final houses and the work center.

Bram shook his head and said they should wait one more year. Then they would decide whether to Fold the work Center to Mataia or to some other location.

Erica said that fit her plans. She wanted to get more involved in the work going on in Mataia.

Bram asked whether she would be interested in partnering with Pat in looking into the future political, social, and economic direction happening on Earth and then taking appropriate actions in the present to guide the Earth through any turmoil that might end up making it look like the three Alien planets they had just found.

Erica replied that it sounded like something she would enjoy and that she might even be good at. She said she would meet with Pat and see how they would work together.

Bram complimented her on the splendid work she had done in transforming the Fold site at Dallas and he would pull her back in when it came time to finish the job.

Once Erica left, Bram asked Linda to come into his office.

Linda came in the door as Erica left. She knew that something other than Bram's normal work was going to come on to her "to do" plate.

Bram asked her to talk to her father to get his thoughts about getting the land transferred to the Dallas city. He wanted to make sure it was low key and did not make the news.

He then asked her to set up a meeting with the General so he could negotiate a few of his Marines to finish the transformation of the Dallas Fold site. He wanted the park ready to transfer in the next few months and would like all evidence of their presence gone.

He asked to have a meeting with Remi, Luke, Lori, and Orlando to discuss the use of the existing Fold work center and warehouse. He was wondering whether a more appropriate location might be on Terimund.

He smiled and then asked if everyone was ready for lunch.

Ron Mueller

Chapter 19: The Way Forward

Bram asked Linda to arrange a meeting with the General and the Admiral. He made sure to ask her to use their first names.

He then entered his office and took Isaac, Ada and Einstein Jr. from their tunnel kingdom and placed them on his desk.

He told them that he needed their guidance.

He asked them if providing food was all the help that Mataia should provide the Aliens.

The three mice shook their heads in the negative.

He said asked them whether the Aliens should be helped to survive. He was pleased that they indicated that they should.

Zoe gave them some cookie crumbs and praised them for giving the right answer.

Bram then asked whether the Aliens should be provided the means to communicate with each other.

Once again, the three mice shook their heads in the affirmative.

He then asked whether they should be taught their language.

Again, the three mice shook their heads in the affirmative.

Zoe petted the three mice and complement them on their wisdom and compassion.

She asked if they should help the aliens improve the structures of their homes and to provide better clothing.

The three mice shook their heads in the affirmative.

Bram then asked if he should stop Zoe from spoiling them.

He and Zoe both laughed when the three mice shook their heads to indicate No.

After putting the mice back in their tunnel kingdom Bram commented that the last question was a test question to prove to himself that they were really answering his questions.

Eric had been watching and jokingly commented that he was now convinced that Bram had only achieved fame and fortune because he had met the right mouse out on the desert.

Bram said that he agreed because the guidance of the mice was something of which he had never dreamt.

Linda came in and let him know that the General and Admiral were on their way over from the Main Work Center.

Bram thanked her and asked her to set up a meeting with Mallica so he could see how the team working to learn the Alien language, alphabet and the shape of their characters was progressing. He suggested he meet them in the Viewing Room.

Linda replied that she would arrange it and walked out.

Bram asked if either Zoe or Eric had anything they wanted to ask the General and the Admiral. He let them know that he was going to ask the general to maintain the pretense of guarding the Fold compound on Earth for the next year. He would also like them to remove all the concrete or black top around the building and plant trees and grass on the lot area.

He asked them where he should be considering Folding the work area and hangar.

Zoe was the first to reply and said he should consider Folding it to Terimund.

Bram asked about her quick reply.

Zoe commented that she had overheard Orlando discussing the need for a facility there.

Bram said that he liked that idea and that he would engage Orlando and see what he thought of the idea.

Linda called in and said that Lester and Dennis had arrived, and she was bringing them in.

Bram went to the meeting table in the center of the office and greeted the two of them. He offered them coffee, tea, or some other drink from the refrigerator.

It was black coffee for both of them and after serving them the coffee, Bram sat down with a bottle of sparkling water.

He thanked them for taking time to meet with him and said he had three objectives.

One was to arrange for Marine guards to remain at the Fold compound at Dalles.

The second was to share his thoughts on how to lift the Aliens up from their current dismal condition to the point where they could be working together to restore their planet.

The third was that he wanted to learn more about the Alien past and to get Pat and Amy involved in using the past to accelerate the recovery of the current Alien planet.

The General said that all the objectives fit well with the thinking and discussions he and Dennis had been having.

The first objective was easy. He would ask for volunteers to continue to play being Marines. He was sure he would have no trouble getting that fifty or so people that would be needed. He would sweeten the pot by offering to pay the expenses of Fold vacations.

He asked what Bram had in mind to lift the Aliens up.

Bram replied that he would like to provide the capability and the means for them to make better shelters and better clothing. The next step would be to provide the means for the various Alien groups to communicate with each other. And the third involved both Pat and Amy Folding plants, animals from the past to the present to help the Aliens improve their environment.

Dennis commented that he liked giving the aliens the means to communicate. He asked what they were going to do about the huge quantity of ash that covered the land, was in the seas and even in the air.

Bram smiled and replied that he was not sure how to handle it all. He suggested they set up an isolated processing plant that was located on the planet that had no Aliens living on it and process the ash into building materials that could then be used in the rebuilding. They could also place several filtering plants in the ocean to remove the ash from the water. He had no suggestion about cleaning the air.

Lester said he liked the two ideas and would have his team work on the details. He added that the air would most likely clear as the amount of ash on the land was reduced. He would have the team locate where the winds were the strongest and begin removing ash in those locations.

He commented that the level of activity would be hard to be kept from the Aliens.

Bram said that when the Aliens had reached the point where terraforming was to be introduced, they should be contacted and informed that humans were helping them recover. He added that by that time their team should all be fluent in the Alien language.

He was not sure what the Alien reaction would be, but he felt that the ARRT team would be able to set up the situation that would ensure a positive outcome.

The General agreed that they should take the critical steps first and worry about Alien reaction later. He figured that they should at least learn what the planet was referred to by the Aliens and what they called themselves.

Bram nodded as said that he was meeting with Mallica later in the day to see how her team was progressing in deciphering the message and in learning the Alien alphabet. Her team would help the ARRT team to get a better understanding of the Aliens.

He suggested that ARRT enroll Mallica and her small team and have them extract the history of the alien population.

Both the General and the Admiral said they would love to have Mallica join their effort. They both commented in how pleased they were to get the help of everyone that had so far stepped forward. It allowed them to keep the permanent members of the ARRT small at the beginning. They felt that the team should grow as the actual implementation of the improvement work went into place.

They asked how they were going to continue to recruit people to come to Mataia.

Bram thanked them for the question and replied that he needed to take up that subject with Erica, Elizabeth, and Melisa. Erica was ready for new work and was a great recruiter. He was not sure how they would attract new blood but figured the three of them would come up with the way.

The General agreed and said that one of his Marines had been a recruiter for several years and might be of help.

Bram asked the General to connect that ex-Marine with Erica.

The General and Admiral both thanked Bram for getting them focused on how to handle the Alien Research and Restoration Team. In the very near future, they would contact him and schedule a review of their plans.

Bram thanked them and wished them a productive day.

Bram was quiet for a moment and then asked Zoe and Eric if they had any friends that they thought might be interested in moving to Mataia.

Zoe nodded and said that she had several and she was sure that both Bob and Thomas would have friends that would welcome the opportunity as well.

Eric said he like the idea of recruiting friends and maybe they should include the family members of those friends.

Bram agreed. He said he would work with Erica to set up a recruiting process so they could recruit people in a way that introduced new people into the Mataian society in a smooth even pace. It was clear to him that they needed many more people than they currently had.

Linda called him and gave him the ten-minute warning that he was scheduled to meet with Mallica and her team next and that the meeting was in the Viewing Room.

Bram got up and said that he thought the meeting might be interesting.

Eric said he thought it might because he had been in her Swooshian language class and Mallica was one of the few people that worked almost at Bram speed.

When he entered and Mallica began talking to him in a language that was very singsong but seemed to have an outward flow of air he knew that she had broken the code. He saw a strange cube enclosed in one of the retrieval bubbles and figured she had also retrieved an alien artifact. Linh and Duong were sitting with their Chinese friends, and they were all smiling and provided the rest of the positive atmosphere in the room.

Mallica said that going to the Alien School had given them all about a sixth-grade education. They had learned the name of the planets, the name of the city where the school was located. They had also learned the name of the planets because there was a mobile with all the planets hanging on it and all cities were shown on each of the planets.

Bram asked what the Aliens were called.

Mallica commented that the word human was first recorded in the mid thirteenth century and owed its existence to the Middle French humain that meant "of or belonging to man."

That word, in turn, came from the Latin humanus, thought to be a hybrid of homo, meaning "man," and humus, meaning "earth." Thus, a human is an individual firmly rooted to the Earth.

She said that the Alien equivalent seemed to have a similar connotation. Since the fourth planet was the origin of all the Aliens and their equivalent of Earth is Kutika. So, they are Kutikans.

Bram smiled and complimented the team in naming the intelligent beings. He said he felt much more comfortable talking about helping the Kutikans. He asked that the team share it broadly.

He pointed at the bubble with the cube inside and asked what it was.

Mallica shook her head and said that she did not know. She went on to say that the team had translated the Kutikan message, and it was a forlorn one saying that their world was coming to an end and that they had put all of the history of their race on to an information cube and had launched it toward their star in hopes that some intelligent race would make it to their system in time to intercept the cube and learn about a race that had achieved a marvelous way of life but had not learned to get along with each other.

Mallica said it was the story of Superman where his parents had sent their child toward Earth to give him a chance to survive but in the case of the Kutikans they only had the ability to preserve their history.

She had worked with Marcus to send out a capture bubble that had retrieved the history. She said that he and Eric ginned up a piece of software that guided a bubble to the cube. He was able to calculate how far the cube had traveled and from the speed of the cube and the location of the third planet they were able to determine that the destruction had taken place about one hundred Earth years ago.

She said that Linh and Duong had contacted Remi who had demonstrated that he could figure out how to power up almost anything and had asked him for help. Once the meeting was over, they were going to take the bubble to him and let him try to figure out how to power it up so they could retrieve the history of the Kutikans.

Bram said that Remi would most likely get it powered up and they should consider asking Marcus to figure out how to extract and copy the information. He commented that Marcus had become a master at leveraging the supercomputer to investigate other computers.

Mallica said she would certainly engage him.

Bram asked Mallica to learn what kind of food was eaten by the Kutikans. He asked her to get a wide variety of food samples and bring the samples back to the present. He would contact Marial in the far future and see if he could get one of the food generators and set it up so the surviving Kutikans could eat food that they would have eaten had they lived before the destruction of their worlds.

Mallica said that she would make that a priority and by the end of the week she would have as large of a food sampling as possible.

Bram said that he was going to see if Chef D'Carluca wanted to get involved. He could learn how to use the food generator and perhaps calibrate it for what he prepared and then send the settings to the future so that his creations could be duplicated in the far Mataian future. He could also learn how to prepare the food that the Kutikans used to eat. Once he did that, The General and Admiral could get duplicate food generators built and distributed to the surviving Kutikans. This approach would greatly accelerate giving the Kutikans a diet that would sustain them in a healthy way.

Mallica smiled and said that the Kutikans were about to experience the Bram speed at getting them back to a place where they would be enjoying their lives.

Bram nodded. He said that he would like to be living when the Kutikans established their first city in the sky.

Ron Mueller

Chapter 20: Primeira

A few days later he was meeting with Castor and Donna. He had asked them to give him a tour of the dry planet that they were figuring out how to transform.

The tour began with the bubble looking down at the huge pile of dirt that had been Folded there from Mataia by Pat and Amy.

Then it went out around the planet. He was surprised by how dry it was. It indeed was a desert world. There were quite a few oasis like water holes that had plants around the edge. The biggest plants he had seen so far were bushes that topped out at about two feet. There seemed to be small shrimp-like creatures swimming in the water. He asked if the creatures had been studied and received a no.

There were three very large lakes that were about the size of the Great Lakes, but Castor said that all the lakes were only twenty feet at their deepest. This meant that any slight breeze raised fairly large waves that sucked the water out from behind and bared the bottom of the lake. Then the water would flow back, and the lake would level out again. This seemed to have kept life from developing in them.

Donna pointed out the large amount of Mataian dirt that was neatly piled up in one spot. She said that it was really very good dirt as compared with the rest of the world that it had been deposited on. However, they were still trying to figure out how to use it.

Bram asked whether they had yet named the planet and got the reply that they had several candidate names and they wanted his input at to which name they should pick.

He asked for the list and got; Storskal, Dorren, Paaaole, Esteril, Pulvis and Miska. Bram laughed and asked what the two had been drinking when they had come up with the list.

Castor said they had gone online and researched names for dry land and desert.

Bram then rattled off several suggestions: Trezo, Triu, Tertia, Terimund and Trecera. He was aware that he and several others were referring to the planet as Terimund.

This time it was Castor and Donna that laughed and the said that Bram was throwing out different versions of three.

He said that indeed he was. The planet they were going to populate, and transform was the third dry planet.

Castor said he disagreed. He pointed out that the Earth and Mataia were eight percent water whereas the planet he and Donna had been cast out on was ninety percent desert. It was one of a kind. It should get a name such as: Prima, Primeira, Primisa, Primera.

Bram smiled and said that he liked Primeira because it was indeed one of a kind.

Castor let out a "Hurrah" and he and Donna repeated it three times.

Bram suggested that the two work with Pat and Amy to determine where they should start the transformation process.

He said that he had an idea how to stabilize the lakes. They could put in water breaks across the lakes and use the energy of the water passing through them to both generate electricity and control the size of the wave traveling across the lake. Then they might be able to populate the lakes with some rugged fish and plant life.

He then asked if they might be able to utilize the hangar and work center that was currently on Earth at the Dallas site.

Both Donna and Castor asked if he had someone monitoring them because they had been discussing how they could establish a work center on Primeira but thought they were daydreaming.

Bram asked how soon they could use such a facility.

Donna asked how soon it could get Folded into place.

Bram said as soon as they determined the optimal location and worked with Pat and Amy to get the footings excavated. They should work with Marcus to determine the Fold coordinates.

Castor said that he and Donna had already pick a location by the up-wind side of one of the lakes.

They would make getting with Pat, Amy, and Marcus a priority.

Bram said that they had just set the timing for the total disappearance of the Fold community from Dallas.

He was going to leave the meeting and work with Erica, the General and Ted to arrange for the final Dallas site final folds.

He asked if they were contemplating having people live on Primeira.

Donna replied that they had talked about it. They thought that getting firsthand knowledge about the weather, changes in the conditions of the environment, doing analysis of the water, air and land would be enhanced by having people living on Primeira.

Bram said that he agreed with them, and they should work with Amy and Pat on developing the living areas since the two of them had city planners on Earth that they were working with. He suggested they also establish Fold transportation on Primeira.

He would make sure they had adequate funding for their team.

Donna and Castor thanked him for helping them name the planet and for inspiring them as how to proceed.

Castor said that he had a ditty, though it was not necessarily pretty. He held up a note and he and Donna chanted.

Thought we were lost in the desert.
No water, no life, nowhere to go.
Lost in the desert with nowhere to go.
Hot sun, hot sand, hot water, hot damn.
Wham, Bam and then there was Bram.
Wham, Bam and then there was Bram.
Not serving ice cream but serving a dream.
A dream, a life, the way to survive.
A dream, a life, the way to survive.
A place to live, a place to work.
And he made sure we would not go broke.
Wham, Bam, Thank you Bram.

The two stood up and left at a fast walk reciting their ditty.

Bram smiled and went back to his office.

Linda asked what he had done to get Donna and Castor so pumped up.

Bram smiled and said that it was a mystery how he sometimes did almost nothing to get folks excited. In their case he had loaded them up with a lifetime of work.

He asked Linda to set up a joint meeting of the General, Erica, Melisa, and Ted. He said that she was welcome to sit in.

Linda asked what the focus of the meeting was about.

Bram said that it was the elimination of all trace of the Earth Fold Facility.

Linda said that she would arrange it, and she thanked him for the invitation, and she planned to sit in.

Bram went back into his office. He asked what Zoe and Eric had thought about the meeting with Castor and Donna.

Eric said that he was ready to go jogging off with the two of them. It had been a very up lifting session. He was now excited to work with them to get their buildings and homes Folded into position. He was going to ask Marcus to let him be the primary person to do the Folding of the buildings into place.

Zoe commented that she had also been energized. She said that eliminating all traces of Fold on Earth had gotten accelerated and she was very interested in moving on. She was now interested in working with Amy and Pat in helping restore Kutikan to its former glory.

Bram said that he was also interested in focusing a good portion of his effort in getting the Kutikans back to living a life that let them develop.

He said that he was going to ask some questions of their little advisors. He walked over to the little door and rang the doorbell and opened it. A few moments later the three mice came scurrying out and got in his hand.

He placed them on the desk.

Zoe came over and gave them some cookie crumbs.

Bram asked them if it was the right time to erase all signs of the Fold facility on Earth and got a positive head shake from the three.

He then asked if Eric should place the Hangar and Work Building on Primeira and again got a positive head shake.

The next question was if he should set up a series of trips for the people that had worked and lived on the Earth Fold compound to visit the park that their work and living area had been transformed into.

He got a third positive head shake.

He asked if Zoe should work with Pat and Amy to bring forward the past plant and animals to the current Kutikan time.

This time the mice shook their heads in the negative.

Zoe gave a little moan.

Bram then asked if Zoe should be involved in restoring Kutikan.

The three shook their heads in the positive.

He asked if she should focus on cleaning Kutikan of the ash.

The three mice gave a very energetic positive head shake.

Zoe smiled. She said it made sense. The plants and animals needed a clean environment to be able to survive in the present.

Bram pointed to the three mice as they shook their head in the affirmative. He commented that it was the first time he had seen them respond to a statement versus a question. He gave them another cookie crumb and said that he would give their advisors a break. He picked them up and put them at the door to their kingdom and watched them scurry in.

Linda said that in fifteen minutes they should be in the Viewing Room. She would have everyone online and on the screen.

Bram called Linda in and said that he wanted them to agree on the order of the meeting.

He went on to say that he was going to ask the General to get his folks ready to finish the park after Eric folded the work center and hangar out.

He was going to asked Erica to arrange the Folds of the remaining houses and to ensure that the fence to the apple orchard was in place.

He was going to ask Ted to arrange for a quiet transfer of the land to the Dallas City. He wanted the title transfer to occur at a quiet ceremony at lake side at the park. He was going to have Stetson Catering providing food and drinks.

And he was going to ask Melisa to manage the visits of any Fold community person that wanted to take a Fold Trip on a weekday to visit the park. The limit at any one time would be five people.

He would ask the General to have his folks put in a chamber where the Fold vehicle could deliver the visitors.

He asked if there was anything else that needed doing.

Eric commented that Folding out the facility would require that the power to the Hangar and Work Center was removed.

Zoe asked about the security fence around the facility and the gate.

Linda asked about the no-fly air space over the Fold compound.

Bram said that he was glad that he had held a quick meeting before getting online.

Linda pointed at the clock and said it was time.

Bram greeted everyone and let them know this was the Fold shutdown meeting that was to take place next year, but recent events had dictated a more aggressive disappearance.

He then said that each of them would play a critical role in turning the site into a beautiful park owned and maintained by the Dallas City.

He asked Ted whether he and the lawyer were ready to execute the transfer.

Ted replied that they could do it at any time. He added that the clause that offered to cover the cost of maintaining the park for the next ten years was the lever to making the transfer a quiet one.

Bram asked if arranging the removal of the no-fly zone might add some additional leverage to the deal.

Ted thought that might be more important than the maintenance cost. It would open up the sky for additional flights. He said he would work with his lawyer to add this to the transfer paperwork.

Bram then said he would like to have the transfer be a ceremony by the lake and that he would like Stetson Catering to facilitate a top end lake side picnic. He asked whether Stetson Catering was willing to do that.

Ted replied that he would only do it if the person asking would go fishing with him.

Bram smiled and said that he would love to go fishing and it was a deal.

He then asked if Erica would be able to work on getting the no-fly zone removed. He also needed to have all the power remove from the buildings being Folded out and the fence around the facility removed. The only fence to be left standing was the one separating the apple orchard from the park.

He asked if Erica could handle those items.

Erica replied that she had been using the supervisor that had initially managed the installation of the Fold power system, and he lived and loved Mataia. She said the power would be no problem. She said that if Lester supplied a work detail she would get the fence Folded out on some dark night.

She then commented that he had forgotten removing the road that led up to the compound. She would get it Folded out at the same time as the fencing. Then once again she would need help in getting the large trees Folded into place.

Eric spoke up and said that he would work with her to ensure that the Folds would take place at the times she specified.

The General said since she had correctly used his name he had no choice but to deliver the help she needed.

Bram said that he was going to ask one additional piece of work that Lester needed to supply manpower for. He would need a hole excavated where Amy and Pat could Fold a receive and transmit chamber that would be underground.

This would be the chamber where Melisa would allow four to five people who were willing to visit the park on a weekday to Fold in and out.

He asked if Melisa was willing to manage the weekday visit to the park.

Melisa said that she could and suggested just one visit per week so that it would not draw attention. She said that everyone was currently so busy that she had seen a significant drop for the weekend Fold vacations.

Bram thanked her for the heads up about the weekend vacations and said that he wanted to meet with her and figure out how to get the weekend vacations up to their past levels.

Linda asked about the team that had been originally started out as a Lacy team but had been transferred to Lester. She wondered where they were.

Lester smiled and replied that they were mostly on his current team that was focused on how to restore Kutikan. He went on and said that a couple had chosen to get under Chef D'Carluca wing and had found out that he was a tough boss. One of them had just become the Chef in the Fold Work Center and was experimenting on Bram.

Bram smiled and added that he was finding it hard to bear the pain of eating so well.

Erica commented that she had recently worked with Senator Etaing who had inquired if there might be a spot in the Fold organization for her younger brother the lawyer.

Bram said there indeed was room, but he wanted to discuss the opportunity directly with Senator Etaing's brother because there was not a traditional career spot for a lawyer. The opportunities were many. He said he recalled that her younger brother had a talented wife and two kids, and they were all welcome.

He asked that the two of them meet with Melisa to organize the approach to recruiting new people.

Melisa commented that she had multiple inquiries from a variety of people asking how they could get a friend or a relative onboard the Fold program. She added that the time to organize how to keep a slow steady flow of new recruits coming in was now.

Bram made the point that the meeting had gone past the original objectives. He asked Linda to set up two additional meetings. One to brainstorm the final disappearance of Fold from Earth. And the other to focus on setting up a recruiting strategy and process.

He thanked everyone for participating and it was now time for he and the people in the Viewing Room to go to the cafeteria and suffer their Chef's torture. He waved goodbye and cut the feed.

Linda commented that she was happy about Bram agreeing to go fishing with her Father.

Bram replied that if every bargain was as easy as that one, he wanted to bargain more often with her father.

Ron Mueller

<u>Chapter 21: Weddings</u>

Donna had reminded Bram about the upcoming Rushing River weddings and that she and Castor had both wedding parties ready. They were going to practice their wedding in the chapel on Mataia, but they were still ready to Fold to the Rushing River location for the Wedding. The folks who were Earth located on Earth would practice virtually but then would attend physically.

Mike and Mary were please to hold the wedding and pleased that once again the catering would be done by Stetson catering. They commented that the Fold weddings were keeping them in business.

The weddings reminded Bram that the fence with the laser shield needed to be removed and he would need a suitable Fold arrival and departure site near the Rushing River.

Bram contacted Ted and arranged to go fishing after the weddings. He asked if Ted was ready to list his fishing expeditions as one of the weekend Fold vacations. Ted replied that he thought it would be a great way to establish his fishing business. He asked how that could be arranged.

The answer was that he should get Melinda involved and let her set up Dallas as a Fold vacation site.

Zoe had heard the conversation with Ted and said that she was looking forward to go fishing with no gun battles on the horizon.

Bram said that such an occasion would be welcome.

She then shared the fact that both Thomas and Bob were getting to the point where they were going to be the next to get married. They both said that they wanted to be the first to get married on Mataia. They were working on getting their two brides to be cleared so they could migrate to Mataia before the wedding. They figure that would give the two a chance to experience the Mataian culture and then if there was an issue they could decide to back out.

Bram smiled and said that he was sure that both Bob and Thomas would make sure their two brides would love Mataia.

Eric piped in that he knew that the two had already set up three weekend Fold vacation each. They were hitting the locations on Earth that they knew their significant other had mentioned as places that were on their bucket list.

Bram said that those weekend vacations were a key element that had made the transition to Mataia an enjoyable one.

He would need to suggest to Erica that they get used as part of the recruiting of new people to Mataia.

Linda buzzed in and asked what he had done to get her father interested in working with Melisa to set up Stetson Fishing as part of a Dallas weekend vacation. She added that her father had said he had a new secluded river side home that would be a great purchase. It was a home built for a family of ten. The family was a well to do one and the home was gorgeous.

"I have done nothing other than agree to go fishing with him," Bram replied. He was pleased that Ted was acting so fast. He was sure that one of the catalysts was Rita, Ted's wife. She had often mentioned that she wanted him to set up a fishing business.

Linda then added that Luke had let her know about the Fishing business and that he was planning to use his weekends to Fold back to Earth and use his boat as one of those that was earning money.

Bram replied that seemed to be a terrific way to both relax and be productive.

Linda replied that Bram was having too much of an influence on her family. She then shared the fact that she was going to Fold with Melisa to Dallas on the morrow to tour the house in question. Melisa had commented that she figured she needed to move fast to get a large luxurious waterfront home.

Bram chuckled and said he agreed with her and said that he agreed with Linda that he was having too much influence on the Stetson family.

Linda replied that she was Mrs. Evender now and hung up.

Zoe asked if Linda was mad.

Bram shook his head and said that she had mentioned that she had often tried to get her father to set up a sports fishing business and had been turned down every time.

He called Melisa and asked her to find a house on the highway near to the Rushing River Resort. It didn't need to be fancy, but it should have a space where a Fold vehicle could deliver and pick up people. She might also consider making the place attractive enough to put it in her weekend vacation list.

Melisa said she would see if she could meet his request. She said that the purchase of the large luxury home on the Columbia River was almost in her pocket. She had made an offer and was meeting the Realtor and the owner when she visited. Linda knew the realtor and was accompanying her to facilitate the purchase. She said she would ask the realtor what might be available on the highway to the Rushing River.

Bram asked Melisa that if she made the purchase to contact the general and cancel the building of a Fold chamber at the park.

Melisa replied that she would do that.

He thanked her and hung up.

He asked Zoe if she knew how much Melisa's Weekend Fold vacation business made each year.

Zoe said that she had no clue.

Bram said that Melisa had let him know that the business was taking in close to three million a year. It had ten million invested in the stock market and the income that was currently coming in was at about two million each year. He said that Melisa spent several million each year to maintain each of the vacation locations.

Melissa also had the business gifting about two hundred thousand a year to a fund called the Fold Miracle Child that helped disabled kids and young adults.

He felt that he had the right person managing a well-oiled machine.

Zoe smiled and asked how the Fold Miracle child was doing.

Bram smiled and said that their miracle child was now a clamorous young woman who had just contacted her parents and let them know that she was engaged to one of the Marines who was residing on Mataia and working in Remi's lab doing analysis of materials coming from some place called Kutikan.

Zoe smiled and said that it would be good to have Zuri on Mataia and involved in an activity that interested her.

Bram agreed and he was wondering what activity there might be that would be challenging enough.

Linda came on over the intercom to say that her snoopy sister had just let her know that she had snooped out more aliens and was standing at her desk wanting to talk to him.

Bram told her to send Lacy in and that three people were eager to hear what she had to share.

Lacy came in and went to the fridge and got a bottle of water. She said that she had found the evidence of some intelligent aliens, but she was not sure what she had found. She said that the object was definitely a rocket or spaceship and was moving at close to the speed of light and headed toward a distant galaxy. She had identified the distant galaxy, and she had identified the potential starting point of the space going object. She said that she had come to see him because she was resource strapped and was looking for help in going to the objects launch location and the objects destination location.

Bram asked her if she was monitoring his office because she had arrived just in time to offer up a very unique opportunity for their miracle child that was coming home to get married and would be looking for something interesting to work on.

Lacy smiled, everyone in Bram's inner circle knew that Zuri was the miracle child. She asked who the lucky person was that Zuri was planning to marry.

Bram smiled and said that he was the Marine that had danced with her during the quadruple marriage.

Lacy said that figuring out what her team had just discovered would indeed be a unique opportunity.

Bram asked if there was anything that needed to be immediately done.

Lacy replied that she had assigned one of her team members to keep an observation bubble Folding along the same path as the spaceship so they could keep track of it but, even at close to the speed of light at which it was moving, it would be another few thousand years before it arrived at the solar system where it seemed to be going.

Bram nodded and said that she should continue to track the object, and he would work on staffing a team to develop the details of what her team had discovered.

He commented that it was now clear that other sapient life forms existed in the vast universe. They now had contact with two sapient populations. One that was as different from the human form as could be but was as intelligent and one that at a peak, was beyond what the human had achieved, had it not destroyed itself.

He went on to ask where in the discovery spectrum Lacy's new discovery would land.

Lacy replied that Zuri might tell them the rest of the story in the near future. She said she was relieved that her team could continue to focus on finding other life forms and that the follow up of the teams most recent discovery would be in good hands.

Bram said that he had to get refocused on weddings because he figured that one more would soon be added to the list. He knew that Zuri and her husband to be would most likely want to be married where they had first met.

A few days later Elizabeth came to his office and said that she was the liaison for a young ex-Marine who was afraid to go to the BOSS and asked her for her help in arranging for his wedding.

Bram smiled at Elizabeth emphasizing boss. He asked if it was the lucky guy that was marrying the person that had been their miracle child who she had coached through college.

Elizabeth smiled and said that "yes our miracle child is now a beautiful young woman." She said that the two wanted to get married where they had first met.

Bram asked if being part of a three-wedding ceremony might work?

Elizabeth nodded and said that it would be appropriate. She said that Zuri had one special request that after the wedding and the wedding dinner, she would like to go to fishing with Ted and his crew.

Bram said that fiction could not be any better than real life, he had just made arrangements to that effect with Ted. He commented that Ted would most likely say that he would be honored to take Zuri fishing as her first big step in her marriage.

He added that he was sure that Rita would insist on having a picnic in the park after the fishing trip.

Elizabeth asked who the other two getting hitched were and when was the date for their weddings.

Bram replied that Donna and Castor were the two getting married and the date was still fluid, but it was about a month away.

Elizabeth said that was close in, but doable. She said she would let, Zuri and her husband to be, Weylan know. She then added that the two wanted him to preside over their wedding.

Bram said he would be most honored to marry them. He then added that he would handle setting up the fishing trip. He asked if the two had selected a honeymoon location.

Elizabeth said the two were thinking about vacationing some place on Mataia.

Bram suggested she contact Pat and Amy who he was sure would come up with several suggestions and videos that would help Zuri make her choice.

Zoe excused herself for interrupting, but she wanted to share that she had been looking at the video's that Amy and Pat kept taking of the various places. They had just recently found a place where the Mataian Plate Tectonics had created one of the few water falls that existed on the planet.

She suggested that Elizabeth share that with Zuri.

She smiled and added that she wanted to make sure that the only other person who had a first name starting with the last letter in the alphabet would end up taking the best honeymoon on Mataia.

Elizabeth said she would make sure Zuri viewed Zoe's suggested honeymoon location.

Bram asked if Elizabeth would act in the same role as she had in the previous weddings.

She said that she had been asked to do so by Zuri, but she would need to see what Donna and Castor had planned.

Bram said he thought she was a shoe in.

Elizabeth nodded and said it was time for her to get going.

After she left, Bram was about to get ready to review the restoration work going on Kutikan when Zoe reminded him it was getting close to lunch time and it was their turn to go over to the Main Work Center and have lunch with Pat and Amy.

On the way-out Bram invited Linda to go to lunch with them.

Linda replied that she never missed going to lunch when it came to going to the Main cafeteria.

Bram called Marcus and Remi to let them know about the new Alien discovery and that he wanted to see if they could locate the home of the Alien. He asked if they would join him in Lacy's teamwork center.

Pat watched as Bran entered the cafeteria and commented to Amy that, by the look on his face, he was thinking about more than the wedding.

Amy asked why she though that.

Pat said if he was only thinking about the wedding he would be all smiles, instead he had a serious work face.

Bram looked over at Amy and Pat and smiled as he went to get his food.

Pat said that at least he had noticed them and come up from whatever the new focus happened to be.

Amy again asked how Pat knew that it was a new focus.

Pat replied that once he had organized a new focus area, he never got that deep faraway look. She was sure it was a new focus.

Bram sat down and asked how everything was going.

Amy commented that he should develop a way to clone people so they could continue to handle the work load he kept pushing at them.

Bram smiled and replied that as he recalled, everything that she and Pat were working on was work that they had each requested or volunteered to do. He added that he personally knew that self-control was extremely difficult, but it was the only remedy that he knew for her condition.

Linda laughed and said that she was pleased to learn that he was just as tough on his other good friends as he was on her.

Pat asked what was new with him.

Bram replied that the Stetson sisters were both trying to give him a hard time. The oldest was complaining about the fact that he had too much influence over the Stetson family and the other kept finding new Aliens.

Amy reacted first and asked if he were joking.

Bram said that he was not and that after lunch he was going to go to Lacy's work area to investigate it a little farther but in the long term he was going to see if Zuri would take on the longer-term investigation of the newly discovered aliens.

Pat commented that it would be a great assignment for Zuri. She added that she was really curious what Bram would discover.

He smiled and said that only the person willing to curl up with him on the recliner would learn every detail.

There was a chorus of voices volunteering to curl up with him.

Bram raised his two arms, laughed, and said he only wanted Pat to curl up with him, but he would share the details of what he found with all of them.

Ron Mueller

Chapter 22: Amoral Aliens

After lunch, Bram left Pat and Amy and headed to Lacy's work center.

When he entered, the work area went silent. Lacy immediately asked for the time.

Bram asked if he was arriving at an inconvenient time.

Lacy smiled and replied that someone in her group had just earned a paid Fold vacation because the work team had a bet on the time that he would come to their work area.

Bram asked if this was a standing bet or just on this day.

Lacy replied that the bet and the prize had been made on her return from her meeting with him.

Bram shook his head and said he was getting too predictable. He asked who the winner was.

Lacy turned to the person who had written down the time and asked him who had the closest time. He called out the time and one of the technicians jumped up and down whooping it up and said she was going to spend a weekend in Jamaica.

Bram congratulated her and said he would throw in a hundred for her knowing him so well.

He then asked who was tracking the new alien spaceship. As he got to her station, Marcus, and Remi both showed up and Lacy again asked for the time

Bram smiled and asked if the team always spent their work hours gambling.

Marcus looked confused and asked what was up.

Bram explained that he had just won someone in the room a prize.

When the person who had taken the time called out the winner, the person who was following the alien spaceship yelled out a loud, YES. She looked at Marcus and Remi and thanked them.

Then Lacy said there were several additional winners because the second part of the bet was that Remi would be with Marcus.

This time the person that had been logging the time read four names from the list and said they had all earned a day off or an extra days pay.

Bram asked if Lacy could afford to give anyone time off.

Lacy shook her head and said she couldn't but said that the time off would be held until there was some time available. She added that is why she had added the choice of a day's pay because they could all use a couple of extra dollars on the Fold vacations.

Bram complimented Lacy on running a fun work area then he asked the lady he was standing behind if her name happened to be Clair.

The young woman stopped and asked how he could possibly remember her.

He smiled and replied that she was one of the persons sitting by the pool on the day the three shooters had shot and almost killed one of the people at the pool. He said he had studied that situation and had learned who everyone was. He shared the fact that she had been born in Tennessee. Her mother was a technician, and her father was in the automotive business restoring, maintaining, and selling cars.

He went on to say that her family name was Alpharad, and it means queen of everything.

She shook her head and said that everything she had heard about him was true.

Bram smiled and asked what everything she had heard implied.

She shook her head and said that people claimed that he never forgot anything and knew almost everything.

Bram said that such talk was an over exaggeration and that in fact she probably knew just as much as anyone.

He asked if she knew the origin of the spaceship she was tracking.

She shook her head negatively.

He asked Marcus to back track the rocket path and see if he could locate the origin.

He asked Clair is she knew if the spaceship had passengers, and she again shook her head negatively.

He asked Remi to send a prob into the spaceship.

Almost immediately Remi said he had lost the observation bubble. It must have Folded into something solid. He said he was Folding a second one in toward the front.

It was obvious to Bram that the second met the same fate as the first one.

After the fifth loss Remi said that it seemed that the rocket was a solid and seem more like a very large missile than a spaceship.

Bram asked how large the missile happened to be.

Clair said that was something she did know. It was roughly six football fields in diameter and twenty football fields long.

Bram shook his head and said that if it was an explosive with the power of C4 they were looking at a planet killer.

Lacy said that if that was true then she and her team had bad news because they had just found three more planet killers all leading back to the same source.

Bram asked how far away each of the rockets were from the source.

After a moment someone in the room called out that the rockets were all about one light year from the source and two light years away from the targets.

Bram said that he remembered Lacy saying that the first missile was traveling at half the speed of light and that meant that the missiles were about two Mataian years from hitting their targets.

He announced that he was setting up a team to study and resolve the situation that had been discovered. It would be a separate team that he was going to call The Eliminators, and they would have two main objectives. One was to eliminate the four planet killing missiles and the second was to investigate the civilization that was so amoral that they would send the missiles to eliminate entire worlds.

He was asking Lacy and her team to get a closer look at what the four targeted planets had in common and let him know. Their primary mission remained to find additional intelligent beings and he would determine how each of the four planets would be investigated.

He then commented that they must be looking into a region of the universe that was closer to its center and older than they were. He pointed to the fact that Earth was at the edge of the Milky Way galaxy and that the Milky Way was at the edge of the Universe and traveling away from its center.

Mataia was in a galaxy almost one hundred light years closer to the center of the universe. Primeira was a light year away but at about the same distance from the center. Kutikan and the two other planets were again about fifty light years closer to the center. He went on to say that he would not be surprised if the Amoral planet was only a few light years from the center of the Universe. He then asked what they thought might be on the side opposite from where they were looking.

Lacy smiled and replied that she would wait for him to answer that question and when he did she would ask him to share it with her.

Bram shook his head and said that they all had enough exploration that when their lifetimes were over, the next generation would wonder why they had explored so little.

Bram Nielson Collection

Marcus spoke up and said that he had the galaxy and the solar system where the Amoran Aliens resided. He reinforced Bram's discussion by saying that it was in toward the center in what seemed to be a very old galaxy.

He suggested that they plan a visit for the next day.

Bram said that would be a good time. He asked Lacy if she planned to join in on the trip.

Lacy asked what time and where should she be.

Bram replied eight sharp and at the Negative Fold launch pad.

He then left Lacy's work center and returned to his office.

Linda smiled as Bram approached her desk and let him know that her sister had called to let her know that she was going for a ride with him the next day.

She asked who else he had in mind.

Bram replied that Marcus and Remi would be going with him. He added that he would also like to the get the General, the Admiral, and Mallica to go. He added that Zoe and Eric would also be going.

Linda asked whether she should include snacks and a lunch.

Bram said that she should since he did not know exactly how long it would take.

He looked around and realized that Remi and Marcus were not with him. He called Marcus and asked him to have the coordinates of the five planets that had been discovered with intelligent life on them.

He contacted Remi and asked him to have a twelve-person Fold craft ready to Fold at eight in the morning.

That evening Bram shared the events of the afternoon and asked if Pat wanted to ride along.

Pat responded with a negative shake of her head. She said that she and Amy had discussed the possibility of a Fold expedition to examine the new find, but they agreed that they had their hands full with the effort to provide food for the Kutikans and getting ready to bring forward the plants from the past.

Additionally, they were working with Donna and Castor to get started on getting the work center and the hangar from Earth into position and powered up on Primeira. She commented on the fact that structures would be powered up and managed just like the buildings on Mataia. And for the short-term Mataia would be the location for the treatment of waste from the buildings on Primeira. The water use there would be processed and Folded to the top of the buildings at Primeira by some portable water preparation system that had been Folded to Primeira. The work was getting rapidly done but the list of things to do was extensive.

She shared the fact that Erica was just as swamped with the request coming from Donna and Castor. The big-ticket item was the across the lake wave breaks that he had suggested to the two of them. They felt that getting the lakes calmed would be a big step forward to getting on with terra forming the planet. She said that the two were referring to terra forming as Prima Forming.

Bram said he like the sound of the new term. Prima Forming was what it was and what she and Amy were doing on Mataia should be called Mata Forming. And what they would do on Kutikan should be called Kuti Forming and on Walelhan it should be Wale Forming and on Vultlhan it should be Vulti Forming. That way each one of the planet transformations the two of them was doing could specifically referred to and progress tracked.

Pat said that she would share the names with Amy, and she was fairly certain they would take up the names and begin reporting progress using the names. She admitted that the two of them had already gotten their actions confused because of the lack of not having clear names.

Bram said that the same was beginning to happen to him. They needed everyone to be able to clearly and easily distinguish where and what in the Universe they referring to.

He then shared the fact that the Amorans seemed to only be able to reach out some three hundred light years with their technology but evidently the technology was rigorous enough at that range to discern intelligent life. He was referring to them as Amorans because he felt their action were those of a coward and they were amoral. Their approach was not one of embracing other intelligent life but to eliminate it so they would not have to have competition in an infinitely large universe. He felt such behavior was the most despicable actions that any civilization could take. He said that he was going to ask the team that would study them whether the Amorans should be isolated and kept from using their technology in the way they were currently doing.

Pat said that by selecting Zuri to lead that team he had put the best person to determine if that was appropriate.

Bram agreed.

He then said that he wanted to set up four more teams to study the four new planets with intelligent beings on them.

Pat asked if he had team leaders selected for those teams.

He replied that he had not had time to think who was ready to lead those teams.

Pat suggested he ask the current team leaders to suggest individuals that were ready to be promoted and capable of leading the new teams. She said that she felt that asking the current team leaders would empower them and it was a good way to surface new talent.

Bram agreed and said he would put out the word after he got back from the upcoming Fold trip.

The next day as he jogged in to work he almost fell down when Zoe sang out a new ditty.

> There's dirt in Fold city.
> Amoral action, sinful and degrading
> There will be judgement in the waiting.
> There's dirt in Fold city.
> It ugly when things could be pretty.
> But Amoral actions, Judgement in the waiting
> Four victims unknowingly about to be hit.
> Being sent a wallop so devastating.
> It is Amoral action, it's the dirt in Fold City
> Action will be taken; Fold City has awakened.
> Fold city will react against Amoral action.
> There will be no dirt tolerated in Fold City.

They all entered the hangar and were surprised to hear the ditty being repeated by a chorus from other people at the Negative Fold center.

Bram knew that Pat had likely written the ditty and had sent it to Linda who had posted it in everyone's in box.

He thought about the atmosphere that was so positively charged and energized not only himself but everyone around him. He thought he would miss the jogs that he had so enjoyed on Earth when he went into work, but he now knew that he was having just as much fun on Mataia as at the Dallas site. The Dalles site that was now a lush green park for the members of the Dallas community to enjoy.

Linda asked what he thought of his greeting as he entered the hangar.

Bram thanked her for getting everyone that had made it to work involved. It had set a positive tone for him.

Linda said he should thank his mate because she had sent it over to her.

Bram said he would certainly do so. He asked if she knew if everyone was ready.

He said that he was going to take fifteen minutes to converse with his advisors and then head down to the launch area.

Linda replied that the General and the Admiral were in the cafeteria having breakfast. They had asked her to give them a five-minute warning. She added that Orlando was having breakfast with the General at the request of the General. She said the general had asked for him to be part of the Fold to Amoral.

Bram replied that Orlando was welcome, and she should pack an extra lunch for him.

Linda nodded and said that was easily done.

Bram went into his office and took out Isaac, Ada and Einstein Jr. and put them on his desk.

He asked them if he should ask the current team leaders for names to lead the new teams needed to study the newly discovered Alien planets.

He got the positive head shakes he expected.

He asked whether there was any hope at changing the Amoran culture.

This time he got two no head shakes, but Ada did not respond. A moment later she moved her head in a circle. The Isaac and Einstein Jr. joined her.

He asked if they meant maybe. This time there were three positive head shakes.

Zoe came over and gave them all some additional cookie crumbs and praised them for expanding the language that they shared. She received three positive head shakes.

Bram asked if he should destroy the missiles now.

He got three positive head shakes.

He thanked the three and carried them to the small door leading to their tunnel system.

Eric shook his head and commented that each time he watched the two of them converse with the mice he wondered about the world around him and if he really understood any of it.

Bram replied that all of them lacked the sensitivity and the ability to grasp the totality of the environment that surrounded them. They lacked the additional sensory organs that would give them a clear vision of the reality they live in.

He got up and led the way out of his office.

Ron Mueller

Chapter 23: Amora

When Bram got to the Fold area, everyone going on the expedition to Amora was ready and standing by.

Bram said good morning. He then walked over to Orlando and asked what his role was going to be.

Orlando smiled and replied that the General had asked him to come along so a proper ditty about the trip would be written.

Bram chuckled and said he was glad there was someone accompanying him that would find some humor in learning about Amora.

Marcus suggested that they first visit the four target planets and then approach Amora from the area of one of the planets. He pointed out that Amora had demonstrated that their sensing technology was a superior and long range one. He did not want them to be able to back track them to Mataia.

Bram agreed with Marcus and said that the four planets were already targeted and traveling from their location to Amora might frighten the Amorans, which he said was very appropriate.

He asked Marcus to make sure they were not detected by the four worlds they were going to visit first. He wanted to look and gain some understanding of the four worlds but did not want them to know about the visit at this point in time.

Marcus put them well outside of the solar system of each planet and then sent in some observation bubbles that Folded swiftly back in time like a rock skipping across the still water of a placid lake. He was able to capture the desired information and images in a matter of a few minutes. In less than an hour the team had visited all four planets and were ready to skip to Amora.

Marcus stopped and had the supercomputer back on Mataia received the information. He then had it do a comparison between planets.

He reported that all four planets were roughly the same size, had almost the same rotational velocity, traveled around their star at about the same rate and all had an advanced technical capability that had them exploring their solar system via rockets that were similar to the ones Earth was currently using. Their skies were full of flying airplanes.

Bram thanked Marcus for the quick analysis and the comparison of the three to each other.

He said he would like get the same information about Amora.

Marcus said that he would Fold to some location well outside the Amoran solar system and send his bubbles in.

He had no sooner Folded to the location he had chosen than his sensor warned that they were being hit by some sort of unknown rays.

Marcus immediately Folded. He announced he was Folding back one thousand years into the Amoran past.

This time he Folded to a thirty-thousand-foot altitude above the planet.

He sent in his bubble scouts and then began a series of one hundred year forward Folds. When he was within one hundred years of the present, he received a signal that he believed was a challenge and he immediately Folded back fifty years and waited to see if he would get a challenge as he reduced his Fold skips to ten second Folds that in essence kept them invisible.

He explained that the ability for the long-range sensing was about one hundred years old. He speculated that during the following hundred years the sensing technology was significantly improved. He reported that his scout bubbles had not recorded any flight ability nor any rocket action. He speculated that the Amorans had not developed flight or space travel. Their long ranging sensing technology was most likely exposing them to technology that they saw as a threat.

Bram thanked Marcus for his quick analysis. He asked him to remain in their past but send his scout bubbles to the present time and have them skip backwards in time long enough to get a complete picture of Amora.

It turned out that going back through time was the appropriate technique because they got challenged at each point of exposure, but no action was taken because the scout bubble was on to the next point in the past.

It was noon and they decided to relax for a short time before following Marcus's recommendation to return to Mataia.

This time Marcus said that he was already having the supercomputer process the data they had gathered, and he would organize it so they could have an assessment review in the late afternoon.

Bram complemented him for the rapid work. He thanked Remi for having the bubbles and the transport ready.

He then asked the General what Gary Tatum, Art Baratta and Matt were doing and for whom they were working. He said that he wanted to get those three to lead three of the four teams that he was going to create to investigate the four targeted alien planets.

Mallica spoke up and said that Matt had been working with her on translating the various alien languages and if Bram was asking about him to offer him a position, she would support getting him in the position to lead a team. She commented that translation work and learning new languages was going to take an upswing. It would give her an opportunity to recruit some new folks. She added that the translation work was irregular and more like part time work and most of her members were on other teams.

The General replied that he was not sure who each of the other three worked for. He was in contact with them, but they mostly discussed how much they loved living on Mataia when they had a beer together. He said that he encouraged them to keep the conversation away from work.

Bram nodded and agreed that keeping it social made for a more relaxed periodic meeting. He said he would follow up with Erica who kept track of everyone's assignments and made sure everyone's compensation was competitive versus their Earth counterparts.

The Admiral commented that he didn't realize that law enforcement personnel got such low pay.

Bram reminded him that the compensation was based purely on the take home pay minus the taxes the various governments extracted. What the Admiral was experiencing was what the typical worker on Earth experienced.

The significant difference was that on Mataia he had no expenses and the money he did earn was all his to spend as he saw fit. He could spend it all on Fold vacations or on Earth shopping sprees.

The Admiral smiled and said that life on Mataia was a phenomenal experiment in easy living.

Bram asked the Admiral what team he wanted to lead. He was surprised when the response was that he was ready for any additional work, and it did not need to be in a leadership role.

He asked if the Admiral would consider taking the role of coaching the four new team leaders and their members as they took on the study of the four new Alien worlds.

The Admiral nodded and replied that he would love to do something like that.

The General spoke up and said that he would like to add coaching to his resume.

Bram was pleased to have the two volunteers to coach the new teams. It would allow him to focus on the rehabilitation and fresh development of Kutikan and working with Zuri on studying and dealing with Amora.

On return to his office, he immediately put in a call to Erica and asked about the status of the four people he was interested in naming as leaders of the four new teams.

Matt Simple, working for Mallica, had already been selected and would hear about the opportunity from her.

Gary Tatum, one of the Marine divers, was now working for Amy and Pat in the capacity of feeding the surviving Kutikanians. Moving him over was just a matter of timing.

Art Baratta was a graduate Chef trained by Chef D'Carluca. This meant that he was really not a candidate.

The alternate name that popped up was Duong Tran. He felt that Duong would make an effective team leader.

The final name was Charles Ford the science advisor that had been on the Oversight Committee. He was currently under employed working for Elizabeth.

He put in a call to Elizabeth and asked her about Charles and learned that she though highly of him and enjoyed working with him. She commented that his partner was also a great fellow. Bram asked her if putting him in the lead of one of the new teams he was creating would be appropriate.

She said that it was a very good move. Bram asked her to attend the afternoon update that Marcus was holding at four and then afterwards she would be ready to let Charles know. She asked where she should be at four and then said she would see him there.

Bram then put in a call to Duong and invited him to attend the meeting that Marcus was having at four in the Fold Center Viewing room.

He then put a call into Amy and asked her about Gary Tatum and was told he was one of the leaders on their team. He asked her if she could fly her chopper without him. She asked what he had in mind. He suggested that she and Pat attend Marcus's meeting being held at four that afternoon in the Fold Work Center Viewing Room.

Amy hung up and asked Pat what Bram was up to. Pat shook her head and said that he had left in the morning to investigate five separate newly discovered Alien races. All she knew was that Marcus was having a meeting at the end of the day. She speculated that they would get an overview of each of the alien races. Other than that, she had no idea what Bram was up to.

Bram asked Zoe and Eric what they knew of the four people he was thinking about.

Zoe commented that Duong would be a great team leader.

Eric agreed with her and then said that Charles was exceptionally sharp and fun to work with. He also liked his partner who was a little less outgoing but pleasant to talk with.

They both said that they had not followed what Gary had been doing but expected that he would be well thought of by whomever he worked for or with.

And they both agreed that Matt, who was like a brother to both of them, was exceptional.

They both ended by saying that Bram could have picked a dozen other people that would be qualified to lead. They commented that there were no followers but only talented and capable people to pick from.

Bram smiled and asked if they were the critics or the endorsers.

Zoe shook her head and said that they had so little critique because everyone tried to follow his favorite saying to treat others as you wish to be treated.

Bram commented that he had seen the final draft of the Mataian Constitution, and it began with that phrase.

He then commented that thought had triggered the fact that the weddings were on the coming weekend.

Zoe asked how that would have triggered such a connection.

Bram replied that he did not know how his brain got triggered but what had happened, was that she had mentioned those words, and he had seen her catching a fish out on the Lake and he had seen Zuri sitting on the bow of Ted's boat and that had reminded him of her Wedding request to go fishing.

Zoe shook her head and said that it was time to go to the meeting and deal with reality and that as strange as that might be it was not as strange as trying to figure out how his mind worked.

Bram followed her and was still chuckling when they got to Linda's desk.

Linda got up and followed them. She said that if the meeting was making Bram chuckle, she was not going to miss it. She said that Lacy said she should not miss the meeting. She said she thought they would be the last to get to the meeting.

Bram did not reply but continued to follow Zoe.

They all went in and sat down in their seats.

Marcus stood up at his desk and welcomed them. He commented that he and some of them had taken a very successful trip out to five new Alien discoveries. He had a story to tell that he found uncomfortable and that went against everything that the Mataian society lived by. He asked Elizabeth what the first sentence in the Mataian Constitution was.

Elizabeth responded, "Treat others the way you wish to be treated."

Marcus then displayed four missiles and the four planets that were the targets and explained that Bram had labeled them Planet killers.

He then zeroed in on Amoral. He commented that he agreed with the name that Bram had given the planet and its society.

He then displayed what was a very pleasant world with a landscape that was similar in variety to what would be found on Earth. The land mases had different unique shapes, but it clearly showed that the planet had gone through the plate Teutonic activity similar to Earths and it had mountains similar to those on Earth.

The plant life was abundant and there seemed to be a variety of animals. The beings were bipedal and were similar to a human but looked more like the Denisovans but were amazingly like them than he had anticipated.

He highlighted the fact that they had not developed flight or any rocket capacity. Their major technical achievement had until just recently been their exceptional sensing capability. They had been able to discover and study four alien cultures that were three light years away. What they discovered must have alarmed them to an extreme. They had rapidly developed, built, and deployed the largest missile that he had ever seen. It was extremely large, but it was simple. It was an engine pushing a tremendous amount of explosive material and a guidance system.

He pointed out that Lacy's team had discovered the missiles and then he and Remi had found the location of Amora, and later the location of the four targeted planets.

This morning Bram had led them on an exploratory Fold journey, and they had visited all five planets. He commented on the fact that they had not done a close in Fold on the four planets. Remi and he had sent their scout bubbles in to get a closer look at all four planets and had the close ups that needed a lot of study. The top line was that they were all similar to Earth, they had developed flight and rocket technology and had cities and living areas.

He said that was all he had ready as an overview.

Bram Nielson Collection

He asked Bram if there was anything that he wanted to add.

Bram thanked Marcus at having been able to give such a thorough overview so quickly.

He then said that Amoral would be the focus of investigation by a team that would be led by Zuri.

He was also naming four teams to study and analyze the four other Alien civilizations. He had identified the leaders for those teams and their bosses were all sitting in the room and would let those individuals know of their new roles.

He commented that the next couple of years was going to be exciting and that eventually they would communicate with the newly discovered intelligences.

He said that dealing with the Amoral aliens was going to be personal for him. That society had to change, or he would need to figure out how they could be isolated.

He called the meeting to an end and stood up and led the way out of the Viewing room.

Every time he thought about the actions that the Amoral aliens had taken; it shook his belief system. He knew they were going to test the limits of each of the principles he held dear.

Ron Mueller

<u>Chapter 24: Mole</u>

Pat was sitting next to Bram on their dual recliners when she asked him whether he was ready for the coming weekend weddings.

He jokingly asked whose wedding they were going to attend. Then he gave a small laugh and said that he was actually looking beyond that and anticipating the fishing trip. He said that he had asked Castor what he was looking forward to and he had answered the chance to go fishing and not having to carry his entire field kit and weapons.

Pat agreed that she was looking forward to fishing as well, but she was really happy to be the Matron of honor for Zuri. She felt like a younger sister was getting married.

Bram agreed that being asked to preside over all three marriages was an honor that he would remember for his lifetime. He felt that having been able to watch Zuri blossom was the sweet honey of life.

He said that he had lunch with Nuro and Jina and they were happy beyond belief. They said that Zuri had picked a mate that was very much in love with her, and the Marine Corps had made him strong enough to withstand Zuri's ways. She was proud that he was a Chef and was now the Chef that boasted of serving the smartest man on Mataia and soon he would be making the dinners for the smartest woman on Mataia.

He said that as far as Donna and Castor was concerned, the two of them had saved him so many times that he considered them not only very good friends but two people that had been and were still willing to take a bullet for him. He was pleased that Orlando was the best man for Castor. He was surprised that Donna's husband had chosen Duong to be the best man as the fill in for his best friend who would attend remotely.

The dinner and dance afterward was going to be close coupled to the Wedding as it had been for their wedding and then there was the fishing expedition and an early evening picnic at Celilo park. Zuri was honeymooning on Mataia.

Donna and Castor had chosen to honeymoon on Primeira. They said that some strange women had Folded in two beautiful homes to their lake side lots and had arranged for a yard crew to landscape the yards using the foliage available on Primeira.

Pat smiled and said that she and Amy had managed to expedite the two homes getting constructed on Earth. Erica had arranged for the interior decor. The General had arranged for the digging of the foundation. Amy and I determined the center coordinates of each structure and Marcus Folded the homes into place. Water and waste service was being handled by the system on Mataia.

This was their present to the two couples. They would be the first to honeymoon and live on Primeira.

Pat went on to say that the water wave reducers were considered Bram's gift that allowed them to live near the water.

Bram asked whether she and Amy had stocked any fish there.

She said that doing so was more difficult than it sounded because just throwing them in was not an option if they were to have food to survive. She and Amy were learning how hard it was to build an environment from the bottom up and had been working for some time to get some sea life for Mataia and had yet to get up to the fish level of the food chain. It was really a bottom-up system and there was no skipping steps.

She said that fishing with Ted and fishing on Earth was going to be happening for a long time and maybe when he retired, he might be able to go fishing on Mataia.

Bram said that he was in no rush and accepted the fact that there was no past to go get the natural stuff that existed before like on Kutikans that had brunt their world out of existence.

Pat nodded but clarified that even with the abundant availability of past resources, re-establishing the Kutikan environment was going to take a very long time. The Kutikans that were alive at the moment would be long dead before Kutikan would be reestablished. She estimated it would take several generations to reestablish the environment.

Bram asked if she knew what had happened to the environment. She shook her head and said the team was still looking into what triggered the doomsday weapon.

Pat answered her phone.

It was Jina calling to let her know that Zuri had just Folded in. She was wondering if it would be possible to give Zuri a tour of her home to be.

Pat said that after breakfast the next day she could meet Zuri and give her a tour and the keys to the house. She could also suggest what to stock up on so that it would be move in ready after the wedding.

She asked whether Weylan would be touring as well.

Jina said that neither of them was sure since her arrival was a few days early.

After Pat hung up, Bram commented that it was going to be hard to resist getting Zuri started but he was going to wait until after her honeymoon to get her rolling in her new assignment. He said that he was currently in the process of staffing her team so it would be ready to roll when she began.

Pat said waiting until after the honeymoon was a good idea. She was sure that Zuri would find out all she needed to know on her own.

Bram said that he was taking the next day off and going out to look in on Einstein and spend the day walking the desert.

Pat chuckled and asked what he was going to do the day after to avoid Zuri.

He laughed and said he might go visit Mike and Mary and do a little river fishing with the excuse of seeing if things were ready for the wedding.

And then on Friday he could tour the new house by the lake that should be in Melisa's possession and see if fishing off the pier was any good. And finally, he could inspect the house near the Inn that he had asked her to purchase.

Pat laughed and reminded him that he had a lunch date with her the next day.

He replied that he was going to lock himself in his office and have Linda refuse to let anyone in.

Linda laughed when Bram asked her to keep everyone away from his office. She said that rumor had it that Zuri was on Mataia, and she was eager to learn about her new assignment.

Bram said that it was not fair to put the Amoral assignment on her shoulders just before her wedding.

Linda shook her head and suggested that he leave the filtering to Zuri and that Zuri would be distracted by love and romance for the entire time she was on her honeymoon.

Bram said that he was not good at judging such things. His mind would be working both situations at the same time.

Linda commented that Zuri had mentioned that she did not have a warped nonlinear unconventional mind like his. She said she had a strong mind, but it was linear and hers to command.

Bram laughed and thanked Linda for describing a person on the verge of being taken away in a straight jacket.

She laughed and said that she was glad to be of help.

Bram went in and took Ada, Isaac, and Einstein Jr. out and put them on his desk.

Zoe came over and gave them a few cookie crumbs and warned them that Bram was going to unload his worries on them.

Bram said that Zoe was right. He asked if he should tell Zuri about the terrible action taken by planet Amoral.

All three gave a positive nod.

Zoe asked if Bram should visit the rock in the desert before the wedding?

All three gave a positive nod.

She then asked if he should tell Zuri about Amoral before going to the rock.

And she got three positive nods.

Bram smiled and asked if the fact that Zoe was giving them extra cookie crumbs had biased their answers.

The three mice shook their head in the negative.

Eric commented that the two of them had gone off their rockers.

Both Bram and Zoe laughed when the three mice shook their heads in the negative.

Bram picked up the three mice and returned them to their kingdom entrance in the bookshelf.

He commented that the reason that they never needed to see Dr. Windal was that they had three mice that regularly relieved their stress and erased all their doubts.

Eric smiled and said that maybe he should be the one going to sessions with her after all he was beginning to believe in mice that understood English.

Bram said that he was going to get a snack from the second most famous Chef on Mataia and asked who was going with him.

Zoe laughed and said that she should stay and work on her nails, but she would join him and took the lead while Eric took his usual spot behind Bram.

Bram had challenged the two multiple times about the fact that he thought their protection was no longer needed but they always responded, "someday."

It turned out that Chef Henslier was celebrating the arrival of his bride to be by making a special desert that he was giving out for free. When Bram walked in, he realized he was walking into an enthusiastic crowd that was in a celebratory mood. He was soon surrounded. Suddenly he saw one of the technicians with a gun in his hand. He stepped in toward him, grabbed the gun, and then realized that there was no place to aim it without the risk of someone being shot. He spun into the attacker's chest and brought the gun barrel to his chest just below his collar bone and pulled the trigger twice. The bullet went through him and hit the gun man twice in the chest. The gun man let go of his weapon and fell to the ground.

It was all over in less than a few seconds.

Bram turned and watched as Zoe examined the fallen technician.

Zoe shook her head and said that he was gone.

Bram walked over and sat down at a table. He looked at Eric and asked if Zoe was always right about the fact that danger was waiting to happen.

Zoe asked if he was bleeding.

Bram replied that he was not bleeding as much as he thought but he was sure that two bullets passing through most likely had done some damage.

The next thing he knew he was put in a wheelchair and rushed down the hallway to an examination room that also had an x-ray and cat scan equipment.

The Fold Work Center doctor did a quick external examination and sealed the wound and then put him in the cat scan.

A few minutes later he said that there was no internal damage. The bullets had traveled through and not hit any arteries or any organs.

Bram thanked him for his quick examination and said that he was going back to the cafeteria to have some of the goodies that the Chef had prepared.

The doctor suggested he take it easy.

Bram replied that he would walk slowly, chew carefully and refrain from laughing.

The doctor asked Zoe if Bram was always so nonchalant.

Eric replied that he was seeing Bram at his best.

Bram smiled and walked slowly out and back toward the cafeteria behind Zoe. He saw a table open near the window and sat down.

A few moments later Chef Evender came out with a cart that had every dessert that had been made for the occasion.

Bram looked over the cart and asked if it could be left there because he was planning to ruin his lunch.

Chef Evender suggested that he save his stomach for a Spaghetti de Mare that was in the process of being prepared for him.

Bram nodded and replied that he would limit the amount of dessert, but he really could use a tall mug of coffee.

Zoe said she could go for a large mug of coffee as well.

The coffee had just arrived when Pat, Zuri, Amy, Elizabeth Donna, and Mallica came rushing in.

Linda ran in right after they had entered.

Bram smiled and asked if they had heard he had a cart full deserts prepared by the second most talented Chef on Mataia.

Pat shook her head and asked if he had really shot himself.

Bram nodded, and replied it was the only thing he could think of to prevent someone else from getting shot. He had not intended to kill the shooter, but he had intended to take him down.

Zoe shook her head and said that it all happened so fast that Bram had already killed the shooter before she or Eric had a chance to take their weapons out of their holsters.

Donna commented that both Orlando and Castor swore that in his previous life Bram was either a Barbarian or the first Marine hero. In either case they said that they never got to shoot when Bram was on the attack.

Bram Nielson Collection

Bram replied that his Aikido coach had also claimed that he felt a presence of the past when watching him practice. But what he remembered most was what he had been told to do. It was to act then talk. In this case there was no one to talk to after he had acted.

Pat had listened and knew that Bram was himself and feeling fine.

She said that she had a ditty for the occasion.

> A mild man, a somewhat crazy mild man
> The hero of long ago was one today.
> He is a mild man who to shoots himself.
> To save all those around
> Saving those he enriches and cares for
> He sits and laughs enjoying sweets.
> And says its nothing, just two small holes.
> One in front, one in back, what, the heck
> The sweets are great and the coffee a strong deep black.
> Hey, let's celebrate the weddings, let's celebrate
> Zuri's back and her soul mate is no hack.
> He makes the best sweets and that's a fact.
> And there is a man, a somewhat crazy mild man.
> For sure a hero on this day as he is on every other day.

Donna took up the ditty and soon everyone in the cafeteria was repeating the chant and stomping their feet in rhythm to her cadence.

Zuri had come into the cafeteria and came to Bram and gave him a hug and quietly told him that she loved him like an older brother.

Bram replied that he was looking forward to the wedding, but he was really into going fishing with his younger sister.

He had just finished his desert when the attending Dr. walked in and asked how he was feeling.

Bram apologized about not having been more cordial and able to greet him earlier. He was about to ask his name when Linda introduced him as Dr. Edwin Marzurka who arrived two days ago.

Bram said that his arrival was well timed and that the handling of his first gunshot victim had been well handled.

Dr. Marzurka shook his head and said that he had been a trauma doctor for five years and had never met any gunshot patient that had walked out of his office and gone to have some sweets and a cup of coffee. He said that he had come in and listened to the ditty and then joined in. He said that a couple of words needed changing and that instead of mild man it would be more appropriate to say wild crazy man.

Bram laughed and asked if that was just a reaction or was, he giving a diagnosis?

Dr. Marzurka shook his head and said that he was really happy that he took Dr. Sewal up on coming to Mataia. His wife was in love with the house, the ease with which she was able to get the things she needed, and his two kids loved the school and all the new friends they were making.

He said that what had convinced him to accept was when Dr. Sewal read him the opening paragraph of the Mataian Constitution and now that he had met the person who repeated that phrase often enough for it to be the first line of the constitution he knew he had made the best decision of his life. He shook his head and finished by say, "even if that person is a wild and crazy man willing to shoot himself."

Bram thanked Dr. Marzurka and said that he planned to spend the rest of the day sitting on a boulder out in the middle of the desert with his mental phycologists and advisors.

He smiled when the Dr. said that he didn't think he had met them yet and asked where their offices were.

Bram replied that their offices were at a secret location out in the desert and only the most privileged ever got to meet with them.

Pat smiled and commented that she agreed with the suggestion that the word that should be emphasized was a crazy man.

Bram asked Linda to arrange for a Fold transport to take him to the desert after lunch. He said that until then he planned to relax and enjoy the scenery from his office window.

Chapter 25: Recovery

The Spaghetti de Mare lunch turned out to be served to a fairly large group. Pat, Amy, Elizabeth, Zuri, and Donna joined him, and the cafeteria was filled.

He found out later that a lot of other people had planned to come for lunch, but Linda had asked them not to.

When he found out he thanked her.

The flavor of the spaghetti was somehow enhanced. He had several servings and finally ask Chef Henslier what he had done to make his Spaghetti de Mare the most delicious that he had ever eaten.

Chef Henslier smiled and yelled, "Hurrah!, Hurrah!, Hurrah!," and he saluted Bram and then shouted he is not only a hero but also a top food critic with excellent taste.

Bram was all smiles and glad that he had praised the taste of the food. He was surprised at the reaction.

He thank the Chef again and said that he was off to his relaxing afternoon.

He followed Zoe back to his office where he picked up Ada, Isaac, and Einstein Jr. and then they walked down to the Fold Launch pad.

It turned out that Pat and Zuri were coming along.

Once they got to the boulder, he took the three mice out of his pocket, and they scurried down into the hole in the rock.

He noted that Zoe and Eric had each chosen to stand on opposite sides of the boulder.

While they were waiting, Zuri asked if they should postpone the wedding.

The three returned with Einstein and his mate and two new little ones who looked robust and normal in size.

Bram greeted them and said that they were looking healthy.

He pointed to Zuri and said that she was getting married on the weekend and had come to say hello before she went on her honeymoon.

Einstein seemed to understand and went over to Zuri and stood on his hind legs until she lowered her hand. He got in and curled up for a moment and then got out.

Bram explained that Einstein had just approved of her marriage.

Zuri smiled and thanked Einstein who shook his head up and down.

Bram said there was no need to postpone the wedding. His shoulder might be a little sore, but his mouth would work just fine. He would be able to officiate the three weddings.

Zuri smiled and said that he had really made Weylan's day by praising his signature dish.

Bram smiled and said that he realized that almost immediately and the spaghetti was the best that he could remember. He had outdone Chef D'Carluca.

He then said that he was taking a walk through the desert before going back home. He wanted to see if the plants on the island had adapted to Mataia.

Pat asked if she could walk along.

Bram replied yes, and said that Zuri should join in. He said that he planned to come back often to relax and think about how to guide the teams that were addressing problems that none of them had anticipated.

Zoe took the lead and said he could guide her by simply calling out right or left.

Zuri asked about the main problem with the planet and the aliens that her team would be focused on.

Bram replied that she and her team would be studying how an advanced society could be so amoral that they would launch four planet killing missiles at four civilizations that were at least three light years away and most likely had no inkling that Amoral existed.

Zuri shook her head and wondered if she were up to being neutral until she learned more.

Bram replied that it would be really hard. Additionally, the Amorals as he was referring to them had developed long range sensors able to reach out and study the details of planets at the three light year range. That would make studying them extremely difficult. He wanted to make sure they never located Mataia.

He suggested that her team begin their studies back before the Amorals developed their sensing technology. He let her know that Marcus had that time, and he had extensive imagery of the planet. Bram also said that they should learn the language and identify the actual name of the planet.

Zuri replied that she thought her team would have their plate full.

Bram agreed and suggested they go slow. One of the first tasks was to eliminate the planet killer rockets.

Pat brought the discussion back to the desert on the island and said that it seemed to be returning to full life like it had on Earth.

Bram asked why she thought so.

Pat pointed to several cactuses that were blooming and commented that the last time they had walked the desert those cactuses seemed to be having trouble. She said she would get one of her team to figure out what had changed.

Bram asked whether knowing that would help her with the rest of Mataia-forming the planet.

Pat said that she felt like it would.

Zuri commented that she had heard that the General and the Admiral were leading a team studying the planet Kutikan. She asked if that population had actually almost totally annihilated themselves.

Bram nodded and added that Pat and Amy were heavily into bringing the past environment forward in time in an effort to re-establish the planet.

They were working with Remi and the lab to figure out how to recycle all the ash that had been generated by whatever wiped out all living organisms and plants.

Zuri commented that it was hard to accept an advanced civilization committing seppuku.

Bram said he agreed and bet that it had all happened because of some accident and some sort of automated retaliation response.

Zuri agreed and said she was putting her money on a monumental planet killing accident. She added that it was one that the Earth seemed to be setting itself up for.

Bram stopped and said that it was time for him to get back to the office. He wanted to launch one of the four teams before going home.

Pat agreed that it was time to get back but that the two of them should go home and relax.

Bram knew that Pat was not making a suggestion and that she was insisting he call it a day. He knew instinctively that she was right.

Zuri said that she was having dinner with her parents. She said that Weylan was bringing a Lemon Meringue pie for dessert.

Bram asked if he could come over for dessert?

Zuri shook her head and said that Weylan was sending a blue berry pie over to Pat.

Zoe said that she and Eric would plan to come over and have some hot blue berry pie and a scoop of vanilla ice and asked Pat what time they should plan on arriving.

Bram stayed out of the exchange as Pat gave the time and asked Zoe to bring vanilla ice cream.

Pat looked at Bram and asked if having company for desert was OK.

He nodded and replied that once he got home he was going to sit down on their couch close his eyes and think for a while.

It was not long after they sat down when Pat smiled when it was clear to her that he had fallen asleep. She got up and went to the kitchen and decided that a cheese, lettuce, tomato, and egg sandwich would be supper. A large piece of blue berry pie and vanilla ice cream would be desert. She put a bottle of Spumanti into the refrigerator to cool and then returned to sit in the recliner.

Bram was breathing in a steady rhythm. She was glad that she had insisted they come home when he had wanted to go to his office to finish the day.

She shook her head when she thought about the fact that he had chosen to shoot through his body in order to prevent someone in the cafeteria from being shot by the gun man. She was amazed that he had done so with the intent to shoot his attacker. She knew Bram was the person that ran toward a problem when most would freeze or run. In this case he had done more than run toward a problem.

The doorbell rang and she realized that she had not awakened Bram for his sandwich.

Bram woke up and gave a light laugh and said that he had done a thorough examination of his eyelids, and they had no holes in them.

Pat got up and went to the door and let Zoe and Eric in,

Bram asked if he had missed dinner.

Pat replied that she had made a large salad for them, and it had been waiting to make sure he did not find holes in his eyelids. She led the way to the dining room and then brought the salads in. She served coffee that was on the refreshment bar.

Bram realized that his body had chosen to focus on working on the bullet wound and that Pat had let him sleep through the normal dinner time. He looked at the size of the salad and said that he only wanted half of it.

Pat had left the dressing to the side, so it was easy to cut Bram's salad in half.

Zoe smiled and said she would cut his piece of blue berry pie so that it was only half as large as hers.

Bram smiled and replied that he was cutting down on the salad so he could double up on the blueberry pie and ice cream.

As he ate, he decided to get to bed early. He knew that the next day was going to be heavy. He wanted to work with Zuri to get her team set up and be functioning while she was on her honeymoon. He also wanted to get the four other team leaders in place and give them their starting goals.

He wondered whether Pat might like to stay an extra day at the Inn. He figured that getting to fish out on the lake and then doing some river fishing would be great.

He asked if staying an extra day at the Inn would interest anyone.

Pat nodded and said she thought it would be a great idea. She knew that if they returned Bram would be back into his intense work. She figured one more day of relaxation was what he needed.

Zoe replied that she and Eric would love that and if they had anything to do, they could do it from there.

Bram nodded then smiled and asked if shooting himself meant that she was going to start protecting him from himself.

Zoe shook her head and said that she did not possess the ability to provide that kind of protection. She pointed to Pat and said that that kind of protection came from her.

Pat was in the process of pouring a glass of wine for everyone. She said that she had an impossible responsibility in that area. She pointed to the sling that Bram was using and said that she lived with someone willing to shoot himself. She finished with the question, "How was she ever going to protect him from his mind?"

Bram knew that there was no answer he could give. Instead, he proposed a toast to a calm, great wedding, and the best fishing that they had ever enjoyed.

Zoe and Eric left shortly after they all finished desert. She commented to Eric that Bram probably should take the next day off, but she knew he would not. She suggested that they make sure that Linda arranged to have those that Bram planned to interact with come to his office.

Shortly after Zoe left, Bram said that he was going to go to bed early.

Pat let him know that she thought it was a great idea. She would be right up after getting things ready for the morning.

Bram did not remember falling asleep but when his eyes opened next the sun was shining through the window. He knew he was late for work. He shook his head and knew that his body had done what it had to do to recover.

The spot next to him was empty and no longer warm so he knew that Pat had been up for some time.

He got up showered the best he could without wetting the bandages on his right shoulder.

He then made his way toward the great smell of pancakes and sausage.

When he entered the kitchen both Pat and Zoe greeted him.

He asked Zoe if she had moved back into his house.

Zoe shook her head and said that he was so late that she had come over to make sure he had survived.

Bram smiled, poured himself a cup of coffee and sat down next to Eric.

He asked him if Zoe was on something or was, she always so hypomanic.

Eric replied that he refused to answer on the grounds that he wanted to remain married.

Zoe smiled and said that Eric wasn't answering for that reason but because he didn't know what hypomanic meant and yes watching someone shoot himself had taken her to the edge of her controllable level of stress.

Bram smiled and said that the only other person who he would have had a clear shot at was his most trusted female bodyguard.

Zoe laughed and said in that case she felt much better about the choice he had made.

Chapter 26: Guns and Bible

Bram arrived at his office an hour later than normal.

Linda greeted him and said that she had arranged for all the people that he had wanted to meet to come to his office. She asked if he wanted to have lunch brought in.

Bram knew that she was trying to ease the workload for the day. He accepted her arranging for folks to come to his office, but he felt like going to lunch was something he needed to do. He knew this time Zoe would be clearing the path if the lunchroom was crowded. He figured it was like getting back on a horse after getting thrown. Then he smiled at his analogy since he had never been thrown from a horse.

He thanked Linda and went into his office. He went to the bookcase, opened the little door, and brought Ada, Isaac, and Einstein Jr. to his desk.

Zoe had brought over some cookie crumbs and said that she wanted to ask the first question.

She asked if Bram should work that day? The three mice shook their head in the affirmative. She shook her head and called them little slave drivers.

Bram said the mice knew that it was better to keep going than to pamper oneself.

He then asked if he had picked the right leaders for all the new teams.

He was pleased with the affirmative head shakes.

He then asked if Zoe was too protective of him.

All the mice shook their heads in the negative.

This caused Bram to ask whether he would need her protection in the future.

He was surprised when the headshakes were all in the positive.

Zoe reacted as well. She said that she was going to alert Bob, Thomas, and Orlando. She said that she would also consider Castor and Donna, but it was their wedding weekend. She asked if the fence around the Inn was still in place.

Bram replied that it was. He asked if she thought something would happen during the wedding weekend.

Zoe commented that so far all of the weddings had been consummated with a gun battle. She was going to be prepared for it.

Bram asked her who would be instigating such an action.

Zoe said she would contact Lacy and see if she had any ideas. She then asked if she had actually been successful in removing all traces of Fold from Earth at the present time and in the future. She said that it had to be a miss that she had not foreseen.

Eric quietly asked if they knew how they sounded reacting to the headshakes of three mice.

Zoe replied that yes, they were reacting to the headshakes of three mice that had so far batted one thousand per cent.

Eric nodded and said he agreed but still wondered how the mice did what they did.

Bram said he had no idea and that maybe they talked to the wind and the wind gave them the answers.

He decided to have a talk with Orlando and get him to have all his Marine friends at the ready.

Linda called in to give him a ten-minute warning before the stream of people would arrive. She let him know that Zuri and two folks she had selected were ready to come in.

Bram organized his thoughts and then pulled his white board to the end of the meeting table. He always felt that the ability to write on it allowed him to concentrate better than working on his computer. He had an updated wide board version that automatically took in his writing and put it into his computer Word document.

He welcomed Zuri.

She introduced Jan Rattle who would act as the leader for the week she was on vacation. Then she introduced Valentina Vogler who preferred to be called Val and who had an engineering degree from Cal Tech and had attained the rank of Ensign in the Navy.

Bram welcomed them.

Zoe asked if they cared for any refreshments.

Bram waited a moment and then he shared his expectations of the team. He then let them know that he wanted them to deal with the fact that they were to determine how to manage an entire planet of beings that were intelligent and at the same time amoral. They were willing to kill four populations on planets that were three light years away and who had no clue that each of their planets had been targeted for annihilation.

He said that in the coming week he would work with the team to eliminate the missiles that were a third of the way to those planets.

Zuri interjected that she did not want the missiles destroyed. Instead, she wanted the missiles turned and to begin their return back to their launch origin. She asked if Bram could get that done and then prevent the Amorals from changing the return course.

Bram smiled and said that Zuri had the right thing in mind and yes, he would work with Remi to make sure that once they turned the missiles, they would not be able to be turned again.

He complimented her on choosing to use their own weapons against them. He suggested that she and the team step back in time to the point when the Amorals did not have the super sensitive sensing technology and study the planet in detail. They should focus specifically on what would make an intelligent society be willing to condemn another world to death with no provocation.

Zuri nodded and said she would be very interested in discovering that motive. She said that she could not imagine what it might be.

Bram then said he would like to suggest two more people to round out the team. He said that Linh had suggested that Simone Lisitsa, one of the IT specialists on her team be named to the new team. He then added that a recently recruited sociology student named Vasily Wit seem to be a good fit on her team. Both were ready to be interviewed that day.

Zuri said she would get them to come to a meeting where all of them could talk about the objectives, the strategies and outline an initial work plan that afternoon. Then when she returned from her honeymoon, they would finish their planning and get on the project full time, and she added with a vengeance.

Bram remined them that they should approach their effort with his favorite saying and now the lead in to the Mataian constitution.

Zuri nodded and thanked him for that reminder. She then stood up and said that it was time for her to get her team organized so he could easily guide them during the next week.

Bram asked if Linda could get the other four team leaders to come in together while he went to the cafeteria for a break.

Linda said she would agree if he stayed in his office until Zoe and Eric checked out the cafeteria first.

Bram gave a small a laugh and said that lightening seldom hit in the same spot twice, but he would wait in his office.

He had just finished preparing for the next four team leaders and whomever they might bring with them when Zoe returned and said that they would be early, and the cafeteria was relatively empty.

Zoe took the lead and they all walked to the cafeteria.

Bram was pouring himself an iced tea when one of the kitchen staff came out to where he was and said that he would take the drink to the table and bring whatever he wanted from the snack bar as well.

Bram looked to the kitchen door where Chef Henslier gave him a salute. Bram raised is left hand and waved. He then selected a bear claw and went to an empty table that was in the far corner near the windows. He sat down with his back to the wall.

He took note that Zoe sat facing the cafeteria entrance and Eric sat facing him. The chair that faced the window but had its back to the door was empty.

The kitchen aid put Bram's drink and bear claw down and said that if he wanted anything else he would be at the counter ready to respond.

Bram thanked him and after he had left, Bram asked Zoe what she was thinking about for the upcoming wedding weekend.

Zoe said that she was going to meet with Orlando, the General and the Admiral after work to decide how to prepare for an attack.

Bram shook his head and said someday he would like to understand what continued to fuel the desire to kill him. He wondered if there was such a thing as an undiscovered organ that was an attack magnet.

Zoe shook her head and then smiled and said that the attackers were just jealous that he had such a good-looking bodyguard.

Bram chuckled and said he would have replaced her, but he had never found a person more homely to do so.

Eric stood up and said that he thought it was time to get back to work and led the way out of the cafeteria.

Bram asked Eric what was bothering him.

Eric replied that every time there was a gun fight, he always ended up in back and Zoe ended out running in to the shooters.

Bram replied that he remembered very clearly that Eric was at Zoe's side as they both jumped the swimming pool fence in their skimpy swimsuits, and he remember very well that the two of them stood side by side responding to the incoming barrage of bullets coming from the speed boats bearing down on them and he remembered the two of them leaping into the hail of bullets when the future sent assassins back to kill him.

Bram stopped and asked if he remembered all the many times Eric had saved him or was it that the two of them talked to mice that irritated him.

Eric started laughing and said that as always Bram had changed his mood for the better. He said he was not sure what was bothering him. He figured that it was the fact that they were always fighting back and seldom did they attack or even suspect whom to attack.

Bram said that he could understand that situation. He too was constantly frustrated about getting attacked by people that he did not know and whom he had never negatively affected. It was hard for him to come up with the rational logic to clarify that situation.

Zoe said she kept it simple. She said she talked to mice and relieved her frustrations.

Eric said he was going to do that as well.

Bram stopped by Linda's desk and asked if things were set.

Linda said that everyone was going to come in after lunch.

He asked her to check with the General, Admiral, Lacy, and Orlando to see if they could meet online in fifteen to discuss the upcoming wedding situation.

Linda said that she would set it up.

Bram then went into the office. He asked Zoe if meeting with them early would be acceptable.

Zoe thanked him for freeing up her after work hours. She figured that everyone would feel better about getting it done earlier.

Bram agreed and he would feel better as well. He wanted to hear what each of them thought of the situation and to evaluate how they would determine the source of where the order and the munitions for the attack had originated.

He felt that the source had to be Earth bound and it had to be because of residue Fold information still existed somehow, somewhere.

Linda called in and let him know that she had everyone on and was ready to start the meeting with the folks he had requested.

Bram welcomed everyone and then stated his objective of setting up the defenses for the weekend.

The General smiled and commented that all they had to do was to provide him with enough ammunition so that when he shot himself through the body to kill the attackers, he would be able to keep firing. He then went on to say he was happy to see that Bram had recovered enough to think about and plan on countering any additional attacks.

He said that every ex-marine attending the wedding would have access to the weapons they were used to using.

Bram thanked him and asked Lacy if she could have the attack bubbles on call.

Lacy replied that they would be on call and would be using the latest weapons available. She said that she had the bubbles refurbished and rearmed with the latest weapons that her contact in the army had provided.

Bram thanked her and commented that she had always used the skill with her air attacks to confuse and defeat the attackers.

The Admiral said that he had six ex-Navy Seals that he had recruited and brought to Mataia. They would be arranged around the higher ground and provide sniper capability to the defense.

Bram said that the Admiral was providing a surprise capability. He commented that he had not been aware of the arrival of the six.

The Admiral nodded and said that he had planned to introduce them just before the discovery of the Amoral planet and the other four planets. Then he hesitated again when he learned that Bram had shot himself in the most amazing self-defense move that he had ever heard of. And now Bram was organizing for a potential attack at a wedding. He said he was lucky to be on Mataia where he did not have to explain the sequence of events to anyone else.

Bram nodded and said he would like to meet them before they provided their support.

The Admiral said that the six were anxious to meet the person that the ex-Marines were claiming that was tougher than any Seal would ever be.

Bram laughed and replied that he figured they were in for a disappointment.

Orlando smiled and said that he had greeted them for Bram and had shown him in action and the six had all agreed that they were looking at the mild-mannered person who turned into a toothed attack monster when it got into a fight. He said they were even more impressed when they learned that Bram was also a non-dimensional minister registered to perform marriages.

Orlando said that the six were calling Bram the pistol packing preacher that carried a bible in one hand and the instrument of death in the other, always offering to treat others as he wished to be treated but willing to give back better than what he received.

Bram smiled and said he should have kept Orlando busier, but he then thanked him for having his back and that it would allow him to greet the six without having to bring them up to date.

He said that he wanted to make sure they understood that he never initiated any of the actions when he had to retaliate against the attackers. There was no religious righteousness involved.

Orlando said that he had made the point that there had never been a time when the creator of the Fold effort had acted preemptively.

Bram thanked everyone for being ready and he added that he hoped that it was preparation that they would not need to activate.

He then said that it was time for lunch and afterward he had four team leaders and their members to meet with before the end of the day.

He asked the Admiral if the six new ex-Seal team members might be able to join him for lunch.

The Admiral replied that the six would be quite pleased to join him.

Bram thanked him and declared the meeting over.

Linda disconnected the feed and then asked Bram if there was any special order for his lunch.

Bram said since he was dealing with a bunch of Seals he wondered if the Chef had fish on the menu.

He asked Zoe and Eric how they felt about the meeting.

Zoe commented that she felt sorry for the potential attackers.

Eric said he agreed that the attackers faced certain annihilation if they attacked and did not immediately surrender.

Bram said that he agreed and hoped that the preparation was all it turned out to be. He then declared it was time to eat.

Ron Mueller

Chapter 27: The Inn and More

Bram kept the lunch with the six ex-Seals low key. He welcomed them and asked if they had any questions and asked what type of work they were looking for. He was glad to hear that they would work with anyone wanting their help. He said that they should make sure they found work that they would want to do in the long term. He suggested they work with the staffing folks that Erica led.

Zoe saw that the six were a little overwhelmed. She asked each where they were from and to share some high point in their life.

Without exception every one of the six said that their Navy stint was the highlight.

Zoe asked whether they had any girl friends or sweethearts back home.

Bram listened and knew that Zoe was doing what he would not have been able to do. She was drawing out what made the six valuable to Mataia. He would have to thank her later.

After the lunch back in his office, he met with the leaders that he was putting in place to study the four new civilizations that had been discovered. He gave them his initial objectives but suggested they organize their teams, and all together develop a strategy and detailed plans on how to study, learn and later engage the people of those planets.

He stressed the point that their approach to the four planets should always be from their past before the Amoral planet had developed their long-range sensors. After they were at the planets they could then come forward in time to the correct current time. He wanted to ensure that the Amoral planet never knew from where the Mataians were coming from.

That evening he once again fell asleep on his recliner. Pat had gotten an update from Linda that Bram had gone all out throughout the day. This time when Bram woke up, he said that he didn't feel like eating but Pat insisted that he at least have a bowl of pomegranate seeds and glass of milk. He asked about making it chocolate milk and Pat said that would be OK, but they did not have any and the local quick pick-up store was closed.

They both knew that no such store existed, and Bram said that he would settle for the milk.

The next morning the Fold to the receiving location along the highway that was about three miles from the Inn included Orlando, Castor, Donna, Bob, Thomas, Zoe and Eric and a large box that Orlando said carried a significant number of arms for the Marines who would come later and who would bring more weapons and ammunition.

Bram and Pat both asked about the would-be spouses.

Castor and Donna replied that they would be Folding down shortly, and they would all be ready for the afternoon wedding walk through. They added that Zuri and her Marine beau, Bram's personal chef, were escorting them down.

Bram asked when had Weylan become his "personal" Chef.

Their Fold happened and they were inside an old barn.

Bram said that they should unload and then proceed out the back door away from the highway and then call for the transport that Ted had arranged. He said that Ted had set it up so that it would wait in the Inn parking lot for a pickup call. Ted had stressed that the folks arriving should be outside and ready to get into the transport.

Once the process started, the driver would make a continuous loop that always started at the Inn. The driver knew nothing about the Fold system, and he might ask questions that most likely should not be answered.

Once they were all out and the weapons box was ready, Bram pointed to the call box mounted on a post and clearly labeled, "pickup call phone." He pressed the call button and asked to be picked up.

The pickup vehicle was a minibus that had a large back carrying space. It could easily carry twenty people and a significant amount of luggage.

When the minibus stopped and while Orlando and Castor loaded the large weapons box, Zoe did a quick inspection of the under carriage and the interior before allowing Bram to enter.

Bram went to the front door of the van so he could check out the driver. As soon as he saw who it was he started to laugh. He asked how long Cedric had been a minibus driver and did he have a license to transport weapons and ammunition. He knew immediately that Ted had set him up.

Cedric laughed said that he had started working at his new profession at about six in the morning when he had picked up the minibus from the rental car office.

Bram said he refused to ride in the front suicide seat and got in and sat down next to Pat.

Orlando got in the front seat and said that he knew exactly how Cedric drove and had no fear of sitting next to him.

The transport never stopped. By lunch time all of the wedding party and a healthy number of guests had Folded in.

Bram had positioned the laser shield so that it was above the top of the two fences but could be dropped down in just a few seconds. He had walked the fence to ensure that there were no obstructions that would be in the way when the barrier was lowered to the ground. He tested and an additional feature that had come to him from watching a movie depicting the defense of an ancient castle where the archers fired their crossbows through narrow slits called balistraria. He had programed the controls of the laser shield so he could raise the front part of the top cover from the wall section and raise the top up two feet and provide an opening that the snipers could shoot through. He had created a horizontal balistraria for the snipers to shoot from.

He then asked the ex-Navy seals to take up positions in the top floor of the rooms that faced the front. He suggested that if they were attacked he would activate the opening and it would open for two seconds allowing them to shoot and then it would close automatically, and they would need to activate it to be able to shoot again.

The leader of the six said he loved the idea of setting things up so they could lay to the side of the windows and roll into position as the shield went up and then roll away as the shield went down, and they all reloaded.

Bram said that the rooms were theirs and they should enjoy the best rooms in the Inn.

A few minutes later the Admiral came to Bram and commented that he had just made lifetime friends of the six ex-Seals.

Bram smiled and said the Navy was much easier to make friends with than the Marines.

Orlando was standing with Bram laughed and said that he had told his Marines not to trust anyone so brainy and handsome but when pretty boy out did him in the first major attack, he put out the word to give him a break and the Marines now loved him.

The Admiral laughed and said the General had told Bram so much that his men were trying to take Orlando's job.

Orlando shook his head and said that competition was about going to lunch with Bram who had Chef D'Carluca wrapped around his little finger and was always trying to impress him with some special lunch. It was a lunch that those guarding Bram got to share.

Bram shook his head and said that they needed to make sure that all the guests got into the Inn safely by six in the morning and anyone that was late would not be Folded to Earth. He said he planned to put the shield up during the practice and that everyone already at the Inn was to be inside the shield.

Mike came over and said he and Mary had just arranged to have some of the guests that were staying overnight moved away from the rooms he had arranged for the Seals.

He then let them know that Stetson Catering were done getting their food serving tables set up and they were ready for folks to get their lunch.

Bram used the portable microphone he had in his hand and let everyone know lunch was ready and it was a first come first serve event.

He watched as all the young men rushed over to form three lines in front of each serving table. He approved of the fact that the Stetsons had come prepared to handle a large crowd of eager eaters.

Pat waved to him from the table that she and Amy were sitting at.

He walked over and saw that they were holding a seat for him that had a plate with a little of everything on it. He noted that the plate was a heavy-duty disposable. He sat down and took a bite of the slice of pink roast beef and knew he was in for a great lunch.

Elizabeth had watched the arrival of all the wedding party and had talked to all three brides and grooms and had walked them through the wedding ceremony. She had made the point that Bram would preside but if there was any disruption, he would then take action in the manner he thought would be most appropriate and they should do as he instructed otherwise, she was in charge and would keep things on track.

The lunch was a leisurely one and Elizabeth hated to break it up, but she stood and gave everyone the ten-minute warning and asked that the food be removed from the Inn.

Bram watched as the Stetson crew transformed the main floor into the arrangement for the wedding. He noted that Orlando had moved the majority of the ex-Marines to the veranda and was giving them instructions.

He also saw Ted had his team put up a table at the end of the veranda and put the extra food and desert on it.

He would have to give him and Marial a hard time about spoiling the young men.

Elizabeth then called the wedding practice to order and had everyone walk slowly through it.

Bram took the three rings from the ring bearer. He realized that Elizabeth was using plastic copies for the practice.

He noted that Elizabeth had everything flowing smoothly. He looked out the windows to the veranda and realized that Orlando was still instructing the men on how to defend the Inn. He noted that they all had an updated version of the field weapons that they had previously used. It was clear that the General's connections with the gun industry was still strong.

Elizabeth declared the practice over. She reminded the wedding party that they would all go immediately to their tables after the ceremony and be served by Chef D'Carluca and his team. The rest of the wedding guests would be sitting at tables that would have a number on it that let them know the serving table and the order they had in the line to that table.

Bram went to the Veranda and asked about the new weapons. Orlando said that they were the latest version of the Marine field weapon. Bram asked where they would be stored in the long run.

Orlando looked at him and replied that he would make sure they were stored wherever Bram suggested.

Bram said that he wanted them to be stored on Earth and that the house down the road should be modified to have a vault that would hold an array of weapons.

Orlando nodded and said he would personally work on getting that done.

Bram saw that Pat, Mike, Mary, and Amy were sitting and enjoying an iced tea. He was also aware that Zoe, Eric, Bob, and Thomas were standing along the veranda wall looking like they were enjoying the scenery.

He walked over near where Mike was sitting and smiled as his former FBI bodyguards took new positions with two of them on one side and two around the corner of the Veranda that faced the Rushing River.

It reminded him of all the previous times that they had faced adversity.

This time he felt that by having developed the laser shield he was doing his part at keeping those around him protected.

Marcus, Mylan, and Marcus Jr. came out on the porch. Mylan smiled and announced that she had convinced her Dad to take Monday and Tuesday off and go on a two-day Fold mini vacation to Easter Island. She said that Melisa had just told them about having purchased and prepared a house on the island for Fold vacations. Melisa said that she was putting it on the list on Monday, so I ask Dad to be the first to go there.

Mylan said that she was going there to evaluate the guide that Melisa had hired.

Bram looked at Marcus and said that there was no way to get out of going with his daughter on a business trip. He said they should all have an enjoyable time. He then asked if they were going to stay after the wedding to go fishing and got a resounding yes from all of them.

Marcus Jr. immediately said that he had refused to go to Easter Island if it meant missing the fishing trip. He said it was great to come to the wedding, but the fishing trip was the real reason that he had come.

Bram asked if the two of them knew the flower girl and the ring bearer.

Mylan reminded him that the school on Mataia had a small population, and it was taught similar to a Montessori school with everyone in the same room and often working on the same projects. They all knew each other well.

Bram smiled and said he envied them. They were getting the best schooling possible, and they had a dad that went on many vacations with them.

Marcus said they were going to watch a movie in the television room and guided the way back inside.

The six ex-Navy Seals came out to where Bram was standing and said that they wanted to thank him for arranging for them to have such great rooms. They commented that they were impressed with the Marine band and the Pop Music group. It was great to dance and enjoy a drink at no expense. One of them said that Mataia had to recruit more young women so that the women wouldn't have to dance so much and get worn out.

Bram pointed to where Erica had just sat down and said that they should go and let her know that she had to do a better job recruiting young women.

One of the young men shook his head and said that he was afraid to do that. She had interviewed him, and he figured that he was lucky to have made it to Mataia.

Bram walked over to where Erica was sitting and asked her if she had been tough on the young man standing with him.

Erica nodded and then pointed at each one and said she would introduce each one of them to Bram.

Bram Nielson Collection

She began by introducing Dan Karajin that started off with her on the wrong track by saying the Admiral had approved him to come to Mataia and wondered why she was interviewing him. She said that his attitude had made the rest of his interview much more intense, and she had almost refused him. She said that she had called Dennis and let him know that she was considering rejecting him.

She then went down the list, Art Solti, a Bostonian who had earned a metal of merit for his service. Easy to get along with and a person who did not seek to use an Admiral for cover.

She then named Herib Hahn and said that what stood out was his love of skiing on the small family ski slope in the Rockies. She admired the fact that he had worked on the slopes while still going to school. He admitted joining the Navy was his way to see if he could get out to the bigger world.

Leo Barenbon, the lion of the six. She described him as the quiet leader who seems to also be the thinker. He impressed me with his careful answers. He grew up in the rural south but has a liberal view of race and gender.

Then there is Coro Atemis, the shy one but willing to risk his life for what he thinks is important. Erika made the point that he felt that having a just government was important.

Finally, Krys "the black Seal" a quiet hero that had only praise for the other five of his team. He made the point that they had always stood up for him whenever color entered negatively into the picture. She said that his support of Dan was why she had finally decided to accept him because she was not satisfied with the Admiral saying he would have a talk with Dan.

Bram smiled and pointed at Erica and made the point that she was not so tough she was just thorough.

Someone spoke up and said that she had saved his Naval career, and he had come back to her and pleaded his case so he could get on Mataia. He said that he had turned down a promotion to Lt Commander.

Erica smiled and greeted Stanley Lecter who was standing with Gerry, who had been a part of what Bram called the Magnetron Romance and was now Erica's husband.

Stanley went on to say that he looked back and was lucky to have met someone who told him to treat others the way he wanted to be treated.

Bram said that he was glad to see the US Navy so well represented.

He then pointed at the six and said that they wanted Erica to recruit more young women so they would be able to dance with them.

He said he was going to go inside and see who was dancing and make sure the wall flowers got off the wall.

That evening Pat listened as Bram shared his thoughts about who might be the instigator of any attack.

Bram said he was confident that Zoe and her team had been thorough in erasing the Fold information. He said that the only way the history of the Fold program would resurface was if one of his attackers had prepared an information time capsule and left it for his children to find. That child now grown would be given the time capsule and learn about the enemy that had killed their parent. They in turn might be able to organize and get the funding from others that might have been named in the time capsule.

Pat smiled and said that she would leave getting the proof for his theory of how an attack might be staged. She said that she was thinking about the wedding of the miracle child. She said that she and Jina had spent time sharing how the Fold program had changed not only Zuri's fate but also Nuro and her life for the better. Jina felt that it was providence that the person who had developed the Fold technology was the person who would perform the marriage of their daughter.

Bram said that was a good note on which to get into bed and get re-energized for a busy wedding day.

Chapter 28: Amor and More

The next morning Bram had a quick breakfast with Mike, Mary, Pat, Elizabeth, and Amy. His bodyguards were standing around the room. Each had prepared a plate with waffles and had a cup of coffee nearby.

Mike had made enough waffles and fried sausage links that there was plenty for everyone. He had plenty of butter, a variety of jams and maple syrup.

They were all quiet as they ate breakfast. The plan was to get dressed after breakfast.

Pat broke the silence and asked about all the guests and where they had all stayed.

Bram said that the new house where they had arrived had more than fifty of their former Marine personnel. The wedding party had all stayed at the Inn. The other guests had stayed on Mataia and were in the process of arriving as they spoke.

He said that Chef D'Carluca, his crew and the dinners for the wedding party had arrived and were in the viewing room that had been taken over to hold their meal.

Elizabeth said that she had made sure the wedding party members were up for breakfast that was being catered by Stetson Catering. Who had already positioned all their food against the wall of the Inn's ballroom.

Mary smiled and commented that once again she and Mike could take it easy since Chef D'Carluca and the Stetsons were doing all the catering. She said that it didn't get much better than that.

Mike said that it did because he had gotten an invite from Ted Stetson to go fishing in the afternoon.

Orlando came into the kitchen and let Bram know that all the marine guard were on the veranda enjoying a hearty breakfast. He said that the Minibus was making a constant circle, and all the guests were arriving form Mataia early as they had been requested.

He asked Bram what else he could do.

Bram stood up and took out a controller. He showed it to Orlando and said that it was the activate and deactivate controller for the laser shield. At the moment the laser shield was activated but he had raised it so that the bottom was currently at the height of the top of the twenty-foot fence. He explained that once the shield was down, there was not much that needed doing. He felt it was better for Orlando to hold the controls while the ceremony was underway.

Orlando nodded and said that he would hold it but if anything needed to be changed he was counting on Bram to do that.

Bram said that it would be no problem. They would both be at the altar.

Cedric came in and let Bram know that he had just completed the last run of the shuttle. He had checked with Linda to make sure all the guests that were coming were here.

She had reassured him that no more Folds would occur.

He added that she had shared the fact that the auditorium in Mataia was set up to broadcast the wedding and that those on Mataia would be watching.

Bram asked Orlando to ensure that everyone was inside the fenced area.

He followed Orlando out.

He asked Cedric to park the minibus at the opposite end of the parking lot as far away from the Inn as possible.

Cedric did one better and parked the minibus on the other side of the bridge across the river. He then jogged back to the lodge.

Once Cedric was in, Bram lowered the laser shield. He walked out to the fence and made sure that the bottom of the shield was all the way down in the two-foot-deep cement trench by throwing a few pebbles down into the trench to see them sparkle and get folded into the negative Fold realm.

He then walked up to the six rooms and made sure the six ex seals were awake, and in position. He verified that the leader understood how to activate the raising of the top of the shield and that they had three seconds to shoot.

He was reassured that they could get two shots off in that amount of time and if they could see their targets clearly they would have two hits each time.

Bram then went and got dressed and went down to the hall to the lectern. He had everything written out. He didn't need what was written, he had everything memorized but should the action distract him he would be able to get reoriented quickly by using his notes.

Elizabeth approached him and let him know that the wedding party was ready. She walked over to the leader of the group providing the music and let him know that she would signal him when it was time to bring out the brides.

Bram saw that Lacy was sitting at the back and she had her headset on and knew she was in communication with her Fold attack team located back on Mataia but controlling attack bubbles located somewhere high in the sky and taking small Fold skips in time so they would be invisible to any sophisticated monitoring group on Earth.

He wondered if any movement of people, drones or other means of attack had been spotted.

The thought that maybe all of their precautions were for naught crossed his mind.

But Elizabeth's signal for the processional music to start brough his attention to the fact that bridesmaids and the groomsmen were coming up to the stage.

Elizabeth then walked up and stood at a podium set up at the corner of the stage and greeted everyone and then smiled and said that she was simply going to advise them in simple Mataian of two facts. One they should each have each other's back and they should apply the first sentence of the Mataian constitution and change the words slightly and "treat each other as you wish to be treated."

That brought an unexpected cheer from those in attendance. She then wished them a lifetime of happiness.

Then the music change to "here comes the bride"

Bram turned his attention to the brides being escorted in. The General, wearing his formal Marine uniform escorted Donna in. Castor's bride was Escorted in by Orlando, who was wearing a Dark Green suit with a white hanky and a white boutonniere.

Then Zuri appeared Nuro was beaming as he brough his daughter up the aisle. Zuri was stunning in her plain white wedding dress. A blue sapphire necklace on a gold chain accented her chest and matching dangling earrings accented her ears. He knew that her husband to be had spent a small sum to purchase her the matching sapphire engagement ring. He and Pat had gifted the necklace and Nuro and Jina had gifted the earrings.

The hush in the room spoke volumes as he watched the Fold miracle child, now a woman walk up the aisle to take the hand of a young ex-Marine, now a graduate Chef from the Chef D'Carluca school.

Bram had each of them read their marriage vows.

Bram Nielson Collection

Then as Zuri finished exchanging vows, the sound in the hall changed and it sounded as if it was raining. Then several explosions above them seemed to accent Bram shouting out that he declare them all married, and the bride and groom should kiss. The sound of rain intensified and the explosions around the Inn intensified.

Orlando had rushed out to the veranda and realized that the attackers had bullets that were penetrating the screen, but they were being evaporated down to dart sized needles.

Bram realized that the bullets were made of some superior kind of metal. He increased the power of the lasers. He knew that this would be a drain on the batteries that powered the laser shield but figured he had about twelve hours of power. If needed he would replace his bubbles.

He watched as the six snipers were firing and saw that they were taking out twelve attackers every time the shield opened.

The rockets being fired hit the laser shield, sent up huge sparklers and blew up. A couple got through only to fall on the ground and explode. The explosions shattered the windows.

Lacy came out to the Veranda and said she was losing a considerable number of bubbles. She said that the drones being used against her were very sophisticated. She had taken out twenty drones and had lost twelve bubbles.

Bram asked if she had enough fighter drones.

Lacy replied that it depended on how many of the sophisticated drones the attackers had.

Bram said that he was going to join the snipers and add a little more pain to the attackers.

Orlando, Castor, and Donna said that they were going to join him. Orlando handed Bram one of the new sniper rifles he had in the gun case.

He then led the way to the second floor.

Bram began slow but in a few moments every time the shield opened; he was able to get three shots off. It seemed to him that the battle was going on forever.

He noted that Pat, Amy, Marial, and Linda had set up an ammo delivery service.

The General had made some calls and suddenly the sky seemed to be full of helicopters firing their Vulcan gatling guns.

Bram continued firing and watched as it became apparent that the attackers were being defeated.

Lacy's fighter bubbles were no longer facing the sophisticated drones. She had broadcast the command that the attackers lay down their weapons and surrender or they faced certain death.

Orlando shouted that he was going to lead his men out and round up the enemy.

Bram followed him down to the shield and opened the gate and watched fifty fully battle armored men follow Orlando out toward the attacker's position.

He was pleased to see the sky fill with at least fifty attack bubbles that laid down laser fire in front of Orlando and his men. The laser then took out a couple of attackers that had chosen to fire their weapons.

Lacy once again announced it was surrender or die. This time she had use a deep based voice that sounded like the voice of God from one of the biblical movies.

He was surprised how effective it was. He saw hands go up and fighters go down on their knees.

Orlando had his men bring the attackers into the parking lot and lay face down. They then zip locked their hands behind them. There were close to one hundred prisoners.

Bram asked what they were going to do with one hundred prisoners.

689

The Admiral smiled and said that he was going to send them on a slow boat to some island in the Pacific and drop them off.

Bram nodded and said that would be a great way to handle the situation. He then asked about the dead ones.

The general asked if there was a way to Fold them to a location where they could be buried or left for eternity.

Bram nodded and said that they could be folded in to the very distant past long before the human existed.

Elizabeth announced that it was time for the wedding party to have their reception dinner.

Mike and Mary had brought out the brooms and cleaning equipment and the General had asked a number of his ex-Marines to help him sweep the glass off the floor.

Bram asked Lacy to work with Marcus and Amy to move the dead to some ancient time. He then went in and joined the Wedding party and for the meal that Chef D'Carluca had prepared.

Pat sat down next to him and put her hand on his and asked if he was OK.

Bram nodded and said that he needed to follow up and learn who had instigated the attack.

He watched the three brides and grooms get up for their first dance.

Once they had the floor and everyone cheered, he took Pat's hand and led her to the Dance floor and soon the dance area was full.

Lacy finished her dance with Ray and then came over to Bram and said that all the bodies had been, ID'd photographed, and Folded to a distant past of the Earth. She had the weapons, the ammunition and the personal belongings stored in the barn of the house down the highway.

The Admiral had used his connections and had called in some transport and the prisoners were on the way to the coast where they would be put on a US Navy ship and taken to some remote island in the Pacific and dropped off.

She said that Linda had limited the fishing trip to ten fishing boats that were all full and ready to go. Those Folding back to Mataia would have until six in the evening to take a Fold.

Bram thanked her for the update. He said that he was ready to go fishing.

He looked around at all the people in the room and felt good about the fact that he had been proactive in preparing for the attack.

Pat saw Bram relax. She knew that he had spent a great deal of time working on the attack scenario. She also knew that he would be relentless at finding out who was behind the funding and organizing of the attack and would not relent in the search. Those organizers would rue the day they had decided to challenge Bram.

Bram spent the rest of the afternoon and early evening fishing and thinking through how to move forward on his personal journey.

He knew that he had unfinished work in learning and embracing new beings and intelligences that would enrich everyone.

He was determined to end the attacks from those on Earth, though he was not sure that it would be possible. He was aware that he had improved his technology but so had those who had attacked.

He smiled as he remembered the day he had been pulled over for speeding through a small town and the officer that had stopped him was bubbling with enthusiasm because he had just caught his first speeder with his new radar system that could accurately clock a car while he sat on a side street. The officer had been so happy that he had only written him a warning ticket.

Bram felt that way, he had been given a warning about the improving technology and knew that his current laser shield would need to be improved.

He smiled as he thought about time. In his world it did not stand still. In the Fold world it existed in both the positive Fold and the negative Fold realms but in the negative Fold realm it was not linear and in that realm all of history was fluid. He had stepped in several times, and he was sure he had created ripples in time.

He planned to remain active and affect both past history and future history in as positive of a way possible, but he knew that he would not always have control of the size of ripples he would create.

The End

Ron Mueller

Bram Nielson Collection

<u>About the Author</u>

Ronald E. Mueller
remwriter95@gmail.com
Ron grew up in what is now Flint River State Park in Southeast Iowa. The 170-year-old house Ron lived in is built into a hillside. It faces a 125-foot-high cliff towering over the little Flint River. The house and the land talked to him about; the passing of time, the struggle to conquer the land, the struggles people faced and the wonder of nature.

He climbed the cliffs, crawled into the caves, dove from the swimming rock, collected clams from the bottom of the pond, gigged and skinned frogs for their legs. He trapped muskrats for fur, hunted raccoon in the dead of night, and with only a stick hunted rabbits in the dead of winter.

His young life was outdoors, and nature tested him.

He walked to a one room stone schoolhouse uphill both ways. A stern but warm-hearted teacher, Mrs. Henry was instrumental in shaping his character as she shepherded him from the fourth to the eighth grade. A Montessori before its time. It was a wonderful way to grow up.

His experiences inter-twined with snippets of fantasy lend themselves to the adventures he leads the reader through.

Ron Mueller

<u>Characters in the Stories</u>

Amy	Wellington	NASA astronaut
Aanon	Zann	Swoosh Leader of the Alien's
Ada	Mouse	Einsteins children mice
Angela	Newton	Olivia Newton's Daughter
Bob		FBI body guards
Bonank	Etaing	Senator Senate Oversight Committee
Bram	Nielson	Protagonist
Castor	Suarez	Marine guard
Cedric	Stetson	Fishing boat
Celilo Park		Fishing point launch area, along Columbia River.
Charles	Ford	Science Advisor Senate Oversight Committee
Dalles		site in Oregon along Columbia River.
Danial	Bascom	Senator W Virginia Senate Oversight Committee
Daryl	Nazda	Backup Pilot Bubble 1 Pat Pilot
David	Conden	Utah Senator's partner
Dennison	Newton	Olivia Newton's Son
Donna		New Marine guard
Edward	Sharp	Site Marine Commander
Einstein	Mouse	Bram's first mouse
Einstein City		City on the Mataia
Elizabeth	Miller	Humanist philosopher
Eric		FBI body guards
Erica	Wilson	Initial arch rival
Ester	Mannerly	Nasa quality inspector for the two wheels.
Gerald	Gerry	Sooner Captain Erica's husband
Harold	Redat	Backup Pilot Bubble 2 Amy Pilot
Isaac	Mouse	Einsteins children mice
Jeffrey	Mikelson	Boss that is patient,
Jina	Juma	Mom
John	Morgan	NASA director Jefferies Boss
John	Stately	Senator Utah Senate Oversight Committee
Jose	Estrada	project manager wheel one and two
Lacy	Stetson	first office support. Ted's daughter
Lester	Tilson	Marine Major General in charge of Fold security
Linda	Stetson	Ted's oldest becomes Brams support.
Lori	Middleton	Lab, workshop supervisor
Luke	Stetson	Fishing boat Ted's son
Mallica	Evenston	World class mathematician
Marcus	Smith	World class astrophysicist
Marial	Stetson	Brought Picnic lunch, Cedric's wife
Mary		Rushing River Inn Owner
Mataia		(Ma ta ee ah) New world to which Bram moves
Melisa	Etrius	Organizer of the Fold neighborhood activities
Mike		Rushing River Inn Owner
Mt. Jefferson		location to hike & go fishing, near Rushing River
Myla	Smith	
Nuro	Juma	Dad
Ohaan	Toon	Bram's Alian equivalent

694

Bram Nielson Collection

Olivia	Newton	Senator Maine Senate Oversight Committee
Orlando	Gutieres	Marine guard
Patricia	Fleming	NASA astronaut Brams mate
Primeira	Planet	New Dry world to be used
Raymond		Daedlus Husband to be of Lacy
RCID		rhombicosidodecahedron-Geometric shape
Remi	Hardwood	Direct bubble assembly Lab technical
rhombicosidodecahedron		RCID shape of time & distance in negative Fold
Rita	Stetson	Brought Picnic lunch, Ted's wife
Samuel	Natorly	US President
Serena	Windal	Fold phycologist -Marine Therapist
Swoosh	Water Planet	Name of Alien Water world
Ted	Stetson	Fishing boat
Thomas		FBI body guards
USS Hood Wheel One		First Fold vessels
USS Rainier Wheel Two		First Fold vessels
Woo-an	Ang	Ohaan's mate
Zoe		FBI body guards
Zuri	Juma	Wheel chair bound autistic mental giant savant,

Ron Mueller

Published by: Around the World Publishing LLC.

QR Links to
ATWP.US web site

www.ingramcontent.com/pod-product-compliance
Lightning Source LLC
Chambersburg PA
CBHW070706100726
47907CB00001B/71